W9-CNA-200

PHILLIP E. JONES

12-31-09
Big Dog

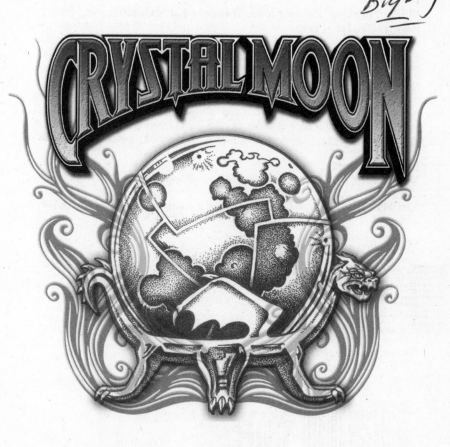

CRYSTAL MOON

Magic of Luvelles

The Worlds of the Crystal Moon
Book 2 Crystal Moon, Magic of Luvelles

View a high-def, printable – MAP - of Grayham
www.WorldsoftheCrystalMoon.com

Phillip "Big Dog" Jones' blog and answer Fan's Questions at,
www.PhillipJones.com

Copyright © 2009 by Phillip E. Jones. All rights reserved.

No part of this publication may be reproduced, stored in a retrieval system or trans-mitted in any form or by any means, electronic, mechanical or otherwise without the written permission of the publisher. If you have purchased this book without a cover, then be aware that this book is stolen property—and reported as "unsold or stolen" to the publisher; neither the publisher nor author has received payment for this book.

Illustrations done by:
Ian Ferrebee, Cindy Fletcher, Kathleen Stone and Angela Woods

Special thanks to Georgia Carpenter and Bill Zavatchin for their patience and invalu-able input.

This printing was done in 2009 by:
Worzalla Publishing Co., Stevens Point, WI • 866-523-7737

This novel is a work of fiction. Names, characters, events, incidents and places are the product of the author's imagination. Any resemblance to actual persons, people or events is purely coincidental.

Library of Congress Cataloging-in-Publication Data
First published in 2009 under ISBN — 978-0-9816423-1-4
Crystal Moon, Magic of Luvelles

ISBN: 978-0-9816423-1-4

9 780981 642314   52499

Printed in the United States of America
10 9 8 7 6 5 4 3 2

Shapeshift Productions, LLC

For readers of advanced seasons.

CRYSTAL MOON

Magic of Luvelles

Big Dog

Phillip E. Jones

Crystal Moon Magic of Luvelles

Book 2

I would like to thank the illustrators for their hard work!

Ian Ferrebee
www.tigereyegraphics.com

Cindy Fletcher
Cinfl37@yahoo.com

Kathleen Stone
www.vangosmedia.com

Angela Woods
www.angelawoodsfineart.com

Stop

Soul to Soul

Hello again, fellow soul,

I'm truly pleased to see that you've decided to join me for the second of many stories. When last you visited the Worlds of the Crystal Moon, there were so many questions, most of which will now be answered to the best of my abilities.

If I can warn you of one thing, it would be to say that this story isn't for the faint-hearted or a mind without the proper wit with which to follow the manipulations of not only the gods, but also those who were involved in the events which allow for the telling of such a story.

Even I have found the revelations—which have been said to be fact—to be disturbing, and have struggled to determine the truth... if there is such a thing any longer.

I beg you to give me your undivided attention as you continue forward. Let us begin again with the second of many stories— Crystal Moon, Magic of Luvelles. I do hope you enjoy my recollections.

Your friend and fellow soul
inside the ***Book of Immortality,***
Phillip **"Big Dog"** Jones

Glossary

Dawn
The moment when the sun rises just above the horizon.

Morning
Period of the day between Dawn and Early Bailem.

Early Bailem
When the sun has reached the halfway point between the horizon and its highest point in the sky, the Peak of Bailem.

Peak of Bailem
The moment when the sun has reached its highest point.

Late Bailem
The moment when the sun has passed the Peak of Bailem and taken a position halfway between the Peak of Bailem and when the sun disappears behind the horizon.

Evening
The moments between Late Bailem and when the sun is about to disappear behind the horizon.

Night
The moments after the sun has disappeared behind the horizon until it once again rises and becomes Dawn.

Midnight
An estimated series of moments that is said to be in the middle of the night.

————————— SEASON or SEASONS —————————
There are different uses for the words *season* and *seasons*.

Season
The common meaning referring to winter, spring, summer, and fall.

Seasons
People can refer to their ages by using the term *season* or *seasons*. For example: if someone were to be born during a winter season, he or she would become another season older, once they have reached the following winter. They are said to be so many winter seasons old.

Table of Contents

Gabriel - Book of Immortality

Illustration by Ian Ferrebee

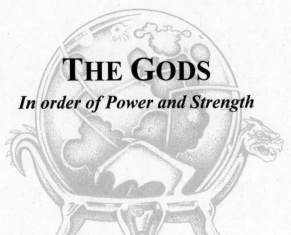

THE GODS

In order of Power and Strength

Bassorine—The Late God of War

Bassorine, prior to his destruction, instigated wars on the worlds and in that way helped to control the population growth on each. He was rugged-looking, an outdoorsman with human features. He was the oldest of all the gods who managed to survive the God Wars. Bassorine was, **by far**, the most powerful of all the gods and has been replaced by a new God of War... Mosley.

ଔ

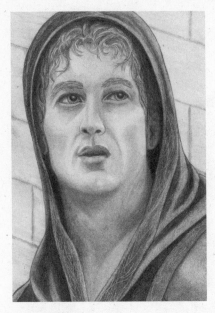

Lasidious—God of Mischief and Deception

When Lasidious's eyes are not glowing red and his teeth aren't sharpened to fine points, he's actually quite debonair-looking. He has short sandy brown hair, blue eyes and a chiseled chin. He has tremendous sex appeal and was human before ascending to become a god. Lasidious is charismatic, charming, witty, and a liar who loves mischief. He is nearly six feet tall with an athletic build beneath his robes. He normally keeps the hood of his sleeveless robe up no matter what color he wears, only occasionally putting it down.

Alistar—God of the Harvest

Alistar is thin with human features. His hair, sandy brown beneath a hooded green robe, complements his thin face. Pleasant-looking with soft brown eyes, Alistar is in charge of the world's harvests and determines if there will be feast or famine. He is known to the other gods in the *Farendrite Collective* as having a good nature.

෧ଓ

Hosseff—Shade God of Death

Hosseff wears an assortment of different-colored robes and can transform from a human to his normal appearance as a shade. When in shade form, the form of his birthright, no facial features can be seen. Instead, a mist, haze or emptiness fills the hood. His hands also look like smoke and have no definition. Hosseff loves Death and helps to return the souls of the dead back to the Book of Immortality's many pages.

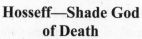

Mieonus—Goddess of Hate

Mieonus, a beautiful goddess with human features, has long brunette hair and soft brown eyes. She isn't as elegant-looking as the goddess, Celestria, but she tries awfully hard. She wears an assortment of different gowns and loves the look of lifted heels beneath her feet. With a heart full of hate, nothing gives her more pleasure than to watch the pain of the world's populations as they struggle through life.

ෆ

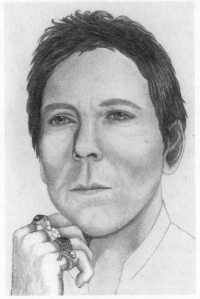

Mosley—The New God of War

Mosley is a Night Terror Wolf. It is now his job to take over Bassorine's duties as the God of War. His breath has the ability to make mortals sleep. His furry coat is solid black and he is intellectually superior to many of the gods. He now lives on the god world of Ancients Sovereign in Bassorine's old cabin home on top of Catalyst Mountain.

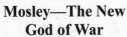

Yaloom—God of Greed

Yaloom is a pompous god who thinks of nothing but himself. He loves the finer things the gods have created and surrounds himself with them. His home lies beneath a giant waterfall on the Hidden God World of Ancients Sovereign. His appearance is plain, despite his rich robes and his ring-covered fingers. Although he thinks he is a leader, Yaloom is easily manipulated by others within the collective of gods and they consider him to be nothing more than a sheep.

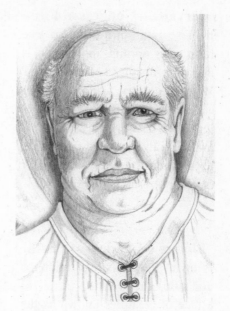

Celestria—Goddess of Evil-Natured Beasts

Celestria, the most stunning of all the gods, has elven beauty without a flaw. Her every curve and gesture are perfect. The blue of her eyes could have been stolen from the ocean and her hair cascades over her shoulders and ripples gently as she walks. Her voice, an angel's voice, is soft and sweet to the ear. Celestria is worthy to be called goddess, even if only judged on her physical features, but beware—her heart is evil and she loves only Lasidious.

❧

Bailem—God of the Sun

Bailem is the only angel to survive the God Wars. Short, chubby, and balding, his remaining brown, short hair is on the sides of his head. This angel god wears white robes with golden trim. His pure-white wings are stunningly beautiful and lay elegantly down his back outside his robes. His tail sticks out through his robe and moves wildly around when excited. Bailem can be a little too serious at any given moment, but has the ability to lighten up when the mood strikes him. All in all, he is a peaceful being.

❧

Jervaise—Goddess of Fire

Jervaise is a spirit with no true form. Her normal appearance is that of a floating ball of energy. When necessary, she can materialize into a beautiful ghostly being when dealing with the others in the collective. However, she doesn't make it a habit to appear to her followers on the worlds.

C３

Lictina—Goddess of Earth

Prior to Lictina's ascension to godhood, she was the queen of a race of creatures known as the Lizardians. A peaceful being, her job is to make adjustments that will ensure the land masses on each world continue to shift the way they need to. This constant shifting ensures that each world remains stable and serves to release the tension that builds at the center of each world's core. Many of Lictina's followers live on the World of Trollcom. Lictina, as you can imagine by the name of her race, looks like a lizard. She does, however stand erect on two legs and wears elegant looking robes lined with gems. She keeps her hood up at all times. The goddess is self-conscious of her appearance while around the others of the collective.

C３

Owain—God of Water

Owain is responsible to govern the worlds' water supplies. He is very short with long dark hair. His eyes are black and he wears soft blue-colored suits, not being a fan of robes. Owain's parents were also dwarfs and gods, but held little power compared to many of the other gods prior to the God Wars. His mother and father were destroyed in the wars but had enough foresight to place Owain in the protective custody of the collective prior to their destruction.

C３

Calla—Goddess of Truth

Calla has always been a god and is almost as old as Bassorine. But despite her age, she is not nearly as powerful as some of the others. Without accepting the collective's offer to join, she would have perished during the God Wars. She is human in appearance and wears dresses of lace. Calla is not stunningly gorgeous, but she is far from ugly. Calla's title is also her function among the gods.

C３

Helmep—God of Healing

Helmep was a human healer before his ascension. He lived and died nearly 900,000 years ago on a world called Gosslain in the Helgias Galaxy billions of light years from old Earth. He ascended just after his death because of Bassorine's desire to keep him around. Helmep was one of Bassorine's faithful while living on his world and it was this faith that gave him the blessing of godhood. Helmep is the weakest of all the gods within the *Farendrite Collective* and serves as the deity which many of the healers on the World of Harvestom serve. He is handsome, well-built, has short blonde hair, and hazel eyes. In white robes with dark trimmed accents, Helmep is known for his kind heart.

C&#x3;

Keylom—God of Peace and of Good-Natured Beasts

Keylom was a mild-mannered centaur prior to ascending to godhood. Part horse and part elf, his long dark hair covers his pointed ears and runs down the back of his vest-covered torso. His elfin face is handsome with a small goatee. The bottom portion of his body is that of a beautiful black stallion with a golden blanket draped across his back. Keylom keeps his anatomy well groomed and has the responsibility of establishing peace in times of distress.

C&#x3;

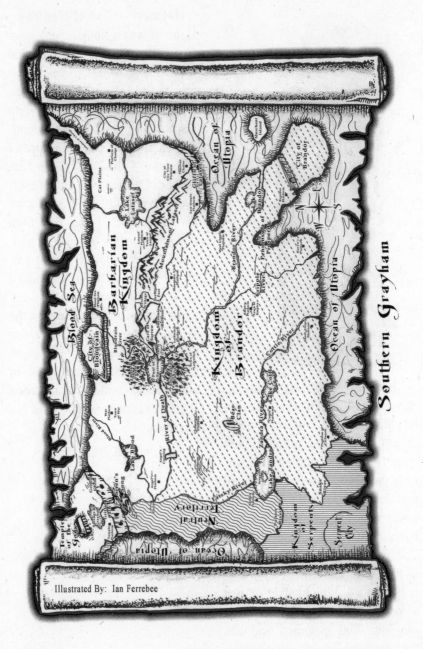

Southern Grayham

All Maps

Illustrated by Ian Ferrebee

Boyafed - Leader of the Dark Order

Illustration by Kathleen Stone

Introduction

The night was a miserable collection of moments in which to visit the forest... the sounds of anything that moved echoed between the hardened trees, their petrified trunks acting as sounding boards, making it nearly impossible to tell which direction the noises were reflected from. The slightest flap of a wing, skitter of a beetle, snapping of a twig... all heightened the tension within the warrior's mind.

With each step, Boyafed nervously pushed forward, aimlessly looking for the tree of Balecut. With his elven eyes, he searched the shadowy outlines for the beasts he knew were hidden in the darkness.

They were called Tricksters—devious creatures with the ability to teleport so rapidly, it was nearly impossible to bury a sword deep enough to kill one. Hideous game players with the features of gremlins, only taller than most of their cousins by a foot or so, they toyed with their victims before administering a grisly death... thus their descriptive, if gruesome, name.

Shalee Goodrich - Queen of Brandor

Illustration by Angela Woods

Chapter 1

𝔄 𝔏𝔦𝔱𝔱𝔩𝔢 𝔓𝔞𝔶𝔫𝔢

Black skies threatened the land below as the clouds continued to rumble with rage-filled curses. The morning had been unkind to Western Luvelles, punishing the terrain with pebble-sized hail and earth-scarring strikes of electrical fury. The forest had taken the brunt of the storm, the high winds abusing many of the tall evergreen trees, causing their branches to fall heavily to the ground. Countless mud-filled puddles could hardly be avoided, staining the white dress of a severely injured woman.

Shalee Goodrich, powerful sorceress and queen to the Kingdom of Brandor, gritted her teeth in agony. Her moans could be heard as she crawled along the muddy road leading away from the Swamp. The open wound across her abdomen marked an easy trail to follow for the dark figure stalking her. Her flight had slowed and now, the once-sporadic speckled drops of blood were turning into smaller coin-shaped areas of saturated earth.

The hunter knew his prey was beginning to tire. He smiled as he bent down, rubbing his hand across the stained dirt.

"You can't run forever," he whispered. "Your blood gives you away! It didn't have to end, but I'm going to miss you!" Methodically, he rubbed the essence of her life between his fingertips and tasted it.

Shalee crawled off the road and into the forest. Her forearms were torn from the gravel embedded in her skin. Her teeth chattered uncontrollably as her body continued to lose its heat, but she managed to force herself into an upright position against a large stone. The blade of her assailant had made a clean cut. She tried using her magic to cauterize the wound, but failed.

Why can't I use my magic? Her mind screamed for answers, but none could be found. Again she closed her eyes and tried to teleport. Nothing—there was no escape. *I've got to get out of here. He's going to kill me.*

It wasn't long before her attacker stood above her, looking down with eyes full of evil intent.

Allow me to take you back 80 Peaks of Bailem

Early Bailem
The City of Brandor

Southern Grayham

The city of Brandor, an architectural wonder despite its lack of certain creature comforts—electricity, running water, and so much more—reminded both the king and queen of what they both would have imagined King Arthur's Camelot to look like prior to each of them being stolen or rather, ripped away, from their true home, Earth.

The rest of their kingdom, a hodgepodge of many different forms of architecture, suffered in grandeur. All, that is, but the city of West Utopia, an elegant city with a Romanesque feel. Because of this, it had a much higher class of people living there than the rest of the kingdom. It was as if King Arthur, Caesar, and Robin Hood all got together and said: "Let's make a mess while building a kingdom!"

Both Sam and Shalee agreed that this lack of consistency needed to be fixed once the war George Nailer had instigated was over, and even then, only after the Crystal Moon's pieces were joined together again and resting inside the Temple of the Gods. This renovation of the kingdom would put Shalee's education as an architect—back on earth—to the test.

But since Earth had been destroyed, thanks to the 'so-called' gods and their ridiculous God Wars—a series of wars which destroyed the entire cosmos—this rugged world of Grayham was now their home, whether they liked it or not, and they would need to find a way to leave behind the past and do whatever it took to make do in their current situation.

But hey… easier said than done… right?

"My king… my queen," Michael said confidently as he took a knee. A strong, bold man, well-groomed and the General Absolute of Brandor's army, he wore his best chain armor with a black cape draped across his back. The Crest of Brandor was positioned at the cape's center—a red shield with gold outlined edges and a golden scale at the shield's center to symbolize the kingdom's belief in justice.

"Speak, Michael. What news do you bring us today?" Sam pushed himself clear of his heavy royal chair. The king was large, or at least considered large for a human, but still seemed small in stature compared to most of the barbarians of the north. Sam's short, dark hair and brown eyes complimented a strong, handsome face which rested atop a 6'4", 275-pound, well-defined frame, all thanks to a god's gifts—Mosley—the new wolf-god of War.

Michael answered. "The news I bring is all good, my king. The army's advance on Bloodvain is going well. The Barbarian people are surrendering as news of Senchae's death is spreading. Of course, there are those who've chosen to fight, but their numbers are scattered. They're disorganized with no real battle plan. They've proven to be no match for our forces. It's only a matter of moments before all of Southern Grayham lives in service to you, my king."

Sam leaned forward. "And have the two missing pieces of the Crystal Moon been found yet?"

"No… we've searched everywhere and still continue to search. Seth's underground kingdom is massive and the Serpent King had no idea George hid the crystals there. But there is news I believe will benefit our kingdom."

"And… this news is?"

"Seth himself, in an effort to show his willingness to cooperate, has led the army to a deep shaft full of coin. Apparently, the serpents have no use for coin."

"What…why would Seth have a shaft full of coin in the first place, and why would the snakes care about saving coin if they have no need for it?"

Michael grinned as he responded. "Seth's kind has always sold their poisons and various forms of plant life, which grow in the marsh, to Merchant Island. They do this to keep men from crossing their borders. For them, it's not about the coin… it's about being left alone. Because of this, for thousands of seasons they've just been throwing it all into a pit after selling their goods. I've ordered it all to be brought back to Brandor and put into the royal vaults. But I fear we won't have enough room to hold it all."

Pushing his hands through his hair, Sam began to chuckle. "This is what I consider a pleasant problem to have. I'll order new vaults to be built. How many do you think we'll need?"

Again, Michael grinned.

"I would say that another twenty-five or so should do, but you may want to make them twice as large, my king."

Sam leaned back in his throne. "Holy garesh… there's that much? If this is indeed the case, our kingdom will never lack for anything again. We'll be able to make the upgrades not only to Brandor, but the rest of the kingdom as well."

Sam rose from his throne and motioned for Michael to stand from his kneeled position. Moving to look out the window to the city below, Sam sighed as he watched the everyday common man moving along the meticulously placed cobblestone streets and enjoyed the thought that their pain would soon be over. Their loved ones would return to them and life could now move forward, hopefully in peace.

Sam pushed his hands through his hair again and enjoyed a deep breath full of Grayham's crisp, clean air as a gentle breeze found its way through the heavy stone window and onto his face.

"Finally… some good news, General," Sam said while exhaling methodically. "This coin will be a blessing for everyone. I was worried there would be more needless bloodshed before the barbarians stopped fighting. The families of our men will be happy to know it's only a matter of moments before their loved ones return home. I imagine there's enough coin to reward each man for their service, based on what you've just told me?"

"There is more than enough to reward the men for a hundred lives lived, my king."

Sam shook his head in disbelief. "It's hard to envision that kind of coin. I look forward to seeing this myself. We'll need to get the new vaults built quickly."

"But what about George?" Shalee interrupted, wanting answers of her own.

The queen, as always, was stunning, her fashion sense impeccable. The soft blue gown she wore only managed to compliment the natural glow caused by her pregnancy. She stood from her throne, pushed back her long blonde hair and, after taking Precious into her hand, tapped the staff's butt end on the throne room's stone floor. She continued to speak as she looked at the General through her beautiful blue eyes.

"The coin sounds great, General, but do you know where George is? Does anyone know where Kepler is? How about both of his brothers, for that matter? They are enemies to all of Southern Grayham. We need to find them and keep them from hurting anyone else. This whole war was their creation in the first place."

Michael's mood changed as his report of the kingdom's new-found fortune was instantly overshadowed by George and Kepler's disappearances.

"My queen, I have assigned five hundred men to hunt down Kepler and his brothers, and I have assigned another two hundred to do nothing but search for George. It's only a matter of moments before they turn up."

Shalee moved next to Sam.

"Michael, I want to make sure everything is peaceful before our baby is born." She touched her stomach. "I don't want any child of mine being born into a world with this kind of hate existing in it. Two hundred men aren't enough to fight against George's power."

"Yes, my queen, I understand. I'll double the numbers in the search party." He turned to Sam. "What other orders would you give, my king?"

Sam motioned for everyone to clear the room except for Michael and Shalee. Once the castle's staff was gone, he continued.

"There's no one here now. Let's talk as friends for a moment."

"Okay... what's on your mind, Sam?"

"You know I've commanded all the members of the Senate to come to Brandor. I want to discuss how we should proceed before giving any more orders. I've called the Senate here because I personally think we need to have the members of our government go into the Barbarian kingdom of Bloodvain and spread the word that we wish to live with them in peace. They'll need to take an offering of some kind and give one to each of the Barbarian nobles. I think it would be wise to make sure their royal families are still treated as royalty."

Michael cut in. "You want us to treat them as royalty? Sire, this sounds outrageous, if you ask me. I don't think Senchae Bloodvain would have done the same for Brandor's nobles if he had been the one to win the war."

"Exactly. That's why it's important for us to do this. I want them to see that we respect their people. I also want to meet with each of their nobles and determine who among them would be the best choices as new members of our Senate. I plan on selecting ten of them myself and give each one of them their own personal seat within the courts of Brandor. It's important that the Barbarian people are represented within a newly united Southern Grayham."

Michael just stood silently. Shalee saw the confusion on his face.

"What's bothering you, Michael? Why so quiet?"

"I suppose I've never thought of the Barbarians as becoming members of our Senate. The senators themselves will have much to say about this. I'm sure your ideas won't be welcomed with open arms, Sam."

The king thought a moment. "Let me ask you something, Michael. If you were a Barbarian and you hated the people of the south, not to mention the fact that you were taught to hate them since childhood, wouldn't you hate them even more if your people were left out of the day-to-day functions of a government that had been forced down your throat? Think about it for a moment. How would you feel? Don't you think you would find it easier to accept the changes in your life if you had a voice within this new government?"

After spending a while pondering his king's opinion, Michael finally responded, "I think your logic makes sense. I agree with what you've said. I don't like it, but I agree. It will take some moments for my mind to adjust. I'll make the men of our army understand because I trust the two of you, but this is going to be a tough picture you'll need to paint before the Senate buys off on your ideas."

"Don't worry about them," Shalee said with a faint smile. "After Sam reminds the Senate that it was the gods' decision for us to come into this world and create a peaceful empire, they'll see things our way. Besides, we're still at war until Sam declares otherwise. Sam can do as he pleases, and the Senate will have no choice but to comply."

Michael patted Sam on the shoulder. "I do hope you handle this matter with far more tact than our lovely queen has just suggested."

Sam laughed as he pulled Shalee close.

"Our queen is definitely spirited. I'm sure I'll figure something out before I address the members of the Senate."

Michael sighed. "I often forget the two of you have such powerful friends backing your positions as king and queen. Not many men have the gods on their side. Please forgive me... I don't completely understand how the mind of a woman from Earth works. Shalee, forgive my anxiety when you talk assertively. I still find myself getting used to you!"

Shalee moved to Michael and gave him a hug, followed by a quick wink.

"There's no forgiveness necessary. I'm sure it's not just the women from Earth that the men from Grayham don't understand. Women are pretty much the same here as they were back home, and as all good women do, we should keep our men guessing. You know, keep you wondering if you'll ever figure us out."

Michael gave a half-hearted smile, and because of his discomfort with the queen's demeanor, he turned to Sam and brought the tone of the meeting back to formality.

"As for me, my king, you both have my full support and I agree that it's best to give the Barbarian people a voice. I believe this will work to change their perception that the people of Brandor are nothing more than common swine. But as I've already said, you have your work cut out for you."

"Let's hope we're right, General. Let me know when you've found George and Kepler."

"Yes, my king."

Late Bailem, Three Days Later
The Griffon's Platform
The Temple of the Gods on Southern Grayham

Sam ordered four men to go to the Temple of the Gods after asking Shalee for a scroll the men could use to teleport there. When the queen asked why, all the king would say was that he had a surprise for her. After Shalee explained how the scroll worked, the king took the men out into the royal garden and gave his orders.

Both Sam and Shalee now sat at a small wooden table close to the edge of the Griffon's Platform which overlooked all of Southern Grayham. Cooked hen was on the menu and the royal chef was personally there to serve them. Once the meal was uncovered, Sam watched the smile appear on his queen's face.

"I'm glad you like it, Shalee. I'm also glad you were able to teleport us here. We haven't had many moments to ourselves since our arrival on this world. I just wanted you to understand how much I love you. I couldn't think of any place more romantic."

"This was a lovely idea! You've outdone yourself."

She stood from her chair and moved to him, holding his eyes within her gaze as she approached. She leaned over and the passion she felt for her king could be seen as she prepared to thank him. The men standing guard at the edges of the platform quickly turned their backs to allow for privacy, but the royal chef simply smiled and quietly moved to a better position to enjoy the romance of the moment.

Her lips were soft and tasted like melon. Her tongue gently accented the mood and Sam's heart melted as she softly nibbled not only his bottom lip, but the top of his right ear as well. He trembled and forgot everything around him. When finally Shalee moved back, she once again held his eyes with hers until she settled back into her seat.

The chef could not contain his excitement and he spoke, ruining the mood. "Well done, my queen," he shouted. "Bravo! It's nice to know that my king and his lovely queen share such an incredible love between them!"

Shalee blushed as Sam turned to give the chef a look. "Thomas, don't you have something better to do than spend your moments watching us?"

"My apologies, my king... I shall fetch some wine."

As Sam watched Thomas move to the far side of the platform, he took a moment to marvel at the gigantic temple doors beyond. His genius mind could remember in vivid detail how he felt the first moment he saw the massive hinges. Each door was nearly seventy-five feet tall and formed an arch toward each other at the top. He remembered thinking how heavy they must be. At almost two feet thick he could only imagine the sound they would make if one of them were to slam into the wall when opened.

Shalee lifted her glass from the table and moved to take a look around. The view was breathtaking, one of those moments where her soul had to take it all in. The Temple of the Gods sat back from the edge of Griffon Falls quite a ways. The water of the falls fell over 3,500 feet to the land below and was fed by a series of natural springs that surfaced all across the top of the plateau and eventually pooled together before flowing over the edge. Many different types of beautiful flowers, as well as other forms of vegetation which she had grown accustomed to seeing since their arrival on Grayham, bloomed around each of these pools. The sight was glorious and set the perfect mood for a wonderful date with her incredible husband.

After dinner, Sam had the men clear the table. Once they teleported back to Brandor as ordered, Sam moved to the edge of the platform and rang the bell.

"I have a surprise for you. Do you remember the first time we rode the griffon and you were sound asleep? You know... the day you threw your fit after our arrival?"

"How could I remember something I slept through? I've always regretted missing out on that experience."

"Well, now you'll have the chance to make up for it."

Shalee smiled and pushed up against him. "Just take a look at you, Sam Goodrich. Who would have ever guessed you had a romantic bone somewhere inside that delicious body of yours?"

Sam used his genius intellect to remember Shalee's exact words when she found out they would need to ride the griffon to get to Brandor for the first time.

Shalee had shouted at Mosley, "If you think I'm going to ride some giant whatever-it-is, you've got another thing coming. I'm not about to get on some creepy winged thingy. I don't know how to ride stuff like that. Do they bite? I just bet they bite! Oh, my gosh, do they smell? What if I can't handle the stench?"

Mosley had become sick of Shalee's ranting that day. The wolf breathed on her face and she immediately fell asleep. Her body slumped onto the same platform where they now stood.

The wolf had said, "She will sleep for a while. I'm sure she'll be far more pleasant when she's had a chance to adjust. Are all the women from Earth like this one?"

Sam had smiled at the wolf that day and responded, "Only the ones worth keeping. I have to admit, I find her very attractive. I like her sassiness. You'll grow to like her, Mosley... besides, she's just a tad bit stressed right now. That's all."

"I hope you're right, Sam."

Sam's thoughts returned to the present.

He grinned at the pleasant feeling of the memory and pulled Shalee close. He was kissing her when Soresym crested the cliff's ledge. The king reacted quickly and grabbed the railing surrounding the platform as the massive wings of the Griffon stirred the evening air with tremendous force. The majestic beast lowered himself to the landing platform. Shalee couldn't contain her excitement and ran toward Soresym, touching his feather-covered neck as he knelt down.

"It's good to see you, Soresym! I think of you often."

"And I you, child. Are you ready to enjoy the flight you missed?"

"Thank you for doing this for me, Soresym," Sam said as he approached. "I cannot express how much I appreciate you for this."

"You're welcome, King of Brandor... anything for a friend."

Sam lifted Shalee onto the griffon's back, and then climbed up. He tied both himself and his queen in with heavy leather straps and pulled her close to prepare for takeoff. Majestically, the beast walked to the edge of the platform. Sam smiled as he looked down. Shalee lifted her arms in the air and screamed as they fell from the cliff's ledge toward the land below.

Soresym - A Griffon

Illustration by Kathleen Stone

Soresym kept his wings tightly folded as the ground approached, waiting until the last possible moment before he spread them and allowed the wind to be captured beneath his feathers. They swooped to a position just above the mist of the falls. Both Sam and Shalee enjoyed the adrenaline rush and the coolness of the mist was refreshing.

Shalee shouted, "Oohhh, my gosh, Sam... this is the best date ever!"

Sam reached around her waist and pulled her tightly to him. He looked out across the countryside as it passed swiftly beneath. After a while, the king leaned in and put his mouth close to the queen's ear.

"I love you, baby!"

Shalee turned her head and after tasting his lips, responded, "I love you too, hon."

Western Luvelles
The Dark Chancellor's Dark Tower-Palace

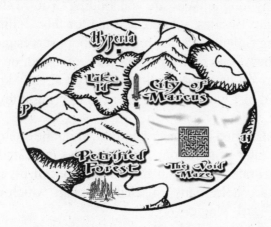

Chancellor Marcus Id stormed into the highest level of his tall dark tower-palace. He threw his black cape, marked with the Order's symbol, and watched it fly across the room. Despite the evil Chancellor's desire for the cape to hit the wall, the magic cloth refused to be abused and adjusted its own course, peacefully hanging itself up.

Marcus grunted with disappointment, his brown eyes cold, tension filling his lanky limbs beneath the confines of his golden shirt. His long brownish-black hair fell across his elven features as he shouted at the top of his lungs, "My brother's self-righteous attitude is becoming tiresome!"

After a moment of silence, Marcus turned and realized he was yelling at an empty room. He grunted again before lighting his pipe and shouted some more, "Gage, get your good-for-nothing backside in here before I decide to have you skinned!"

Another few moments passed before a dark-coated badger, covered in a short-fitted red robe, patiently entered the room, walking erect. He ignored the Chancellor's threat and tapped his tiny wooden cane on the cold stones of the tower-palace floor, taking his own sweet moments. "Would you stop shouting? Just relax a bit, will you? Stick to the plan. Acting this way will accomplish nothing."

"Careful, Gage. You should watch your tongue. I'm not in the mood to be argued with!"

"Watch my tongue! Who are you kidding? You're always in the mood to fight. Besides, you created me for this. Telling you that you're acting ridiculous is my job. If memory serves me right, and it always does, you created me to speak my mind, or rather, our mind, when you have these idiotic fits. You already know you're acting stupid or I wouldn't feel the need to bring it to your attention."

Marcus slammed his boney hand down on the stone table resting at the center of the room. The table was large and sat within a coldly decorated, private bedroom chamber of his palace. The stone's surface held many chiseled markings which represented the ways of Dark Magic.

"Then you obviously know what I'm thinking now!" Marcus said as the smoke from his pipe drifted past the anger in his eyes.

Gage's furry face instantly showed his concern. He hurried across the floor—a task hard for a badger to do while walking upright on his hind legs—and jumped onto the table. The badger pounded the butt of his cane hard against the stone surface.

"It's too early to try 'n kill your brothers—either of them, no matter how badly you desire this! You don't have the power yet!"

"Gregory is no match for my power. I could kill Gregory with little trouble. I should also destroy his precious city of glass while I'm at it! Why someone would want to live in a glass palace is beyond me… his goodness sickens me!"

Gage growled at Marcus, and then looked up at the dark, petrified wood rafters spanning the length of the room. "Would you stop this? We both know it isn't Gregory you're worried about. It's the Head Master you fear."

Marcus snapped his head around and stormed toward the window. He took a long deep breath and looked toward the temple's roof, which completely surrounded his tower-palace below. Taking a moment to admire the dismal-looking city which he had named after himself, he finally responded.

"I fear no one, not even Brayson! I think I could defeat him."

The badger just gave Marcus a look and waited for a response.

"Well... so what if I am afraid of Brayson! I don't need to have you pointing it out to me. My powers have grown, and maybe it's the right moment to challenge him."

The badger sat down on the table's stone surface. Tracing the etched makings with his claw, he responded, "You must wait. If you're wrong about your ability to defeat him, then you'll be dead, and for what... simply because you have no patience! Head Master Brayson hasn't taken a new Mystic-Learner in over twenty seasons now. You must wait for this to happen. I'm sure it will be soon."

"How can you be so sure? Brayson doesn't seem to be in a hurry to find another student. How am I going to get my hands on his spell? Without it, I can't open the chest that holds the key."

Marcus thought back to the confrontation he'd had with Brayson's last Mystic-Learner.

Hettolyn, a young Halfling, was making his way to Brayson's shrine after receiving the secret spell from the Head Master. The shrine, located on the southern end of the Head Master's Island, served the most important purpose throughout all of Luvelles.

Marcus stopped Hettolyn just prior to his arrival. The shrine housed a magically-locked chest and the spell was the only thing that would open it... the key to the Source was inside.

"Where do you think you're going, boy?" the Dark Chancellor asked, appearing in front of Hettolyn.

"Aahhhh... you startled me! Who are you, sir?"

"*Who* doesn't matter. You and I have something to discuss."

"I see," the young Halfling responded with nervous conviction. "Then I suppose it doesn't matter what I'm doing here, or where I'm going, if it doesn't matter who you are."

Marcus laughed. "You're right, it *doesn't* matter. It's what you have that matters and what you have, you're going to give to me."

Marcus remembered the fear in Hettolyn's eyes as he lifted his hand and bound the young Halfling with his magic.

"Please, let me go! I have nothing of value to give you. I have nothing other than the clothes on my back."

"How could you possibly not know who I am, boy?"

"I'm sorry, I've never heard of you. Or at least, I don't think I have, since you won't reveal your name. I've never seen you before. You have the wrong man. You must be waiting for someone else."

"What's your name, boy?

"I'm called Hettolyn, from Equality."

"Ha, Equality is a city full of weak minds. Are you also weak, Hettolyn? Is your mind strong enough to resist me?"

"I believe that I'm strong, sir. You have my name, now why do you bind me?"

"How about we find out how strong you are, Hettolyn? Today, you're going to recite for me the spell my brother gave you to unlock his precious chest. Today, you're going to die if I don't lay my hands on the key to the Source."

"I have no idea what you're speaking about! I have a family. Please... they need me!"

"Don't lie to me, boy. I know you seek the key resting inside your precious Master Brayson's chest. You seek your chance to meet with the Source. You wish to look into the Eye of Magic. I think we both know I have the right man."

"As I have said, I don't know anything about these things!"

"We shall see." Marcus lifted his hands.

Marcus shook his head. The Halfling had proven to be unforthcoming. He gave his life to protect Brayson's secret spell and the Dark Chancellor destroyed his body.

"Gage, that spell is the gateway to all my desires. Once I have it, I can get the key and gain access to the Source. Only then will I be able to rule all of Luvelles."

Gage showed all his sharp teeth and once again tapped his cane hard against the table. His tone was firm as he spoke. "You know the key is worth the wait! Controlling this world means everything to you! Only the Source can give you the power you seek and without this power, you'll be unable to kill the Head Master."

"I already know this, Goswig!"

"Then why are we talking about it?"

"Because all this waiting around, while my brother basks in his glory, is killing me! Brayson is so pompous… I want to rip that arrogant smile right off his face and feed it to the Krape Lords. It's absurd that he remains neutral in all things. I don't understand how someone could avoid choosing a side. At least Gregory, no matter how vexatious he is, has chosen to wallow in all his goodness."

Gage shook his head before responding. "Your impatience solves nothing. It won't be long before he has a new Mystic-Learner and he'll do the same thing he's always done."

Marcus smiled wickedly. "Yes… he'll give his Mystic-Learner the spell. And, as always, the spell will only be able to be spoken once before it's forgotten. All I need to do is force Brayson's Mystic-Learner to speak the spell's words to me. Once I have them, I can get past his magic and gain access to the key."

"You're right," Gage snapped, "but you might want to be a bit more patient when the moment presents itself. You're supposed to get the information before you kill them, ya know!"

"You're really testing me, Goswig! I already know this," Marcus said before taking another drag of his pipe.

Gage ignored him. "Ha! Your anger will subside. Besides, once you've spoken with the Source, you'll be all powerful—without rival." The Goswig swallowed hard at the thought of his words and shook his furry head in disgust, careful not to allow Marcus to see his disapproval. He would have continued to dwell on his dislike for Marcus's evil ways, but he was distracted and managed to capture another thought from Marcus's mind. The thought was ridiculous, the badger had to laugh.

"What's so funny?" Marcus sneered.

After collecting his thoughts, Gage responded. "Well… I guess I find it humorous you call your brother pompous, when you were just thinking that you're the only brother vain enough to name a city after yourself. I would call that fairly pompous—not to mention, completely vain, wouldn't you?"

"Careful, Goswig, you're walking on thin ice with me right now."

"Don't get mad at me! You're the one who thought it."

Marcus gave Gage a look of warning and pointed his boney finger in the badger's direction.

"Okay, okay, okay!" the badger said.

Gage watched as Marcus left the room. The Goswig breathed deeply and thought, *I don't like this job! There's too much hate in your heart. Marcus... you make my head hurt.*

Kebble's Kettle
The Village of Floren

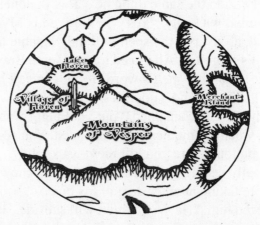

George Nailer rushed into his room, his deep blue eyes full of anxiety. The day had finally come to leave Kebble's inn.

"Athena... Athena, where are you?" Shutting the door, the mage scanned the empty room. "We need to hurry. This is the day we've been waiting for."

"Honey, just relax," Athena said from behind the washroom door. "I'll be ready in a moment. Besides, you don't want to look over-anxious... you said so yourself."

Athena's light-blue eyes carried a sense of joy. Her rounded belly was starting to show the life the couple had created back on Grayham. She could only smile as she brushed her long blonde hair with an ivory-handled brush, gazing in the mirror.

"I know what I said," George barked, "but that doesn't change the fact that I am anxious and want to get going! We've been stuck here at this damn inn far too long! It's about time that piece of garesh sent word for us to come see him."

Athena - Mrs. George Nailer

Illustration by Kathleen Stone

Athena poked her head out the door. "George Nailer, you watch that mouth of yours! You know I hate it when you speak so foul. And there you go again, using that word 'time' again. You know there is no such thing."

"Bah," George whispered, careful not to allow Athena to hear. "Yes, dear. I'm sure I meant to say, I'm glad the 'moment' has arrived for the Head Master to send word for us. We're supposed to meet and find out where the families' new homes are going to be."

Athena looked back into the mirror and smiled. She knew it was hard for her husband to change his old habits after a life filled with such nasty language. Taking a deep breath, she continued to brush her hair and responded, "I know... you're right... I agree, I'm also glad the moment has come, but the family has enjoyed our stay here. Kebble has been more than pleasant. I thank the gods you had enough coin to keep us sheltered for so long. I can't imagine what my family would have done if you didn't."

"The gods had nothing to do with it," George said as he shifted from one foot to another. He knew his wealth had come at Amar's expense. He also knew it was Lasidious who, acting as Amar, convinced the Head Master to give him the dead mage's riches.

He had killed Amar on Grayham just outside the City of Champions's gates and eaten Amar's heart. This brutal night of murder had given George the powers he currently possessed. Eating the heart before Amar's soul left for the Book of Immortality was the only way to steal his power. Despite the foul taste, he had managed to choke down the bloody meal without incident.

"Coin isn't an issue," he continued. "I've told you that more than once. You need to stop worrying. I'm just ready to move on and get settled. This inn has been an okay place to crash, but I think we need to have our own space. I want to get past this damn pit stop."

"What's a pit stop? And I'm sure we haven't crashed into anything. Some of the things you say are so strange. I have trouble understanding how you talk at moments. Did all the people from Earth talk like you?" She laid down her brush and smiled. "Mother said you confused her the other day. She said you spoke of how much you missed your car and something called a plane. I've been meaning to ask you about them."

Rolling his eyes, George sat heavily on the edge of the bed and threw himself back with a flop. "Babe, you're killing me! It's nothing worth talking about right now. Don't worry about it. Just hurry up so we can get going. I'm sure you look stunning. Can we go now?"

"Yes, but this doesn't mean I won't ask again later."

"Well, later is better." He stood up, moved into the washroom and pulled her close. "I love you."

She smiled and lowered her head against his chest, her favorite spot to be. "I love you, too. I'll be ready soon. I want to look beautiful for you."

As Athena and George left the inn, they said goodbye to Kebble. As always, the short, plump elf lifted his pipe into the air and happily bid them farewell. "Be careful... come back in one piece," he joked. His rosy cheeks and yellowish smoke-stained mustache complemented his jovial smile.

Kepler, George's solid black, undead, demon-jaguar friend with red glowing eyes was napping outside. As the couple exited the front doors, the demon stood up and stretched his massive form, his powerful muscles rippling beneath his coat. The top of the giant cat's back was eye-level with George, and his weight, when standing, bent the planks of the porch everywhere his giant paws rested.

"Where're we off to?" the demon said with a yawn.

"The Head Master sent for us," George responded. "We're supposed to meet him at his school at the center of the village."

"Finally, some action. Let's get going. I hope he's got something for us to do. If I spend another moment lying on this porch, I'll lose my mind!"

George nodded. "I agree with you, big guy. I'm sure things are about to change."

The Village of Floren had been their home for the last 115 Peaks of Bailem. After George and Athena's family left Grayham, George and Kepler had maintained a low profile on Luvelles. It was necessary to stay out of the spotlight since the collective of the gods had no idea where they had gone—all, that is, except Lasidious and Celestria.

After George killed the witches Celestria had stayed with during her pregnancy, there had been no need to use any form of powerful magic. He had successfully retrieved Lasidious's newborn son from the witches' home and had been playing uncle ever since. Today was the day he had been waiting for.

Susanne, Athena's sister, had done a wonderful job adapting to motherhood, despite the fact she had never given birth. A perfect deception had been placed in Susanne's mind and she believed with her whole heart that she was the true mother of a god's son.

The rest of Athena's family had also been given a vision to create the same belief. There was no doubt in anyone's mind that Susanne was the child's mother, and the façade had worked perfectly.

These visions had been projected into their minds by the rat, Maldwin, at George's request. He hated lying to Athena and her family as much as he hated leaving Maldwin behind on Grayham, but knew it was for the best. The rat was now living happily with his large rodent family in his new home, and as for Athena's family, well, they never seemed happier.

George had given Lasidious and Celestria's son the name Garrin. Garrin's birth broke the most sacred rule within the Book of Immortality—a rule created by the gods to avoid a power struggle between those of the collective. The rule forbade two gods from having a child, and Gabriel, the Book of Immortality, was in charge of enforcing this rule. But the Book could not enforce a rule without the knowledge of a rule being broken.

Lasidious, staying true to form and doing what a God of Mischief does best, had found a way to break this rule with his evil lover, Celestria. Both the conception and the birth of their son had been planned for more than 14,000 seasons and special precautions had been made to keep the Book of Immortality from knowing of the child's birth.

A being created by two gods with enough power between them could possess the ability to control the Book of Immortality. Gabriel would no longer be able to protect the gods from one another.

Instead, the Book would now serve only one. Chaos would be the result. All that was left for George to do was hide Garrin's existence from the gods until the baby was old enough to command his powers.

The theft of the Crystal Moon had been brilliant. Hiding its five pieces and scattering them throughout the worlds provided a beautiful distraction which would keep the gods busy while Garrin matured... or so Lasidious and Celestria hoped.

George was the other part of Lasidious's master plan. Until now, he had worked with George to create many other distractions—distractions that had caused a war on Grayham. It was now the right moments to do the same on Luvelles and once again capture the gods' attentions.

Lasidious's pact with George—the promise to retrieve his daughter's soul from the *Book of Immortality* and allow her to live once again—would continue to motivate the ex-Earthling. Lasidious had already managed to show George the way to attain large amounts of power, but on Luvelles, this level of power had been attained by many. Further attention to George's growth was necessary to achieve the god's goals.

George and Athena's family had settled in Floren. The Village of Floren was an area of highly concentrated magic. The village air smelled of it. The strongest of all who commanded the arts—both good and evil—came to Floren to begin their training. But, true to the nature of these conflicted paths, they parted ways once their training was complete.

The Head Master's school was only for those with exceptional skill... skills like the ones George had stolen from Amar. Very few were allowed to attend this school and even fewer were allowed to train under the Head Master's personal supervision.

It wasn't uncommon for a student to become severely injured while trying to command too much power. As a result, Floren had some of the finest healers available within all the worlds. Healers were given passage to Luvelles from the World of Harvestom by the Head Master himself in order to keep his students alive.

It wasn't long before George stood with Athena and Kepler at the base of the Head Master's school. The building was invisible to the naked eye. If it hadn't been for some very specific directions and detailed instructions, George would never have known they had arrived. The words to the spell which revealed the entrance were written in the Elven language. Without Kebble's help, George would not have been able to pronounce any of it.

Now he spoke with a forceful voice: ***"Aa' menle nauva calen ar' ta hwesta e' ale'quenle,"*** which meant—*May thy paths be green and the breeze on thy backs.*

When the door appeared, the mage reached out and opened it. The way inside was now revealed to the rest of the group. Once the door shut, the entrance once again vanished to the outside world.

The inside of the school was massive. A circular staircase stretched up for what seemed to be forever. Bookcases full of endless knowledge lined every wall and stretched up just as far. The furniture was made of dark heavy stone with chiseled etchings filled with gold that represented both the paths of White and Dark Magic. The floor beneath slowly changed color as if different sources of light had been placed beneath to shine through.

"They're so beautiful," Athena said as she watched many different pairings of fairies carry books from one shelf to another. "It looks as if they are reorganizing. Look, George... look at how many it takes to carry that big one. I bet there are at least seven of them."

George agreed, although he was still fascinated with the floor. He bent over to see if the light created warmth, but before he had the chance to touch it, a silver-sphere, no bigger than two fists, quickly flew up, stopped, and hovered in front of them.

"Looks like they know we're here," Kepler growled, sensing a threat.

"Finally," George said, studying the object. "Maybe it will lead us to the Head Master."

Kepler stayed guarded. "Say something to it... see if it responds. I don't get a good feeling from this... this thing!"

Athena tugged at George's robe. "I agree with Kepler. Something isn't right here. Let's leave. We can come back when someone else is here to greet us."

George rolled his eyes. He put on a smile and softly said, "Babe, don't worry. I'm sure everything will be just—"

George was unable to finish his sentence. Small electric shocks began to shoot from the ball. Kepler roared in pain as the first of these charges hit his nose. George quickly responded by throwing up a wall of force to protect them, but the ball moved through the invisible barrier as if it were not even there and once again began to shoot. Athena was hit. She cried out, begging George to protect her.

George lifted his hands. Fire erupted from the mage's fingertips. The ball quickly absorbed the magic and used the power against him, redirecting the fire at George's face. It cut through the air at a high rate of speed. George barely managed to get out of the way.

The books resting on the shelves behind him exploded from the intensity of the impact. The force knocked the visitors across the room and as they landed on the floor, it changed to the color purple. George and the now-unconscious Athena slid to a stop, but Kepler, taking the brunt of the explosion and sliding in a different direction, hit his head hard against the edge of the stone table near the spiral staircase, letting out a hellish roar. The sound was deafening. George jumped to his feet, chills running down his spine as he heard the demon's cry. Quickly, he shouted to capture the sphere's attention.

Again the sphere began to shoot its charges. and now, George was hit in the leg. Now pissed off, he screamed, "Take this, you S.O.B!" The mage blasted the ball with hundreds of magical arrows that sent the sphere crashing hard into a bookcase located at the far side of the room. The severity of the impact sent pieces—of not only the shelf, but the books as well—flying in every direction. George used his wall of force to keep Athena from being hit again, but his act of heroism left him vulnerable. The edge of a heavy book binding caught him on the temple. Dazed, he fell hard to the floor and struggled to stay alert. A moment later, the silver menace lifted from the floor and resumed its offensive.

Kepler growled as he stood up. His head was bloodied and his dark black coat was singed and saturated with his own demon blood. The cut created by his impact with the stone table's heavy leg was not deep, but it was a bleeder.

"We can't take much more of this, George," he shouted, but George was unable to respond. Knowing now that it was up to him, and without hesitation, the giant cat launched into the air. As he came down, the demon hit the sphere hard with one of his powerful claws. The ball bounced and rolled across the now yellow-colored floor, which reflected off the sphere's shiny surface. A metallic clanking pierced the air as it did. Kepler followed. Covering the distance quickly, he pounced hard onto the enemy, putting all his weight on top to hold it down. He turned to yell, "George, get over—"

Suddenly the demon cat roared in pain, unable to finish his call for help. He pulled his massive claws clear of the ball's surface as blood began to pour from the many punctured holes in his right front paw.

Kepler's painful scream filled the room with such powerful reverberations that many books fell clear of their shelves. The roar served to clear George's mind and helped him to regain his composure. The mage grabbed the bookshelf nearest him and used it as a crutch to get to his feet. As he did, he saw Athena lying motionless behind the wall of force. His anger was now hatred for his enemy. Finding the ball, he shouted for Kepler to stand clear. The giant cat moved, quickly limping across the room and leaving a trail of black demon blood.

Before George could take the offensive, the sphere retracted its large, thick needles and moved to hover just outside the invisible wall protecting Athena. Waking from the pain, Athena screamed as another electrical charge passed through her pocket of invisible protection and hit her belly. Seeing this, George's emotions took over and fueled his powers to a level he had never experienced.

Kepler, sensing that George's use of magic was going to be dangerous, leaped skyward and with his massive claws, ripped into the spiral staircase. He hung suspended, twisting his massive head around, and watched as George's hands lifted to release his wicked magic. A powerful wave of water blasted from George's fingertips. The force of the gush was tremendous. The anger George felt, knowing his wife and unborn baby were in danger, only added to the magic's velocity.

The torrential force pushed the ball backward, smashing it hard against the bookshelves before allowing it to fall. The orb landed with a splash and sunk to the now pink-colored floor, illuminating the water with an eerie glow as it sloshed around. The wave had not only destroyed the ball, but also everything which had been sitting on this lower level of the tower.

Debris covered the water's surface, waist-high. Beneath the now burgundy-colored liquid, the damaged sphere exploded, sending a powerful fountain of water and debris skyward. Kepler was the one to suffer. Besides becoming drenched, the demon was clubbed with many solid objects and, as a result, fell heavily, landing with a huge splash which displaced enough water that a finer cannon-ball could not have been performed if practiced over and over.

George, seeing the fight had ended, quickly lowered his pocket of protection and pushed through the debris to get to Athena. He submerged beneath the water and, to his delight, found his beautiful wife sitting well-protected within her bubble of force. He gave Athena a wink, stood up, and checked on the gigantic wet pussy-cat. Seeing that the jaguar would live, he used his magic to open the door and siphoned the water out of the school. Once he was completely certain there were no other threats coming, he released Athena from her protective barrier.

From high above, a voice called out, "Well done… ha, ha, ha… well done, George!" A figure in a red robe began to slowly descend, not using the spiral staircase, but floating towards them in mid-air. The man removed his hood and George could see he had short brown hair and a goatee. He appeared to be an older man, maybe fifty-five or sixty seasons, with elven features, something George had become accustomed to seeing since the families' arrival on Luvelles. George could only imagine how old this guy actually was, since other elves—elves that also looked his age—were already hundreds of seasons old.

"Not bad for your first lesson. I think you've handled yourself wonderfully. Amar said you would be a worthy Mystic-Learner. I'm sure you can understand my desire to see this for myself."

George trudged through what was left of the watery mess, now only ankle-high with a red glow. He pushed Athena's hair clear of her face to make sure she was okay before responding.

"Who the hell are you?" he shouted, turning back to the red-robed man.

"I don't know of this hell you speak of, but I think you already know who I am, George."

"Yeah, I suppose I do. Well, that's just great! My wife is pregnant, you son of a—"

"Now, now, now, let's not be so hasty, George. You're assuming I didn't know she was pregnant. I know plenty. I would never send you up against something strong enough to do any real damage, to you, or your wife... well... well, to your wife, anyway. The sphere knew to use its weaker magic on Athena. The charges that hit her would not have done any real damage to her or the baby.

"The powerful magic was only directed toward you... and Kepler, of course. In fact, it was your own power that did all the real damage. Looking back on it, maybe I should have taken away the sphere's ability to deflect your fire. I was concerned when the explosion from the blast knocked Athena unconscious. I'll need to remember that for later encounters. Look at my bookshelves, they're a mess! I do hope you're okay, Athena!"

Athena stayed quiet, but Kepler didn't hesitate to jump into the conversation. "Don't forget me! I'm sure you hope I'm okay as well? I'm bleeding, ya know! My head and my right paw are riddled with holes!"

Brayson laughed. "Yes, Kepler, you too. I'm sure you won't bleed out before I can get you fixed up. Stop whining. I don't think I've ever seen a beast your size cry so."

Kepler growled, but Brayson ignored the giant cat's threat. "Let's retire to my office, shall we?"

He waved his hand and the group began to float upward.

Athena squealed as her feet left the floor, but Brayson took hold of her arm. "Relax, young one. There's nothing to fear. I'm sure that by now you've all figured out that I'm the Head Master. My name is Brayson Id."

George, still angry, reached out to shake hands in a political manner as he watched the distance between them and the floor expand. "Well, Brayson, I'm sure I should feel like it's a pleasure, but you're going to have to forgive my lack of enthusiasm at the moment."

The Head Master frowned, "I said my name is Brayson Id. I didn't say that you could use my name, George. You will call me Master Id."

"I'll what? You must be out of your freakin' mind if you think—"

Before the mage could finish his sentence, he began to fall to the floor below. As he fell, he screamed, "Master, Master!"

His descent suddenly stopped and once again George began to lift slowly toward the others.

"Ha ... now that was a beautiful thing to see," Kepler said with an evil grin. "He sure put you in line! George, you should've seen your face. It was a moment I won't forget!" A drop of blood fell from the giant cat's paw and narrowly missed George before landing into what was left of the now orange-colored water below.

George snapped angrily, "Don't forget, Kepler... I may not be able to fight off the Master here, but I can give you a look to match Kroger's!"

The demon stopped laughing. The idea of being turned to stone wasn't pleasing. He whispered to the others, "What a grump!"

Everyone laughed, except Athena. She had never seen George command the powers he had used to defeat the silver sphere. His power bothered her and she would need to speak with him later, but now was not the right moment. She put on a strong, happy face and joined the conversation. "Honey, you're so cute when you're angry."

Despite his anger, George had to smile. Athena always had a way of softening his mood, no matter how disgruntled he became.

When finally they approached the ceiling, the group passed right through it and reappeared in the Head Master's office. In awe, they all moved to the windows and stared out.

"I can see everything from here," Athena said. "It's all so beautiful. This building must be very tall—I can see the mountains below us. Honey, look, it's the island the Merchant Angels left us on! I had no idea Western Luvelles was so beautiful."

Brayson responded. "Very good, Athena. Your sense of direction is impeccable, but you're not in my School of Magic any longer. My office floats high above the lands of Western Luvelles and is invisible to those who live below. Only a few know of its existence, and when you leave this place, you'll remember everything you've seen, but will be unable to tell anyone about it. This spell is how I ensure my secret stays safe. Only those I invite can come back."

Athena pointed toward the water. "What's beyond the oceans?"

Brayson smiled, enjoying her curiosity. "Good question, Athena, allow me to tell you a little more about our world. There are four large areas of land which are populated on this world, and I'm responsible for keeping in touch with all their leaders. You already know that you're on Western Luvelles, which is divided into two territories. We call these lands Kerkinn, but you may not know that there are other lands. Eastern Luvelles, which I'm sure you can imagine by the name, lies far to the east. The territories which make up Eastern Luvelles are called Doridelven. Doridelven is an area known for abusing slaves, and the leaders of these territories have fought against each other for many, many seasons. Eastern Luvelles is mostly populated by Halflings, but there is one special race of Elves who live there, known as Wood Elves, and they have a very unique ability."

Athena was intrigued. "What kind of ability, and how does it affect their lives?"

Brayson pulled a book from one of the heavy wooden shelves which held many ancient tomes. After carefully ruffling through the pages, he handed it to Athena.

"Wood Elves have the ability to take the form of different animals. Usually their personality determines what kind of animal they can shape-shift into. This special race of elf is able to use the senses of their animal form, even while walking as men. So, I would have to say this would be how their ability affects their lives. Now, as a whole, Wood Elves are known for producing some of the finest students of healing. I've sent more than one of them to Harvestom to train with the High Priestess."

George looked over Athena's shoulder. "This ability to shape-shift is intriguing, and something I want to learn more about some-day. Is their ability to change magical or natural?"

"This ability is magical. It's a magic that no other elf has ever been able to master... not even myself. Even though my magic is far stronger than theirs, I still cannot understand this special power. The Wood Elves have managed to keep this secret well-guarded and it is only passed down within their race."

George turned the page, skimming the tome further. *Can you imagine how something like this could help a guy throughout his life? Maybe I'll have to eat another heart someday!*

Brayson decided to change the subject. "Now, as I was saying before, there are two other large land masses. The first lies far to the south. This area is called the Unmarked Territory and has been unmapped due to the savagery of the people who live there. Over the seasons, every man who has tried to study the area has perished. No one even tries any longer. Perhaps, when my days have passed as Head Master, I will map this area myself since I have the power to avoid a similar fate.

"The final area is located far to the north. This area is called Desolation and a small population lives there, maybe a few thousand or so. They have adapted to the intense cold and keep to themselves, causing no harm to anyone. This land has been mapped, but there's really nothing of interest other than the animals which roam the area."

It was easy to see George's excitement as he responded. "This whole world is incredible. I must learn everything I can while I'm here. Can you tell us some more about Western Luvelles? I know very little and can't wait to learn. And, I love your office, by the way. How do I get this kind of power? I want an office like this of my own someday."

Brayson had to smile. "I'm glad you like the idea of my floating office. Come take a look at this."

The Head Master waved his hand and one of the windows be-gan to zoom in on some of the farther areas of the land below, acting as a large telescope of sorts while Brayson took the moments necessary to point out many places of interest.

"As I have said before, Western Luvelles is called Kerkinn, and there are two Kingdoms which exist within it."

The window settled on one of the many cities.

"Look here... this is the City of Marcus, my brother's City of Shadows which he has named after himself. The lake just west of his city is called Lake Id... and it would take a man 63 Peaks of Bailem to walk there if he were to begin his journey from the entrance of my school."

Athena grabbed George's arm. "We should travel there some-day and look around."

Brayson chuckled.

"That's a bad idea, definitely a bad idea, Athena. Let me explain. My brother Marcus is the Chancellor of Dark Magic. I would sug-gest you stay away from him at all costs. He doesn't take kindly to outsiders and he hates even himself. His city is located in the Kingdom of Hyperia and there isn't much about this kingdom which is appealing to men with goodness in their hearts. All the lands within the Western Territory are under the rule of the king, Gedlin Hyperia, but my brother and his army rules even him, by fear. But enough of this! I find it depressing to speak about. Let's change the subject, shall we?"

Brayson adjusted the window's angle to another area of the land below.

"Just to the north of Lake Id is the City of Hyperia, and if you look straight to the east, there is a large strait that divides both kingdoms. The Eastern Territory is controlled by the King of Lavan, Heltgone Lavan... and, this territory is called the Kingdom of Lavan. If you're thinking that it's not very original, I agree completely, but kings do tend to be vain.

"Now, within this kingdom lives my youngest brother, Gregory Id, and he's the Chancellor of White Magic, or all magic that is considered to be good or neutral in nature. Both the kings and my brothers answer to me. I'm one of but a few things that keep them from going to war with one another. I'm sure you understand that with great power comes great responsibility, George."

"I do, Master Id."

George hated the way the name sounded as it left his tongue. He thought to himself, *It won't be long before you're calling me Master... you piece of garesh.*

He filed the thought away in the back of his mind and said, "So, what else can you tell us?"

"As I was saying, Marcus is the Chancellor of all those who command dark magic. He's the brother that many fear. If it were up to Marcus, every living thing would answer to him or die. He isn't the one you would want to befriend."

Marcus sounds like my kind of guy, George thought. *Maybe I'll have to look into this some more.*

Once again, Brayson redirected the group's attention. "Now... if you'll look far to the east, I'll show you one of the finest cities on Western Luvelles."

Brayson moved his hand and the window on the east side of the room began to zoom in across the world. "Now you can see the city of my youngest brother. Look closely." The window zoomed in further with another wave of the Master's hand.

"My youngest brother, Gregory, calls this his City of Inspiration. It's made of solid glass. The glass has been magically altered and protected from damage. It has been colored many different ways to give the people their privacy, but even more importantly, the color gives the depth necessary to outline the edges of the buildings. We wouldn't want the inhabitants to constantly be running into clear walls, now would we?"

Athena giggled, "I suppose not. That would be terrible. Your brother's city is so beautiful. I would love to visit someday." She hesitated. "I hate to be rude, but where are my families' new homes going to be?"

Brayson smiled.

"You're a woman who gets right to the point, I see. Come here, young lady."

The Head Master walked to one of the other windows and waved his hand.

"Do you see the first island north of the one the Merchant Angels left you on?"

"I do," Athena replied, with George looking over her shoulder.

"This is my island." Again he waved his hand and the window zoomed in on the northern shores. "If you look closely, you'll see that I've prepared a home for each of you and your family's individual needs."

Athena gave Brayson a hug. "Thank you, Master Id. My family will be very happy there, I'm sure."

"I'm glad you like them. You may call me Brayson."

"What?" George redirected his attention. "So we can call you

Brayson now?"

"No, no... I said Athena may call me Brayson. You, on the other hand, will still call me Master Id, as we have already discussed."

George rolled his eyes and turned back to the windows. Kepler hid his smile, but enjoyed every moment of George's irritation.

Brayson moved to the center of the room. "In the morning, I'll take your entire family to your new homes. This will be where you'll stay until George's training is complete. Very few people have had the privilege of training under my supervision, George. If you hadn't come so highly recommended by Amar, you wouldn't have been given this privilege either. I'll see you bright and early, before Early Bailem. Athena, please make sure that George has a full belly and a pack full of food. These rations will need to last him for a while. You won't be seeing much of your husband. Let's hope that he won't miss anything important."

Athena responded. "I'm fine with this... as long as he's there when I need him for the baby."

"I wouldn't worry. I'll keep an eye on you and help if anything unexpected happens."

George tried to interject. "Why can—"

Before the mage could finish his sentence, Brayson waved his hand. The next thing the group knew, they all were standing on the ground outside the school.

"Damn it, this guy is going to drive me absolutely crazy!" George snapped.

Athena winked at Kepler and started walking. "Let's go, boys!"

Kepler thought a moment as they began walking towards the inn. The giant cat hobbled from his wounds. "Well, at least my bleeding has stopped. I thought Master Id was going to give me something to help, but I guess he must've forgotten. I left blood on his floor to remind him."

"Serves the chump right," George snapped.

After walking a bit, Kepler thought of something that perplexed him. "So, George... why does Brayson think Amar visited him? How could he have done this when you—"

Quickly, George cut him off. "Kepler, buddy, maybe we could

save this conversation for later. I'm sure you'll agree that it's too long of a story and maybe something we could chat about after we've started on our journeys."

The demon understood and dropped the subject without further comment.

"You boys sure know how to keep secrets," Athena said, poking George lovingly as she walked beside him. "Maybe you should allow me in on some of your boy talk."

George looked at Kepler, then to Athena.

"Nope, I think we'll just leave it as guy stuff, babe."

"Suit yourself. Geeeesh!"

Meanwhile, Shade Hollow
Western Luvelles

"Payne... the moments have come," Lasidious, God of Mischief, said after appearing inside a large cave full of bat-like creatures. Icy blue stalactites hung from the ceiling above a deep pool of fresh water. Light found its way into the cave, despite this particular spot being hidden deep within the earth. It reflected off the pool's watery surface and shimmered against the cave's walls.

Payne, on the other hand, was not one of the bat-like creatures. He was a fairy-demon—the only fairy-demon in existence. Each moment a bat approached his meal, the demon side of Payne snatched it up, bit its head off, and spit it on the ground.

"Go away... eating," Payne growled, not knowing or, perhaps not understanding because of his young age that, the being in front of him was a 'so-called' god.

The birth of Payne was a successful manipulation, or better yet, a suggestion successfully planted by Lasidious into the open mind of Payne's father just over four seasons ago.

"The human I told you about is here on Luvelles. Are you ready to find some new friends? I know how important it is for you to find friends. You do want to have friends... right, Payne?"

Payne's red face lifted with his mouth full of freshly shredded throat from a female elf. "Now... you want Payne go now?" He growled childishly and began to pout. "I want eat because... because... um... it took forever."

"What took forever, Payne?"

"Errrr, for her to be... uh... uh, the right heat... yeah, the right heat. I eat now... good now. Won't taste good again... gotta eat it now!"

"Are you saying that her temperature is just right and she won't taste this good if you eat her later?"

"Yeah... you leave... I eat."

Lasidious smiled inside and took a deep breath. Payne was important and he was too young to argue with. He needed to be patient with the fairy-demon.

"By all means, continue eating. I would hate to ruin your dinner. I can wait a while longer."

"Don't watch... don't like that!"

Lasidious turned and stood next to the pool. "I will wait over here. You continue eating, but you do need to get going."

The fairy-demon was solid red from head to toe. His mother, Sharvesa, a Carver demon, was the Queen of Demons on the World of Dragonia. Payne took after his mother for the most part when it came to his looks. Tiny horns rested on his forehead. Claw-like hands, both razor-sharp, served him well when killing, and he had a whip-like tail that ended in a fine point. The little fairy-demon also had many of Sharvesa's natural abilities but, unlike his mother, Payne was an outcast, unable to live among the other demons that were of a pure bloodline, all thanks to his father. Payne's white fairy wings rested on his back and served as a constant reminder to Sharvesa's subjects that he was an abomination to their race.

To satisfy a desire placed in his mind by Lasidious, Defondel, the Fairy King of Luvelles, set out on a personal quest to create a new race of fairies. After arriving on the demon queen's World of Dragonia, Defondel found Sharvesa. He used his fairy magic to cast a powerful spell on the demon queen and, while Payne's mother lay in her slumber, Defondel took advantage of her. The fairy's four-inch tall frame disappeared inside the queen as he crawled around within her. It didn't take long, but when the Fairy King slid out and back into the open of the cave's floor, Payne's mother was pregnant.

The demon world would have killed Payne if not for his mother's decision to send Payne to be raised by his father—a decision made only after the queen requested a visit to the World of Luvelles and was denied. Sharvesa's anger toward Defondel was quite evident to the Head Master. Brayson turned down the demon queen's request, knowing full well that vengeance would have been the sole reason for her presence on his world.

In order to cause the Fairy King some discomfort and spare herself the irritation of raising an unwanted child, Sharvesa sent Payne with the Merchant Angels to live with his father. This decision—one also encouraged by Lasidious in his manipulative way—was a welcome suggestion and acted on quickly. The choice avoided a sure death for her mutt of a son. Payne would have been devoured by the demon world. Sharvesa's subjects, though loyal to their queen, would not allow an impure demon-fairy-midget to live among them as a constant reminder of the disgrace they felt by his miserable existence.

Payne's small red body and his size, compliments of his tiny father, functioned without imperfection. Although only three feet tall, he looked like a miniature red bodybuilder with wings and possessed the agility of a gazelle. He kept his tiny horns sharp. The youthfulness of his face reminded Defondel of a cute demon-cherub.

Of all his natural abilities, Payne's favorite was to polymorph and shape-shift. On many occasions over the last season, he used this talent to create company. He would rip off a finger, sit it on a rock or any other flat surface that seemed acceptable, and watch it change into various different creatures. He then used these moments to argue with his creations whenever something was on his mind. Many of their conversations ended in large childish tantrums due to his juvenile mind.

Payne was initially accepted by the Fairy King's people... for a while. Eventually, he was misunderstood because his demon half loved to be mischievous. Before his segregation from his father's kind, there were many occasions when Payne had flown around the fairy kingdom dusting the armies of his father with their own magical powders stolen from the fairy army's armory. Then, he would sit back and laugh at the intoxicating effects the fairy dust had on them. The sight of the male fairies kissing on one another in a drunken state never seemed to get old. Payne was warned by the council that such acts weren't considered welcome. The fairy council explained that the safety of all fairies was in jeopardy when the army could not perform their duties properly. Finally, at only two seasons, Payne was asked to leave and live in a cave that rested at the center of Shade Hollow. He had lived the last full season of his life alone and was left to fend for himself.

Since Payne's natural immunities were many, the magic of the fairy army was not strong enough to force him out. King Defondel was left with no choice but to uphold the council's wishes and banished his son to a life of solitude. Payne's heart was crushed, but he obeyed his father and left the Fairy Kingdom for his new home. This life of solitude was something Lasidious had hoped would happen when he began his evil plotting of the fairy-demon's creation.

Payne knew no other way to feed... killing was his only option. But despite all this, there was good in Payne and even with his ancestral heritage, killing made him feel bad. He was a block of clay just waiting to be molded into something special, and Lasidious knew it.

"Have you considered my proposal, Payne?" Lasidious said after giving him enough moments to eat.

"Yep!"

"So what have you decided?"

"I don't know... seems okay... I guess... Payne don't know!"

The god rolled his eyes. "You guess? Why are you hesitating?"

Payne ripped into the belly of the female elf and, after a moment, pulled out a handful. The fairy-demon quickly cleared away the fat and tore into the intestines—his favorite part. As he began to eat, Lasidious held his nose in disgust. He was a deity, but he had never imagined that the manipulation of Payne's birth would have turned out to be so foul.

"Listen to me, Payne. If you want to get out of this cave, it would be wise for you to befriend this human."

"Befriend... what that mean?"

Lasidious took a deep breath. He had to remind himself he was dealing with a child. "It means to become his friend."

"So, say that, that... um... that way then."

"Payne, let's focus. You're getting sidetracked. Okay?"

"Fine, gosh, you say them big words... not Payne."

"Payne, listen to me. Please, try to focus. This human will be seeking power within this world and if you're at his side, those that hurt you will have no choice but to bow down to you someday."

The fairy-demon growled as if confused. "Don't need bowing... Payne like fun. Payne want friends." He fumbled to keep every last bit of the intestinal delicacy from running down his chin as he continued. "So... um... the human, the human come get Payne?"

"No, if you want to travel with him, you'll need to seek him out in the Village of Floren. You can find this man at Kebble's Kettle... the only inn within that village."

"What's 'inn' mean?"

Lasidious rolled his eyes. "It's a place where people pay to sleep. Many people stay there and they can eat there as well."

"Eat... Payne like to eat. Why not sleep on ground? What 'pay' mean?"

"They pay coin to sleep because most humans don't like to sleep on the ground!"

"What's coin?"

"You'll see what many things are, including coin, as you travel with this human. You'll learn and can ask this human your questions."

"The human feed Payne?"

"Yes he'll feed you... but not elves. This is your decision to make. Only you can decide if you want to go. But if you want to have friends, I would go and find this man if I were you. His name is George and he travels with a large black cat named Kepler. I would imagine that you'll find Kepler to be helpful in learning the ways of your mother. Kepler is also a demon. Maybe someday, with training, you can become powerful or better yet, strong enough to go back to your mother's home world and punish those who forced her to send you away."

"But, Payne's no angry. Maybe Payne make them like Payne a lot. Do you think... um, I mean... they might like Payne, a bunch?"

"Of course they would, but you would need to travel with this human first."

"The human do for Payne so Payne do this? How... um... how make friends with him?"

"He will help if you listen to him! Have I ever lied to you, Payne? I've been your friend for over a season now. Don't you trust me yet? I want you to tell this human that you have been sent to be his Goswig."

"What a Goswig?"

Lasidious took a deep breath. "A Goswig is an animal or a creature that assists his master and does whatever the master asks of it. Goswigs can come in all shapes and sizes. Some have both natural and magical abilities, much like you, Payne. It's an honor to be a

Goswig, and very few beings are chosen to be one."

"Honor... what's honor?"

"It's a good thing. It means you're special."

"But Payne want a friend. Does Payne gots to be Goswig? Do I gotta do stuff he says for Payne to do?"

"You don't have to do anything that you don't want to do. But, this is a way for you to finally meet friends. This human will accept you no matter what happens, no matter what you do."

"So, all Payne do... is umm... what do Payne say again?"

"Pay attention or you'll mess this up. And stop talking about yourself in third person. It sounds ridiculous."

"What 'third person' mean?"

"Bah... never mind. You need to tell this human that you've been sent to be his Goswig."

"Ok... his Goswig... got it, and Payne gotta do what he says... got it. You promise him be Payne's friend?"

Lasidious impatiently held the smile on his face. "I promise. Do you have any other questions before I continue?"

"Payne can't remember your name. Tell Payne!"

"My name is Friend," Lasidious said, forcing another patient smile that showed all his teeth. "Payne, you won't see me again after this. The human you'll be looking for goes by the name George Nailer. I'll show you where to teleport."

"George Nailer... silly name. Payne make fun with that name. I've never seen no human before."

"No, no, no, Payne, you're to be his Goswig, remember? Goswigs don't make fun of their masters. Goswigs call the one they serve Master."

"Master...yuck. Payne don't want to say that. Payne want be friends. I like George gooder."

"It's better, Payne," Lasidious snapped—his patience now having run its course. "You like the name George better. That's how you say it. You really need to listen when people talk. You need to learn how to speak intelligently."

"Sorry! Don't be mad to Payne."

"Uuggg... Do you want to have friends or not?"

"Yes!" The fairy-demon lowered his red head the way any

child does when scolded. He kicked a small rock. "Payne want friends."

"Then maybe you should choose to call George Master! If you don't, he may not want you around. It's up to you. I personally don't care any longer!"

"Ummm... all right... fine, um... stop yelling to Payne. I hate his name. It's stupid, stupid, stupid, stupid. He better feed Payne, gooder!"

"I'm sure he will feed you very well, but you better get going."

Lasidious touched the fairy-demon's head and gave him the vision of Kebble's Kettle. "This is the inn I told you about, and this is what George looks like."

"Yuck, humans ugly!"

"Payne, focus... the jaguar's name is Kepler and here's how the cat looks. You best get going now."

"Kepler, I like him. Wow... him have red eyes, that's weird. Nice kitty."

Lasidious had to smile. He knew Kepler hated the word 'kitty.' This meeting was going to be fun to watch.

"Weird? Payne, your whole body is red. How can Kepler's eyes be weird?"

"Payne don't know... just cause... well... ummm... ya, just 'cause... I guess!"

Lasidious's patience was now completely gone. "Just be good to George! You want him to like you. If George likes you, then you'll have a new friend and some really good food!"

"Yes... um... I want George..."

"His name is Master. Concentrate, Payne, or you'll mess this up!"

"Uuhhh... yeah, yeah, yeah, ... I want Master to like Payne. Food... good... I'll go to George... I mean, to Master... thanks, Friend!"

"You're welcome, Payne," the God of Mischief said as he vanished.

Payne quickly grabbed a few more mouthfuls of elf before disappearing himself.

Chapter 2

A Whole Lotta Glass

Gregory Id, the Chancellor of White Magic and those who command it, stood from his bed and walked across the transparent floor of his bedroom chamber. As always, he enjoyed the sight of the torrent of water as it rushed swiftly beneath the glass under his feet.

The City of Inspiration was his creation and white magic was responsible for perfectly forming every building within it. Each structure, no matter how large or small, was made of glass and Gregory's bedroom chamber, located below the main level of a 200-foot-tall shimmering tower-palace, was no exception.

To provide privacy, the glass walls of each building were created to keep wandering eyes out and an array of colors was used to add to perfection's glory. If there was a flaw to be found, it would not be discovered by the naked eye.

Crystal Lake, Western Luvelles's largest body of water, sat high above Gregory's city. The area it covered was vast—so vast, in fact, it could have been named a sea. The clear blue water cascaded down the steep cliffs to the north and worked its way underground toward the city. After rushing beneath Gregory's tower-palace, it once again surfaced and flowed through a crystal moat before continuing on to Lake Lavan.

Gregory was an elf of average height with a thin frame. He was known for his strong will and tremendous charisma. His hair was long, sandy-blonde, and covered his pointed ears. His eyes were a deep blue and accented his pale complexion. He was beloved throughout the Kingdom of Lavan. His kindness, not to mention his charitable use of magic, had served him well while creating this beautiful relationship with the people.

On many occasions, Gregory had used his powers to provide homes for the less fortunate... the less fortunate primarily being those who could not command magic. Luvelles, though populated by mostly Elves, Halflings, and Spirits, was not a completely magical world despite the magical nature of these races. In some areas, the very air smelled of magic, but not everyone could summon its uses.

Elves, Halflings and Spirits were the three dominant races on Luvelles. Many other races also lived on this world, but they were not included on the list created by the gods. The gods, in fact, had decided to keep them separated from one another, and special permission had to be granted before a member of one of these three races could visit another world.

Gregory looked at his naked body as he stood in front of the mirror. He looked over his shoulder to make sure he was alone, only to quickly turn back around and flex what little muscle he had. He shook his head with disappointment and shouted, "Mykklyn, I would like to wear my green robe today. Please bring it to me, and my yellow belt also."

"Who would have ever guessed?" a voice responded while the speaker entering the room. "You always wear the same thing," the Goswig said as if annoyed. "I'll have them brought to you. But it does get rather old, you know. Wearing the same old thing is silly. I can't believe you're the one who created this perfectly fabulous city, a city full of so many beautiful colors, and yet you fail to have the ability to dress yourself in a proper manner."

The lioness turned and began to leave the room.

Gregory stopped her. "Mykklyn... you know, on second thought, let's change it up a bit. How about I wear my green robe and my black belt?"

"Wow... you best be careful, you're really stretching your boundaries on this one. You might find yourself venturing too far out onto a thin limb." The lioness shook her head. "Green and black it is. One of these days I'm not going to allow you to dress yourself anymore. Why don't you just run around without your clothes on? At least that would be a change, and far less boring."

Mykklyn growled as she left the room. It wasn't long before she returned. A servant entered behind her with the Chancellor's clothes. "Shall I have your normal prepared for breakfast?" The lioness jumped onto the glass table and lowered her heavy, golden-coated body into a comfortable position. She began to move one of her sharp claws along the symbols of white magic that had been etched into the table's surface. "You're on a roll today. Maybe we should try something new. I think a Bergan egg, with Greggle hash, Corgan blood steak and some Poppel bread would be perfect."

"No, no, no... I'll just have my usual. Why must we do this every morning? It's not like I don't have enough to worry about already!" Gregory turned toward the mirror and adjusted his belt.

"We do this because you're boring and I'm trying to fix you. You have a perfect eye for beauty when it comes to this city, but you're nothing more than a sad, sad man when it pertains to matters of fashion. Your predictability with your diet is, well, it's just tiresome. Eating the same thing every day is completely ridiculous. You're broken and you don't even know it."

"Just have them bring me my oats and let's get the day going! I have to meet with my brothers at the Peak of Bailem and there are things I must do before I go."

Mykklyn jumped down from the table. "I'll go fetch your breakfast, Your Boringness." The lioness vanished.

"Uuggg... that Goswig is going to drive me crazy."

Meanwhile, Kebble's Kettle:
The Village of Floren

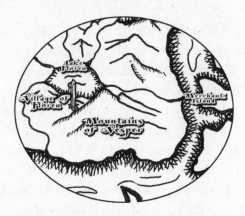

Mary, Athena's mother and mother–in–law to George Nailer, kept her eyes eagerly focused on the teleportation platform as she approached. The dark-haired, blue-eyed woman had been summoned to the front desk of Kebble's inn to retrieve yet another gift. She had absolutely no clue where they were coming from, but someone had their eye on her.

As she opened the box, she smiled. It was perfect—a beautiful, light blue sun-dress and, as always, just her size. This made fifteen different dresses she had received since the families' arrival on Luvelles.

The stay at the inn had been a pleasant one for the most part, but she was glad the moment had arrived to move on. Mary had not ventured past the front porch of Kebble's establishment due to her son-in-law's request. George said it wasn't safe to go out until he had been informed that the moment was right. The air within this village smelled strange and something as simple as sitting on the porch made her nervous.

Countless individuals of questionable character had checked into the inn over the past 115 Peaks of Bailem. Many of these individuals traveled with different forms of intimidating-looking beasts similar to Kepler, George's giant feline companion. The family had become restless waiting for this day, and a change of environment was a welcome one.

Mary hurried back to her room. She put on the new dress and stood in front of the mirror in the washroom to bask in the glow of how it made her feel. It was not long before she was interrupted by George, knocking on her door.

Mary - Mother of Athena and Susanne

Illustration by Kathleen Stone

"Mother," the mage shouted through the heavy wood, "we need to get going. Are you packed? I hope you're ready to go."

"I am. Come on in here and carry my bag, please."

George opened the door. "Ahhh, now that's just the sweetest thing, another new dress," he chided with a hint of sarcasm. "You look absolutely stunning. I think someone is still trying to get on your good side. I wonder when you'll meet this person."

Mary moved close and whispered in his ear like a child, "I don't know, but I hope he's handsome."

"Who said it's a man?" George joked.

Mary turned up her nose. "It better be. I would never—!"

Amused at her response, he laughed. "I hope so too, for your sake."

As they left the room, George headed towards the teleportation platform, but Mary hesitated and took a few moments to lean over the balcony's wooden rail. This would be the last chance she would have to look down at the dining area and the bar below.

She had never gotten used to how the walls and this railing felt. From a distance, Kebble's inn looked to be made of many normal types of building material, but once a person got right up close, they could see that the inn was alive.

As she passed her hand across the railing's surface, she could feel the tiny little prickly hairs that tickled her palm. The heart of the organic structure could be felt as a pulse shot through the railing like some sort of vein or artery. She pulled her hand away and thought, *Oohhh, that's just so unnerving.*

Many nights she had watched the diverse characteristics of Kebble's patrons from this very spot and on one occasion she had seen something, something that had scared her—a man had died. The cause of his death had been unexplained. It was as if nobody cared, that the gentleman was expendable, without importance—almost as if he had been expected to die. One minute, the man was laughing and the next, he was burning from the inside out. She would never forget his cries as his body reduced to nothing more than a pile of ash before her very eyes.

Everyone had continued eating, not bothering to give his remains anything more than a casual glance. Kebble had been the only one who seemed to care. She didn't know if it was because he was a good man, or if it had more to do with the fact that it was his inn and now there was just another mess to clean up. But despite her confusion about the short elf's actions that night, she had made friends with Kebble and would miss him.

Mary took one final mental snapshot of the place before making her way to the teleportation platform. As she stood on it, she disappeared from the fourth floor and reappeared near the front desk.

"Goodbye, Kebble. I don't know if we'll see one another again. You've been a gracious host."

The short, chubby, rosy-cheeked elf removed his pipe and kissed the top of her hand before bidding her farewell. "I shall miss you, Mary!"

"And I you... you've been wonderful. I do hope this isn't the last moment we'll see each other. I haven't made any other friends since our arrival, you know."

Kebble smiled and winked as he responded. "Oh, I think you're about to meet someone special, Mary, and I'm sure this won't be the last chance for us to see each other. I want a full report of your adventures when next we meet."

"Oohhh my, I do hope you're right. I could use someone special in my life. But I do promise to keep you informed. Goodbye, Kebble."

"Goodbye, my lady!"

Payne was enjoying the morning sun as it fell across the village. Sitting on top of the inn's roof, the fairy-demon lifted his face into the air and absorbed its warmth—all while childishly bouncing one of his legs. He was anxious, and waiting patiently for George to exit the building was hard for him to do. But, as usual, the fairy-demon had created company.

Payne had torn off one of his fingers and allowed it to morph into a small rabbit. The animal had a perfect cotton tail and gray fur. It twitched its pudgy nose, waiting for a response.

Payne - Fairy and Demon

Illustration by Kathleen Stone

"Would you stop shaking your leg? The human will come out soon."

"I know... I know, stupid," Payne growled.

"Who're you calling stupid, idiot?"

"Payne is no idiot."

"Well, you're the one bouncing your leg all over the place."

"So?"

"So, relax, this George will come out."

"Don't say that. Payne won't relax. Shut up!"

The bunny scratched the back of one of its long ears before responding. "I'll say whatever I want."

"No."

"Yes, I will, and you're an idiot."

"No, no, no, no... Payne's not... um... not an idiot... you're making Payne angry."

"Oh, forgive me. Whatever will I do? I best run and hide. The mighty fairy-demon is angry."

Payne ground his teeth, "Stop... or... I'll... I'll—"

The rabbit turned, lifted up onto his back legs and raised his front paws in defiance. "You'll what?"

"I'll do this." Payne grabbed the animal and lifted him towards his mouth.

"What're you doing?"

"Eating you... geeeesh... and you think Payne's so stupid."

"If you eat me, you'll lose a finger."

"Oh... um... yeah... forgot. Then... then...Payne will..."

"Just shut up. You'll do nothing. I have grown bored with you. Goodbye!" The rabbit began to melt away and once again attached itself to Payne's hand.

The fairy-demon growled, "Stupid finger!"

Not long afterward, George and Athena's entire family exited the inn. Payne was now more nervous than ever. He whispered to himself, "Great... can't talk... can't talk to humans. There are many, too many of them, too many to talk... those other ones... oh, too many with the human... not good. Payne wanna go... got to go... go home."

A voice from behind Payne spoke—a voice from someone Payne couldn't see.

"Yes, you can. Payne. You can talk to George. It'll be okay!"

"Who's there?" the demon said, quickly turning, ready to bite. "Is that you, Friend?"

"It's okay, Payne. You can do this. Go down there and say hello."

The fairy-demon shouted with excitement. "I'm not going, I'm... Payne's scared. Can't go nowhere. I won't talk to the human!"

"I think you will, Payne. You have been discovered. Look below."

George looked up as the fairy-demon looked down. "Hey Kepler, what the hell is that thing?"

"I have no idea, but it's small...ugly, too."

"Eeeek," Athena shouted. "George, what's that?"

Now the whole family was looking.

"Is it dangerous?"

"Beats me! Kepler, are you sure you haven't ever seen anything like it?"

"No, nothing quite like *that*. I would remember. It appears to be a demon of some sort, but why so tiny, I have no clue. It's odd, if you ask me, but it's definitely an ugly little thing, don't you think?"

Payne yelled at the invisible voice. "Now look... you made Payne... eerrr, um... they know now. The humans knows." Payne reached out to feel the air, but found nothing. "Hello... um... voice... you there? Pssst, hey voice... you there, can you hear Payne?" The fairy demon shouted. "Great...hearing stuff!"

Payne turned back around and looked at George. "What? Ain't you never seen no one talk before!"

Kepler laughed and sat down. He answered before George had the chance. "I have, in fact, but not something as odd as you."

"Odd...me...um, Payne not odd. Who you calling odd... furball! And I'm not a something, I'm Payne...I'm Payne!"

The jaguar stood and began to walk away. "Clearly. You're definitely odd and you are a pain, a pain in my rear end."

The demon cat was not interested in learning anymore, but Payne was not done with him. The fairy-demon teleported onto Kepler's back, grabbed both his ears with his claws, and hung on.

"I said Payne not odd! I can bite... I can bite you, furball."

The giant cat began to shake wildly, trying to hurl the fairy-demon off, but when Kepler moved, Payne only dug his claws in deeper to keep from being thrown.

"You can't get me off, kitty. This is fun. Friend said I would like you, kitty."

Kepler let out a roar. "George, get this damn thing off me!"

It took a moment, but the mage managed to stop laughing and waved his hand. Both Kepler and Payne froze in place. George then walked over to the tiny annoyance and plucked him from Kepler's back, moving away before releasing the giant jaguar. Once the demon cat could move, he began to walk toward Payne.

"Stay there, Kepler," George commanded.

"Why? He'll make a great meal. Let me have him. You know I hate being called a kitty."

George's mind was working fast. He wanted to know more before he let Kepler at him. "What are you, and what's your name? Don't lie to me, or I'll feed you to the furball over there."

"Not funny, George," Kepler growled.

Smiling, the mage waved his hand again and released only Payne's mouth. "Speak, and be quick about it!"

"I'm Payne. I'm... um... um, a fairy-demon."

Kepler growled. "There's no such thing. He lies."

"There is so."

"No, there's not."

"There is so!" Payne shouted even louder.

"No, there isn't!" Kepler roared.

The mage lifted his hands and shouted. "Hey! You two are acting silly. Stop this and let's talk civilly."

"George, who are you going to listen to, me, or this... this thing?"

"Payne's not a thing. I'm a fairy-demon. Payne's mother is the queen... Queen of Demons on... on... eerrr, um... I forget."

"Ha, there is only one Queen of Demons, and she lives on another world. I doubt that your mother is the Queen of Dragonia."

"That's it... Dragonia... Payne's mother... the queen."

"You lie."

"No lie... I swear."

Kepler growled and his eyes began to glow a brighter, deeper red than normal. "And your father, what of him, I suppose he's a king?"

"Yes... um, he's... he's the Fairy King. He's here... on Luvelles."

"George, he lies. Let me eat him. I don't have the moments to waste on this."

Payne showed his pointed teeth. "Then... then why does Payne got fairy wings, stupid?"

Kepler began to respond, but George spoke over the top of him.

"Stop this. Let's take a look... shall we?" The mage turned Payne's little red figure over and examined his wings."

Susanne, Athena's younger sister—pretty, but not fabulous-looking—jumped into the conversation.

"Hang on a second!" She turned and handed baby Garrin to Mary, who was still dwelling on the fact that George had used magic to take control of the situation. Slowly Susanne moved closer to take a look.

"George, they do look like fairy wings. I've seen them in drawings before, but never would I have thought I'd see a pair. Maybe the little—whatever he is—is telling the truth."

George took note of the stunned look on Mary's face. As he acknowledged Susanne, he was glad he had informed Athena's family that he could command magic. As he looked past Susanne and toward the rest of the group, he could see how shocked they all were at his use of it, despite the knowledge that he could do so. George had kept a short leash on everyone and had asked them to stay inside the inn until they received instruction on what to do next. Looking back on this decision, he now thought it might have been better to break them all in and expose them to it slowly over the past 115 days.

After a moment, George said, "Athena., maybe you could help them find a way to close their mouths. They look stunned. We wouldn't want any bugs to take up residence in there."

"Ha, ha, ha, very funny, George. What did you expect? I told you they haven't ever seen magic used before. Go about your business and give me a moment."

As Athena turned to address her family, she had to smile. She had thought about this moment and what it would be like for them. She was still having trouble dealing with their run-in with the silver sphere. She had seen magic before, but had no idea her husband was so powerful, and it scared her. Athena remembered what it was like to experience the fear of seeing magic for the first moment. Many moments she had thought back to their wedding night, when George teleported her to their home in his arms. She knew full well the anxiety her family was feeling and, at this moment, her strength was necessary to help ease their minds.

"I'm inclined to think he's telling the truth," George finally said as he touched Payne's wings. "What did you say your name was again?"

"Payne."

"Well, Payne, tell me why I should stop the big kitty here from eating you."

Again Kepler growled. "George, come on. Stop saying that word."

The mage had to grin as he waited for Payne's response.

"Because... um... cause Friend said I'm to be your Goswig," Payne said, anxious to find a way out of the trouble he was in. He hated being frozen and the idea that he couldn't teleport while in this condition really ate at him.

"Goswig? And why would I want you to be my Goswig?"

"Friend said come. Friend said I got to call you Master. He said Payne got to do the stuff you say, and... um... I got to be... um... good, I guess."

George looked at Kepler, puzzled. He sat Payne down and lowered himself to the ground beside him, pushing his new robe into a more comfortable position as he did. Once sitting, he continued to question. "You said your friend sent you? Who is your friend?"

"Yes... my friend... um... eerrr... he is Friend. Friend sent me."

"I know, you said that. But what's your friend's name?"

"I told you," Payne replied, frustrated. "Friend."

"No, you said your friend sent you. I want to know his name."

"His name is Friend."

"Friend!"

"Yes, Friend."

George shook his head. "You're saying your friend sent you, I get that. Now what's his name?"

"Friend."

"Yes, but what's his name?"

"Rrrrrrrr, his name is Friend."

"Friend... really, it's just Friend. He's got to have a name."

The fairy-demon growled and snapped back. "His name is Friend. Please stop making me say it. My friend, his name... um... it's Friend. He told Payne to come. He said you be good to Payne."

George thought a moment. He knew he was missing something. None of this made any sense. He would allow Payne to come along until he could figure the little guy out. He could make a decision on what to do with him later. The mage turned and looked at Kepler. "Come with me, Kep."

The two walked away from the group. George was the first to speak. "None of this makes sense. Something tells me that we should take this red little midget with us until we know more. If he turns out to be useless, you can eat him, okay?"

"I hate this idea. This little freak is going to be a pain in my furry black ass. I won't be responsible if he comes up missing."

"Look, I understand your feelings. I'll tell him he needs to chill out. I'll tell him he's got to act right. I'll tell him to stay away from you. I'll tell him—"

"George, stop already!" Kepler grinned as a jaguar would. "You're not really going to do the tell him, tell him, tell him, tell him thing again, are you? You sound like a babbling idiot."

"Bah... shut up, will ya? Look, I just need you to look at the bigger picture here. Someone has sent him to be my Goswig. Why, I don't know, but it's happened. I think I have an idea who, but I'm not sure it's wise to say it out loud. Come here." George leaned over and whispered in Kepler's ear.

"Really? Why would he send this—this, whatever it is?"

"Hell if I know. But when I talk with him, I'll ask. For now, we need to tolerate this little guy until I know for sure. I'm asking you to be patient. I think this little fairy-demon may come in handy if I'm right about who sent him."

"This isn't what I signed on for, George, and you know it."

Kepler turned and made his way back to Payne. "I suggest you stay away from my ears. Touch them again and I'll eat you for dinner."

"Geesh, okay, kitty."

"And don't call me kitty!"

"Okay, furball."

"Or furball either, or anything else you think of that you find amusing or clever. You will call me Kepler, and only Kepler."

"Geesh... why so pissy... kitty?"

Kepler let out a hellacious roar. Athena's entire family backed away. Baby Garrin woke from his sleep and began to cry. Kepler lowered his mouth around Payne's head and was about to bite down, but George froze him.

George stomped his foot hard against the ground.

"You have got to be kidding me!" The mage shouted as he walked over and pulled Payne from under the jaguar-demon's jaws. He lifted the fairy-demon up in front of his face. "If I were you, I would do as he says or I'll freeze you again and allow him to eat you. You may have been sent to be my Goswig, but you will call me Master, and the jaguar, Kepler. Do we have an understanding?"

Payne rolled his eyes. "If Payne do... um... will you feed Payne good?"

"I will, but you must eat what the rest of us eat. I'm not a restaurant."

"Restaurant? What's a restaurant?"

"Never mind. You'll eat what we eat, got it?"

"Do you eat elves? They are tasty... um... the small girl ones, mmmmm. I can kill them! Payne likes the part that holds the brown stuff. You know... down here." The demon pointed to his abdomen.

George looked at Kepler, then back at Payne. "You mean you like to eat their garesh? Oh man, that's just nasty. That's just sick and wrong. How could you be any more repulsive? You'll eat what we eat. Don't even think about putting something in your mouth unless you ask me first. Do you understand me? And stop calling yourself by your name. You sound stupid."

George did not listen to anything else Payne had to say. He was fighting off his need to vomit. He would need to pay close attention to their new little companion—killing elves was not a good idea. He released his magic and began to walk with the family towards the Head Master's school.

"Let's go, everyone. Mary, let me have Garrin. I'll calm him down."

On his way past the fairy-demon, Kepler thumped Payne on the head with the backside of his large paw and sent the little guy flying into the side of Kebble's inn. It took a while, but once Payne collected his bearings, he shook out the cobwebs and flew to catch up with the group.

Meanwhile,
Head Master Brayson's Floating Office in the Sky

"Amar, it's good to see you again, my friend," Brayson said, hugging his old Mystic-Learner.

"You also, Master," Lasidious responded, perfectly disguised as Amar once again. The God of Mischief was dressed in black robes and his hair was long and gray, just as Amar's had been before his unseasonal death on Grayham, a fact Brayson knew nothing about.

"Master, I've come to tell you I've sent Payne, the fairy-demon, to be George's Goswig. I know this is abnormal and I also know it's not my place to do so, but I think it will be a good fit for him. I hope this is okay with you?"

Brayson frowned. "Why would you do something like this? I had planned on giving him a Goswig this morning. This is highly unusual and crosses the boundaries of our friendship."

"Please forgive me, Master… I have traveled with this human. He's one of the few who can handle such a powerful Goswig. He's also the only one who will be able to put up with Payne's immaturity. This is the perfect chance for Payne to get out of his cave and become useful."

Brayson thought a moment. He walked around his office and eventually waved his hand across one of the magical windows. It did not take long for it to zoom in on George's position. As he watched the mage's family walk towards the school, Brayson continued. "Amar, you're really going out of your way to help this human. I want to know why—I don't know that I necessarily agree with what you've done."

Lasidious moved toward the window and took a look. "I see much of myself in him. He's going to be stronger than I am. George doesn't understand how he can do the things he does, but yet he does them. He does them naturally, without words or a staff. I find this fascinating. I think with your guidance, he could be extremely powerful. Not only could he be powerful, but George is loyal to those he chooses as friends. He could prove helpful when your brother Marcus becomes more of an annoyance than he already is."

The Head Master turned to look into Amar's eyes. "How do you know of the struggles between us?"

"Let's just say I pay attention. You're my friend and I would do anything to help you. It's clear to me that your brother is becoming more agitated as the days pass. He carries a tremendous anger in his heart, though I don't know the reasons why."

"I didn't know you paid such close attention to what's happening here on Luvelles. I assumed that you were happy living with your brother on Grayham. How is your brother, anyway?"

"He is doing well, and I make it my business to pay attention to Luvelles. We are friends, after all." Lasidious looked out the window and cleverly pushed his hair behind his ears as Amar would have done. "It looks as if Payne has already found George. Maybe you could trust me on this and allow them to stay together. I know I should've come to you first, but I just didn't have the moments necessary. If I'd waited, you would've assigned him a different Goswig. I will mind my place in the future, I promise, Master!"

"Well, like I said, I don't know that this is a good idea, but maybe you're right. After all, you do know him better than I do. But do nothing further without my knowledge. I'll allow Payne to stay with George. This is an odd pairing to say the least... I hope you're right and George is indeed able to handle him. Once he bonds with the fairy-demon, I can't give him a new Goswig, so your decision better be the right one!"

"I'm right, but if I'm proven wrong, it will only serve to remind me why you are the Head Master and I am not."

Brayson pulled Amar close and put an arm across his shoulders. "Flattery will get you everywhere. Now, get going before George arrives. The things I let my favorite Mystic-Learner get away with—it's criminal, I tell you. Keep in touch, Amar, and I'll keep you informed of how things are going."

"I will."

With that said, the God of Mischief vanished.

Brayson watched as the family arrived at the base of the invisible school of magic. With a wave of his hand, one of the windows of his office adjusted as the magic manipulated the vision. The faces of the family appeared and with another quick motion the window adjusted further and zoomed in on only Mary's face, leaving a soft glow about her head as if she were some kind of an angel.

"Your beauty is beyond compare," Brayson said softly as he gazed at the image while standing in the empty room. "I have looked forward to this day... but now I find myself suddenly nervous. You must have been molded by the goddess herself to have such grace."

"Finally... we're here," George said as he stopped the family at the base of the invisible tower.

Mary looked quizzically at him for a moment before questioning. "What do you mean, George? There's nothing here."

"I know. That's what's so great about this place. Just watch and see. I mean it! This is really cool, so watch closely. Man, I love this world!"

He began to speak the words that would reveal the front door, but before he could finish, Brayson appeared next to him. Mary, astonished, was the first to speak.

"Oh my, you startled me, sir. The use of magic on this world is overwhelming. It doesn't feel normal and it's somewhat unnerving."

"Ha, ha, ha... don't worry yourself with such concerns, Mary," Brayson responded. "I welcome you all to my School of Magic. You'll become familiar with the uses of magic soon enough. This world is where the Source of Magic resides. Where I'm about to take your family, you'll experience many different uses of magic. Many of the creatures that will be living near you use these different forms of the arts on a daily basis."

Mary replied, "I see no school. All I see is a field. And just who are you anyway, and how do you know my name, sir?"

"I know many things, Mary, and you will see my school in a moment. My name is Brayson Id," he continued. "I am the Head Master of all the lands of Luvelles which make up this world. It's a pleasure to meet you. I have looked forward to this day for quite a while now. I see you're wearing one of the dresses I sent you."

Mary gasped, "You're the one who sent me this dress?" It was hard for her to fight back the smile. "Do you always keep a woman waiting? I've wondered on many occasions about who was sending me these wonderful gifts. You should be punished for making me wait so."

Brayson reached out and lifted her hand to kiss the top of it, watching Mary's eyes as she trembled with excitement. His goatee tickled and his blue eyes held her gaze affectionately.

"You're absolutely right… I should be tortured for my abuse."

"Yes, yes you should, sir!" she responded, fighting back her desire to scream ecstatically. This was the first moment she had been flirted with in many seasons and to say that it was hard for her to hold back her excitement, would be an understatement.

Brayson's smile was full of charm as he spoke in the language of the Elves.

"Khila amin, voronwer!"

"Oh my, I don't know what you just said, but it sounded beautiful."

"I said, follow me, lovely one!"

The remark was a welcomed advance that Mary would file away in the back of her mind as unforgettable. "You just know all the right things to say to make a lady smile, Mr. Id! Lead the way."

The family stood in silence. Glances were exchanged between them. It was as if Brayson and Mary had completely forgotten they were present. They simply stood in awe as Brayson continued.

"It will be wonderful to have such a beauty on my island. I've been watching you and have done so since your arrival on Merchant Island. I can't ever recall seeing such grace in any other woman."

Watching Mary smile, Brayson changed the subject. "I have prepared many homes for your family to live in. I do hope you like them."

Mary responded with a hint of sarcasm. "Then I shall be sure to let you know if I approve when I see them." She winked and put her arm through Brayson's.

Grinning, Brayson moved his hand through the air in a big circle. The door to the school appeared, and after enjoying the shock on Mary's face, he guided the speechless woman inside with the rest of the family in tow.

It only took a moment for Mary's shock to disappear and be replaced by another emotion. A big smile crossed her face as she looked over her shoulder at Athena and Susanne. Both girls giggled as they watched their mother disappear inside.

George and Kepler remained outside while Payne stayed close to Athena and vanished inside with the others.

"Well, that's just great!" George sighed in frustration. "He just put the moves on my mother-in-law. Damn, Kep... this guy is smooth. You know she's gonna fall for him. He looks like Tom Selleck, for hell's sake. You've got to be kidding me. This clown and his red power-robe are just oozing with charm. I want to puke. He's been sending her dresses this entire time. If this isn't a conflict of interest, I don't know what is."

Kepler looked up at him. "What do you mean? Why is this so bad? And who's this Tom Selleck, anyway?"

"Other than being my favorite private eye on one of my favorite shows on Earth, just forget who Tom Selleck is. If Brayson butters Mary up, how could I ta—"

The mage thought twice before finishing his sentence out loud. He whispered into Kepler's ear.

The demon cat's red eyes lit up. "Aahhhh, I see your point. We'll have to cross that bridge when we come to it... agreed? Oh, and by the way, you called him Brayson. It's Master Id to you, Mr. Mystic-Learner!"

"Shut up before I make a statue out of you."

"That's not funny, George!"

The mage grinned and gave his large feline friend a hug around the neck.

"Okay, George... you can stop that now... you know I hate it when you act so disgustingly nice to me. It's not natural for me to be seen this way, I tell ya!"

After a short pause to enjoy the demon's discomfort, George continued.

"I don't like how this looks. Let's keep our eyes open for a way to stop this. We can't have him getting too close to Mary. If he gets too close to her… then he's too close to us!" Both of them entered the school and shut the door; again it vanished to the rest of the world.

Mary slowly walked about the room. The beautiful detail of the school's design captured her fancy, especially the spiraling staircase. The mess created by George's fight with the sphere was gone as if it had never happened. Everything was returned to normal.

"My, my, Mr. Id, I've never seen such a place. May I look around, sir?"

"Mary, please call me Brayson. By all means, feel free to explore."

George rolled his eyes. "Great, everyone gets to call him Brayson but me!"

"Oh, honey," Athena said as she took his arms, pulled them around her waist, and kissed him. "You're forgetting that you're here to learn from Brayson. He must have a reason why you must call him Master Id."

"Yea, it's to piss me off."

"Stop that," she said with a touch of harshness. "You might want to change your attitude! Make me proud, honey!"

George had to smile, and pulled his wife close. After some moments passed, Brayson gathered everyone into a tight group and teleported them to the northern shores of his personal island. Once there, he addressed them all.

"This is where you'll be living until the completion of George's training."

As the family turned to look, their faces expressed their delight. Eleven different structures had been created and formed a perfect circle. The four children who were old enough to play ran for the large rocks at the community's center and began a game of follow the leader, jumping from stone to stone.

Brayson spoke. "It appears the children like it. I trust you will all enjoy your stay here. George, Amar took the opportunity to explain your tastes when I met with him. I have to admit that it took many, many moments to understand how all the details should look. He said it would remind you of Earth. I quizzed him on how he knew such things, but all he said was that I should speak with you. I would very much like to know about your Earth someday. I have tried to create something similar to his descriptions. I hope you find this place to your liking."

George scanned the area. It looked like a nice, family-friendly subdivision. It did indeed feel like he was back on Earth. Granted, there were no roads, no sidewalks, or fancy landscapes, but the homes did have style: rock-covered exterior walls, good lines, and heavy wooden door entrances.

"Amar told you I would like this?"

"He did. I trust you find this acceptable."

"I believe this will do just fine. You have outdone yourself, Master Id. You have given me a true taste of my old home. Thank you."

"I'm pleased that you're happy, George. You're more than welcome."

Brayson cleared his throat, then continued. "We have much to discuss. We will begin your training this evening. I would like you to meet me in my office by Late Bailem. You may bring Kepler and Payne. Amar informed me that he sent Payne to you and I have agreed to allow him to be your Goswig. I do hope you can handle him once you've finished the bonding ritual."

Payne tugged on Brayson's robe. Once he had George's attention, he showed all his fairy-demon teeth. "Payne a Goswig?"

Brayson laughed and quickly picked Payne up. "Not yet, Payne, but you will be soon, I promise. You'll need to listen to your Master, though."

"Um... my master... um ... ahhh ... George, right?"

"Yes, Payne, it's George."

George knew now that Lasidious had been plotting and it looked to be in his favor. He appreciated the god's gestures, but wondered when he would be able to speak with him. He interrupted the moment shared by Payne and Master Id.

"I'm sure I'll find out soon enough if I can handle Payne, but what type of Goswig do you have, Master Id, and where is it?"

Brayson spoke with pride. "My Goswig is known as a Phoenix. He's the most powerful Goswig on Luvelles. The essence of a Phoenix lies within its feathers. This is why they are so glorious to look at. He's a marvelous creature, and his crimson-colored feathers make him majestic. I keep him someplace safe. You'll meet him one of these days, George, if you ever manage to prepare yourself to go through the trials."

"What trials are you talking about, and what is this bonding ritual that you're referring to?"

"We can discuss all of this later tonight, I think."

Without saying another word, Brayson walked over to Mary and took her by the arm. "Allow me to guide you to your new home, my lady. I have added something very special just for you... something I hope you'll use often. It will allow you to contact me whenever you want. I do hope we'll become well-acquainted."

Mary's beautiful blue eyes accented her blushing cheeks. She moved her dark hair clear of her face before responding. "You do know how to make a woman feel special. I hope for this as well."

Brayson smiled and guided her to the front door. After showing her how to contact him, he kissed the top of her hand once more.

"Tenna' ento lye omenta!"

Brayson vanished and Mary turned to the rest of the family, who had followed out of curiosity. "I think this magic thing is kind of sexy, don't you? I don't know what he just said, but it was beautiful, I'm sure!"

George whispered into Kepler's ear as the commotion of the family grew. "This isn't looking good. I have a gut feeling this is going to be a huge problem."

Payne appeared on Kepler's back. "Let's eat!"

Kepler growled. "Get off me, freak!"

𝔅𝔯𝔞𝔶𝔰𝔬𝔫'𝔰 𝔥𝔬𝔪𝔢
The Head Master's Island

The Peak of Bailem was approaching and Brayson was waiting patiently for his brothers to arrive. His home was hidden within a heavily-wooded area of his island, somewhere near the center. When sitting inside the dwelling, it appeared to have no walls, but they were there. From the outside, the home appeared to be nothing more than a massive mound of boulders with plants growing between the many cracks—the door was invisible to all.

Once inside, the magic's illusion provided for the perfect atmosphere. The mound of boulders had been hollowed at its center, but Brayson's furniture looked as if it sat within the middle of the forest. The trees appeared to cast their shadows across the home's floor, which in reality was a perfectly smoothed rock surface. Subtle key points defined the boundaries of the magic's illusion that hid the walls. Only Brayson and the Kedgles knew exactly where to look to avoid running into them.

The Kedgles were fascinating creatures—only eight inches tall—but handy to have around. They had a human head with human-looking eyes, a mouse-like nose with whiskers, a tiny human torso, elf ears, and a full head of hair. The rest of their bodies from the waist down resembled a large tarantula. Wings rested between their eight legs attached to the top of their spidery back. The Kedgles were a magical race, proficient in creating illusions and maintaining those illusions indefinitely.

Brayson had entered a pact with the Kedgle King long ago, allowing the Kedgles to live on his island. The island itself was protected by Brayson's magic and because of this, the Kedgles were free from threat. The pact would stay in effect as long as they maintained his home's cleanliness and the illusion the Head Master had come to enjoy within it.

Brayson was waiting at his table when the door opened. "Hello, brother," Marcus said as he moved across the room, the smoke from his pipe trailing behind him as he walked. "I see you're still living inside this miserable mound of rocks. I'll never understand why you insist on such a simple existence."

"There are many things you'll never understand, Marcus. You spend far too many of your moments thinking about trivial things. I much prefer this over the darkness and the shadows of your city."

Marcus leaned over the table and lowered his pipe, his brown eyes filled with disgust beneath his long hair. "How typical... you'll never change. You think you're better than me."

"No, not better. Just more pleasant."

Before anything else could be said, Gregory entered. "Gentleman, how are we today?" He vanished, only to reappear in the seat next to Brayson.

Marcus grunted and sat down. Brayson leaned back in his chair and smiled. "I'm well, Gregory, and yourself?"

"Busy, very busy. I've been working on a set of plans to build a glass bridge across Lake Lavan. It will connect the shores just west of my city to the shores just north of the City of Lavan. The king and I have been working on this idea for nearly a full season now. We're about ready to break ground."

"You're so pathetic," Marcus snapped. "Why do you feel the need to connect your precious city of glass to the King of Lavan's? Why share it with a people who can't command even the simplest of magic? They're beneath you, brother. They are but mere Halflings. How could you associate with those of impure blood?"

Brayson shook his head.

"You'll never get it. It's hard to believe we come from the same mother. How you ever became so angry, I guess we'll never know."

Marcus wanted to cuss their mother. He knew he did not share this half of their bloodline with them. Clearly they did not know this, or they had simply forgotten what they had heard as children. Only their father's blood was common between them. He would not divulge this forgotten secret. It would only serve to hurt his future plans. Any edge that this belief—the belief that they were of the exact same blood line might give him—was worth keeping.

Brayson looked at Gregory before responding. "Marcus, you asked for this meeting. Why are we here? I don't have all day to listen to your negativity, so get on with it!"

Welcome to the first edition of

The Luvelles Gazette

When you want an update about your favorite characters

Lasidious and Celestria are now home on the Hidden God World of Ancients Sovereign. They are discussing the next part of their plan. The moment to call for a meeting of the gods is at hand and the next piece of the Crystal Moon will be hidden at a location soon to be revealed.

Brayson, Gregory and Marcus are still inside Brayson's home. The conversation has become heated and from the looks of things, it may prove to be a useless gathering.

Payne is with Kepler. George has requested they talk. Kepler, although reluctant, agreed and is trying to find a way to tolerate the fairy-demon.

Susanne and Athena are in Susanne's new home. Susanne is feeding baby Garrin, but he won't stop crying. Athena is doing everything she can think of to help her sister find a way to make him happy.

Mary is anxious to use her mirror to contact Brayson. The only thing stopping her is the short amount of moments it has been since his departure.

Sam Goodrich, King of Brandor, and his queen, Shalee, are discussing what to do with Kepler's brothers back on the World of Grayham. Sam's army hunted them down and brought them to the City of Brandor in two large cages. Southern Grayham has changed a lot over the past 115 Peaks of Bailem.

There are two other major issues to be deal with: The first is the queen's health. Shalee has started to bleed sporadically and is nearing the end of her second trimester of pregnancy. The city's best healers have been summoned to keep an eye on the queen until she delivers.

The second issue is the meeting Sam has called with the Senate. He plans to explain his decision to allow ten Barbarians to join the Senate as members of a newly reformed government. He will also explain that these barbarians will have a voice while voting on the laws to govern the kingdom's daily operations. Sam will leave Shalee and head to Brandor's version of a courthouse.

Mosley, the God of War, is watching Sam and Shalee without their knowledge. The wolf is invisible to all those within Sam's castle and is listening in on their conversations to get an idea of how recent events may unfold.

On the Hidden God World of Ancients Sovereign—the other gods have watched carefully to see how the Kingdom of Brandor would change. Brandor's army has defeated the Barbarians of the north and is now in control of every area within Southern Grayham. Brandor, as ordered by Sam, has spared many barbarians' lives as they surrendered and swore their loyalty to his crown.

Thank you for reading the Luvelles Gazette

Chapter 3

𝕭𝖎𝖙𝖙𝖊𝖗 𝕸𝖊𝖒𝖔𝖗𝖎𝖊𝖘

The World of Grayham,
Brandor's Court

Sam has taken his position at the head of the court. The room is wide, spacious, and large enough for nearly one hundred and twenty members of the Senate to come from all over Grayham and take their seats on either side of a wide open area covered with a large red rug. The only thing resting in the middle of this rug is a good-sized circular table made of heavy, dark wood, which both the defense and prosecution would walk around while presenting their cases to the court.

The Leader of the Senate, who also acted as a judge, had been moved from his normal spot and asked to join the others to make room for the king's throne. Once everyone had settled down, Sam stood and moved to the center of the room, standing next to the table.

The king removed Kael from his sheath and shouted for the Sword of the Gods to bring forth his flame. Once Sam had everyone's full attention, he addressed the group.

"I have called you here to inform you of the changes I'm going to make in the Senate. This will be implemented before I declare the war to be over. Each of you will be required to do your part. Those of you who wish to argue with me will be given the chance to step down from your position and allow another, much wiser, man to fill your spot."

Mosley watched from his invisible position as the murmurs of the Senators filled the room. Not a single soul dared to stand and object. The tone Sam used in the delivery of his opening set the mood of the meeting. The king grabbed the end of Kael's fiery blade and lifted both arms to move the sword into a position resting against the back of his head. The men of the Senate watched in awe, noting the fact that he had not been burned.

"I will be adding ten new members to the body of this Senate. These men will not be your normal members. They will be Barbarian nobles." He took Kael from behind his head and extended the blade's point in the direction of the Senators as he slowly turned around. "Does any man here wish to voice an objection to my decision? If so, speak now so I can fill your seat with another Barbarian."

After a long period of absolute silence, Sam continued. "Allow me to explain my decision. This will happen with or without your support. I suggest you try to wrap your minds around this new idea. This kingdom will find a harmony and you, you, you, and the rest of you, will work hard to make this happen. Does everyone here understand me?"

Brayson's Home
The Meeting Continues

"You had your chance to speak with the Source, Marcus. I gave it to you more than a hundred seasons ago. If you had been considered worthy, you would've been given the chance to look into the Eye of Magic. But it's a good thing the dragon didn't find you worthy. The Eye would have swallowed your soul. You'd be dead!"

"What a pile of garesh, Brayson. I'm much stronger now, almost as strong as you! Even without looking into the Eye, I have become the Chancellor of Dark Magic and I'm sure the Source will find me worthy now." Marcus took a puff of his pipe and blew it in Brayson's direction.

Brayson shook his head and stood from the table to avoid the smoke. Grabbing his glass, he breathed deep and took a drink. "I don't doubt that you're capable. I'm sure the dragon would allow you to look into the Eye. But it's my job to determine who sees the Ancient One and frankly, the hate in your heart sickens me. If I allow you to stand before the Source and you somehow manage to look into the Eye, and live, who knows what kind of havoc you would bring to Luvelles."

"It's not for you to monitor what I do!"

"You're right. Monitoring your actions isn't normally my concern, until it becomes a problem for the wellbeing of many. It's my job to determine who meets with the Source, and you won't be getting another chance. You would abuse this power."

Gregory spoke up before Marcus had the chance to explode. "I agree with Brayson. I wasn't considered worthy to look into the Eye, either. I also think you would become a threat if given the chance to do so. Your heart is full of darkness, and for the life of me, I can't figure out why."

"Who cares what you can't understand, you imbecile? I don't owe you an explanation for my actions. You should watch yourself, Gregory. You aren't strong enough to speak to me this way. I could kill you where you stand."

Brayson had enough. "And you aren't strong enough to make threats of this nature in my presence. I think you should leave. If you try to hurt Gregory, you'll deal with me. I'll kill you myself if you cross that line."

"Ha... you don't have it in you! Besides, I believe I could defeat you. My power is strong!"

Brayson's face turned cold. His blue eyes darkened as he leaned across the table toward Marcus. "If I were you, I would not test my resolve!"

"We will see, my brother. Someday... we will see." Marcus vanished.

After a moment of silence, Gregory spoke. "Should I be worried? He's making me nervous. I can't defend myself against his magic. He's stronger than I am."

"I know... I know! I'm also scared for your wellbeing. I need to think and find a way to figure out what he's up to. If he stands in front of the Eye, he'll receive the power to defeat me as well. I can't let him meet with the Ancient One. He has overcome his weakness. The reason the Source didn't allow him to look into the Eye before now no longer exists."

Gregory moved to stand near the cold fireplace in thought. He leaned over and touched the logs—a strong fire began to burn.

Turning back to Brayson, he sighed. "Exactly what is the key to getting past the Source? I have no desire to look into the Eye, so tell me the secret."

"Doubt. You must not have any doubt that you're worthy, or the Source won't allow you to pass."

"After all these years, I've never figured this out. It's disturbing to know that I was held back because I doubted myself. I wish I would've known."

"I wish that, too. We could use the extra power you would've received right about now. We need to figure out what Marcus is planning. This is a matter of urgency. I'll come see you when I know more. Until then, I want you to wear this amulet."

Brayson opened a small chest sitting on his bookshelf. He removed the amulet and waved his hand across it. The diamond-shaped stone burned bright red within its leather strap setting. "Put this on. It will protect you until I can figure things out."

The Kedgle - Hepplesif

Illustration by Kathleen Stone

Brayson moved across the room and clapped his hands. Three Kedgles hurried across the room, their spider legs making little clicking sounds on the illusion of the forest floor. He bent down and picked up one named Hepplesif, who sat in the palm of his hand.

"Hepplesif, my friend, I need your assistance."

The Kedgle twitched his mouse-like nose and listened closely with his tiny elf-ears.

Brayson continued, "I need one hundred of your kind to go with my brother to live in his palace. We need your help. Your illusions could prove useful. This would only be a temporary situation. Will you go and speak with your king and tell him I need his approval?"

Hepplesif spread the wings that were attached to his hairy spider back and responded, "I'll go now. What shall I tell the king you're offering in return?"

"What would he king want?"

The Kedgle lifted his tiny hand to his chin in thought. "Maybe a case of Froslip ale would do the trick."

"Hepplesif... you ask too much. You know how hard it was to get that kind of ale here from Harvestom? I had to pull a lot of strings to get it brought to me by the Merchant Angels. It is, after all, the rarest ale on that world."

"Okay, then maybe a bottle would do. Oh, and I get a mug for myself also, since I am delivering the message."

"Ha ha... my friend, you drive a hard bargain. Tell your king that a bottle is his, and I will give you two mugs full, but they will be mugs of your own size. Agreed?"

"Bah, you know me too well. I would have chosen one of your mugs. It would have lasted much longer that way, but... agreed!"

"Like you said, I know you too well. Please hurry and go find your king." Brayson opened the door and let the Kedgles fly out.

Gregory sighed, "Thank you Brayson. You're a good brother." They embraced, then Gregory vanished.

𝕾outhern 𝕲rayham
The City of Brandor

Sam stood from his throne. Asking everyone to leave, he then turned to speak with Shalee, his queen.

"How are you feeling?"

"I'm okay, I guess, but the spotting won't stop. I'm scared for the baby. These cramps are killing me. This has been going on for over six days now, and it isn't getting any better."

"Dang it, Shalee, how many times do I need to tell you that you should be lying down?"

"Stop yelling at me. I don't need the extra stress right now."

Sam softened his approach. "You're right, but I can handle this on my own, and I want you to go lie down. Michael will be here soon with Kepler's brothers, and I'll dispose of the jaguars quickly. I'll come fill you in when it's over."

"I want to see this. I want to see if I can get any information out of them. I want to know where Kepler has gone. If we find Kepler, George shouldn't be far away."

Neither Sam nor Shalee knew it, but Mosley was listening in on their conversation with his wolf ears lifted high. The God of War was invisible to the mortals.

The king rubbed his hand softly across his love's face. "I agree this is important, honey, but I can get the information you want without risking your health. Will you please go lie down? I promise to tell you everything. I love you. I don't want you to push yourself too hard. The baby needs you to take it easy right now."

Shalee thought a moment. She realized she needed the rest and she also knew Sam was worried. She couldn't understand why she was having so many problems. Mosley had told her that Bassorine himself had chosen her to be Sam's mate. The wolf said she was perfect for childbearing. He further said Bassorine had met with the gods of Earth and this was one of the requests he asked of them before her soul had been sent to join with her fetus. But now, the blood and cramping suggested otherwise. This was a conversation she planned on taking up with Mosley as soon as she saw the deity.

"I think I'll go and lie down after all. Wake me when you're done, please."

The king smiled and kissed her. Three healers who had been summoned to keep a constant watch over her gently assisted their queen from the throne room. Not long after, Michael entered.

"Sire, both demon cats are outside. What would you have me do with them?"

"Take them to the courtyard and don't allow anyone near them. Keep them in their cages. I want to question them myself."

After checking on Shalee and ensuring she was okay, Sam made his way to the courtyard. He didn't waste any of his moments once there. "What are your names, demons?"

Koffler, the mentally-challenged of the three brothers, began to laugh. "We're not going to tell you anything."

Sam thought a moment before responding. "I will offer one of you your chance at freedom in return for the information I'm after."

Koffler laughed again, but Keller, with a mind equal to that of his brother Kepler, took a different approach. "My name is Keller and this is Koffler."

Koffler became angered. "What—"

"Shut up," Keller growled. The giant cat turned and looked at Sam. "What guarantee do I have that you'll honor what you've said and spare me once I've given you this information? What will keep your army from coming after me again?"

Sam moved close to the cage, but stayed far enough away to avoid the demon cat's powerful claws. He held up his sword. "This is Kael, a sword given to me by Bassorine himself. I don't need you to tell me anything. I'm asking you to tell me what I want to know. I could always have my men pin you down and cut you up a bit. Once you're near death, I'll touch Kael to your head and you'll be forced to give me the information. Which would you prefer?"

Koffler shouted, "Don't tell. He'll destroy us anyway."

"Shut up, idiot. I have no desire to be destroyed. I'll tell you what you want to know, King of Brandor. I don't seem to have much of a choice. Killing me is impossible since I'm already dead, but I suspect you know my weakness, and my destruction would be inevitable."

"Don't do it," Koffler roared. The giant cat threw himself against the side of his cage to make his point.

Sam walked over to Koffler's cage. "You have exceeded your usefulness. Allow me to demonstrate that I do, indeed, know your weakness."

The king commanded Kael to bring forth the blade's fire. Once this had been done, he spoke the words of power to extend the length of the blade as he pointed the tip in the jaguar's direction. The demon cried out in pain as the sword skewered his undead heart. The men backed away from their king as the sword's heat intensified and Keller moved to the far side of his cage. It didn't take long before the undead cat was reduced to nothing more than a large pile of ash.

The King now redirected his attention to Keller. "I assume you're ready to talk?"

"I am, providing I have your word that you'll allow me to walk out of this city without being harmed. I also want your word that you won't send your army after me once I've gone. Once I have this, I will tell you all I know."

"You have my word that my army will not come for you. Once you are past the city gates, you are on your own. Are we agreed?"

"Agreed. What would you like to know?"

"Where is your brother Kepler? I want to know if George is with him."

"And if I tell you this, I'm free to go?"

"You are free once I know where they are. I will open your cage myself."

"What's the catch?"

"There isn't one. I'll escort you myself to ensure your safety to the city's gates. Beyond that, you're on your own, and my army will not set foot outside this city to come after you. I'll personally walk you to your freedom."

Keller studied Sam's face before responding. After a moment of silence, he finally spoke. "My brother and George left together. They went to the World of Luvelles. They caught a ride with the Merchant Angels and I haven't seen them since."

Sam looked hard into the demon's eyes. "Come to the edge of the cage. If you're telling me the truth, the sword will confirm it and you'll be free."

Keller moved toward Sam. Once Kael was put against the jaguar, Sam spoke. "Say everything you told me again, demon."

"My brother and George left together. They are no longer on this world. They went to Luvelles."

Kael took a moment, but eventually spoke. "He's telling the truth, Sam, but this creature's heart is dark and he could become an issue for you later if you let him go."

Sam moved to the end of the cage. "I suppose he could, but a promise is a promise." Sam looked coldly into the demon's red, glowing eyes. "When I open this door, I expect you to be on your best behavior. Look around; there are many sharp objects aimed at you right now. You'll stay with me until we get to the city gates. If you make one false move, I'll personally separate your coat from the rest of your body and make your hide my new bedcover."

The demon rolled his eyes. "Okay, you don't need to be so dramatic about it. I will do as you command."

It took a while to get there, but once they arrived at the gate, Sam turned to Keller. "I would run if I were you. I really want you out of my sight."

Without saying a word, the jaguar took off. A moment later, Sam asked Michael to bring him his bow, the same bow he had been given by Bassorine. The general did as instructed. He removed the weapon from his mount and tossed it through the air to his king.

Sam held the bow to his side. "General, if my memory serves me right, I promised the army would not set foot outside the city's gates to go after him, right?"

"Yes, Sire, you're correct."

"I also said that once he gets past the gates, he's on his own, right?"

"Right again, my king."

"But, I did not say that I wouldn't kill him myself."

"You're correct again. Here's to good shooting, Sire."

Sam raised his Bow of Accuracy. Five arrows with burning hot tips were handed to him. The king waited until the jaguar was almost out of sight, then shot the five arrows without pause—one after another and waited. Moments later, the demon fell hard to the ground and tumbled head over heels.

"General, it appears I've kept my word. But the cat has somehow managed to die anyway. Who would ever guess that a tragedy such as this would happen to our feline friend? I find it rather convenient that burning hot arrows would fall from the sky and pierce the heart of our undead enemy. I'm truly broken up about it. But I still would hate to lose the chance to have a nice new bed cover. Will you see to it that his pelt makes its way to my room once it has been prepared?"

"My king, as always, your sarcasm is amusing."

Michael signaled his men to follow him.

One of the castle handmaidens rushed toward them on horseback, shouting as she approached. "Sire... the queen! The queen is screaming and the baby—"

Before the servant could finish, Sam ordered the general to hand him the reins of his new mount. He threw his weight on top of the beast and directed the ghostly, now-tamed, water mist mare toward the castle.

The Hidden God World of Ancients Sovereign
Beneath the Peaks of Angels

"Brayson is going to allow George to keep Payne as his Goswig," Lasidious said as he walked up behind his evil lover. Celestria was sitting at the large stone table of their home, deep within the Peaks of Angels. The goddess had added many feminine touches to make their home warm, full of bright white accents which contrasted perfectly against their dark, cave-like walls. She had been staring into the green flames of their fireplace when Lasidious entered.

Celestria leaned her head back and allowed him to kiss her. The god was quite debonair with his short sandy brown hair, blue eyes, and chiseled chin. His sex appeal excited the beautiful goddess.

He was a tad less than six feet with an athletic build. But it was his charm that won her heart over 14,000 seasons ago.

Celestria stood and moved into Lasidious' arms. The goddess was absolutely beautiful. Her eyes could have stolen the blue from the clearest ocean and made it their own. Her brunette hair fell elegantly over her shoulders and down her back as she moved. If an imperfection was to be found anywhere on her, it wasn't on the outside. Every curve and every gesture was flawless within her bright yellow dress. The voice—an angelic voice— was sweet and soft to the ear. She was worthy of being called goddess.

"How did our baby look? Did you see him?" Celestria leaned in and nibbled on Lasidious's ear.

The god trembled as the wetness of her tongue left its mark. He struggled to focus, but somehow managed to answer her question. "I did... Garrin is well. He cried out when Kepler became angry, but he's well taken care of. He was just startled a bit."

"We need to be careful. Garrin has some growing to do before he'll be able to command the power necessary to control the Book of Immortality."

"Which is why we've been working to create tension between the brothers. Marcus's anger is becoming stronger by the day. His dreams are becoming nightmares. All he thinks about is how much he hates his siblings."

Celestria cupped the god's face and kissed him softly. "Your evil mind simply amazes me. How you ever thought to plant the seeds of resentment all those seasons ago is beyond me. I would have loved to see Marcus's face when he heard his mother tell the other two boys that he was worthless. I can only imagine how bad it stung to hear her say she didn't love him. To hear that she only cared for Brayson and Gregory just had to rip his little heart out of his chest. I so enjoy his pain. If you push him harder, he'll start a war. This should keep the eyes of the gods off our son for sure."

Lasidious smiled and lifted Celestria into his arms. He spun with her and set her down, only to kiss her once more. "I don't need to push him any farther. Marcus has already decided to go after his brother's position as Head Master. He just needs to figure out how. The great thing is that George is standing in Marcus's way, and George will stop at nothing to get his daughter's soul out of the Book of Immortality. All I need to do is give George some simple guidance and he'll do the rest."

"When does he meet with Brayson again?"

"I don't know, but I'm sure it will happen soon. George will be bonded with Payne and if he lives through it, the fairy-demon should be able to help George when the moment comes that he's neded."

"What of the others? I hear the gods are talking. They want to know when you'll reveal the location of the next piece of the Crystal Moon."

Lasidious smiled, took Celestria by the hand, and guided her toward their bedroom as he answered. "I will call a meeting with the gods tomorrow and I'll meet with the Book of Immortality shortly. But first, I have better things to do and you have a piece of crystal to hide." The so-called deity slowly shut the door as he pulled Celestria close.

Marcus Id's Dark Tower-Palace

Gage kept his distance as Marcus threw most everything he could get his hands on around the bedroom chamber of his dark tower-palace. Books, scrolls, quills, chairs, and even his pillows now lay scattered across the cold floor. The badger was feeling a whirlwind of emotions as the Chancellor's mind screamed with unorganized thoughts. It was clear that Marcus was hurting and he sucked on the tip as his pipe as if he wished to pull the tobacco right through it. His heart was not only full of hate, but was now also full of a tremendous, agonizing sorrow. All Gage could piece together were many small bits of Marcus's past. After many moments, the Chancellor finally settled down. His exhaustion consumed him and sleep followed not long after.

The Goswig walked over to the side of the bed and jumped up. He lowered himself down, put his small wooden cane to his side, and took a deep breath. He knew what he was about to do was forbidden, but he had to know the reasons Marcus acted the way he did. He began to search his master's memories. Something had to be the cause of all this hate, resentment, and fear, whatever was tormenting the Chancellor's soul... it was not long before Gage had discovered the root of the problem.

The memories presented themselves to the badger in a vision—a vision as clear as if he were actually there.

"Mother, Mother," a young boy's voice, full of excitement, shouted as he entered the School of Magic. Gage recognized the boy and the school. The boy was a memory of the past, a young Brayson Id who looked no older than 13 seasons. The school was the school of the boy's father, Hedron, the Head Master whom Brayson would replace as an adult.

A moment later, another boy ran in, but this child was younger by nearly four seasons. The badger also recognized this child. It was Gregory Id.

"I'll be right down," a stout female voice shouted. "Stay on the rug and off the floor—it's just been polished." A heavy woman began making her decent down the spiral staircase. She was an elf, but clearly out of shape. Her outfit, although nice, did not hide the weight. She waddled as she walked. Her face was broken out, and scarred because of it.

Gage looked for Marcus, assuming he must be nearby. When he did not see him, he noticed a small crack in the door leading outside to the village. He moved to take a look, passing through the door as if it were not even there. On the other side was the child, now only about 11 seasons old. He was waiting, crouched down, ready to jump out and yell. It appeared he had intentions of scaring his brothers once they came looking for him. His ear was pressed against the door close to the crack. He was listening for their footsteps and to the conversation inside. Gage could also hear everything that was being said.

"Mother, Gregory cast his first spell today," Brayson shouted.

"Yeah, I turned a frog into a mouse. It was neat."

"That's wonderful. Your father will be proud of you. I'll tell him once he has finished the lesson with his new Mystic-Learner. I'm proud of you too, Gregory."

"Thanks, Mom. Where's Marcus? I've got to show him."

What Gage heard next out of Helen's mouth was unbelievable. He couldn't believe the boys' mother would say so many hurtful things.

"How many different occasions have I told you boys to stay away from Marcus? He's not your real brother. He's a mistake your father made with the local whore. You boys need to stick together. Marcus isn't worth our love. He's an abomination, an ugly little thing that won't go away."

"But, Mom!" both boys said, almost at the same moment.

"No, no, no, I'll hear nothing more of this. You two stay away from Marcus and hopefully he'll leave us someday."

Gage watched as Marcus lowered his head and walked down the village road. He could feel the rejection and the pain.

The vision began to fade and a moment later, the badger found himself in another, completely different memory.

For this series of moments he watched Marcus, still only 11 seasons old, as he crept into his father's bedroom. The Head Master was not home, but Helen, now nothing more than another fat Corgan he hated with everything in him, lay sleeping. The badger could feel the boy's heart aching as he approached the bed. The thoughts of Helen's words were playing over and over in his mind as her snores filled the night.

Stay away from Marcus ... he's not your real brother. He's a mistake your father made with the local whore. He's an abomination, an ugly little thing. Hopefully he'll leave us someday.

Gage watched as Marcus slowly lifted the covers. The boy pulled out a Cossenger from his pack. The snake was the deadliest reptile on Luvelles. Once bitten, the venom would take only a moment to kill its victim.

The badger desperately wanted to cry out for Marcus to stop, but this was only a memory. The past could not be changed and Marcus could not hear him no matter how loud he screamed for his attention. All he could do now was watch. It was only a matter of moments before the bite happened. When it did, Marcus covered Helen's mouth so she couldn't scream. The boy looked into her eyes until she was lifeless. Gage's heart ached for Marcus as the boy put the snake back into the pack.

"I hate you, too," was all he said before leaving the room.

Many other memories of pain filled Marcus's mind as Gage sat next to his sleeping figure, but after a while, another very specific memory surfaced.

Now they were in the Head Master's office. All three boys had become adult elf men and stood in front of their father.

Hedron spoke.

"Brayson, the moment has come for you to visit the Source... you too, Gregory. Let's see if what I've taught you has sunk into those brains of yours."

"Am I also going, Father?" Marcus asked. "I'm ready and will make you proud."

"You won't be going. Only your brothers are ready."

"But I can do everything they can do. I'm better than they are, and my magic is stronger."

Hedron waved his hand across the top of Brayson and Gregory's heads. Once the brothers had vanished, the Head Master responded. "You're not ready. Something isn't right with you, boy, and until you figure it out, I cannot send you to speak with the Source."

"But—!"

"But nothing—you're not ready. We'll continue your training tomorrow. Now go and fetch my dinner."

Gage could not believe how cold Hedron had been to Marcus. It was as if he viewed the young man as an irritation, not a son.

The vision faded and after a moment, another memory surfaced.

It was clearly many seasons later and again they were in the Head Master's office. But Marcus didn't stand before Hedron—in this vision it was Brayson, the new Head Master. Gregory was not present.

"I don't know what to say, Marcus. I can't help you anymore. I allowed you to speak with the Source—it's not my fault you were found lacking and denied the opportunity to look into the Eye."

"It *is* your fault. You knew I wouldn't be allowed to pass. You could've told me the secret. All you had to do is tell me how to get past the Source."

"Why would I do that, Marcus? That's not how it works, and you know it. It wouldn't be much of a test if I told you the answers, now would it? Some things need to remain sacred."

"Of everyone, brother, I thought you would be the last person on Luvelles to hold me back. You could've helped me. You're the Head Master. You can do whatever you want. Tell me the secret and allow me to speak with the Source again."

"No, you've had your chance. I won't give you another one. There are clearly things you must learn before you deserve the power you seek. The only person holding you back is you!"

The memory faded.

Gage stood up on the bed and looked at Marcus as he thought to himself, *Master, you are a mountain about to erupt. I'm sorry, but I don't wish to be around when this happens. I'm not strong enough to share the feelings of your hate. When you wake, I will be gone. I must get away, far enough away to avoid sharing your thoughts. I wish you the best, Master.*

The badger vanished.

The Luvelles Gazette

When you want an update about your favorite characters

Lasidious is planning to meet with the Book of Immortality in the morning. He plans to address the topic of a meeting of the gods.

Celestria plans to visit Grogger's Swamp to secure a hiding place for the third piece of the Crystal Moon.

Head Master Brayson plans to meet with George. There is much to discuss and he needs to talk about the responsibility of taking on a Goswig. Other matters of George's training are also necessary subjects of conversation.

George is now with Kepler and Payne. He is going over a few last-minute instructions with them before teleporting them all to Brayson's floating office.

Athena and Susanne are once again inside Susanne's new home. Garrin will not stop crying. They are finding it hard to comfort him. Both women feel the addition of Payne to George's little group is an odd one, but Athena was quick to point out that her husband has a tendency to pick strange companions. The subject of conversation turned to the absence of Maldwin, the rat.

Mary has stopped again in front of the mirror Brayson gave her. She can't stop looking at herself. She has been feeling beautiful ever since the Head Master's advances. This is the tenth dress she has tried on, of the fifteen given to her. She wants to look perfect before she activates the mirror to summon Brayson.

Sam is making his way back to Shalee in the City of Brandor, on Southern Grayham. The situation is grim.

Mosley plans to go to Luvelles. He wants to see for himself what George and Kepler have been up to.

Gregory is inside his glass palace. The confrontation with Marcus has left him on edge. He appreciates the amulet Brayson gave him for protection, but he is still increasing the security within his city. He hopes the Kedgle king will accept Brayson's offer of Froslip juice in exchange for their help.

Marcus is still sleeping.

Gage has left the Dark Chancellor's palace. He has teleported to the far west side of Crystal Lake, located in the Kingdom of Lavan. The badger is hoping to find a temporary place of refuge there. To do this, he must seek the permission from a race of beings called the Ultorians.

Thank you for reading the Luvelles Gazette

Chapter 4

Sam Junior

The Head Master's Island

The homes Brayson provided the family were sturdy. A modest combination of natural colors, throw rugs, and magical lamps, which at the time of George's departure from Earth would have been considered in style, was placed throughout each structure. The furniture was elegant and, to George's surprise, Lasidious had done a wonderful job of studying his finer tastes. The wood looked as if it had been stained, something he had not seen until now, but just another fascinating use of magic. Compared to the World of Grayham, the class and style of living on Luvelles had proven to be far more enjoyable.

This world's idea of refrigeration was also accomplished through the use of magic. As Athena went into Susanne's food closets to find something to settle Garrin down, she was blasted by a burst of cold air. As she opened the door, she saw many frozen items that rested on hard wooden shelves. Quickly she shut the door and continued her conversation with Susanne.

"I have not asked George about him lately," Athena said, shouting upstairs. "I don't know if we'll ever see Maldwin again. Hey Susanne, is there another food closet in this house?"

"Not that I know of," Susanne's voice echoed back. "Mother said her food closet changes. She was very excited and wanted to tell me about it."

"What do you mean, it changes?"

"I don't know. I didn't get into it with her. Garrin has started to cry again and needs to be changed. I swear, this child must be full to the top of his head. It's like he never stops going."

Athena turned and looked again at the food closet door. After a moment, she reopened it. The frozen food was gone and the temperature had went up. Now she saw grains, rice, and other nonperishable items. She shut the door.

"Okay, this isn't normal," she said softly, talking to herself. "What else is in here?"

Again she opened the door, only peeking in. Through the crack, she could feel that the temperature had dropped, but it was not cold enough to freeze anything. Now there were Bergan eggs, Corgan milk, Greggle hash, Hogswayne (or rather, pigs' fat), and many forms of fruits and vegetables.

"Susanne," Athena said, shouting up the stairs again, "you've got to see this. Your food closet is the most amazing thing I've ever seen."

"I'll be right there. Go check out the bathroom. Say the word 'illuminate.' The whole thing fills with light, just like it did back at Kebble's inn. I never get tired of that. There's also a platform near the front door that teleports you upstairs. Mother said the beds even make themselves."

"What? Our beds will make themselves? How?"

"How am I supposed to know? Magic, I guess!"

"I hope our clothes will clean themselves, too."

"Wouldn't that be nice!"

George shook his finger. "Payne, you need to listen. If you're going to be my Goswig, you must pay attention. That's all I need you to do."

"Quit picking on Payne."

Kepler rolled his eyes. "No one's picking on you, freak. Shut up and do what you're told."

Before George could say anything else, Payne disappeared.

"Where did he go?" Kepler said, scanning.

"I don't know!"

Suddenly the giant jaguar cried out in agony. Payne had reappeared, grabbed the tip of the undead cat's tail, and bit down hard. The look on Kepler's face was classic.

"Ha, ha, ha, oh my lord, Kep, your face... you should see your face!" George said as he continued to laugh, despite the fairy-demon's obvious disregard for his former instructions.

"Get this damn thing off me, George!"

Payne released his bite and backed off, but Kepler was not done. His massive paw swiped through the air, aimed at Payne's head.

"You missed... kitty... too slow... too fat!"

Kepler's mighty roar filled the air and Athena heard it from inside Susanne's house. The jaguar began to chase Payne around the clearing in the center of the community of homes. Payne was enjoying the excitement, but Kepler was dead set on killing him.

"Come here, you little freak!"

"Come get Payne, kitty."

"Stand still a moment so I can bash your head in."

Kepler was adjusting to the quick changes in Payne's direction. His powerful muscles rippled under his dark coat as he moved as fast as he possibly could, but it was not fast enough.

George tried to get their attention, but had a hard time speaking. With as hard as he was laughing, the words took a moment to form. "We've got to go guys. HEY... HEY... HEY, DANG IT, we've got to get going!"

Athena walked up behind him. "I think the whole family heard Kepler's roar. The baby's crying again. What's going on with those two?"

"Well, Payne bit his tail. Now Kepler's pissed off."

"I thought you were going to have a talk with them?"

"I did, but I don't think it sank in. Kepler called Payne a freak and it was on. I swear to you, Kepler is going to kill him."

Athena shook her head. "I'm glad I'm not in your shoes right now. I don't think I'd have enough patience to put up with them acting this way. You can't let Kepler hurt Payne—he's just a baby. He's young, and how do you think you acted at three seasons old..."

"I know... I know. I kind of find this all extremely humorous, to tell you the truth, but I need to put a short leash on Payne. I don't fully understand what a Goswig does yet, but I'm sure it'll require better behavior than this. But right now, I need your help with Payne, babe."

Nothing else could be said before Payne flew over and stopped next to the side of George's new home. He taunted the jaguar as he waited in front of the stone-covered wall.

"Come on, kitty... come get Payne. Fat kitty... slow kitty!"

"Bad idea, Kep..." George shouted, but could not finish his sentence before Kepler launched into the air. He watched as the giant cat stretched out, completely zeroed in on the fairy-demon's position—ignoring the stone-covered wall beyond. Just before contact, Payne vanished, and Kepler smashed face-first into the granite.

"Oh, my goodness! Go see if he's okay, George." Athena turned and shouted. "Payne, you come over here right now and take a seat on the porch steps. Don't you dare move a muscle. You do as I say, right now!"

George watched as Payne did as he was told, the little guy's head lowered after being scolded. Then he turned to look at Kepler's motionless form. "I think it's a bad idea to walk up on a demon-jaguar when his pride is hurt. I don't think he wants to be asked if he's okay right now."

"But he's not moving!"

"I know. Relax a moment, will ya? Let's give him a second!"

After a moment, Payne began to antagonize Kepler from the steps. "Ha, Payne bet kitty won't call Payne freak no more!"

George bound Payne with his power. "Stay there and don't say anything else. If he's dead, I'm going to kill you myself."

"But—"

The mage pointed, "Not another word."

Slowly George approached the giant cat. "Kep, you okay?"

"Uuggggg... ohhhh... my head. I really hate that little freak!"

"You scared me," Athena said as she shoved past George. "Let me have a look at you. I think you'll be okay. You have a nasty cut, but it's nothing that some healing mud won't fix, but I think that, between your ears and your face, you're gonna look frightful for a few days."

"Damn, Kep, look at the hole you put in my house. It's a close call, but I'm pretty sure the house won."

"Not funny, George. Do you see me laughing? I'm not laughing, am I? I really hate that little freak."

"Okay, okay, I get it. You don't like him!"

"No, you don't get it. He's going to drive me insane. Maybe you should take me back to Grayham if you're going to allow him to stay. I could be lying around comfortably in my pass right now. I could be eating people in peace."

George was caught off guard. He didn't expect Kepler to react this way. He had a decision to make—it was either Payne or Kepler, and he needed to choose right now.

"I'll tell Payne to go. Your friendship is more important to me. Just give me a moment, okay?"

"Fine, I'll be inside with Athena." The giant cat pushed past George, nearly knocking him over, and slowly walked past Payne without as much as a single glance. The door of the home slammed behind him once he was inside, emphasizing his hatred for the fairy-demon.

George walked over to Payne and released his magic. "Payne, I don't want you around any longer. I can't afford to have a Goswig that doesn't listen. I'm sorry that I've got to say this, but you need to leave now."

"Payne don't wanna go. Payne be really, really good. I like here... um and... Athena nice to Payne."

"I understand, little guy, but you don't listen and you're creating problems. I'm sorry, but you have to go. Goodbye, Payne."

George shook his head with disappointment and went inside.

Payne stood quietly for a while and stared hopefully at the heavy wooden door that had shut him out. Tears began to flow from the corners of his eyes.

Eventually, he lowered his head and vanished.

George and Kepler appeared in Brayson's office a little while later. The left side of Kepler's head was swollen. The brown healing mud Athena had administered stuck out like a sore thumb on his thick, black fur.

"What happened to you?" Brayson said as he stood from his desk. He closed a large, heavily-bound book and walked across the room to the two.

Kepler responded with a grunt and moved to a comfortable spot to lie down.

"A wall hit him."

"What do you mean?"

"It's a long story. Don't ask."

"Where's Payne?"

"I told him to go home. He's more trouble than he's worth."

Brayson sighed. "Too bad you couldn't handle him. He has the potential to be the strongest Goswig a mage could possibly have. He could have been a real asset to you someday. But if you're unable to control him, it is best to know now."

"What?" George said, caught off guard. "I could've handled him! The problem was the relationship between Payne and Kepler. I was put in a position of choosing, so I chose someone I knew I could count on."

Brayson thought a moment as he looked out the window to the land below. "Loyalty is important, I agree, but if you are able to handle Payne, then maybe Kepler needs to try harder. Like I've already said, the fairy-demon has powers that could be useful to you."

Kepler cut in. "I can't stand the little freak. Power or not, I don't want him around."

Brayson smiled. "Kepler, when you met George, did you like him at first?"

"No, not at first, but he was much easier to stomach!"

"Ha, I'm sure he was, but look at the two of you now. Your relationship with George has grown and two friends stand before me, choosing each other's friendship over any other. If you take the moments necessary, perhaps, just perhaps, you and Payne could find a similar relationship."

"I doubt it!" Kepler sneered.

The Head Master moved over to the jaguar and looked closely at his face. Kepler winced as Brayson touched a sore spot, then went to a bookcase at the center of the room and removed a small vial. Opening the lid, he poured a drop of the potion under Kepler's tongue. Instantly the swelling began to reduce, the cuts mended themselves shut, and it wasn't long before he was good as new.

"I trust that feels better?"

"Yes, much, thank you."

George was amazed. "I've never seen anything like that. He healed in a matter of moments. How's this possible?"

Master Id handed a different type of vial to George. "The healers in Floren are the best at what they do. You'll find no stronger magical cures than what they possess. If you have a pulse, they can fix you. I want you to keep this vial with you. It's not as powerful as what I've just given Kepler, but it will do the job. It will just take longer for its effects to work. The vial I have is very rare and I don't wish to part with it. I'm sure that you will need something to keep Kepler healthy. I'm not going to allow you to quit on Payne."

"What?" Kepler shouted and stood up. "I'm not going to hang around with that little freak."

Brayson looked Kepler in the eyes and moved to a position which was only a matter of inches from the deadly beast's snout. Brayson spoke with authority. "Yes, you are going to find a way to get along with Payne! This conversation is over and the matter is settled."

Kepler tried to object, but found his ability to argue—and move, thanks to Brayson's power—was gone. The giant cat could only watch as Brayson waved his hand across one of the windows. "Seek Payne," he commanded. A moment later, the window zoomed in on the fairy-demon's position. He was sitting on top of George's house, waiting for the mage to come home.

"George, come and take a look at this."

George moved to the window. He couldn't believe it.

"Kep, look at this. Payne hasn't left the house."

Brayson had to release the cat's bonds before he could respond.

"So what? He'll leave. Just give him enough moments and he'll go away. I'm sure he'll leave. That's what freaks do."

Brayson looked at Kepler. "You need to change your attitude. You're not getting out of this. You're going to learn to work as a team."

"Easy for you to say. You're not the one getting your ears ripped off. He hasn't taken a bite out of *your* tail, has he? Which, by the way, could use another drop of that potion you gave me."

Brayson administered the elixir and it wasn't long before Kepler's tail was mended.

"George, I want you to leave Kepler with me. Go home and allow Payne back in your good graces."

George hesitated, looked at the demon-cat, and shrugged his shoulders as if he had no say in the matter before responding. "Okay, but he might not be willing to come with me."

Brayson looked back out the window and waved his hand. Payne's face came into focus. "Look at him. I'm sure he'd like another chance. The little guy has lived alone for the last season of his life and he's still very young. You need to be a mentor to Payne. He'll be your Goswig, and Kepler will just have to learn how to get along with him."

"And if I refuse?" Kepler growled.

"I don't think I've given you the option to refuse," Brayson said as he looked the demon-cat in the eye. "I'm sure we understand one another. Would you say I'm correct in my assumption?"

Kepler didn't answer. Instead, he lay back down. He wanted to object, but knew it was pointless. Like it or not, he was stuck with the little freak.

George was impressed by the way Brayson handled the situation. He was also glad he could explore the uses of Payne's skills. The Head Master had given him the perfect place to put blame. When it came to having the fairy-demon around, he would now be able blame Brayson every instance Payne made Kepler angry. It was perfect.

When George appeared outside the home, he had a plan.

"George!" Payne shouted from the roof top.

The mage ignored the call and continued inside as if he heard nothing. Again Payne shouted, and again George ignored him. He pushed open the large wooden door and called out, "Babe, I'm home."

Suddenly, the fairy-demon appeared in front of him, his wings flapping wildly as he hovered.

George acted surprised. "Payne, what're you doing here? I asked you to go."

"Payne be good. Let Payne stay. Payne be bad no more."

"You won't be good. You've ignored me when I asked you to get along with Kepler. How can I trust you to be good now?"

"No, Payne really, really, really, really, really promise to do gooder. Payne be better."

Athena walked up to them. She was a welcome sight. George knew she had a soft spot for Payne already and understood the child's mind. Though Payne was not your normal child, she would still treat him the way she would any young one, and this meant giving him a second chance. George knew he could use this to his advantage.

"I thought you were meeting with Brayson." Athena said, kissing him on the cheek. "Miss me?"

"I always miss you. I am meeting with Brayson, or rather, I was. I had to come home for a bit first." George didn't want Athena to quiz him further, so he quickly turned the conversation around and redirected it towards Payne. "Payne is asking me to give him a second chance. Do you think I should? I don't think he'll be able to behave."

"Oh, oh, oh... Payne is so, so good... Payne promises... Payne really, really will!"

"Aw, honey, he's sorry." She turned and looked at Payne. "Will you try real hard and do as you're told?"

"Payne promise, promise, promise!"

George smiled within himself. He knew exactly what his wife would say next, and he'd be able to use this as leverage to control Payne in the future. All he needed to do was play it out a little longer, and Payne would do everything he said.

"I think you should give him another chance."

"I don't know. I don't think he'll behave. Maybe I should think about it a while."

Payne turned and looked to Athena for help. Like a child, he rubbed up next to her in order to gain favor. While his eyes were on hers, he gave his best "forgive me" look.

Athena looked up at George and he winked at his wife so she would play along. Athena understood what he wanted. She raised her voice and barked out a command. "I said to give Payne another chance. I don't want to hear another word about this. Payne, you'll behave and George, you'll allow him to stay with you. Do the two of you understand me?"

Payne lowered his head, not liking the scolding, and shuffled his feet. "Okay, fine … geesh!"

George could not have been any happier with Athena's performance. He looked at Payne, then back at Athena. "Yes dear!" The mage touched the fairy-demon on the back, and both of them disappeared.

From the window of Mary's home, Brayson watched George disappear. A smile crossed his face as he turned around. "Well, Mary, I must go. It's been a pleasure to see you again. I'm glad you used the mirror to call me." He lifted her hand and kissed the top of it. Mary sighed. "It seems that my moments have run out and I must get back to my office. I would like to come and see you again. I could take you someplace special."

"Yes, please do. Come as often as you'd like."

Brayson kissed her forehead and as he did, he spoke with passion in the language of the Elves.

"Vanimle sila tiri."

"Oh my, that sounded glorious. What did you say?"

"I said, 'Your beauty shines bright!'"

Brayson vanished.

"Aahhhh, I'm really going to like this magic thing." Mary giggled and retired to her room.

Back on Southern Grayham
Sam and Shalee's Bedroom Chamber

Sam had ridden his mist mare as fast as it could carry him to get back to the castle. His jaguar problems were over and he now knew where George was hiding, but the news paled in comparison to what he was about to find out as he walked through the door of his bedroom chamber. The king adjusted his mindset and prepared to call upon the medical knowledge he had acquired on Earth before its destruction. Calmly he sat on the edge of the bed and assessed the situation.

Shalee was pale, fatigued, her forehead cold to the touch, eyes bloodshot and full of tears. "Shalee... sweetheart, I need you to tell me what you're feeling. I need you to explain everything that's been happening since I left."

The queen pulled back the covers before speaking. Her voice was weak and full of sorrow. "It's the baby."

Sam moved to the end of the bed. As he looked between her legs, it took every ounce of strength to hold back the heartache. The infant had been expelled and the baby's skin was blue from the lack of oxygen within the womb. Little Sam Jr. was motionless—lying lifeless within his own afterbirth. Shalee had been near the end of her second trimester and the baby looked to be nearly three pounds. Every finger and toe was accounted for, but unable to grab hold of Sam's finger. The king ordered everyone to leave the room.

Quietly he gathered a clean cloth and spread it out on the corner of the bed. He lifted the baby and placed him gently at its center.

The edges were folded to cover his lifeless son. Sam moved to the center of the room and placed the infant on the table.

Moving to the edge of the bed, Sam pulled his grieving wife into his arms. He held her close to provide a safe place to grieve. After many moments had passed, Sam pulled back.

"Shalee, we need to get you cleaned up. There are things we need to do to prevent any further complications. I need to check inside you to see if all the afterbirth has passed, and I'll place some padding to absorb the drainage."

"Sam, I'm so sorry! I'm so very sorry! I let you down!"

"No, honey, you didn't. This kind of thing can happen to any woman. We'll get through this, I promise, but first, we need to get you cleaned up."

Shalee shook her head and allowed Sam to take charge of the situation. It would not be long before the queen was sleeping, exhaustion finally overwhelming her.

With the situation well in hand, tears now began to roll down Sam's face.

Brayson's Office in the Sky

When George appeared back inside the Head Master's office, Kepler was sleeping and there was no sign of Brayson.

"Kep, where's Master Id?"

The demon opened his eyes and yawned. "I don't know … who cares! We were talking about Payne when suddenly Brayson excused himself and vanished. I see you brought the little freak back with you!"

Payne looked at George. He wanted to fight with Kepler, but did not want to risk upsetting him.

"Well that's just great," George said, ignoring Kepler's comment. "I bet he went to see Mary. Damn, Kep, this isn't good…"

"What's not good?" Brayson responded, appearing behind the mage.

George whirled around. "How long have you been standing there?"

"Long enough to hear something isn't good. What're we talking about?"

"Oh, it's nothing that I can't handle someday."

George changed the subject. "So, what're we supposed to do now? You said something about beginning my training. And you were going to explain how to bond with a Goswig. What did you mean by that?"

Brayson moved to sit at his desk. The heavy wood was carved with a large image of a dragon resting on the front of it, the image of the Source. He opened a giant book which sat heavily on top of it.

"George, you and Payne come here a moment, I want you to see this."

George did as he was told and looked at the book. "This is fascinating. I've never seen anything that looked so ancient. But I don't understand the Elven language, so I can't read it."

"It won't matter. Just concentrate."

George began to focus, but his lack of comprehension of the language frustrated him. "Master Id, what does this phrase mean?"

Brayson leaned over and took a look. He took a moment to explain some of the phonetics of the Elven language. "Now try to sound it out. I'm sure you can do it."

The challenge was intriguing. George focused harder now than before, and slowly he began to sound out the phrase. *"Uuma ma'ten' rashwe, ta tuluva a' lle."* The magic of the book's pages began to stir and it wasn't long after that both George and Payne were sucked in, vanishing with a misty trail that followed them inside the many pieces of parchment. A new story of bonding had begun.

Kepler quickly jumped up from where he lay and began growling at Brayson. "What have you done? What did your magic do to them?"

"Relax, Kepler! Everything will be okay, providing George is able to find a way back. The book is taking them on a journey. The phrase meant, 'don't look for trouble, it will come to you!'"

"What do you mean... providing he can find a way back? And what kind of trouble is he in?"

"George and Payne must take this journey together. If they don't work with one another, they could end up lost or even dead. This is how he will learn to bond with Payne."

"What do you mean... lost, and why would he die?"

"I mean they may never return! He could die because the trials are dangerous."

"Athena isn't going to like the sound of that," the demon-cat scoffed.

Brayson smiled. "Athena doesn't need to know unless George fails and doesn't return... agreed?

"Bah, I suppose!"

Chapter 5

𝔄 𝔉𝔬𝔯𝔟𝔦𝔡𝔡𝔢𝔫 𝔉𝔯𝔲𝔦𝔱

Grayham: Sam's Throne Room

Southern Grayham

Sam spent most of the night consoling Shalee after he had cleaned her up. When finally she fell asleep from exhaustion, the King gently lifted the cloth that held the expired life of their infant son and sought solitude within the confines of his throne room.

As Sam cradled the child, tormented tears began to flow. He would never know the joy of Sam Junior's company. He was empty, his heart ached, his mind was anguished, and he trembled with every breath. He sobbed, wishing with his whole heart to trade his life for the opportunity to give Shalee the chance to know their son.

The memories of everything lost began to flood his mind. He missed Earth, his family, Helga and BJ—especially BJ—and he could only imagine how much the people of his kingdom missed the thousands of men who were only just recently lost in the war.

Sitting on the throne, Sam put both of his legs tightly together and laid the baby on his lap. Slowly he peeled back the layers of the blanket hiding the infant's tiny form. It only took but a look for the king to lose what was left of his composure and he began to wail.

The World of Luvelles,
Grogger's Swamp, Northwestern Hyperia

Celestria appeared in the middle of Grogger's Swamp. It was a miserable place, cold, dark, and murky, the air smelling of half-rotted corpses. The goddess levitated above the moss-covered water and watched as the back of a large creature skimmed the top of its surface.

The swamp was full of many forms of reptiles, amphibians, insects and birds—most of which had been deformed or altered magically, then discarded to live out the rest of their days here in misery.

A large bird with reversed wings flew past her. Its long neck was rolled under its body to see where it was going, since it flew tail first. The goddess shook her head at the ridiculous concept that some powerful wizard would waste his moments on such a childish manipulation.

The swamp covered a tremendous area of Northwestern Luvelles and had become a magical garbage dump, of sorts. These were the experiments of those who sought to strengthen their control of the dark arts. Many of these hideous creatures wandered the swamp badly mutated, but one was like no other.

This was the home of Grogger, a fifty-foot-tall, seventy-five-foot-wide giant, deformed shapple toad. Shapple toads, in general, were not a threat. Normally they were small, about the size of a man's fist. They ate tiny bugs and hopped away from anything larger than themselves that approached. Once an insect had been swallowed, it was slowly digested for days.

Grogger, on the other hand, was not your normal shapple toad. He had been transformed by the darkest of magic—magic commanded by Marcus Id. The Chancellor of Dark Magic had performed many powerful experiments on the beast. As a result, the enormous shapple toad now ruled the swamp. Once inside the toad's belly, his prey remained alive, compliments of Marcus's magic, and was digested slowly over 10 seasons. Many brave men and other forms of life currently resided within Grogger's stomach. Each instance where a new victim was added, the toad's overall size expanded a bit more. At the pace the shapple continued to eat, he would eventually be more than one hundred feet tall and twice as wide. The souls trapped inside could be heard whenever Grogger opened his mouth—their screams sounding in a tormented nightmare.

Celestria understood the digestive traits of the acid inside Grogger's belly. This beast was perfect for their plan—the plan she and Lasidious had decided to implement 100 seasons ago. She had been the one to implant the desire to magically manipulate Grogger in Marcus' mind. The Dark Chancellor's lust for power was strong and it didn't take much encouragement before he took action.

The goddess would place the third piece of the Crystal Moon inside the toad's belly. She hoped to speak with those trapped inside and offer them a chance at freedom. They would hold the crystal until someone came to retrieve it. All she had to do was encourage Grogger to swallow her. It had to be the beast's decision to do so. This was critical—the goddess needed to ensure that the rules of Free Will were obeyed within the Book of Immortality's pages.

Grogger - Giant Shapple Toad

Illustration by Cindy Fletcher

The ground shook as Grogger surprised Celestria, landing behind the goddess. The murky, moss-filled water splashed everywhere, saturating her gown. As it turned out, getting inside the beast would not be an issue. The giant toad's tongue lashed out and pulled her in.

The goddess could not move, due to the sheer number of bodies that were compacted so tightly together. Slowly she expanded her invisible shield of protection to allow for some room. Once this was done, she lifted her hand and commanded the darkness to dissipate.

Despite the knowledge of what she would see inside, she was appalled. It took everything within her to fight back the sickness she felt. The partially-digested life forms, all of which were in various stages of decomposition, caused her to gag. The magic acid within Grogger's belly appeared to attack the outermost extremities first and slowly work its way to the main organs of the body throughout the seasons. Many arms, legs, fingers, and toes were missing.

Although alive, none of Grogger's victims appeared to be co-herent. The screams she heard when Grogger opened his mouth to pull her in must have come from a source other than the nearly sixty motionless figures in front of her. She would need to wake one of them in order to solicit the help she was after. Man or beast, it didn't matter—she figured it best to choose one who had not been exposed to the acid for any lengthy period.

Lying not far away was an elf dressed for the hunt. He wore heavy leather boots and gloves, with the rest of his body covered from the neck down. His crossbow had been severely damaged, probably from the force of Grogger's tongue as he was pulled in-side. The only part of his person left uncovered was his face—but due to the way the magic acid worked, the only damage suffered was to his long blonde hair, and even then it was just the ends that had been damaged. The goddess figured that his capture could not have been much more than a few days ago. She extended her field of force to include the sleeping figure and pulled him inside.

"Hello... hello, are you okay?" She gently touched his shoulder. The elf didn't move. She waved her hand to clear the air of the stench. "Sir, wake up."

After many moments, the hunter began to open his eyes. It took a while longer, but eventually he gained his composure. "Where am I?"

"You're inside the beast-toad of the swamp," she replied softly. "We both are trapped in here. Are you okay?"

"I'm hurt. It's hard to move!"

"I can imagine. The beast's tongue carries quite a force with it. What's your name, hunter?"

"My name is Geylyn Jesthrene, from Hyperia." The elf tried to sit up, but pain shot through his chest. "I must've broken a few things. I don't seem to be able to move. I was here to hunt the beast and win the respect of my family. I had no idea that Grogger had grown so large. It appears we have done nothing but assist his growth further. What a fool I was to think a miserable crossbow could kill him."

"What happened?" she asked, pretending to care. She allowed her mind to wander, thinking of many other things while Geylyn, babbled on.

"The beast surprised me. My mount became spooked and threw me to the ground. I should have known I was in trouble. Krapes are known for their keen sense of danger. I thought I was standing in front of a large mossy-hill of dirt when suddenly it opened up. It was Grogger's mouth, and the beast's tongue was the last thing I saw. I should've paid closer attention to the Krape's warning signs."

Krapes are the mounts of all those on Luvelles who are unable to command magic to teleport. The Krapes' appearance is strange. They are extremely hairy with a large portion of their body resembling the shape of an oversized kangaroo. Their upper arms resemble those of an ape. A long heavy tail extends behind them for balance, with a large mace-like hardened mass at the end which they use for protection. The head of the Krape looks to be reptilian—similar to a raptor's, but with three eyes. One of these eyes rests on the back of their head, allowing them to avoid being attacked from behind. It is virtually impossible to surprise one of these creatures.

Krapes are not carnivores, despite the sharp teeth they possess. Their diet consists of fruits, grains, and many forms of tree bark. Their teeth are used as a weapon when in battle. Normally, a wild, untamed Krape stores food inside a large pouch that rests overtop of its abdomen, but once they've been domesticated, the pouch is used to carry their rider's goods. The saddle of a rider always rests on the back, close to the Krape's haunches. This type of mount can cover a large distance in a short amount of moments, both by running like a raptor or hopping like a kangaroo. Fully grown, the beasts are nearly twelve feet tall.

Celestria placed her hands on Geylyn's head. Four ribs were cracked from the force of Grogger's tongue. "I don't think I would

feel bad about misjudging the shapple's size. Many have underestimated the beast, from the looks of it. I'm sure that when you heard
about the giant toad, you didn't expect it would be so large."
The elf began to laugh, but just as quickly stopped and grabbed his
side.

"Your ribs are broken. I can mend them if you'd like."

Geylyn looked into her eyes, "I would welcome the relief, even
if it's only a temporary reprieve before I die. Are you a healer?
Oh, I'm sorry… where are my manners? What's your name, my
lady?"

"You could say I have many talents. My name is Celestria." The
goddess healed his wounds as she spoke.

Geylyn knew the name. He quickly moved to his knees and
bowed. "I didn't know your face. I'm sorry for my ignorance,
Goddess. I wouldn't have expected a god to be in the stomach of a
giant beast."

"It's quite all right, my friend. You appear to have an excuse,
given your current situation. How would you like to be handed a
way out of here?"

Geylyn smiled. "I think it's safe to say I'd wish for the opportunity to win my freedom, if given the chance. Is this why you have
come to me?"

"Yes, Geylyn, I need your help."

"I will help, or at least as much as I can, but I don't understand
why you've chosen me. My family doesn't serve you—we serve
Alistar. Clearly this service to our god appears to be misplaced,
since he doesn't appear to care about the situation I currently find
myself in, as you have."

Celestria smiled. She would use Geylyn's comment to her advantage. "I do care about you, Geylyn. Why else would I come to
such a miserable place? You don't deserve to die this way, or be ignored by your god. Your life should be cherished, as I cherish you.
It is, however, against the rules of the gods for me to take you out
of here, but there is a way I can save you. It is up to you to choose
to help me save your life! I promise that you'll feel no pain, nor
will you smell the foul stench of this place while you wait. If you
choose to live in service to me, I will also leave you with enough
food to keep you satisfied until help arrives."

Meanwhile: The Hidden God World of Ancients Sovereign:
The Hall of Judgment

Lasidious addressed the gods. "I have called you here to establish the rules for retrieving the third piece of the Crystal Moon."

"Where's Celestria?" Mosley interrupted, taking note of the goddess's absence.

"She'll be here shortly. Don't worry yourself about such things, Mosley. We have much to discuss about the continuation of our godly game. The third piece of the Crystal Moon has been hidden."

Yaloom, the God of Greed and once again the team leader for evil, spoke first. "Our game... we haven't played this game for many days now." He stood up and adjusted his burgundy-colored robe and as he did, his many gold rings filled with assorted gems contrasted beautifully, complimenting the robe's cloth. He moved to a more powerful position behind his chair and methodically placed his hands on its back before continuing. "You haven't given us any information about the next piece of the crystal's whereabouts for more than 100 Peaks of Bailem."

Of all the gods in the room, Lasidious hated Yaloom the most. Yaloom had exquisite taste, though plain to look at. His hair was short, eyes blue, complexion fair, and his body fit. But the God of Greed was not an intellectually gifted deity. Lasidious loathed speaking with him and knew it was easy to fluster Yaloom when attacking his character.

"As always, Yaloom, you have managed to annoy me. But despite your many aggravating attributes, evil still has captured the first two pieces of the Crystal Moon necessary to win the game. If you manage to retrieve this third piece, the worlds will fall under your team's control."

Mosley interjected again. "I would imagine this conversation will include the location of the crystal?"

"It may... I haven't decided that yet, my furry friend. First we need to discuss the rules."

The Book of Immortality floated over and lowered himself to the large marble table they all sat around within the Hall of Judgment. He carried with him a mug full of freshly-squeezed nasha—a drink created from the fruit harvested from the god's orchards. Nasha only existed on Ancients Sovereign. It was the Farendrite Collective's version of the Tree of Life—the one similar to the tree used by the gods of Earth when humans were placed on that world.

Gabriel, the Book, took a drink and swished the liquid around within his rosy cheeks before speaking. "It's your game, Lasidious. I, for one, would love to hear the rules you wish to lay out."

"As do I," Mosley affirmed.

Lasidious took a deep breath. "So... as I was about to say, each team needs to pick one person to go after this third piece of crystal. This person can be anyone you choose other than the three brothers in control of Luvelles. There's no need to start another war on Luvelles over the crystal's whereabouts."

The God of Mischief leaned back and put his feet on the heavy marble table. "Of course, we need to live by the laws of the Book of Immortality and observe the sacred right a mortal has to Free Will. Other than that, there are no more rules. You now have the moments necessary to go and determine who your choices will be. I will call another meeting and divulge the crystal's location soon."

"Why not tell us now?" Yaloom snapped.

Mosley shook his furry wolf-head. "Because it's what you want him to do and he thinks you're an idiot. He's doing this to toy with you. Just be patient, and we'll know the crystal's location soon enough."

Lasidious watched Yaloom sit down in anger, then looked at the rest of the gods. "Are there any questions?"

"Yes," Yaloom snidely replied. "What of the first two pieces of crystal? The ones George collected on Grayham. Where is George, and why haven't these pieces been put back inside the Temple of the Gods on Grayham?"

"George is on Luvelles," Mosley interjected. "So is Kepler!"

"And how do you know this?" Yaloom said as he turned his attention to the wolf. "How could George possibly get to Luvelles?"

"I don't know. Maybe you should ask Lasidious!"

Yaloom redirected his stare as Lasidious shifted his feet and leaned back in his chair, putting his hands behind his head. "I have no idea. You might want to ask George that question. Better yet, ask Brayson Id. I had nothing to do with it. I didn't know he was on Luvelles. I've been looking for him since the war on Grayham. Mosley, are you sure that's where he is?"

Yaloom rolled his eyes and listened to the wolf-god's response.

"I'm sure. I heard Brandor's king question Kepler's brothers just before both of the demon-cats were killed. I heard Keller tell Sam that George and Kepler left for Luvelles and caught a ride with the Merchant Angels."

Lasidious continued his deception. "I wonder how he made this happen. Maybe one of us should speak with the Head Master and find out."

"I will speak with Brayson," Gabriel responded.

"Then it's settled. But meanwhile, are there any questions about my rules for the retrieval of the third piece of the Crystal Moon?"

"Seems simple enough to me," Mieonus, Goddess of Hate, replied. She stood and adjusted her royal purple gown. Her features were human, with dark hair, olive skin, and a firm body that filled the dress perfectly. She moved around the chair, her high heels clicking on the marble floor as she did so, and pushed the chair in.

Alistar, God of the Harvest, stood, "I just want to confirm what you've said. We can choose anyone, as long as it's not one of the brothers..."

"That's what I said," Lasidious responded as he began to walk around the table.

"No matter what?"

"Yes, no matter what!"

Alistar was dressed in a brown robe. He turned his narrow face with soft brown eyes toward Mosley. "Are you thinking what I'm thinking?"

"I am! We need to take a trip to Brandor. But we should give it a day or two, as Shalee has miscarried."

"Oh, that's wonderful," Mieonus responded. "She has too much potential to be bothered by something as trivial as raising a baby. It's the best thing for her!"

Mosley growled, "I strongly disagree."

The goddess smiled. "Let's not let differences of opinion spoil the moment. I wish to savor the thought of Shalee's pain."

Mosley shook his head with disgust. A moment later, Celestria appeared in front of the group. "It's done. The third piece of Crystal has been hidden."

The beautiful goddess had cleaned most of the moss and filth of the swamp from her dress—all, that is, except one small spot on the bottom, towards the back. From where she appeared, only Mosley noticed. The wolf slowly lifted himself from the floor and walked methodically past her. As he did, his keen sense of smell took note of the unique aroma. He knew instantly where she had been. The wolf nodded his head and the remains of the spot disappeared.

Mosley spoke. "Well, I for one will be waiting for your disclosure of the crystal's exact location. I request that those on my team meet with me at my home. We have planning to do. Celestria, as always, it's nice to see you again. Maybe we'll have more of a chance to speak with each other later." With that, Mosley vanished.

"Huh, he didn't even give me the chance to respond," Celestria said as she took a seat. "How are the rest of you doing?"

All members of the wolf-god's team quickly acknowledged her and vanished as well. Yaloom's team was the only one left.

Lasidious looked at Yaloom. "I can't believe Mieonus would allow you to take control of the team again. Your last display of leadership was completely lacking any form of real thought. But I have no doubt that you'll mess this up."

Yaloom grunted, "Hmpf, I can handle this with ease! You underestimate me!"

"I doubt it. Face it, Yaloom, you're an idiot. I would venture to guess you're completely dumbfounded about who to choose. I would've expected as much, considering your mental ability to think through a situation. I'm sure you'll—".

Yaloom cut in. "Lasidious, you've made this an easy choice for us. We shall choose George, your little pet creation."

As soon as the god spoke, the Book of Immortality lifted from the table and sent a brutal wave of power into Yaloom. The deity was thrown backward and smashed into the thick marble wall. His body hit so hard, it left a large crack as he fell to the floor as nothing more than a mortal—stripped of all his godly powers.

Gabriel floated over the top of him.

"You have broken the Rule of Fromalla, Yaloom. You are now nothing more than a mortal man and can no longer stay with us on Ancients Sovereign."

Yaloom began to sob as he realized what he had done. The others in the room were astounded and confused. They began to shout wildly with questions for the Book. Mieonus, on the other hand, knew full well the promise that had been made. She was present in the royal theatre of Brandor the day Sam killed Double D. It was on this day that Lasidious, Mosley, Yaloom and the goddess had entered into the pact of Fromalla. Lasidious had told the gods that it had been because of his manipulations that George was able to find his power.

Fromalla was the rule, or rather the law, that was created by the gods and written in the pages of the Book of Immortality. It was created due to the overwhelming lack of trust the gods had for each other after the God Wars were over. Even though the collective had fought on the same side during the wars, once the wars were over, a battle of a new kind had started. Each of them was bidding for as many followers as they could get when the new worlds were created. In the process, they would share each other's secrets to try and undermine their campaigns.

It had been Bassorine, the late God of War, now destroyed, who

called for a meeting. In this meeting he suggested that they vote
to pass the Law of Fromalla. The rule was long and covered most
any angle, but basically meant that if two or more gods got to-
gether and shared secrets that were said to be under the rule of
Fromalla, they could not be divulged to any of the others without
penalty of being made mortal.

The Book of Immortality was responsible for enforcing this
rule and Yaloom had just informed the others that Lasidious had
a hand in George acquiring his powers. It didn't matter if the slip
of this information was subtle, or even an accident—the rule was
clear—this information had been protected under their pact.

Mieonus held her hand up to silence the rest of her team,
"There's nothing for us to question. I was there when Fromalla
was implemented. Yaloom has broken our sacred law and as we all
know, the Book feels this betrayal as soon as the rule is broken. I'll
lead our team from now on. We'll all meet at Yaloom's old home,
and I think I'll claim it as my own."

She turned her attention to the fallen god. "No offense, Yaloom,
but I'm not sad to see you go. I believe you did us all a favor. We
no longer have to deal with your incompetence! I'm so going to
enjoy my new home. I have always envied the way the waterfall
ran through it—now it is mine!"

Yaloom screamed, "This isn't over. I'll have my revenge!"

Lasidious walked over, leaned down and smiled wickedly. His
eyes turned red and his teeth to fine points. He hissed with an evil
that made those in the room tremble.

"Oh, but it is over, Yaloom. You are more than 930,000 seasons
old. In a few days, you'll be nothing more than a pile of dust. No
one will remember your name once those that serve you find out
about your fall from glory. I'll see to it that every trace of your
existence is removed from the worlds."

Lasidious stood and took Celestria's hand. The last thing the
God of Mischief heard before he teleported home was Yaloom's
scream.

Mieonus dismissed herself, "I trust I'll see the rest of you at my
new home?" She vanished, leaving behind an echo of laughter.

Moments later, the rest of Mieonus's team also disappeared without saying goodbye.

The Book of Immortality looked at the fallen god. "How you could have made such a stupid mistake is beyond me. Where would you like to live out the rest of your days? And I would choose wisely if I were you--we both know those days are short. And don't forget, you're also granted one request, according to the laws within my pages."

Yaloom thought for a series of moments. Eventually a smile crossed his face.

"I still have a significant amount of power, despite being stripped of my godly abilities, and I also have my memories. I can turn this to my advantage, I think! Now that I'm no longer a god, I can help to change the balance of power to my favor without recourse. I'm no longer required to observe your laws of Free Will. I may not be able to hurt Lasidious—or Mieonus, for that matter—but I can take what they want. I will do this by assisting Shalee and helping her get the third piece of Crystal Moon. I can also win my life back, once I'm gone."

The Book interrupted. "I agree, you could help her, but this doesn't answer my question. What is your final request?"

"I'm sorry, Gabriel. I would like you to harness what's left of my power and my memories and put it into a vial in the form of a potion. I wish to be left with this vial in my presence and taken to the throne room of Brandor."

The Book frowned. "I don't like the sound of this, Yaloom. Yet again, the collective has failed to address another matter of great significance within my laws. If I harvest what's left of your powers, even though they're no longer godly, and trap your memories within this potion you would have me make, it will cause problems."

Yaloom smiled. "Yes, but, it's in your laws to grant me this request. You must give this to me, and according to the collective's laws, you cannot tell the others what I've done."

Gabriel sighed. "Brandor, as you wish."

Just East of Crystal Lake,
The World of Luvelles, The Kingdom of Lavan

Gage stood on a hillside looking down at the village he hoped to make his new home. The badger was nervous, nearly sick to his stomach with worry. He knew that without the permission of the Ultorians, he would not be able to take up residency here. He decided to make his descent to the shores of Crystal Lake at nightfall. This was when the Ultorians left their underwater city to come ashore.

Many Goswigs lived in this village with no name. Some of these Goswigs had run away as he had done, and yet others simply needed a place to live after the death of their masters. Gage had no idea what any of them had said or done in order to earn the right to live here.

The village was a secret place and only Goswigs knew of its location. Magic kept the village entrance hidden and again, only Goswigs could see it. If given permission, Gage would be living in what appeared to be nothing more than a glorified hut. This was not what he wanted, but it was the only place that would be safe from Marcus. The Dark Chancellor would view his disappearance as a betrayal, and Marcus's power would be weakened because of Gage's absence.

As he looked at the village, there appeared to be no movement. It was as if the place was abandoned. He wondered if he was in the right place, but decided it was wise to speak with the Ultorian leaders before making any further decisions.

Lasidious and Celestria's Home,
Ancients Sovereign

"Do you think Mosley saw the swamp residue on your dress?" Lasidious asked as he sat near the green flames of their cube-shaped fireplace.

Celestria moved over to take a seat in his lap, "It appears the stain on my dress is gone and I wasn't the one who removed it. I would guess that he saw the clue and got rid of it before the others noticed. I'm sure he knows the crystal is somewhere inside Grogger's Swamp."

Lasidious smiled and kissed his evil lover. "You've got to love that wolf. He's definitely perceptive, and can you believe Yaloom's idiocy? How could he make such an enormous mistake? How could he have been so stupid? I knew he wasn't the cleverest of minds, but to be made mortal over something as trivial as choosing his words poorly, is simply ridiculous."

"Yaloom wanted to use your creation against you. He wanted to rub it in your face and get a reaction. It appears you were under his skin more than you originally estimated. We can forget about this part of our plan now. I'm glad it's over. It's just one more piece of the puzzle that has fallen into place."

Celestria glowed with her enjoyment of Yaloom's demise as she continued. "I know that we've spoken of getting rid of him, but I would've never imagined it would've happened without working for it. I just love it when they do our dirty work for us!"

Lasidious could only smile as he replied. "Gabriel won't be able to draw from either Yaloom's or Bassorine's power when the moment comes to take a stand against us and our son. Whoever is chosen to replace Yaloom will be far weaker than he was, and this bodes well for us. We only have one more godly inconvenience to get rid of, and by then, Garrin will be able to hold the book under his control. With Bassorine, Yaloom, and our unsuspecting friend out of the way, the others won't be able to match our combined power. We just need to give Garrin the moments he needs to mature a bit more."

Lasidious enjoyed the thought. He took a deep breath and chuckled. "I believe Mosley will convince Shalee to go after the crystal. I'm glad her powers have grown so quickly. This is an unexpected twist we can use to our advantage. I hope she finds the crystal before the other team's choice."

"Agreed. All we have to do is plow the road in front of her and she'll follow it straight to the piece of crystal. Do you think you'll be able to convince her to abandon the ways of good?" The goddess rolled her hands over top of one another as she moved to stand before the green flames of their fireplace. "I do hope she chooses evil."

"Well, she's very bitter right now. I imagine she'll be vulnerable after the loss of her child. What better moment to tempt her than now?"

Lasidious changed the subject. "Did you find someone to hold the crystal for us—someone who will be grateful to have Shalee save them?"

"Oh yes, and he's gorgeous. His name is Geylyn Jesthrene. He's a hunter from Hyperia. Geylyn is quite debonair and handled himself like a true gentleman—even inside Grogger's belly, he addressed me properly. I gave the crystal to him and fixed his wonderfully perfect head of hair."

"Your enthusiasm for this Geylyn is not shared by me."

Celestria moved to the god and kissed him, "I think your jealousy is attractive."

"Hmmph, I bet... let's change the subject. I imagine Mieonus will want George to go after the crystal for their team, but when she's unable to find him, she'll come looking for us. I think it best to implement the next part of our plan."

Celestria rubbed her hands across his face, "Yes, my lover, but first, you have business to attend to." The goddess grabbed him by the hand and pulled the deity into their bedroom.

"Let me assure you that you have nothing to be jealous of. You know you're the only evil lover for me."

"I better be!"

"Oh... but you are!" Her tongue found his as the door shut.

Sam's Throne Room,
The City of Brandor, Southern Grayham

When Yaloom appeared in Sam's throne room with the Book of Immortality, the king was asleep, leaning against the padded arms of the large royal chair. The lifeless body of his miscarried son still rested in his arms.

Yaloom quickly spoke. "Thank you, Gabriel, this is perfect. Unexpected, but something I can turn into my favor. It won't be long before I'm nothing more than just another soul within your pages. I hope you'll give me good dreams as I wait for my turn to be reborn."

The Book didn't respond and simply vanished.

Yaloom shrugged. "Guess not, no matter, I've got other ideas!"

Yaloom moved to sit next to Sam. As he woke the king, he was careful not to startle him. Speaking softly, he said, "Sam, wake up. We need to talk, King of Brandor."

Sam knew the god's face. He had seen pictures of him in the royal library. Slowly he lifted himself from the floor and sat Sam Junior on the soft cushion of his throne. He kept his back to the deity as he spoke.

"I'm in no mood to visit with the gods today, Yaloom. My son has been expelled and I don't have much faith in any of you right now."

"I understand, but I'm here to help."

Sam's eyebrow lifted as his curiosity was piqued. Slowly he turned to face his visitor.

"Exactly how do you intend to help?"

Yaloom pulled the vial from his pocket.

"I have been stripped of my godly powers. This vial contains the essence of what was left of my power and my memories. If you were to give this to your queen, she'll be able to save your baby. I'll give this vial to you under one condition."

Sam could only stare at the blue liquid inside the glass. It glowed light blue and was intoxicating to his eyes. He stood there for what seemed to be forever before Yaloom snapped his fingers.

"Sam, are you paying attention?"

"I am … I'm just tired. If I give this liquid to Shalee, you're saying that she can bring our son back to life?"

"In a manner of speaking. This potion contains not only a significant amount of power, but it also contains many of my memories, as I have said. It will assist your queen to gain the power necessary to teleport to the hidden god world. Someday, after she meets with the Source of Magic on Luvelles, she'll be able to make the journey to Ancients Sovereign and pick the fruit from the nasha tree. You'll be able to extract the necessary juice from this forbidden fruit and use it to bring your son back to life."

Sam took a step back and sat on the steps leading to his throne. "Are you saying Sam Junior could live a normal life if she does this?"

"I am saying exactly that, but there are many unknowns here. I have no way of knowing exactly how Shalee will react to the potion. I do know it won't kill her, but I don't know how long it will take before my memories begin to fill her mind or when she'll begin to feel the benefits of the additional power. It could happen quickly or slowly, but your guess is as good as mine. All I know for sure is that it will eventually happen."

"Don't you have some kind of an idea about how long it'll take before Shalee could gain the power necessary to be able to teleport between worlds?"

"Like I said … I don't know, but without this potion she'll never develop the power to do so, and your son will never know his father. Without this elixir, she won't gain the knowledge of the location of the Hidden God World."

Sam thought long and hard before responding. He moved to a window and looked over his royal garden. He smirked as he watched two young boys, boys who shouldn't be in the garden in the first place, chase each other through the many twists and turns of the most elegant place to play hide and go seek. Eventually he turned to face Yaloom.

"I know that I'll live long enough to see that day. I have my unicorn horn and I've been using it each night to receive its benefit of an extended life. But my son, on the other hand, could be nothing more than dust by the moment she gains this power… what then? How will he benefit from the fruit's juice when he has wasted away?"

Yaloom put his hand on Sam's shoulder.

"It won't matter what condition your baby's corpse is in. Keep your son's remains protected from the elements, and when the day comes, all you'll need to do is simply pour the extracted juice over his remains. The power of the fruit will do the rest."

"And what about his soul?"

"Your child's soul will be released from the Book of Immortality and returned to his body. This is the power the fruit possesses. After all, this is the reason why the gods chose to make the nasha a forbidden fruit in the first place, and have kept it from the worlds. Your son will live again. He'll live as if nothing has ever happened, as if he had never been expelled. He'll possess the knowledge of the gods—minus their powers, of course, but he will have powers of his own."

Sam thought a moment. "You said there was one condition. What is this so-called condition?"

"I'm dying, Sam. Everything we've spoken of and continue to speak of now is to be kept a secret. I don't want this information that I'm about to give you to be shared with Mosley or any of the other gods. Will you agree to this?"

Sam thought a moment. His curiosity had to know what the god had to say. "I won't say anything, nor will anyone else in my kingdom."

Yaloom sighed with relief. "I request that your wife retrieve a second piece of fruit from the nasha tree and you use that juice on my remains. Please take care of my body as you would your son's, and when the day comes, I wish to be reborn as you pour the liquid of the fruit over what's left of me."

Yaloom took a long deep breath. "There is one side effect of the fruit. I will be alive, but I'll be reduced to nothing more than a helpless baby. I ask to be given to a good family, preferably one of a royal bloodline. I also want you to save half of the liquid in this vial. If you agree to this, I'll surrender all that I am to you. You can have it and all your queen will need to do is drink her share of the liquid inside."

Sam thought long and hard before responding. "I will speak with Shalee. You have my word that if she doesn't want to undertake this task, I'll return the potion to you."

Yaloom knew he had nothing to lose. He was dying whether Sam convinced the queen to drink the liquid or not, so he surrendered the vial. "If she doesn't, you can drink the vial yourself. You won't be able to save your son, but it will give you a substantial amount of power."

"Power isn't something I need right now. I already rule all of

Southern Grayham. I would rather have my son back—I'll try to persuade Shalee to do this."

Yaloom placed his hand on Sam's shoulder again. "You've proven to be a wise king. Where do you want me to be when I pass on? I don't have many moments left... maybe a few days, at most. I can feel my body changing. I imagine that by tomorrow morning, I will be showing the signs of my upcoming death."

Sam called for one of his servants. He ordered the boy to take the fallen god to the castle's guest quarters, but first he was to bring the finest casket available to the room. Once the boy was gone, Sam turned to Yaloom.

"When the moment comes, crawl inside the casket and shut the lid. Until then, my servants will give you anything you ask for. If everything you have said is true and this potion saves my son's life, I'll do everything you've asked of me, I swear to this. I also swear to you that the queen and I will raise you as our own once you have been reborn. I will save your half of the liquid within the vial and give it to you personally once you're old enough. Let's just hope that Shalee agrees to this!"

The Luvelles Gazette

When you want an update about your favorite characters

Gage is approaching the shores of Crystal Lake. He can only hope the Ultorians will allow him to live with the other Goswigs.

Head Master Brayson is meeting with the Kedgle king. The creature of illusion has agreed to send one hundred of his subjects to protect Gregory for as long as they are needed. In return, the king wants an additional bottle of the rare froslip ale from the World of Harvestom to be delivered to Gregory's glass palace. Brayson knew right away that Hepplesif had asked the king to make this a condition of their service, since he would be in charge of the Kedgles that were being dispatched for this mission.

George and Payne are lost within the Book of Bonding that sits on the Head Master's desk. They have been wandering in circles. All the trees within the fog look the same.

Athena and Susanne are helping Mary decorate her new home. Garrin is sleeping as the women discuss Brayson's charm.

Kepler is lying on one of the large rocks within the clearing near the family's new homes. The children were forced to find another spot to play after the demon-cat rudely interrupted their game of follow the leader. He is frustrated and can do nothing to help George finish the bonding process with Payne.

Sam is with Shalee and explaining everything Yaloom spoke of regarding the forbidden fruit located on the Hidden God World. Something about Shalee doesn't seem quite right. She is agitated with Sam and seems to be upset with everything he says. The king is also a bit touchy. The death of their baby is causing a tremendous amount of stress in their relationship.

Mosley plans to go to Brandor, but not until he has given Sam and Shalee some space to deal with their loss. He has no idea that Yaloom visited Sam in his throne room. During their team meeting, the gods concluded they would have the upper hand since Mosley knew where the third piece of the Crystal Moon had been hidden. They all agreed the swamp was a large area to cover, but concluded unanimously that the stain on Celestria's dress was clearly a clue directly meant to give them an advantage.

They could only assume that the answer to the crystal's whereabouts would present itself upon Shalee's arrival. Sam would need to request that his queen be given a temporary blessing of passage to visit Luvelles from the Head Master.

Gregory is inside his glass palace. He has increased his security while waiting for the Kedgles to arrive.

Marcus has been storming insanely around his Dark Palace. He is unable to find Gage and has killed three of his servants for their lack of knowledge of the Goswig's whereabouts. He is also angry that his pipe's tobacco has run out and has sent for more.

Thank you for reading the Luvelles Gazette

Chapter 6

Kiayasis Methelborn
The Shores of Crystal Lake

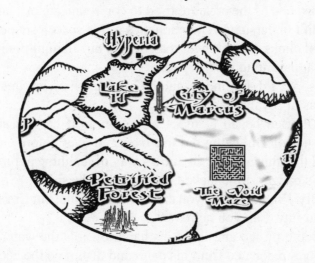

As Gage stood on the lake's shore he could see the clear blue water change as night swallowed the day. It was not the change one would normally expect to see, one where the water went dark from the absence of light. Instead, the lake's surface began to radiate in places. The lights were soft blue and angelic. The glow was not constant, but instead more of a combination of many illuminations that glided through the water at a rapid pace. As the numbers of irradiant figures increased, so did the heavenly feel of the lake's surface.

While in the water, Ultorians, as a race, looked to be translucent, human-like, with giant wings, their internal organs visible. If a man were to look upon them, each organ could be clearly identified and appeared as if outlined.

After a bit, the water began to stir not far off shore. A single figure lifted from the water. Its form changed with each step it took on dry land. The Ultorian's wings retracted within the confines of its back, leaving no biological sign that they had ever existed. Its skin began to radiate with tremendous heat as it changed into a prism of fleshy colors. The water evaporated as the steam rose into the chill of the night air.

Gage kept his eyes fixed as the rainbow-colored figure approached. With each step the being left a trail of gelatinous goo that stained the pebbles of the lake's shore a brilliant white. The badger listened as the creature tried to communicate in a language he couldn't understand. The phonetics of his speech sounded like a series of clicks, some longer than others, but all high-pitched and somewhat painful to his furry ears.

"I'm sorry, I don't understand," Gage said, bowing in case the being was of royal blood.

The Ultorian began to make a motion as if he was about to vomit. The colorful being did this over and over before Gage understood that this was the creature's way of laughing at him.

Gage's badger smile lacked conviction as he spoke. "So you're not royalty. I'm not sure if you can understand me, but I'm seeking a place to stay. Can you help me?"

The being turned and lifted his hand towards the water. Ultra-sonic waves resonated from his palm and disturbed the lake's surface. Not long after, another, smaller Ultorian emerged and moved to stand beside him. This being's face was more childlike, his colors not as bright as his predecessor's, and he failed to leave the gooey trail as he approached.

"My name is Syse. This is my friend, Swill. And you are?"

"Oh good," Gage said, taking a deep, relaxing breath. "You can understand me!"

"I do, but you have ignored my question. Who are you?"

"My name is Gage. I have come seeking refuge."

"Are you claiming to be Goswig?"

"I am Goswig. I have been in the service of Marcus Id for many, many seasons."

Syse shook his head in a negative manner. "You will need to

speak with King Ulitor. Unfortunately for you, under the circumstances, we will not be able to authorize you to live with the other Goswigs."

"Is it because I was created and not born of a normal mother?"

"No, it isn't. I cannot say anything further. You'll need to speak with our king. Only he can give you the permission you seek."

Swill began to speak and Syse turned to give the attention that his mannerisms commanded. His actions were sharp and the rapid clicking sounds of his voice were filled with urgency.

Syse turned around and without an explanation, rushed towards the lake and disappeared beneath its surface. After a moment, Swill turned and lifted the badger from the ground. He began to walk towards the water and as he did, Gage began to squirm.

"Ummm, Swill, I can't breathe down there... Swill... SWILL!"

Meanwhile,
the Outskirts of The City of Marcus

Kiayasis Methelborn patiently set his mother's necessary potion ingredients down on the table. Ever since Kiayasis could remember, he had helped Gwen create the same magical elixir, once every 20 Peaks of Bailem. Today, as always, Gwen was being difficult, refusing to drink the potion and Kiayasis, just as he had done many, many moments before, remained loving and understanding, encouraging her to drink.

"Yes, Mother, I know you're unhappy."

A shallow voice responded from shadows across the room of a rundown home. "I hate myself! I don't want to continue living."

"You don't mean that, Mother. You're just depressed. You'll be okay in a few moments."

"I'll never be okay. I'm hideous. I'm disgusting. Everyone hates me. They all look at me like I'm an outcast." She shouted in Elven. "Amin delotha amin Thanga yassen templa!"

"You know you're not cursed, Mother."

"They all hate me!"

"No one thinks ill of you, Mother. You'll feel better soon. Now stop speaking of such things and take your elixir."

Kiayasis siphoned the potion's liquid from the heavy kettle above the fire and put the necessary dose into a small vial. All Gwen needed to do was swallow the liquid, and watch as the scars covering the majority of her body melted away.

For as long as the potion lasted, Gwen was stunningly beautiful, her long hair brunette, eyes brown, skin olive, and gentle curves that easily turned any male elf's head. But as the potion began to lose its effects, Gwen was left to hide her hideous appearance. It would be nearly three Peaks of Bailem before her body could withstand another dose.

During this period of moments she was nothing more than a miserable reminder of an experiment gone bad during her child-hood. At only 12 seasons old, Gwen had snuck into her father's laboratory and began to play with magic she didn't fully under-stand. Before anyone could stop her, she had concocted a deadly combination of components that had exploded, destroying the lab and nearly taking her life. The only thing that saved her was the instinct to hide beneath the large, thick wooden table she had been working on. She had seen the reaction of the components as they began to build and dove for cover. The table saved her from the devastation of a direct blast, but the intense heat left behind a hid-eous reminder of that day. Gwen felt her face, not to mention the rest of her body, to be grotesque, monstrous-looking.

Kiayasis, now 120 seasons old, had strong Elven features. His eyes were blue, hair straight, flowing, long, and dark black. He stood over six feet tall, was well-built, and much stronger than his father. He was also extremely charismatic and charming. He now lived alone at the center of the City of Marcus, but always returned home to the city's outskirts to let his mother know she was loved during her moments of struggle.

"Mother, it's done. Drink your elixir and you'll feel beautiful again. I hate seeing you like this."

Gwen kept her head lowered and remained huddled in the cor-ner of the room where she always retreated once the potion wore off. Gwen's home was run-down, dirty, and located outside the city. She, like many others, was considered to be one of the city's rejects. A large wall separated Gwen and her type from the people within the walls who were of a pure Elven bloodline, had substantial wealth, and the ability to control the stronger powers of the dark arts.

Only Elves of a pure bloodline were allowed to reside within Marcus's walls, but a pure bloodline alone wasn't enough to get an elf approval. Many of the people in this area, although pure-blooded, were without magical abilities or strong enough power to be allowed to live within the Dark Chancellor's shadowed city. As a result, they were treated as minor irritations and given jobs considered less than desirable.

"Mother, you need to stop sulking. Let me help you up." Kiayasis leaned down and, as he had done on many occasions before, lifted Gwen and carried her to a chair near the kitchen table. As he sat her down, the old wood creaked beneath her weight.

Gwen had never married. She had tried to find a companion, but each relationship had ended because of the depression she experienced when the potion's magic wore off. The longest relationship in her life had been for nearly one whole season, a union that had produced the joy of her life—Kiayasis.

Her baby's father, Boyafed, was a powerful man back then, and still was to this very day. The Order's temple encircled the Dark Chancellor's tower-palace and rested on a hill at the city's center. Boyafed was the leader of this Order—The Dark Order of Holy Paladins. He was charismatic, charming, strong, and handsome. These were just a few of the many delicious traits Gwen had fallen in love with.

It was the best season of Gwen's life, but her happiness was short-lived. Boyafed realized how taxing it was going to be to live with Gwen, and dealing with her ongoing depression wasn't a task he cared to undertake. He took Gwen outside the city's walls and left her with enough coin to pay for the home she currently lived in. This was Boyafed's way of ensuring she had a safe place to give birth and raise their child. And, although not a part of Gwen's life any longer, he did remain a part of his son's life and visited him often. This was over 120 seasons ago.

Kiayasis, despite his mother's inability to use powerful magic, benefited from Boyafed's biological contributions to his genetic makeup. As a result, he commanded strong magic of his own. For the last 20 seasons Gwen's son had been living near his father, training, and praying to the God of Death, Hosseff, to become a Dark, Holy Paladin. Tomorrow would be Kiayasis' graduation. He would receive his first assignment and don the black-plate armor of the Order—a group chosen by Boyafed himself. It was their duty to handle the day-to-day operations of not only the city, but the twenty-five hundred elves in training who held shields bearing the symbol of the Order.

"Mother, open your mouth and drink. You know it will make you feel better. Please don't make me force it down your throat."

Gwen slowly lifted her head and poured the elixir into her mouth. It only took a moment for the magic to take effect. Her skin began to clear and the scars peeled away and fell to the floor. Once again, she was beautiful.

Kiayasis smiled, "Now see, you look wonderful!" He lifted a mirror as he always did to ensure she could see the potion's benefit. And, as always, Gwen seemed to be surprised at the transformation before she began to smile.

"I'm pretty. I'm beautiful. Do you think I'm beautiful, Kiayasis?"

"You have always been beautiful to me, Mother."

"Oh... my boy, you're good to me. You can never leave me. I need you, Kiayasis. Your father is keeping you from me. I don't think I can stand another day without you."

"I miss you too, Mother, but my training is almost at an end and I have enjoyed getting to know my father."

"I can't be without you." Gwen pulled away and turned her back to him.

"Don't be like this, Mother. I have always been here for you."

"It's not the same. Your father has taken you from me. I want you to come home. I demand that you come home! I won't spend another day without you!"

"You know I love you." Kiayasis pulled Gwen close, hugging her tight.

Her ongoing mood swings were a source of contention. Kiayasis knew he would never be free to live his own life because she would always command his attention and, despite his love for her, she would ruin whatever chance he might have at finding any real, lasting enjoyment.

Gwen pulled away from his arms.

"If you love me, you'll come home! Stay with me, Kiayasis! Please don't go back to your father's army!"

He put on a big smile and took a long, relaxing deep breath. "Come here, Mother. I will stay with you. You're right. I should never have left you alone."

"Oh … my baby, do you really mean it? Thank you! I knew my boy would choose me!" She rushed back into his arms.

He held his smile until her head rested below his chin. He caressed her back as he reached behind his own. His hand grasped a bone-handled dagger, a blade known only to the Dark Order of Holy Paladins, and continued to speak.

"Mother, you don't have to worry any longer. I'll come home to you. I've always been here to remove your pain. You're right … I love you more than anything."

Careful to keep Gwen's head tucked under his chin, tears began to run down his cheeks. "You mean everything to me, Mother! You've always been beautiful to me. I can stop your torment."

Without further hesitation, he plunged the blade deep within her gut and lifted it up to ensure a quick death. As he reached around his mother's head, he pulled Gwen's face into his chest to smother her cries. It did not take long for the last bit of air to escape her limp form that remained standing only because of his will to keep her erect. With one gentle swoop, he lifted her into his arms and carried her lifeless figure into the bedroom.

Kiayasis laid Gwen's head on the pillow, adjusting the rest of her body to a position that seemed peaceful. Slowly he pulled the covers over her and took a seat next to her on the bed.

"See, Mother, now you'll always be beautiful. Your scars will never reappear. But I can't care for you any longer... May your soul find the peace it seeks with the gods."

Wiping the tears from his face, Kiayasis closed the door to her room. As he left the house, he bolted the door shut and began walking toward the city's walls.

It was not more than a few moments before the magic hiding Gwen's scars began to fade. Kiayasis was wrong; her beauty faded as the magic did, and her soul left to find its home on the Book of Immortality's pages. His mother would be found as nothing more than a hideous reminder of a once-gentle soul. She would be forgotten.

The Temple of the Holy Order

"Lord Hosseff, to what do I owe this pleasure?" Boyafed, the leader of the Dark Order of Holy Paladins, said as he dropped to one knee before his god.

"Stand up, Boyafed. We have much to discuss. Walk with me."

The temple of the Order encircled Marcus Id's tower-palace. The perfectly polished, white granite hallways were lined with fifteen-foot-tall red demonic statues with large black wings and thick horns. Some of their wings were folded behind them, while others were wide-spread. The monstrous faces looked as if they were crying out for battle. Each demon held a large torch which cast an eerie glow.

Boyafed wore all black except for his gold-colored shirt. His cape carried the Order's symbol at its center—a heavy stone table, also gold in color, represented their belief in offering sacrifices to their god. His eyes were dark brown, hair short, and his rock-hard jaw complemented his strong frame.

"My Lord, how may I be of service?"

Hosseff stopped and looked out the temple window which sat just above the rest of the city below. The only building higher than the temple was Marcus's tower, which stood hundreds of feet taller at its highest point. The whole city rested beneath the shadows of heavy gray clouds, clouds which never moved from their fixed location. They hovered in one spot thanks to Marcus Id's magic, and this depressive atmosphere was how the city became to be known as a City of Shadows.

The god looked to have a human face when in the direct light of the torches, his hood hiding the fact that his ears were not Elven. But as they moved away toward the shadows, his appearance changed. He became smoky or hazy-looking, his robes being the only thing visible in the fading light once it dissipated. On this day, the deity wore a golden robe with black trim. The god spoke as if his voice was nothing more than a windy whisper.

"I need someone to escort a human woman from Merchant Island to the swamp lands of Grogger. She will be coming from Grayham. I'm not here to order this done, but I would appreciate your assistance, Boyafed. I know your son Kiayasis has completed his training and will be given his first assignment as an official member of the Order at Early Bailem tomorrow."

"Yes, my Lord, he's strong and will make a fine addition to our numbers. He plans to make his first sacrifice to you in the morning, my Lord. Would you like me to send Kiayasis to retrieve this woman and act as her guide?"

"I'm sure he'll do a fine job. This woman seeks something within the swamp. She'll need to enter alone. Kiayasis would need to wait for her."

Hosseff put his wispy hand on Boyafed's shoulder. "The woman's name is Shalee. She is powerful—a sorceress who weilds magic great enough to command your respect. The Merchant Angels will bring her to Luvelles soon. Kiayasis will need to make his way there and wait for her arrival."

"My son lives to serve you, my lord."

Hosseff moved back into the direct light of the torch and his features solidified. Again he put his hand on the leader's shoulder, but now his skin could be seen once it finished solidifying.

"You're the foundation of this Order, Boyafed. You have made me proud for nearly 400 seasons. I'm sure you'll continue to do so."

"Thank you, my lord." The Order leader bowed to one knee.

Hosseff lifted him from the floor. "There's something else I wish to discuss with you. It's something of grave importance."

Meanwhile, Back on Grayham,
Brandor's Castle

"Oh my god, Sam, you've got to quit nagging me. I'll drink it when I'm ready!"

"Shalee, just drink the potion. Yaloom said it will give us the chance to save our baby. Why don't you want to do this? Damn it, Shalee, don't you want to be a mother?"

"Just give it to me already! I'll drink it, but you better stop badgering me! You know, you're really starting to piss me off!"

The queen quickly drank her half of the potion and chucked the bottle across the room. It smashed hard against the wall. Sam watched it shatter and thought to himself, *I'm glad that I divided it into two separate vials prior to handing it to you. WOW!*

"Oh, yuck," Shalee cried. "This potion Yaloom gave you tastes absolutely awful! It's almost as bad as this shallow relationship of ours! We were rushed into things—how could we truly love one another in such a short time? And, you know what else... I won't stand..."

Shalee suddenly stopped talking, stood from the side of the bed and pushed hard against her stomach. As she did, she doubled over and fell to the stone floor. Sam rushed to pick her up and laid her on the bed. Before her head hit the pillow, she was out cold.

"Shalee... Shalee, come on—wake up!" He pushed her blonde hair clear of her face. "Wake up!"

The king, relying on his medical training from Earth, began to examine her. The queen's heart rate was elevated, pupils unresponsive, and her skin felt feverish. Sam darted out of the room and moments later, pushed through the door of Yaloom's guest quarters.

"Why did Shalee pass out after drinking your potion? What's wrong with her?"

The fallen god's appearance had changed. He looked like an old man nearing death as he struggled to stand from his chair. "What did you expect, Sam? Your wife's body needs the moments necessary to adjust to her new powers. She'll be okay, I assure you. It'll be hard for her mind to absorb the information my memories contain. She may not even be able to use her new abilities at first, but she will come to understand them. I just don't know when this will happen, as I have told you before. Try not to worry. I would not have given you the potion if she wasn't strong enough to handle its effects."

Sam took a deep breath. "You look like garesh. You might want to consider going to sleep inside your casket tonight. From the looks of it, I doubt you'll be waking up—no offense, of course."

Yaloom tried to laugh, but instead, began to cough up blood. It took him a moment to settle down. "No offense taken … I plan to do just that. The coffin was a nice touch. I hope the next series of moments that my eyes look upon you, they'll be the eyes of a baby."

"I've given you my word."

"Then it appears that we have a pact, King of Brandor, or should I say, Dad." Yaloom weakly patted Sam on the shoulder.

It bothered Sam to hear Yaloom calling him Dad. "I don't think you should call me that. Please, don't say it again. I would rather be spared such words until I know my son lives!"

"I understand. I'll save it for later then. I think I'll retire to my casket now. Will you have someone watch me through the night and seal me inside once I've quit breathing?"

"I will... until later, then?"

"Yes. Until later, Sam!"

Sam turned to leave. As he approached the door, Yaloom called to him. "Sam!"

Taking a deep breath, Sam turned around. "Yes?"

"Thank you. You're a good man, and a better king. Southern Grayham has needed a man like you for many, many seasons. Your wife will succeed. She's strong and I wouldn't worry about the outcome of your son's future if I were you."

"I hope your right, Yaloom... I hope you're right." The king lowered his head and left the room.

Yaloom sighed heavily and whispered "I hope I'm right too. I truly do hope I'm right!"

Inside the Book of Bonding on Head Master Brayson's Desk

George walked through the fog while Payne flew beside him. The haze hovered. It was thick, making it impossible for them to see the ground. The fog did, however, stop near George's waist.

George nervously thought to himself— *I feel like I'm inside some kind of Thriller video. Maybe Michael Jackson will jump out from behind one of these trees dressed as a werewolf.* He chuckled quietly as he continued to remember the fondness he felt for the singer's music before he was taken from Earth. *It's too bad such a great artist had to die!*

The forest trees stretched high into the darkness, yet there did not appear to be a night sky. All they had seen since their arrival was more of the same. They were wandering in circles. Nothing about this place made any sense and how they had gotten here was even more of a mystery. Neither the mage nor the fairy-demon realized they had been sucked into the giant Book of Bonding on Brayson's desk.

"This place is miserable, Payne. We need to find our way through these trees, but I'm not sure which way to go."

Payne thought a moment, "Use magic."

"To do what? We're in a forest, for hell's sake."

The fairy-demon looked confused. "What hell mean?"

George shrugged, "Forget what hell means. How do you want me to use my magic?"

"To find the way... um... gotta find a way?"

"And exactly how would I do that?"

"Don't know," he responded, shrugging his small, bright red shoulders. "You is the master!"

"Bah, how can I find a way when…" George hesitated and began to think. After a few moments of spinning around in one spot, he raised his hands directly in front of him, put his palms together and motioned for the fog to part. The haze began to split, moving with his hands as he separated them slowly. The ground beneath was revealed.

Damn, nothing here... maybe I should try again.

George took a quarter turn to the right and repeated the process. Again the ground bared itself and again there was nothing.

"Damn! Let me try again," he said aloud.

On the third try, a path was revealed.

"That's weird. We've been walking forever, but somehow this path seems to begin where my feet touch the ground. What are the chances of that? Do you think it's magical?"

Payne lowered himself to the ground and touched the path. "It lives."

"What do you mean … it lives?"

"Um... it breathes... you know, like Payne and Master do. He want George to find it."

"What do you mean... *he*? And I've told you to stop talking about us as if we're third parties. You're driving me nuts."

"Okay, okay... grouchy Master." Payne lowered his ear to the ground. "His name... um, um... I mean... um... the, the, the…"

"The path, Payne, the path. It's called a path."

Payne growled with frustration. "The path... name... Follow."

"What? The path has a name, and it's Follow?"

"Yes."

"Well that's the most absurd thing I've ever heard. A path named Follow—you've got to be kidding me. I'm not even sure what else to say. But at least we're getting somewhere! I wonder where Follow will lead us. My hell... I can't believe I'm referring to a path as a person. So let's follow Follow's path." George shook his head. "Holy hell, that's almost confusing."

"Master acting stupid."

"Shut up, Payne. Let me think." He turned to ponder a moment, grabbing his chin. "That's actually kind of humorous. Hey, Payne... ask Follow—"

As he turned to look at the fairy-demon, he was shocked to see that Payne had already begun to move forward.

"Hey, hey... dang it Payne, wait for me. It's bad enough that I have to follow Follow, without following you!" George chuckled. *Wow, I amuse myself sometimes. Damn, I'm good!*

As they moved down Follow's path, the flowers originally hidden by the fog were now visible. What was left of the haze had completely vanished and everything was now in plain sight. The plants paid attention to their movements as if they were aware of their presence. Their stigmas acted as eyes, staring the pair down as their stems adjusted the flower's red-petaled bodies for the perfect line of sight.

"What are these, some kind of creepy tulip creatures or something? I feel like they're stalking us," George said with a touch of mild anxiety in his voice.

Payne flew over to one. "Payne tell you." He snatched it out of the ground and shoved it in his mouth. "Flower thingy tastes good."

Suddenly the earth beneath the flowers began to shift. One by one, leg-like roots began to appear as the rest of their bodies emerged from the ground. Slowly they began to surround George, preparing to attack. The mage had not noticed until now, but they had teeth. Their stigmas were splitting in two and transforming into an actual pair of eyes. Long, leafy arms peeled away from their stems and turned claw-like.

"Payne, I don't like this. Get over here quick... right now, damn it!"

Payne flew beside him. George grabbed the demon and teleported further down the path. Once they reappeared, he shouted, "Run!"

They sprinted down the path as the creatures scurried after them, their petals falling to the forest floor as they gave chase. Payne flew backwards while George looked over his shoulder. But Follow's path was about to end and both of them had failed to observe the large hole that had opened up in front of them. Payne watched as George disappeared into the darkness. Without hesitation, the fairy-demon folded his wings and fell, diving into the hole to catch up.

Chapter 7

𝔜𝔬𝔲'𝔯𝔢 𝔓𝔯𝔬𝔲𝔡 𝔬𝔣 𝔐𝔢?
Inside the Book of Bonding

Payne dove into the hole after George, his demon eyes able to see their surroundings as they fell into the darkness of the shaft. The end of their fall was approaching rapidly and he knew he didn't have many moments left. He was working to keep his body as streamlined as possible to catch up with George, but the mage was too far ahead.

Payne shouted, "Master, teleport," but he couldn't understand the response.

The rock floor was only a few hundred feet away now. His eyes quickly searched for a place to land. He teleported to the bottom and allowed his body to erupt with flames. He burned bright, hoping to shed enough light on the area to clearly define the terrain. The water he now stood ankle-deep in began to evaporate as the flames tore aggressively into it. All the fairy-demon could do was hope his actions were enough. It was now up to George to save himself.

Less than two feet remained before impact. Payne had already covered his eyes and began listening for the splat he knew George would make. After a moment, the fairy-demon began to peek through his fiery claws. George was standing in one of but a few dry spots on the far side of the hole's water-covered floor. He had teleported to a spot safe enough to avoid the heat of Payne's burning body.

Payne began to dance around, singing out loud, pleased that his plan had worked. As he did, each step he took caused a searing sound as the water found his burning hot footsteps and sent small clouds of evaporated moisture floating into the air.

"Master so safe... Master so safe... Master so safe... Master so safe. Payne saved him... Payne saved him... Payne saved him... Payne saved him. You need Payne... you need Payne... ha, ha, ha... you need Payne... you need Payne. Payne so good... Payne so good... na, na, na... Payne so good... Payne so good—yeah!"

Payne stuck out his long red tongue and blew slobbery, fiery spit in George's direction, all of which evaporated as it moved through the air.

George, although shaken from the fall, began to laugh, careful to keep his distance from the demon's flame. "Yes—you saved me, and I'm proud of you, Payne. I'd be dead right now if it weren't for you. I couldn't see anything until you used your flame. I'm very impressed."

The fairy-demon stopped his celebration. "Master proud of Payne?" The fire encompassing his body dissipated and his tiny black eyes began to shed tears that evaporated when they touched his hot skin. "Payne never hears no one say that to Payne before!"

George lifted his hand and a light began to burn within the palm. With his other hand he summoned a breeze to help cool the area. As the heat faded, the mage approached his little companion. "I'm saying it, Payne. You made me proud just now. Without you, I'd be dead."

"Neat, that's neat... um... Payne hungry." True to form, the child's attention span had moved on to something else.

"Speaking of eating, it was your eating habits that got us into this mess in the first place. I thought we agreed you would eat what I do? And stop talking in third person!"

"Nope, Payne never agreed. Payne just listened to Master's order. Payne never did no agreeing. Why Master no do teleport... um... you know... to the top... uhh, the big hole?"

George rolled his eyes. "I tried, but my powers weren't strong enough. I think there was a stronger magic that made it impossible. I think we were meant to fall down here. Something stopped us from teleporting back to the surface."

"So... umm... now what to do, Master?"

The Underwater City of Ultor

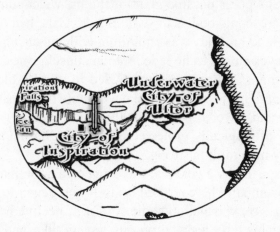

Swill had carried Gage far beneath the surface of Crystal Lake. He had protected the badger by using his angelic water wings to create a perfect pocket of air. They were now approaching a beautiful reef of freshwater coral with colors so vibrant it was like nothing Gage had ever seen before.

The Ultorian headed rapidly towards the reef with no sign of slowing down. Gage was nervous. He had never been under water before, let alone moving so quickly while beneath it. He was unable to do anything. as his magic was not working within Swill's protective barrier. All he could do now was watch.

A pair of fairly good-sized sea snakes emerged from their holes. They moved in a large circular pattern, seeming to indicate where Swill needed to go. The reef was nearly upon them, but the Ultorian failed to change the speed of his approach. Gage closed his eyes, but when the impact with the coral never happened, he opened them just enough to get a peek. The reef appeared to be far away again, but they had not moved. Their bodies had shrunk and were continuing to shrink. The sea snakes now appeared to be many, many times larger than they were only moments ago... giants, titans of a watery underworld.

The closer they came to the coral shelf, the farther away they seemed to get. Gage didn't realize it, but he was now no larger than a speck of sand and the shrinking was not going to stop there.

Eventually their approach narrowed to a specific part of the reef and the coral's pores became giant openings, welcoming their tiny-little-microscopic bodies to swim inside. Gage had never seen such magic, and his body was struggling with the change. Finally, his badger eyes closed as he faded into unconsciousness.

The Ultorians' entire kingdom resided in an area of not more than two square inches. Crystal Lake was more of a freshwater sea than a lake,and covered over 210,000 square miles. Within this small piece of magically protected coral, the Ultorian race numbered nearly nine million strong.

When Gage finally awoke, he was lying on a floor. It took a moment, but eventually he collected himself and began to study his surroundings. He was within some sort of protective barrier. The floor beneath his furry feet was porous, sponge-like, and alive. Beyond his bubble of air, the Ultorians' iridescent blue bodies could be seen swimming all around.

Gage watched intently as his hosts swam past his location. He was now in the middle of a highly populated area. It was as if he was on display. He could not see much past the barrier, but he could tell there was an organized flow in how they moved. Eventually a familiar face appeared.

It was Syse. He swam up to the bubble, settled onto the coral floor and walked through the barrier's gelatinous wall. His wings beat rapidly to cool the area within the bubble while making his transformation. He changed from an iridescent blue to a soft blend of yellows, oranges, and finally reds. The heat from this exchange boiled the water from his skin and sent a cloud of steam billowing up and through the barrier's roof. The badger appreciated the breezy relief Syse's wings provided.

"I see you've finally awakened," Syse said as he sat on the floor and lifted his head towards the bubble's roof, only to make more of the same high-pitched clicking noises he had made while communicating with Swill. Once this was done, he again addressed Gage.

"You'll need to speak with our king. We were warned you would come. I'm sorry, but I had no choice other than to bring you here."

"What do you mean, you were warned?"

"Chancellor Id warned us you might come. Beyond telling you this, I cannot speak of the matter further until King Ultor arrives."

"Am I to be returned to Marcus?"

"This is not for me to decide. The king will determine your fate."

Gage closed his eyes. He tried to teleport, but nothing happened.

Syse sighed. "You're not strong enough to escape. I understand your fear, but I assure you our king is an understanding leader. He will listen to you before making a decision about what to do with you."

"This isn't how I imagined my escape from Marcus's service would end up. I only wanted to find a peaceful place to live. When am I to meet with your king?"

"I don't know. I have sent word that you're awake. We shall know soon enough."

The Next Day, Mary's Home

Brayson Id appeared unexpectedly on Mary's doorstep just after Early Bailem. He knocked and waited patiently for her to answer. When Mary opened the door, she was still wearing a nightgown and her hair was a mess. As quickly as she had opened the door, she slammed it shut. Raising her voice, she spoke through the heavy wood.

"I look awful, Brayson. I thought you were one of the kids. I don't want you to see me this way."

Working hard to fight back a good laugh, Brayson responded, "I remember promising to take you someplace special. I'm sorry for disturbing you, but I assure you that it's okay for you to open the door. I'll ignore the fact that you aren't ready for the day."

"Mr. Id, I need to do my hair! I would love to see you, but do I need to remind you that a woman needs some notice? You'll just have to come back."

Brayson waved his hand across the door. "Mary, please take a look in the mirror I gave you. I'm sure you look stunning. All you need to do is change."

Brayson stood silent, his ear pressed against the wooden barrier, waiting for her reaction. He heard Mary gasp and a moment later the door opened. In her excitement, she completely disregarded the fact that she still wore only a nightgown.

"How did you do that? My hair... it's perfect."

"Magic, my dear... magic!"

Mary took him by the hand and pulled him into the doorway. She gave him a quick kiss on the cheek. "You stay right here. I'll go and change." Thrilled with her new look, she jumped onto the teleportation platform near the front door and reappeared in her bedroom—leaving Chancellor Brayson Id, the most powerful and influential elf on all of Luvelles, standing in her doorway.

The Castle of Brandor,
Sam's Throne Room, Southern Grayham

"No, Mosley, I don't want Shalee going to Luvelles," Sam said as he stood from his throne. His eyes moved from the wolf, and came to rest on Alistar, God of the Harvest. "She just had a miscarriage, for hell's sake! Our relationship is suffering and we need the moments necessary to fix things before she goes tromping off to another world! Shalee isn't acting like her normal self right now. Everything I do is wrong lately. I think the gods need to settle this matter on their own. We need to be left alone!"

The wolf-god sighed. "Sam, I understand your pain and your concerns about the stress your relationship is under. I also understand that you're angry about the baby. But—"

Sam interrupted by shouting. "You're damn right I'm angry about my baby! I'm also angry because the gods destroyed Earth! I'm angry because Shalee and I were dragged into this world against our will and have been asked to do the impossible! We did what the gods asked of us. I fought in the arenas of Grayham... I found a way to become a king, and for what... only to lose the Crystal Moon's pieces to George. I have united all of Southern Grayham under one throne and things are starting to look good for the people. There's peace on Grayham. But that's not good enough for you is it, Mosley? God forbid the gods give us the moments we need to move past the problems we're facing!

"Shalee believes our relationship is shallow. She feels we were rushed into things and I happen to agree. But I'm not willing to sacrifice what's left of our relationship so she can chase your stupid crystal.

"You know what... it amazes me how stupid the gods were when making your laws. The idea that the gods can't fix their own mess with the Crystal Moon because of some ridiculous rule within the Book's pages... ha, what a joke! How could gods be such idiots?"

Both Mosley and Alistar waited patiently as Sam continued to shout.

"Now I find myself sitting here mourning the loss of our son, and you come to me and tell me that Shalee is needed on Luvelles. We haven't even had a chance to grieve yet! Dang it ... I know how the Book of Immortality works, and I also know you can't make her go! I won't allow her to go, and there's nothing you can do about it! I'm tired of the games. Besides, Shalee is in no condition to go to Luvelles, anyway."

Mosley's response would have to wait. Both his and Alistar's attention turned to watch as Shalee gingerly walked into the room, assisted by her team of healers. She was still recovering from the effects of her miscarriage and the consumption of her half of Yaloom's potion. She gave Sam a nasty glance, then looked at Mosley and forced a smile.

"Did I hear the three of you talking about me?"

"It's nothing, sweetheart. Why are you out of bed? You should be resting."

The queen ignored Sam. Both Mosley and Alistar could feel the tension and moved to greet her. Mosley spoke first. "Hello, Shalee. It's good to see that you're up and moving around."

"Yes, child," Alistar added, "I'm sorry for your pain." He pulled a leaf from the pocket of his green robe and handed it to Shalee. "I brought this for you from the God World. Chew on it and it will assist in your recovery. You'll feel as good as new in a day or so."

"What the hell!" Sam shouted. "We don't want to hear that you're sorry. We just want our health and our son back!"
Shalee took a seat on her throne. "Oh, just shut up, Sam... will ya? There's no reason for everyone to yell at one another."

Sam tried to calm himself as he replied, but instead, failed miserably. "I know I shouldn't yell. But dang it... Mosley and Alistar are here to ask you to go to Luvelles. They want you to go after the third piece of the Crystal Moon. This really pisses me off! We did what the gods asked of us once already, and look where it's gotten us. I've killed many men, and so have you, for that matter. Earth is still destroyed and I don't see that changing any time soon. We managed to lose both of Grayham's crystal's pieces to George. And if that's not enough... our son is dead! What have we gotten in return for doing their dirty work? Not a dang thing, that's what! Yea, we live in this stupid castle, but that doesn't replace our son. That doesn't replace our families. I can't handle this any longer! At least they could give us our baby back!"

Shalee began to cry. Sam realized how his tone must have sounded and as all men do who know they have been idiots, he tried to console her.

"No, Sam, *no*. Don't you dare touch me! You need to leave me alone, and I don't want to hear another word from you! I won't stay here while you resent me for our son's death!"

"I'm not resenting you!"

"Yes, you are! You think I let you down! You think my magic is to blame for the loss of our baby! You aren't really mad at the gods. You're mad at me! You're disgusted with me. Maybe I do need to go. I need to get out of here for a while. I'm going to Luvelles with Mosley."

The wolf-god did not respond, nor did Alistar. Instead Sam became enraged.

"Hell, no. You're not going anywhere! You can't go unless I request permission from the Head Master of that world. I won't do it! You belong here with me!"

"I belong where I say I belong... not where you think I belong. We need a break. If you won't get permission from the Head Master, then I'll leave and go find a place to be alone. I need to get away from you. I can't handle your judgmental eyes any longer. The way you look at me makes me feel like a failure!"

"Ha... what a crock of garesh. The way I look at you, my butt! Hell, all I've done since the miscarriage is take care of you. I don't have a problem with you at all! You act like you're the only one hurting here. I have feelings too, ya know! You're acting like a witch!"

"I'm not a witch!"

Sam rolled his eyes. "I said you're acting like one, not that you are one. Maybe you should listen for a change. I also said I don't judge you or think you're a failure."

"Don't lie to me... don't you dare lie to me, Sam Goodrich! You know you're mad at me, and I know you blame me for everything that's happened. I'm going to Luvelles whether you like it or not. If you won't get the approval, then I'll give you this stupid crown I'm wearing, and you can find a new queen. for all I care!"

"What? I don't want anyone else! You can't just walk out on me! You're a queen, for hell's sake!"

Shalee gave Sam a disgusted look as she responded. "Yeah, right, you loathe me now! I don't care about being your queen. It's not like this relationship ever had a chance, anyway. Are you going to ask the Head Master for his permission, or shall I give you this crown right now? I won't spend another night here with you if you don't let me go!"

"Dang it, Shalee. You're really pissing me off. I don't loathe you, nor do I want you to go. But hey... if you want to leave me that badly, if you want to run out on us, I'll make it happen! You can kiss my royal ass! Maybe with some luck, you'll get it through that thick head of yours that I don't blame you for anything. Take your damn time apart. Just come home when you're ready. Just remember... I'll always love you, no matter what! Oh and P.S., you can kiss my butt again for thinking otherwise!" Sam turned and headed out the door.

Shalee called after him. "Just get the approval, Sam! I'll decide what's best for me from here on out... YOU JERK!" She turned to leave out the opposite door. "Mosley, come with me. Alistar, I don't want to speak with you, go away!" she shouted as she stormed out of the room.

Mosley turned to Alistar, nodded, and began to follow her. But before the wolf could leave the room, Sam came back in to make one final comment.

"So help me, Mosley, if she so much as gets a single scratch on her, I'll find a way to pay the gods back for their manipulations. You have taken enough from me already. Don't make me figure out a way to destroy every last one of you, because I won't rest until I do!"

Mosley nodded.

"Sam, you seem to have forgotten that I'm your friend. I only want to save you, not hurt you. Shalee is the only one I can trust to go after this piece of the Crystal Moon. This is bigger than you and this is even bigger than your marriage. It's even bigger than the death of your son."

"Nothing's bigger than the death of my son... NOTHING!"

"Perhaps Shalee is right. The two of you do need a break. She can save many lives. I'm only doing what needs to be done to save billions. I'm sure you'll see through your anger soon enough and we will speak again. I care for you Sam. I always will, and I'm sure Shalee will find a way out of her depression and come home to you once she has the crystal's third piece."

"Yeah, right! Just get out of my face. You're just like the rest of the gods. All you want is to play your little games with the mortals!"

Mosley lowered his head without responding and trotted from the room. Alistar moved to stand beside the king. "Sam, here is a piece of fepple root. I want you to brew this in some water and drink it. It will help to settle your nerves and allow you to think straight."

"Hmpf... whatever, just give it to me." Sam snatched the plant from the god's thin hands and left without saying thank you.

Alistar's soft brown eyes turned cold as he watched Sam leave. He whispered beneath his breath as he rubbed his hands together with satisfaction. "Well, this is all coming together rather nicely."

∽∽ ∽∽

Shalee sat down on the edge of the bed. Mosley was not far behind and entered the room with reserved caution. The queen didn't waste any moments, and the deity quickly created an invisible barrier to protect their conversation.

Shalee looked directly into the wolf's eyes.

"You told me that Bassorine had asked the gods of Earth to bless me. You said I was given the perfect body for childbearing."

"He did... and you were."

"Then why did I lose the baby?"

"Your body is struggling to keep up with the growth of your magic. The fetus was unable to handle the strain. Once you've had the moments necessary to adjust, you'll be able to have a child without any problems. You haven't even commanded magic for one full season. I was concerned that this might happen when I learned of your pregnancy."

"Then why didn't you say something to me? You're supposed to be my friend, Mosley!"

"I think we both know I'm your friend. What would it have changed if I did say something to you? You still would've been pregnant. If I'd told you of my concerns, it would have only served to cause additional, unnecessary stress. I was hoping that I was wrong and you would be able to carry the child to term. I'm sorry for your loss. I really am."

"So Sam is right. It's because of my magic that I lost our child."

"Did Sam actually say this to you?"

"No, not in words, but I can see it in his eyes." She took a deep breath, then continued. "I want to go to Luvelles. I need a break. It may have been a mistake for the two of us to have gotten together in the first place. We should've never gotten married!"

Mosley jumped onto the bed and lay down next to her. "I don't think you mean that."

"Ohhhhhhh, but I do. Did you hear him? It's my fault... all of it, and he hates me. He only says he loves me because I'm the last thing in his life that reminds him of Earth. I can see right through his pile of garesh."

"I don't agree with you, Shalee," Mosley said sharply, "Sam loves you!"

"Oh, of course you don't agree. You need me to go after your crystal. You don't want me to change my mind. You don't need to walk on eggshells while you're talking to me, Mosley. Let's just change the subject. This is really depressing, and I don't want to talk about Sam."

"Okay, but I'm sure you'll look back on this and feel differently soon."

"I don't think so. Anyway... why did you want me to go to Luvelles? Isn't there anyone on that world who could go after the crystal?"

"Yes, but I wanted to ask you to go after the third piece because I trust you. It could be dangerous. In fact, I'm sure it *will* be dangerous. But with the way your powers have advanced, I think it will be a good diversion right now if you took on this journey. Besides, I have faith in you."

"I do need to get out of here, but I'm not so sure I believe in your faith in me."

Mosley growled softly. "Are you really going to treat our friendship this way, Shalee?"

Shalee fell back on the bed and started to cry. "You're right. I'm being too hard on you, Mosley. You're not the one I'm mad at. I just feel so callous and I can't bear the thought of Sam looking down his nose at me. His eyes are full of disgust. Maybe I'll stay on Luvelles and never come back."

"I'm sure those are nothing more than emotional words. I'm telling you that you'll feel differently soon."

The wolf-god's words angered Shalee. "If you don't stop telling me how I'm gonna feel, I might just try to turn you into something other than a dog. Stop trying to make it better. I can't believe how stupid men are! Just shut up and listen—that's all you need to do. You're supposed to be a god. Why don't you know when to just shut up and listen?"

Mosley didn't respond. He simply sat there and waited for her to finish. After a moment of continued men-bashing, Shalee stood from the bed and put the leaf Alistar gave her between her teeth.

While chewing, she continued.

"I'll go to Luvelles, but I'm done with Sam. I doubt our love was ever real in the first place. He won't even miss me!" She waited for Mosley's response, but when the wolf just sat there quietly and his reply never came, she snapped. "God... men are just so... so... ewwwwww!"

The Temple of the Dark Order of Holy Paladins

Boyafed, leader of the Dark Order, stood in front of the council. Behind him, the majority of his Holy Paladins, along with those in training, had fallen into twenty large, columned formations. Boyafed's feet were planted firmly on top of a circular stone pedestal. Two elf men, with heads bowed, knelt at Boyafed's feet with brass chalices in front of them.

The council consisted of ten elves, all strong in the ways of Dark Magic and skilled with the Order's blessed blades. They sat on two separate elevated platforms, each one running diagonally on either side of Boyafed's pedestal. Between these platforms stood an enormous statue of the God of Death, Hosseff, which was nearly sixty feet tall. His arms were outstretched and lowered towards either side of a golden-colored stone altar which rested at his feet, the altar's highest point being nearly waist-high.

Two demons, one on each hand, hung upside down with their claw-like feet holding onto the god's stone fingers. Their arms reached toward the table as if they were looking to collect something. The table, or rather the altar, was nearly nine feet long and half as wide. It served as the symbol for the Order and also as the place to honor their god when making sacrifices to Hosseff.

The chamber was large, easily able to hold all those who served. In total, 4,430 elves filled the great room. The area was lit with many magical torches, their bright yellowish-red flames reflecting off the perfectly polished white marble floor.

With their heads lowered, the two men waited patiently to receive their blessings. The leader of the Order lifted his head and held his arms high.

"Today we honor Hosseff!"

The entire gathering responded in unison, shouting. "Our Lord, the wise and mighty Hosseff!" They yelled, stomping their right foot at the completion of the statement.

"Today the men before me shall become holy servants of Hosseff. They shall don the black plate armor of our Lord's Dark Paladin Army and deliver swift judgment to any who oppose him."

Again the ranks shouted, "Our Lord, the wise and mighty Hosseff," and stomped their right foot.

"These two brave men have completed their training and have earned the right to be called brother."

The ranks shouted, "Hail, brothers!"

Boyafed pulled his bone-handled dagger from its sheath and held it high. "Today these men will spread their blood across Hosseff's altar. Their blood will be cherished by our god. He will take them in as his own children and bless them with his Call of Death. They shall become Holy Paladins of the Dark Order."

Everyone shouted, "Blessed are the Children of Hosseff!"

Boyafed took his dagger and cut into the left palm of each man's hand.

"Brothers, allow your blood to flow into your chalice. Give Hosseff a taste of the blood that will serve him. Lord Hosseff, accept the blood of these men as tokens of their faith in you."

As Kiayasis Methelborn and his companion watched the blood flow from their hands, the entire hall filled with another shouted praise for Hosseff. Both men wrapped their hands, lowered themselves from Boyafed's pedestal and moved to stand beside the golden altar.

They shouted, "Lord Hosseff, my blood is your blood and my service is promised within this offering. I pledge my life to you. Blessed are the children of Hosseff!"

The entire hall shouted, "Blessed are the children of Hosseff!"

Once the ceremony was complete, Boyafed Methelborn pulled Kiayasis aside. They stood near the golden altar.

"You look strong, Kiayasis. The Order's armor suits you."
"I've waited for this day, Father. I want to make you proud."

Kiayasis Methelborn – Elf and Son of Boyafed

Illustration by Kathleen Stone

"And I am proud. Follow me, I have something for you. Something I've given no other before now. Most men must earn this, but I want this to be my gift to you. I've had this animal groomed for you for the last 10 seasons."

"10 seasons? I had no idea you had that much faith in me."

"I've always had faith in you. After all, you're my son. I never expected any less of you. You're a Methelborn, and all Methelborns are strong."

Boyafed led Kiayasis to a teleportation platform. When they reappeared, they stood far outside the city in an area without a population. This place was where the Order's stables had been created. They were like no other on Luvelles, covering nearly four acres. The entire structure, except for the earth floor and ceiling, was made of dark marble. Each stall was nearly forty feet wide and twice as deep. The ceiling was made of heavy wooden logs that had been harvested from the Petrified Forest.

On either side of the stall's entrances were red demon statues with black wings. Each demon had six arms, two legs and stood nearly thirty feet tall, despite being in a seated position. Their six arms were stretched forward with each hand grasping an iron gate, acting as hinges. Each stall was capable of holding just one of the Dark Paladin's mounts inside it.

The mounts of the Dark Paladins are relatives of the Krapes the common elves of Luvelles ride. They are much bigger than the Krapes, but have been given a similar name. They are called Krape Lords and stand nearly thirty-five feet tall, some twenty-three feet taller than their cousins. The Krape Lords are able to carry a saddle large enough to hold three grown adult elves. Instead of maul-like hammers at the end of their tails, the tails split apart at their ends and allow for a deadly poisonous point to protrude from their center, which can be used as a projectile.

Krape Lords have large wings and are hairless, unlike their relatives. Their heads look to be more like a dragon's than a raptor's, but they do still have a large pouch across their abdomen in which to carry things. When fully loaded with the paladin's armor, food, weapons and passengers, the Krape Lords become giant land runners with incredible speed. Due to the excessive weight, they are unable to fly more than a few hundred feet. Instead, they use their massive wings to assist them while clearing large gaps or holes in the terrain. But when the beast is free from excessive weight and only carries a single rider, it flies with grace.

Krape Lords use their strong ape-like arms not only to lift, but also to throw heavy objects. The biggest difference between them and their cousins, the Krapes, is that the Krape Lords are carnivorous and their diets consist of corgan meat, a large cow-like beast. They usually eat one of these 4000-pound creatures every third Peak of Bailem.

Krape Lord Joss

Illustration by Kathleen Stone

Kiayasis stood in front of his new mount. "Father... he's majestic."

Boyafed smiled. "I'm glad you approve. His name is Joss. He has been trained well and is responsive to every command you have learned while in training. Joss will serve you better than any other mount within our ranks."

"I couldn't ask for anything more. Thank you."

Kiayasis stood in awe for a moment before changing the subject. "I was told you have an assignment for me."

Boyafed commanded Joss to follow them out of the stable. The Krape Lord did as instructed after snorting a bit.

"I need you to go to Merchant Island. Our Lord Hosseff has informed me that a woman from Grayham will be arriving soon. You are to take her to Grogger's Swamp. Once there, you'll allow her to go in alone. She has something she must do and must do it alone."

"What of her safety? Grogger will surely devour her."

"Hosseff has commanded this. It's not our place to question our lord."

"I'm sorry, Father, I didn't know!"

"How could you have known? Besides... this woman is a powerful sorceress. I imagine she'll be fine once inside the swamp. There's something else I must tell you, something that will please Hosseff."

"What is it?"

Boyafed put his arm around Kiayasis and led him away from the stable with Joss in tow as they finished their conversation.

Chapter 8

Lord Dowd

The Underwater City of Ultor

Gage sat patiently in his underwater bubble of protection. Syse had been called away and the only thing for him to do was sit there as if on display. When King Ultor finally made his presence known, those who swam outside stopped to acknowledge their beloved leader.

Just as Syse had done, the king used his heavy water wings to cool the area within the barrier as his skin heated up in a prism of colors during his transformation. There was an imposing size difference between the others and their king. He was taller and clearly much stronger than the rest.

Gage had to smile, knowing now after a discussion with Syse that, despite the king's size, they were still within a tiny, single pore within a small piece of coral. Not only that, but there were millions of these beings compacted into this infinitely small spot and yet, there still seemed to be plenty of room. He had to be unimaginably small.

"Why have you come, Goswig? You have betrayed your master... explain your actions!"

Gage swallowed hard. "Sire, I'm here to seek refuge. My master is an angry man. His hate consumes him and his thoughts echo through my mind and cause me great distress. I beg you... please... please, don't send me back."

"Your master told me this day would come. How can I oppose the will of a man such as Marcus Id? He's far too powerful. I can appreciate your desires in this matter, but your presence here puts my kind in danger."

Gage lowered his head. He knew Ultor was right. "Sire, I'm

sorry for putting you in this position. I'm ready to be returned to my master and face his punishment."

The king could see the distress in Gage's eyes. His heart reached out. Ultor was a kind king—beloved by his race. "You said your master's thoughts echo in your mind? Please explain."

"My master's thoughts are mine to share when he is near. I've come all this way in order to escape his mind. His hate is overwhelming, and his pain causes me pain. I cannot take any more of it. If it's your intention to send me back, please allow me to die here. At least my death would be considered merciful."

Ultor thought a moment before responding. "Does your master also share your mind?"

"No, sire, he doesn't."

"You had to travel to the far side of Luvelles in order to escape his mind. Is this correct?"

"It is."

"This is good. I'll allow you to stay. You may take refuge with the other Goswigs. If the day ever comes that you begin to sense your master's thoughts, I want you to teleport away from the others. You must leave us and go into hiding. I can't allow your master to have the knowledge that I've gone against his wishes. But I cannot turn you over to him in good conscience. I know of Marcus Id's coldness. I felt it when he came to see me. He knows Goswigs come to me, but he knows nothing of what I do with them.

"I would imagine that, without you at his side, Marcus won't be able to come visit me. You have been with him too long now, or at least long enough that the loss of your companionship will weaken his powers for a good while. You'll need to assume a new identity. No one can know of your service to Marcus. Can you do this?"

Gage's furry face gleamed with satisfaction. "Sire, I can become a ghost, you'll see. Thank you."

"You're welcome, my hairy little friend. Just remember that your presence here jeopardizes the existence of my entire kingdom. You must leave as soon as you sense him."

Ultor lifted his head and shouted out a series of high-pitched clicking sounds. It wasn't long before Swill appeared, along with Syse, and they began their ascent back to the surface of Crystal Lake, with Gage properly protected.

The Mountains of Oraness

Brayson appeared with Mary at his side. Before them was a pool with fire burning on top of its watery surface. The flames were tall, producing an uncomfortable heat that could be felt from where they stood, though nearly forty feet away. The pool rested within the Mountains of Oraness. To the far side, directly opposite their position, was an entrance to a cave. There was no way around the flames to get to this opening. The mountains were steep, forming cliffs which shot up from the edges of the pool, creating a protective barrier that nearly encompassed its entire perimeter. The spot where they now stood was the only place Brayson could have teleported them both without fear of being burned.

"This place is special to me," Brayson said. "I've never brought a woman here before. Come to think of it, I've never brought anyone here before at all."

Mary studied her surroundings, totally speechless. Brayson smiled as he enjoyed her expression and continued, "I can see you're pleased... Have you ever seen anything like this?"

Mary collected herself. "Never. How are such things possible? How can the fire burn on top of the water?"

"The fire doesn't burn on the water. The fire burns because of the creature at the pool's center. The fire burns as a result of the beast's need to be comforted within the flames. The water beneath isn't affected by the heat—in fact, the water would be boiling if it were. This is powerful magic. This is the home of my Goswig."

"Your Goswig... what kind of Goswig would sit within the flames?"

"Take my hand and I'll show you. Do you remember me telling George that I had a Phoenix?"

"I'm sorry, I must have forgotten."

"It's quite alright. Take my hand."

Cautiously, Mary took hold. She was apprehensive, but once assured that everything was okay, cooperated and began to walk. Brayson led her into the flames and across the top of the water. As they approached the center of the pool, the fire began to dissipate.

They now stood on a small island patch of dirt located at the pool's center. Sitting on top of a stone perch was a small, crimson-yellow bird. A thin layer of flame enveloped its entire body. In total, Brayson's feathered Goswig was no bigger than twelve inches long.

Mary leaned into Brayson. "I remember now. You were right. He is majestic-looking."

"I'm glad you agree." Brayson then turned and spoke to the Phoenix. "Fisgig, I want you to meet someone special. This is Mary."

The Phoenix responded in its own language. *"Hej, de yameso yorkamenta."*

"She doesn't speak your language, my friend. You're going to have to lower yourself to our level in order to speak with us."

Fisgig sighed. "If I must. I was wondering when I would be meeting with you, Mary. You're every bit as beautiful as Master Id said you'd be. It's nice to put a face to the name."

Mary enjoyed the compliment. "Thank you." She was unsure how to act, being out of her comfort zone, but excited to push her boundaries anyway. Being around such magic made her feel alive, yet frightened. Either way, she wanted to see what Brayson Id was all about.

Brayson reached in and took the flaming bird on his hand. "Fisgig is preparing to burn himself to death, and will be reborn from his ashes soon."

"What...why would he do such a thing?"

"With each death, Fisgig is able to command greater powers. This is the end of his fifth life. When he emerges from his ashes four mornings from now, he'll be stronger. His rebirth will add to my power as well."

"How does his rebirth affect you?" Mary asked.

"We are bonded together. While he's dead, I'll be vulnerable. After I take you home, I'll return here and wait until Fisgig lives once again. I've never told anyone this before. I'm entrusting you with my most sacred secret. This is the kind of trust I wish to have with you."

She didn't know what to say. No one had ever wanted this kind of relationship with her before, sharing thoughts, feelings, and trust. Brayson took her hand and lifted it to set the Phoenix on it.

"I don't wish to be burned!" she said with fright and pulled her arm away. "I don't have the magic necessary to protect me."

"Nor do you need magic to protect you," Fisgig responded. "I can control my flame. You'll be safe. It wasn't Master Id who protected you while you walked through the flames above the pool... it was me. Allow me to sit on your hand. It's safe, I assure you."

Mary was still uneasy, but there was something in the tone of Fisgig's voice that sounded truthful. She reached out, willing her hand not to tremble.

Brayson changed the subject as Mary took the Phoenix on her finger. The bird was surprisingly light, and she didn't feel the heat from his flame at all. She breathed in relief and turned her attention back to what Brayson was saying. "The cave beyond this pool is the home of the Source. No one but us knows its true location.

"And what is this true location? I'm still learning my way around, you know."

"You're within the Mountains of Oraness. I send my students here when the moment has come for them to seek the gift."

"What gift?"

"The gift of power... magic's ultimate power!"

Mary thought a moment. "If you send your students here, then how is it that we are the only three who know where the Source is located? And what is the Source, anyway?"

"This area is protected. A man cannot teleport directly into this area unless he possesses the knowledge given only to the Head Master. It's a nice title to have and has its perks. The knowledge of the Source's location is passed down from one Head Master to another. The cliffs surrounding this area are magically protected to keep curious minds from climbing them and revealing the true location of the Source's home.

"When my students come here, they must use a teleportation platform within the Source's temple, located inside the Void Maze. The maze is far from here and isn't a simple thing to navigate. The maze is torturous. A man could become lost for days before finding a way to get to its center, or even a way back out, for that matter. It would take a man nearly 100 Peaks of Bailem to walk from the base of these mountains to the maze. Not to mention, the boat ride necessary to cross the Straits of Ebarna.

"The Source is an ancient dragon said to be the source of all magic, but this isn't really the case. The Source is the protector of the Eye of Magic and has been for ages."

"How old is the Source?" Mary said, cutting in. "How ancient is he?"

Brayson thought a bit before responding. "All I can say is that the Source has seen the creation and the destruction of many worlds."

"You said he protects the Eye of Magic. What does he protect it from?"

Brayson smiled. "I like your inquisitive nature. I can see that talking to you will keep me on my toes."

Mary winked. "I would rather you like me for my wit, not just my good looks." She held out her hand, and Fisgig returned to his perch.

Brayson enjoyed her confidence. "To answer your question, The Source protects the Eye from men. In order for a man to look into the Eye, he must first prove himself to be worthy to pass the Source. If deemed so, the Eye will invite this aspiring mage to look into it. Many men have been swallowed whole by the Eye and lost forever. Their souls are spit out and left to find their way to the gods."

"That's horrible," Mary said. "Why would someone want to

look into the Eye if they could be killed? And why is it only men who get to look into the Eye? What about women? Do you consider women not good enough?" She put her hands on her hips and waited for the answer.

"Power is the reason men look into the Eye," Brayson responded, taking note of her body language.

Brayson took Fisgig from his perch and set the bird on his shoulder. "To answer your question regarding women and why they haven't looked into the Eye, I've never met a woman who has been ready to meet the Source. I have nothing against women seeking this power. In fact, I would welcome the day a woman was able to be the first. Until then, I can only speak of what has happened 'til now."

Mary pondered his answer. "I'm glad you're open to the idea. I admire strong women. I hope to know this woman, someday."

"As would I." Brayson took a moment to find her eyes. He held her hands in his. "I see much strength in you, Mary. I also see a delightful wit and an ability to enjoy the moment. I watched from the bar at Kebble's inn as you and your daughters made your other family members laugh."

Mary slapped his arm. "You mean to tell me that you were in the same bar and never said hello? Why?"

"I had to work up the nerve. I needed to figure out how to approach you. The dresses were intended to buy me the moments necessary to accomplish this. Please forgive me."

Mary laughed. "There is no forgiveness necessary. I find your vulnerability cute." After giving another wink she changed the subject. "You were going to tell me about the men who seek the power of the Eye."

Brayson took a deep breath. "So, as I was saying, many men seek power, but it's also this same search for power that causes doubt. A man may succeed and convince the Source that he's worthy to pass, but it's not the Source they should fear. In fact, every now and then, the Source simply allows a man to pass without questioning him.

"It's the Eye they should be afraid of. When a man is invited by the Eye to look into it, it sees their doubt, and it hates doubt. It devours them and, like I said before, swallows them whole. Only those who believe they're truly ready to receive the Eye's gift survive. These men are granted power far beyond their own comprehension. They spend the rest of their lives as scholars of the arts trying to understand how to use this power. They strive to become immortal... god-like... but to my knowledge, no one has ever managed to attain this level without passing on first."

"And is this your goal, to become god-like?" Mary said, cutting in again. "Do you desire to have so much power that you would forget to live your life and instead, search for it?"

Brayson smiled. "I do enjoy your directness. I have no desire to become god-like, and furthermore, I enjoy living everyday to its fullest. If I had been so focused on attaining greater power, I would have never noticed you, now would I?"

Again Mary slapped at his arm, but now, there was a satisfied twinkle in her eyes. "Good answer, Mr. Id. There just might be hope for you and me."

Taking his hand, she gave it a squeeze. "So tell me more about you."

Brayson cleared his throat. "I am the last man to look into the Eye and survive. Before me, it was my father. He was 1,200 seasons old when he finally died. I still haven't reached my full magical potential and as I have said, I have no desire to."

Removing Fisgig from his shoulder and returning the phoenix to his perch, he continued. "There have been only twelve men over the last 10,000 seasons who have passed this ultimate test. 2,764 men have tried and lost their lives in search of this ultimate power."

Mary stood in shock as she listened. Brayson continued. "Are you okay? You look as if you have questions, or maybe some concerns."

"Well, of course she does," Fisgig responded. "You would too if the situation were reversed. It's okay, Mary. Ask anything you wish."

"I have so many more questions, I'm not sure where to start. Is George going to look into the Eye someday?"

Brayson smiled and took her by the hands. "This is nothing to worry about right now. If the day comes that he's ready, I will tell you. You can always ask me something else as you think of it. But for now, how would you like to meet your first dragon?"

Mary's smile widened. "Dragon? Are you serious? Me... meet a dragon?"

Inside the Book of Bonding

George sat down heavily, careful to avoid the water surrounding his dry spot at the bottom of the hole they had fallen into. He was exhausted and tired of trying to figure out a way to get out. Payne had tried to fly up to the surface, but some unseen force was not allowing him to do so.

"I'm not sure what to do," George said, his voice full of irritation as he stood back up and adjusted his robe. He grunted at the fact that he felt dirty and longed for a bath. He hated being in this rugged atmosphere. The water that pooled at the bottom of the hole made it hard to avoid the filth and was unacceptable. His ragged appearance was a far cry from the neatly pressed Gucci persona he used to sport while on Earth. Eventually he lifted his head, made a conscious decision to stop feeling sorry for himself, and refocused his mind on the task at hand.

"We must be missing something here. Why can't we teleport out of this damn hole? There are no openings for us to go any further. I'm hungry and I'm tired. I wonder what Brayson and his Goswig would do in a situation like this?"

"Sleep," Payne said as he lowered himself to George's side.

"No, Payne, I'm sure Brayson wouldn't sleep. Are you even paying attention to me? What does that have to do with what I just asked you?"

"Master say Master tired. So sleep! Payne keep Master safe. Payne protects the Master while asleep."

"Yes, Payne... I know, you saved my life. I've already told you that I'm proud of you, but we need to find a way out of here or we'll starve to death. We've got to focus. There has to be a way out of here."

George thought long and hard as he scanned his surroundings. Eventually, something popped into his head. "Brayson said he had a Phoenix and from the movies I've seen, I know they command fire. Maybe fire would work on these roots."

"What a movie?"

"Nothing, let's just focus."

"Geez, Master grouchy to Payne."

The mage rolled his eyes and took a look around again. All he could see were the shaft walls and the roots from the heavy trees above that somehow managed to extend this deep into the earth.

"Screw me, this sucks."

Payne snapped his head around and looked at him. "What screw mean?"

"Nothing, forget I said it. Athena doesn't like it when I talk that way, so just forget I said it."

George thought a moment and eventually came up with an idea.

"The flowers up top reacted when you pulled one of them out of the ground. Maybe the plants down here are alive too. Maybe they'll…"

The mage lifted his hand and sent fire all across the roots. They retracted within themselves, and as they did, a small crack near the floor appeared. George smiled, turned around, put his hands on his hips, and enjoyed his success.

"Ha… I knew there had to be a way out of here!"

"Again," Payne said. "Again Master!"

George did it again and the crack widened further.

"This looks promising. Payne, look at this. There's a cave on the other side of this gap, and it's well-lit. It's still too small to fit through. Stand back—let me try again."

He stepped back and again burned the roots, keeping at it until the hole was large enough for them to pass.

"Hurry, Payne, fly through before it closes."

Payne did as instructed and the wall shut behind them. A long, well-lit cave stretched into the distance with no end in sight. The light seemed to come from within the walls, which looked as if they were glowing. George took a deep breath.

"Well, this is freaking eerie. I don't like this one bit. Something tells me we're in for trouble. I have the heebee-jeebees."

"What heebee-jeebees, Master, and what freaking mean?"

George Nailer - Mystic-Learner

Illustration by Angela Woods

Payne asked as he tilted his head in confusion.

"Oh, nothing. It just means that I feel a bit scared."

"I not scared," the fairy-demon said, pushing out his chest. He hovered above the floor with wings flapping wildly.

"That's because you're brave, Payne!"

"Yes, Payne brave."

"Yes, you are, and that's good because we may need your brav-ery someday." The mage thought a bit and then continued. "Well, at least this place is a change of scenery, I suppose!"

"What scenery mean?"

"I swear to the gods, Payne, I'm going to make you study a freaking dictionary one of these days."

"Be nice to Payne. Payne saved you. What dictionary mean?"

"Payne!"

"Okay... okay, geesh."

Suddenly a loud scream filled the air. It sounded like a fright-ened woman. George began to run toward the noise with Payne flying behind. It was unnerving to run in the direction of danger as the screams grew louder. Eventually the corridor came to an end and a large room opened up in front of them.

An old woman had been left hanging, suspended in chains high above a banquet table full of food. Her dress had been shredded, claw marks on her legs, and blood dripped from the end of her foot, falling into a wooden bowl which also rested at the table's end.

Four large creatures, one in each corner of the room, were slow-ly crawling along the ceiling. It appeared as if they had intentions of killing her. The figures were dark, without faces, and almost completely covered with hair. Their claws ripped into the stones to keep them suspended. With every step, the rubble fell to the floor below and broke apart.

George lifted his hands and without hesitation, sent his magic flying. Thousands of needles filled the air in two different direc-tions and, as anticipated, the creatures fell lifeless to the floor with a loud thud.

Again he shot his needles and again they made contact with the two other beasts, but nothing happened. The needles bounced harmlessly off them as the creatures turned their attention towards their new visitors.

The woman shouted. "You must run! They'll kill you. You can't save me... *run*!"

Payne did not wait for George to give a command. He teleported next to one of the beasts and used his claws to cut the creature free from the grip it had on the ceiling stones. Three of the four claws released. Payne adjusted and quickly took a bite out of the arm of the fourth claw before the animal could make the adjustment necessary to fight back. The noise it made as it fell nearly sixty feet to the floor before landing hard on its head sounded helpless and vulnerable.

George quickly ran toward the wounded beast. He removed his sword and buried the blade deep within the center of the animal's mass. Another cry could be heard as the fourth beast scurried down the wall.

Payne tried to attack, but as he did, he found that his claws were no longer able to cause damage. The next thing the fairy-demon felt was a hard claw across his tiny face. He fell to the table below, but was lucky enough to land on a large cooked bird of some sort at the table's center. Food flew everywhere, breaking his fall as the little guy slid to a stop. But the impact had been severe enough to leave him groggy; he would need some moments before continuing the fight.

The beast finished descending the wall as the woman screamed for George to make his retreat. Slowly, the beast began to walk toward him and as it did, three more appeared at its side. The bodies of the ones they had previously killed vanished.

Again the woman shouted. "You must run. Save yourself. You cannot kill them!"

George heard something in her voice. His many years of deception and lies clued him in. He knew a con when he heard one. This was a set-up. She wasn't in trouble—she was the bait.

The beasts slowly moved to surround him. He had to make a choice. Run or fight, but one or the other had to be done and done quickly. The beasts began to charge. They leaped into the air and came down on top of him just as he teleported to the end of the table. The mage lifted his hands and sent a bolt of lightning arcing above him. It hit the woman with such force that she flew upward and hit hard against the ceiling a good fifteen feet above her and was knocked unconscious.

The chains around her wrists coiled with her as she rose. As she fell back toward the floor, they snapped tight against her weight. Her arms gave way under the pressure and ripped off at the elbows. She tumbled wildly as she fell, her head cracking clean open as it smashed into the floor. The scull broke apart and exposed the brain.

Now George redirected his attention, and from the corner of his eye, he saw the creatures hurling themselves through the air. He teleported, but only after receiving a nasty gash across his shoulder. With one good hand, he aimed for the woman's exposed brain from across the room, his needles flying and penetrating the soft tissue. The effects were instantaneous. All the beasts disappeared in an explosion of smoke.

The woman's body began to shake—she was expanding. Something was causing pressure to build from inside of her. George teleported, grabbed Payne, and threw up his wall of force quick enough to save them both. The entire room filled with a green, poisonous gas; they would need to stay put inside the protective barrier until it dissipated.

Marcus Id's Dark Tower

Boyafed, leader of the Dark Order of Holy Paladins, walked into the throne room of Marcus Id's dark tower-palace. He waited impatiently, tapping his foot as Marcus entered the room.

"This better be important, Boyafed," Marcus snapped as he watched the Order leader move to take a seat on his throne. The Dark Chancellor hated the fact that Boyafed would have the nerve to sit in the one spot the Dark Warrior knew would irritate him the most. He held his tongue and acted as if he cared less. "So, have you found Gage?"

"No, but I have other news that may please you, despite his disappearance."

"And what news could you give me that would make me feel so much better?"

Boyafed stood, brushed past Marcus and arrogantly produced a parchment.

"What's this?" Marcus growled as he opened the document. A

smile eventually appeared as he continued to read. "Boyafed, my good man, this is indeed pleasant news. Are you absolutely sure of this information?"

"I am... your brother has taken a new Mystic-Learner. My spies have since lost sight of him, but he does exist."

Marcus began to pace as he thought. "Boyafed, this is wonderful news. I want you to have your finest men look for Gage. Have your son lead the search. This would make a fine first assignment for him."

"I can't, nor would I waste his moments with such nonsense."

"What? Why can't you send him, and why would this be considered a waste of his moments?"

"Lord Hosseff requested that Kiayasis be sent to Merchant Island to escort a woman who's coming from Grayham. She needs to go to Grogger's Swamp. Apparently she has business there and furthermore, it's not my problem that you can't keep your Goswig under control! I will send others to look for your pet!"

Marcus hated his tone but dismissed it. "Lord Hosseff was here? Why wasn't I told of this? Why didn't you send for me?"

"I have come to you as soon as I carried out our god's instructions. This is the first chance I've had to speak with you. Besides, Hosseff didn't ask for you. He came seeking me. I have many men who will be just as capable of finding Gage as Kiayasis."

"You should remember who runs this city, Boyafed. You speak to me as if you have forgotten your place."

"I haven't forgotten whose city this is, but I think you've lost sight of who commands the army you claim to be in charge of. My men respect you only because they follow my orders. It would be wise for you to remember that I'm the only reason you have this perception of power."

It took everything within Marcus to stay calm. "I'll remember that, but why would Hosseff want Kiayasis to escort this woman to Grogger's Swamp?"

"Does *why* really matter? Our god has spoken. I haven't eaten ,so maybe we could speak more of this over a nice Corgan steak and some cold ale?"

"That's a pleasant idea. I am hungry, now that I think of it. We do have plans to make now that my brother has a new Mystic-

Learner. I'll meet you in the dining hall in a few moments from now. I need to put away a few things first."

"Until then."

The dark paladin left the room. As he did, Marcus whispered. "Soon you'll be forced to watch your tongue, Boyafed. When that day comes, you'll bow before me or die... and I could care less which one!"

Marcus teleported.

The Next Day
Gregory Id's Glass Palace

Gregory Id called for the leader of his White Paladin Army to come to a meeting. He was waiting patiently for Dowd to arrive when Mykklyn entered his bedroom chamber. The Goswig's heavy paws thumped against the glass floor as she jaunted gracefully across it and looked at the rushing water passing beneath her.

The lioness spoke. "Dowd has arrived. He's waiting for you in your throne room."

Gregory sighed heavily. "Thank you, Mykklyn. Please tell him I'll be there in a moment."

"As you wish." The Goswig vanished.

Dowd, the white paladin leader, was from a strong elven family. They had been in the service of many different chancellors for nearly 6,000 seasons. Dowd was by far the strongest leader the Paladins of Light had ever seen from his bloodline. He was large, powerful, and diplomatic. His short, dark hair accented his strong-jawed features and his presence commanded respect. He exuded confidence and his men followed him without question.

Dowd's men numbered almost 4,000 strong, with nearly another 3,000 in training. The White Paladin Army served two gods: Keylom—God of Peace, and Helmep—God of Healing. Both gods were glorified among their ranks and Dowd saw to it that no man who served beneath him fell away from this path of glory.

The army was not in existence for the purpose of attaining stature For this reason, they had never been given a specific name. The "Paladins of Light" was a name given by the people nearly

8,000 seasons ago, created when the Dark Order of Holy Paladins had attacked. The White Paladin Army had chased the darkness out of their kingdom. With the darkness gone, they became known as the Paladins of Light.

Lord Dowd - Elf and Leader of the White Paladin Army

Illustration by Kathleen Stone

"Lord Dowd, thank you for coming." Gregory said after appearing on his throne.

"Chancellor," Dowd responded as he lowered his head to symbolize his respect for Gregory. "How may I be of service?"

"I fear that my brother, Marcus, has become more of an irritation than he normally is. I would appreciate it if you would send someone to gather information on what's to come. Head Master Brayson has provided us with some additional security. I would like you to meet Hepplesif."

Gregory pointed up as he moved to look out a window and across his City of Inspiration below. Hepplesif's wings beat violently across his spider back. The Kedgle had been watching from one of the glass beams above. He twitched his mouse-like nose as he slowly lowered to only a few paces away from Dowd. The leader of the White Paladin Army watched in amazement as Hepplesif's spider legs began clicking on the glass floor.

"And what are you?" Dowd said after a moment.

Gregory was the one to answer. "This is Hepplesif. He's a Kedgle, and their king has been kind enough to send one hundred within their ranks to assist you in the protection of my palace."

Dowd was intrigued. He had heard of the Kedgles, but had never seen one. He studied Hepplesif's body. After a moment of staring, Hepplesif spoke.

"Lord Dowd, you're making this introduction uncomfortable. I understand your curiosity, but maybe we could get to the matters at hand?"

"By all means, I'm sorry. I didn't mean to be rude."

"It's quite all right. I felt the same way the first moment I saw an elf. You look as odd to me as I must to you."

"I can imagine." Dowd turned his attention to Gregory. "Chancellor, what exactly is the Kedgles' role in protecting the palace?"

Gregory moved across the room and once again took his place on the throne. The large chair was made of white-shaded glass. Large, soft red cushions had been mounted both on the seat's surface and its back. The throne sat in the center of a large circular area that was completely transparent, without imperfections, unlike the rest of the glass floor which had been intentionally clouded. The throne looked as if it were hovering—as if resting on nothing. A man could look right through this spot. The earth beneath fell away into the darkness for as far as the eye could see.

"The Kedgles will use their illusions to create confusion if the palace is attacked by my brother's dark army. These illusions will give you and your men an advantage. You should be able to drive them out of the city if they attack."

Dowd thought a moment. He turned to look at Hepplesif. "These illusions will only affect our enemy … is this what I'm hearing?"

"Yes, this is correct."

"What do you need from me?"

Hepplesif's spider legs made clicking noises on the glass as he adjusted his position. He climbed onto the arm of Gregory's throne and now, in a better position for conversation, he continued.

"I would think it's best to know what my allies and enemies look like. I need to know how your men will be dressed. I want to know what our enemies will be wearing if they attack. My kind will keep your men from seeing our illusions. The Dark Chancellor's men will appear to be confused. Then, Lord Dowd, you should easily defeat Marcus's dark soldiers."

"This sounds positive," Dowd said as he removed his cape. "My men will be dressed in silver armor, with white markings. Some men wear plate, others prefer chain. If they aren't wearing their armor for any reason, they would be wearing their capes as I do. You can see it's black, with white trim. The symbol for the Paladins of Light will be on it—the Turtle Elf of Healing."

After showing the symbol, Dowd put his cape back on. "Now, as far as the Dark Order goes, their men will be wearing black plate, with black capes and gold accents. Their symbol is a golden altar. This symbol rests on both their shoulders and their capes. You won't have any trouble picking them out of a crowd."

Hepplesif looked at Gregory. "Chancellor, it seems that everything is under control. I'll speak with you some other moment. I'll now address the others and see to it that they understand everything that has been discussed here."

The Kedgle turned again to face the Paladin of Light leader and spoke in the Elven language. "Lord Dowd, *Saesa omentien lle. I'narr en gothrim glinuva nuin I'anor!*"

"And nice meeting you as well, Hepplesif. Let's hope you're

right and the sun finds their bones inviting."

Hepplesif flew out of the room. Once gone, Gregory addressed Dowd.

"Please give me a report, once your spies have gathered any intelligence as to my brother's intentions."

"Tenna' ento lye omenta, Chancellor."

"Until then, Lord Dowd."

Both Gregory and the paladin leader left the room. Once gone, a figure emerged from his invisible position within the shadows. It was Marcus. "Well, well, my little brother has a plan. You're smarter than you look, Gregory—but not smart enough."

With that, the Dark Chancellor vanished.

The Mountains of Oraness

Brayson looked down at Fisgig's ashes. The Phoenix had burned himself to death the night before. It was now only a matter of waiting. He would stay here for a few more Peaks of Bailem. The fiery bird would rise again to begin his new life and Brayson's power would increase substantially because of it. For the moment, he was vulnerable to attack. He would need to hide within the Source's cave until he was made whole once again.

When Brayson took Fisgig as his Goswig, he had been warned by his father, Hedron—the Head Master before him—of the danger he would be in during moments of the Phoenix's death. Hedron had allowed him to choose his own Goswig, a choice his father had never given any other Mystic-Learner. Brayson had selected the one creature with the most power of any other Goswig. Since that day, there had been only one birth of a new potential Goswig that could command powers greater than his Phoenix. This new Goswig was special, but also required the abilities of a very special master to command him. As Brayson continued to dwell on George and Payne's new relationship, he made his way into the cave.

It didn't take long before he stood in front of the Source. He could not see the giant beast since the dragon chose to remain invisible, but he was there nonetheless. Brayson lowered to one knee and spoke.

"Yaaraer... quel re, nae saian luume'!"

A voice responded from within the nothingness... "Hello, Brayson. You're right, it has been too long since we last saw each other... good day to you as well. To what do I owe this pleasure?"

"Ancient One, I'm here while my Goswig prepares to be re-born. I have taken on a new Mystic-Learner. I'm sure you'll meet him when the moment is right. His skills are advanced for someone who hasn't had any formal training. He seems to have been blessed by the gods."

"I'm sure you're right. I look forward to this meeting. What else can you tell me of things?"

Brayson's eyes widened. A smile crossed his face as he looked up at the massive dragon's solidifying form. "The woman I introduced you to has stolen a piece of my heart. I don't seem to be able to keep her at bay. I worry that she'll be a distraction. I need some advice."

"Ahh … love can be a tricky thing. Take a seat. Let's discuss this matter further."

Gogswayne,
The Underground Goswig Village

Gage awoke and lifted his head from the soft pillow he was resting on. As he gathered himself, he noticed an odd-looking creature staring down at him. The bottom half looked snake-like, with fins, while the torso had wings which kept it suspended while hovering in one spot. Two muscular shoulders protruded on either side, covered with scales, except for the clawed talons attached at their ends. The creature's head appeared as any man's. He had brown hair, dark eyes and the pointed ears of an elf. Every now and then a slithering tongue shot out of its mouth and looked as a snake's would.

Gage pulled back his robe and rubbed his eyes against his furry forearm before taking a second look at the creature.

"Where am I?" he said with a raspy voice.

"Ha… he doesn't know where he's at," the creature hissed as it flew out of the quaint little home without saying another word.

He intended to retrieve another log which rested near a group of trees.

Once back inside, the creature threw the log onto the fire and moved to a position far enough away from the badger to give enough room for good conversation.

"I figured as much," he hissed again. "Everyone forgets after coming back from King Ultor's underwater kingdom. You're in the underground city of Gogswayne. You're exhausted from the transition your body had to make when visiting the king's under-water coral kingdom. We've all been through it. I imagine that you'll be tired for a few more Peaks of Bailem before you begin to feel normal again."

Gage thought a moment before responding. "I remember... I remember shrinking and meeting with King Ultor. The last thing I remember after that is being carried to the surface, but not much more. My name is Gage."

"Yes, I know. Syse and Swill told me this before they left. Syse informed me that you spoke with King Ultor himself. You should feel honored. I can't think of another Goswig that has spoken with him other than Strongbear. Usually, we meet with his second in command. I'm sure your story will be one to tell the others."

Gage stood up. His limbs felt feeble. It took most of his strength to stand upright without falling. Slowly he stretched and respond-ed.

"What's your name and what exactly are you, anyway? How many others of us are there?"

"Where are my manners?" the creature said, chuckling, "My name is Gallrum, and I am a Serwin."

"I have heard that name before," Gage interrupted, "but I haven't ever met one of you until now."

"Then I'm glad to be your first," he replied with a quick pose of introduction. "Now to answer your other question... there are nearly a thousand of us living in Gogswayne. You, my friend, just increased our village's population to nine hundred and ninety eight. We've all agreed that we should have a big celebration when we hit an even thousand."

Gallrum- A Serwin

Illustration by Angela Woods

Gage took a moment to look around. He was in a pleasant-looking home. The walls were made of rock, but the décor remained bright and cheerful, despite the rock's cold-looking surfaces. Candles were scattered here and there and cast a warm glow, along with the fireplace which had been chiseled into the wall. The furniture was quaint, made of wood, and the bedding he had been lying on looked as if someone had taken the moments necessary to quilt it. This place was much more pleasant than Marcus Id's dark tower-palace. Gallrum commented as Gage looked at the craftsmanship of the blanket.

"Strongbear is the one who makes such things."

"What? A male made this?"

"Yes... he's quite talented, don't you think?"

"Is he a little... well, you know, on the sensitive side?"

Gallrum began to laugh. "Strongbear hates it when someone makes that mistake. I would be careful not to say that to anyone else around here."

"I'm sorry, I guess I just assumed."

"I wouldn't assume much while living in Gogswayne. Strongbear is always sewing something. He provides most everyone within our little underground village something that he's quilted at one moment or another. He's the owner of the finest establishment that serves the best Quaggle in town."

"Quaggle?" Gage interrupted. "What's that?"

"Well sir, you'll see… quaggle is the finest meal a Goswig can eat. You'll just have to see for yourself."

"You said this place is called Gogswayne. I thought this was a place with no name."

"As I have already said, I wouldn't assume too much while living here."

"What else can you tell me about the others?"

Gallrum flew over to a small table. He reached down and lifted a bound book from its surface with his talons. He tossed it across the room, but Gage failed to catch it. Gallrum laughed hissingly before explaining.

"Inside that book you'll find a record of everyone who lives here. I'll give you the moments necessary to study it. You're weak and still need to rest. I'll take you into our village once you have recovered completely."

Gage lowered himself to the bed and put his head on the pillow. "I'm still feeling so tired. Thank you, Gallrum, I'll be looking forward to meeting the others."

The Luvelles Gazette

When you want an update about your favorite characters

Lasidious and Celestria are within their home beneath the Peaks of Angels. They plan to stay away from the other gods on Ancients Sovereign until the moment has come to reveal the exact location of the third piece of the Crystal Moon.

Head Master Brayson is inside the Source's cave. He has spoken in length with the ancient dragon and is now speaking with the King of Grayham through a pool filled with molten lava. Sam's image is shimmering within the fiery liquid as he informs Brayson of his queen's desire to visit Luvelles. Brayson is continuously wiping the sweat from his brow due to the heat and, judging by the way the conversation is going, it appears that Shalee will be given passage to Luvelles.

George and Payne are still trapped within the Book of Bonding on the Head Master's desk. They are hungry, but George is unsure if it is safe to eat the food from the banquet table.

Kepler has rounded up a number of swassel gophers. He happened across them while searching the woods around the families' new homes. The demon jaguar plans to have these gophers dig him a lair beneath the large rocks the children have been playing on at the center of the clearing.

Athena, Susanne, and Mary are visiting with one another inside Mary's home. Baby Garrin has finished cutting his first tooth and seems to be much happier. The women are enjoying hearing the adventures of Mary's first date with Brayson.

Shalee has arrived on Grayham's Merchant Island. She plans to teleport back to Brandor once she has familiarized herself with the area. When Sam receives permission from the Head Master, she will teleport back to Merchant Island to catch a ride to Luvelles with the Merchant Angels.

Mosley is with the gods on his team. They have agreed that Mosley will inform Shalee of everything she needs to know about Grogger's Swamp. The wolf plans to have this conversation while Shalee is riding inside the container the Merchant Angels will carry her in while bringing her to Luvelles. The gods can only hope the answer to the crystal's whereabouts will present itself once she arrives at the swamp.

Mieonus, Goddess of Hate, is with her team of gods. She has been looking for George. They intend to use him to go after the crystal. Since the mage cannot be found, the gods have decided to speak with Lasidious in order to get an idea of where George might be.

Gregory is with the King of Lavan. They have agreed to break ground on the new bridge between their two cities. It was decided that the supports of the bridge will be made of heavy stone, while the undercarriage (substructure), traveled pathway (roadbed), and the uppercarriage (superstructure) will be made of magically created glass in three separate colors to give the bridge ample definition.

Marcus is meeting with Boyafed. He has a mission for the leader of the Dark Order but worries about the friction within their relationship. He hates the idea that Boyafed doesn't respect his authority.

Gage is still sleeping. His strength is increasing but he is still not ready to be up and about. Strongbear has called for a meeting of the Goswigs. The large brown bear plans to announce Gage's arrival to the others.

Lord Dowd has met with three of his finest Paladins of Light and dispatched them to spy on both Marcus and the leader of the Dark Order. The men are to return once they have information about the intentions of their enemies.

Yaloom has been sealed in his casket and put inside Brandor's royal crypt only after Sam ensured that the ex-god's body was well-preserved. He will be kept there until Shalee is able to retrieve the nasha fruit from the hidden god world.

Kiayasis is making his way to the Merchant Island of Luvelles. He intends to wait for Shalee's arrival and carry out his orders. Since he is the only one riding Joss, the Krape Lord is able to maintain flight. Once loaded with the queen and all her belongings, extended flight will no longer be possible due to the extra weight.

Hepplesif is with his small battalion of Kedgles. The tiny commander is working on the best way to protect Gregory's palace and various other key areas of the city.

Thank you for reading the Luvelles Gazette

Chapter 9

Quaggle

5 Peaks of Bailem Have Passed, The Merchant Island of Luvelles

Shalee stepped out of the transport container and took her first look at the Merchant Island of Luvelles. The place was busy, crawling with many rugged-looking elves as they both loaded and unloaded containers that were easily twenty, in some cases, thirty times larger than the one she had just stepped from.

She knew full well from what she had learned since becoming a queen that each world shared many different forms of merchandise between them. It was this constant flow of trade that helped fuel each world's economy, no matter how barbaric some of them seemed.

Mosley visited Shalee during her trip and discussed the dangers of Grogger's Swamp. She now knew where she had to go, but the wolf-god had said nothing about an escort. It was just prior to her arrival on Merchant Island that Mosley had vanished. Shalee sat in the dark until morning and waited patiently for the docking crew to open her container.

For the last few hours she had been dwelling on her thoughts of Sam. She was angered at how her selfish husband could be, so cold, and if that wasn't bad enough, she believed he judged her for the loss of their baby. Many tears had run down her cheeks since Mosley's departure and now, unexpectedly—as if out of no-where—a man claimed to be here to help her.

She now stood in front of Kiayasis Methelborn. She looked horrid, worn out from the trip, and her clothes smelled of human waste since there were no provisions to relieve one's self other than to simply just let it flow.

"Your Majesty," Kiayasis said as he bowed on one knee and lowered his head. "I'm here to assist you with your journey to the Swamplands of Luvelles."

Shalee studied her visitor. She was unprepared for this kind of surprise and felt embarrassed, not to mention completely appalled, at her smelly outfit which also appeared terribly wrinkled from sleeping on the hard container floor.

"Who are you?" she said anxiously, wishing she could run and hide.

"I am Kiayasis, my lady. Allow me to assist you with your things."

"Hold on a just a minute, mister. I had no knowledge you would be coming."

"I'm sorry, Your Majesty, but I have no idea what a minute means. Do you wish for me to go? Shall I leave?"

"I mean, give me a moment... please."

Kiayasis kept his head lowered as Shalee walked back into the container to grab her bags. She quickly decided she should change before leaving and pulled the door closed, careful to leave just enough of a crack to shed the light she needed to choose something fresher and a little more fashionable. She dabbed a few drops of Bledsfull Essence on her neck to cover her odor. Now she smelled like berries and pee—how wonderful was this first impression.

As she threw the bags across her shoulder and stepped back out of the container, she studied her escort once again from head to toe. He was dressed in black pants with a heavy gold-colored shirt. His hair was long and dark black, but his eyes were lowered so she couldn't see them. He was fit—his shoulders held the black cape which draped across them nicely. He did have a soothing voice. Maybe she would investigate this further and allow the escort to happen.

"Who sent you?" Shalee said as she lowered her bags beside him.

"I have been sent by the Head Master," the paladin said, lying without hesitation. "He wishes for you to be taken safely to your destination."

Shalee sighed with gratitude. "Well, this is an unexpected surprise. I had no idea you'd be coming. I must tell the Head Master how much I appreciate his generosity when I see him."

"May I stand, my lady?"

"Yes, yes, by all means. Stand up and let's find a place to bathe and get some rest. These crates aren't very comfortable and I could use a good night's sleep and a nice hot soaking bath."

Kiayasis smiled and as he did, Shalee took note of his blue eyes. They were stunning, what she considered to be dreamy, and his facial features were also perfect. She was so absorbed in thought as she looked him over that she barely heard him as he spoke.

"Allow me to call for a ride," Kiayasis said as he turned and gave a sharp whistle.

Shalee snapped out of her lapse of concentration and found something new to marvel at—Joss emgered from behind a group of crates. The Krape Lord kept his large wings folded and approached swiftly, using only his hind legs.

"Oh my gosh... what's that thing?"

"Don't be afraid, Your Majesty. This thing has a name. He is called Joss, and he will be our ride to the Swamplands. He'll get us there much faster than it would normally take if we were to walk. He's also tame... allow me to have your hand and I'll introduce you to him properly."

"I'm not so sure about this. He looks mean, and I would hate for him to think that I always smell this nasty."

Kiayasis turned and looked directly into Shalee's eyes. "My Lady, I assure you that it's safe, and he won't care about the smell. I'm here to protect you on your journey, not to allow my mount to devour you." He gave her a charming smile. "Besides, I hear queens taste sour anyway."

For a brief moment, Shalee enjoyed Kiayasis's charm. She took his hand and completely forgot about Sam. The dark paladin lifted her arm into the air with her hand held open.

"Joss, vara tel' Seldarine."

"What did you say to him?" she said as she watched Joss sniff her palm.

Kiayasis patted Joss on his snout before the Krape Lord lifted up. "I told him to protect you and ignore the foul smell."

"Well … that was just rude... it's not like I could—"

Kiayasis laughed and stopped her before she could finish. "I was only being clever, Your Majesty. I didn't really tell him that. I told him to protect you. I like to enjoy a good laugh every now and then. I do hope that's okay with you, my lady." Again Kiayasis smiled and again, she enjoyed his charm.

"Was that the language of the elves? I've had to study some of it, but only enough to get by."

"Ta na... Arwenamin."

"And what did that mean?"

"I said... it was, my lady."

Shalee loved his soft voice, and his deep blue eyes softened her mood. She was going to enjoy this escort's company.

Kiayasis took Shalee's bags and put them inside Joss's large pouch, the only place on a Krape Lord's body to have hair. The hair acted as a cushion, protecting Joss from being injured when objects shifted inside. With his large, ape-like arms, Joss adjusted the weight's distribution until he felt comfortable. Between Kiayasis's Dark Plate armor, his weapons, their food, and Shalee's bags, Joss was carrying more than a full load.

Kiayasis commanded Joss to lower to the ground.

"My lady, allow me to assist you. It may take you a few tries to adjust while mounting such a fine animal, but I assure, you it becomes easier as you go."

"I'm sure it will. He's so huge... are you sure about this?"

"I'm sure, Your Majesty, everything will be alright. If you don't like riding Joss after giving him a chance, I can carry you myself, but you have to promise to bathe first."

Again Kiayasis' smile widened.

"A woman doesn't want to hear that she smells. I'm sure I'll be just fine riding on Joss—I'm not as fragile as I look. And please, call me Shalee. I'm sure you'll enjoy the way I smell once I clean up."

"I cannot call you by your name, my lady. To do so would be a disgrace to your crown."

Shalee leaned in close. "Who would know? I certainly don't plan on telling anyone, so just think about it. If you're uncomfortable with it, then just consider it an order and then you'll have to call me by my name. Besides, you already told me that I smell. "

"I will consider it, Your Majesty. We best get going. It will take many moments to get to an inn. The one here on Merchant Island is full, but they'll allow you to bathe before we cross the Ebarna Strait. We will head to the Merchant Ferry after you're done cleaning up. I will pay the toll to cross and once we get to the other side, there's a small village with a well-cared for little inn. You'll be able to rest there."

The Queen of Grayham held tight to Kiayasis as they departed. In the back of her mind she enjoyed how he felt. She would have felt guilty for enjoying this pleasure, but her anger towards Sam welcomed the diversion. At least she was now being viewed as a woman—not a failure in this man's eyes.

The Mountains of Oraness

Boyafed entered Marcus Id's throne room. Just like the rest of the Chancellor's palace, this room was a dismal one and stunk of Marcus's nasty habit. The tobacco's smoke seemed to linger everywhere he turned, making Boyafed ill and irritable.

Many symbols of Dark Magic had been carved into the palace's stone walls and the heavy pieces of wooden furniture made from trees taken from Wraithwood Hollow were placed strategically throughout.

"What do you want, Marcus?" the Order leader snapped as he came to a stop.

Marcus bit down hard on his pipe, annoyed at the way Boyafed spoke. Before turning around to acknowledge the dark paladin's presence, he forced a smile to cover his mood.

"I have some news. I overheard my brother speaking with Lord Dowd. He has sent spies to live among us. You may want to look for any new faces within your ranks. They seek to gather information of a possible attack."

"Why would they be seeking this sort of information? I have no intention of sending my men to attack your brother's city of glass. Our forces are equally matched, and to attack without cause would be a senseless loss of life."

"I agree with you, but why would he send spies? I would think you would want to deal with these imposters. Maybe Gregory intends to give you cause for an attack."

"How were you in a position to overhear such a conversation? What reason could you have to spy on your brother in the first place?"

Marcus snapped with irritation. "I don't presume to know everything you do, Boyafed. How and why I do things or come across information is my business alone! Maybe you should concentrate on getting rid of the intruders and spend less of your moments scrutinizing my affairs!"

The leader of the Order moved close. His eyes grew cold and his fist tightened. "If I were you, I would only speak to those who fear you in the manner in which you have just spoken. Now answer the question! I'm in no mood for your games and I won't allow that kind of tone to escape your lips again when it's directed at me. Do we have an understanding?"

Marcus was dying inside, debating whether to challenge Boyafed's advance. But after a moment, and only after biting his tongue, he answered with a bold-faced lie, and all the while he managed to keep his composure.

"I was at a meeting with both of my brothers. Gregory spoke as if he has plans to march against us. He's growing brave and is tightening the security within his city. If you don't believe me, send someone to check it out. After hearing him speak, I chose to spy on him further. I went to his throne room and listened from the shadows. If he has sent his spies, and I'm right that he will be doing so, I thought it was best to tell you. I wanted to make sure you were, or rather, we, were prepared."

The dark paladin leader backed away. He thought a moment before responding. "I'll send some of my men to gather intelligence. What else can you tell me?"

"The Kedgle king has sent one hundred of his kind to help Gregory protect his city."

"What...why?"

"I don't know, but they are planning to use illusions on your men to cause confusion while Dowd's men strike them down. Dowd himself explained to the Kedgle commander what your men would look like. They plan to use their illusions in a specific manner and give their visions to those who wear the Order's colors. You'll need to figure out a way past this magic."

Boyafed lowered himself to the steps leading to Marcus's throne. After a bit he looked up. "I know of these creatures. Getting past the Kedgle's magic seems simple enough. I may need to attack your brother's city after all."

Marcus smiled within, then feigned his concern by putting his hand to his chin as if in thought. "Hmmmm ... well, maybe you're going about this the wrong way. Don't you think that a smaller strike without a large confrontation would be more appropriate?"

Boyafed thought before responding. "Agreed—a few men should be able to dispose of the Kedgles simply enough. Once they're dead, their king won't be so willing to send reinforcements. These men could leave Gregory's city of glass and return when I'm prepared to launch a full assault. I would imagine most of these creatures will be housed in one building or maybe even a large room, since they are so small. It'll be best to dispose of them all at the same moment. We will need to survey their posts and determine how they plan to guard the city. I'll send two men to gather the intelligence I'll need to formulate a plan."

"How do you plan on dealing with the spies within your ranks?"

Boyafed stood from the steps and headed for the door. He responded without looking back. "Don't worry about it—I've got it under control!"

Once the paladin leader was gone, Marcus sat on his throne. He looked at the door and grinned. *Well, that went better than I expected,* he thought.

Brayson's Desk
Inside the Book of Bonding

George and Payne had decided to take their chances a few days earlier and partook of the feast they stumbled upon after killing the old woman and her beast protectors. The food on the long banquet table had proven to be a blessing in disguise, but there seemed to be no specific reason for the table or the food to have been there. However, despite the puzzle, their need to eat outweighed their need to understand why the table had been there.

At first, George had been worried that the green gas which filled the room had settled on the food, but after he became hungry enough, he used his magic to summon the water necessary to wash the food off and began to chow down. George made sure they grabbed everything they could and stuffed it into a purple tablecloth. He threw it over his shoulder and waited for something bad to happen, but nothing ever came.

They had been walking for the last few days, following a winding corridor which eventually led them back to the surface. They were beyond the outskirts of the forest they had originally appeared within, and were walking towards a mountain range.

The landscape was beginning to change. As they walked through the hills, they followed a small stream that had been created from the snow melting on top of the mountains.

Many large rocks and ditches surrounded the area. The vegetation had not grown in this spot and scorch marks darkened much of the area around them. Eventually they found themselves in front of a small statue. The figure was exactly Payne's height. The stone replica looked exactly like the little guy, right down to his fairy wings and tiny demon horns. Even the new scar across the side of Payne's face, the one caused by the beast's claw, had been chiseled into it.

Payne flew over to his gray-colored counterpart and stood next to it. "It's Payne… neat! Let's eat." Yet again, his attention span failed to focus on something bigger than his stomach.

George played with the growth of his beard while he thought. He never would have allowed his appearance to get like this, but since appearing in the forest, he had not been able to clean up. His body odor was making it hard for him to concentrate.

"Something is telling me this isn't good, Payne."

"Why… Payne likes Payne. He's me... like Payne."

"I'm sure you do like him, buddy, but this isn't right. I think we're in trouble."

"Why?"

"I don't know, but something tells me this isn't where we want to be."

A voice from behind them responded. Both Payne and George whirled around to face this new presence.

"Now I know this is bad," George said as he moved toward his alternate self. "What are you? Who are you? Why are you here? What do you want and why do you look like me? Damn... I look like hell!"

"I am you... or rather, we are your opposites," he responded while pointing at the statue. As both George and Payne turned around, Payne's opposite had become animated—its color had changed from stone gray to the normal red of Payne's natural appearance.

"I don't like him no more, Master. That Payne bad." Payne quickly moved back and hovered next to George. "I hate Payne now!"

George's duplicate self continued. "This is your final test. You won't be able to leave this place and return to Luvelles until I've decided that you're ready." He lifted his hands. A wave of force knocked both George and Payne to the far side of a small mound.

"That piece of garesh just attacked us... I knew this was gonna suck!" George lifted himself from the ground and released his magic. Fire covered his alternate self, only to be defended by a bubble of protection.

"Take that... you garesh piece sort of Master," Payne shouted, and followed with an attack of his own. The fairy-demon teleported behind his duplicate self and grabbed him. He ripped into its shoulder with his claws and carried him skyward.

The fight was on.

The Hall of Judgment:
Ancients Sovereign

Mieonus, Goddess of Hate, called for a meeting with Lasidious and Celestria inside Gabriel's hall. The Book of Immortality was present. Sitting around the large heavy stone table within the

Book's home, Mieonus was the first to speak.

"Lasidious, I thought George was on Luvelles," Mieonus said as she pushed her long dark hair behind her ears. She adjusted her elegant white gown as she waited for a response.

"He is."

"I have been unable to find him. Is this some sort of a trick you've decided to play?"

"No, Mosley was the one who said he was on Luvelles, not me. I don't think Mosley would lie about such a thing."

"Then why can't I sense his presence? I should be able to, now that I know where he is."

Celestria decided to speak up. "George is inside the Book of Bonding on Head Master Brayson's desk. I wouldn't worry about it. We didn't intend to share the location of the crystal's where-abouts until George has had a chance to find his way out. I under-stand that you deserve the chance to manipulate him into going after this piece of the Crystal Moon."

Mieonus seemed to be satisfied with Celestria's explanation. She stood from the table and prepared to leave. "It sounds like everything is under control. I will visit the Head Master and see what I can learn. Gabriel, as always, it's good to see you. I'll speak with you later." The goddess vanished.

Gabriel floated across the table and lowered his heavy binding to the table in front of Lasidious. "I must say that you're playing with the gods as if they are mere puppets. It's my opinion that this game you've chosen to play is a diversion for something much larger. I don't know what it is yet, but I'll find out."

Lasidious was about to respond, but before he could, Mosley appeared.

"I'm sorry for my interruption. I have things I wish to say to you, Lasidious. I would like to do them under the Rule of Fro-malla. I would also like to have this conversation in the confines of your home within the Peaks of Angels. I would like to have the benefit of a conversation without interruption."

The Book of Immortality floated over to the wolf-god. "Am I to be part of this conversation?"

"I'm sorry, Gabriel, but I wish to speak with Lasidious and Celestria alone."

The Book grunted and floated out of the Hall. After a moment, Mosley continued.

"If you're okay with this, Lasidious, we will meet right now in your home."

Celestria looked at her evil lover and after another moment of exchanged glances, they agreed, and then vanished. Mosley quickly followed suit.

Once everyone arrived, they sat around the table near the green flames of the god's fireplace, which cast an eerie glow, setting the mood. Mosley turned one of the chairs into a platform and jumped on top of it. Celestria quickly lit some of the candles she had placed about their cave-like home. Lasidious waved his hand. A feast of assorted foods and refreshments appeared before them.

"Well, Mosley, I have to admit I'm curious," the God of Mischief said once everything was in order. "What could be so important that it requires the Rule of Fromalla to be enacted before we can speak?"

Mosley jumped down off his platform and began to pace. "Shalee is on her way to Grogger's Swamp. Something unexpected has happened... something I never would have expected. The leader of the Dark Order has sent his son Kiayasis to provide Shalee an escort. I was there on Merchant Island when Kiayasis introduced himself. He told Shalee the Head Master sent him, but I know better. He was sent by Boyafed. My question is... why? Why would the Order care anything about a sorceress from Grayham? I spoke with Hosseff to see if he had anything to do with it, but it was clear he had no idea what I was talking about. After I left, I came to the conclusion that it was you. You were the one who made this happen. I know I'm right, and there's no sense in denying it, so level with me..."

Celestria interrupted before Mosley could continue. "Why is Shalee going to Grogger's Swamp? What could possibly be there that she would want... or even find remotely interesting?"

Mosley sighed and jumped back onto the platform. He looked her in the eye. "I know the two of you intentionally left me the clue as to where the crystal is. I smelled it on your dress. I know

Lasidious was the one who convinced Boyafed to send Kiayasis to escort Shalee. Lasidious, we have had an understanding between us, though it has been an unspoken one. I have given you the respect that both of you deserve by coming to you first, and in return, I would ask you give me the same. I've come to you in order to invoke the Rule of Fromalla. Your secret stays safe with me and I know this information will be unable to leave this room. I'm asking you to level with me and let me in on the reasons for this manipulation."

Lasidious chuckled as he stood from the table. "Mosley, of all the gods I like you the most. You're perceptive and relentless. I did ask Boyafed to send Kiayasis to escort Shalee. I figured you would choose her to go after the crystal, and we did intentionally leave you a clue on Celestria's gown."

"Why would you want to help me?"

"Because, my furry friend, your team needs to capture this piece of the crystal in order to keep our little game going. If Mieonus's team captures this last piece, the Book of Immortality would require me to surrender the entire Crystal Moon back to the Temple of the Gods. Evil would rule for all of eternity. I'm not naïve, Mosley. I know we need a balance of both good and evil. This is how things should be. I don't want this piece of the crystal to be captured by anyone but you and your team."

Mosley began to pace again. "Why would you send Kiayasis to provide Shalee an escort? He's an evil man and serves Hosseff."

Lasidious looked at Celestria. "Would you care to answer this one?"

Celestria lowered her glassful of wine to the table. "We sent Kiayasis because the Order is feared. This will ensure that Shalee makes it safely to her destination. We all know Luvelles is full of magic much stronger than what she commands. She is traveling through the Kingdom of Hyperia, and this is where much of the darkness on Luvelles resides. Beyond what help we've already given to Shalee, your precious little sorceress can find her own way home to Grayham after she captures the crystal. If she stumbles across someone who would harm her, then so be it."

Mosley swallowed a piece of meat before responding. "It seems that my questions have been answered. Something isn't sitting right with me, though. I haven't quite figured out what it is yet, but I'm sure it will present itself during some other moment. I'll speak with both of you again. Thank you for answering my questions." The wolf vanished.

Celestria began to shout a wave of questions. "Do you think they are putting it all together? Do you think they know we're stalling? Are we losing our advantage? Do they know about our baby?"

The God of Mischief pulled her close and pushed her hair back from her face. He kissed her softly and spoke with a tender voice. "If they knew anything, we would be dead already. They can suspect all they want. The Book can do nothing unless he has evidence that we've done something wrong. Our baby is safe and we're still alive. All we need to do it stay the course. Soon our baby will be old enough to release his powers. Garrin will be able take control of Gabriel, with our help, and we'll have nothing to worry about. It doesn't matter if they suspect anything. By the moment they put it all together, it will be too late."

The goddess cupped his face. She kissed him softly and said, "Your confidence is intoxicating. Maybe you should demonstrate some more of this."

Lasidious lifted her from the floor. "Maybe I will."

Their lips met again, soft at first, and then the pressure built as their heartbeats rose. Lasidious pinned his evil lover up against a wall and... WELL… the rest will be left to the imagination.

The Village of Gogswayne

It was a new day on Luvelles. Gage awoke and stretched his furry body. The badger jumped down from the resting spot he had been lying on since his arrival. He's had more than one conversation with his new flying Serwin friend, Gallrum, since he came, but his body was simply too weak to venture out of the home.

Serwin was the name for Gallrum's reptilian race. They primarily occupied the forest of Shade Hollow. Gallrum had left Shade Hollow and been bonded to an evil wizard named Balecut. Like many of the occupants of this hidden village, Gallrum left his master and sought refuge to avoid the constant abuse he had received. But despite the Goswig's absence, Balecut still was one of the most powerful wizards on Luvelles, third only to Brayson and Marcus. Gregory Id was also more powerful than Balecut, but the White Chancellor was considered a warlock and commanded a different kind of power. All in all, Balecut was the fourth most powerful being on Luvelles, but the absence of his Goswig kept him from growing stronger.

Unlike every other morning, Gage was alone. Gallrum was nowhere to be found within his quaint little home. Gage took a deep breath and opened the door. He was surprised by what he saw as he leaned against his small wooden cane. If he had not known they were underground, he would have sworn that the city had been built above it. The magic here was strong. It was as if they had their own sun. Plants grew, trees blossomed, and a gentle wind passed through the branches. The earth was wet, as if it had just rained, and the gray clouds that filled the clear blue of what seemed to be an actual sky were moving, floating along as any normal cloud would.

Gallrum's home appeared to be at the end of a long cobblestone street. On either side of the road there were many different storefronts. Gage adjusted his robe and began to walk, looking everywhere as he went. There was a building for most anything he could think of—flowers, furniture, a diner, a healer, and even a shop called "The Butcher's Block."

"You must be Gage," a voice called out.

The badger redirected his attention. A large brown bear was approaching.

"I am, and you must be Strongbear ... Gallrum has told me all about you."

"It was all pleasant, I hope. I made you a blanket. I make everyone something when they arrive. I was hoping that you'd be out and about today. I trust you're feeling better. Adjusting to normal life after visiting the Ultorian city can be quite difficult. Come with me and I'll feed you."

"Oh, I don't know that I feel up to moving around too much. Maybe I'll stop here and look around some more tomorrow."

Strongbear lifted Gage from the ground. "I'll just carry you. So are you with me or against me on this one?"

The badger had no idea how to respond so he said, "Ummm... I'm with you, I think."

"Ha, ha, ha, you're gonna make a fine addition to Gogswayne. Let's get you some food. What-da-ya say? Are you with me or against me?"

"Ummm... I thought we already determined that I was with you?"

"Oh yeah, I forgot! Yeah, you're with me!"

The bear began to scratch his big brown head as if lost in thought. Gage could see that he was trying to determine if he really heard the badger say he was with him.

Gage cleared his throat to get the bear's attention. "So, food does sound really great right about now. Gallrum told me about your diner. He said you have the finest quaggle a Goswig could eat. What exactly is quaggle?"

Strongbear's big belly jiggled as he began to chuckle. "I wouldn't listen to Gallrum's idea of good food. He's a Serwin. They consider corgan flies an acceptable meal. Quaggle is an assortment of eyeballs that I pluck out of all the fish before I serve them to my patrons. It takes me about two Peaks of Bailem to gather enough eyes to fill a single plate for Gallrum. I've never told him he's the only one I serve this meal to. He tells everyone when they arrive how great my quaggle is. We just allow him to have this fantasy. I think I'll feed you something far more pleasant."

Gage smiled. "I think something far more pleasant sounds nice."

Strongbear laughed again as he began to trot down the cobblestone street. "I have lived in our underground city for nearly 600 seasons, and although I didn't intend to do so, the population here has a tendency to look to me for guidance."

"Let me guess—they're all with you," Gage said, seizing the opportunity to make a funny.

The bear laughed. "That's exactly right. I suppose it's a good position to be in when you want something done. But for the most part, I simply feed everyone and make blankets and other pleasantries to give to the others."

"I don't think I have ever met a sewing bear before."

Strongbear lifted a brow and stopped jogging. "I do hope that you're not judging me because I like to craft."

"No, no, I would never do such a thing. I apologize if it sounded that way."

"Don't judge this old bear by the fur that covers him. I have many skills other than sewing." He leaned over and whispered. "My other skills aside, I make my own special brew of ale and a wonderful corgan jerky. Are you a drinker? Come on, you've got to be a drinker, aren't ya? Are ya with me, or against me?"

Chapter 10

𝕬 𝕸𝖔𝖒𝖊𝖓𝖙 𝖔𝖋 𝕻𝖆𝖘𝖘𝖎𝖔𝖓

Kiayasis held Joss at a steady pace. The Krape Lord's energy and desire to run made this task a difficult job. Shalee rode behind Kiayasis as they worked their way north along the western edge of the Mountains of Vesper. They hoped to be following the western shores of Lake Iple within three Peaks of Bailem.

"Tell me about your family," Shalee said, holding her arms around Kiayasis as Joss moved quickly across the hilly terrain.

"My father is a good man. He's the leader of the army I belong to. My mother, I'm sad to say, is dead."

"I'm sorry."

"Don't be—she lived a good life. She was an incredible woman. She taught me how to treat a lady and how to be a good man. Her name was Gwen, and I remember her for her beauty."

"You make her sound like an angel. I wish I could say the same thing about my mother. As much as I would like to, I can't think of anything to say, other than she was a little irritating. I suppose there were moments when we bonded, but it all seems to be outweighed by her annoying ability to ruin a moment. I did love her, though."

Kiayasis twisted around just enough so that he could see Shalee's eyes.

"It seems to me that despite your mother's stated shortcomings, a bit of perfection was born the day you came into the world." He winked and turned back around.

Shalee was unsure how to respond. Instead of ruining the moment, she squeezed her arms about his waist to let him know of her satisfaction with his comment. Kiayasis put his hand on hers and caressed it with a single soft stroke. Once done, he commanded Joss into a bouncing, wing-flapping run.

The Krape Lord had been trained to use his large wings to assist in this form of travel. The beast sprang into the air with his hind legs and used his massive wings to cover a large distance before the weight he was carrying forced him back to the ground.

Mary's Home

Brayson knocked on Mary's door. When she opened it, a bright smile crossed her face. She quickly pulled him inside and threw herself into his arms. The embrace was passionate. Brayson took the opportunity to steal his first kiss. Neither of them wanted the moment to end. After several moments, Mary drew back and found his eyes.

"You're back... does this mean Fisgig is alive?"

He kissed the top of her forehead once more before responding.

"He is. I left him with the Source. It will be a few more days before he has gathered all of his memories, but my powers have returned. And you, my lady, were the first one I thought of visiting once I could leave the cave."

Mary nestled into his arms. "You make it sound so romantic. So where are you taking me today?"

"I'm afraid I must go to my office. By chance, has George returned?"

"No... was he supposed to?"

"Not necessarily. He must still be working on his mission."

"What mission is that?"

"It's nothing to concern yourself with. You're welcome to come with me. I'll see to it that you get home once I've completed my work."

"I would love that. Let me freshen up and we'll leave."

After arriving at Brayson's office in the sky, it wasn't long before the Goddess of Hate, Mieonus, made an appearance.

"Oh, you scared me," Mary said after jumping with a start and quickly moving behind Brayson. "I haven't gotten used to the way people just show up on this world."

Brayson knew full well who stood in front of him. He bowed.

"Goddess, how may I serve you?" he said, keeping his eyes lowered to the floor. He pulled Mary down with him. "What brings you here? I live to serve." *(With all his knowledge and all his goodness, the Head Master had no idea the deity he served was the most hateful of them*

Mieonus spoke completely out of character. She sounded gentle and sweet. "Hello Brayson, it's a pleasure to see you. You're looking well. I have come looking for George. Is he still inside your Book of Bonding?"

"He is."

"I would like to speak with him when he returns. I'll leave this crystal with you. Would you please have George use it to summon me when he's completed his test?"

"I will, but I don't know when he'll be back."

"I understand. Please just see to it that he gets the crystal, if you don't mind." The goddess forced a pleasant smile, then continued. "Of all my subjects who live in service to me, Brayson, I'm the most proud of you." Mieonus vanished.

Mary stood and moved back out from behind Brayson. "Who was that?"

"That was the one I serve. Her name is Mieonus, but I call her Goddess to show the proper respect."

"I gathered that from the conversation. What I meant to say was, why would a god come here to see you, and why would she be looking for George? She said something about a test. What did she mean by, is he still inside of a book?"

Brayson gathered his thoughts before responding. "The mission George is on is a test to see if he and Payne will be able to bond with one another. If he's unable to complete this test, he could be lost to us forever. He could die."

"Forever, die... what about my daughter Athena and her baby? If he doesn't come home, she'll be left raising a child on her own. This is not a good thing!"

Brayson pulled her close. "I don't expect this will happen. George is a smart man. It's a necessary step for a mage of his caliber to take on a Goswig, who will allow him to grow and eventually become a wizard or warlock, depending on the path George chooses to take.

"I'm not sure why a deity would want to speak with him, but this is a conversation I intend to be present for when they meet. It's intriguing that my new Mystic-Learner has a connection with the gods."

"Well, I think it's unnerving! My son-in-law is playing with some very powerful beings and that's downright scary."

"I'm sure George knows what he's doing. I wouldn't worry about such things. Maybe you could help me with some of the organizing I need to do. It'll help to take your mind off George, and give me a chance to teach you some of the elven language."

Mary smiled. "As long as you promise to say something beautiful to me."

Inside the Book of Bonding

George rolled over slowly, his robes charred, forearms burned. Payne lay next to him, face down and motionless. All George could do was watch as his alternate self moved to stand overtop his exhausted body. This being, although it looked just like him, was far more powerful, but how? It was hopeless.

"You win," George cried out. "I can't fight you any longer. My power's drained. You're the better man. Just kill me already, damn it."

With a cold voice the duplicate responded. "You're weak. I would've expected more, much more. You don't deserve to be bonded with such a powerful Goswig. Your little friend has succeeded in beating his adversary, but he was unable save you. He's close to death, as are you. I didn't wish to hurt him. He had the fighting spirit necessary to earn the right to leave this place. Unfortunately you needed to defeat us both in order to be released. It's because of your failure that Payne will perish alongside you. I imagine he'll pass on not long after I'm finished with you. Too bad, because this little fairy-demon could've given you an incredible amount of power."

Tears flowed as George began to beg. "Please, allow me to die without the use of magic. I don't want to be left unrecognizable. Your magic will scar my face. I don't want my wife to see me that way. Please, just give me this request. It's the least you could do!"

"Your wife will never see your face again. She'll live a life without the satisfaction of saying goodbye."

George began to sob. "You can't do this... please... please!"

"Oh, but I can. It's funny how the harm you've caused so many others has left you in such a pathetic position. You have failed and will die alone as a consequence of your crimes. You have failed to destroy your own weaknesses. Without your magic, you can no longer fight. It's over—just accept your fate and die with whatever dignity you can find from such a miserable life."

George couldn't argue—he had used and abused so many people who had deserved better in his life. All he could do was beg for a quick death.

"At least allow me to die without the use of magic. Please, I beg you… just use my blade. Either way, I'll die, and you'll win. I mean, what could it hurt?"

"An interesting request... it's a good way to die, I suppose. I'm sure I can make it just as painful as the torture I could administer with my magic!"

He lifted his hands in the air and turned to look at the horizon. "What better way to die than to release your last breath to a setting sun? Your eyes will capture the glory of such wonderful colors before they close forever."

After a moment, George's alternate self turned to face his victim. A sharp cracking sound filled the evening air. The alternate being's right eye exploded as the bullet passed through it and into his brain.

George shouted, "I bet you didn't see that coming, chump!" Watching his enemy fall lifeless, he managed to scramble to his feet. Blood continued to leak out of the alternate's eye as George moved to stand above him.

"You shouldn't talk so much, moron! Everyone knows that's how you get yourself killed. You took the bait and now—well, just look at ya—*you're dead!*"

He leaned over to put the small pistol away beneath his pant leg, the same pistol he had on him when taken from Earth, the same one he had used to threaten Maldwin, the rat, the day he met him. He continued to talk to the corpse as he did so.

"I bet you've never seen one of these. It's called a .22. It only fires one bullet at a time, so I'm glad I didn't miss. I thought I would never need it with magic and all, but something told me to keep it handy. I guess now that I think about it, some Earth magic just saved my ass. Kind of ironic, now that I think about it."

He moved to take Payne into his arms. The little fairy-demon's body draped limply as he looked down at him. "This is bad, real bad!"

Brayson's Floating Office

George appeared with Payne hanging across his arms. He set the fairy-demon down on the floor. "Quick, I need your help. Payne's in trouble and he's not breathing!"

Brayson assisted Mary from his lap and stood from the chair behind his heavy wooden desk. He teleported to the far side of the room, grabbed a vial from the bookcase, and teleported next to Payne.

"George, open his mouth. I need to get the liquid below his tongue in order for it to work."

Once the light blue droplet was administered, Brayson sighed. "There's nothing more that can be done. It's up to the gods whether he lives or dies."

George rubbed his hands across his face as if in disbelief. "He can't die! He saved my life. If he dies, it's my fault... I let him down."

"It's not your fault, son," Brayson said as he moved toward him. Mary watched as Brayson extended his hand to help George to his feet. "We can't always control the outcome of things. Some-things are just simply bigger than we are."

"Is that supposed to make me feel better?" George snapped as he pulled away. "What kind of crappy logic was that?"

"It's just the way of things," Brayson responded, remaining calm.

"Bull crap. I don't believe that. I should've been there for him."

"You can't save everyone. If he dies... it simply wasn't meant to be."

"Hell no, I won't believe that. You weren't there. It's my fault and I should've saved him. Your logic sucks... it's a pile of garesh, I tell ya."

Brayson was about to respond, but a faint voice filled the air.

"Yeah... garesh, crappy logic," Payne said as he struggled to sit up.

George pushed past Brayson and knelt at Payne's side. "You're alive. I thought you were a goner. That vial must be some have some vicious healing mojo in it."

Payne grinned. "I'm hungry."

"Ha... that sounds like the Payne I know. My hell, it really sucked where we were. I never want to go there again."

"Yeah, sucked," Payne affirmed.

Mary instantly began to scold them both. "George, what have I told you about speaking that way? It's foul and definitely not something I wish my future grandbaby to hear. Payne, you won't speak like that either. Do you both understand me?"

George had been so caught up in the situation he hadn't realized Mary was in the room. "I'm sorry, Mother, you're right. Master, I was just frightened. I owe you both an apology. Thanks for saving him."

Brayson walked over and put his hand on George's shoulder, only to pull away. "George, you need a bath. You smell something awful. We have much to discuss, but first, go home and clean up. We can meet in the morning."

Mary interrupted before George could respond. "Aren't you going to tell him about the goddess's visit?"

Brayson moved close to Mary in an attempt to avoid George's nasty odor. "I will, but I think it can wait until morning. I'm sure we all have many questions, but I'm equally sure that a good night's rest will give us all clear heads. We'll meet again in the morning. Maybe you could make us some breakfast, Mary."

Mary enjoyed the tenderness of Brayson's arms as he put them around her from behind. "I would love to make breakfast."

Before anyone could speak another word, Brayson teleported

them all to the clearing in front of their homes. There was no more conversation beyond the normal goodbyes. George and Payne went inside, calling for Athena.

Mary took a moment to rub her hand through Brayson's short brown hair and played with the tips of his small, pointed ears. "You, Mr. Id, are a handsome man. I just love hair on a man's face. You can tickle my neck with it whenever you wish."

After giving Mary a long kiss goodbye, Brayson returned to his office.

The next morning, Brayson knocked on Mary's door. She gave him a warm welcome and instructed him to take a seat at the kitchen table. Mary had put on her best dress—one that Brayson had sent as one of his many gifts. It was a yellow gown that hung low across her chest. Her long hair and smooth skin complemented the ensemble. At 44 seasons, she looked absolutely radiant to Brayson's old eyes of 730 seasons.

It wasn't long before George walked through the door and killed the mood. "Mother," he shouted from the front door. "What's for breakfast?"

Athena slapped him across the back of his arm. "Don't be so rude. You don't have to yell."

"Yes, dear." He grinned. "You know... I think that as the baby gets bigger inside of you, you seem to be slapping me harder and harder. That one stung a bit, babe."

"Then I suggest you start minding your manners."

"Yes, ma'am."

Payne was not far behind. Before George could get to the kitchen, he remembered they were missing someone important. "Athena, where's Kepler?"

She took him outside and pointed at the mound of rocks at the clearing's center. "Go to the other side of the stones. Kepler had a family of swassel gophers dig him a new lair. He's probably sleeping. All he's done since your departure is lie around and sulk. I think he misses you!"

George gave Athena a quick kiss and made his way to the stones. He lowered himself into the large hole and used his power to clear the darkness. Sure enough, Kepler was lying with his head tucked beneath his paws.

"Kepler, wake up... I'm home."

As soon as the demon-jaguar heard his voice, the giant cat's spirit was lifted, but despite his excitement, Kepler downplayed his emotions. He slowly stood, stretched his powerful black body, and methodically turned his red glowing eyes toward his friend.

"Finally, your back, I've been extremely bored. Please tell me we're going somewhere."

George moved toward him. He hugged the demon's large, furry neck.

As always, Kepler squirmed while inside the mage's embrace. "Must you hug me so much? I keep telling you it's not natural for a demon-jaguar to be so close to one of you humans. Maybe we should have boundaries."

"Ha... not a chance, big boy. You'll just have to get use to it. Besides, I love ya, buddy."

Kepler cringed. "Love is such a strong word, don't you think?"

George smiled and changed the subject. "Anyway, I'm not sure what's going on, but Master Brayson said there was a god looking for me. Usually this means something's about to happen. Maybe Lasidious has something for us to do, though I don't know why he would approach Master Brayson about it."

"Maybe it's not Lasidious."

"I don't know, but I'll find out. Mary is inside making breakfast. Master Brayson is here and intends to speak with me about it. I'll come back and get you once I know more. It's good to see you, my friend."

"You're not leaving me anywhere. If someone is making breakfast, I'd better be invited."

After breakfast, George took the crystal Mieonus had left behind and met Brayson inside his floating office, Payne and Kepler tagging along.

Brayson was the first to speak. "George, use the crystal to summon the goddess."

The mage did as instructed. It wasn't long before Mieonus appeared. George recognized her instantly. "I know your face," he said.

"Yes, George, we've met before in Bloodvain's throne room and again on Scorpion Island. I see you're adjusting well to life on Luvelles. I trust that your bonding with your new Goswig wasn't difficult."

"Ha—I wish that was the case. I was nearly eaten by a bunch of pissed-off plants and then I about fell to my death and that's all before we barely escaped with our lives. I wouldn't call anything about the bonding process easy."

Payne piped in. "Payne saved Master!"

The goddess took a good look at Payne. She had no idea the fairy-demon existed. "And what are you?"

Payne was about to answer, but George stopped him. "Don't get him started. Once he gets going, you'll regret it. Tell me what it is you want with me."

Brayson couldn't believe how direct George was with the goddess, but he stayed quiet since she didn't seem to be bothered by his approach.

Mieonus took a seat behind Brayson's desk, lifted her feet on top of it, and carefully adjusted her gown.

Brayson watched as the one he served acted as if she were one of them—as if it were normal to be speaking candidly with George. He was still shocked at how his Mystic-Learner had spoken to her—it was as if she were his equal—as if a friendship existed, or worse, as if George didn't care she was a deity. Never would he have spoken to his god in such a way, but she seemed pleased to be speaking with him.

Mieonus looked through the Book of Bonding's pages while resting it on top of her curvy legs. "I wish to speak with you alone, George." She turned to look at Brayson. "May we use your office? This is between just the two of us."

The Head Master wanted to object, but he could not fathom going against the wishes of the one he served. "By all means... I will leave." he vanished.

Mieonus waved her hands. Kepler and Payne also vanished, only to reappear outside the School of Magic.

Kepler let out an angry roar. "Garesh… that makes me mad, and I'm tired of being left out! This is really starting to get on my nerves!"

"It okay, kitty," Payne said as he stood next to the demon. "Payne talk to ya."

"Well, that's just great. Just teleport us home, you little freak."

Back inside Brayson's office, Mieonus continued. "A piece of the Crystal Moon has been placed on Luvelles. I would like you to go after it, since you have the first two pieces already. If you capture this piece, Lasidious will return the rest of the Crystal Moon to the Temple of the Gods on Grayham and everything will return to normal."

George began to laugh.

"You can't be serious! I'm tired of running around, gathering the crystal's pieces. Since it was Lasidious that took the Crystal Moon from the Temple of the Gods in the first place, maybe you should speak with him about this. This isn't my problem—this is your problem. I'm just a normal guy trying to learn the ways of magic."

Mieonus didn't like his response, but she didn't want to cause tension. She could clearly see George was closed to the idea for the moment. She decided to take another approach.

"George, my dear, dear friend, I think both of us know you're the best man for the job. I would pay you well for your service. I only ask that you think about it. Considering your competition, I would think after you know everything, you just might want to go after this piece. There's no one else who understands Shalee the way you could. You know how Earth women think."

"Shalee is seeking the crystal? And what about Sam?"

"She is, but Sam is still on Grayham."

"Well now, this changes things. I have a debt I would like to settle with her. She did, after all, try to kill me on Scorpion Island the day Brandor invaded. At that moment, I was in a hurry to leave that miserable cave and my power was drained, but I've never forgotten that she sent her magic flying in my direction. I could have been killed if not for my power to deflect hers. I will think about it. This may be something I want to do after all, *but,* you're going to pay me well if I do. I don't work for free!"

Mieonus's brows tightened. "Since when did you become so bold that you feel free to speak to a god this way?"

George allowed an evil, smug grin to cross his face. "I would imagine I feel so bold since I know there's nothing you can do about it. You may have your servants fooled—but as for me, I could care less about your powers. I know you are bound to the laws within the Book of Immortality's pages. You'll need to pay me, and pay me well, or I won't go after your crystal."

Mieonus stood and tossed him another one of her crystals. "We shall see how confident you are when someone who serves me is breathing down your neck for the way you've spoken. Maybe then you'll learn some humility and beg for forgiveness once you've suffered enough blood loss. If you choose to go after the crystal, just summon me with this... it could save your life if you choose to do this for me."

George sneered at her. "So you threaten me and then expect me to go after your damn piece of the crystal?"

Mieonus sighed and calmly responded. "No—there's no threat being implied here, George, *but* there is a promise that if you don't start rethinking how you speak to me from now on, it will be sure death from those who command greater powers than you! I personally don't need to hurt you. I've many others who can do it for me, and all it takes is a little promise and a simple suggestion. You're not stupid enough to think I don't have the upper hand in this conversation. Please tell me you're smarter than this, George. And don't allow your faith in Lasidious to give you unjustified overconfidence. It will only end up getting you killed. I imagine you understand where I'm coming from, and if you wish, after you've thought it through a bit... just summon me once you have made your final decision. Your death, or retrieving the third piece of the Crystal Moon, but either way, I will win. I always win, make no mistake about that!" She took a moment to laugh and then vanished.

George lowered himself into Brayson's chair and began to think as he wiped the sweat from his brow. *Damn... well, that sucked and didn't go how I imagined it would. I've got to be smarter than this from now on. Somehow, I need to get on her good side before she has me strung up. Dang it, George! Why did you have to go and be such an idiot? I mean, how stupid could I get?*

George's Home

That night, Lasidious appeared to George in his dreams. It had been nearly 140 Peaks of Bailem since the last moment the God of Mischief visited him in this manner.

"It's about time I heard from you," George said as the visions of his daughter, Abbie, faded away and were replaced by Lasidious's face. "I thought you forgot about me."

"I'm sure you didn't feel put out. You've been doing just fine without me. I see you've bonded with Payne...you're welcome, by the way."

"So it was you who sent Payne to me. I figured as much. I could only assume you were the one Payne calls Friend."

"I am, and Payne is strong, though he doesn't realize it yet. He has the potential to be the most powerful Goswig a man could have. Even I don't know his full potential. He could become a dominant force while living in service to you. His mind is young. You can mold him into what you need him to be. Be good to him and he'll be loyal. Treat him with kindness and he'll never turn on you.

"You need to remember that if your Goswig were to ever perish, your powers would be affected also. Listen carefully to what I'm saying. The death of other Goswigs weakens the powers of their master when they die, just as your powers would be weakened if Payne dies."

"Okay, I get it... your little hint is not so subtle. I'll remember that when the moment comes."

"Good, George. Now that you're bonded with our little fairy-demon friend, you can draw from his power. You can do things now you couldn't do before. Take the moments necessary to experiment with this. Learn how to channel his energy. Become one with Payne and use his energy as a way to boost the power within you."

George began to laugh.

"What's so funny?" Lasidious asked, puzzled.

"Oh, nothing. You just sound like an old television show I used to watch back on Earth. I almost feel like you should be calling me Grasshopper."

It was clear Lasidious had no idea what he was talking about. The god changed the subject.

"I have something I need to tell you. It's about the piece of crystal hidden here on Luvelles."

"Yes, I know... Mieonus wants me to go after it. And she threatened to have me killed if I don't. She said she would have someone come after me."

Lasidious took a moment to ponder. "It appears we have much to discuss. This is going to be tricky, and we need to make sure we do everything just right."

The Next Morning,
Mary's Home

George walked through the door of his mother-in-law's home without knocking. "Mary, is Brayson here?" he shouted. "I went to his office, but he's not there."

There was no response. He headed up the stairs. "Hello... Mary... are you in there?" he said, speaking through the bedroom door.

When the door to the room opened, it was just enough for Brayson to slide through. He wore nothing but his underpants. "What do you want, George? I'm kind of busy at the moment."

The mage grinned. "We need to talk."

"Okay, but give me a while. I will come and find you."

"This can't wait. It involves what Mieonus has asked me to do. I'll be out front."

Brayson rolled his eyes. "Your timing is simply terrible."

George grinned again and turned to head down the stairs.

Brayson whispered to himself. *"Yes, Master... I'm sorry for the intrusion, Master. Oh, no, no, no, don't worry about it, George... I always like to be interrupted... anything for my new Mystic-Learner, anything at all."*

George sat patiently on the front steps of Mary's home. It wasn't long before Brayson appeared beside him.

"What could possibly be so important?"

"I'm sorry, but Mieonus has given me an assignment. But it will require that I stand before the Source."

"The Source! Why would she want you to do such a thing? You're not ready to look into the Eye of Magic yet."

George threw his hands up as if to say he didn't know, and then responded. "Look... I know this is unusual. Heck, I have been led to Luvelles by the gods and for whatever reason, they seem to have a plan for me. Apparently Amar was just a way for you and me to meet. Mieonus said I am to speak with the Source and there's a war about to happen on this world. Apparently, you alone won't be strong enough to put a stop to it. You're going to need my help and as I have said already, Mieonus wants me to meet with the Source and acquire the power necessary to assist you."

"But you're not ready for this!"

"I understand your concern, but I'm ready. You just don't realize it yet. Mieonus has prepared me for this day."

"George, if you only knew what happens when you meet with the Source. If the Ancient One allows you to look into the Eye of Magic, you could be lost forever. You're soul could be swallowed and I imagine Athena, not to mention, Mary, would have my hide for letting you do something like this. This isn't something you should try before you're ready."

"I know all about the Eye, and I assure you I'm ready. How many of your Mystic-Learners have had gods as friends?"

"I suppose I see your point, and Mieonus is also the goddess I serve. Who better to know your skills than her? Maybe I am worried over nothing."

"There you go—that's how you know I'm ready. Mieonus said I am, so that means you have nothing to worry about... *right?*"

Brayson stood and began to pace. "This just doesn't seem right. Why would the goddess wish to send a young boy of only 23 seasons to risk so much?"

"Master... you doubt your god?"

"No, I don't doubt her. I believe she is a wise deity and knows what's best. But this isn't something I would normally do without giving the proper training first. Look at what happened when you bonded with Payne. Both of you nearly died. If you go to the Source before you're ready and he allows you to pass, you could very well finish what the bonding process was unable to do. You could be sacrificing your life for nothing."

George shrugged, then said, "I appreciate your concern, but how do we tell the goddess no ... and how many men could have lived going through the bonding process with Payne in the first place? It was a near impossible situation, but somehow I pulled it off."

Brayson rubbed his hands through his hair and his eyes seemed to carry the weight of all Luvelles within them. "The way to the Source is filled with many perils. You would need to go through the trials no matter what. I cannot allow you to pass by them. The Source won't speak with you unless you've passed these tests."

"Master, Mieonus knows something we don't. I have faith in my abilities. I don't doubt that with Payne and Kepler at my side, I'll pass with ease."

Brayson smiled uneasily as he sat down to put his arm around his Mystic-Learner.

"I want you to remember these words. I would never say this to anyone, but considering the circumstances, I will give you a helpful hint. Don't ever forget what I'm about to tell you. It's your belief in yourself that saves you. Belief is the key."

"I won't forget, Master. I'll make you proud, I promise."

"If there is indeed a war coming, then I shall need you at my side. I've never given anyone advice on passing the Eye. You're the first and I'll just have to put my faith in my goddess's hands."

Brayson patted him on the back and stood up. "I need a few days to prepare the trials for your journey. I'll meet you in my office at the Peak of Bailem in three days. You may want to gather the things you think you might need. I cannot tell you what to take with you, so choose wisely."

"Thank you... I'll be there." George watched as Brayson walked back inside Mary's home. Once the door was shut, he allowed an evil grin to appear on his face. "What a sucker! That went better than expected. It's all coming together."

An unexpected voice snuck up from behind. "What's all coming together?" Athena said, "and who's the sucker? What is a sucker, anyway?"

"Oh, it's nothing to worry about, babe. A sucker is a good thing. It's just an Earth expression." He turned around, put on an innocent face and moved to take her in his arms. "I was just thinking we should spend some quality moments together."

"Ahhhhhh... you're so adorable."

As he pulled her close, he felt guilty for the lie he had told her. He was compromising his vows and hated himself for it. He thought, *Somehow I need to keep our love sacred. I need to do better than this. Lying to you isn't acceptable, and you deserve better from me. I'll find a way to be better... I swear it!*

George lowered to her belly and kissed it. "How's my little guy doing in there? What do you say we go and have a picnic?"

"What a lovely idea," Athena responded with a giggle.

Two more Peaks of Bailem have passed and Late Bailem has come and gone.

Kiayasis assisted Shalee as she slid from the top of Joss's saddle. The Krape Lord had lowered its massive form, giving the sorceress some much needed assistance as she descended to the grass below. Kiayasis' strong hands embraced her waist as he set her down gently.

The past four days had proven to be enjoyable. Shalee had nearly forgotten about her problems with her king on Grayham. Thoughts of Sam had been put to the back of her mind. Kiayasis's company had come at a moment of need and had proven to be a wonderful diversion, providing her mind with a much-needed distraction.

Shalee was feeling beautiful again. Her long blonde hair had been pinned up behind her head and she had used her magic to transform one of the dresses in her bag into a perfectly fitted pair of pants. The idea of using the dress's material to create such an item had seemed unfashionable, but after putting on the finished result, she had been pleasantly surprised at the new look. She could now straddle the Krape Lord's saddle without fear of being exposed.

Since this morning they had been following the western banks of Lake Iple. Joss had been an effective means of transportation and now, Kiayasis was emptying the Krape Lord's large pouch. After he pulled the heavy leather saddle from Joss's back, the mighty beast spread his wings and took off.

"Where's he going?" Shalee asked with her eyes fixed on Joss's graceful movements. "That's incredible... when he flies, he looks like a dragon."

Kiayasis began to polish his armor, systematically clearing away the hair from inside the Krape Lord's pouch as he responded. "He needs to feed, but he'll be back by morning."

"What does he eat?" she asked as she watched Joss fly across the smooth waters of the lake. It was a peaceful evening and the sun reflected off its surface, casting a magical feel as the warmth of the setting sun found her face. She took a long deep breath as she listened to Kiayasis's response.

"I'm sure he'll find a large animal of some kind, or maybe even a corgan from a farmer's field."

"So he eats meat. I would never guess that after being with him over the last few days. Joss seems so gentle and sweet, now I've gotten to know him. I guess I just assumed he ate something else, since you treat him like a pet."

Kiayasis chuckled. "No, Joss is a killer, alright. It's in his nature, but don't worry, he's been trained not to attack unless given the order. He has left one other night while you slept to go and eat. You just didn't see him go."

"How do the farmers feel about him eating their... their... what did you call them, again?"

"Corgans...they're called corgans, and the people of this world slaughter them for meat. The farmers don't say much of anything, since the law allows the Krape Lords to feed whenever they want. They are compensated by my father, but I imagine it's not as much as they would make when taken to Merchant Island."

Shalee took note of Kiayasis's long dark hair as he continued to polish his armor. He was gorgeous. She continued to be thankful that, at least in this man's eyes anyway, she wasn't a failure. He knew nothing of her inability to carry her pregnancy to term. She could be herself and it seemed as if he was enjoying her company.

"Is there someone special in your life?" she said after studying him more.

"What? Women shouldn't ask such questions of a man!"

"Oh, I'm sorry... I meant no offense. I was only trying to get to know you better."

"Well, I suppose since you're a queen, I should answer your questions."

Shalee felt stupid and didn't know how to react. "Please, if it's improper to speak about this, don't tell me anything."

"It was an aggressive question and completely against the custom of the Elven people. This is the type of question a man should initiate, and then, it should be done in a more subtle manner, and only if the male is interested. But I shall answer your question; I would like you to know about me. There is no one special in my life, no one at all. I have dedicated my life to attaining my position of service within my father's army. I have only just recently acquired the goals I set for myself 25 seasons ago. I've longed to be with a woman, but until now, I haven't had the moments to do so. I suppose I'm ready for something to happen if the day comes that I should meet the right one. What about you? I assume your king is a good man?"

Shalee's mood changed. She began to withdraw within herself, but Kiayasis reacted and moved to sit beside her. He took her hands and placed them between his.

"I didn't mean to upset you. Clearly there's something wrong. I'll listen if you share with me."

The queen looked at his hands. They were strong, yet they held her perfectly sculpted hands gently between his. She decided to confide in him.

"The king blames me for the loss of our child. He looks at me like I'm diseased. It wasn't my fault. I had no idea my magic would hurt the baby. I don't think I can ever go back to him. I cannot live with someone who thinks I'm a failure. He hates me now!"

"Your king said all of this?"

"No, but he doesn't have to. He actually denies it, but I can see it in his eyes. It's in his every expression, and I can hear it in his voice. He hates me now. I would even go so far as to say he loathes me."

Kiayasis stood and pulled her next to him. His voice was soft and his eyes carried a tenderness Shalee longed for. "I cannot imagine a woman with your beauty being a failure. Your grace alone should bring joy to the heart of your king. *Tula sinome, lle naa vanima, cormamin lindua ele lle.*"

"That sounded wonderful. What did you say?"

Kiayasis made sure he held Shalee's gaze as he responded. "I said... come here. You're beautiful and my heart would sing to be with a woman like you. Well... that's a rough translation any-way."

Shalee melted and allowed Kiayasis to pull her within his arms. He held her close as she began to cry. He did not let her go until the last tear fell.

When morning arrived, Joss landed and Kiayasis once again loaded the Krape Lord's pouch.

"Shall we get going? It will take us a little more than four Peaks of Bailem to get to the Village of Bestep. There's something I must do there before we head north to the Swamplands."

Shalee smiled as Kiayasis lifted her onto the Krape Lord's sad-dle. "Good morning, Joss," she said as she settled down onto the heavily padded leather surface. "I hope you enjoyed your meal."

Joss grunted and responded by releasing a massive fart that vi-brated the saddle. The smell nearly caused her to throw up. Gag-ging, she pinched her nose and yelled, "For heaven's sake, Joss, and to think I thought you were growing on me."

Kiayasis could only laugh as he climbed up and took hold of the beast's reins. He commanded the Krape Lord into a powerful run across the pebbles of the lake's shoreline, creating a wake of stones as his massive, clawed feet struck the ground

The Dungeon of the Dark Order

It is now the Peak of Bailem, but despite the day being pleasant outside, the dungeon of the Dark Order remained cold, damp, and miserable. Four Paladins of Light have been hung by their arms and wait in agony for the leader of the Dark Paladin Army to arrive. They have been beaten, their flesh torn apart from being whipped, each receiving over twenty lashes. Once the information had been spread that there were spies hidden within the Dark Order's ranks, Boyafed's commanders hadn't taken long to single out Lord Dowd's men and they had been left hanging since just before Early Bailem.

When the leader of the Dark Order finally made his decent down the dungeon steps, he commanded his men to leave. He now stood in front of his bloodied enemies. They were weak and barely conscious. Boyafed moved to the far side of the cell and proceeded to revive each one with a cold bucket of water. Once they were fully aware of his presence, he spoke.

"All I wish to know is why you've come." Seeing there would be no answer, Boyafed decided to start with the basics. "We are all military men here... there's no harm in sharing our names with one another. I am Boyafed, the leader of the Order. Who among you is your superior?"

Spitting blood to the stones of the cold floor, a fit elf with short blonde hair spoke out. Blood dripped from the end of his toes as he struggled to gather the air he needed to do so. "I am their superior. My name is Tolas... there's nothing we will say to answer any of your questions. You know we've been sworn to secrecy and have been ordered to surrender our lives if need be. We're prepared to die for our gods and we're equally as prepared to die for Lord Dowd."

Boyafed admired Tolas's strength. He knew the elf would indeed give his life to serve not only his gods, but his lord as well. He could only hope the others were not as strong. He moved to stand in front of another of his enemies.

"Tolas is strong... a fine leader, to be sure. What's your name, son?"

"I'm not your son," he responded, lifting himself up to capture his breath, his strong, muscled frame, rippling as he did so. "My name is Kollis and I'll tell you nothing!"

The Dark Order leader pulled his bone-handled dagger from its sheath. He put the point of the blade against the elf's chest. He could see the fear in the elf's brown eyes as he methodically began to carve the symbol of the Order into his skin. The white paladin screamed as the rest of Tolas's men shouted for Boyafed to stop as they watched Kollis' blood flow down his muscular abdomen. But Tolas, on the other hand, remained silent.

"If you won't give me the answers I'm seeking, then it appears I have no choice but to send each of you home with a reminder or your moments spent with me. I'm sure your army will be happy to welcome each of you home with the symbol of Hosseff carved into your chests."

The man hanging at the far end of the lined group, a man much weaker and thinner than the rest, spoke out. His red hair and freckled nose stood out like a sore thumb. Boyafed could practically smell the fear as he began to spill their secrets.

"We were sent to see if you had plans to attack the White Chancellor's city. Please... I beg you; I don't wish to be scarred with your god's symbol. I don't wish to dishonor the one I serve."

Tolas shouted. "Grolan, be quiet. You dishonor yourself, you dishonor Lord Dowd, and you dishonor our gods by speaking out. Say nothing further or I'll kill you myself."

Boyafed moved to stand in front of Grolan. "I'll let you live! I would not want your god's symbol carved into my skin, either. What else have you been sent here for?"

Tolas shouted, commanding Grolan's silence, but Grolan didn't listen, his voice quaking as he spoke. "Nothing... we have been sent for no other reason than what I've given you... I swear! We were only sent to see if there were plans to attack the White Chancellor's city."

"That's it... I believe you, Grolan, but this is a job for one man, not four."

Again Tolas shouted and warned Grolan to say nothing further, but his light blue eyes gave away his terror. He had pissed himself, the yellow liquid running down his inner thigh as he trembled. This was the first situation he had faced any real danger. Prior to this day, he had only stood up to his counterparts in training exercises. He was weak and he now knew it, this realization breaking his spirit as he began to cry.

"I swear to this... I swear it to the gods I serve. There's no other reason we're here."

Tolas lowered his head and shook it. He knew Boyafed would not allow them to leave and if he did, they would not leave without being punished first.

Boyafed lifted Grolan's chin. His dark eyes burned right through the frightened paladin's soul. "You disgust me. There's no honor in betraying your leader. Lord Dowd would kill you himself if he were here. But... no worries, I'll send you home with a reminder of your failure. I'm sure Dowd will deal with you properly. Why he would send someone so weak is beyond my imagination. If I were Tolas, you wouldn't leave this dungeon alive."

Boyafed began to carve the Order's symbol into his chest. Grolan screamed in agony. Boyafed repeated the process on each one of them until he came to Tolas. Slowly he wiped the blood from his dagger and only after it had been sheathed, Boyafed removed Tolas's bonds and lowered him to the floor.

"Of all your men, you're the only one worth respecting. You held strong to your oath and didn't waver. There isn't fear in your eyes. You spoke with courage. I respect this. You can take your men and leave. Tell Lord Dowd I said to fight one another would accomplish nothing. It's a senseless loss of life, and further, tell him to stay on his side of the Ebarna Strait. I better not find any more of his men within my ranks. If I do, they won't be as fortunate to arrive home in one piece."

Boyafed thought a moment. He unsheathed his dagger and handed it to Tolas. "I can only assume you have business that needs attending to. Leave the blade with the guards on your way out."

"Thank you, I'll deliver your message," Tolas responded. He lowered his eyes in respect as Boyafed exited the cell. All that could be heard was Grolan's screams as the leader of the Dark Order ascended the dungeon stairs. "Ah, the beautiful sound of death!"

Chapter 11

Three Little Words
Ancients Sovereign The Hall of Judgment

The gods gathered and those able to sit around the large marble table within Gabriel's Hall of Judgment had taken a seat.

"I've called you here to announce the location of the third piece of the Crystal Moon. Each team has made their choice as to who will be seeking this piece. Mieonus, your team has chosen George, and Mosley's team, as we all know, has chosen Shalee. The crystal is hidden within these three words."

Lasidious tossed two pieces of parchment onto the table.

"Another riddle," Mieonus said, standing from her chair. She leaned over the table to take a look. "This is ridiculous. Your last riddle was practically impossible to understand. This isn't a riddle. It's only three words."

Lasidious took a deep breath. "There are only two possible answers. Both are full of danger. The rules are simple. You will give the riddle to your team's choice. Both Shalee and George will be required to figure out where they need to go in order to find the third piece of the Crystal Moon. You're not to offer them any help. If there is anything said that will assist them in any way, I will destroy the Crystal Moon and allow the worlds to be destroyed. It is up to them to determine which way they go."

Mosley jumped onto the table and read the words aloud.

A Soul Swallowed

The wolf-god jumped from the table. "Interesting, but it seems simple enough. I'm sure Shalee will enjoy the challenge." He vanished.

"Well, this is simply aggravating," Mieonus shouted. "How do you expect anyone to understand what this means? How do you expect them to find something so small with a clue like this?"

Keylom's hooves clapped against the marble floor of the hall as he moved to a position to see the words for himself. The centaur looked at Lasidious. "As always, your wit has provided some entertainment."

"Oh, just shut up, will ya?" Mieonus shouted. "He's toying with us again."

Lasidious took Celestria's hand, ignoring Mieonus's comment. "Good luck," he said as they both vanished.

Mieonus rolled her eyes. "Can you believe this? Talk about a needle in a haystack."

Hosseff stood and pulled his hood overtop his shadowy head. "Just give the parchment to George, Mieonus, and stop complaining. I'm sure the others of our team feel the same way. I've got better things to do than listen to your constant nagging." Hosseff vanished and the others followed suit.

All that was left with Mieonus was the Book of Immortality.

"Gabriel, I think—"

"I don't care, Mieonus... I don't care." The Book disappeared.

"I hate it when they all do that," she said, stomping the lifted heeled shoe of her right foot on the floor before vanishing herself.

George and Athena's Home

Mieonus appeared inside George and Athena's home. "George, we need to talk."

Athena was startled by her appearance. She quickly moved behind George as he turned to face the goddess.

"Ever hear of knocking?" George snapped. "You should try it sometime!"

"Careful how you speak to me, George. I'm in no mood to deal with your sarcasm anymore."

"My sarcasm... who gives a garesh what you're in the mood for? I will act how I wish in my own home. Maybe you should leave, or better yet, you could go and get your friends to come and hunt me down. I have a little surprise for them, so bring it on!"

Mieonus could not believe his confidence was so unshaken. She could have sworn she had left him with a sense of desperation when last they spoke. She was about to confront the mage when Athena spoke out.

"George, your manners... where are they?" Athena said as she tugged at his new, royal purple-colored robe. "I'm sorry for my husband's tone. I'm sure if you had knocked, this conversation would—"

Mieonus waved her hand and Athena's voice was silenced. "I'm in no mood to listen to you, either. I should destroy you both for your husband's arrogance!"

"Ha, ha, ha, as if you could," George said. "I now know something you don't. Spare me your babbling threats and get to the point of why you've come. I assume you have knowledge of the crystal's whereabouts and wish me to go after it. I have decided to go, but it has nothing to do with what you want. I do hope you decide to send your goons after me. I will use it to my advantage and ensure I take their power from them. You have no idea how much power I can command now. How about you give me the information and take a hike?"

Mieonus wanted desperately to destroy him for how he spoke, but instead, she calmly responded. "It appears Lasidious has taught you something more than I'm aware of. No matter, I'll just have to find a way to destroy *you* later." She threw the parchment at him. "I have come to give you this note. You should use this to help you find the crystal. I do hope the journey kills you!"

Athena was gripping her husband's arm tightly. She knew he could feel her distress, but she also knew his personality wasn't about to back down now. She was frightened by the fact that Mieonus's power was forcing her to keep silent. Tears began to run down her cheeks as she waited for George's response.

After a moment he looked up and smiled as he found the goddess's eyes. "This seems to fit what I've just learned. Master Id is a better teacher than I thought. He said the Eye of Magic can swallow a man's soul if he isn't ready to take on the responsibility of handling great power. It seems your note couldn't have come at a better moment. I will go through the trials and speak with the Source. With a little luck, I'll be able to look into the Eye and pass its test. Maybe the crystal's location will be revealed if I do?"

Mieonus was stunned. "You got all that out of three little words? How convenient it is that you find yourself in the position to be Brayson's new Mystic-Learner. It appears we have an advantage. I can only assume your desire for power will strengthen your desire to go after the crystal for me?"

George could see the fear in Athena's wet eyes. He had to let Mieonus know he would go for the crystal and find a way to make his wife feel better at the same moment.

"I will go after your crystal, but I will do it only after you give me the Promise of Sovereign that you will leave anyone I love alone. You must promise me you won't send anyone to hurt them, or myself, for that matter. You and I need to call a truce and start this relationship over again. I'll give you the respect you deserve only after you've given me this promise."

"Lasidious has taught you well and I will agree to your terms, but only on one condition!" Mieonus put her hand on George's shoulder and pushed him aside. She looked Athena in the eye. "You will bow on one knee before me when I show up. If you do this. I will make the promise. Do we have a deal?"

George wanted to bash her on the head, but instead he said, "We have a deal!"

Mieonus smiled as she wiped the tears from Athena's cheeks. "You should be proud to have a husband who will bow to a god he hates just to protect his wife and his family from a horrible death. It seems I won't have to come back here to watch your family die after all. Pity though, because I would've enjoyed it!"

Again the deity wiped another tear from Athena's face. "I do hope your baby is every bit as beautiful as you are, my dear. I will take my leave." She vanished.

Once gone, Athena's voice returned. She didn't hesitate as she began to poke George on the chest. "You and I need to talk right now! You're coming with me and you're in more trouble than I can even express right now! How dare you bring danger into this home!"

"Babe—"

"Don't you even think about saying babe to me right now… you don't say a word unless spoken to, you got it, Mr. Nailer?"

"Yes ma'am," he said softly, not wanting to anger her further. He thought to himself… *Damn, this is going to suck… she's pretty mad!*

As they walked out of the kitchen, a dark bird which looked much like a raven was sitting on the window sill. It took flight, only flapping its wings for a few strokes before disappearing.

Marcus Id's Dark Tower-Palace

Marcus's face was full of concern. He needed to speak with the Ultorian king and would have teleported directly into the king's throne room, but the magic necessary to protect him within the confines of the Ultorian's microscopic coral castle required more power than he currently could muster without the assistance of his missing Goswig.

He had been pacing within the confines of his bedroom chambers for the last few days, waiting impatiently for the Ultorian king to return his request for a meeting. The smoke from his pipe created a haze above his head. Just when he thought he was about to go insane, a crystal sphere, sitting on the heavy stone table at the center of the room, lit up with the Ultorian king's face inside. Marcus snatched his pipe from his mouth and moved to take a seat.

The Ultorian king spoke first. "How may I be of assistance, Chancellor?"

Marcus collected his thoughts. "I trust everything is going well, Farun?"

"Everything is fine, thank you. Why have you requested this meeting?"

"Have you had any visitors I would have interest in? I'm sure you know of whom I speak."

"As we discussed many seasons ago, I would send any such visitor back to you if he made his presence known to me or any others of my kind. I would imagine you're missing Goswig is smart enough to know you would seek him here. There must be a reason why he hasn't come. I wish I could help you, but I cannot."

Marcus leaned toward the crystal's image of Farun Ultor. "If you're protecting him, I'll destroy your tiny kingdom. Are you sure you haven't seen Gage? Think hard before you answer."

"I have not seen your Goswig! Your threats are unnecessary. Goodbye, Chancellor!"

The crystal's vision faded.

"Damn!" Marcus shouted as he grabbed the sphere and threw it against the wall beyond the table. The ball exploded into hundreds of small pieces, landing scattered about the room. He cried out, "Lord Hosseff... please .. hear your loyal servant. I just need one good piece of news."

Moments later his prayer was answered.

"Caw... Caw," the same dark bird which had been sitting in George's window sill called out as it flew through the open window and landed on the table.

Marcus took a seat. "Well, well, and what news do you bring?" He leaned forward and looked into the bird's eyes. It wasn't long before a smile spread across his face. "This is indeed good news."

The Home of Mosley,
The Hidden God World of Ancients Sovereign

Mosley called for Alistar, God of the Harvest, to his home on top of Catalyst Mountain. Bassorine, the late God of War, had left this home behind after his destruction and Mosley found it to be to his liking. It was a perfect home for a wolf. Mosley looked down into the valleys below from the porch of his cabin as he waited for Alistar to arrive. He took a deep breath. The fresh air smelled wonderful to his canine senses. The wild flowers were in bloom all across the hillsides.

It wasn't long before Alistar appeared in front of him. "Have you given Lasidious's note to Shalee?"

"I haven't... it's not necessary. She already knows where the crystal is, and the three words on this parchment won't give her the exact location. I plan to keep clear and allow her to continue on her journey to Grogger's Swamp. I'm sure the answer will present itself once she arrives. Beyond that, there's nothing else we can do."

"Lasidious may not like your decision."

"Lasidious trusts my judgment. He respects me and won't have a problem with it. I have called you here for other reasons. Something else is going on here... something larger than this game we are playing with the Crystal Moon. I want to look deeper than what we see on the surface."

"What are we looking for?"

"I don't know. What I do know is that Lasidious is up to something big. I would look into this by myself, but Lasidious is keeping an eye on me, I'm sure of it, and I'm going to need your help."

"Do you have any suggestions as to where I should start?"

"Start with George's family—maybe you can see something I've missed. It is hard for me to investigate when I'm worried I will be discovered. I think you could do it secretly without Lasidious's knowledge."

"I will find you once I know more," Alistar said as he vanished.

The Next Day, Early Bailem

Lord Dowd entered Gregory Id's throne room. His face carried a harsh look of agitation as he stopped in front of the White Chancellor's glass throne. Hepplesif was sitting on the arm of the royal chair next to Gregory as Dowd addressed him.

"Chancellor, my men have returned from the City of Marcus. Boyafed has no plan to attack. In fact, Tolas informed me he has a genuine desire to avoid war. He informed Tolas it would be a senseless loss of life to fight one another. Apparently he seemed to be surprised we would think he wanted war."

"Then it sounds as if Marcus was making empty threats. This is good news. I'll keep the Kedgles around for a while longer until I can be sure this threat is behind us. Thank you, Lord Dowd."

"You're welcome, but the news isn't all good. One of my men perished because of the mission. He has dishonored himself and the gods. I feel that, despite this man's weakness, we should see to it his family is well taken care of. Will you please see to this for me?"

Gregory nodded. "I will visit the family myself. Leave the information I need with Mykklyn and I'll take the family enough coin to make a smooth adjustment within their home. If need be, I will offer the wife a job within my palace to see they stay fed."

"As always, Chancellor, you lead by example!" Dowd turned and left the room.

The Luvelles Gazette

When you want an update about your favorite characters

Shalee and Kiayasis are approaching the Village of Bestep. They plan to stay at the local inn. Kiayasis has business he must attend to before continuing their journey to Grogger's Swamp.

George, Payne, and Kepler are making their way to the shrine located on the southern end of the Head Master's island. The shrine houses the key to the Source's temple located at the center of the Void Maze.

Marcus has been stalking George's group since their departure from home the night before. He has been watching the group from the shadows of the forest on Brayson's Island.

Athena, Mary, and Susanne have decided to take baby Garrin shopping. Brayson has given Mary a scroll in which to teleport the girls to the City of Inspiration. All three of the women are excited to see Gregory Id's city of glass.

Boyafed is meeting with two of his finest dark paladin warriors.

Gregory Id has met with Hepplesif, the Kedgle commander. They have determined Marcus's threats were empty, but still commanded enough concern to leave a small group of Kedgles behind in order to guard Gregory's palace. Only twenty Kedgles will stay behind while the rest of these creatures of illusion return home to Brayson's island to be with their families.

The goddess Mieonus plans to find Mosley. She has questions to ask the wolf-god about Shalee's travels on Luvelles.

Thank you for reading the Luvelles Gazette

Chapter 12

The Easy Way or The Hard Way

World of Grayham,
The City of Brandor, The King's Royal Garden

Michael, how could the queen just leave like this? How on Grayham could she possibly allow our baby's death to come between us?"

"Sire, may I speak freely?"

"Of course you can. We're alone and I need a friend right now. Forget about being a general, and talk with me."

"As you wish… I think the queen is acting like any other woman would act if she were thrown into an unfamiliar world and asked to do the impossible."

"Okay… I'm listening."

"Try and see things from the queen's point of view. Take a look at everything that's happened since your arrival from your Earth. Both of you lost your families, and you were asked by the gods to kill and fight your way into positions of power within a world you had no idea existed until you woke up in the Temple of the Gods. The queen's best friend, Helga, was taken from her, a loss I heard the queen myself describe as something she'd never completely heal from. She loved Helga as if she were her own mother and I'm sure you must've felt something similar when BJ took his own life."

Sam sighed. "I did feel terrible about his death and I remember it was hard on both of us, heck… I bet it was hard on you too, for that matter!"

Michael sat down on one of the many benches within the garden. The flowers were still in bloom, a fact that under normal circumstances would not be the case. They should have wilted by now and lay dormant for the winter, but these were not normal circumstances. The theft of the Crystal Moon had many side effects, taking away each world's ability to properly rotate through the seasons. All of Southern Grayham had been stuck in this extended season since the Crystal Moon's disappearance.

Michael responded, "You know... the queen will come back when she's ready. She's lost her way and soon, she'll remember how much you love her. The loss of your baby must've been all it took to take the last ounce of strength she had remaining within her. She has never been quite right after Helga's death, and now the added loss of your child must be devastating."

Sam moved to take a seat next to Michael. "I know you're right, but I'll be damned if I have any idea about what to do. This isn't just some kind of problem my intelligence can fix. I feel out of my element on this one. What would you do if you were me?"

Michael put his arm around his king. "If it were me, I would take another approach. If you don't mind, I will give you a suggestion, but it will require you to put a tremendous amount of faith in me."

Sam turned and looked Michael dead in the eye. "I trust you and I'm listening. Let me hear your ideas!"

The Glass City of Inspiration

Mary, Athena, Susanne, and baby Garrin appeared next to the crystal moat leading away from Gregory's glorified city of glass. They had used a Scroll of Teleportation, but had done so only after spending the proper amount of moments listening to Brayson's instructions on how to properly use it.

The girls had come to the City of Inspiration with a few goals in mind. The first: to spend the day shopping, followed by sightseeing and learning as much as they could about the city's creation.

As they walked through an enormous pair of gates, they marveled at how this city made of glass had been magically altered. The gates appeared as if they were actual pieces of wood, only to have its secret revealed as they shimmered beneath the sun's light when standing at just the right angle. No matter where they looked, it was impossible to avoid the constant need to gasp at the next beautiful wonder. Cobblestone streets, merchants' carts, ornate lamp posts, and fountains that flowed outside of nearly every storefront—all glass, holding within them many colors they had never seen before. Large prisms had been placed strategically throughout the city, causing a rainbow to be cast against the side of Gregory's tower, only to slowly pass over its surface as the sun moved across the sky.

The vegetation had been given access to the earth below in order to retrieve the nutrients necessary to survive. Massive coranran trees lined the streets, their heavily leaved branches cast shadows to temper the sun's reflected light which came from many of the city's taller structures.

"Can you believe this place?" Mary said, finally managing to utter a few words. "I would never have been able to imagine such a place could exist."

Athena took Mary by the arm and pulled her mother close. "I have to admit... I really like your new man. This is going to be the best day of shopping. How thoughtful it was of him to send us here."

"Really," Susanne cut in, her voice also full of excitement. "I need to find me a magic man. It's not fair. You two can't have all the fun, ya know. Let's find me a handsome one while we're here. After all... this is a city full of magic. How hard could it be?"

Both Mary and Athena laughed. Mary responded. "We'll just have to add that to our shopping list."

After a few more pleasant giggles, the women came across a beautiful elven woman sitting on a fountain. This fountain was much larger than the others they had seen. The glass had been altered and held a canary yellow hue. The sign above the door was written in the language of the elves.

Mary reached into her small handbag and produced a book. "Brayson said we could use this to translate anything we don't understand. I guess this sign qualifies."

"Wow... he thinks of everything." Susanne look over Mary's shoulder, adjusting baby Garrin's weight to rest on her opposite hip. "So what's the translation?"

"Give me a moment, will ya! I'm working on it. I think that... if I'm reading this right... it says... 'The Future's Vision'."

Athena tugged at Mary's dress. "That sounds interesting. Maybe we should check it out."

The store was full of crystals, potions, and many jars of odd-looking creatures. At the center of the room sat a circular table which rested low to the floor, a single symbol engraved at its center and covering much of its surface.

"What's it mean? Look it up, Mother," Susanne said, lowering Garrin into the padded wagon George had created after the night he brought the baby to Kebble's inn.

Athena took note of Garrin's heavy eyes. She rubbed his head for a moment before moving to stand next to Mary.

"Haven't you figured it out yet? What does it say?"

A voice sounded from the store's entrance with an answer. It was the same woman who had been sitting on the fountain's edge. "It means future."

As she entered, the woman's steps were filled with grace. She wore a soft blue dress that flowed well against her figure and hung low enough to cover her feet. Her brown hair was covered with a long white cloth which hid much of her back and was held in place with an elegant woven rope, its color matching her dress. Silver earrings matched her thick bracelets, the ensemble accenting a thin chain around her neck. The chain carried the same symbol as the table's center.

"Hello, my name is Mary, and these are my daughters, Athena and Susanne. The little guy here is Garrin, my grandson."

"Bryanna is my name. Fate has brought you to me. You have many questions... questions of love... questions about your future. I can see all and I can see you. I can speak to you of things unknown. Do you wish to have revealed that which is unknown?"

Glances were exchanged, shoulders shrugged, and a desire to know more filled the ladies' eyes. "Of course," Mary responded, "we would like to know more. How much will it cost?"

"Coin matters not. Fate has demanded this of me and I shall speak of your destinies without compensation."

Bryanna lowered to her knees, leaned toward the table, and

waved a hand over the symbol. A mist appeared and slowly the face of Brayson filled the haze as it lifted towards the ceiling.

Bryanna and Head Master Brayson

Illustration by Kathleen Stone

Mary had to catch her breath. She could not believe her eyes and moved to sit next to the table.

"Are you okay, Mother?" Athena said, moving to pull Mary close.

"What kind of trickery is this?" Susanne whispered from Mary's other side.

The green hue of Bryanna's eyes had vanished and they now looked milky white. Her voice trembled as she spoke. "Love, a true love... a union of between elf and human... a union blessed and also doomed. Beware the danger around you."

Brayson's image was replaced with George's face as Bryanna continued. "A heart cries for a soul's release. She is trapped, waiting to be reborn. Evil surrounds this family."

Bryanna began to shake. "Evil guides the head of this family... and is testing a father's love." She began to shout, waking Garrin, who started to cry. "The worlds, death, destruction, sorrow... Aahhhhhhhhhh... ALL IS LOST!"

Mary'd had enough. She grabbed Garrin and ran from the store. Athena and Susanne were not far behind. They did not stop until they were all winded.

Mary tried to console the baby. He was screaming something awful. Susanne and Athena watched, trying to catch their breath, as Mary rocked him in her arms. The motion seemed to help. Eventually Garrin settled down and fell back asleep.

Mary lowered him into his padded wagon. "I hate to speak as George does, but what the hell was that?"

"Mother," Athena said, covering her mouth. "You're really angry!"

"I am! What did she mean when she said evil surrounds our family? She said it guides the family's head. Why was George's face shown when she began to shake? Did she mean evil controls him? She said Brayson and I were a union. Does this mean he is to be my husband and if he is, why is our union doomed? What is all this death and sorrow she is speaking of? Do you think all this is going to happen?"

Before the girls could answer, Mary pulled an emerald from her handbag. "Brayson said I could use this to summon one of Gregory's servants. They will take us to see him. Let's hope he can give us some answers. I have never been so scared in my entire life."

Susanne cut in, "Why don't we just go home and talk with Brayson right now? He could tell us everything we want to know. We can always come back later."

"Because we can't use the scroll to teleport home until after Late Bailem. That's when Brayson said it would be safe again."

Mary rubbed the gem. It was only a matter of moments before a glimmering crystal carriage appeared as if out of nowhere. A tiny little Halfling, no larger than a few feet tall, jumped from his seat and climbed up the side to open the door. *"Amin naa lle nai,"* was all he said.

Athena looked at them. "What did he say?"

Mary moved to the carriage. "I don't know, but get in. We need to find Gregory."

The Hidden God World of Ancients Sovereign,
Mosley's Cabin

Mieonus appeared on the front porch of Mosley's cabin. The wolf-god was lying in the sun and didn't bother to move to acknowledge her presence. With his snout tucked beneath his front legs, Mosley spoke in a somber voice. "What do you want, Mieonus?"

"Is that the way you greet your guests, Mosley? I only wish to have a simple conversation."

"Again... what do you want? A guest is someone I wish to have around. You wouldn't qualify as a wish of mine."

"Your words wound me, Mosley."

"Spare me the drama! What do you want?"

Mieonus shrugged. "I've noticed Shalee is traveling near the Village of Bestep. She is with one of the Dark Order's paladin warriors."

"And..."

"So... why is she with him? The third piece of the Crystal Moon is nowhere near that particular part of Luvelles. I would like to know where she's going."

"Ha... as if I would tell you."

"Must you be like this, Mosley? I would like to start over. Let's try to be friends."

"Friends, you say. Are you prepared to tell me where George is going?"

"I am. I think it would be more entertaining to know everything. I mean, what could it hurt? According to Lasidious's rules, we can't help either of them anyway, so why not share information with one another?"

"So prove to me you're sincere. I'm listening... where is George going, and what conclusion did he come to when he read the three words on Lasidious's note? Did they give him an idea of where he should go?"

"They did."

"Okay, so where's he headed?"

"I'm sincere and I do wish to start over. I also wish to become better acquainted so I will start by telling you this. George has determined that the answer is to go before the Source. He thinks the crystal will present itself once he has looked into the Eye of Magic. I think he's right... the words did speak of swallowing a soul, and the Eye does swallow souls."

Mosley finally lifted up his head. "Maybe he's right and maybe he's not, but we'll never know until it's all said and done, will we?"

"I feel pretty good about it. So now it's your turn. Where's Shalee going and why?"

Mosley stood and stretched his furry body before responding. "I said it seems like you were sincere about being my friend. I didn't say I wished to be yours. I suppose you'll just have to wait and see where Shalee is going."

Mosley vanished.

"Damn that wolf!" she shouted, stomping her foot.

The Village of Bestep,
Late Bailem

Kiayasis assisted Shalee once again as she slid from the Krape Lord's back. He took a moment to put his armor on and turned to face her.

Shalee took a cloth from her sack and moved to stand in front of him. She polished away the smudges that had been created while inside Joss's pouch. "You look handsome in black. The gold that has been used as an accent has been well-placed."

"Thank you," he responded with a wink. "I'll have to thank you properly later!"

"Are you flirting with me?"

"And what if I am?"

"If you're going to flirt," she pulled him close. "You best be willing to follow it up with a nice dinner."

"I shall do just that. Is dinner followed with a kiss?"

Shalee took his chin into the palm of her hand. She leaned in and whispered in his ear. "You're being awfully presumptuous, don't you think?"

Kiayasis blushed and took Shalee's hand. They began their walk into the village. An Order's servant had taken Joss and led him into the stables which had been prepared especially for the dark paladin's mounts. Most every city, town or village throughout the Kingdom of Hyperia had special stables which had been built large enough to hold these giant beasts. It didn't take long before the 4000-pound corgan tied up inside Joss's stall began to scream as the Krape Lord tore into his meal.

"Oh my," Shalee said, turning back to look. "That sounds absolutely terrible. He must have been extremely hungry."

"I told you Joss is a killer!" Kiayasis looked down the dirt road toward the village. "I have some business to attend to. I'll take you to the inn and meet you for dinner once I'm done. I'll make sure the meal is extra special."

"I hope so!" She winked flirtatiously.

Kiayasis had to catch his breath before responding. "Um... ahh... we'll need to leave in the morning. I think just after Early Bailem should give us the moments necessary to recover from a night of drink and fun. We have a long journey ahead of us before we arrive at Grogger's Swamp."

Bestep was a dark place, full of darker people. Many of the village's inhabitants were mercenaries, evil magic for hire. It was as if Bestep was a war zone. Hot tempers had all but destroyed many of the structures not far from the inn. One of the building's stone walls had been scorched and the outline of a body had been burned into it.

But Shalee would be in good hands and Kiayasis knew this as he headed for his destination. The owner of the inn, a man named Tygrus, was an ex-soldier of the Dark Order. He was well-known as a merciless killer and all those who came to Bestep avoided confrontation while in his establishment. He would ask Tygrus to watch over Shalee until he returned.

When Kiayasis arrived at his destination, he knocked on the rickety door of an old rundown shack which rested on thick stilts over the Id River. The door's wood was not solid and the fire inside could be seen through the cracks. Eventually a figure peeked out.

"No one's here... go away, I say," a hermit of a man shouted.

Kiayasis' eyes were cold as he responded. "Open in the name of the Order... answer or die!"

"Open in the name of the Order, he says. Answer or die, he says. What else will the mean man threaten, I say?"

The bottom of the door scraped across the wooden floor. A tiny midget with arms covered in sores and dirty matted hair scurried away from Kiayasis and sat next to the fire at the far side of the room.

"How do you live like this, Gorne? Not too smart to have a fire going in a structure in this condition."

"How do I live like this, he says? Better than me, he thinks he is, I think. What does the mean man want from Gorne, I say? He wants something, he does? The fire isn't real, I say. A stupid man stands before me, I think."

Kiayasis ignored his comment and stepped into the room. His foot passed right through the rotted wood.

"Hee, hee, ha, ha... heavy the mean man is, I say. Lose weight he should, I think. Fat, the Order has become, is the word I will spread!"

Kiayasis gathered his thoughts, still ignoring the irritating mannerisms of the hermit. "I have business we need to discuss, Gorne. I need you to sell me the Knife."

"Eewww, hee, hee, ha, ha... the Knife, he says. The Knife of Spirits he wants, I say. Why does the mean man think Gorne has the Knife, I want to know, I say?"

"I'm in no mood for games. Sell the knife to me so I can leave!"

"Why, I say?"

"The Order needs it. You shouldn't question my authority. I have the lawful right to take what I need as long as it's for Order business. You can sell it to me or I could just always take it, but either way, I'm going to leave here with it."

"Don't have the Knife, I say. Go away, you should, I think. Shut the door, I say. Leave Gorne alone, you should."

With his blessed sword of the Order drawn, Kiayasis responded, "Give me the Knife and do it quickly. I don't wish to kill you, but I will."

"Grrrrr... kill Gorne, he will. Hate the mean man, I do. Give you the Knife of Spirits, I will. To kill something magical you need to do, I think. Strong this magic must be, I say."

Gorne tossed the sheathed blade across the room. "Leave Gorne alone now, I say. Please go now, I beg. Given you what you want, I have. Hate you Gorne does, I say! Leave your coin on the floor, I beg!"

Kiayasis shook his head in disgust and pulled the door shut after dropping a pouch full of coins on the rotted wood. He headed for the inn. After cleaning up and making himself presentable, he knocked on Shalee's door. His long black hair fell across the muscled shoulders of his golden shirt. The blue of his eyes gleamed with anticipation as the door opened.

Shalee had used her magic to create a beautiful white gown. Her blonde hair was pinned up to expose a gold necklace that closed tightly around her neck. Earrings, also made of gold, held assorted gems of many colors.

Kiayasis spoke. "I have never seen anything so beautiful. Your shoes, they hold the back of your feet high off the floor. Your face has color on it. How is this possible? I can't seem to take my eyes off you."

Shalee grinned. "I will tell you after dinner."

Kiayasis face showed a spirited pleasure as he responded. "It will be a shame to take such a wonderful gown off such a beautiful body."

"What?" Shalee said, taking a step back. Her hands moved up and down in front of her body as if she were putting herself on display while continuing. "You're not going to see this dress fall from this body that easily! Maybe, if you're lucky, I might allow you to kiss me goodnight... MAYBE!"

"A kiss, you say! I have prepared quite the night. It is being set up as we speak."

"Ah, you've come prepared to spoil me." Not a single thought of Sam entered her mind as she took his arm and squeezed.

The Next Day,
Just Before the Peak of Bailem,
Brayson's Island

George, Payne and Kepler had arrived at the shrine located on the south side of the Head Master's island. The key to the Source's temple rested inside a chest sealed within the shrine.

"What kind of a place is this?" George said. "This is more like a crypt, not a shrine. Brayson definitely has a flare for the dramatic. Sticking this thing out here in the middle of a forest is kinda creepy."

George dropped his bag of supplies to the ground. He adjusted his purple robe to a more comfortable position. The robe was split, both in the front and the back just below his waist and a loose-fitting pair of pants covered his legs. With his pistol strapped under his right pant leg, loaded with his last bullet, and a short sword hanging from his left hip, George was ready for the trials that would begin as soon as they entered the shrine and retrieved the key to the Source's temple.

Payne flew overtop the structure. He planted his small, red fairy-demon butt down on top of it and lowered his wings to a rested position before looking down and shouting, "I'm hungry."

"Shut up," Kepler responded. "Be quiet while we think a bit."

"Geez, fine, kitty," Payne growled back.

Ignoring the fairy-demon, the large jaguar began to sniff around the shrine's base. After a few moments had passed, the cat lifted his head, questioning, "What are you waiting for, George? You have the words to Brayson's spell. Use it on the door and let's get going already."

The mage was about to respond, but a voice from behind within the forest spoke out. "Well, well, well... the day has finally come."

Kepler was the first to react. The demon-jaguar prepared to attack and lowered into a position which would allow him to spring into action. As for the rest of the group, George methodically turned to find the source of the voice while Payne stayed put, hoping this new person would have some food.

A gentleman with a thin frame dressed in all black and a golden shirt slowly walked toward them. His long brownish-black hair fell across his shoulders as he continued to speak.

"I have been waiting to meet you," Marcus Id said, his brown eyes cold. "We have business to discuss, George."

Kepler growled. "How does he know your name? Who is this guy?"

"His name is Marcus Id... Brayson's brother, better known as the Dark Chancellor."

"I'm flattered... it's good to know we'll be able to move past such useless introductions. They bore me anyway, don't you agree?

"HEY... you got food?" Payne shouted. "Payne hungry!"

Marcus ignored the fairy-demon and continued to hold George's gaze. "You have something I need."

George leaned against the shrine and thought a moment. Kepler waited for his response, but when one didn't come, he growled. "Well... aren't you going to say anything?"

"Yes, when I'm good and ready. I'm still sorting out how little I care about what this chump has to say. He's been watching us for a long while now."

Kepler was shocked. "What? When were you going to tell me?"

George was about to respond, but Marcus cleared his throat to command their attention. "It seems you don't understand exactly who I am and what I want."

Kepler kept his red glowing eyes fixed on George as he waited for his response. The mage casually pushed clear of the shrine and found Marcus's stare. "I'm pretty sure I know who you are. I also know what you want. I think you should go, because you're not going to get what you came for."

Marcus leaned forward, his voice filled with hate. "We can do this the easy way, and you'll all live, or we could do it the hard way, and you'll all die. So, what will it be?"

Kepler didn't wait to hear anymore. He lunged for Marcus. George had no chance to stop the demon-jaguar's attack and could only watch as Kepler's large paw cut through the air, aimed for the chancellor's head. Instead of connecting with its target, Kepler's massive body was thrown hard into the trees with just a simple wave of Marcus's hand. The demon-cat cried out as he fell limply toward the ground. Before he landed, fire shot from Marcus's finger and buried deep into Kepler's chest. Kepler tried to lift his head, but instead, his red eyes lost their glow and slowly closed as he fell into unconsciousness.

Payne teleported behind Marcus and dug his claws into the back of both the Chancellor's legs. He ripped downward, causing two severe gashes before he was also sent skyward into the trees. The fairy-demon fell hard, landing headfirst not far from the cat.

George rushed in and punched Marcus on the side of his head. The Dark Chancellor fell to the ground. George followed his fall and threw his weight on top of him, straddling Marcus with a leg on either side.

The wizard waved his hand, but nothing happened. George smiled and smashed his fist hard into the Chancellor's chest. Marcus managed to wave his hand again, but still nothing happened. George delivered another solid shot to his face and now, Marcus was stunned. He tried to defend himself, but George's punches were now coming in waves. Eventually a few of the blows found a solid target and sent Marcus into a temporary darkness as his eyes shut.

Leaving Marcus out cold, George stood and rushed to Kepler's side. He lifted the demon-cat's head and poured a drop of the light blue liquid Brayson had given him under the jaguar's tongue. He repeated the same process with Payne. After the healing liquid fell into the fairy-demon's mouth, he rushed back to gather Marcus's legs and arms to bind them.

After dragging the Dark Chancellor's lanky body to a tree, George secured him with a woven rope he had brought along in his bag. All he could do now was hope Kepler and Payne would wake up. He began pacing anxiously back and forth, waiting for the elixir's healing power to cure their ailments.

Marcus opened his eyes. Realizing he had been tied up, he spit blood from his mouth to the ground. "You should release me or I'll—"

"You'll what? You won't do anything but sit there and shut the hell up! Open your mouth again and I'll finish killing you." George held the elixir up in front of Marcus's face. "This better work... they better not die or you're a dead man! But I can't have you bleeding to death before I know what's going on. The cuts on your legs are bad, so open your mouth."

The Chancellor did as he was told. The drop of potion found its target and was swallowed without pause.

George moved to check on Payne. The little fairy-demon was beginning to move. George lifted his tiny red body from the ground, carried him over to Kepler's motionless figure, and set him down.

"I'll be right here, Payne. I need to check on Kepler... don't worry, little guy." George lifted the demon-cat's head and set it in his lap. "Kepler... come on, wake up. Come on, Kep... we've come too far. You can't die on me now."

George knew fire was the only thing that could kill the giant cat. Marcus's magic must've struck Kepler's heart. As George continued to encourage the jaguar, Payne finished gathering his senses and moved to sit next to the mage. It only took a moment for his tiny mind to understand the severity of Kepler's condition. With his claws outstretched, he carefully rubbed the demon-cat's neck.

"Kepler," he whispered, leaning in to lie against the giant cat's black coat, "Live... Payne like you. Don't want you dead. You

Payne's friend. You Payne's favorite kitty!"

Tears filled George's eyes. No matter what Payne said, Kepler continued to lie motionless on the forest floor. George reached into his pouch and administered another drop of the healing elixir.

"Come on, Kep... I need you!" he whispered. His mind continued to speak silently. *You're my best friend. I can't lose you, too. I've already lost too much. Fight this, Kepler, fight this!*

Payne sat silently and listened as George stared hopelessly at the closed eyes of the beast.

George shouted, "Get up ya big lug! Things just wouldn't be the same without you."

He tried frantically to search for the cat's pulse and found a shallow one on his neck. It was faint, but there nonetheless. He held his fingers over this spot and waited for the elixir to strengthen the frequency in which he felt the next pump. But this would not be the day for recoveries and eventually, Kepler's heart stopped.

"No, no, Kepler, no, no, no, you can do this! Fight it for hell's sake, fight it... fight it!" George fell forward across the giant cat's body. Unable to control his emotions, the mage wept uncontrollably.

The sun lowered behind the horizon before Marcus decided it was a good idea to finally break his silence. "I can help, George!"

The sound of the Dark Chancellor's voice angered the mage. He lowered Kepler's head gently to the ground and moved to stand in front of Marcus. With all his hate, he sent his magic flying. Lightning hit Marcus, but failed to cause anything other than minor discomfort.

George closed his eyes and concentrated. He channeled Payne's power to amplify his own. A firestorm filled the morning air. The trees all around Marcus turned to ash, but the intense heat only managed to give the Chancellor a slight tan.

George took a step back, exhausted. He had never tried to summon that much power before. "What... how..."

Marcus cut him off before he could finish. "Your magic isn't powerful enough to harm me."

The top of the tree behind the Chancellor had disintegrated. He was now only bound to a stump. His body had shielded it from damage. But yet the ropes around Marcus had failed to burn.

"Why didn't the rope burn?" George said, noticing it hadn't been damaged.

Marcus looked down and took note before responding. "It's because the rope is touching the skin by my hands. Everything I'm wearing was also protected. These are things a Mystic-Learner of your ability should already know."

"Who are you to tell me what I should know? I wouldn't talk anymore, if I were you!"

Marcus shook his head. The ash in his hair created a small cloud before settling on the ground. "I have to admit... your skills are progressing quite well. I have underestimated you. You're far more powerful than Brayson's last Mystic-Learner. I'm sure you wouldn't hesitate to finish me off if you could."

"I don't need magic to kill you. I could always beat you to death with my own two hands."

Marcus sighed. "You could, but you won't."

"You don't know me. Don't think I don't understand how to screw with someone's mind. You're not gonna get into my head. I'm the master when it comes to that. Let me demonstrate how to kill someone." George began to walk toward him and pulled his hand back into a striking position.

Marcus spoke quickly. "If you kill me, you won't be able to save Kepler."

The mage stopped his swing and thought a moment. "He's dead already. That's bad for you, I think."

"I can fix this!"

George hesitated and after lowering his hands, he responded, "What do you mean... you can fix this? He's already dead? There's no saving him now."

"You're wrong. I can bring him back to life. I serve the god, Hosseff. This means I command the Touch of Death, but it can only be used once a season."

"I'm listening. Tell me more about this so-called touch..."

"If I tell more, you'll have an advantage."

"Ha... you actually think you have cards to play! What a fool! You must think I'm stupid? Maybe, just maybe I know how to take your power from you. I will just cut your ass open and eat your damn heart. I'll take your power away from you and keep it for myself."

Marcus started to laugh. "I had no idea that my heart was located in my ass. I bet it would taste like garesh if this is indeed the case."

"Ohhhhh, so we have a wise guy here. You find this funny, do ya? Only a fool would laugh... or maybe there's something you know that I don't."

"The power you need isn't mine to command at will. I know you could kill me and take my powers. I have stolen more than one person's powers myself when I was younger. I'm surprised a human would have the knowledge of how to do this. Only the most ancient of elven families have found a way to pass this knowledge down to their ancestors. The gods took this information from the worlds many, many seasons ago. Somebody powerful must have shared this secret with you... someone worth my respect. I'm positive it wasn't Brayson. He wouldn't share this kind of information with a student of the arts."

Marcus took a deep breath and continued. "Unfortunately for you, the power you need wouldn't pass to you with my death. It just doesn't work that way! The one power you want to control the most would be lost with my last breath. Your large feline friend would remain cold and lifeless."

"I'm listening... explain!"

"You must be a servant of Hosseff, and not just any servant. You must be blessed by my lord himself before you can summon the power to raise the dead. The Touch of Death is only controlled by the chosen of the Order. With this single Touch, we can take life or give it."

George stood and looked hard into Marcus's eyes. "I think you're lying. I should just kill you!"

"You could, but what if you're wrong and I'm telling the truth? Could you live with yourself, knowing you had the chance to save your friend?"

Payne walked over and stood next to George. He had heard everything Marcus said. He tugged at the bottom of George's robe.

"Umm, let help kitty."

George lowered himself to eye-level with Marcus. "I knew you would come here. Your brother warned me about his last Mystic-Learner. He has known for many moments now that you were the one who killed him. I think Brayson said his name was Hettolyn. Your power won't hurt me either. I have been given something to protect me. This power is the same reason you have been unable to escape your bonds. It's why you have been unable to teleport home. If I set you free, what guarantee do I have you'll use your Touch of Death to save Kepler?"

Marcus adjusted within his bonds. The ropes were cutting into his wrists. "You have something I want. Since I can't take it from you, it appears I have no other option but to help you."

"Brayson told me you would try to force me to give you the words to his spell. He also said you would kill me if you had the chance. I'm not a stupid man. I understand your desire for power. I understand why you wish to speak with the Source and look into the Eye of Magic. Maybe you're going about this all wrong. Maybe you should take a different approach."

Marcus thought a moment. "I'm curious as to what you have in mind. How could I go about getting the power I want without getting the spell from you?"

George leaned in and whispered to keep Payne from hearing. Marcus's facial expressions slowly changed. After a long while of listening, the Dark Chancellor finally responded.

"Ahhhh... I like it. I like it all, but there is much we need to discuss if this is to work. All angles will need to be considered."

George took a seat. "I'm the man when it comes to covering the angles. Tell me everything you know."

"What?" Payne said, feeling a little left out. "Tell Payne... you gotta tell Payne! Are you talking food? Payne hungry!"

Chapter 13

𝕻𝖆𝖘𝖘𝖎𝖔𝖓𝖆𝖙𝖊 𝕸𝖔𝖒𝖊𝖓𝖙𝖘
Village of Solace

Brayson woke with Mary at his side and looked out across the ocean to watch the sun as it began to creep over the horizon. He had teleported them both to the Village of Solace for an evening of dining and quiet relaxation within the mountains of Crystal's Peaks. Dinner had gone well the night before. The relaxing massages by torchlight had set the mood. The feeling of romance led them into each other's arms.

Solace was a peaceful village, sitting high on top of the tallest peak which happened to overlook the Ocean of Agregan to the east. The village itself was meant to be an escape, a place of relaxation and meditation. Every visitor received the same view of the coastline far below the cliff's face, as every room was built into the side of it. The east walls were facing the ocean and had been left open with nothing more than a stone railing to keep those who stayed the night from falling. Thanks to the extended season, the weather had remained warm enough to bring Mary here for a quiet getaway, a getaway that had turned passionate.

Mary rolled over and put her chin on Brayson's chest. She reached up and played with his pointed ears and his goatee as she spoke. "Your ears are just so cute. I can't stop playing with them."

"I'm glad you approve."

Brayson rolled her over and brushed the hair from her face before kissing her soft lips. "I was hoping you would enjoy this place. Solace was only just recently created. The man responsible for this beautiful magical wonder nearly killed himself in the process, but the outcome was worth the risk, I would say. He has since recovered and maintains a residence here."

"I have never seen places as nice as the places I've seen on Luvelles. Even Kebble's inn makes the town I'm from seem less than desirable. I still have a home in Lethwitch. I can only assume my neighbor is keeping an eye on it for me while I'm gone. It's a rugged town... farmers mostly, and magic is, well, it's not like it is here. As far as I know, there are only two men, or rather were two men, who could use it.

"The eldest is named Morre. He's a good man, very kind, and I'll never forget the day I met him. He looked different than the rest of the townspeople. His gray beard and dirty-looking robes gave me the creeps. Ha, that's something I learned from George... the creeps. He speaks so strangely every now and then. Anyway, after I got to know Morre and found a way to look past his foul smell, he grew on me, I suppose. I heard he had a brother, but I never met him, nor did I ask Morre about his family. I should have been more sensitive but I'm not sure why I didn't ask—"

"Amar," Brayson said interrupting her. "His name is Amar. He studied here on Luvelles under my supervision many seasons ago. He's also a good man, but has a tendency to lean towards the darker side of magic. He's only limited because of his fear of failure. I wasn't able to allow him to meet with the Source. He just never matured enough."

Brayson rolled to his back and continued. "Amar is still a friend of mine. In fact, he's the reason why I allowed George to come to Luvelles in the first place, a decision I'm glad I made ever since seeing you step onto Merchant Island.

"George could be very powerful someday. It seems to me he's been blessed by the gods. I was speaking with Amar about this the other day. He visited me in my office. He suggested I make Payne George's Goswig. I wasn't fond of the idea, but it just may work after all. I imagine Amar has gone back to Grayham by now."

Mary sat up straight. Concern filled her eyes as she pulled up the covers to hide her breasts. "That's impossible! Amar couldn't have come here—you must be mistaken!"

Brayson sat up to match her position. "I wouldn't lie about something as trivial as Amar's visit. Why would you say this to me? Is there something I should know?"

"Amar is dead! If you're saying Morre's brother was named Amar... then he's not alive! There's no way he could've been in your office. Morre came into the inn one night while I was working. It was just prior to my family leaving Lethwitch to make the trip to the Merchant Island on Grayham. He was crying and drinking heavily. After a few drinks he told me his brother's body had been found in a barn of some sort just outside the City of Champions!"

Brayson stood and began to pace. His mind was racing and he didn't bother to cover himself. Mary could not help but notice his ass. It was right there, impossible to ignore. It was perfect and worth her admiration. She enjoyed the moment while she waited for him to respond. Brayson turned to face her.

"Are you sure about this, Mary? If he's dead, then…" Brayson could see she wasn't hearing him. Her attention was elsewhere. Quickly he pulled the covers around him. "Mary, this is serious. Pay attention to these eyes, not that one!"

Embarrassed, she looked up. "Go ahead. You have my full attention now!"

After a brief smile, the concern reappeared on Brayson's face. "If what you're saying is true, there's something going on. I need to speak with George."

"But how? You said he's already started the trials to meet with the Source. I thought you wouldn't be able to speak with him until after he's looked into the Eye of Magic. From the way it sounds, if the Eye swallows him, you may never have the chance to speak with him. I just hate the thought of that!"

"You're right, I can't speak with him, not now, anyway. You're also right that I may never be able to. I need to investigate Amar's death further. I swear to you he was just here."

"I believe you … maybe there's a good explanation for this."

"There must be. I'll search for the answer after I take you home."

"I don't want to leave just yet. I like it here."

Brayson thought a moment. "One more day won't change anything. We could stay until tomorrow."

Mary smiled, and then thought of her daughter. "What will I tell Athena if George doesn't return? I didn't have the heart to tell her he was going on such a dangerous journey. If he doesn't return, she'll be left to raise their baby on her own."

Brayson lowered to sit beside her. "I'll be there. If he doesn't make it, I will personally help raise the baby with the rest of the family. After all... you and I should make good grandparents."

Mary gasped. "Do you know what you're saying?"

"I do, and when this is all over, I intend to make you my wife."

Mary grabbed his arm. "But I will age and die long before you do."

"I have knowledge of something that will extend your life. I haven't waited my whole life to have you leave me so quickly. We will take the journey to Dragonia to accomplish this. The trip will be dangerous but worth the risk. It would allow us to be together forever."

Mary grabbed Brayson, pulling him close. "Are you immortal?"

"Ha... I wish. I either used the term forever too loosely or you could be taking it too literally. But either way, we would live another 2,000 seasons or so once you drink from the Well of Covain."

"Oh my, a magic well that gives longer life? Come here, you, I need to show you something. Tell me more of this magic while I make you smile."

"As you wish!" he said, and pulled the covers over the top of them.

"Oh my... you naughty boy... stop that... no, no, no... do it again. Stop that... Eeeek! Ahhhhhhh! Brayson Id, you better... Oh me, oh my... I dare you to do that again. I'm gonna have to start loving you! Oh wow... do that again! Oh my gosh, oh my gosh... oh my... Eeeek... I love you Brayson Id."

North of Bestep,
The Beach of the Volton Ocean

The morning on the western shoreline of Luvelles was brisk, yet still comfortable with the assistance of a small fire which Kiayasis had made the evening before and kept going throughout the night.

Shalee sat close to the fire, holding her hot cup of jasin. She was impressed at how the roots of a scrawny-looking bush Kiayasis had ripped from the ground made a wonderful replacement for the coffee she missed so much from back on Earth. She could think of nothing better than to be sitting here on this beautiful beach with the sand between her toes and looking out across the ocean. The only thing missing was the sun, which rested behind the mountains to the east, and the warmth of Kiayasis's arms around her. Unfortunately, there was nothing she could do about the sun, since it was coming up on the other side of Luvelles, but she could do something about Kiayasis's arms, since they were only a few feet away.

After cleaning up from their meal, Kiayasis lowered down next to Shalee. He leaned in and gave her a soft kiss on the cheek. Aside from holding one another near the fire the evening before, the cheek was as far as Shalee had let him go. "I trust everything was to your satisfaction?"

"I think I've died and gone to paradise."

"Paradise... I've never heard this word before. What does it mean?"

"It means, a place so beautiful you would be crazy to want to leave."

"And who says we have to leave?"

Shalee leaned into him, took another sip from her cup, and reached up to touch his face. "I've never snuggled on a beach before. Thank you. It was a beautiful memory I'll always cherish."

"As will I," Kiayasis said, then changed the subject. "But, if we are to get you to Grogger's Swamp, we best get going."

"Well, you're definitely a man. Only a man would take the perfect moment and talk about work. How about we take a day off and stay here? I'm tired of riding on Joss's saddle and my butt still hurts. Let's take a mental health day for our bottoms." She leaned in and kissed his pointed elf ears. "I'm sure we could find plenty to do."

Kiayasis stood, removed his clothes and headed for the water. He shouted as he ran, "I'll be waiting!"

"Are you out of your mind? It's too chilly to go in there, and I'm not going to allow you to see me naked. Nice try, though!" She continued to think, *However, I have no problem looking at that cute butt of yours.*

"Aw, come on, Shalee! I promise to warm you up afterwards. Come swim with me."

Shalee stood and shouted, "No, I told you already you're not getting my clothes off. We barely know each other!" She did, how-ever, kick off a cute pair of pink cozy-slippers she had created with her magic the night before, hiked up her dress, and waded out, knee-deep. *Oh... I'll play, big boy, she thought. I'll play! But not with my clothes off!*

Brayson's Island,
The Shrine

Kepler opened his red glowing eyes slowly. Marcus stepped back and allowed George to move in. The Touch of Death had taken nearly a full day before the demon-jaguar's breath finally returned to his large body.

Marcus collapsed from exhaustion. Payne rushed over and handed him a pouch full of water. The Chancellor took a drink and lay down on the ground, flat on his back. "I need to sleep. I need to sleep." It was almost instantaneous—Marcus was out cold.

After a brief period of grogginess, Kepler lifted his head from the forest floor. "What happened?"

George began to laugh and quickly wiped the tears from his eyes. "You had your ass handed to you. Marcus knocked the crap out of you. You actually died."

Kepler rose to his feet. After noticing Marcus's figure on the ground, he responded, "If I died, then why am I standing here while he's lying flat on his back? Did you revive me? Did I kill him before he hurt me?"

"Ha! If only that were the case," George said, giving the giant cat an even bigger hug.

Kepler squirmed. "Okay... that's great... just great. I die and now you have a need to hug on me. It's bad enough I have to put up with you in the first place. Okay, you can let go now... George... George... this is awkward!"

George laughed and released his hold on the jaguar's neck. "You died alright, but you never touched him."

"So how did he die?"

Payne jumped into the conversation. "Not dead... Marcus sleeps... and um, Payne's glad you not dead no more, kitty!"

"Uuggg, can someone just put me out of my misery! George, please kill me again so I don't have to keep hearing that word. I've had nightmares about that word ever since meeting this little freak."

Payne laughed. "You like Payne. I'm good freak... right, kitty?"

George gave Kepler a look. "Come on… cut the little guy some slack. He's trying to be nice."

Kepler moved to Payne and nudged him. "If you're going to call me kitty, then I'm going to call you freak. We'll call it even, a fair trade, I think."

George moved to stand over the Chancellor's sleeping figure. "Marcus brought you back to life. He used a power given to him by his god in order to do it."

"Why?"

"Let's just say we came to an understanding after I knocked him out cold with my fists."

"Quit lying … now I know you're full of garesh."

"Seriously, no lie."

"So how did you avoid his magic? Tell me what happened."

"We will talk about that later—we need to get going. We've lost too many moments already and need to get started on the trials. We need to open the shrine's door and find the key to the Source's Temple."

"What about Marcus? Shouldn't we kill him, after what he did to me?"

"He'll be okay… just leave him be. I have plans for him and I've already told him we're going to get going once you awoke. He has things to do… things which will stir the pot a bit."

"What kind of things? And what pot are you referring to?"

"Let's go, we'll talk about it all later! I'm sure you'll get a kick out of my little agreement with Marcus. I think it will benefit us nicely."

The Luvelles Gazette

When you want an update about your favorite characters

Four more Peaks of Bailem have passed

Shalee and Kiayasis are now left to walk on foot. Joss has injured his leg and flew back to the stables in Bestep to be cared for. They would have arrived at Grogger's Swamp by now, but with the loss of Joss's ability to travel quickly, they were still a good ten Peaks of Bailem away and have been walking ever since. Kiayasis was unable to carry his armor, their camp supplies and Shalee's bags all at the same moment. As a result, he has been wearing his armor and carrying their camp supplies while Shalee has been carrying her bags and his clothes all strapped to her back. She has also taken along a few pieces of the food. She plans to use her magic to multiply what they need when they eat. She has also used her magic to make their loads feel lighter.

George, Payne, and Kepler have set up camp. They can see the entrance to the Void Maze. It took most of the last four days to cross the Ebarna Strait. Other than the boat ride, they had to walk the entire distance necessary to get to this spot, since none of them knew the terrain well enough to teleport safely.

Athena, Mary, and Susanne have decided to take another trip to the City of Inspiration. They have agreed, after having a small get together with both Gregory and Brayson, that the woman, Bryanna, who scared them was wrong and there was nothing to worry about. They do plan, however, to avoid her store and any conversations of doom.

Boyafed is scheduled to meet with Lord Dowd. He has summoned the white paladin leader to meet with him alone just outside the City of Marcus near the shoreline of Lake Id. The Dark Order leader wants to assure Lord Dowd that the Order's dark paladins have no plans to attack his city.

Gregory Id plans to meet with the King of Lavan. There are issues which need to be addressed concerning the bridge connecting their two cities.

The goddess Mieonus has been watching Shalee and Kiayasis. She now knows of their plans to head to Grogger's Swamp. She has sent word requesting to speak with Lasidious and Celestria.

Mosley has plans to meet with Alistar. The God of the Harvest is pretending to look for clues as to what Lasidious and Celestria are up to. He agrees with Mosley that there is something larger going on than just this simple game involving the Crystal Moon. But he agrees with the wolf for reasons of his own... evil reasons.

Hosseff, God of Death has been watching Marcus ever since the Dark Chancellor summoned his gift, the Touch of Death. After watching Kepler's resurrection, the shade has been curious about the new alignment Marcus has made with George and figures the events that should unfold in the near future as a result of this union will be worth watching.

Brayson is waiting for Morre, Amar's brother who lives on Grayham, to respond to his request for a simple conversation. He has been in his office since the Peak of Bailem yesterday, constantly checking his Mirror of Communication.

Thank you for reading the Luvelles Gazette

Chapter 14

𝔓oorly 𝔄imed 𝔄rrows
Two Peaks of Bailem Later,
Ancients Sovereign

Lasidious and Celestria, after considering Mieonus's request to come speak with her in her new home, finally decided to show up. The Goddess of Hate had made only minor changes to Yaloom's fashionable style of decorating. The home rested within the Great Falls on Ancients Sovereign and the deity was looking forward to her first set of guests.

When they arrived, they found Mieonus watching Shalee and Kiayasis from a massive indoor waterfall that fell like a sheet of glass into a large pool far below. Yaloom added this feature to the home many, many seasons ago when he created it. The perfect sheet of water was a lot like watching a giant movie screen.

Yaloom had exquisite taste which also represented many of Mieonus's ideas of what perfection truly was. The pool far below the fall's projected image had thousands of diamonds that shimmered from the bottom of its depth. The water from the pool continued on and cascaded over many other smaller falls before exiting the structure. The base of this mansion, built at the center of a 1,100-foot drop, had a hole that opened near the cliff and released the water down the remaining 500-foot drop below.

Every ounce of the falls funneled into the home before it exited at the bottom. Despite the massive amount of force that poured into the top of the structure, it was pleasant where they stood. Yaloom engineered this exotic mansion in such a way that the deafening sound was carried away from the main level where they were speaking. He smoothed the walls inside to quietly direct the water peacefully around them, allowing for good conversation. Now Mieonus enjoyed this serenity at Yaloom's loss.

"What did you want, Mieonus?" Lasidious asked.

"I thought you would find it interesting that I've figured out where Shalee is going. She thinks the crystal has been hidden within Grogger's Swamp. What I can't figure out is why one of the Dark Order's paladins is escorting her. It doesn't make any sense."

Celestria moved to look into the fall's image. She watched as Shalee and Kiayasis walked hand in hand. "Lasidious, come look at this."

Lasidious could only laugh. After a moment he collected himself and responded. "I wish Sam was here to see this. How wonderful would it be to watch his reaction? Better yet...how fun would it be to watch a fight between Sam and Kiayasis? I'm not sure, but I think I would put my coin on Sam's blade."

Celestria leaned into him. "I'm not so sure. The Order's paladins are trained under the harshest of circumstances. Kiayasis is Boyafed's son. I wouldn't be surprised if he sent Sam's soul to find its place within the Book of Immortality's pages."

Mieonus cut in. "Aren't you two the least bit curious as to why Kiayasis is with Shalee in the first place?"

Both gods answered as if sharing the same mind. "No... should we be?"

"Yes, you should. The Order is an evil army and Shalee represents everything that is good. How could she be traveling with someone like Kiayasis?"

Lasidious took Celestria's hand. "Mieonus, maybe you should consider the fact that Shalee doesn't know about the Order or their evil ways. Maybe she thought he was charming. Kiayasis could have found her beauty appealing and simply offered to assist her on her travels. Why are you so worried about these trivial things? You should be more concerned about the missing piece of the Crystal Moon."

"The crystal is all but mine. George is on his way to speak with the Source. Once he looks into the Eye of Magic, the crystal will be under evil's control and we will rule the worlds as you have promised."

Lasidious and Celestria began laughing.

"What's so funny?"

Lasidious responded. "The crystal hasn't been hidden within the Source. George has misunderstood the three words on the parchment and it appears Shalee is on the right path."

"What?" Mieonus shouted. "How could this be? The words spoke of a soul swallowed. The Eye of Magic does exactly that when a person fails to show their belief in themselves. What else could it be?"

Celestria answered. "Look at it this way, Mieonus. If we were to put the crystal inside the Eye of Magic and the Eye decided to swallow George, he couldn't very well return the crystal to us, now could he? But, on the other hand, if we were to put the crystal, oh, let's just say... somewhere inside Grogger's Swamp, more specifically, inside Grogger's belly... a person with the power necessary to handle such a job could retrieve the crystal and get back out without being harmed. It appears Shalee is closer to finding the crystal than George is."

Mieonus stomped her foot. "This is really irritating. By the moment George finally finishes the trials and figures out the crystal wasn't there, he'll never learn about Grogger's special digestive traits quick enough to beat Shalee to it."

"I'm sorry, Mieonus, but it appears you'll have to try for the next piece once we've hidden it."

"This is ridiculous. I have a mind to stop playing your stupid game."

Lasidious smiled. "You can always keep yourself entertained while watching Shalee and Kiayasis. It would seem that their relationship could provide some wonderful confrontations. Besides, Celestria and I have been watching the three brothers. It looks like there's something big building."

"What do you mean?"

Both gods vanished, leaving Mieonus standing alone in front of the images within the falls. "Damn, I hate it when they do that! No one answers my questions any more!"

The City of Inspiration,
Lord Dowd's Home

Spirit Bull Shaban and Lord Dowd

Illustration by Kathleen Stone

Lord Dowd stood behind his home and next to his ghostly mount. He had worked hard to create this courtyard garden. This was his place of solitude, a relaxing escape in which he had sat silently on many nights while winding down after a day of intense training with his men.

Despite the abrupt nature his men had come to know so well, Dowd had a green thumb and it was the simple things in life that made him happy. Everywhere he looked something beautiful grew—roses, daisies, and many other exotic flowers and bushes known only to the World of Luvelles. His favorite of all within his self-planted world was the Cordanrian Corgel, an intoxicatingly fragrant bush, which, when fully grown, stood almost eye-level. The plant was covered in royal purple blooms with white lacey leaves and emitted a natural opiate which temporarily gave the person smelling it a short-lived buzz.

Dowd was a proud man. His silver-plated armor was polished to perfection, resting perfectly on his large, powerful frame. His short, dark hair had been freshly cut and he felt confident about his upcoming meeting with Boyafed, the Dark Order leader. He was summoned to the meeting on the shoreline of Lake Id and had just finished making all his preparations. As he finished attaching a cape to a special set of snaps on top of his shoulders, he took a deep breath.

"The moment has come to go, boy," Dowd said, looking up at the hazed outline of his mount. "Let's hope this meeting is a good thing! There's no telling what he's thinking after releasing Tolas and his men."

Dowd rode the same type of mount as the rest of his white army. There were no stables necessary to house these creatures. They were carefree and required no special provisions.

Shaban was a spirit-bull, nearly six times the size of a bull on Earth. At approximately 15,000 pounds of ghostly flesh when materialized, Shaban had been the Paladin of Light's mount for nearly 100 seasons. The bull had the ability to use both defensive and offensive magic while Dowd remained mounted or touched him in any way. But, when the warrior dismounted or fell from his saddle, the spirit-bull would slowly dematerialize and eventually became nothing more than a smoky-looking figure objects could pass right through. He would stay this way until touched again by his rider.

Dowd pulled on the spirit-bull's reins. "Come down here. Let's have a look at you today before we go, shall we?"

Shaban responded and lowered his gigantic head, allowing his master to rub his snout. As soon as the paladin's hand made contact, his ghostly form turned to flesh. The weight of his 15,000 pounds instantly made four large impressions beneath his massive hooves.

This simple exchange of affection was yet another one of the small things in life Dowd looked forward to, but this moment was to be short-lived.

Suddenly, from a location unseen, an arrow or a bolt flew past Dowd's head and into Shaban's left eye. The spirit exploded, the shock wave sending Dowd flying backwards into the opening of a well's mouth at the garden's center. His armor filled with water and the weight of the metal pulled him deep beneath the surface with relative quickness.

From the far side of the courtyard, Marcus lowered the crossbow to his side. "That was unexpected. Hmmm... they blow up; I would've never guessed that could happen. I suppose an adjustment to our new plan is in order." After a few more moments passed, he vanished.

From deep beneath the surface of the well's water level, Dowd worked frantically to remove his armor. He could not seem to move fast enough. He felt helpless and his air was now in short supply. Eventually his mind began to turn clouded as he struggled to fight the need to gasp for air.

Something hit his shoulder. Dowd turned and located a rope with a stone attached to its end. Quickly, he tugged. It was secure. Without further hesitation he pulled himself to the surface. The air was like a drug when it filled his lungs. Never in his life had he realized how much he appreciated the simple act of breathing.

After catching his breath, he methodically removed each piece of his armor, his arm draped through a lasso he had created to free both hands. When finally he climbed out and over the top of the well's glass walls, Dowd rested for only a moment before pulling up his armor to the surface.

There was no one around. He scanned the area, but no one could be seen. *Who would throw a rope in to save me and leave without the reward I would give them,* he thought.

Something caught his eye. He moved to the area where the spirit-bull had stood. A bolt from one of the Dark Order's cross bows rested in one of Shaban's hoof prints. Leaning down to inspect the projectile further, he scanned the area. He stood and said only one single word. "BOYAFED!"

Dowd had no idea the God of Death was standing near him— invisible, not more than five feet away. Hosseff smiled as he watched the white paladin leader take the Dark Order's arrow and head inside his home of glass.

"This should make for some wonderful entertainment. With war, comes death," the shade-god said as he waved his hand. The rope lifted from the ground, floated over to the spot where the god had found it and hung itself up.

"It looks as if war is about to make itself known here on Luvelles!" Laughing, the deity vanished for his home on Ancients Sovereign.

The Underground Village of Goswigs

Gage quickly realized that living with the Goswigs was not going to be an easy thing to do. Strongbear kept everyone busy. The large brown bear was constantly working on something and for the last few days, he had decided to expand their hidden underground world far beneath the surface of Luvelles.

The badger couldn't fathom where Strongbear found the energy to run his diner, make the blankets he gave to other Goswigs, and if that wasn't enough, the energy to make their village grow.

"Good Morning, Gage," Strongbear said, tossing a new blanket in the badger's direction as he entered the diner for breakfast. "So are you with me today... or are you against me?"

Gage rolled his eyes. He was sick of hearing the bear's stupid statement. All Strongbear ever said when he wanted anything was, "Are you with me... or against me?"

"I'm with ya, big guy," Gage responded softly as he took a seat.

Strongbear smiled and continued, "I think we're going to continue working on the area south of the city. We have a lot of dirt to move before we'll have our new lake."

"Let him wake up, will ya? No one is with ya when they're half-asleep," Gallrum shouted. The Serwin flapped his wings and hovered over to join Gage at his table. "The poor thing hasn't even had the chance to breathe yet this morning and you're already barking your orders." His serpent scale-covered body lowered to the seat and coiled his tail to lift him high enough for good conversation. "So how are you this morning, Gage?"

Gage looked around before answering. The diner was pleasant, but rugged-looking, the same style in which Strongbear kept his cave which sat just behind the diner. Many of the Goswigs he had met at the city meeting after his arrival were having breakfast and enjoying a good chat.

Strongbear was known for his ability to serve each Goswig what they enjoyed most. There were beavers who feasted on bark, chickens eating grain, eagles ripping apart raw fish, billy goats gnawing on straw, lions devouring Corgan meat, fairies nibbling on fruit, bats drinking the blood drained from the Corgan, wolfs, boars, and many other forms of animals and other mythical creatures.

"I'm fine thanks... doesn't Strongbear ever just take a day off? Why does everyone listen to him anyway? It's not like the village will fall apart if he just enjoys a day every now and then. I should find a way to get him to relax."

Gallrum laughed. "Well, normally Strongbear would be hibernating by now, but for some odd reason, the end of summer has continued to drag on. We usually enjoy ourselves when he's sound asleep."

"I heard that," Strongbear shouted from the far side of the room. "You're all gonna need your strength today. I would eat up if I were you." As if instructed to do so, nearly every Goswig moaned and started complaining at the same moment.

"Hey... knock it off and eat!" The bear turned and went into his cave-like kitchen.

They lowered their heads as instructed and began eating. As usual, Gallrum ate his quaggle, but Gage didn't have an appetite for fish eyes. The badger had adapted many seasons ago and enjoyed normal everyday elven food. He ate strips of ham, which irritated the boars, eggs which made the chickens nervous, and followed them up with a small loaf of freshly baked bread which seemed to sit well with everyone.

After breakfast was over, Strongbear ordered the group in a strong growl to report to the dig site. "I want that lake to be finished before I die. That's one big hole we need to dig, so we can't afford to waste the day. There are just too many projects to be done in this city before we're done. Let's get moving everyone! Are you with me... or are you against me?"

Gage rolled his eyes.

The Void Maze

Kepler was planning to lead the group into the maze after sitting down for a good meal. With each bite, George studied the tall, leaf-covered bushes that shaped the maze's many walls from a safe distance. Since their arrival, something had been bothering him, but he couldn't figure out what it was or why he had such a sick feeling in his stomach.

"Kep, this place gives me the creeps... even from here."

Kepler swallowed a mouthful of half-eaten Corgan he had killed the night before. With the assistance of George's magic, they had moved the heavy cow-like body to a spot just outside their camp.

"I don't know. I suppose you could be right, but it just doesn't look so bad to me."

Payne looked at George and then back at the maze. "Why go in?"

"Because, Payne, we need to get to the temple at the center of it."

"Ya... um, but why go in?"

"I have told you this already. We need to see the Source. This is the only way to get to him."

"No... um... no... no, it's not."

Kepler growled. "Look, freak, it is the only way. You're wasting our moments by arguing with us."

"No, kitty... Payne show ya!"

The fairy-demon spread his wings and flew towards the maze. George watched and once he understood what Payne was going to do, he turned to Kepler.

"He just might have a good idea. He's going to fly over the top of it all and teleport back to us. Once he sees the temple, I'll be able to teleport us right to it once I look into his mind to see where to take us."

Their moment of excitement was short-lived. Payne smashed hard into an invisible barrier high above the maze's entrance and fell hard to the ground below. Both George and Kepler jumped to their feet. They would have rushed in to see if he was okay, but before they could take a step, a small furry creature, the likes of which neither of them had ever seen before ran out, picked

Payne's tiny red body off the ground, and darted back inside.

George raised his hand, a single magic arrow shot from his palm. The missile cut through the air only to miss its target by a narrow margin as the creature turned the first corner.

Kepler covered the distance quickly. He darted inside past the maze's entrance and turned the corner to pursue. He stopped, crouched in a guarded position and stared down the empty corridor. He growled deep and then shouted.

"There's no one here. He's gone." His eyes had changed from their normal glow to an intense, bright red. "George, don't come in here," he shouted, raising his voice even louder than before. "You won't be able to see!"

George slid to a stop just before breaking the barrier of the entrance. He took a moment to calm himself. "Why?"

Kepler moved to find the entrance, but as he rounded the corner, it was gone. All he could see was a heavy stone brick wall. "Where are you? Can you hear me?"

"What do you mean? Yes I can hear you, and I can see you standing there yelling at me. Why are you acting so damn strange?"

"I can't find you. Everything has changed."

"What... what do you mean, everything has changed. Are you losing it?"

Kepler growled. "I think you know me better than that. Of course I'm not losing it. Everything has changed, I tell ya. I can't see you from where I'm standing. It's like you've disappeared."

George thought a moment. "So why can you hear me then?"

"How should I know? You're the magic user... you tell me!"

"Okay... start by telling me what you're seeing."

"It's pitch black in here—your eyes aren't made for this. Use your magic on them before you come in."

"I'm not coming in there until I know what you're talking about. What do you mean, it's pitch black? It's only morning. There's plenty of daylight left."

"When I passed the entrance, everything went dark. There's powerful magic being used here once you've past the barrier."

"What barrier? I swear I'm looking right at you!"

"That may be, but the entrance isn't normal."

"Explain!"

"It must be some sort of barrier. From out there... or rather, from where you're standing, I also saw a maze with leaf-covered walls, but now... now I see heavy stones stacked on top of one another and I'm standing here in the dark. It's like some kind of underground dungeon."

"What the hell are you talking about? Can't you see the sky above?"

Kepler growled in frustration. "If I could see the sky, then I wouldn't have said the words underground dungeon, now would I ... dumbass!"

"Okay, okay... sorry... so tell me what else you're seeing."

"Just use your magic on your eyes and come look for yourself."

"Why would I do that? We need to get you back out of there."

"Because it's the only way to get to the Source's temple... remember?"

"Bah... smart ass! Okay, I'm coming in!"

George waved his hands across his eyes and stepped through the entrance. The light changed to darkness as he passed the invisible barrier. The magic assisted his vision as he studied the area. Just as Kepler had said, the sky had faded away. The corridors of the maze were cold-looking. The gray stones were stacked perfectly on top of one another like giant bricks. Many places along the narrow passageways were covered with moss, moisture from the ceiling above feeding its growth. Vines emerged throughout and disappeared through the floor.

"Damn, Kep... this place is dreadful."

The jaguar turned and looked back down the corridor. "I don't have a good feeling about this place!"

George slapped his forehead. "Ya think! Maybe now you'll trust me the next time we're sitting around our camp fire and I say, Kep, this place gives me the creeps!"

Kepler ignored his tone and moved ahead. "It's easy to see how that thing disappeared with Payne so quickly."

George thought a moment. "This is gonna suck. Just watch where you're walking. I've seen places like this on Earth."

Kepler stopped dead in his tracks. He turned and looked at the mage. "You've been in places like this? You should be the one leading the way, then."

"Um... not exactly, but I have seen movies like this."

"Hmpf... you're just as lost as I am, then! The movies you've told me about sound ridiculously fake."

"Oh... I forgot... you're right, and all this just seems so real. Anyway... they were all good movies and I don't care what anyone says. Let me tell ya some more about it. It'll keep our minds off the creepiness of this place. See... there's this one movie, and it's about a wickedly powerful mummy. You know... the kind that curses everyone..."

Brayson's Floating Office

Brayson impatiently paced back and forth within his floating office high above Luvelles and had been since the Peak of Bailem yesterday. Three days had passed since the Head Master sent word through Brandor's mirror on Grayham for Morre, Amar's brother, to contact him. He had spoken with Michael, Sam's General Absolute, and was assured that Morre would receive his message and be allowed access to the king's mirror.

Eventually Brayson's personal mirror, framed with the same wood his desk had been made from, filled with an image. It was Morre. The mage had prepared for their conversation and taken the moments necessary to clean up, something he normally didn't do. It was Morre's way of showing his appreciation and respect for Brayson. His long gray beard had been trimmed, hair brushed, and his charcoal-colored robes were new. The only thing he had forgotten to do was clean what was left of his teeth. His entire body fit within the mirror's size and the wrinkles around his eyes could be easily seen.

Morre lowered his head and bowed on one knee. "Head Master... I teleported to Brandor as soon as I received word of your request to speak with me. I'm sorry it has taken so long. The general has seen to it that our conversation will remain private."

"Please stand up, Morre; it's been too long since last we spoke. I trust things are well for you and your brother."

Brayson took mental notes as he watched Morre's reaction carefully. He could see the pain as it appeared on his face. "I take it you haven't heard. I should've found a way to contact you, Master Id."

"Please, call me Brayson. I'm your brother's friend. We should also talk as friends."

"I would like that, but I fear my news is grim."

Brayson swallowed hard. "So tell me what I haven't been told..."

A single tear fell from Morre's eye as he responded. "My brother was murdered by someone who left him lying in his own blood. They found him mutilated in a smith's barn, not far from the City of Champions. A chisel and a hammer had been used to pry his chest open."

Brayson moved closer to the mirror and waved his hand. The heavy wooden chair behind his desk floated over to him. Once in a sitting position, Brayson responded, "His chest was ripped open?"

"Yes!"

"What of his heart?"

"It was missing."

"It was?"

"Yes, it was, but—"

Brayson interrupted. "Who on Grayham would have this knowledge?"

Morre looked confused. "What knowledge are you speaking of?"

"I'm sure you understand there are things I cannot speak of. I need to know how long it has been since Amar's death."

The mage lifted his hand to his face in thought. "I have lost track of the days, but if I were to venture a guess, it has been nearly a half a season of my life."

Brayson now knew he had been deceived. His mind filled with rage as he thought about the imposter who had visited him in this very room not long ago. The most powerful wizard on Luvelles stood from his chair and with an aggressive wave of his hand, sent the heavy object flying across the room through one of the large windows only to begin its long fall to the land below.

Morre responded, "I'm also angry about his death. I had no idea you cared for Amar this much!"

Brayson took a few long deep breaths. "I'm sorry, my friend. I'm going to find the person responsible for Amar's death. I'll bring him to you myself and allow you to have your revenge. Somebody came to my office just the other day and looked exactly like your brother. He even spoke as Amar would have. I fear I have been lied to. I have made many decisions thinking it was your brother who requested these favors. I'll find this impostor and he'll regret the day he ever met me."

"I would cherish the chance to meet my brother's killer. I want to know what kind of man would do such a thing. I hope I have the power to do something about it when the moment comes!"

"Don't worry, you will, my friend... you will!"

Brayson waved his hand and the mirror's image faded before he vanished.

Far below, just outside the School of Magic's entrance, two male elves, both students, were having a conversation about the day's lessons. Brayson's chair slammed hard into the dirt behind them, splintering into many pieces which went flying in all directions. Both elves grabbed hold of one another, frightened. But once they realized how it looked, they quickly released their embrace, straightened their robes and turned to walk in opposite directions as if nothing had happened, stepping over debris as they went.

The Coastline of Lake Lavan
West of the City of Inspiration

The White Chancellor appeared with the King of Lavan on the north shoreline of Lake Lavan, due west of the City of Inspiration. It was from this spot that the two leaders intended to extend their new bridge of glass toward the southwest across the lake's waters and to the shoreline of the king's city, the city of Lavan. Many workers were standing around, waiting for a decision to be made.

The king was a heavy Halfling, fat from his many years of sitting on his throne. His hair was short brown, with a trimmed beard and mustache. His dress was normal for a man in his position. The king's symbol, a sordan sparrow, rested at the center of his jeweled crown of gold.

Gregory, as always, wore green robes and a yellow belt to cover his thin frame. His long hair had been pulled up into a ponytail, exposing his small elven ears.

The two men moved toward the area of trouble as the workers parted to let them pass. Gregory started the conversation. "So what seems to be the problem, Heltgone?"

The king pointed toward a boat floating a good distance off shore. "The workers have run into a problem. Their magic isn't strong enough to hold back the water. It's stopping them from moving forward with the construction of the bridge's supports."

"Have they tried combining their power?"

"They have… on many occasions, in fact, but there's simply too much magic needed to push this much water aside and hold it in place long enough to set the stones."

"Well, we can't build our bridge of glass without the proper support, now can we? Let me think on this a moment."

Heltgone leaned over, grabbed a few pebbles from the shore and tossed them in, disturbing the crystal blue of the lake's surface. "Whatever solution you come up with needs to be safer than what we've already tried. Six men lost their lives in the last attempt. The weight of the water crushed them when the magic failed."

"Have their families been properly compensated for their loss?"

"They have. I've seen to it myself."

"Maybe we're going about this the wrong way. I think I know of a way to increase the magic needed to finish the job. We could always speak with the Ultorian king and ask him if he would offer us any assistance. They have more than enough magic for a job such as this."

Before anything else could be said, Gregory's Goswig, the lioness Mykklyn, appeared with Lord Dowd at her side. The Paladin of Light leader held the arrow that killed Shaban. Dowd didn't waste any moments. He tossed the arrow at Gregory's feet.

With a simple motion of his hand, the arrow lifted from the

ground and into Gregory's palm. "What's this?"

"It's a bolt from one of the Order's crossbows, intended to kill me!"

"What? How?"

"The Order tried to kill me at my home. They obviously missed, but managed to kill my spirit-bull."

"What ... Shaban is dead?" the king of Lavan said quickly, knowing of Dowd's mount.

Dowd looked directly at Heltgone and responded. "Yes ... Shaban is dead, and he was my mount for nearly 100 seasons. I was supposed to meet with Boyafed earlier today, but I found myself at the bottom of my well fighting for my life. Someone dropped me a rope and I used it to climb out, but when I made it to the surface, they were gone."

"When was this?" Gregory said.

"This morning, just before Early Bailem."

"Then my brother does intend to go to war!"

"This wasn't the work of your brother. Marcus wouldn't wield such a weapon—he would use his magic. This was an order given directly by Boyafed himself."

Mykklyn interrupted, moving between them as she spoke. "If the Order wants you dead, then they must've been planning this for a while now. An attack of this nature isn't something you just do unless you wish to weaken an army. With you out of the way, they must feel they would have an advantage."

"It seems there are larger problems here to worry about than the construction of our bridge," Heltgone said. "I'll return home and have my Argont Commander put the city on notice. I'll wait for your call. If my army is needed, we'll be ready."

Dowd lowered his head. "I appreciate your willingness to fight, sire. I'll be sure to let you know if this is indeed a sign that war is approaching. I've missed my meeting with Boyafed. I must try to figure out what his true intentions are before I react."

The king patted Dowd on the arm. "I'm sure as long as you're around, we'll all be in..."

Before the king could finish, another bolt flew past Dowd's shoulder and pierced Heltgone's right eye. Death was instantaneous as he fell to the ground. Dowd took a defensive position and turned to find the projectile's origin. Gregory crouched and put an invisible wall of force around both himself and the king's body.

The workers were shouting from a location not far away. Dowd and Mykklyn moved quickly to see what the commotion was about. It was clear to the Paladin of Light leader they had seen what happened.

A large elf male, also the project leader, made sure he had Dowd's attention.

"Lord Dowd... Lord Dowd... I saw him, I saw him."

"Speak, man! Who did this?" Mykklyn growled.

"We saw a warrior, dressed in the Dark Order's armor, appear right over there." He pointed to an area near a section of stone that had been stacked on the shoreline. "It all happened so fast. He appeared, shot his bow, and then disappeared just as quick. He dropped this before he left."

Dowd took the crossbow and examined it. The rank of a high ranking officer had been engraved on its stock. It was definitely a Dark Order weapon. Angry, he moved back to where the king's body lay.

"This makes twice today they've tried to kill me." He pulled the arrow from the king's eye. "This was meant for me."

Mykklyn responded. "How could an attempt on your life be so amateurish?"

"What do you mean?"

"Boyafed's men are trained better than this. They wouldn't miss, nor would they leave their weapons behind. I find it odd they've failed to hit you on both occasions but somehow hit the same spot on both victims."

"You're right! They hit the eye on both occasions. Could this be some kind of warning? Is Boyafed toying with us?"

"I don't know, but we have a dead man here. He needs to be honored and taken home for a proper Passing Ceremony," Gregory said as he stood and commanded the king's body to be moved. A number of Halfling men rushed in and lifted Heltgone's lifeless figure above their heads. "Take him to my palace and prepare his body. I'll take him back to Lavan and light the fire myself."

Brayson's Floating Office

Boyafed tossed his long sword onto the large golden alter resting beneath the statue of Hosseff. His voice echoed within the great hall as he looked up past the demons hanging from the God of Death's fingers and lifted his hands into the air.

"Hosseff, give me guidance!"

Marcus watched quietly from the shadows as Boyafed's second-in-command entered the hallway and rushed to make his way to Boyafed's side. He lowered his head to symbolize his respect before speaking. "My liege..."

"Dayden, my friend, you have come at the perfect moment. I could use your guidance."

"I wish I could say I've come with good news. You may not wish to have my guidance once you hear what I have to say."

Boyafed studied the face of his Argont Commander. Dayden was a larger man, strong, fit, confident, and wielded magic nearly as strong as his own. He wore all black, except for a gold shirt, and a cape with the Order's symbol at its center. His rank had been molded into the buckle of his belt when it was cast just as every other member of the Order's army had been, and then again engraved on each of his weapons.

The men had been friends since childhood. Boyafed put his hand on Dayden's shoulder before responding, "What is it? Your eyes carry the weight of Luvelles within them."

"Three of our men lay dead as we speak."

"What ... how ... where?"

Dayden produced three arrows and handed them to Boyafed. "Lord Dowd apparently has decided he wishes war!"

"Damn him! I was to meet with him this morning, but he never showed. My message must have fallen on deaf ears. I should have killed his men when I had the chance. What more can you tell me?"

"I have the bow used in the attack. The killer must have dropped it when making his escape."

"Did anyone see this man's face?"

"No, but they saw enough of him to give chase. The men who pursued said he wore the colors of the Paladins of Light."

"And the rank on the bow?"

"It's the same rank as a simple sergeant. The same rank as Tolas, the man you let return home with his men."

"What are you saying—that the man I let go is responsible for this attack?"

"No... all I'm saying is that the rank on the bow is the same rank as the man you allowed to return to Lord Dowd after you tortured his men."

Boyafed moved to lean against the golden altar. He lifted his sword and unsheathed its finely polished blade. "It appears that Dowd has issued a challenge, Dayden. Do you think we should answer it with war?"

"My liege, with all due respect, this isn't a decision I should be asked to make! It isn't my place to question or second-guess your command!"

Boyafed stood and secured the blade to his side. "I'm not asking for a decision, my old friend. I'm asking you for an opinion."

"Then it's my opinion that only three men aren't worth killing thousands for. I think we should try to resolve this another way. Many other men rely on you to have a full understanding of events before you send them to war. If I were you, I would send men to investigate Lord Dowd's intentions further before making a final decision."

Boyafed moved to Dayden and pulled him close. After a brief hug was exchanged, he kissed his forehead and responded. "You are wise, my friend. This must be the reason why our friendship has lasted for so long."

Dayden jabbed Boyafed playfully in the ribs. "I love you as well, old man!"

As both men left, Marcus stepped from the shadows. "It seems a little more persuasion is in order," he hissed. His eyes were cold beneath the torchlight of the great hall. "War will come, Boyafed... war has come knocking at your door. Soon I'll have the power to force you to kneel at my feet."

Chapter 15

𝕬 𝕳𝖊𝖆𝖛𝖞 𝕳𝖊𝖆𝖗𝖙

Two Peaks of Bailem Have Passed, Ancients Sovereign

Mosley and Alistar sat on the porch of Mosley's cabin home on top of Catalyst Mountain. They had been enjoying the view of the valleys below during their conversation. The slopes leading away from the cabin were covered with many blooming colors.

"I have looked for anything that could suggest that Lasidious and Celestria are up to something."

"And did you find anything?"

"I haven't."

The god turned his narrow face in Mosley's direction. His brown eyes found the wolf-god's before continuing. "There's nothing suspicious, but I still share your concern. They're up to something! This game isn't really a game at all. All we do is watch and wait to see who'll capture the crystal's pieces first. If only this game were something, oh, I don't know... something more hands-on. As it stands right now, this game is simply boring and a complete waste of my moments."

Mosley closed his eyes and lifted his snout into the sunlight. "It's beautiful up here. I just can't bring myself to move from this place some days. Do you think Bassorine would have cared if I decide to stay here permanently?"

"Bassorine spoke highly of you for more than 300 seasons before his destruction. If he hadn't cared for you, he wouldn't have left the Book with instructions that you were to take his place. If he were to have any problem with anything you have or haven't done, he would say you don't act as a God of War should."

Mosley's furry ears lifted and came to rest in an attentive position. "How so? I have done nothing against the gods."

"It's not the gods you're failing. You're failing the people of the worlds. You don't seem to care that it's your job to create war. It's your job to act as a form of population control. With nothing more than a few simple suggestions, you have the power to make kings fight for each other's lands, take each other's food, and force the faith of their gods on the people they conquer."

The God of the Harvest stood and moved to the porch's railing. After a moment he continued. "Look at what I've done on the World of Harvestom. Why do you think I've started to initiate a famine across the Kingdom of Kless? It's to set up a desperate situation so you can go in and place the desire for war in their hearts. The king of Kless believes the Tadreens have stolen the Seeds of Plenty. With your help, war will consume the Centaur king's lands and make room for the Book of Immortality to release many of the souls within his pages... souls who deserve another chance at life, a chance to be reborn."

The God of War stretched his black-coated body and moved to stand beside Alistar. He lifted his front paws up to the top of the railing and used them to stay balanced in an upright position.

"I see your point. I need to get past my own issues with death. I know I need to do my job. I just hate to see the people die. I realize it's necessary to create these wars as a part of the cycle of life. I've been trying to avoid this issue, but I understand it must be done and I can't avoid my duties any longer."

Hosseff appeared on the ground below within the flowers. The light of the sun passed right through the shade-god's shadowy head. Once the effect of his appearance had been felt, his face materialized. He looked human, his eyes golden brown, hair long and dark and the gold robe he decided to wear was trimmed in black and hung to the ground, covering his feet. His windy voice sounded like a whisper as he spoke.

"Mosley, there are matters on Luvelles which require your attention."

"What matters are you referring to?"

"The Light and the Darkness on Luvelles are in distress. The timing is perfect for your suggestions of war."

Alistar laughed at the irony of Hosseff's timing. "How interesting it is that you would appear at this very moment, and with news of war, no less. Mosley and I were just discussing his responsibilities as the God of War."

Hosseff lifted his hood from his back. His face dissipated and returned to its shadowy form as the light failed to penetrate the robe's heavy cloth. "Then such news should give the wolf some enjoyment. Mosley, you need to ensure that this war happens. I will relish walking through the battlefields of death. I'll collect the souls who have perished and return them to the Book's pages. I'll do my job as a God of Death should; now you need to do yours!" The shade vanished.

Mosley jumped from the porch and turned to face Alistar. "It is moments like these that make being a god seem less than desirable!" The wolf disappeared.

Alistar sat down, put his feet up on the rail, threw his hands behind his head and lifted his face toward the sun's warming rays. He spoke aloud, despite being alone. "But it's also at moments like this, when I'm alone, surrounded by such incredible beauty that, as a god, I can sit back and enjoy all we've created. I can also enjoy how well the plan is coming together."

The Dungeon Catacombs,
The Void Maze

Fire erupted from George's hands and as a result, the small creature coming after them fell to the ground, burned and unrecognizable. The mage moved to stand over the monstrous site, only to kick what was left of the small body to the side of the corridor and into the wall. One of its legs separated upon impact and as it fell toward the floor, a nail from one of its clawed toes made an eerie scratching noise which sounded a lot like nails on a chalkboard.

"Damn... I hate that sound. Kep, we've been lost in here for, for... oh, hell... I've got no idea how long we've been walking through this stinking place. If I have to kill anymore of these little turds, I'm gonna go crazy."

"It's not like they're hard for you to kill. Quit complaining. I'm the one with all the scratches."

"I'm just sick of wandering aimlessly!"

Kepler knew relief was in sight. "I do have some good news."

"And what would that be? No wait... don't tell me. I bet there's another corner just ahead. We'll be able to make the turn and get lost down that corridor, just like we have in all the rest of them!"

"Well, I guess you can look at it that way, or I could just tell you I can smell Payne's scent. He's around the next corner."

"Ya know, Kep, sometimes you really know how to lift a guy's spirits. Come here, ya big lug."

"Bah, don't go getting all sappy on me again. I don't need another hug, dang it. You're so stinking sensitive sometimes!"

George rummaged his hand through the black fur on the top of Kepler's head. "Let's get moving."

"Yes, let's... at least that way you'll keep your grimy hands to yourself!"

George carefully peeked around the stone wall of the dungeon's corner corridor. To his surprise, the area ahead opened up into a field. "We've made it through. The temple is sitting on the far side of the clearing."

"I can see too, ya know," Kepler growled. "We need to get Payne out of that cage."

Payne had been suspended just above a large bonfire at the field's center. His cage was glowing from the intense heat and the length of moments he had been enveloped within the flames. Hundreds of creatures, similar to the ones they had been killing for the last couple of days, danced around the fire. Most of them seemed agitated that the fairy-demon wouldn't cook.

Payne was singing. He appeared to be happy and didn't seem to understand that the situation he was in was serious. The little guy acted grateful, as if he appreciated the flaming hot bath.

Kepler shook his head. "What an idiot... only Payne would sing while in captivity."

"He's too young to understand. I don't think he knows his life is in jeopardy."

"Wait... what's he doing?"

They watched as Payne lifted his arms and extended them toward the thick iron bars of his cage. One of the creatures dancing by the fire lifted from the ground and flew through air. The beast slammed hard against the side and was pinned.

The screams it made as the fire began to consume its flesh were hellish. Even Kepler's evil heart was bothered by the sound as Payne continued to hold his arms steady until the magic sucked the lifeless form through the narrow gap and into his claws. He began to eat the scorched flesh quickly before the heat completely burnt the flavor from it.

George whispered. "I think the fire is feeding his power."
Kepler thought a moment. "At least we know now why he's happy, but I don't agree with you. I think his hunger has caused him to use resources that even he himself didn't know he has. It's just like what you described to me after he saved you inside the Book of Bonding. You said he let his body burn. He did it without thinking. All he knew was that he needed to save you. He knew you needed light in order to teleport to a safe spot. Who knows how powerful he is, or even how powerful you are for that matter, since you share his power now."

"Do you really think so? If this is true, then who knows what we can accomplish."

"I agree. Let's think about it for a moment. We've walked through this dungeon for what feels like days now, and every time one of those hairy creatures got their claws on me, you had to use the vial of elixir Brayson gave you to heal my wounds.

"Now you, on the other hand, have simply held up your hands and destroyed them with your magic as if they were nothing more than minor irritations. I think your powers are growing. This must be the benefit of having Payne as your Goswig."

"I think you're right. I bet that was hard for you to admit."

"Bah...he's still a freak!"

George smiled and turned to look around the corner. "Maybe Payne will eat them all if we give him long enough!"

"Ha... I don't doubt it, but I'm hungry myself and we're out of food."

"Agreed. You need to stay behind me when we go out."

"Why?"

"Just trust me, Kep!"

George took a deep breath and turned to walk out into the open with Kepler at his heels. As they passed the end of the dungeon's stones, dark clouds lined the night sky.

George's steps were filled with purpose. He focused on Payne as he approached the hundreds of hairy creatures surrounding him. He stopped when he felt Payne's magic begin to surround him and shouted, "Hey you little pieces of garesh... come get me. Daddy brought dinner!"

Kepler lowered to the ground, ready to pounce. "Wow, how clever you have become. You sound like an idiot. Which reminds me... do you want me to tell them something once they get here? Should I tell them I don't think you know what you're doing? I could tell them you told me to tell them we are both crazy."

"Shut up, I'm concentrating! Tease me later, for hell's sake!"

Payne became excited and shouted from his cage. "Master... you came for Payne!"

The sounds the creature's claw-like feet made as they pounded against the earth were intimidating, but George held strong. Focusing on Payne, he closed his eyes and pulled magic from the fairy-demon's power. He raised his hands. Thousands of needles shot from his fingertips. He moved his arms back and forth to ensure he covered the spread of bodies as they began to fall lifeless to the ground.

When George opened his eyes, they were blood red. The beast's bodies were lying on top of one another, many of them cut clean through. George began to sway. He fell to the ground, but Kepler managed to move beneath him and used his large body to soften his fall.

"George, are you okay? Your eyes... they're filled with blood."

The mage could not respond. His eyes shut, his body relaxed, and a moment later, he fell into unconsciousness.

Kepler knew he did not have any moments to waste. The power George used was simply too much for his body to handle. He tried to retrieve the vial from the mage's robe, but his massive paws weren't built for such things.

I have to get Payne out of that cage, he thought. The demon-jaguar turned his giant black body and ran hard towards Payne's prison above the flames. He launched into the air.

"Hold on!" he shouted. Payne managed to grab the bars just before contact as the demon-cat smashed into the cage. Kepler's body easily surrounded the entire structure. The thin chain holding the cage snapped easily, allowing his momentum to carry them clear of the flames.

Kepler lifted himself from the ground. To his surprise, the bars of the cage collapsed, leaving Payne pinned inside. "Are you hurt?"

"No, not hurt, kitty."

"Can you teleport out of there?"

"No... um... can't."

"We have to get you out. I need you to give George a drop of the potion Brayson gave him."

"No... can't get out. Bite hand off."

"What?"

"Bite hand off. Payne help Master."

"How will biting your hand off help George?'

Payne shouted, "BITE!"

Kepler lowered his mouth towards the fairy-demon's hand. "Ugg, you stink!"

"Bite, kitty... bite!"

"Consider it a pleasure!"

Kepler chomped down hard and severed the hand with ease. Payne screamed in agony as the jaguar spit it to the ground.

"Now what do I do, freak?"

With tear-filled eyes, the fairy demon responded. "Payne help Master now."

The hand began to change. It wasn't long before a much smaller likeness of Payne had morphed and began to fly towards George, with Kepler not far behind. The vial was retrieved and set on the ground with the lid up.

"I need help kitty," the tiny little morphed Payne shouted.

Kepler covered the lid with the tips of his teeth and twisted. The lid slid out. Reaching inside the bottle, the smaller Payne cupped some of the liquid with the palm of his claw and flew above George's mouth. He reached in and lifted the mage's tongue as he emptied his hand beneath it. He repeated the process once more to ensure enough of the elixir had been used. The only thing they could do now was wait.

One Peak of Bailem
South of Grogger's Swamp

Kiayasis finished setting up camp for the night. They had stayed close to the shoreline. After eating and ensuring the fire was burning strong, he sat next to Shalee, pulling her close. This would be their final night together before Shalee made her way inside the swamp. The weather was peaceful and the sun was beginning to set.

"This is hard."

"What's hard?" Shalee responded softly.

"I have been with you for the last 31 Peaks of Bailem. We've spent so many moments together and I've never done something like this before."

"Am I really so bad? Are you tired of my company?"

"That's not what I mean. I'm saying it's hard because when this is over, you'll be leaving. You'll need to return to your king and to your duties as a queen. I don't think I can bear the thought of being apart from you. You've captured my heart and I wish desperately to be with you."

Shalee turned and stroked his face. "I don't know that I wish to go back to Grayham. I'm happy where I am. I'm happy with you."

They watched as the sun disappeared behind the horizon. The waves of the Volton Ocean crashed against the shoreline, amplifying the mood.

"I wish you to stay. I would cherish you. *Manka lle merna amin merna quen mela en' coiamin.*"

"What did you say?"

"I said ... I would make you the love of my life, if you wish it."

Shalee couldn't believe her ears. "You think you could care for me that much?"

"I don't think... I know! I would love you... I do love you!"

Fear rushed through her as her mind went wild with thought. *What would Sam think? How would he feel when I tell him I'm not coming home? How will I tell him? Will he use his power as king to force me to come home?*

A moment later, a whole new, fresh set of thoughts ran wild. *What's Sam going to do about it? He can't do anything. My powers are strong enough to fight any demand he'll make for me to return to Grayham. I'll use my magic to stay where I'm loved and not looked at as if I'm a failure. He doesn't truly want me, anyway.*

"Shalee... hey, are you okay?"

"I'm sorry. I was just thinking of how I'm going to tell Sam I'm not coming home. I want to stay here and be with you!"

"Are you serious?"

"I am! I can't believe this is happening."

"Nor can I, but this news makes me an extremely happy man!"

"Will you love me if I stay on Luvelles?"

"I already do... and always will."

Shalee pushed into him. "Then show me how much."

Kiayasis stood, lifted her up and moved to a small pile of furs he had laid out on the beach. He kissed her softly while respecting the boundaries she had set. He rubbed the small of her back until she was sound asleep.

Kiayasis slowly pulled away, quietly put on his shirt and began walking along the beach. When enough moments had passed to put a considerable distance between himself and the camp, he removed a small mirror, about the size of his palm.

He spoke to it as if alive. "Find my father." Eventually the image of Boyafed appeared.

"Kiayasis, my son, how are things going on your journey?"

"It has gone well, but Joss was injured."

"Yes, I know, I have received word. He should heal quickly. I wouldn't worry about him. He's one of the finest Krape Lords in my army."

Boyafed could see the concern on Kiayasis's face. "What bothers you?"

"Father... the woman I travel with is a good woman. She's done nothing to deserve the end you've ordered me to give her. She is kind, and this isn't an order I wish to carry out."

Boyafed sighed. "If you were any other man, I would have you beaten for questioning me. This isn't an order I've given lightly. This was a request from our lord, Hosseff. Who are we to question his wishes?"

"But I love her!"

"You what? How could you fall in love with a woman you've been ordered to kill? How could you allow yourself to become so blind, so gullible? What's wrong with you, boy?"

"Father, I know you're angry, but—"

"But nothing... she's a queen! Her king would not allow her to stay with you. Even if it were possible for you to be with her, you cannot! She doesn't have elven blood. The Head Master would not allow her to stay. You must honor Hosseff and fulfill your order. Our lord requested you for this mission! You should feel honored!"

"Please... can't you speak with Hosseff? Maybe—"

Boyafed shouted over the top of him. "Kiayasis, you have a job to do! I won't bother Hosseff with my son's inability to follow orders."

Kiayasis lowered his head. "I don't wish to shame you, Father. I will carry out my order and ensure Hosseff is pleased with my actions."

"That's better! I knew you would come to your senses. I'm proud of you, son. I'll be sure to reward you well. Now, finish your task. Did you retrieve the Knife of Spirits from Gorne while in Bestep?"

"I did."

"Then you're nearly done. When the queen has finished her task within Grogger's Swamp, use the knife to temporarily steal her powers. The knife isn't meant to kill. You must cut across her abdomen. Once this is done, you'll be able to finish her from there."

"I won't fail you, Father!"

"I know. You're my son, the son of a Methelborn. I couldn't be any prouder of how you've turned out."

"Thank you, Father."

"We'll speak again soon. I'm going to grab some ale with Dayden. Goodbye, boy."

The mirror went dark. Kiayasis fell to his knees, his heart heavy... he began to cry.

The Luvelles Gazette
When you want an update about your favorite characters

Just Before Late Bailem, The Next Day

Shalee and Kiayasis have arrived at the entrance to Grogger's Swamp. She plans to enter the swamp in the morning. Kiayasis plans to set camp and wait for her return. As they sit beside the fire, Shalee calls Kiayasis, baby.

Kepler and Payne are still waiting for George to come out of his state of unconsciousness. Payne used his magic to move the sleeping mage into his current position. Since then, Kepler has been acting as a giant cushion and has allowed George to rest against him. A few wandering creatures from inside the maze have attacked, but Payne slew them quickly.

Athena, Mary, and Susanne are currently at home, but plan to use the Scroll of Teleportation to visit the City of Nept in the morning.

Boyafed is inside the Order's temple. He plans to meet with Marcus. The Dark Chancellor has requested his presence and will be leaving soon.

Gregory Id has returned home from the king of Lavan's Passing Ceremony. He plans to attend the meeting Lord Dowd has called with his military leaders. It is to be held at Late Bailem tomorrow. With the unexpected slaying of the king, he feels Lord Dowd will have no choice but to call for war.

Mieonus is inside her home on Ancients Sovereign. She has been watching Shalee and Kiayasis's relationship develop. The goddess enjoyed the order given to Kiayasis by Boyafed and looks forward to the sorceress's misery once she has been cut by the Knife of Spirits. But something unexpected has happened and now the goddess is anticipating a potentially larger confrontation. A new player has joined the game and has learned Shalee and Kiayasis's location. This bold figure has tracked them down and is watching from a distance, close enough to hear Shalee and Kiayasis's conversation. Mieonus could only smile when she heard Shalee use the word, 'baby.'

Mosley plans to attend Lord Dowd's meeting.

Brayson plans to travel to Mogg's Village. He needs to speak with the visionary about many of the current events which have recently transpired.

Gage and the other Goswigs within the hidden underground village of Goswayne are hard at work. Strongbear has been relentless with his order to finish their new lake. Everyone was with the big brown bear and not against him.

Marcus is standing over a man's dead body. This was the last person who needed to be killed. War is sure to follow once Boyafed hears the news.

Lasidious and Celestria are inside their home beneath the Peaks of Angels. Celestria is nervous about Mosley and Alistar's investigation into the fact that they are up to something larger than the game for the pieces of the Crystal Moon.

Thank you for reading the Luvelles Gazette

Chapter 16

A Secret Revealed

Lasidious and Celestria's Home
Beneath the Peaks of Angels

Celestria paced back and forth in front of the fireplace with green flames within their cave-like home far beneath the Peaks of Angels.

"They're going to figure things out. Alistar has been snooping around and Mosley is too smart to keep our secret from him. It's just a matter of moments now. Between the two of them, they're going to find out about our son!"

Lasidious stood from his chair next to the heavy stone table and moved to take hold of her. With a hand on each shoulder he looked into her beautiful blue eyes and spoke in a soft, relaxed voice. "Take a deep breath."

"How can I? We're going to be made mortal. Once they discover Garrin's existence, they'll kill our son and then our end will be no better than Yaloom's."

Lasidious pulled her close. "I have things under control. You worry too much. There's nothing for them to find out—there's no reason for them to look for Garrin. Mosley doesn't have any idea we're willing to go against the Book's law and have a child."

"How can you be so sure? The wolf is clever... and Alistar will find out, if Mosley doesn't!"

"None of the others would ever guess we're foolish enough to go against the Book of Immortality's power! Alistar and Mosley are looking for something sinister, not something that cries and soils a diaper."

"But—"

"But nothing... everything is under control. Mosley's attention is now focused on Luvelles. With both the Dark and White Paladin Armies resting on the brink of war, he has no choice but to focus on his duties as the God of War. He must ensure that the leaders of these armies choose war over a diplomatic resolution."

"What about Alistar? He has the moments necessary on his hands to look for something to cause us problems."

Lasidious began to laugh.

"What's so funny?"

"Alistar isn't a threat."

"What do you mean? How can you be so sure he won't find anything? He isn't stupid. He's every bit as smart as Mosley, and we've already had to dance around that wolf's snout being stuck in places we don't want it to be."

"There's something you don't know about Alistar."

"I think I know plenty. I have known him for well over 13,000— or maybe it's been over 14,000 seasons—now."

"Yes, and who was he with when you met him?"

"He was with you, so what does that mean?"

Lasidious pulled out a chair from the table and motioned for his evil lover to take a seat. Celestria tucked her cherry red-colored gown between her legs before sitting.

Lasidious also sat before continuing. "It was the two of us who decided to recruit you to join the collective. We both wanted you to fight with us and help to put an end to the God Wars. When the Farendrite Collective was first formed, it was Alistar and me who started it."

"Yes... I know all this, but what're you getting at?"

"Well… there's a big secret Alistar and I have kept from all the gods. I have also kept this secret from you."

"Me, why me? I thought we shared everything."

"We do... well, almost everything."

"This better be good. To say I'm a little angry right now is an understatement!"

Lasidious smiled. "You won't be mad for long. I'm sure you'll find this very intriguing."

"So spit it out already!"

Lasidious leaned back in his seat. "What I'm about to tell you needs to be under the Rule of Fromalla."

"What? Why would I need to enter into the Pact of Fromalla with you? I'm your lover, not your enemy!"

"I'll explain everything once you've agreed."

"This better be really good. Okay, so I agree to the damn rule. Fromalla it is, but this better be the explanation above all other explanations or you'll be spending the rest of your existence without me in your bed!"

"There's no need for threats. I assure you, you'll be quite happy when I'm done."

"So get on with it!"

Lasidious took a deep breath and leaned forward across the table. "Alistar and I have known each other since birth. We're brothers!"

Celestria gasped. She sat back in her chair and turned to look into the green flames, watching them dance within the fireplace. After many moments passed, she turned and found her evil lover's eyes. "This is an enormous secret! I'm not sure what to say."

"Allow me to explain why I didn't tell you."

"Please do, because I'm feeling betrayed."

"I understand how you could feel that way, but I assure you there's a reason. You see, after Alistar and I put the idea of the Farendrite Collective together, we realized it would be easier to get others to join us if we were selling the idea that a perfect balance of good and evil was necessary for the survival of those who fought together during the wars. It was also necessary for the creation of new worlds, since everything was being destroyed with each battle that passed. With the destruction of both Heaven and Hell, it was more important than ever to create a group that represented both sides. Evil and Good had to be a part of the collective, and it was an easy sell to make the others see this.

"Both of us knew we weren't powerful enough to live through the wars if we only fought side by side. We needed help and there were a few gods we had our eye on to join our little collective. But since both of us were evil, one of us had to take on the role of being good. We agreed to never tell anyone. We couldn't afford the secret to get out, since it would ruin our chances to have any kind of an advantage over those we intended to recruit."

Celestria stood and shouted, "So I was a piece of your game? I suppose you think this is okay with me?"

"No, no, no... you're wrong to think that way. Alistar and I never intended to recruit you. In fact, I never knew you existed until we met each other in your father's heavenly Kingdom of Challic. It was your father we intended to recruit, but he was destroyed before we could approach him. When we arrived, all we found floating in space was your unconscious figure among the debris. Your father had to be powerful, to keep you from perishing!"

Celestria began to cry. "My father was extremely powerful. He could have easily defeated his attackers if it wasn't for his desire to protect me. I'm the only reason he was caught in a bad position. His destruction was because of me... I miss him so much."

Lasidious gave her a moment to collect herself. "The strength of your father's power was the reason we planned to recruit him. It was only after I laid eyes on you that I convinced my brother to allow me to bring you into our group. If you remember right, Bassorine and Mieonus had already joined the collective by that moment. I can remember being taken by your beauty. I approached you only because I wanted to know you and learn who you were. The fact that you were evil was only a bonus."

Celestria wiped the tears from her face. "So how does all this fit into our plans, and how does this get us to where we are now?"

"Great questions... you see, Alistar and I knew Bassorine was powerful enough that with the assistance of a small group at his side, we could handle anything that threatened us while the God Wars continued. All we had to do was continue to put together a team that would easily defeat all those who opposed us.

"But Alistar and I agreed we had a hurdle to jump. We knew Bassorine was going to become a problem once the wars were over. He was too strong to overpower, and all of us would be required to live by his rules. We agreed to manipulate the others within the collective into thinking that the creation of the Book of Immortality was a good idea. There were enough of us that Bassorine would have to consider the concept."

"Why?" Celestria said, interrupting.

"Because if Bassorine were to fight against the Book's creation, he would be alone after he destroyed us all, and he knew it. He would be alone within the vast expanse of an empty universe with no one to talk to, no one to love and no one to serve him. He would be miserable.

"Once the others were on board with the Book's creation, Alistar and I decided to give Bassorine the confidence that his sword would be able to destroy the Book. We did this for two reasons. The first was to give him peace of mind about its creation and the second was to protect us from the Book if the moment ever came where we needed to destroy it."

Celestria stood from the table and spoke in a tone Lasidious had not heard for nearly 3000 seasons. "You lie... I was there when the others had the conversation about the weaknesses the Book of Immortality would have. Do you think I'm stupid?"

"No, of course not... do you think I'm foolish enough to lie to you now with all we've done, not to mention with as far as we've come? You know I can't lie to you. You made sure of that. We are closer now than ever to having complete control over the others. Just think about it, Celestria. Who brought up the idea of the Book's creation in the first place?"

Lasidious watched as her expression changed. "Alistar... it was Alistar. You're telling me the two of you knew before the creation of the Book that you planned to use it against Bassorine to kill him?"

"I am!"

"But why... you only bound yourself to the rules agreed upon by the gods when the Book became more powerful than us all. You created something stronger than Bassorine."

"Yes, but we created something with a limited amount of power. We created something neutral and with no alignment to either good or evil. We created a being whose only desire is to do the job assigned to him by the gods. Gabriel was the balance we needed until we could put our plans into effect.

"Our baby will be strong enough to take control of the Book. With Alistar working with us, we'll be able to keep the others from learning of our little deception. Garrin will be able to grow without fear of death."

Lasidious moved to pull Celestria to him, but she held up her hand. "How could you have known I would be willing to have your child?"

"I didn't know how you would react. This baby was a backup plan and you were the only piece of the puzzle I had to figure out in order to implement a second plan. All I knew was that I wanted you. I knew you had a piece of my evil heart and I was willing to do anything to be with you. I took a big risk drinking the potion you gave me many seasons ago. I knew it would stop me from lying to you, but you were worth it. Alistar and I both felt that my desire to love you would win your affections. We hoped you would avoid asking me anything that would reveal our relationship as brothers. We also hoped you would grow to love me, and you did. Together, you and I have given birth to a baby who'll take control of the Book. The other plan Alistar and I have cooked up is also being implemented and will soon be known to the gods.

"You know your potion keeps me from lying to you. You know I'm telling you the truth. Now you can relax and know our son is going to be okay. There's nothing to worry about. Alistar is going to keep Mosley busy. The wolf won't have the moments necessary to figure anything out."

Celestria pulled him close. She held his eyes in hers before asking more questions. "Since my potion won't allow you to lie, I want to know if you and Alistar have plans to dispose of me after our child is in control of the Book."

Lasidious laughed. "No, of course not. I told you how I feel! You know what the plan is! I will also explain all the details of our backup plan, as well."

"Do you really love me?"

"Yes, of course I do!"

"Then why are we talking when we should be having fun?" The goddess cupped his face in her hands and kissed him gently. Lasidious trembled with excitement.

"You can explain more once you have apologized to me properly." She took him by the hand and smiled. "I want you to take me on a date and I want you to be clever!"

The Dark Chancellor's Tower-Palace,
The City of Marcus

Marcus appeared inside his large bedroom chamber within his tower-palace. He was in a hurry and needed to meet with Boyafed in the dining hall. His servants had prepared a hot bath. The blood covering his body needed to be removed and he had to change to a clean robe before joining the dark paladin leader for dinner.

Eventually Marcus appeared and moved to take a seat. Boyafed had already arrived and had taken it upon himself to sit at the head of the table.

Boyafed smiled, knowing full well his choice of seats would irritate Marcus, but the Chancellor, despite his anger about Boyafed's nerve, decided to handle the situation with humility. He had come to this meeting with an agenda.

"Good evening, Boyafed."

"What do you want, Marcus? Why am I sitting here having dinner with you? I have better things to do with my evening."

Marcus shook his head as if frustrated and lowered his pipe from his mouth. "You and I have clearly started out on the wrong path. We've irritated one another for so many seasons now. I wish to call a truce. I wish to apologize for speaking to you without the respect you deserve. I understand you're the heart and soul of this city, and without you, the strength of this city would pale in comparison. I need to give you the same respect your men do. I owe you this much. I want to let you know I intend to work with you from here on out."

Boyafed pondered his words before responding. "These are words I never expected from your lips. What happened to cause such a change of heart?"

"I have realized if I'm to achieve my full potential as a leader, I need to find an example and strive to better myself. I see the men and how they treat you. I see how powerful you are. I want to feel respect from those I command, as you do."

Boyafed stood and moved next to the hearth of a cold fireplace. The dining hall was large and his voice echoed as he responded.

"Your goal is admirable and I accept your apology. Please take your seat at the table's head. Consider this my first act of our new agreement."

Marcus moved to take his seat. He smiled and gestured his appreciation before signaling the servants to bring them their food. There's big news coming your way, Boyafed, he thought. *I'm sure you won't be so arrogant when your men find the body of your best friend, Dayden, your precious Argont Commander!*

Mogg's Village

Brayson now stood just outside a tiny little hole which acted as the entrance to Mogg's tree. The sprite had lived for nearly 300 seasons within this ancient haspelyan spruce. All of Mogg's kind had made their homes within this small community of hollowed trees and were buzzing around, anxiously watching him.

Mogg - And her family of Sprites

The Head Master knew his presence was a threat to this tiny race of beings, but he was here for a specific reason and this reason outweighed their anxiety. Mogg was the only creature on Luvelles to master the magic of the past and Brayson needed this magic to gather the knowledge he desired.

When Mogg finally returned from her outing to gather the village's dinner for the evening, she was with two companions. All three sprites struggled to carry a single blushel berry through the trees and eventually, they managed to place it on the ground. They were breathing heavy and had worked tirelessly for most of the day to pick just this one piece of fruit from a nearby bush. The berry was only an inch and a half in diameter, but still it managed to cause a fair amount of stress.

Mogg instantly recognized their large elven visitor and flew into a hovering position only feet in front of Brayson's face. Her wings hummed rapidly back and forth while many dazzling colors fell from them in a shimmering glitter that dissipated prior to reaching the ground. It wasn't long before Brayson had hundreds of these tiny one-inch-high beings hovering all around him.

"When have you come for, Head Master?" Mogg said, her voice small and high-pitched.

"I need your help."

"I didn't say *why*, wizard. I said... *when!*"

"I don't understand."

"I know you seek knowledge of the past. I know you desire my help. When are the moments from which you seek answers?"

"I seek to know the truth of a friend's death. The moments of when this happened are still unclear to me. I do know it's been nearly half a season."

"What can you offer for my help?"

"I don't know... what do you want for helping me?"

Brayson watched as Mogg's eyes moved away from his and began to follow a beautiful red and yellow butterfly. The entire village of sprites began to follow it as if hypnotized by the fluttering of its wings. Brayson snapped his fingers to capture their attention. He knew the sprites were notorious for their short attention spans and their insatiable love for butterflies.

"Mogg, please don't lose focus. I need your help."

"I apologize... they are beautiful, yes?"

"They are... now what can I offer you that would help your village?"

"We need to gather berries. Your magic is strong. You could gather them for us. Your magic will protect them from rotting. My family would be spared such hard labor. If you do this but only once a season, I will help you."

"You want me to pick berries?"

"Yes... it's a hard task for us, but you are large and it will be easy for you."

"I'll pick your berries, but only this once. I'll pick enough to fill a single tree. I'll protect this tree with my magic and keep them from rotting. If you don't agree to this, say so now and I'll leave."

Mogg thought a moment. She knew even a single treeful would feed their village for at least two seasons. "These terms are acceptable. I'll help you with the answers you seek, once the task has been completed."

Brayson bent over and picked up the berry off the ground. He held it between two fingers and dropped it into the tiny hole of Mogg's tree. "I'll return in the morning and begin filling the tree of your choice. I hope you enjoy your dinner." He vanished.

Grogger's Swampland,
The Next Morning Before Early Bailem

Shalee and Kiayasis stopped the night before just beyond the outskirts of Grogger's Swamp. Camp had been set and after a wonderful night of strong-armed embraces, Shalee smiled as she finished her breakfast. Kiayasis's advances were becoming increasingly harder to resist. She now found herself desiring to do more, but this desire had been held at bay.

The morning air carried a chill. The sky was growing angry and threatened to make Shalee's entrance into the swamp miserable. Lightning filled the sky in the distance and the wind was slowly increasing in force. From the far side of the fire, Kiayasis tossed another log into the flames and resumed his early morning tasks.

"I've been thinking about making a few changes in my life. I get tired of constantly sharpening this knife," Kiayasis said, stroking the blade of his bone-handled dagger across the stone's coarse surface. "I'm always living by the rules of my father's army. He always says... 'You can't carry a dull blade, son!' Maybe the moment has come for me to move on and settle down."

Shalee didn't respond. Her attention was elsewhere.

"Shalee... did you hear me?"

"It looks so dark... so dreary... so ugly!"

"What does?"

"The swamp... it's feels like I'm about to go into some kind of cemetery. It looks haunted."

"What do you mean, 'some kind of cemetery,' what's that?"

"Oh, I apologize. I forget I'm not home anymore. I know you burn the dead to celebrate their passing, but where I'm from, a cemetery is a place where we bury the bodies of the people who've died. We put them in the ground and cover them with dirt."

"Why would you do something like that? Doesn't this dishonor the dead? And exactly where are you from, anyway? You say it as if it isn't Grayham."

"I'm not originally from Grayham. The place I'm from is called Earth and many of us had a belief that a person's body would rise again when our god came back to collect his faithful. We laid the dead facing east so that when they rose again, the first thing they would see was our lord's face as he came for us. I can only imagine what that would've been like."

Kiayasis set the dagger down. "Do you still have this belief?"

"No... now I'm finding my beliefs are lost to me. I had faith once, a strong faith, or at least as strong as it could be, considering my upbringing."

"What do you mean by upbringing?"

"I mean how I was raised. The problem is that after coming to these worlds and seeing the things I've seen, I'm not so sure I believe in much of anything any longer. I find it strange to believe in gods that are so flawed, so imperfect, so opposite of the concept I used to believe in. A god is supposed to be perfect. In my mind, they should be an all-knowing entity, a figurehead worth praising and now, well... I suppose that now I think it's all just a big crock of garesh."

Kiayasis sighed and shook his head with disappointment. "Then you haven't served the one true god. Hosseff is powerful and he is all-knowing... just as you said a god should be. He possesses power beyond our comprehension and you would be wise to serve him!"

Shalee began to laugh uncontrollably. Kiayasis instantly felt uncomfortable and lifted his eyes toward the sky as if worried Hosseff would strike her down. After a moment of the dark paladin questioning why she found his statements to be so humorous, she calmed down and responded.

"I'm sorry, but I think it would be best if we changed the subject. I don't wish to offend you about your beliefs."

"Fair enough—I feel the same way. Why don't you tell me why you left this Earth of yours?"

Shalee looked at the swamp's entrance and again her mind began to wander.

"Shalee, I asked you a question! Shalee... Shalee, where are you... hey, I'm over here."

Struggling to pull her eyes away from the fog, she said, "It just hangs there, threatening to suck me in." Chilled, she eventually managed to find Kiayasis's glare. "I'm sorry, but it just looks so evil."

"I wouldn't worry about it. The swamp always looks like this. I would be more worried about what's inside if I were you. I would go in with you, but my orders are to allow you to go in alone. I can't go any farther."

"Is this your way of cheering me up? How could someone be so cute and so ignorant at the same moment?"

Kiayasis smiled. "You're right. I wasn't thinking. Let's talk of other things. Tell me why you left your Earth."

"Because I had no choice. I was—"

Kiayasis interrupted. "We always have a choice. Choices are what make us who we are. Choices give us character."

"Ha... if only that were true. You think you know, but you don't. We don't always have a—"

Kiayasis stopped her. "We always have a choice. I recently have had to make one of the hardest choices of my life. I think you'll like what I have to tell you. The—"

Shalee decided to return the favor and cut him off as he had done to her. "You don't even know what a hard choice is. Everything was taken from me and, no... we don't always have a choice in what happens to us! Things just happen! They get forced on us, and... and... oh! You're making me mad! You know what? You're not really scoring too many points with me right now!"

Kiayasis tilted his head as if confused. "Points, what points?"

"Hmph... men... just forget it. Like I was saying before you so rudely interrupted, I had no choice. I was taken from my home by the gods. Did you hear that? I said... THE GODS! They gave me no choice in the matter!"

"I'm sorry, please continue. I would love to hear how the gods took you away from your Earth! I won't say another word!"

"Good... that would be the best thing for you to do right now!"

After a long, awkward moment of silence, she finally continued.

"This just chaps my hide. As I was saying... I had no choice in the matter! I was stolen from my home, MY EARTH... and placed on Grayham with Sam. We were asked to do so many horrible things, I still have nightmares because of them. I have killed so much and so has Sam. Life here has been stressful for us. I would've never chosen to leave my family and neither would Sam, no matter what we were offered to come here. I never wanted to be put in a position where I had to kill anyone. I can only imagine how Sam must have felt... oh, my gosh... how he must be feeling!"

Shalee lowered her eyes. Tears began to slowly roll down her cheeks. Kiayasis moved to sit beside her, but she refused to be comforted and stood quickly to move away.

"Oh no... what am I doing? How could I be so selfish?"

"What are you talking about? You're not being selfish. You said yourself, your king has treated you poorly. You have only done what was right for—"

"Right for who?" she shouted. "Is this really what's right for me?"

Kiayasis stood and moved to her. "Of course this is what's right for you. It's what's right for us. I have decided to leave my father's army for you. I believe we could have an incredible life together.

I can build us a wonderful home. My father's army isn't a healthy way to begin a life together, anyway. I love you, Shalee!"

Shalee shook her head. "No, Kiayasis! Don't say that!" Tears ran freely. Her voice trembled and filled with an uncontrollable sobbing as she continued. "Sam... oh my heavens, Sam has done nothing wrong. I've betrayed him. How could I be so awful... so selfish? This is not how a queen should act. How can I lead others if I cannot even lead myself?"

Kiayasis cut in. "You won't need to lead others. This is about you and me! You said your king loathed you. You said he looked down his nose at you!"

"I know what I said," she snapped, "but he never actually said those things. I only felt like he viewed me that way. This is all my fault!"

Shalee moved to her bag and put on the pair of pants she had created with her magic. She pulled them up beneath her dress and began to walk in the opposite direction, away from the swamp. Kiayasis pursued and after grabbing hold of her sweater-covered arms, turned her around to face him. "What about us?"

"Kiayasis... aren't you listening to me? How could you ask me a question like that? I need to think! Leave me alone so I can gather my thoughts!"

"Leave you alone... *no*... I won't do that! You have said things you just can't take back. You have allowed me to hold you in my arms! I respected your boundaries and it was the best thing I've ever done. You can't just let a man tell you he loves you and then walk away! What kind of a woman would that make you?"

Shalee stopped and with a harsh voice began to scold Kiayasis. She lifted her arm and with one finger extended, began to move it back and forth. "I don't know! Why don't you tell me what kind of woman it makes me! I've already done it once. I left Sam and he told me he loved me. In fact, his final words before I left were... 'Come home when you're ready. Just remember... I will always love you, no matter what!' So tell me, Kiayasis, what kind of a woman does that make me?"

Kiayasis stood in silence. Shalee could see he was at a loss for words. She continued. "The problem is self-created. I was too self-absorbed. I felt guilty for losing our child and now... I've thrown everything away... and for what? For—"

Kiayasis now shouted back at her. "Go ahead... say it! You would be throwing away your life for someone like me. You don't think I'm good enough, do you?"

Shalee took a long, hard deep breath. "It's my fault... this is all my fault! If I hadn't been so selfish, I would never—"

"What, Shalee... you would never care for me? You would never have said the things you have to me? How do you expect me to react to this?"

"I don't know! But we cannot continue this relationship. It's wrong and both of us know it!"

Kiayasis fell to his knees. Shalee moved to stand in front of him—she could feel his pain. The sorceress put her left hand on his right shoulder and spoke with a tender voice. "I believe we could have been a good couple. I do love you, but I should return home once I'm done here and beg Sam for his forgiveness."

Kiayasis mumbled something beneath his breath.

"I didn't understand you. Kiayasis, please don't make this harder than it already is. What did you say? Come on... let's not be like this with one another."

The dark paladin quickly grasped the Knife of Spirits and slashed hard across Shalee's exposed abdomen. He stood quickly, kicking her to the ground. He shouted as he watched her raise her hand to use her magic. "I said you've made this decision easy for me! You're a fool. You should never have turned your back on me!"

The sorceress began to scoot backward, away from her attacker, the pain shooting through her entire body with every little movement. She continued to hold her hand extended toward him, but the magic wouldn't come when summoned. Kiayasis began to taunt his new prey.

"Ahhhhhhh... your magic has left you! I will give you a headstart. I want this killing to have some sport."

"Why? Why would you do this?" she screamed. She pushed hard against the wound to ease the pain.

"I think you know the answer to your own stupid question, Shalee. You are clearly a tease. I would have expected this sort of rejection from a common wench... but you... you've hurt me deeper than any other. I'm going to show you the meaning of pain. I'm going to kill you! I suggest you run!"

Kiayasis turned and walked over to the fire of their camp. Once Shalee's blood was wiped from the Knife of Spirit's blade, he sat down and continued to sharpen his dagger.

Shalee struggled to stand. She had to hunch over in order to keep from ripping the wound open further. Her white pants were absorbing the blood as it ran down her legs. She tried to use her magic again, but the power failed to flow through her. She had no choice... she needed to escape. Kiayasis watched as she hobbled towards the forest in the distance.

Chapter 17

𝕿raitor

The Void Maze, The Source's Temple

Kepler was sound asleep when George finally woke in the field just outside the Source's Temple. The demon-jaguar had figured out a way to remove Payne's tiny red body from the cage that had collapsed beneath his weight, and Payne had used his magic to move George against Kepler's hairy body. The little guy had also managed to kill a few more wandering strays which attacked as soon as they exited the maze dungeon.

They wanted George to be comfortable and warm and Kepler had stayed put, refusing to move until the mage recovered. Payne was the first to see the color of George's blue eyes. He flew over and held up a piece of one of the small creatures George had killed just over a day and a half ago.

"Master hungry? Payne cooks it like kitty say to! It's meat."

Kepler opened his eyes and rolled his head to look over the top of his shoulder. "It's about time you woke up. How're you feeling?"

George took a minute to gather his thoughts. He leaned back against Kepler's black fur and stretched. "I feel like I've been hit by a train."

"What a train?" Payne said, plopping down on George's lap.

"Don't start, freak! Let him breathe a moment and get off him!"

"Fine... geesh," the fairy-demon responded and began to pout.

George managed to get to his feet. He took the piece of meat from Payne's claw and took a bite. "I'm starved. I could eat a horse. Thanks for allowing me to lie against you, Kep."

Kepler stretched before responding. "You're welcome, but

please, please, don't start with the hugs again. I know that's what you're thinking and you don't need to show me your appreciation."

George had to laugh. "Okay... I won't. Don't worry, big guy."

"Good! Can we get on with things, and why are you looking at me that way? What are you grinning for?"

George turned and his smile grew as he looked at the fairy-demon. "Payne."

"What, Master?"

George turned and gave Kepler an evil grin. "Payne, I want you to hug Kepler for me."

"Bah... dang it George, keep that freak away from me!"

"Come to Payne, kitty."

"George... stop him, this isn't funny. I'm going to have to kill someone in a moment."

Kepler began to run to avoid Payne's advances. "Don't run, kitty. Kitty, come back to Payne. Master said got to hug kitty."

"GEORGE… George. I swear I'll pay you back for this!"

The Underground City of Goswigs

Gage removed the harness. His fur was covered in dirt and the removal of the earth necessary to create Strongbear's new lake was beginning to wear on his patience. He was tired of hearing the brown bear shout his favorite phrase. *"So are you with me... or are you against me?"* Gage was feeling like he was now against him.

The badger had been working with Gallrum at his side, along with many of the other Goswigs. They were all just as irritable as he was and it was the perfect moments for a break.

Gage climbed to the top of a large boulder and plopped down by his personal basket of food. He brushed aside the colorful cloth which Strongbear had placed over the top of it and reached in. The large bear had provided each Goswig with a lunch of their own, each holding their favorite flavors. After a few bites of freshly cooked Corgan beef, he finally lifted his head and motioned for Gallrum to join him.

The Serwin flapped his wings and made his way over to the top of the rock. Once he had lowered into a partially-coiled position next to Gage, Gallrum spoke as he reached into his basket and retrieved a bowl of fresh fish eyes.

"I can't be sure, but I think every scale on my body is sore." He lifted the bowl to his mouth. A long, thin, snake-like tongue shot out and scooped up one of the eyes. "Would you like some?" he mumbled with his mouth full.

Gage turned up his nose. "I'd rather not."

"You just don't know what you're missing!"

Gage secured a tin full of water between his paws and took a drink. "You know... I've been doing some thinking."

Gallrum slurped up another eye and hissed a response. "Oh yeah, what about?"

"The other day you said something about Strongbear hibernating when the season changed. I assume you mean that when winter comes, he goes into his cave and sleeps."

"Yep... oohhh, mmmmmm... you've got to try one of these!"

"Gallrum .. pay attention. I have an idea that will benefit us all."

The Serwin swallowed the eye, and then burped it back up. "Oops... guess I didn't chew that one up enough."

The badger fought the need to gag and after a moment of Gallrum looking at him like his reaction was misunderstood, he decided to put his disgust aside and continued.

"I was thinking that Strongbear has accumulated enough fat, he can now start his hibernation."

"I agree, but the season hasn't changed. It isn't cold enough for him to sleep yet."

"Yes, I know, but I have a solution to this problem. There are enough of us living here within our underground hideaway that if we all concentrate and combine our magic, we could create a change of season."

"Ha, ha, ha, you expect us to change the seasons of all Luvelles? Only the gods can do such things."

"No... not on Luvelles. I simply want to change the season here."

"You mean change the weather just within our village?"

"Yes, this is exactly what I mean! Once we cool it down around here, Strongbear will begin his hibernation and he won't be able to boss everyone around."

"This is brilliant!" Gallrum's wings began to flap. He lifted from the stone and hovered to a position eye-level with Gage. "How do we inform the others without Strongbear finding out about it? I would hate to see how a bear of that size would react."

The badger took another bite of Corgan beef and thought a moment. "How often do you go topside and speak with Swill?"

"Every seventh day... I must be standing on the shores of Crystal Lake just after sunset. Swill swims up from the Ultorian city and takes a report from me back to their king. It's my job to inform him about any significant events which may transpire within our village."

"Well, who goes in your place when you're sick?"

"Strongbear does, of course." Gallrum began to grin. "Aahhhh... you want to do it when I'm sick. You want to have our meeting while he's reporting to Swill."

Gage chuckled, "I think you're catching on. When's your next report?"

"Tomorrow night... there's going to be one problem with tomorrow, though."

"And?"

"I don't feel sick... how can Strongbear go if I'm not sick?"

Gage growled! "You pretend, you fake it, you act sick! Do I have to spell it all out for you?"

"Aahhhh, I can do that. This could be fun. You know... I've always pictured myself as a thespian."

Gage grinned as he enjoyed the thought of Strongbear's future slumber. "So are you with me... or are you against me?"

"Oh, I'm with you alright!"

Both Goswigs began to laugh uncontrollably.

Mogg's Village in the Trees

Brayson made his way back from the blushel berry bushes not far from Mogg's village. The sprite had chosen a tree just behind her personal residence for Brayson to fill with the sweet fruit. He had filled two baskets with thousands of berries, and judging by the size of the hallowed hole within this tree, a single trip would be more than sufficient to fill it.

Many of Mogg's tiny family surrounded Brayson as he sauntered into their village. Their excitement could be heard as their voices cried out in song. Many glorious showers of sparkling colors fell from their wings and dissipated just prior to hitting the ground.

Brayson stopped in front of the tree which had been designated to hold the fruit and waved his hand across its surface. The small hole opened up, allowing the Head Master to pour the berries inside. Once the task was complete and the spell had been cast to protect the fruit, the hole reduced to its normal size and Brayson moved to stand near Mogg's tree.

The tiny sprite emerged and hovered in front of him. "Follow me, wizard."

"To where?"

"No... not where... when! Follow me to your when!"

"How do I follow you to the past?"

Mogg shook her small head. "You ask many questions, wizard. How is it you talk so much and still manage to learn? Just follow me... you'll see. Your when is about to become your now."

"But how do you know what when I seek?"

"I always know, wizard... stop talking now and follow me!"

The other fairies quickly flew away and disappeared within their holes. Brayson followed as she began to fly slowly through the trees. He watched as the scenery changed before his eyes. When finally the images slowed down, the daylight had faded away and a barn, or rather a large shed, now stood in front of them in the dark of night.

"This is your when, Head Master."

"How can you be so sure? Where are we? When are we?"

"Your when is the night of your friend's death. Your where is on the World of Grayham. This place is a smith's barn, near a place of champions. I think the answer you seek is walking this way."

"Can they see us?"

"No, wizard, we aren't truly a part of this when. We can only observe."

Brayson turned and looked down the gravel road. It was too dark to make out the figures at first, but as they grew closer, the torches lighting the road eventually showed their faces. The City of Champion's gates were brightly lit in the distance and to his surprise, walking toward him, alive and well, was Amar. But someone unexpected was with him—someone he would have never imagined to see at this particular moment. It was George, his new Mystic-Learner.

"Mogg, are you sure this is the when I'm seeking? I don't think this is it. The other man shouldn't be here."

"Yes, I'm sure, wizard. Just watch, see, instead of talk. My magic to seek out moments is strong. I have brought you to the right when."

"Can they see us?"

Mogg giggled. An increase of sparkling colors fell from her wings as she did so. "You have already asked me this! You lack so much intelligence for such a powerful elf!"

Brayson ignored the sprite's tone and moved in close to listen to the conversation. Both men stopped in front of the smith's barn. George started the conversation.

"I need a hammer from inside. Amar, why don't you use some of your hocus pocus to unlock this?"

Brayson watched as Amar laughed and held up his staff. He spoke the simple command and the lock released. Both men entered and Brayson was quick to follow them inside. George took a seat on a wooden bench near the forge and continued their conversation.

"Sometimes I feel like I'm going crazy. I miss my family, Amar. I want to tell you something. When I first met you, I didn't like you very much, but I've really grown fond of you over the last few days. You remind me of my uncle back home, and I really need someone I can trust in my life. I was wondering if you needed a friend, and how you felt about being friends with me. If you don't want to... hey, I'll understand and I'm really sorry I've bothered you."

Brayson watched as George began to cry. He moved to a better position and waited for Amar's response. He watched as his friend sat next to George on the bench.

"I don't have any problems with being your friend. I would actually prefer to travel this way and I have also wanted this as well, but I've had my doubts. I didn't think you cared for me much. I'm surprised at your request. What made you decide this?"

Brayson knew something wasn't right. He wanted to say something as George hugged Amar and continued talking.

"I've been so alone since my arrival here. I can't tell you how grateful I am that we'll be friends. It makes me happy to know I won't be lonely any longer. I have some news for you that will make you happy as well, my new friend."

"What kind of news?"

"Well, it's like this. I know where you can gain a significant amount of power above what you already command. I know of your power, Amar. I also know this woman will increase your power if you seek her out and take it away from her."

Brayson was floored and his elven ears couldn't believe what he was hearing.

"How do you know of my power? I have said nothing of it."

"I'm a smart man, Amar. Now that we're friends, I'll tell you her name if you want to know it. This is my way of showing you that it's my true desire to be your buddy."

"George! This is valuable information you're giving me. I definitely would like to know her name."

"Friends for life, right? Let's take this foursome all the way until we rule this world!"

"I agree the four of us will dominate."

This is a trap, Brayson thought. He stood close so he could see George's eyes, but they held no sign of deception. *What are you up to, George? I can see through your smile.* He was angered. "Amar, don't fall for this," Brayson shouted, but his call fell on deaf ears. He anxiously began to pace as George spit in his hand and stuck it out.

"Where I'm from, this is how we become friends. You spit in your hand and I spit in mine. Once we shake, we become brothers. We'll become true friends. You do still want to be my friend, right?"

Brayson shouted again. "Stop smiling, Amar. This is a trap. Can't you see it, you fool?" He turned and faced the sprite. "Mogg, can't you allow me to say something to him?"

"We cannot change the past, wizard. You know this to be true. Maybe you should finish what you came for, or we could move on and return to the when from which we came."

"No! I need to know what happens. I wish to stay. I have to know the truth."

"As you wish."

Brayson watched as the two took one another's hand. He could see George's eyes change as the evil appeared within them.

"Amar, I'm so glad you fell for this line of garesh."

Brayson saw the change. It was instantaneous. Amar's eyes widened and he tried to speak, but it was too late. His tongue and lips were now stone. He ripped his hand away and tried to move, but his feet were heavy. They were also now stone and both of his hands were beginning to change.

"Mogg, he's in pain. George is killing him. I need to help him. You must allow me to help."

"I cannot... you can only watch the things that happen during this when. We cannot change it for our own personal reasons. If we do... our own now, the now from which we came, will not be as it was. Stop complaining and watch, wizard."

"This is wrong. How can you just stand by like this?"

"I do nothing because my nothing is somebody else's something in our now. You don't wish to take someone else's now from them, do you?"

Brayson stopped arguing with the sprite. He turned and listened to George deliver his evil words of hate.

"I guarantee you, Amar, you won't feel a thing. Just lie back and relax for a bit. It'll all be over soon. Yuck, I hate a hairy chest. Allow me to get rid of this for you."

Brayson began to cry as he watched George peel the skin back to expose Amar's rib cage.

"Ya know, I hate to say this, Amar, but I'm not really a doctor. I'm not even qualified to be doing this. This may leave you a little bit out of it when you wake up. Ha... who am I kidding... you're not ever going to wake up! I should probably say I'm sorry, but I think

you already know I would be full of garesh. You wouldn't have any idea how I should bust your chest open, would ya? Maybe this hammer and chisel will work. Aw... you don't like that idea. I can see you're a little upset with me. Stop giving me the silent treatment. Geez... you act like you've got a tongue made of stone or something! Ha, ha, ha, ha, ha..."

Brayson could not believe his eyes as he watched George pry Amar's chest open. He began to vomit as George ripped out his heart and took the first bite. He stumbled out of the barn with Mogg hovering behind him as the structure filled with a storm of flashing lights.

What Brayson saw next was also unexpected. A man dressed in robes stood in the failing torchlight at the center of the gravel road. His face was hidden within the shadow of his hood, but it was clear he knew what was happening inside and appeared to be uninterested in doing anything to stop it.

Brayson was taken back at the thought that someone could care so little about a murder, but to the Head Master's surprise, the figure vanished a few moments later.

"Mogg, I wish to follow that man, the one who just disappeared. I want to know the next thing that happens in his when!"

The sprite moved to hover in front of him. "We cannot follow his when. I cannot find his trail."

"What do you mean? His trail begins right over there."

"I'm sorry, wizard... his trail is too powerful for me. I would perish if I were to attempt to take you there. His when is untraceable."

"Then let's follow George. I wish to know more about his when."

Mogg closed her eyes and after a moment of silence, she responded. "George's trail beyond this when has been blocked and is no longer something I can follow."

"What... why?"

"I'm sensing that the man who stood on the road knows we're here to visit George's when. He must have hidden the trail from me. He's made George's trail from this when forward, untraceable... hidden somehow. I fear it isn't safe here any longer. We best leave."

"Mogg, how can a man from the future block another man's trail from this particular when... especially when that same trail is now a part of his own past? How could he know we're here?"

"I don't know this answer, wizard."

Brayson thought a moment. "You said his when from here forward has been blocked. What about his when farther back into George's past? Is this also blocked?"

Mogg closed her eyes again. After a moment of complete silence she opened them. "The when further into George's past is still an active trail which I can follow."

"Mogg, I need you to take me to the most significant event in George's past, the past prior to this when we're currently visiting."

"Follow me, wizard!" Once again the scenery changed, but now there was nothing that seemed familiar to Brayson. They now stood in an old rundown home of some sort. The furniture was nothing like he had ever seen. There was a box sitting on top of a small table with pictures constantly moving within it. Brayson moved to touch it. He expected to be able to reach inside, but found he could not.

"Mogg, what sort of magic is this? I cannot reach the objects inside." He tapped the glass. "What sort of barrier protects the—"

He moved back and watched as a man ran toward the screen and dove in his direction as an explosion blew up a building in the background. The flames appeared to disappear and travel beyond the box's picture, but when Brayson moved to see if any had escaped, he could not understand how the box still felt cold to the touch. Brayson quickly lowered himself back in front of the box and tried to reach through the glass again.

His voice was filled with frustration as he shouted, "Mogg... we need to save this man! He could be dying! The building behind him burns and... and..." He could not believe his eyes as the man stood up as if nothing had happened and dusted off his clothes.

"He lives... how is this possible?"

"Shut up, you fat cow..."

Brayson turned as a grumpy man with a pot belly entered the room. He lifted a thin paper full of a tobacco-smelling substance to his mouth and sucked on it. The way its red cherry lit up on the end reminded him of Marcus's pipe.

"I told you to have that little mistake take out the trash. And get me another damn beer while you're at it!"

Brayson watched as the dark-haired man plopped his weight down in a seated position on an old worn out-looking chair. He leaned back and forced a lever to lift a cushion-covered surface to hold up his feet. After setting his metallic-looking container on a circular side table, the man once again shouted.

"Woman... you better tell George to get his little butt in here. I need to handle some business!"

Brayson watched as a woman ran into the room. Her skinny, unhealthy-looking face was full of panic. She screamed as she spoke.

"You said you wouldn't touch him again! He's your son, Nathan! You can't do this, ya know. You can't make him do these awful things. He's still recovering from the beating you gave him last night. I'll call the cops on ya... I'll do it!"

Brayson rubbed his hands together nervously as Nathan stood from his chair. He grabbed her frail frame and slammed her hard into the doorway leading into another room. Nathan hit her across the face with his fist. For a brief moment her brown eyes rolled up into her head.

"Look atcha, you're a complete waste of good air... if I wanted your opinion, I would give it to you. Do you want me to call your probation officer? I could always tell her where your stash is. Do you really want to go back to jail?"

The woman fell to the floor and began to cry. Brayson badly wanted to help her but couldn't.

"Please... You don't have to do this. I'll do whatever you tell me to. He's just a child. Please don't do this to my baby!"

"Your baby... he's an irritating piece of crap. He's ruined our lives. Look at you... you're pathetic. You're just a crack whore. Why would I want you? Go find your stash and leave me alone. I'll send the little mistake crying to you once I'm done with him. Now get out of my face before I decide to kill him!"

Brayson moved to stand beside Nathan and looked into his eyes. They were cold, full of hate and his breath reeked of an ale smelling substance and his tobacco. "Mogg, I cannot allow this man to do this! How could he do such things?"

The sprite flew over and lowered into a sitting position on Brayson's shoulder. "I understand your frustration, wizard, but we cannot change George's when. You can only watch."

He took a long hard deep breath as he saw Nathan lower himself back into his chair.

"George, get your butt in here and bring a hot towel. I have some business to handle. I need to get this over with. My favorite show is on in an hour.

Brayson watched as the frail woman did as she was told and left the room sobbing. He could see the pain in her walk and after some moments passed, a very young-looking George entered the room.

"Oh no, no, no... Mogg... he's just a child!"

"Yes he is... you said to bring you to the most significant event in George's when. I did as you requested? Just watch, wizard!"

Brayson did as instructed and watched as George spoke.

"What did you want?"

Brayson could not believe the lack of respect Nathan had for his son. It was clear to see George hated him. Nathan's back was to the boy and he didn't bother to turn his head away from the box of pictures as he responded. He held up the container which he had referred to as lotion.

"Watch your tongue, boy! Get in here, I need to hurry."

Brayson was surprised at how strong George sounded in his response, considering the situation.

"I don't want to. I hate doing that. It hurts me... it makes me bleed and you stink. You freaking disgust me!"

Brayson couldn't believe how Nathan kept his eyes focused on the box of pictures.

"Look, you little no good for nothing reason my life sucks... get in here or I'm gonna kill ya!"

Brayson could see the fight in the child's eyes. "Mogg, I think he is going to make a stand. I can see it in his face."

George darted across the room and struck Nathan hard against the temple. It was as if he was berserk, swinging wildly without any hesitation. Nathan cried out in pain and shouted for help as George's punches continued to connect. George screamed.

"You're a piece of crap! You're nothing but an abusive loser, I hate you! I'll make sure you never touch me again or anybody else! I'm not your toy! Who do you think you are? I hate you!"

The fight continued for a long while. Many of the items scattered throughout the home had been thrown and windows were broken. George lifted a metal object with a light at its end and hit Nathan hard across the face. The man fell to the floor and balled up.

Eventually the door burst open and four men in blue clothing rushed in and subdued George. They pulled him from the top of Nathan's body which lay in a fetal position covering his face. The whole way out the door, George shouted. *"Let me kill him—that scum deserves it... let me put him six feet under! Let me kill him! Let me kill him!"*

Brayson stood in silence and scratched the sides of his head just above his elf ears. He moved to the door leading out and watched as the men put George into a metal beast with wheels. Lights illuminated from the beast's back and it cried out with a horrific noise as the metal monster moved away from them and through a wall of people who had gathered to see what the disturbance was all about.

Mogg lifted from his shoulder and flew to the far side of the room. "Do you wish to know anything else, wizard?"

"I do... what is the name of this place where we stand?"

"It is called Orlando, Florida. This is a world not like ours. We have traveled over 14,000 seasons into the past to see this when of George's."

Brayson was speechless, Mogg continued. "Your Mystic-Learner is very old... much older than you are, wizard."

After a while had past, Brayson finally spoke. "I wish to visit another part of George's past. I wish to see the when of his arrival on the world of Grayham prior to Amar's death. I wish to know when George came to our now."

Mogg began to move her tiny sprite wings rapidly back and forth. The normal shower of colors which fell from them was increased substantially. The scenery once again began to change and after a considerable wait, they finally stopped at a place Brayson knew all too well.

"Mogg, I asked to see George's arrival, not the Temple of the Gods on Luvelles. George came to Luvelles from Grayham. We need to go to Grayham!"

"Yes, wizard, I know. You're standing inside the Temple of the Gods on Grayham. I've brought you to a when which happened nearly one season ago."

"What... what about the last 14,000 seasons? Are you telling me George only recently came to our worlds?"

"I'm telling you nothing other than this is the when you requested to see."

Brayson began to look around. Not far away, standing just behind a large pillar, was a group of people moving around the statue of Bassorine and Mosley. After looking a little closer, Brayson rushed over to stand near them.

"Mogg, this is the king of Brandor and his queen. Why are they dressed in such ridiculous clothing? Why is George with them? I need to know why they are together."

The sprite closed her eyes and began to concentrate while Brayson waited impatiently, listening to every word Sam was saying. He listened to the prophecy which had been written on the statue's base.

When finally the sprite opened her eyes, George was already standing on top of the statue's base. Brayson watched as he leaned over and took the first piece of the Crystal Moon. The rest of the pieces vanished. He watched as George reacted.

"Holy crap, man, did you see that? The damn thing just disappeared. What do we do now? That just freaks me the hell out!"

The statue began to shake. Brayson watched Sam move his queen to a safer position. The floor beneath the statue opened up and George fell through a large hole, along with the statue's base. He listened to Sam scream George's name, but nothing could be done to save him.

All of a sudden, the temple went dark. All Brayson could see was Mogg's glitter of colors falling toward the polished marble floors beneath his feet. The darkness strengthened the sparkling shower's decent, rather than dissipating as he was used to seeing. The colors burst into quiet little explosions of intense light as they hit the marble surface.

Mogg was scared. Brayson could hear it in her tiny voice. "It's not good to mess with the gods. We must return to our own now. We must leave before we perish in this when."

"What do you mean? How are we messing with the gods?"

"We don't have many moments left. You must follow me, wizard."

Brayson wanted to argue, but knew it was pointless to do so. "So lead the way!"

The scenery once again began to change and eventually they stood in their own now from which they had left. Mogg stopped and hovered in front of the entrance to her tree. Her anxiety was clear and the fascinating colors of sparkling light were continuing to fall heavily towards the forest floor.

"Mogg, you said something about the gods."

"I don't wish to talk about this further. I fear for our lives. George's when is the reason that our now will end if we investigate your curiosities any further."

"What... how?"

"You're not a very smart elf for your position, wizard. If you wish to tempt fate by challenging a god's warning, then you do it without my help. I'll not speak another word about this night. I wish you to leave!"

"But—"

"NO! I said leave my village or I shall be forced to trap you within another when from which you cannot escape."

Brayson took a long look at the sprite's tiny little face. He could see that she was serious. "Goodbye, Mogg!"

Brayson vanished.

The City of Marcus,
Inside the Temple of the Dark Order

Boyafed stood looking down at his Argont Commander's mutilated body. Dayden had been found on the outskirts of the city. His head had been severed, along with both his arms and legs. His privates had been shoved inside his mouth and sewn shut. It was all the leader of the Dark Order could do to control himself and keep from killing the messenger who delivered Dayden's body to the great Hall of Sacrifice.

Boyafed's best friend since childhood now lay on Hosseff's golden stone altar beneath the statue of his god's outstretched arms. There appeared to be no rhyme or reason for the killing. After clearing everyone from the hall, the dark paladin leader lowered to his knees and tears filled his dark brown eyes.

Memories flooded his mind as he remembered many fond moments of their past together.

"You two boys better dress nice. I won't have any young lady attending the ball with the likes of you if you can't dress appropriately."

"Yes, Mother," Dayden shouted. "We'll be sure to make you proud."

"You better... I'm telling ya... no proper young lady wishes to be escorted by a pair of dirty mongrels."

"Yes, Mama."

A young Dayden, now only 71 seasons old, turned and faced Boyafed. "Did you find it? I swear it's there. I put it under there last night. My dad has been searching for it all day."

Boyafed, also the same age, pushed back from beneath the bed. "I got it!"

"Shhhh, we need to get it out of here. How're we going to do it without my mother knowing? She has extra eyes, you know."

"Let's just get dressed. I'll put the bottle under my pant leg and we'll walk out of here calmly. She'll never expect a thing."

After properly being inspected by a pretty, but petite elven woman, the boys hurried down the long pathway leading away from Dayden's family estate. After running the entire distance, the boys stopped at the entrance to the ball. The dance was being held in a farmer's barn and many magical decorations filled its interior.

Glow spirits, a small bug found only in Wraithwood Hollow, had been captured, transported in, and released to fly around the barn's ceiling. These tiny insects were special. They released a soft burst of blue light which lasted only a moment. When they were put together in a large group, the frequency in which these lights appeared naturally increased and created a magical mood.

"Pssst... Jennikas, come here and bring Corissa. She's in the barn," Boyafed said as he whispered from the shadows on the side of the barn. Dayden was above him as they both peeked around the corner.

Jennika's keen elven eyes looked into the shadows and responded. "Boyafed... Dayden, is that you?"

"Shhhh, don't say anything. Just get Corissa and meet us by Farmer Bedgess's stump."

Without saying another word, she walked into the barn. She was dressed in a beautiful red gown. Her elf ears were exposed and her hair had been pulled back and pinned to the top of her head.

When finally the girls arrived at the farmer's stump, Jennikas and Boyafed embraced. Corissa and Dayden quickly kissed one another and took a seat. Corissa loved green and her eyes, also green, only complemented the gown's color.

The stump was the remains of a massive jedsolip tree, the godfather of all trees on Luvelles. It rested on the banks of the River Id which flowed south away from Lake Id. Twelve men could easily sit together and still have plenty of room.

Boyafed removed the bottle full of mesolliff wine, a sweet-tasting, silky smooth vintage, made from the vineyards of Nept and held it high.

"Ahhh, you got it," Jennikas shouted with excitement.

"We did, and you two lucky ladies are gonna share it with us," Boyafed said with an adorable smile. "Are you sure you're ready for what will happen next if we drink this?"

Both girls huddled together and after a moment of whispering back and forth they turned to face the boys. "We both agree that we're ready!"

Dayden clapped his hands. "Tonight we drink to the sweetness of love. Tomorrow we will be men and you will be women."

Corissa giggled. "Don't be silly. We'll still be girls and you will still be young boys, but we won't be virgins."

Boyafed's mind managed to find its way back to his current situation.

The Dark Order leader stood from the side of the altar. He looked down at Dayden's body and said his goodbyes. He lifted his hands toward the statue of Hosseff.

"Lord Hosseff, please accept your servant's empty vessel. His soul no longer fills it with life. He has served you well and I ask you to honor him. Take his body from this world. I beg you to provide him a place of honor amongst the loyal who have died before us. I beg you for this."

Boyafed moved back from the altar and watched as the demon statues hanging from the god's fingers animated. Their clawed feet released their hold and fell with wings spread to land at the altar's ends.

Both beings held their dark red hands above Dayden's body as it erupted in flames. The paladin leader watched in absolute silence until his friend's body was nothing more than a pile of ash.

The demons returned to their rightful spot and once again grasped the ends of Hosseff's fingers with their clawed feet. They lowered into an upside down position and stretched their arms towards the altar. A moment later they solidified.

Boyafed lifted his hands towards his god. "I will serve forever!"

As he slowly scooped Dayden's ashes into a golden, gem-covered urn, a high ranking officer of Boyafed's dark army rushed into the hall. The man was next in line to replace the fallen Argont Commander.

"My liege, I have news of how the commander died."

"So speak, Christopher... speak before I cut it out of you."

Christopher dressed as Boyafed did, wearing all black except for his golden yellow shirt and his cape bearing the Order's symbol. His hair was long and pure white. His eyes were without color and looked as if they were made of a fogged crystal with a grayish-looking pupil resting at their centers. His voice was strong and his fighting skills were well-respected throughout Boyafed's army.

"Word has returned from the spot where Dayden's body was found. They found this." Christopher tossed the White Army's dagger to him.

Boyafed unsheathed the ivory-handled blade and lifted it in front of his face. The markings on the blade were the same as the ones the arrows had carried. He screamed and filled the air with an intense hatred. "TOLAS!"

Christopher waited only a moment. "What are your orders?"

"Call for the council. I want them to be seated and ready for my arrival by Late Bailem."

"Will that be all, my liege?"

Boyafed's eyes sent chills down the future Argont Commander's spine as he spoke. "Unless you wish to be offered up to Hoss-eff, I would get out of my sight!"

Christopher turned and fled from the room while Boyafed simply vanished.

From the shadows, Marcus smiled. "How interesting... both councils shall meet tonight. I couldn't ask for better results." The Dark Chancellor disappeared.

Just South of Grogger's Swamp

The morning had been unkind to the lands of Northwestern Luvelles, punishing the terrain with pebble-sized hail and earth-scarring strikes of electrical fury. The forest had taken the brunt of the storm. The high winds had abused many of the tall evergreen trees and many of their branches had fallen heavily to the ground. Countless mud-filled puddles were scattered both on the dirt road following the tree line and throughout the forest floor.

Shalee grit her teeth in agony and moaned as she crawled along the muddy road. The open wound across her abdomen had been torturous and was leaving a trail for Kiayasis to follow. The sporadic, speckled drops of blood were beginning to turn into smaller coin-shaped pools of saturated earth. She had used her sweater to try and pack the wound, but nothing seemed to help. She was tired and the loss of blood was making her sleepy. Her desire to live was beginning to be replaced by her desire to end the pain.

Kiayasis knew Shalee was approaching the end of a valiant effort to run for her life. He had intentionally stalked her from a distance and allowed her to wallow in her misery. He smiled as he bent down and rubbed his hand across the blood-stained earth.

"You can't run forever," he whispered, "Your blood gives you away! It didn't have to end this way. I will miss you!" Methodically, he rubbed the essence of her life between his finger tips and tasted it.

Shalee pulled herself off the road and into the forest. Her forearms were torn, bloodied from the gravel embedded in her skin. Her teeth chattered uncontrollably as her body continued to lose its heat. She managed to force herself into an upright position against a large stone. The knife had made a clean cut. She tried using her magic to cauterize the wound...but failed.

Why can't I use my magic, she thought. Her mind screamed for answers, but none could be found. Again she closed her eyes and tried to teleport... nothing; there was no escape. *I've got to get out of here. He's gonna kill me!*

It wasn't long before Kiayasis stood above her, looking down with eyes filled with evil intent, and now dressed in the Order's armor. "You betrayed me, Shalee... you tossed me aside as if I were no better than the slop trudgeboars eat!"

Shalee's voice was weak. "I'm so sorry. Please, I beg you... stop! I don't want to die. What can I do to make you stop this?"

"The moments for talking are over. You could have had a wonderful life with me. I was prepared to give up everything for you. I was sent here to kill you, but as we went along, I fell in love with you. I was going to let you live and start a new life together, far away from my father's army."

"I'm sorry... Kiayasis, please don't do this!"

Kiayasis unsheathed his long sword. He lifted it toward the sky and shouted, "Hosseff, accept this sacrifice as a token of my faithful service. Her blood shall cover the blessed blade of the Order's faithful. We are your children and as your child, I wish to please you. You are a wise and almighty god."

As he lowered the blade, a voice from the side of the road called out from behind him.

"If it's a sacrifice you're seeking, then maybe you should claim your honor before taking the life of a helpless woman!"

Shalee couldn't believe her eyes. "Sam... oh my God, Sam, help me!"

The king of Grayham was dressed in leather hunting clothes. He wore no armor, but Kael hung from his hip. His crown was missing and his hair was a mess from the storm's high winds. The front of his shirt was only tied halfway up and his broad shoulders pulled the material apart, exposing his muscular chest beneath.

Kiayasis began to laugh. "How poetic... the king of Brandor has come to Luvelles searching for his queen. There's much you don't know about your woman. She has been quite the naughty girl. Do you wish to know—"

Sam spoke over him. "Why does everyone talk when the moment has come to fight? Ready your weapon and pick on someone your own size!"

"What honor is there in fighting with a sword of the gods?" Kiayasis said, and watched Sam's surprise. He knew his sword was no match for Sam's weapon. "You didn't think I would know of such things. I have been informed of your skills. I'll fight you, but not with swords. We will fight with daggers, if you're man enough to accept the challenge, that is!"

Sam lowered Kael to the ground and pulled his dagger from its sheath. Kiayasis tossed his sword to the ground and grabbed the bone handle of his weapon. The two men made a quick exchange of metal-clanking slashes and lunges before Kiayasis's fist found its mark, splitting the king's lip wide open.

Sam didn't allow the punch to faze him. He grabbed Kiayasis with his free hand and pulled him forward to the ground. Sam's knee smashed into the ground as the dark warrior rolled to avoid the paralyzing effects of the failed attempt.

Kiayasis quickly stood to his feet. "Very nice, solid moves for a king. I'm going to enjoy this."

"Again... more talk. Not enough fighting!"

Shalee managed to shout out a few words. "Sam, he has—"

Kiayasis attacked before she could speak further. The dark paladin made two quick stabbing motions which were defended. The warrior quickly rolled to the side and managed to bury his knee into Sam's kidney. The blow sent Sam falling forward, but the king reacted and rolled to his feet quick enough to defend a downward stab meant for his head.

Sam secured Kiayasis's arms and rolled backward, pulling the paladin with him. He pushed hard with his legs and threw the dark warrior hard into the side of a tree. His plate armor made a loud thud against the bark. He fell in an awkward position on his shoulder and head, dropping his dagger. Sam followed and stomped on the blade with his foot before the dark warrior's reaching hand could grab the handle. The king brought his fist down hard across the side of Kiayasis's face. Blood began to pour as two teeth fell to the forest floor.

Sam grabbed Kiayasis's dagger, stuck it deep into the side of the tree and pushed sideways to snap the blade. Throwing the bone handle to the ground, he shouted, "Get up and fight!"

Kiayasis stood and wiped the blood from his chin. Shalee once again tried to speak, but the dark warrior shouted above her. "Shut up, woman!" He turned to face Sam. "Does your queen always run her mouth so?"

Sam ignored Kiayasis' snide remark and began to methodically remove his shirt. The dark warrior watched as Sam clinched both his dagger and his shirt, one in each hand.

The skies above opened up once again and the rain began to fall. The water ran down the skin of the king's bare chest. Shalee had never seen her husband look so intimidating. Sam studied the paladin's face.

After watching for any sign of intimidation on Kiayasis's face and not receiving any, Sam threw both the knife and his shirt to the ground. The dark warrior had been trained not to show weakness. It was best to step things up a notch or two.

"Now it's a fair fight!" Sam shouted as he moved his head side to side, popping his neck. "I have no blade and no armor! Maybe you'll stand a chance!"

Sam Goodrich - King of Brandor

Illustration by Kathleen Stone

Without waiting for a response, he darted in and motioned as if he was going to bring up a left knee, but instead of following it through, he sent in a right hand above the paladin's lowered arms and connected hard against the bridge of Kiayasis's nose.

The dark warrior rolled backward and Sam stopped his attack to allow Kiayasis the moments necesssary to recover. "You don't seem to be much of a warrior. Do all your father's men fight as you do? I bet he's ashamed to have you as his son. I bet Boyafed would be sick to his stomach right now."

Kiayasis stood and removed his hand from his nose. The blood ran freely as he responded. Every emphasized word sent a spray of blood flying through the air. "You don't know me! You don't know anything about my father! You know nothing of the Order and you know nothing of my father's feelings for me!"

The paladin lifted his arms. Fire erupted from the palms of his hands. Flames enveloped Sam's body. For a period of moments the king couldn't be seen. His agony-filled screams filled the forest but, as the flames dissipated, Sam's screams turned to a hysterical laughter. He pointed at Kiayasis and mocked his efforts. The heat hadn't damaged him at all. Even the hair covering his body had escaped harm.

Kiayasis couldn't believe what he had just seen. "How—"

"Does how really matter? I think the moment has come for you to die." Sam rushed in and threw a series of punches and kicks which Kiayasis defended. He kept at it, relentlessly pushing forward to overwhelm the dark warrior until finally, Kiayasis made a critical mistake. The paladin failed to block a hard right hook. The impact buried deep into his left temple. The dark warrior stumbled backward and fell hard to his ass.

Sam followed quickly, pushing his enemy to his back and mounted Kiayasis with a leg on either side, pinning him down. He continued to punch him as the dark warrior tried helplessly to avoid the damage. Eventually a shot landed which sent the paladin into unconsciousness. The king continued to punch over and over again and would have continued until life left his enemy, but Shalee called out to him. It took every last ounce of strength she had to get his attention.

"SAM! You have to stop!"

After one more solid punch, Sam stood. He looked down at Kiayasis's bloodied face. After spitting on him, he moved to stand above Shalee. Realizing her condition, the King ran out to the road and grabbed his bag. He produced a vial and crouched next to his queen.

"Open your mouth and lift your tongue. I need to put a drop of this under it. It'll stop the bleeding and you'll begin to heal."

Shalee did as she was told. Sam's eyes failed to show his love for her. His movements were tense and his actions cold and precise. In her heart, Shalee knew Sam was aware of her lack of faithfulness.

She watched as Sam dragged Kiayasis across the forest floor. He bound both his arms and legs. He pulled the dark warrior by his feet and after throwing them to the ground, he grabbed hold of his shirt and threw him against a tree where he could keep a better eye on him.

"How did you find me?" Shalee said in a shallow voice as she watched the bleeding begin to stop. The magical, healing properties of Brayson's personal elixir were starting to work.

"The Head Master met me on Merchant Island and I have been tracking you ever since."

"Since when do you know how to track someone? And how did you withstand his magic?"

"I made a few requests for my arrival. I'm wearing rings which protect me from certain things. As for tracking, I don't know how to do it, but the tracker I hired did. Once I had you in my sight a few days ago, I told him he could leave. I've been watching you ever since. I wanted to wait until you were alone. I really didn't want to confront you while you were curled up with your little 'baby' over there. I was going to return home without speaking with you after hearing that, but as it turns out… it looks like changing my mind has saved you! How could you call him 'baby' anyway, especially after the death of our son."

Shalee lowered her eyes to the ground. She could not bear to look at him. "You heard that? Then you know I didn't sleep with him."

"You did everything but sleep with him. You allowed him to hold you. I saw you kiss him, Shalee! Damn it, how could you be so selfish?"

"Sam... I'm so sorr—"

"Don't, Shalee! Your regret isn't something I care to hear right now. I'm leaving for Grayham. You'll have to continue your search for the crystal without me. I want you to know that before I go, I'm going to kill the arms that comforted you! This guy makes me sick! Did your parents forget to teach you what faithfulness was, Shalee?"

"Sam, you don't have to kill him! I already told him I wasn't going to continue with the relationship. That's why he tried to kill me. I was so messed up in the head when I arrived here. I felt like you hated me. I was selfish and I know that now. I wish I could fix it all and make it go away. You don't need to kill him. He isn't a threat to us any longer."

Sam thought a moment, stood, and without saying a word, moved to pull Kiayasis clear of the trees. He untied the dark warrior's bonds and after lifting him to his feet, began to smack the sides of his face until the paladin was fully awake. Once sure he had Kiayasis's full attention, he said, "You should leave! Tell your father no man will be killing my queen, not today, or any other! Don't let me see your face again... because the chances of you finding me in a forgiving mood when next we meet are highly unlikely! NOW GO!"

Sam watched as Kiayasis turned to go. Once confident the dark warrior would not return, Sam turned to face Shalee. Kneeling, he took one final look at the queen's wound to see the progress the magical elixir had made in her recovery. The bleeding had completely stopped but it would be a while longer before the cut would fully mend—she would live. Now, he could leave.

Suddenly, Shalee cried out. Sam was barely able to spin fast enough to stop the downward force of a large stone meant for his head. With both hands open, Sam's palms caught the deadly object and used the bend of his arms as springs to repel the stone's intended path. With a thud, the forest floor took the damage, landing next to where Sam's right knee rested. As quick as the attack happened, Sam's right fist was now on a collision course with Kiayasis's groin. The blow was severe, stopping any further advance. The paladin stumbled backward and fell to his knees. Quickly, Sam stood and with a lunging, powerful right-boot to the dark warrior's face, his muddy sole left a nasty imprint, breaking Kiayasis's nose and jaw.

Kiayasis fell to the forest floor.

After sitting him up, the king knelt behind his limp figure. "What am I going to do with you? Do you have a death wish?"

"I live t... t... to serve... Hosseff," he stammered, grunting in pain as blood poured from his nose, across his lips and down his chin before falling directly onto his battered armor. "I cannot return to my father's good graces. I will not stop hunting you until you're both dead!"

Sam shook his head and with a powerful strike to Kiayasis' temple, he sent the dark warrior back into unconsciousness.

He stood and ran his hands through his hair. "This guy is leaving me no choice!"

Shalee knew what was coming. She wanted to say something, but the words were no longer available. She knew Kiayasis had sealed his own fate.

Sam calmly knelt again behind Kiayasis after sitting him up. "Shalee, I have tried to give him his life. I have no choice. He will keep hunting us if I let him go. You heard this yourself. I want you to watch closely… our actions have consequenses!" Shalee cringed as the bones in the dark paladin's neck filled the air with a horrid cracking sound.

Sam's eyes were cold as he moved to stand above his queen. "I told you, you could come home when you're ready. I also told you I would always love you. I'll be there when you get back. I suggest you try to be faithful from here on out."

Shalee tried to say something, but Sam stopped her. "I don't care right now, Shalee… I don't care!"

He reached into his bag and tossed her a package. "You should eat. You're going to need your strength." Pushing his hands through his hair, he sighed before continuing, "I do still love you! The problem is... I'm not sure I can trust you anymore!" Sam pulled a scroll from his pack and after a few words spoken aloud in the elven language, he vanished.

Shalee began to cry. She was left to sit only feet away from Kiayasis's lifeless body. She was too weak to move and would have to bear the agony of both Sam's disappointment and the sight of Kiayasis'corpse.

City of Inspiration,
The Circle of the High Council

Lord Dowd stood at the center of a large circular building made of glass. There were many different tones and shades of color that had been magically applied to the different areas within this domed meeting hall. The design was official-looking, governmental if you will, and specifically created for the White Paladin Council.

Lord Dowd had taken his position as the rightful head of the council and now stood inside a waist-high enclosure which allowed for a fairly significant amount of freedom while addressing the council's esteemed members, all of which had served in the White Paladin Army.

The council surrounded Dowd from all sides and took their seats. They numbered eighty men in total and were dressed in white with silver accents, each bearing the symbol of the White Paladin Army, the Turtle Elf of Healing. These men were responsible for making the decision of how the Kingdom of Lavan would handle situations of war, and on this day, the council gathered to specifically address Lord Dowd's call to begin one.

Mosley, Alistar, and Hosseff the Shade have taken positions behind the council and are looking down at both Lord Dowd and the White Chancellor. The deities are unable to be seen by all present and have come for reasons of their own.

Gregory Id took his seat only feet from Dowd, inside the same enclosure, and assumed his rightful position as the Chancellor to the Kingdom of Lavan by lowering himself onto his throne.

With Heltgone Lavan's life ending so unexpectedly, his throne remained empty and Gregory was responsible to fill his position temporarily until the Head Master could call for a meeting with the City of Lavan's republic leaders. The White Chancellor was expected to handle the duties of both offices until this had happened.

The King of Lavan was infertile and had left behind no sons or daughters. His wife had died only a few seasons ago and his only living relative after the last war between the Dark and White Armies was a sister, but she was deaf and dumb, far from capable of running a kingdom. Brayson was required to determine, with the republic's help, who were the five most powerful families within the Kingdom of Lavan and choose the one which best fit the position as the new royal family. The head of the family would be named king.

"Councilmen, I want to thank you for coming," Lord Dowd said as he opened the meeting. "I've summoned you here to answer my call for war. In the past few days there have been two separate attacks on my life. Three of our paladins lay dead and the king of Lavan has perished from a poorly fired crossbow which was crafted specifically for the Dark Order warriors."

Dowd watched as the members of the council began to murmur and continued. "I wish to gather our forces and call for the Dark Army to meet us on the battle fields south of Olis."

An older man, retired from his commission, stood and made his presence known. His belly was now rounded from his lack of training and the five pints of ale he consumed each night. His nose looked like a cauliflower with a strawberry hue and he had allowed his graying beard to lengthen, but when he spoke, all on the council listened intently.

"Lord Dowd," Heflon said as he bowed his head to honor the White Army's leader. "You said four men have died. I understand one of these men was a king and this is tragic to be sure, but to call for war would kill thousands. Is there no other way to settle this matter between the two armies without having a war? Have you tried to contact Boyafed? Have you tried to find out what his feelings are and what he plans to do?"

Dowd took a deep breath. He didn't like the passive sound of Heflon's question. Dowd respected Heflon by bowing his head to satisfy the politics of the situation before responding, "To answer your question, Councilor, I was scheduled to meet with Boyafed approximately five days ago now. It was at this moment that the first attempt on my life was made, but instead of killing me, they missed and my spirit-bull of nearly 100 seasons perished from a bolt to the eye from one of the Order's crossbows."

Heflon thought a moment. "I was told the bolt responsible for killing the king was also meant to kill you, but this shot hit his eye as well, is this correct?"

"It is. Both bolts missed my person by only inches and killed an unexpected target."

"Lord Dowd., don't you find it odd that a man trained by the Order would fail to hit a stationary target on two separate occasions, but was able to hit the eyes of the beings standing near you? The Dark Army doesn't make these types of mistakes. I'm sure you would agree with me—these are intentional misses and the bolts killed who they were meant for."

"I would agree that whoever this man was, he missed me on both occasions. If the bolts that were fired did indeed find their intended targets, this means war! I say this is an act of war no matter how you try to explain it, Councilman. This is the Dark Order's way of spitting in our faces and such disrespect requires a lesson to be taught. If the king of Lavan were your brother, I doubt you would feel to object."

Heflon looked around the room. "War will kill many. We don't even have any real proof the Order is responsible. For all we know, this man who attacked could be an amateur who simply got his hands on one of their weapons. I don't believe a dark paladin trained by the Order would miss on two separate occasions. I believe this to be trickery."

Many in the room seemed to agree with Heflon, but there were still others who agreed with the white paladin leader. Dowd began to argue his objections to Heflon's logic. The room instantly became angry as the men started to shout at one another to make their cases.

The gods began to converse as they watched the proceedings grow out of hand. Alistar addressed Mosley. "I think the moments have come for you to do your job as the God of War. It looks as if Heflon will talk the Council out of any aggressive action and they'll look for a diplomatic resolution. He does have a point. This doesn't seem like the work of the Order, but of an amateur. The Council is sure to agree with his logic. You must make them feel the proper course of action is war."

Mosley lowered his wolf head. "I've been dreading the day this moment would come! If I had any other choice, I wouldn't do such a thing."

Hosseff responded and Mosley looked into the emptiness beneath the shade-god's hood as the wispy words found their way out of the shadowy darkness which had taken the place of his face.

"Mosley, you should take solace in the fact that war is necessary to control the world's populations. The souls waiting in the Book of Immortality will be given their chance to live again. When you do your job as the God of War, you're working to create a new cycle of life. This is a good thing. It isn't evil to do what's necessary!"

"Well, it doesn't feel like a good thing, but I understand your reasoning." Mosley began to move through the men to stand near Heflon. As he passed, they felt chilled by his presence. They looked to one another for an explanation as they rubbed themselves for warmth. The invisible wolf-god breathed on Heflon's body and began to whisper.

"War is necessary. The Order has played a trick on this council and wants you to think these attacks are the work of an amateur. Heflon, you're far too clever to allow such deceptions to fall on this council's ears. Lord Dowd is right in making his call for war... only you can make these men see that war is a necessary action to rid Luvelles of the evil which plagues this world."

Once finished, Mosley moved to stand beside Alistar. Again the men grabbed themselves as if chilled as he passed right through them. "Let's see how that worked."

Alistar nodded. "I never tire of seeing how people act as we walk through them. I'm sure many of them will come down with colds tomorrow. That was a fine bit of suggesting, Mosley."

"How could you be so blind, Heflon?" Dowd continued to shout. The council as a whole was enraged and many of the men were arguing their points of view. After a moment, Heflon raised his hand. It was as if he commanded their voices and without saying a word, the room quieted.

"My fellow Councilmen, I think there may be another side to this situation we should consider. What if the Order wanted to kill Heltgone? Maybe the Order wanted us to think an amateur was responsible for the two bolts which missed Lord Dowd by passing them only inches from his person. If the Dark Army wished to kill a king, how better to do it than to make us think it possible an outsider could have done this? It would be a fine deception if we were to believe another man has stolen their property and wore the colors of Boyafed's paladin army. They could get away with murder and not worry about retaliation from our army. It would be stupid for us to believe an imposter has mistakenly killed the king of Lavan instead of Lord Dowd. I fear the truth will never be known. We cannot trust the Order. This has been proven throughout history. I hate to say this, but Lord Dowd is right. The moment for war... IS NOW!"

The room erupted with the calls for war. Dowd seized the moment and lifted his blessed blade of the White army high above his head. He shouted with all his might. "I call for war! What say you, Councilmen?" The decision was unanimous.

Mosley turned away from the frenzied cries of the Council. The wolf looked at both Alistar and Hosseff. "It appears we have our war. It won't be long before you'll be collecting the souls to return them to the Book's pages, Shade."

The shade responded. "You have done your job well, Mosley. But there's another war which needs your attention, on Harvestom. Maybe you should go and see to it that it happens as well."

Mosley turned to Alistar. "Shall we go see what the leaders of Harvestom are thinking?"

Alistar put his hand on the God of War's furry head. "Mosley, I

understand how this makes you feel, but I assure you, you're doing only what's necessary to ensure a continuous cycle of life. I'll
stay with you until the job is complete."

"Thank you! It'll take a while for me to learn how to deal with
the sick feeling such decisions put in the pit of my stomach."

Hosseff laughed and both Alistar and Mosley stared hard into
the shadowy nothingness which should have been his face. "Eventually, Mosley, you'll learn to deal with such emotions." The shade
vanished.

Alistar looked at Mosley. "I don't think it's necessary to visit
Boyafed. I'm sure he'll also call for war with his council, after the
recent events which happened there."

Mosley sat on his haunches before responding. "What events
are you referring to?"

"Hosseff told me Boyafed's Argent Commander is dead. Apparently, Boyafed feels Dayden was killed by the White Paladin
Army."

Mosley shook his head in amazement "None of this makes any
sense! How could both armies be manipulated in this way?"

"I don't know, my hairy friend, but this is the case and I think
Hosseff knows more than he's telling us. The Order will accept
Dowd's challenge to meet them in battle and I believe this will be
a war worth watching."

Mosley thought a moment. "I must learn more about how Hosseff thinks."

"Ha... that could take many seasons. But you'll eventually adapt
to the decisions you've had to make when bringing wars to the
worlds, but I seriously doubt I'll ever be able to adapt to the eerie
feeling I get when I try to find a face beneath Hosseff's hood. It's
simply unnerving, don't you think?"

After a brief exchange of laughter and a mutual agreement between the two, both gods left for Harvestom.

The Luvelles Gazette

When you want an update about your favorite characters

The Next Day Just Before Early Bailem

Shalee has managed to slowly work her way back to the camp which Kiayasis had left intact just outside Grogger's Swamp. She has removed the Knife of Spirits from the dark paladin's lifeless body and now carries it high on her right thigh beneath her dress. Sam's disappointment and the pain on his face before he vanished have been haunting her thoughts. She plans to find the missing piece of the Crystal Moon and hurry back to Grayham to beg for forgiveness.

Kepler and Payne are waiting outside the Source's Temple. George has opened the temple's doors and the key he retrieved from Brayson's shrine vanished after opening the magical lock. After going inside, he stood on the teleportation platform. He is now looking at Fisgig's fiery pool of water within the Mountains of Oraness.

Kepler and Payne tried to pass through the entryway of the temple, but George was the only one allowed to pass. An unseen force made it impossible for the pairing to continue any further. All they can do now is wait and Payne has teleported them back to the families' homes.

Mary, Athena, Susanne and baby Garrin woke early. They have eaten a hearty breakfast and have gathered in Mary's kitchen to read from the Scroll of Teleportation Brayson gave Mary. The Head Master stayed the night and avoided talking about George. He did, however, help the girls devise a plan. The ladies are going to visit the City of Nept and take a sip of the many wines of the countryside's vineyards. Athena is now only 36 Peaks of Bailem from giving birth. Brayson left immediately after breakfast, kissing Mary goodbye before he left.

Boyafed and Lord Dowd are speaking by mirrored communication. Dowd has delivered the Kingdom of Lavan's call for war and Boyafed has accepted. The conversation was short. Both the Dark and White armies will meet for battle near Olis. The battle will begin in 50 Peaks of Bailem, once each side has gathered their forces.

Gregory Id has been asked by Lord Dowd to go to the City of Lavan. The Chancellor is to issue the call for Lavan's army to meet and join up with the White army in 40 Peaks of Bailem, just north of Lake Tepp. From there it will be a four Peak of Bailem march to the battlegrounds. The armies will rest and prepare for battle over the next five days.

Lord Dowd has also asked Gregory to travel to three other places in search of support for the war. The first is the shores of Crystal Lake. He is to call on the Ultorian king for any assistance he may be able to offer.

The second is the enchanted woods of Wraithwood Hollow. Gregory is to ask the Wraith Hound Prince, Wisslewine, to call forth his pack of ferocious canine warriors from the center of the Under Eye and bring them to the battlegrounds of Olis.

The third is to visit the Spirit Plains. The Chancellor is to find the king of a race of spirits called the Lost Ones. Gregory will need to capture Shesolaywen, their king, to gain the ability to use the Call of Canair.

Mieonus, the Goddess of Hate, watched Sam save Shalee's life. The entire event was seen by simply watching her waterfall from inside her home on the Hidden God World of Ancients Sovereign. The goddess enjoyed the pain Shalee's actions caused the king of Southern Grayham. Shalee's betrayal of her vows and the death of Kiayasis have given Mieonus a wonderfully evil idea.

Mosley and Alistar are on the World of Harvestom. The famine is slowly spreading across the Kingdom of Kless and desperate moments are beginning to turn the Centaurs against one another. Hunger is responsible for the current cases of cannibalism which are beginning to occur. Neighbors are afraid to open their doors to one another within their forest homes and now live in fear for their lives.

The king of Kless is now completely convinced the king of Tagdrendlia is the one who ordered the Seeds of Plenty to be stolen from him. Without the seeds to produce the crops for his lands, Lasolias's brown-coated centaur army will starve. The king of Kless also believes his men are no longer strong enough to fight for him, but if they do not fight the Black Coats, the Seeds will be lost to his kingdom for good.

On the other side of Northern Harvestom, in the Kingdom of Tagdrendlia, Boseth has recently collected a bountiful harvest and his black-coated army of centaurs is healthy and strong. The King of Tagdrendlia believes his race of Black Coats can easily withstand an advance by Lasolias's Brown Coats. The Tagdrendlia king tried telling Lasolias more than once that he doesn't have his bag filled with the Seeds of Plenty, but Lasolias won't listen.

The Brown Coat and the Black Coat kingdoms have enough hatred between them over one another's flawed appearances without the missing seeds being an issue. The racial tension between these two breeds of centaur only adds to the problem.

Brayson has arrived at his floating office and is waiting to meet with the king of Southern Grayham. Sam is expected to arrive shortly.

Gage and the other Goswigs are now free from Strongbear's constant shouting of orders. Once they voted to pool their magic together and bring winter into their underground city, the large brown bear grew sleepy and now slumbers inside his cave behind his diner. He is expected to hibernate until the season ends.

Marcus is watching Gregory. The moment is nearly right to carry out yet another step of both his and George's evil plans. He just needs to get Gregory alone, but something unexpected is about to happen.

Lasidious and Celestria are inside their home beneath the Peaks of Angels. Lasidious plans to visit George in his dreams. There are things which need to be said. George will need to work quickly to avoid some of the potential problems which could arise as a result of Brayson Id's snooping around with the sprite, Mogg.

Thank you for reading the Luvelles Gazette

Chapter 18

𝕬 𝖁𝖊𝖗𝖞 𝕺𝖑𝖉 𝕯𝖗𝖆𝖌𝖔𝖓

Just outside the Source's Cave,
The Mountains of Oraness

Holy crap, that's hot, George thought as he stood looking at the flames. *These cliffs are so tall, they surround the water. What the... look at that... is that...? The damn water is on fire. Wait... no it's not... it isn't boiling. Something's up with this place. Where the heck am I anyway?*

Focus... I need to think. Okay... George, pull your head out of your ass and let's figure out what the deal is here. The way is completely blocked. There's no way around. So what now?

He could see the cave's entrance on the far side of the pool. He closed his eyes and tried to teleport, but nothing happened.

Okay, I can't teleport. If I walk any farther, the flames will burn my ass up. There's got to be some way I can get across. Think George, think... what kind of magic could I use to put out a fire? How about ice... yes ice, that's worth a shot.

He lifted his hands and a blizzard erupted from his palms. The ice covered the pool's surface and for a brief moment George saw some sort of bird sitting on something at the pool's center.

Okay... now I know a little more. But what's causing the fire? What's the bird doing sitting in the flames? Could it be controlling the flames? No, that's just plain stupid. How could a bird do something like that? Wait... oh man oh man oh man... what if it's... no way... you've got to be kidding me. Have I just seen my first Phoenix? That's Brayson's Goswig.

Okay... let's think here, Georgy boy. If it's a real Phoenix, then why isn't it attacking? I did just cover it with ice. Why isn't it pissed off? Shouldn't that have pissed it off at least a little bit? The ice did affect its flame... or did it? Maybe the magic wasn't strong enough to bother it. Maybe it's not supposed to attack. Maybe this is just a mental game for me to figure out. Maybe I need to hit it with something a little stronger... something a little more harmful to fire. What's fire's worst enemy? Water... yeah, water... but not just any water. Let's give this little guy a tidal wave to deal with. Perhaps a little shock as well. What if this doesn't work and I only manage to piss it off? What if it kills me and picks my eyes out with its beak?

George... come on, you've got to stop this. You're standing here talking to yourself like a bleeding idiot. I bet the Phoenix is sitting over there thinking he's spotted himself a moron. You can't let a bird think that way about you. How can you let this feathered freak psych you out like this? Oh my hell... I'm a moron! I'm sitting here talking with myself, about myself, on what a damn bird thinks about me. I must be going insane.

Okay... pull your head out, Georgy. If I don't do something, I won't get to the other side. I need to get there, so I've got to try something. The Source is inside. Okay... sack up... grab them like you got a pair and put it all on the line. Let's see what this little freak is made of. "Try this one on for size, you little piece of garesh!"

Again he lifted his hands, but this time instead of ice, a massively-huge wave of water rushed across the entire area and managed to extinguish not only the flames, but drenched Brayson's Goswig as well, forcing the Phoenix to cling to its perch with all its might.

George followed the water with a quick bolt of lightning that hit the base of Fisgig's perch. The shock traveled up the wet surface and surged through the bird's crimson-colored body. The Phoenix fell to the ground and convulsed while smoke billowed from its charred feathers. Eventually the wave of water rebounded off the far side of the cliff walls and headed back in the mage's direction, covering not only the Phoenix but everything in its path.

Oh crap, I overdid it. I didn't think of that, George thought as the wave headed his direction. George threw up his wall of force to keep from being swept away. *Way to go, idiot... you could have killed yourself. I mean... where else was that much water gonna go? You're sitting in a damn toilet bowl made of cliffs. Use your head, George... geesh.*

Eventually the water managed to funnel into the cave's mouth. Heavy steam billowed from within. Again George began to think. *Okay... so it must be hot in there. I wonder what's causing the steam.*

The Phoenix was nowhere in sight. Slowly George moved toward the entrance. As he did, he saw the small Phoenix lying next to the base of the cliff near the cave's opening. The bird's flame was extinguished and he was now lying motionless.

George quickly moved to pluck one of its feathers and put it inside his robe. He remembered Brayson's comment the day he took the family to their new homes. *"The essence of a Phoenix lies within its feathers. This is why they are so glorious to look at."*

Fisgig winced when the feather was pulled, but remained unconscious. George didn't wait around to see if the bird would finish dying. Instead, he quickly dredged through the mud and made his way into the mouth of the cave.

Fisgig eventually began to move. He managed to lift himself off the ground. He shook his feathered head in order to collect his bearings. Then he whispered, "Clearly, I wasn't prepared for his magic. This Mystic-Learner is far more advanced than any other. I need to speak with Brayson."

The cave was dark for the most part, but still navigable with the naked eye as small pools of lava surfaced and ran along the floor before disappearing back into the mountain. The glow from the molten liquid created an eerie feeling. Steam still billowed along the rocky ceiling and the condensation was beginning to drip. Each time one of these droplets hit the lava, it created a much smaller puff of steam and lifted back up towards the ceiling.

Again George's thoughts ran wild. *I would've been afraid of this not too long ago. But now something this creepy seems almost like a second home. Hell... living on these worlds has really been screwing with my head. Could I really be this brave, or am I just a dumbass with no common sense? I can't be insane... insane people don't know they're insane... do they?*

Eventually, after working his way deep into the mountain, George came to an area which opened up. It was as if the mountain was hollow. The top of the cavern could not be seen and the walls to the far side were hundreds of feet away and were barely visible. The water from his wave had made it this far. Many more pools of lava funneled into one another and again vanished within the rock. More of the same droplets of condensation were falling everywhere into these tiny molten rivers. A large booming voice filled the cavern.

"I've been waiting for you, but I didn't appreciate the unwelcome bath!"

George lifted his hands and readied himself to strike, but failed to see a target. Again the booming voice could be heard, but this time it laughed. The sound echoed off the stone. George had to cover his ears to stop the pain. Eventually the laughter subsided and the voice spoke.

"You have nothing to fear from me, Mystic-Learner. I am the Source. I am the one you seek."

George didn't waste any time before responding. "Show yourself. I wish to see my first dragon. Do you always greet the ones who seek to speak with you with laughter? Not the manners I would've expected from someone as ancient as you are."

"You're a confident one, aren't you? I can see you're not afraid. A good quality to have, but also a weakness, don't you agree?"

"Confidence is only a weakness if backed up with nothing more than ignorance. I know what your purpose is. I know you're not here to harm me. You're also not the main reason why I've come to this cave. I do, however, have a few questions. Please show yourself so we can have a decent conversation."

The Source chuckled. Again, the mage grabbed his ears and waited for the dragon to speak. "Apparently, young Mystic-Learner, you're under the same belief many are when they come here to stand before me. It seems you think the Eye of magic is always responsible for swallowing the souls who never return. Maybe I use this test to sample one or two of these tiny morsels for myself... and use this misplaced knowledge that all souls are swallowed by the Eye as a cover to do as I please. You might want to consider that, I too, have swallowed a few."

George swallowed hard and held his breath as he saw the sheer size of the dragon as it appeared. The same cavern which had felt enormous now felt as if it were cramped. The Source rose up to spread his wings and stretched. The wings' ends managed to touch the walls on either side with an impressive span of over four hundred feet. And, as this magnificent beast folded them, a large wind filled the cavern. George was blown to the ground, tumbling over and over before coming to a rest. When he finally stopped, he had just missed landing in one of the lava streams.

Again the Source spoke. "You know of me, George. I shall let you breathe now. I was only kidding about eating those who seek the Eye's ultimate power. You don't know this, but you looked upon me for much of your pathetic life back on Earth."

George stayed seated and struggled to collect his thoughts. "How… how umm… how could I not know I looked at you before today? Were you invisible when I looked in your direction? And, how did you know I was from Earth?"

George meets the Source

Illustration by Kathleen Stone

"I was not invisible. In fact, I was in plain sight. I'm older than your Earth. I'm nearly 29,000,000 years old."

"Did you just say years? I haven't heard anyone say that word since my arrival on Grayham."

"As I have said, I know your Earth and I watched as the God Wars finally destroyed your planet. Granted, there wasn't much of it left once the humans shot their weapons of destruction at one another, but I saw it explode nonetheless! It was sad to see such an advanced race of people destroy each other. They never did figure out how to apply their vast amount of knowledge to find a constructive way to resolve issues. I never did understand why your gods of Earth allowed them to treat each other so. But, I suppose you weren't much different than the people of these worlds and the way they fight with one another for power. It's as if the gods simply don't care or they wished war to happen. I suppose I don't really care much one way or another. I just simply fail to comprehend the god's logic."

George thought a moment before responding. "So you're not a god?"

"No, I'm not a god. I chose to live a simple existence. I wouldn't have chosen to be here now except for my desire to live through the God Wars."

"What do you mean?"

The dragon cleared his throat. George had to grab his ears as the sound once again echoed off the stone walls of the cave.

"I had taken my place amongst the stars with my ancestors. The star you came to know on your Earth as the North Star was how you once knew me. I was beautiful and my light captured the attention of your entire solar system, but when the gods began their wars, many of my kind had to surrender their place within the heavens and we were forced to return to our solid form... this pathetic body you see before you now is all that's left of my being."

George was blown away. "Well, from where I'm standing, what you call pathetic is what I call majestic!"

"Your flattery is received with open wings. Thank you!"

George could only stare as he responded. "I can't imagine how you must feel. The idea you were a star just trips me out, and not just any star... you were the star everyone on Earth knew about.

Do you realize the role you had in our earlier ways of navigation? I have to tell you, I did more than one report about you when I was a kid in school."

Again the dragon chuckled and again George covered his ears. Once the noise subsided, the Source spoke. "I know of your daughter. I also know you wish to see her again. I can read your mind and hear your every thought. I can see you'll do whatever it takes to retrieve her soul from the Book of Immortality's pages. I believe you're strong, but you do have many weaknesses. Do you not fear these weaknesses?"

George stood to his feet. "It's hard to fear something I cannot point out to myself. I appreciate your concern, but all I care about is getting my daughter released from the Book's pages. You're right, I will do anything I need to do. I'm sure you would do the same for a child of your own."

"You presume much, mage. I'm a dragon, and I would find it far easier to release my own child's soul than you would. One bite would do the trick, don't you think?" The dragon winked his massive eye.

"Humor... I wouldn't have expected humor. I had no idea a star could be so funny."

The Source lowered his giant head to a position just above George. "Be careful not to allow the hate in your heart to cloud your judgment. The evil running through your veins could be your undoing. It's clear to me you're much stronger than many of the others who have come before you, but strength is nothing without wit. If you allow your anger to control your mind, then all is lost.

"There is much in your past that I can hear running through your mind. I can feel the pain these moments in time have caused you. I understand how you could resent those who hurt you and how you've let the pain turn you into the killer you've become. I would ask you to reevaluate what's important. I can hear your daughter's soul, and I know she wouldn't want her father killing those he came in contact with in order to get her soul released."

George lowered to the floor and lay on his back. "You can hear my daughter? Can you speak with her as well?"

"I can hear her, but I cannot speak to her."

"Is she happy, does she have good dreams? Does she think I

come home to her every night?"

The dragon tilted his massive head. "How do you know such things? How could a mortal have any idea of what…" The dragon hesitated, and then continued. "Ahhhh… I see… it seems someone has given you information far beyond what the gods normally share with mere mortals. You have found favor with this god. I shall speak with him further on this matter some other time, perhaps. As for you, George, you already know the answer to what your daughter's soul envisions within the Book's pages. It's time for you to look into the Eye."

George was torn. He wanted to change, but his agreement with Lasidious was the only way to get his daughter's soul released from the Book of Immortality's pages. "How do you suggest I retrieve her soul without having to kill those who stand in my way? I am open to any suggestion."

The Source moved his head away as his large figure began to dissipate. "Only you can decide how to handle your own issues of morality. I can see there's good in you. I can also sense that you'll struggle to find your way. I do hope the Eye of Magic finds you worthy of its gift. I do hope we meet again someday, George. You may also want to get some sleep before entering the Eye's chamber. You will want to be fresh and have your wits about you."

George moved past the ancient dragon's lair and eventually came to a heavy-looking metal door at the end of a long corridor. *This must be the place, he thought. I will sleep here before I go inside.* He removed his pack and used it as a pillow.

Once asleep, Lasidious made his presence known within his dreams. "George… we need to talk."

"Holy crap, man, where have you been? I have a million questions."

"I'm sure you do, George. I have a few things to tell you first. But you're going to have to think quickly."

"Okay… nothing new with that concept, so lay it on me… what's up?"

"Brayson knows you killed Amar!"

"What? How in the hell did he find something out like this?"

"Celestria was spying on Brayson and she heard your mother-in-law tell him about it. Apparently she spoke with Morre before you left Lethwitch. She knew of Amar's death and when Brayson mentioned Amar had visited his office, Mary told him his friend was dead."

"This is bad. So tell me how Brayson figured out it was me who killed him. Has he said anything to Athena and Mary yet?"

"I don't think Brayson will talk with Mary until he understands everything. You need a plan, George."

"Ya think... do you really think so, Lasidious? Bah... what a pile of garesh I'm in!"

Brayson's Floating Office

Brayson watched from high above Luvelles through one of the windows of his floating office as Sam made his way into the Village of Vesper. He posted one of the students just outside the School of Magic's invisible tower in order to greet the king of Brandor and show him the way inside.

As Sam entered, he could only marvel at how high the spiral staircase shot up into the distance for what seemed to be forever. The fairies moved quickly between the walls of bookcases and as always, were rearranging the books from one shelf to another in an organized fashion. Sam moved to stand beside the same heavy table where Kepler had been injured when fighting the silver sphere. He moved his hands across the etched markings of magic.

It wasn't long before he found a symbol he recognized. It was the same symbol that rested on one of the rings Brayson had given him when arriving on Merchant Island. He moved to one of the bookcases and began to search for a reference in which to study the symbol's meanings, but his knowledge of the elven language was minimal at best and would not have taken much for his genius mind to become lost in thought if it hadn't been for the Head Master's appearance.

"Sam... it's good to see you again," Brayson said as he appeared behind him. "I trust you found your queen and will be returning to Grayham soon?"

Sam's mood went from one of extreme interest to one of enormous irritation upon hearing the reference to Shalee's well-being, but he somehow managed to keep this fact from Brayson as he responded. "I did find her. She's safe and will continue her journey to find the missing piece of the Crystal Moon."

"I do hope your queen is right about the crystal's location. I have recently found out some grave news... news which has left me with many questions for you, if you will."

"Where shall we talk... somewhere more comfortable, perhaps?"

"Of course."

Brayson waved his hand and before Sam knew it, both of them appeared inside his office. Brayson took the moments necessary to explain the layout of the land and showed Sam how the windows of his office could zoom in on most any spot on Luvelles. After many moments passed and Sam's initial questions had finally been answered, Brayson readdressed the subject he wished to discuss.

"I would like to know how you came to Grayham."

"I suppose there isn't any reason to keep the truth from you. Why do you ask?"

"My new Mystic-Learner is traveling to meet with the Source. Although you never said anything when you arrived on Luvelles, I think you may know him."

Sam moved across the room and took a seat in Brayson's new chair. "Let me guess... George is the one you're talking about?"

"He is. So you know him?"

"I do know him, and I will tell you everything I know. But first, what is the Source and why would George go to meet with it?"

Brayson sighed heavily. He explained the Source's function and what would happen if George looked into the Eye of Magic and survived.

Sam became angered. "This isn't good. George is a master manipulator. He is a liar and a thief. Before he left for Luvelles, he managed to start the largest war Grayham has ever seen. Many died and almost as many will spend the rest of their lives as feeble reminders of the men they used to be."

Brayson had to work up the courage for his next question. "Are you from the same world George was from?"

"You know of Earth?" Sam responded as if caught off guard. "Who gave you this information?"

"I don't think it really matters who gave me this information. I suppose whether you came from this Earth or not tells me nothing other than you are alien."

"Ha… alien… me an alien… I've never been called that before. You'll have to forgive me for laughing."

"No offense taken. What else can you tell me of George?"

"Why are you asking me so many questions about him? What has George done now? Has he screwed you over as well?"

"No, he has done nothing to harm me or anyone else I know of since his arrival on Luvelles. I'm more concerned about the person he killed on Grayham. This person was a friend of mine, an old Mystic-Learner to be more precise, and it was the way George killed him that has me concerned."

Sam stood from the chair. "You say that as if there is a way to kill someone that wouldn't cause you to be concerned?"

Brayson gave a shallow smile. "I see your point and I assure you, I'm not a fan of death. But the particular way George killed this man is something to be worried about. Only the most ancient of elves know the secrets of such ways and it is forbidden to speak of them."

"Forbidden… it isn't forbidden for you and me to share information. With my position as the king of Brandor or rather, all of Southern Grayham now, you're allowed to speak of anything that is necessary to prevent war from happening on your world or mine. I studied your laws before I came and I know this to be true."

"I'm impressed and you are correct, but as of right now, George hasn't done anything to cause a war. The two kingdoms on the world below are at odds with each other as we speak. But this has nothing to do with George."

Sam moved to look out one of the office windows. "Your lands are beautiful. I wouldn't be so sure your Mystic-Learner isn't involved somehow. He's a man who looks for every angle of attack. I studied his tactics after he went missing on Grayham. After gathering the full story, George used those around him to do his dirty work. He did it without lifting a single sword himself and he managed to create a war he never fought in. I assure you that if George is on this world, he'll be looking to gain as much power as he can, and you'll be looking at the face of a war with his name written all over it."

Brayson took a seat in his chair. "If what you say is true, then I need to stop George before he speaks with the Source. Come with me, Sam."

Brayson began to reach for the king's shoulder, but before they teleported, Brayson's Goswig appeared. "Your Mystic-Learner gave me quite the shock. He has been visiting with the Source for a while now. His power is even stronger than yours was before you received your gift so many seasons ago."

Brayson sat down heavily in his chair. "Then we are too late. It is now up to the Eye of Magic to determine whether George will receive his gift of greater power."

Sam's irritation with the situation looked past the Phoenix's presence. "What do you mean, it's too late? Let's barge in there and kill him before he has the chance to finish his visit with this so-called Eye."

Brayson sighed and responded patiently. "The Eye isn't just something you can barge into. Once the Source has initiated his conversation with George, no one can enter his cave. The dragon's magic is far more powerful than mine and I cannot pass through it."

"Damn... we need to find a way to level out the playing field. And I think I know just the way to do it. Brayson, take me to the swamps of this beast you call Grogger. I'll go in after the Crystal Moon's missing piece and you can send Shalee to meet with this Source. She's very powerful and she'll be able to kill George once she has looked into this Eye and receives this same gift George will."

Brayson leaned forward. "How could your queen possibly be ready for such a task? Has she also eaten the heart of another?"

"What the heck are you talking about? Why would someone want to eat another person's heart? Her power is growing because of a god's blessings which were placed on her fetus before being sent to our Earth. She also carries around the memories of Yaloom within that irritating brain of hers."

Fisgig spoke. "How are such things possible?"

Sam continued to look out the window. "When I was on Earth, if a bird began to question me the way you just have, I also would say, how are such things possible? I have come to understand that it doesn't matter how... it only matters that it just is. So shall we go get my wife?"

Brayson stood from his chair, waved his hand and the group vanished. Once they were gone, the shade-god Hosseff removed his hood. He had been listening in on their conversation and remained unseen. His shadowy figure materialized into his human form.

He thought to himself, *Bassorine must've been the one to bless Shalee's fetus. If he didn't do it himself, then he's definitely the one responsible for this blessing. So Yaloom's memories are now Shalee's to call upon... how intriguing it is to be the only god who knows this information. I wonder how long it will be before she's able to summon these memories and find her way to Ancients Sovereign. Very clever, Yaloom... very clever. I would have expected far less from you. Someday the nasha fruit may be used to retrieve your soul from the Book. Using Sam and Shalee's infant son's death to find a way to live again was brilliant. You may just find a way back to godliness, my old friend.*

Brayson's Floating Office

Shalee had entered the swamp the night before. She had to make many magical adjustments to her clothes to keep the leeches from finding their way to her skin as she waded through the marsh. Many mutated creatures now lay dead as a result of the countless attacks they had made to devour her, some of which had teeth the size of her head.

On one occasion, a large bird-like catfish-looking thing had swooped down from the fog and tried to stab her with its sharp spearfish point. She had managed to deflect the attack only to have the creature continue on and stick into another beast that had been stalking her from behind. This place was absolutely miserable and she needed to be at her best to survive.

She was now walking within a protective barrier of magic. The water around her started to move as if it was displacing itself and revealing the ground below. Brayson appeared with both Sam and

Fisgig at his side. They stood within Brayson's magic to give Sam the chance to speak with Shalee.

"What are you doing here Sam?" Shalee said as she studied his companions.

Sam's voice was still cold as he responded. "You need to go with the Head Master. Your skills are needed elsewhere. I will go after the missing piece of crystal."

"What... why?"

"Just go with Brayson and he'll explain everything to you."

"Are you still angry with me?"

"Look... this isn't the time to play 'Let's Make Shalee Feel Better.' You're in trouble and you know it. Just go! Save me the irritation for now. We'll speak again once I've had the chance to calm down!"

Brayson decided to speak up. "Shalee, you should already know who I am. This is my Phoenix. His name is Fisgig. Come into my magic. It will keep you safe."

Shalee did as instructed. Sam turned to look at Brayson. "Is there anything I should know about this Grogger creature?"

Fisgig answered. "The creature will try to swallow you whole if he finds you. I'm not sure where your crystal could possibly be, but if you're swallowed by the toad, the acid inside his belly will slowly digest you over 10 seasons. It will be torturous."

"That's disgusting," Shalee said, staring at the Phoenix. "So you can talk?"

Sam was irritated by her surprise that a bird could speak after all they had gone through since their arrival of Grayham. He ignored the queen and turned to Brayson.

"Okay, the acid is no problem." He lifted the sword of the gods. "Right, Kael?"

The blade responded. "This is correct, Sam." Kael lifted from the king's hand and floated over to Brayson. "Head Master... I may be able to feel the crystal's presence if you were to magnify Sam's senses. I should be able to draw from this power and use it to rule out large areas within the swamp and narrow our search for this missing piece."

Brayson waved his hand over Sam's head. "It is done... will there be anything else?"

Sam thought a moment as Kael returned to his sheath. "Maybe something more suitable to wear while trudging through the swamp—I don't care much for leeches. I was covered with them the last chance I had to walk through a swamp on Grayham."

"I got this," Shaleé said as she moved to stand in front of her king. She leaned in and motioned for him to bend down. She whispered in his ear. "I'm so sorry... I do love you!"

Standing back, she lifted her hand and motioned for his clothes to alter their appearance. Sam now had a tight seal which protected his skin.

"The leeches won't be able to get to you, but the water will eventually seep in." She moved next to Brayson. "Just be safe!"

Sam wanted to say something kind to Shaleé, but his anger wouldn't allow it. Instead, he barked an order which Brayson took no offense from. "Get her out of here. She needs to get started on the trials."

The Underwater City of King Ultor

The leader of the Ultorians stood in front of a shimmering-watery image of Gregory Id. The king's coral castle was cleared of the element and remained dry inside. Magical barriers kept the water out of his organic, porous structure. The prism of colors in which his flesh had changed into were marvelous to look at as the White Chancellor looked through his own personal mirror from the other side. He could see through the Ultorian's colored skin and marveled at how each organ appeared as if outlined.

Ultor bowed to show his respect for Gregory as did the Chancellor from the other side of his mirror.

"How may I help you today, Gregory?"

"Thank you for visiting with me. I have come seeking your assistance. War is approaching and I need your help to keep the evil of the Dark Order from spreading across the land. There is no telling what my brother will do if he is allowed to take control of all of Luvelles with his paladins."

"I understand, but we are a peaceful race, and we are unable to fight a battle which is land-based. Unless you bring the battle to us, I fear there is no way in which to help you."

Gregory thought a moment. "Perhaps the Goswigs could help. Would you speak with them and ask them to join Lord Dowd's men north of Lake Tepp? Their combined magic would bring a powerful force with it. They can march with Dowd to the battle-fields of Olis."

Ultor thought a moment before responding. The pressure of his hand displaced the colors within his chin as he pressed against his face. Once he removed it, the colors once again returned to this area. "I will speak with Strongbear. If he chooses to go to war with you, then the Goswigs will rise to the occasion. But if he chooses not to fight I won't make him go!"

"Understood," Gregory said as he bowed in front of his mirror. "This is all I could ask of you, great king. I will hope my answer shows up ready for battle."

The king bowed. "Let's hope!"

Gregory watched as the mirror sitting in the center of his bed-room chamber went dark. He had no idea he was being watched. Marcus's evil smile crossed his face as he peeked around and stared at his younger brother from behind Gregory's mirror. He stood quietly within a spell of invisibility and was about to strike his brother down when Brayson appeared with Shalee and his Go-swig.

Without offering Gregory an explanation, Brayson teleported them away from the White Chancellor's tower of glass and reap-peared in an area where Marcus couldn't follow.

"Ahhhhhhhhhh," Marcus shouted. "Damn you, Brayson!" Af-ter a long moment filled with agitated swears, the Dark Chancellor eventually began to laugh. "What irony... Brayson has just saved your pathetic life, little brother."

Brayson appeared with the group inside the shrine on the south-ern end of his personal island, which once again held the magic key to the Source's Temple inside it. He motioned for the darkness to dissipate and it was quickly replaced with a soothing light.

"What's going on, brother?" Gregory said as he took note of his company. "Why have you brought me here? I have much to do and very few moments to do it in."

Brayson moved to introduce Shalee, and then explained.

"I'm sending the two of you to speak with the Source. I'm going to teleport ahead of you and let the Ancient One know you are coming. You both need to look into the Eye of Magic. Let's hope you both are able to do this and live."

"What... why would you do this, Brayson?"

"I need you to trust me, Gregory. You're going to need the extra power to fight the forces which will come out of the Kingdom of Hyperia. Boyafed will send his new Argent Commander to rally the forces of the mercenaries of Bestep. He'll continue into the forest of Shade Hollow and ask the Serwin king to send his army to follow them into battle. I imagine Boyafed himself will meet with Kassel, the king of Hyperia. Both of us know the numbers of the Hyperian army. But the one thing I fear most is that Boyafed will call upon the debt Balecut personally owes him."

"Oh no... not Balecut... this is bad, really bad!"

Shalee spoke up. "Who is this Balecut and why is he so bad?"

Fisgig responded. "He's a powerful wizard who lives within the Petrified Forest. He can summon the power to bend the moments in which we live. Even though this power will not work against another wizard or even another warlock who commands stronger magic, this ability is feared by most everyone on this world."

"So you're saying this Balecut guy can manipulate time?"

Fisgig's feathered face appeared to be confused as he responded, "I'm not familiar with this term, 'time,' Shalee. Please explain its meaning."

"It means the same thing as the moments which you just referred to as being bendable, but it will be easier to explain when we have enough time or rather, enough moments in which to explain it."

"I think I understand, but as I was saying... Balecut can slow down this concept of time, or rather, the moments in which we live and give the Dark army an advantage while in battle. This is why it is so important for one of you to successfully look into the Eye of Magic. Hopefully Brayson will be able to teach you how to summon this cherished power once you have received the Eye's gift."

"I understand," Gregory responded, but Shalee was deep in thought. Brayson moved to get her attention.

"What has your mind tied up, child?"

Shalee took a deep breath. "So it's safe to say one of us may never return from this journey."

Brayson lifted her chin and looked hard into her eyes. "Both of you may never return from this journey. You can have no doubt in your abilities, Shalee. You must find the courage to go before the Eye and look into the gem's light. The Source won't stop you from looking into the eye once you arrive, I'll see to that, but you'll still need to find your way through the Void Maze in order to get there."

Gregory nudged Shalee. "This will be easy. I've done this before. I'm far more powerful than I was the first series of moments I went through the Maze. We will be standing before the Source's cave in timed moments. Just stay close to me."

Shalee sat down on the floor, ignoring Gregory's flawed use of the word, 'time,' and said, "Head Master, Sam told me you possess the strongest magic on all of Luvelles. Why don't you stop this Boyafed from recruiting this Balecut guy in the first place?"

"My position as the Head Master, though powerful, does not allow me to choose a side in a war. I don't wish for this war to happen, but if I were to force those on Luvelles to stop this war, it would be an abuse of my power. All I can do is try to act as a peacemaker. You are not bound by my same rules. You will be able to use your new powers to help stop this war. I am, however, going to try to find what is causing all the tension between both armies. I plan to start by speaking with your friend George."

"He is no friend of mine," Shalee snapped. "Is he behind all this?"

"I can't be sure, but if what Sam has told me is true... and George was the one responsible for your war on Grayham, then I think he would be the best place to start my investigation."

"Oh, it's true alright." Shalee said, then standing, she looked at

Gregory. "Shall we go?"

Gregory looked at Brayson.

"I need you to tell Lord Dowd he'll have to finish gathering the forces for the battle. I already spoke with King Ultor. He'll need to do the rest of what was requested of me in my absence."

Gregory took Shalee's hand after securing the key to the Source's temple within his robe. The next thing Shalee knew, she was standing outside the Void Maze.

Chapter 19
"I'm Drunk as a Skunk and Need Some Lovin"
The Dark Order's Temple

Boyafed was preparing to leave and go to the Petrified Forest. He was standing in front of a mirror located inside his personal chambers within the Order's Temple when the goddess Mieonus appeared before him. He jumped back with lightning reflexes, grabbed his blessed long sword and quickly took a defensive position, ready to strike. His muscles rippled and were uncovered as they stood at attention.

"Relax, Boyafed! I'm not here to harm you. Do you know who I am?"

"I suggest you tell me before I decide to cut this conversation short."

"Ha… how clever you must consider yourself. I'm Mieonus. You may kneel before me now."

The Order leader knew the name and quickly took a knee and bowed his head. "Has Hosseff sent you, goddess? What must I do to serve my lord?"

She hated the way his statement sounded. The thought of being the shade-god's personal errand girl made her want to puke. Dismissing her irritation, she moved across the room. Her cherry red gown flowing gracefully as she moved. Her black lifted heels clicked against the white marble of his bedroom floor, as she sauntered to the side of his bed. She sat in a comfortable position and studied the powerful warrior before responding. She was amused at how trained Hosseff's followers were. He had kept his head lowered and waited patiently for her to speak.

"Hosseff didn't send me. Come to me and relax!"

Boyafed did as instructed. She watched him closely as he walked across the room, then she patted the bed beside her for him to sit. He did so without question and kept his head bowed once seated.

She enjoyed his strong elven features and found him to be attractive. His eyes were dark brown, hair short and he had a strongly-defined jaw which complimented the masterpiece which served as his frame.

She seductively reached over and lifted his chin until his eyes found hers. She could feel him tremble and his skin quickly covered with goosebumps. With her sweetest smile she spoke.

"Have you ever touched a goddess before, Boyafed? Would you enjoy being with a woman of my beauty?"

Boyafed was unsure how to respond. He sat quietly, trying to find a way to gather his thoughts. The goddess leaned in and gently kissed him, but he didn't kiss back. She kissed him again and kept at it until he responded. After a few moments passed, he found the courage to reach in and pull her to him. She was intoxicatingly beautiful and he could feel his heart pounding.

He stood, lifted her from the bed and took complete control. She allowed the exchange to happen and once the mood had finally died down and both had been completely satisfied, the goddess delivered the bad news while still in his arms.

"Boyafed...I wish with everything in me I could say my visit was solely for the benefit you have so graciously blessed me with. But I cannot say this without it being a lie. I hate to tell you but, something awful has happened. I don't wish to hurt you, but I have also come to deliver bad news... news I'm sure will make you wish to seek vengeance. I assure you I truly don't wish to be the deliverer of such grave news."

The Order leader rolled toward her, kissed her and with a rejuvenated attitude replied, "I'm a big boy. I'm sure I can handle it."

"I don't doubt your ability. I have no doubts in you at all. I wouldn't be laying here beside you if I did."

"So tell me why it is you've come."

"You must first promise to hear me out before getting upset."

"I promise... please continue."

"Your son Kiayasis has been killed by the king of Southern Grayham. I have come to tell you that he broke your son's neck and left him lying in the forest just to the southeast of Grogger's Swamp. I don't like this one bit. I have always admired you, Boyafed, and a man of your stature deserves better."

Boyafed rolled clear of the bed and stood up, failing to cover himself. "Kiayasis was supposed to kill the queen once she made her way through the Swamp. What would make the king decide to kill him? He would have had no knowledge of Kiayasis's order to kill her."

Boyefed-Elf and Leader of the Dark Order

Illustration by Kathleen Stone

"The king saw his queen within Kiayasis's strong arms. He watched them hold one another on their journey to the swamp. I've come to tell you this so you can have your vengeance. I'm truly sorry for your loss. I wouldn't want any child of mine lying lifeless on the forest floor."

"Where is the king now?"

"He's inside the swamp. If you hurry, you can catch him and if you wish... I'll return to comfort you when you have received your payment for your loss with the king's life."

The goddess watched as Boyafed donned the black-plated armor of the Order. He sheathed his sword and assisted her to stand beside him. He took one last glance of admiration at her godly body before kissing her goodbye.

"I must go. I have a king to kill and a sacrifice to give to Hosseff. I would enjoy your company when I'm done." Boyafed said, and then vanished.

Mieonus smiled wickedly as she put her dress back on. She spoke softly to the empty room and pretended for her own amusement that Boyafed was still standing in front of her. *"Aside from my attraction to you being fictitious, Boyafed, you're an idiot, and how could you really believe that I, a goddess, would truly want to be with someone like you? You'll just have to finish your grieving process without me. I must give credit where credit is due, however, you were good.*

Boyafed now stood just outside the Order's stables which held his personal Krape Lord. Before the dark warrior had the chance to enter, Hosseff appeared. Boyafed quickly dropped to a knee. "My lord, to what do I owe the pleasure?"

From within the nothingness beneath the god's hood, Lasidious altered his voice to match Hoseff's whispery tones. "Be careful and do not to allow yourself to be deceived by Mieonus, Boyafed. What she told you about your son is true and Kiayasis is dead. Your desire to avenge his death is acceptable... but Mieonus has desires of her own far beyond just taking you to bed. Her desires are to manipulate you for her own purposes. I don't wish to see you turned into the goddess's personal puppet. You're far too strong of a man for this."

"I shouldn't have laid with her, my lord. I beg your forgiveness. It won't happen again."

"Nonsense—I understand the desires of a man. You did what any man would have done considering the situation, and I applaud you for taking advantage of the opportunity while it existed. The goddess is indeed a beautiful woman, is she not?"

"Yes my lord... and a good lover, to be sure. But I'll avoid her in the future, my lord."

"There's no need to avoid her. Use her how you will. Turn her into a plaything of your own. Just remember the god you serve when the moment comes that she tries to manipulate you further. We have many things to discuss. Your desire to avenge your son's death may give you yet another chance to make me proud."

"I live to serve you, my lord. What would you ask of me?"

The City of Nept,
Just after Late Bailem

The City of Nept had a heavy population, but it was the outskirts of this city that called out to many of those on Luvelles to come and see its beauty. This was the home of some of the finest vineyards throughout the world. Yes, there were other vineyards on these other worlds, but none with the sweet taste of a wine called mesolliff.

The three women were now sitting in an old countryside inn. This was the first place the ladies had seen that reminded them of their farming community back home in Lethwitch. Both Athena and Susanne were glad to finally get off their feet after chasing Mary around the countryside in her drunken state.

For the most part, Susanne had been taking care of baby Garrin while she watched Athena assist Mary to walk between the farms. There wasn't a lot of fancy magic being used around here—in fact, it was quite the opposite, and most of the locals failed to command any sort of real power at all. The grapes grew naturally and were used to produce many different forms of wines, but one special wine was made from a magical vine which grew not far from this inn, the only one within all of Luvelles or better still, in all of the worlds, and its cost was considerably higher than any other wine. The amount of coin to buy a single bottle was quite steep.

With but one taste, Mary had taken a liking to it. The mesolliff wine was all it took and she would have nothing to do with tasting any other. She had been drinking for most of the day, but with just a tiny sip, she had become intolerable. Mary quickly opened her bag and took out the coin Brayson had given her for this trip and slammed it on the bar.

Athena and Susanne refused the drink and were completely embarrassed as the effects of the wine made their mother say things she would never normally say: "I'm drunk as a skunk and need some lovin'." She said it over and over, loudly announcing to the entire establishment that she was quite anxious for some very specific attention. She leaned up against Athena. "I so need some lovin'... I NEED SOME LOVIN', EVERYONE!"

"Mother, shut up, will ya? You're embarrassing us. Let's take her home so Brayson can shut her up." Susanne wanted to die as she watched the owner of the inn finally walk over to speak with them.

"These must be her first moments tasting mesolliff, I see. It's easy to spot a woman who's had her first taste of nature's seduction. I suggest you take her home before she starts to make out with the furniture. It'll get worse before it gets better. I would hurry if I were you."

Mary lifted the bottle and took a big swig. The man behind the counter smiled and crudely said. "I hope you don't have any pets at home. She's in for a crazy night."

The girls quickly gathered around Mary. After Susanne lifted Garrin into her arms, Athena read the spell from the Scroll of Teleportation. In an instant they were back home and standing in Mary's bedroom next to the mirror which Brayson had given their mother.

Mary didn't waste any of her moments. She tossed the corked bottle to the floor, stumbled up to the mirror,and evoked its power. Athena grabbed the bottle from the floor and headed for the door. The girls didn't even have a chance to leave before Brayson's image appeared. As they shut the door behind them, all they heard him say was, "I'll be right there!"

Mary had left her window to the outside world open. The girls felt as if they were completely out of their element as Mary's screams of passion filled the night air once Brayson began to satisfy her needs. Kepler and Payne poked their heads out of Kepler's den beneath the rocks.

The demon-jaguar shouted, "Athena, what's all the commotion about?"

"Payne go see, kitty."

Athena screamed at Payne. "You move and I'll skin ya alive. You go back into that hole right now or I will beat you both. I'm already embarrassed enough, now get some sleep… both of you, do you understand me?"

Kepler lowered back into the hole without saying another word, but Payne waited until Athena and Susanne went inside before he teleported to hovering position far enough away from the window but still able to look through and see everything.

The fairy-demon's head tilted back and forth in many different directions as he became confused as to what was happening. After many, many moments passed and her screams continued to fill the night, all he said after teleporting back into Kepler's lair was, "Kitty, why they do that… it's yuck!"

Kepler didn't look up, but he did have a grin crossing his furry face, which was covered by his front legs. "You will understand someday, freak, but for now why don't you get some sleep."

Athena closed the door to her home and thought. *Well, I'm glad Brayson likes mother's adventurous side. But how can I be expected to look her in the eyes tomorrow?*

The Source's Cave
Outside the Eye of Magic's Chamber

George began to stir. He felt rested and his dream visit with Lasidious had been informative, extremely informative. He grabbed a quick bite to eat from his pack and stood to face the heavy metal door. Behind it, the Eye of Magic waited.

He reached out, but the door opened itself before he could touch it. A chill ran down his spine as the heavy hinges squealed from their many seasons of going without proper maintenance. Beyond the door, sitting attached to the top of a thick wooden staff at the center of a cubed-shaped room was a ruby-red fiery gem. It was large, about the size of his fist. Nothing else occupied the room.

That's it, George thought to himself. *How anticlimactic is this? It's just a stone on a piece of wood. I was expecting something... well, more, I suppose.*

He walked into the room and the door slammed hard behind him, the heavy metal making a thunderous noise. He rubbed his ears, trying to stop the ringing as the room filled with a blinding red light. He had to cover his eyes to protect them and before he knew it, he was standing in front of an angelic being. The light had softened and was replaced with a soft white—everywhere, that is, but for one spot.

The being's face could not be seen due to the light which took its place. Beneath this illuminated face, a ghostly body shimmered while large feathered wings extended on either side. The mage had absolutely no idea what to say or do. Some moments past before the silence was broke.

"I have been waiting for you, George."

He watched as the light of the illuminated face began to fade and was replaced by a large eye. There was no mouth, no lips, no anything to go along with it. It was just a big eye sitting on top of the shoulders of an angel's body.

"Does looking at me displease you?"

George swallowed hard. "I wouldn't say I'm displeased. I would say I'm kind of unsure of what to think right now."

"Your first honest answer. I trust you're prepared to look into my Eye? Do you feel you're ready? Do you worry I will steal your soul from you and swallow it?"

"I'm not worried about anything. I do have questions, though."

The eye blinked. "I've never had a Mystic-Learner come before me and request to have his questions answered. Do you not fear for your soul? I have taken the lives of many of those who were not ready!"

George shrugged his shoulders. "I have nothing to lose. I figure that if I die, you're just doing me a favor and I won't have to deal with this place any longer. Other than that, I feel pretty good about my chances and I can handle whatever it is you're gonna throw at me."

"Your confidence is intriguing... I will allow you one question."

George had to think. He had many, but needed to narrow it down to the most important one. After a short while he finally spoke. "I have listened to Master Id speak of using his power to try to become god-like. He said no one has ever been able to obtain this ultimate power, even though your gift would allow for this to happen. I would like to know why they have not been able to take the gift you gave them and use it to accomplish this ultimate goal of becoming a god. I guess what I'm really asking is, what's holding them all back?"

Again the eye blinked. There was a long silence before its voice filled the room. "Even the most confident have failed to realize they have no limitations to their new power. It is their own inability to believe in the magnitude of the gift which keeps them from moving to a higher level of existence. You are the first to stand before me and have the confidence to pursue a higher level of knowledge. The others simply looked into my eye when asked if ready, and most surrendered their lives because of it."

"What about Master Brayson?"

The Eye blinked. "That would be another question, but there is no harm in answering it. Even your Master Brayson didn't carry the presence of mind with him that you do when he looked into my Eye. Step forward, George, and receive your gift."

George did as instructed. He looked into the massive pupil and suddenly began to feel light as he floated from the floor. Images appeared before him as his mind filled with the knowledge of the most ancient of mystics. Eventually he lowered to the floor and closed his eyes.

The Eye looked down at George's motionless figure. "Sleep, warlock... you need your rest! Your confidence has made you extremely powerful."

Grogger's Swamp

Sam held Kael in his hand. The trail of death the king left as both he and the sword of the gods moved through the murky waters was long. Now they came to a good-sized hill and were finally able to crawl clear of the water for the first time. Walking up the steep embankment, Kael ordered Sam to stop.

"Why?" Sam whispered.

The blade responded. "It's the crystal. I can sense its power. If I'm right, it is just beyond this hill. I would suggest we use caution. We have no idea what we could be facing."

"Agreed."

Sam lowered himself to the ground and finished climbing the hill on his belly. Once at the top he peeked over, but there was nothing but a big mossy mound in the middle of more swamp. The king rolled over and lifted Kael close to his mouth.

"I see nothing; it all looks the same as everything else we've seen."

"Trust me, Sam, I know the crystal is here somewhere. Look again. Maybe you're missing something."

Sam rolled back to his belly and peeked over the hill. Nothing was there. After thinking it through, he picked up a small stone which lay nearby. He rolled to one side and chucked it. Moving to his belly once again, he waited for the pebble to disturb the water below... and what he saw next gave him great concern.

The large moss-covered mound was not a mound at all—it was a creature of some sort. It quickly turned around, opened its mouth, and a large tongue lashed out in the direction of the pebble's disturbance. The tongue was huge, displacing much of the swamp's water as it tore into its surface.

Sam slowly rolled to his back and whispered, "My lord, Kael... they said Grogger was big, but that's an understatement. I wouldn't call him big... I'd say he was enormous."

The blade responded. "I have news, but it won't make you happy."

"And what would that be? Let me guess. The crystal is inside the toad."

"Yes, it is, and you need to get it out."

"Damn, you could have said no!"

For the first time, Sam heard the blade laugh at his humor before responding. "So what is the plan?"

"Beats the hell out of me," Sam shrugged. "It's not like I go charging into the belly of a toad all the time. Let me think a bit." Sam rolled back over to take another look. Grogger was gone. He looked up and to his surprise, the shapple toad was falling from the sky, intending to land on the back side of their position.

Sam quickly commanded Kael to bring forth his fire and further commanded the blade to protect his skin from the toad's acid. He tucked Kael tight to his body to ensure he didn't drop him and kept the point of the blade toward the ground. He closed his eyes, balled up tight, and waited. He could hear the screams of the souls crying out from inside the toad's stomach as his large mouth opened. The force with which Grogger pulled them in nearly knocked Sam unconscious, but somehow he avoided getting any broken bones. In fact, the toad swallowed them so quickly, the flame of Kael's blade didn't have a chance to burn the creature until they were inside.

Grogger began to hop around wildly as his insides started to cook from Kael's heat. The motion helped Sam regain his composure. When he opened his eyes he found himself in a pocket of protection. A man dressed for the hunt and holding the crystal's missing piece was staring at him. They both were being bounced around, but quickly Sam discarded his surprise and pain and buried Kael deep into the base of the beast's stomach to have something to hang onto.

He could hear Grogger's horrific cries and suddenly the pile of bodies beyond the protective barrier began to shift. The toad was going to barf. Sam reached over and pulled the hunter close.

"Hang on... this is going to get interesting!" he shouted. and followed this up with another command for Kael to extend his blade.

Like they were projectiles, every creature and every being inside Grogger's belly was thrown out and into the open, all of them landing on the side of the hill. Sam held tight to Kael as they were pushed out. His command for the sword to extend its length had provided the effect Sam had been after. Kael sliced the toad from its belly all the way out of the beast's mouth. The size of Grogger instantly shrank once the mound of bodies filling him had been expelled, while the brutal cut left him lifeless and nearly split in half through the lower portion of his body.

Sam stood and commanded Kael's flame to dissipate. He wiped the blade clean as best he could under the circumstances and extended his hand toward the hunter. Once on his feet, Sam spoke while looking around at all the partially digested bodies.

"What's your name?" he asked as he reached down and picked up the crystal from the ground. "This is what I came for. I hope you don't mind—I need to take this bad boy with me."

"Uummm... yes, yes, go right ahead. My name is Geylyn Jesthrene. I'm from the City of Hyperia."

"Well, Geylyn, looks like this is your lucky day. How long were you sitting inside the toad's belly, and how did you keep yourself protected from the acid?"

"I'm not supposed to say anything. I was asked to give you the crystal when you came for me and then return home without speaking further. I hate to be rude, but I must go. Thank you for saving me, sir." Geylyn pulled a small scroll from beneath his shirt, read the words from it and vanished. Sam watched as Geylyn's invisible body made tracks along the hillside working his way toward the waters of the swamp.

Sam lifted Kael up to his face. "Well, how's that for gratitude? He wouldn't even answer my questions. Let's find my pack, help as many of these people as we can, and get them out of here."

Before a step could be taken, Mosley appeared. The wolf-god said nothing at first and gave the king a moment to think.

Sam swallowed his pride and then said, "I suppose I owe you an apology for how I spoke with you in my throne room. I was out of line and I'm sorry for speaking to you in that tone. Are we still friends?"

"Of course we are, Sam. I told you you would eventually calm down. A brush with death will make anyone think about what's important. I know you're struggling with Shalee's unfaithfulness and I want you to also know it doesn't sit well with me either, but with enough moments passing, this pain too shall pass and your anger will once again be replaced with love. Stay the course and I'm sure everything will turn out how it should. Once you leave this swamp, you may want to make your way back to Grayham. War is coming to Luvelles and it won't be safe here much longer."

"What about Shalee? I can't just leave her here."

Mosley tilted his furry wolf head as if confused. "Why... where is Shalee, anyway?'

"She has started the trials to meet with the Source. Brayson has sent her to look into the Eye of Magic." Sam could instantly see Mosley knew something he didn't. "What are you not telling me?"

"I wish I could tell you, Sam. I can't tell you all I know. It was Bassorine's wish that I stay silent."

"Well, what the hell does that mean?"

"I need to go, Sam. I will come to you at a later moment. I must go and join this piece of the crystal with the others." The wolf-god vanished.

"Damn the gods," Sam snapped. After a moment he redirected his attention elsewhere. He removed the small vial Brayson had given him and after a close inspection of all the motionless figures, decided he could save only ten of the souls who lay on the side of the hill.

He would lead them to safety once they recovered and had been fed.

The City of Gogswayne

That night, the Goswigs couldn't believe their eyes as King Ultor himself made his way to the banks of Crystal Lake. He had sent Swill and Syse ahead to summon them to a meeting. Everyone was present except for Strongbear, the one Ultor wanted to speak with the most.

The king's skin finished changing and he now stood in front of nearly a thousand different creatures that held the title Goswig. He looked at Gage. "Where is Strongbear?"

Gage swallowed hard. "He's hibernating, Your Majesty."

"Why would the bear be hibernating when the season has not yet changed?"

The entire Goswig population began to murmur, all of them unsure how the badger would explain the situation. They had all agreed to have Gallrum conveniently avoid telling the king about the uniting of their magic to bring winter to their underground village.

Gage decided to tell the truth. "Your Majesty, Strongbear was driving us all crazy. We were tired of listening to him order us around, so we pooled our magic to bring in the new season only within our village."

The reaction they received was not the one they expected. Instead, Ultor began to laugh. Gage still wasn't sure how the gagging motion of the Ultorian race made him feel when they laughed. Every occasion the king leaned forward as if to hurl, Gage wanted to vomit himself and leaned forward.

Eventually the king settled down. "Who organized this use of power?"

Every single one of the Goswigs pointed at Gage. Again the king began to laugh. The badger watched and again, every occasion the king lunged forward, he did too. He found his stomach cramping as a result of the tension he felt from the king's actions. Eventually his laughter subsided again and he said, "We have much to discuss, Gage, but you will need to wake Strongbear. The White Army needs you all to fight beside them in the upcoming war and Strongbear's power will be needed. I will be back tomorrow night." Ultor moved into the water and disappeared beneath the surface. His skin once again changed to an iridescent blue as his large water wings propelled him through the water.

Gage tapped his small staff against the ground. "Well, that's just great! Now we've got to wake him up!" He turned and looked at the mass of Goswigs. "So are you with me... or against me?" he mocked.

All the Goswigs grumbled as they headed back home.

The Luvelles Gazette

When you want an update about your favorite characters

The Next Day Early Bailem

Shalee and Gregory are working their way through the Void Maze. The job George did before them, killing most of the creatures once inside the dungeon's many corridors, has left the pair a fairly simple task of just finding a way through. The trial of the maze has now become more of an effort just to avoid getting lost.

Kepler and Payne are still waiting for George. Kepler has been working with Payne to teach him how to speak more efficiently. Something strange is happening with Payne and he seems to be learning at a rapid pace. The demon-cat has decided to embrace the little freak and accept his company as permanent. Kepler hates to admit it, but Payne is growing on him.

Mary, Athena, Susanne and baby Garrin are inside Mary's home having breakfast. The events of the night before last are still fresh inside Mary's mind, despite the hangover she has from the effects of the mesolliff wine.

Boyafed has set up camp and is waiting for Sam to exit the swamp.

Brayson has given Lord Dowd the message that Gregory will not be able to finish gathering his forces. Dowd has sent Krasous, his Argont Commander, to meet with Wisslewine inside the enchanted woods of Wraithwood Hollow. Krasous is to ask the Wraith Hound Prince to call forth his pack of ferocious canine warriors from the center of the Under Eye and bring them to the Battlegrounds of Olis.

Krasous will also go to the Spirit Plains to find the king of a race of spirits called the Lost Ones and capture Shesolaywen so they can use his Call of Canair.

Brayson is now sitting outside the entrance to the Source's cave waiting for George to make his exit.

Mieonus is watching as Sam guides those he managed to save from Grogger's belly out of the swamp. The magic inside the swamp will not allow for teleportation. Once they make their exit they'll all be able to teleport home. She is looking forward to the confrontation between Sam and Boyafed.

Mosley and Alistar have returned to Ancients Sovereign. They have called for a meeting of the gods to be held inside the Hall of Judgment.

Mosley managed to successfully leave an impression on the minds of the leaders of the World of Harvestom that war is the only course of action. The king of Kless has called for this war with the decision solely based on the theft of the Seeds of Plenty. He ordered the leaders of his Brown Coat army of centaurs to march against the king of Tagdrendlia's Dark Coats by Early Bailem tomorrow. What is left of the food supply in Kless will be used to feed the army as they march into battle.

Many souls will be returned to the Book of Immortality's pages from the devastation and Hosseff, the shade, will be busy collecting the souls and returning them to the Book.

Gage and the other Goswigs are waiting for Strongbear to exit his cave. They have used their magic to reverse the change of seasons and the bear has been slow to wake. The badger and Gallrum are expecting him to be quite grumpy once he has been told everything.

Marcus is waiting inside his dark tower-palace. He is hoping George will return soon so they can implement the last part of their plans. Soon he will be able to stand before the Eye of Magic.

Lasidious and Celestria are inside their home beneath the Peaks of Angels. Both are getting ready and plan to teleport to the Hall of Judgment for Mosley's meeting. And, despite this being Mosley's meeting, Lasidious is about to deliver some heavy news which will change the course of everything.

Lasidious's meeting with Boyafed outside the Order's stables was everything he hoped it would be. The God of Mischief would no longer need to take the form of a shade to manipulate the Dark Order's leader. The last thing Boyafed said to him when ending their little meeting was, "I live to serve you, my lord."

Lasidious had returned home to Ancients Sovereign afterward and celebrated the deception with his evil lover Celestria.

Thank you for reading the Luvelles Gazette

Chapter 20

A Pair of Eyes Closed Forever

The gods assembled within Gabriel's Hall of Judgment. As always, Keylom's heavy hooves clacked against the marble floor as his majestic centaur body entered the room. Lictina's ugly lizardian face, which hardly complimented her elegant robes laced with gems, followed next as her reptilian tail brushed against the floor to take her normal seat.

Bailem appeared behind his chair, adjusted his robe covering his portly belly and spread his beautiful angel wings just enough to allow for him to sit. The rest of the gods either appeared or walked into the room one after another and as always, Lasidious and Celestria were the last to make their presence known.

Mosley moved to begin the meeting once Gabriel floated his binding over and lowered to a comfortable position on the heavy stone table. "I have the third piece of the Crystal Moon, Lasidious. The moment has come to join it with the others."

"Then do it, no one's stopping you," Lasidious said in a snide tone. "We didn't need to come to a meeting just to join the crystals. Go to the Temple of the Gods on Grayham and place it with the other two pieces George collected while on that world."

The room filled with questions. Mosley spoke over the top of them all. "I thought George still had the crystals. Since when did you place them back into the temple?"

"They have been there for nearly 20 Peaks of Bailem. I suppose I just forgot to mention it."

Mieonus stood and shouted at Lasidious. "How could you possibly forget to mention this kind information?"

"Shut up, Mieonus," Mosley snapped. "Your anger won't solve anything. When will you ever figure out that he does this to irritate you, and yet you keep allowing him to get under your skin? Sit down and be quiet."

"I will sit when I wish." The goddess looked around the room, but when every eye looked at her as if she were an idiot, she stomped her high-heeled foot and sat with a huff.

Mosley could not help but enjoy the goddess's embarrassment. After a moment he continued. "I'm assuming you've protected the crystal from being taken and all we can do is add to its pieces."

Lasidious stood and assisted Celestria from her chair. "Mosley is correct. The pieces can be added to, but you won't be able to remove the crystals from the new statue they will rest upon."

Hosseff stood, his wispy voice escaping from the nothingness that was his face as he spoke. "Exactly what kind of statue is it?"

"I suggest you go and take a look for yourself. The statue will be the new resting place for the Crystal Moon from now on." Lasidious and Celestria vanished.

Without further discussion, every god disappeared, only to reappear in front of the new placeholder for the crystal. The statue was made of the most precious gem that could be found in the mines on the World of Trollcom. It was called Diamante and was clear as crystal with a slight yellow hue, but very slight. The light within the Temple reflected from it and produced a glorious glimmer. The image portrayed was that of Lasidious. He stood with his hood down and his hands extended toward the sky. Both hands had been placed together to act as a cradle for the Crystal Moon. The first two pieces of the crystal had been placed in his palms. With the heavy, pure black marble base that the god's feet rested on, the total height of the entire piece was about twenty feet. It rested exactly where the old statue of Bassorine had been.

Mieonus was the first to speak. "I say we destroy it. Who does he think he is to change everything like this? He didn't speak with us and get our approval. This is an outrage!"

Alistar stepped forward. "He doesn't need our approval. We cannot destroy it. If we do, Lasidious will destroy the Crystal Moon. He doesn't need to ask us how we feel about this. He's the strongest of us all now and he holds the power to govern the worlds in the palms of his hands—no pun intended, of course. We can do nothing but allow him to glorify himself. It would seem he has found a way to capture the eyes of the worlds without manipulating the free will of others. I personally think his plan is brilliant. I think it's safe to say we understand what the bigger picture is now, Mosley."

"And what would that be?" Keylom asked. His centaur hooves clacked against the floor of the temple as he moved to a better position to speak. "How does a statue explain a bigger picture?"

Mosley spoke out. "You may be right, Alistar. This makes perfect sense. Lasidious must've stolen the Crystal Moon in order to implement a plan to get rid of Bassorine. He knew that with Bassorine out of the way, he would be the only one powerful enough to control the Crystal Moon."

The wolf turned to look at Gabriel. "Lasidious knew you would be unable to take the crystal from him even after the pieces were put back together. It's his free will to hang on to it and since the laws within your pages keep you from taking away his own personal free will, then he'll be able to hold the Crystal Moon over our heads as a bargaining chip of sorts.

"He knows that without Bassorine, we don't have the power to create a new Crystal Moon. He never has had any intention of destroying it, and this game of his is nothing more than a big diversion. He simply wishes to be the centerpiece for all the worlds to see and it looks as though he has implemented his plan perfectly. I think there's an even bigger picture here, though. I would be willing to bet he hopes to increase the numbers of his followers on each world substantially. This whole thing has been about his desire to get the masses to worship him and take over the Book."

Alistar spoke up. "I agree with Mosley, but I suspect Lasidious is still prepared to destroy the Crystal Moon if we don't continue to play his game." The gods watched as Alistar clearly had something else to say. When he leaned forward, he whispered.

"Everyone, touch one another. We need to combine our power and protect the next part of what I'm about to say. We can't afford to have Lasidious listening in. This is critical and I'm evoking the Rule of Fromalla."

The gods did as instructed. Agreeing to Fromalla, they touched each other and surrounded themselves with a field of protection.

Alistar put his hand on Bailem's shoulder and the other on Mosley's back. He continued, "Clearly we didn't take everything into account when we created Gabriel. We overlooked something very important."

"And what would that be?" the Book of Immortality responded. "I know of every law and I have overlooked nothing. Some of your laws aren't written to completion, but there's nothing that would pertain to this conversation."

The others agreed, but Alistar remained patient. "I'm not referring to a law that has been written. I'm not referring to a law at all. I didn't think of it until now and even then, I didn't put it all together until Mosley said Lasidious plans to take control of the Book. Gabriel doesn't have the ability to grow in strength."

Hosseff's voice whispered from within the emptiness of his hood as he interrupted. "Why would this be necessary? The Book is clearly stronger than us all. I'm not following your logic."

Alistar nodded. "The Book is powerful to be sure, but Gabriel's power is limited to what each of us has given him when we poured a part of our being into his many pages."

"So what are you getting at?" Mieonus snapped in her normal irritating manner.

Alistar looked at her a moment, shook his head in disgust, and then continued. "All of us know we seek followers to increase our power. Just look at what Lasidious has accomplished so far. His powers have grown steadily for the last 10,000 seasons. He's surpassed all of us, but the one he wasn't able to surpass was Bassorine. And now that Bassorine has been destroyed by Gabriel, Lasidious is the strongest of us all. There were many who served Bassorine who no longer have a god to serve.

"Think about it! Mosley is right in his observation. We have watched Lasidious grow because of the sheer number of those on the worlds who worship him. Nearly the entire World of Dragonia now bows to him when he appears before them. The trolls of Trollcom and even the vampires worship him, and we all know how significant their numbers are. This is just the start of what he has accomplished. I think Lasidious plans to gain enough followers to eventually grow more powerful than Gabriel. I think he's going to do this by putting himself in front of all the worlds and glorify himself until they all kneel before him and choose to serve him."

Mosley cut in. "This makes perfect sense." Again he looked at the Book. "Lasidious wouldn't need to break the laws within your pages to become strong enough to control you. With the way your laws are written, we cannot stop him from outgrowing your power. We cannot fight against him because your laws require you to protect him. If we try to destroy Lasidious to stop this from happening, you'll destroy us because if you don't, you'll be destroyed for your failure to do your duty! Your own pages hold the power to destroy you and Lasidious knows this. If you don't do your job, the laws on your pages will invoke this power and he still wins. I hate to admit this, but I admire Lasidious's genius. He's using our own laws against us. It's brilliant—not very nice, but still, brilliant nonetheless—and there's nothing we can do to stop him."

"Hang on just a moment," Bailem said, quickly adjusting his robe to a better position on his chubby belly before adding to the conversation. He once again touched the back of the centaur and with his other hand he placed it on Alistar's shoulder. Once the conversation was protected again, he spoke.

"This is all very disturbing. So how should we proceed? It doesn't appear we have any options. If we fight Lasidious we'll be destroyed by Gabriel. If we don't fight him he'll be able to destroy us all someday soon. I see no other solution. We should surrender the Book to Lasidious and allow him to govern Gabriel while we still can. We need to allow him to control the worlds as well. All we can do is hope he's gracious enough to allow us to continue existing."

"I agree with Bailem," Alistar said. "I have no desire to be destroyed! We should vote on this right now!"

All the gods erupted into a large argument over the different ways they could possibly try to foil Lasidious's plans, but none of their ideas sounded as if they had any merit. Eventually Mosley managed to get their attention. He did so by lifting his head and howling, allowing for the temple walls to reverberate his call. Once he had their full attention, the wolf spoke. "I may have a solution."

Mieonus snapped, "Oh, here we go... as if you could possibly be our savior."

Almost as if everyone shared the same mind, they all shouted, "SHUT UP, MIEONUS!"

Mosley once again enjoyed her irritation for a moment before continuing. "As I was about to say... I may have a solution."

Alistar gently pulled his hand away from Bailem's shoulder as the wolf began to speak. The Rule of Fromalla was only allowed to be broken by the one who implemented the rule. With his hand removed, Lasidious could now listen in and Bailem was listening so intently to what the wolf had to say, he didn't realize the absence of Alistar's hand.

Lasidious and Celestria watched the images of the gods from within their home as the group stood in the temple, hovered together. The green flames of their fireplace beneath the Peaks of Angels on Ancient Sovereign projected each of them clearly.

Lasidious smiled as Alistar removed his hand and he was once again able to listen in on the conversation.

"As I was about to say, I may have a solution." Mosley cleared his throat, and then continued. "It's clear we have a big job in front of us. All of us—and I do mean all of us—will need to work hard, and together, to save ourselves. If it's Lasidious's intention to gain the followers necessary to increase his power, and by doing so take control of Gabriel, then we must act to counter his efforts.

"We must concentrate on keeping the people on each world from changing the gods they serve. I highly doubt we'll be able to convert those who serve Lasidious to serve one of us, but we should try. He's the God of Mischief for a reason, and he's far too cunning to allow for something like this to happen. But what we can do is stop those who are able to be manipulated from serving him. We need to become a part of the people's everyday lives. If we appear to them the way Lasidious appears to his followers or the way Hosseff does to his, for that matter, they'll be less likely to be persuaded to serve him.

"There's something else I think it's best to bring up. I would never share this information, but in the light of current events I feel it necessary to do so."

Both Lasidious and Celestria leaned toward the flames as they waited in anticipation for what the wolf-god had to say. "This is going to be good. I can feel it," Lasidious said as he pulled Celestria to his lap.

Mosley had everyone's full attention. "When the Book of Immortality was created, Bassorine allowed its creation, as we all know."

Gabriel stopped Mosley. "Are you absolutely sure it's wise to reveal Bassorine's plan?"

The emptiness beneath Hosseff's hood whispered, "I find it intriguing that the two of you share the knowledge of Bassorine's scheming and yet the rest of us seem to have been left in the dark. Perhaps it's best for us to know everything."

Alistar added, "We should know this plan, Gabriel. If we can't find a way to stop Lasidious, everything will be his to control."

"I agree with Alistar," Keylom added while stomping one of his centaur hooves on the floor.

Mosley thought a moment. "I think I have a better way of saying this. What you all don't know is that Bassorine developed a backup plan to take back the control of the Book if one of us was ever able to take control of it, a failsafe, if you will. After all, he was the God of War, and tactics was what he did best. As of this moment, this backup plan isn't powerful enough to stop Lasidious from controlling Gabriel, but with the proper grooming, it will be."

Alistar broke into the conversation. "You use the word 'it' as if it isn't a being. What are you referring to when you say… 'it?'"

"This plan needs the moments necessary to mature and until it does, we need to keep Lasidious from gaining the power necessary to control the Book. It's now more important than ever for us to keep Lasidious from gaining control of Gabriel before the plan is strong enough to protect his pages. We need to work hard to stop any additional followers from serving Lasidious. I think this will keep us busy."

Alistar spoke up. "Mosley, I wish to know more about this plan. Does it involve a being or not? It would make sense if it did. Share this with us so we can help them to acquire the power to stop Lasidious… this could save us all."

Mosley thought long and hard about his answer. The gods waited patiently, anticipating his reply. The wolf decided to lie to Alistar. "The plan does not involve a being. It is something much larger. I'll say nothing further."

The room erupted with agitated voices. Mosley looked at Gabriel and winked. The Book smiled and vanished. A moment later, Mosley turned to face the others. "I know you don't approve of what I've chosen to divulge, but there's planning that needs to be done. Let's all meet at the Hall of Judgment and begin."

Lasidious lifted Celestria from his lap as Alistar appeared at the far end of the table inside their home. There was fear in the God of Harvest's voice. "Did you hear what Mosley said? I have to get to the Hall of Judgment. What plan could this possibly be?"

Lasidious smiled. "Go to the meeting, brother. There's nothing to worry about. We will speak later." He watched as Alistar vanished.

Lasidious chuckled. "Well, it appears everything is in order. If not for Mosley, they all would have taken the bait and surrendered Gabriel's power to me. It was worth the effort to try. Mosley is a worthy opponent. I'm enjoying our little game of strategy. Good thing I have many backup plans of my own. I imagine the others will be quite busy while they are running between the worlds to stop me from gaining the additional followers I need to control Gabriel."

Celestria was agitated. "What about Bassorine's plan... doesn't this bother you? It bothers me! How are we going to deal with something we have no clue about? If it's not a being, then what could it possibly be? What will have the power to take back the control of Gabriel once you control him? Somehow we need to find this information out!"

Lasidious chuckled again.

"What's so funny? I fail to see the humor in this situation."

"Don't you see... it is a being. There's nothing else it could be. Mosley must've sensed it wasn't safe to tell them Shalee is the one who'll be able to take control of the Book. I think he knew I was able to hear them, though I don't think he knows it was because of Alistar's deception. I'll encourage Alistar to keep the gods busy while I prepare George for his new role."

"How do you know it's Shalee? You seem so sure of it."

"How else do you explain the growth of her powers? She's grown much faster than any sorceress before her ever has. She possesses the power of a woman who has commanded magic for over a hundred seasons. She has done it without the help of the gods. I laugh at this because Mosley feels like he has a secret, but he doesn't. I have everything under control."

"I would love to know how you have it all under control. You can't touch Shalee. She's protected by the Book and we don't have control of Gabriel yet. How are you going to get rid of her?"

Lasidious pulled his evil lover close. He kissed her gently on the forehead. "Who said anything about me getting rid of Shalee? That's what George is for. He's now the most powerful being on three of the five worlds, other than Brayson Id, and I'm pretty sure he knows how to get around Brayson as well. He'll be able to teleport between these three worlds, and Shalee's power still isn't strong enough to match George's... even if she looks into the Eye of Magic and lives... George's confidence and his questions to the Eye have allowed the Eye to give him a taste of the power of the Ancient Mystics. The Eye has never imparted this knowledge to any other until now. I can only hope George understands what to do with this power after our conversation within his dream."

Celestria smiled and allowed Lasidious to pull her closer. With her mouth positioned near his ear she whispered seductively. "I suggest we celebrate the development of your pet. George is becoming everything you wanted him to be. Your cunning makes me hot!"

Just Outside the Source's Cave,
The Peak of Bailem

Brayson had been standing next to Fisgig's perch waiting patiently for George to make his exit when the new warlock finally strolled out and stopped where the shadow of the cave's entrance passed across the ground.

The Head Master was still angry about many things but figured it best to approach George in a diplomatic manner to gather the information he was after. After seeing George's past, there had to be a way to help him find a peace within himself. "I see the Eye hasn't swallowed your soul. That would be good for you, I think," he shouted across the pool.

George didn't respond. Instead he stayed back and allowed the distance to remain between them. He reached under his robe and removed the feather which he had collected from the Phoenix prior to entering the Source's cave. He lifted it close to his mouth, cupping it within his palms, and began to chant with a whispered voice in the elven language—a language learned as a part of the Eye's gift.

"What are you doing over there?" Brayson said, trying to sound positive and upbeat. He knew what he had to say would cause tension and he cared for George, despite everything he had learned. He wanted to help his Mystic-Learner find peace. "Come on over here and let's have a nice chat. I have a few questions for you."

George lowered his hands from his mouth and opened them. A single arrow made of water and cursed with the very essence of the Phoenix's feather erupted from his hand and after launching through the air, it skewered Fisgig's body before the crimson-colored bird could react.

Brayson watched as his powerful Goswig fell lifeless to the

ground beneath his stone perch. The Head Master reacted by waving his hand to slow down George's moments, but the power to do this had died with the Phoenix. George didn't hesitate and sent a wave of force into Brayson that knocked him into the opposite wall of the steep cliffs. For good measure, George sent two other waves of force his direction to ensure the Head Master would be knocked unconscious.

He ran across the opening, trudging through the pool, and quickly pulled Brayson clear of the water. He dragged him by his feet into the alcove in which he had first appeared prior to entering the cave. He bound Brayson with a rope from his pack, then leaned down next to the heavy weave it was made of and spoke yet another chant, but this time it wasn't the language of the elves—this time the language spoken was that of the ancient mystics. *"Tolamea susayan, cun noble spolasemos papaya ress!"*

The rope tightened further and woke Brayson from his unconscious state as he cried out in pain. George methodically moved to a comfortable distance from Brayson and with a wave of his hand, commanded much of the water within the pool to create a shimmering throne in which to sit. Brayson watched, completely shocked at the power George used as the young warlock took a seat.

The two just looked at one another for quite a while before anything was finally said.

"I know you have learned about Amar's death, Brayson! What I'm trying to decide is what to do with you. I also know Mary knows Amar is dead. Have you told her I was the one who killed him?"

Brayson spoke out, despite being fearful for his life. "I have said nothing to her. I wanted to speak with you and try to understand why you did such a horrible thing."

George tilted his head. "Isn't it obvious? I killed Amar and ate his heart to steal his power. I'm sure you already knew this."

"And do you intend to eat my heart?"

George had to laugh.

"What's so humorous about this situation?" Brayson said, reacting to his old Mystic-learner's arrogance.

After calming himself, George responded, "Why would I want

to eat a heart that has less power than I currently command? Eating your heart will only cause me to lose much of the power I have over you now that your Goswig is dead."

Brayson wasn't sure where to go with the conversation from here and fumbled through his next statement. "There must be some sort of an arrangement we can come to. Tell me what you want and I will give it to you."

George laughed again as he stood and trudged through what was left of the water. He lifted the Phoenix's lifeless body from the ground by its claws. Once standing back in front of Brayson, he threw the corpse at his feet.

"You can't give me anything I don't already have the power to take."

Brayson knew his situation was hopeless. "Do you intend to kill me?"

George once again took his seat on his watery throne. "You know what? That is a good question! You see... I have been asking myself that very thing ever since meeting you at your School of Magic. I've got to admit, I originally intended to kill you as soon as I could, but then you became an important part of Mary's life. Now the question I've had to ask myself is, Do I love my wife—and I do—and do I love her family, and my answer is that I also love them very much. So if this is the case, then shouldn't I find a way to spare your life and start treating you as a father and not my enemy? Should I find a way to accomplish my goals and work around you? Should I give you the same love I've given to them? Do you really love my mother-in-law enough that it would matter if you're dead, or for that matter does she really love you enough to miss you once you're gone?"

Brayson cleared his throat and tried to find a more comfortable position within his bonds. "So what have you decided?"

George looked him dead in the eyes. He leaned forward and with a cold stare and responded. "I've decided... I'll find a way to spare your life. I don't wish to hurt Mary or my family. I believe you love Mary and I also believe she loves you, after watching your relationship grow. You have grown on me too, it seems, but there are a few things that will need to change if you're willing to allow it."

Brayson sighed. "And what would these changes need to be?"

"I'll need to take over your position as the Head Master and you'll need to retire. I'll do everything you would've done and try to figure out a way to stop this war. I'm tired of killing and equally as tired of hurting others.

"The dragon told me he saw some good in me. I've got a chance to change my life and I'm going to take advantage of it. I'm truly sorry for your friend's death, but I really didn't even know Amar that well. I know that without your Goswig, you're not powerful enough to stay in your position as Head Master. I would say, if you're willing to work with me to change things, we can fix the problems of Luvelles and live peaceful lives together with the ones we love. So, what do you say?"

Brayson thought through everything for a while, and then responded. "You intend to stop this war?"

"I do."

"You also plan to find a way to make Luvelles a peaceful place?"

"Again, I do."

Brayson fought the tears back as he looked at Fisgig's lifeless body. "You're right--without my Goswig I won't be able to perform the duties as Head Master. I could help you move into this position without objection from the people. Once they understand you command the power necessary for the job, they won't argue. Elf or not, you would be accepted. They respect the power, not the man. You may run into a problem with the gods, however. Humans are only supposed to visit this world, not stay here unless given permission from the Head Master. The gods may not allow you to take this position."

George smiled. "If you knew what I knew about the gods, you wouldn't worry about such things. They'll do nothing to stop me, I assure you."

"Well, if that's the case, then I can only see one more concern. This concern is for my safety, and it also involves the safety of Mary and your entire family, George!"

"I'm listening."

"My brother Marcus will kill everyone I love once he realizes I don't have the power to stop him from hurting them. He'll do it as a way of appeasing his own sick desire to torture me. I would imagine he would make me watch. It might be best to kill me now in order to spare their lives. Once the people know you're their new Head Master, the word will spread. Once it gets to Marcus's ears, he'll come for me!"

George stood from his shimmering throne of water and with a wave of his hand removed Brayson's bonds. He put his arm around Brayson. "So if I told you I have a plan to deal with Marcus, would you allow me to call you Dad once you take Mary as your wife?"

Brayson reached up and played with his goatee. "I'm still pretty angry with you, but I suppose I could get over it if you do everything you say you will. I'll agree to allow you to call me your father on one condition."

George chuckled, "I've got to love a man with the balls to negotiate with me in your situation. Okay... so what's this condition?"

"I want you to allow Fisgig to live. He won't be able to use his powers any longer, but I wish to have his company. He was more than a Goswig to me. He was my friend and I loved him. As the Head Master of Luvelles—once I've given you the secrets of the position—you'll be able to bring him back to life, without his abilities. He'll live a long life and I can still enjoy our friendship."

George thought a moment. "Exactly how does this work?"

"Throughout history, the gods have given every Head Master this power once they have taken the position. The power rests inside the Stone of Life. We're allowed to use the stone only once a season. This is the same power the Dark Order's paladins call the Touch of Death... but it doesn't require the belief in Hosseff."

"I know of this Touch of Death. So are you saying that when this type of power is used, the person or beast it's used on loses all their power?"

"That's exactly what I'm saying."

"Does it strip this person or this beast of all their natural abilities as well?"

"No, it doesn't take anything natural from them."

George touched Brayson's shoulder and teleported them both just outside of Mary's house.

"I need to think about your request regarding Fisgig. I don't fully understand everything, but I think you've given me enough to ponder. As of right this moment, I don't see a problem with letting the Phoenix live, but like I said... I want to think about it."

George leaned in and whispered in Brayson's ear. "As far as your brother goes... I wouldn't worry about Marcus. Like I said, I've got plans for him. Maybe you should go inside and let's work on creating a happy family... okay, Dad?"

Brayson moved to the bottom of the steps. "Save the word 'dad' for after Fisgig lives and after you've shown me the things you've promised are truthful. I still have many concerns. I do wish to marry your mother-in-law and I will uphold my end of things— you just uphold yours!"

"Goodnight, Brayson."

"Goodnight, George... it does sound like you'll do the right thing. I hope my trust in you isn't misplaced, but I seem to be in a position where I have no choice. I forgive you for taking Amar from me."

George touched his shoulder. "And I forgive you for getting on my good side and being such an old fart. Maybe we should avoid discussing this with the girls for now. I'm still not sure I've made all the right decisions. I may need you to guide me. I want to ensure I do the right things for not only Luvelles, but our family as well."

Brayson smiled and nodded. "I think there's hope for you George. I think the Ancient One was right. There does appear to be good in you. I have been told many terrible things about you since last we spoke, but I trust the dragon's judgment. I'm going to spend the rest of the day with Mary and I'll see you tomorrow morning, if that's okay."

"We will speak later then. We can talk more about who said these terrible things about me."

As soon as Brayson closed the door, George teleported inside Kepler's new lair beneath the stones and quickly waved his hand. The darkness dissipated. Both Kepler and Payne had to cover their eyes to keep the brightness from hurting them.

"What do you want, George? I was sleeping!"

"Master, get out of here and let me get some sleep," Payne shouted.

George was floored as he looked at Payne's red figure. The

fairy-demon had grown over six inches since the last moment he saw him. He had also used a complete sentence which had somehow made perfect sense.

"Did I just hear him right, Kep? Did Payne actually make sense?"

"Yes... I've been working with the little freak."

"Hey, stop calling me a freak. I've already stopped calling you a kitty... now, haven't I?"

George took a seat. "Wow... I leave you guys alone for a few days and when I return, I run into Captain Sentence over here. What's got into you, Payne?"

Kepler interrupted. "Don't get him started. He'll go all damn night and won't shut up. He's on this whole... 'I can talk better than you now' kick. Though irritating, at least he makes sense now. He has been eating everything he can get his hands on. I've never seen anything grow the way he has over the last few days. So, how about you tell me the reason you woke us up."

"I need to know if you have any abilities which would be considered a power, and not something that's considered a natural ability, Kep."

"Why do you need to know?"

"I'll explain, but be honest... this is crucial."

"I have one power. Everything else I can do is considered natural. I can hide within the shadows naturally. I can see in the dark naturally, but the ability to control my Skeleton Warriors is a power given to me by the goddess Celestria. This is why my brothers don't have this power. I did meet the goddess once, you know, just before I met you. She was very beautiful for an elf, I suppose."

"Yes I know, Kep. We talked about it after we had our standoff at the Pool of Sorrow. You remember... the day after I turned Kroger's big ass to stone."

"Okay, so why are you asking me this question, then?"

George thought hard for a bit and then responded. "I don't think you can control the skeletons of the dead any longer."

"Ha... why would you think that?"

"I think that when Marcus brought you back to life, you may have lost it. I want you to go out tonight and kill someone evil. Payne will go with you. If you cannot control the corpse, then I'll know what Brayson has told me about Marcus's Touch of Death is true. This will tell me how I should proceed with things."

"What are you talking about? Why would Brayson tell you something like this?'

"Just trust me, okay?"

"Okay, I can go out and kill someone if you want, but this seems like a bother to prove something I know I can do."

"Just trust me and go check. I'm sure you'll enjoy yourself and it'll make me feel better to know if your power is still intact or not. Payne, I want you to teleport Kepler to the City of Marcus tonight. I'm sure it won't be hard to find an evil soul there."

Payne stood up and stretched his wings. "I would be happy to do this for you, Master. Would there be anything else?"

Kepler growled. "Just stop already, freak... he's already impressed."

Grogger's Swamp
Just Before Late Bailem

Boyafed waited patiently for Sam to exit the swamp. He was dressed in his dark plate armor with gold accents. He had set up camp just outside the entrance. He had a debt to settle and hoped to be able to confront the king of Southern Grayham soon— soon, providing the king managed to survive his venture into the swamp.

It wasn't until just before Late Bailem that Sam finally made his way out of the swamp. Boyafed made sure to capture Sam's attention and waited patiently for the king to say his goodbyes to all those whom he had saved.

Mieonus had called the others to her home. She had been waiting for this confrontation and wanted to share her manipulations of the event with them. She informed them all that something big was about to happen and most of the gods had come out of sheer curiosity. They were now standing in front of her waterfall watching the image of Sam say goodbye to the people as Boyafed waited. The only deities not present were Lasidious and Celestria. Mieonus took the opportunity to brag about her handiwork to make the fight happen.

Mosley sat quietly as he stared into the image of the falls. He was sick to his stomach and the worry could be seen in the wolf's eyes.

Once the group surrounding the king had properly thanked him, they all teleported and went their separate ways. Sam turned to face Boyafed. He took a deep breath, gathered his nerve, and moved to join the dark paladin leader within his camp.

Boyafed motioned for Sam to take a seat. He had prepared a comfortable spot for him to sit and a nice meal was cooking over an open fire. Once each man had taken a moment to relax, Boyafed spoke.

"Do you know who I am, king of Brandor?"

"I do, Boyafed. So what's for dinner?"

"I have prepared jackram stew. I took the moments necessary to hunt a few of them nearby. They're quick little critters. If it wasn't for their clumsiness and the fact that they trip over their own floppy ears, I don't imagine I would've been able to shoot them with my bow. They make a fine meal. Go ahead and have some."

Sam leaned forward and scooped a ladle full into a wooden bowl Boyafed set near him. "I know why you've come. I suppose I'm asking myself why the meal and the idle chatting when you have every desire to avenge your son's life?"

Boyafed filled his bowl. After sitting back and taking a bite, he finally replied. "I've heard of your skills. I know of your war on Grayham and the victory you claimed. The news of such things finds a way to travel between the worlds. Both of us are men of war, but this doesn't mean we can't be civil before doing battle. I prefer to get to know the man I intend to kill."

"I like your style, Boyafed. Your son fought well. You should know that as his father. You should be proud. He served you until his dying breath. I know you gave him an order to kill my queen."

"I appreciate the sentiment, but my son clearly failed to follow his orders. If he were any other man, I would not be here to avenge his death. He was ordered to kill your queen, not fall in love with her. I wish, as a father, I could've said my son was a good soldier, but as it turns out, he was weak in both following instruction and in doing battle. I should tell you it was my god who wished for your queen's death. I personally had nothing against her."

Sam shrugged. "What's a guy to do? You must obey your god, I suppose. We also must love our children no matter how much they disappoint us. It's clear you love both your god and Kiayasis. I would imagine we could talk all night about many different things your son did to make you proud despite his shortcomings as a warrior, but I think we should dispense with these pleasantries and get this little fight of ours over with. Besides, I'm really not that hungry anyway and I think your stew needs some seasoning."

The gods were fixated on Mieonus's waterfall as they made comments of who they felt had better skills. Mosley, on the other hand, was in a world of his own. He stared hard into the images and had tuned out the others. Sam was his friend before becoming a god and this was the king's toughest opponent yet.

You can do this, Sam… you can do this… you can do this… was all he was thinking. It ran through the wolf's mind over and over.

Both men stood and moved away from the camp. Sam pulled Kael from his sheath and commanded the Blade of the Gods to bring forth its fire. Boyafed shouted in the language of the elves and his sword also burst into flames.

Sam smiled. "You're the first person I've met with a Sword of the Gods that had the nerve to use it against Kael here. I suppose that commanding their powers won't be necessary. I'm sure we both know how to avoid this kind of damage."

"I agree... this will need to be a fight without the powers of our blessed blades. I can see the rings on your fingers. I know you're well protected from the affects of magic anyway. The markings are those of the Head Master himself. I'll fight with honor... without magic, and a cold blade."

As they began to circle one another, Sam's curiosity got the better of him. He remembered what Bassorine had told him. His blade was to be the only one with the ability to summon the truth from others. He began to question to test the god's truthfulness while he had the chance.

"Can your blade seek the truth in others as mine can?"

Boyafed stopped moving. "Your blade can do this? That's most impressive... what an incredible power to have at your disposal! I can't tell you how many different occasions I could've used something like that. Why just the other day, I tortured a small group of men in my dungeon and I could've used it. I bet it saves you a lot of trouble when seeking the answers you want."

"Ha... yes sir-re-bob... I have used it twice already. Bassorine gave this sword to me himself. I call him Kael." He quickly spun Kael in his hands and made a gesture as he pointed at Boyafed's sword. "What about yours?"

The Dark Order leader tossed his Blade of the Gods in Sam's direction. "Take a few swipes with him. Feel how light he is in your hand. I call him Quel kaima."

"Aahhhh... an elven name... I think a blade called, 'Sleep Well' is rather appropriate for the death you must've dealt through him in your many seasons as the Order's leader... a clever name to be sure."

The king moved the sword back and forth through the air a bit before tossing the blade to Boyafed. "Impressive, but what's his special power?"

Boyafed began to grin. "I just hate cowards, don't you?"

"Most definitely... why?"

"Quel kaima will allow me to throw him for quite a distance to strike down those who would choose to run from me in battle. I've killed many cowards this way. The blade hates a man without a spine as much as I do. It returns to me with a simple wave of my hand. Hosseff himself gave this blade to me. Beyond that, Quel kaima will do anything yours can do... minus your blade's Call of Truth of course."

"I've never thought to name Kael's power before. May I use this name? The Call of Truth has a ring to it, don't you agree?"

Both warriors had to stop speaking while Kael and Quel kaima took a moment to introduce themselves to one another. After the swords finished their chat, Sam turned to look at Boyafed.

"Well, that was a first for me. Never thought I would see the day two swords had a conversation."

Boyafed had to smile. "This was a first for me also. To answer your question regarding naming your sword's power, you may use this name, but I doubt you'll have the chance when our battle has completed. I promise to make it a quick death."

"Again... very clever, but we'll just have to see about that." Sam decided he had done enough chatting. "I suppose we best get this over with and find out who'll be returning home in a casket."

"I agree… but no matter the outcome, king of Grayham, I consider you a worthy opponent."

"And I you."

Without further conversation, Boyafed moved in. The metal blades clashed hard against each other many, many times in a barrage of upward, downward and side-to-side strikes—all of which were defended by both sides.

Both men stopped and backed away. Boyafed took the opportunity to speak. "Your skill is impressive. May I call you Sam?"

"Go ahead... why not... I suppose if I don't like the way you say it, I can always cut you up a bit."

"Ha... and you say I'm clever. I'm going to enjoy this battle far more than any other, I think. I don't believe I've ever had a man stand before me and manage to use humor while anticipating his death. Most men run like cowards."

"Who said anything about anticipating my own death? There will be no running."

Without further delay Sam lunged in and delivered one swift strike after another. Again, each of these deadly advances was defended.

Boyafed attacked as he pushed Sam backwards— swipes, lunges, elbows, headbutts, leg sweeps and a series of attempted stabs were calculatingly placed between them all, but everything was defended.

Both men once again began to circle and Boyafed attacked again. He kept coming until a small opening finally presented itself. Boyafed's blade slashed deep across the upper part of Sam's left arm. He followed this with a strong foot to the side of the king's leg. Sam fell but managed to defend a downward stab and quickly rolled to his feet while sending an arching slash toward Boyafed's head. The dark paladin blocked the attack and moved back to give Sam the moments to regain his composure.

"I can honestly say you're the finest opponent I've ever faced. I would imagine the only man I'll look forward to fighting after this day will be Lord Dowd."

Sam spit on the ground. "You have to get past this day first." Sam searched deep within his soul. He knew he had to call upon his hidden rage; he opened the monster's cage and allowed it to be released as he lifted Kael to prepare his attack. He rushed in and this time he pushed Boyafed backward. Strike after strike, lunge after lunge, elbow after elbow, punch after punch—all defended until finally he managed to find an opening of his own. He lunged forward with a stabbing motion. The blade penetrated Boyafed's left shoulder just below the collarbone and emerged from the other side.

Boyafed's training allowed him to ignore the pain as if nothing had happened. With Sam's blade penetrating through his shoulder, he used his right hand to send his own sword arching towards the king's head while retrieving his dagger of the Order with his left.

Sam reached out and caught Boyafed's right forearm with his left hand to stop the deadly strike, but he failed to account for Boyafed's free hand. With his right hand still on Kael's grip, the Order's dagger penetrated deep into the side of Sam's ribs on his right side. Boyafed released the dagger and quickly reached up and grabbed Sam's right arm with his left hand to keep the king from removing Kael and doing further damage to his shoulder.

The pain Sam was in was excruciating. Boyafed had laced the blade with a deadly poison and the king could already feel the burn as it began to make its way through his body. The dagger had also penetrated his right lung, making breathing nearly impossible.

Sam released Kael and reached in to take Boyafed's throat in his hand, but this last effort was defended with one quick motion to pull his arm free. With each inhale and exhale, the movement of the Order's dagger did further damage to Sam's lung as it attempted to fill with air.

Boyafed knew the fight was over. Sam dropped his arms and Boyafed allowed the king to step back. Boyafed left the blade in his shoulder until he was completely sure Sam would not be able to make any further advances.

Boyafed grunted as he forced himself to reach into his boot. He tossed Sam a small vial full of a red potion. "Drink this quickly, king of Grayham. It will dull the pain and allow you to die in peace. I'll make sure your body finds its way back to your General Absolute. You'll be given a proper passing celebration as per your customs... I promise you this."

Sam looked at Boyafed after drinking the liquid. With blood running down his chin, he spoke. "Please tell my wife I love her... and I always have!" With that, Sam closed his eyes and lay back on the ground. Boyafed watched as the king's chest eventually stopped rising and the last bit of air escaped him forever.

Boyafed drank another vial of the red potion, then pulled Kael from his shoulder. His cry filled the evening air as the anguish nearly overwhelmed him. He quickly poured a few drops of a powerful healing potion directly onto the wound. He then took a seat next to Sam's body, his face full of excruciating pain.

"I shall always remember the man who was the first to wound me. You were a worthy adversary. You were worthy of being a king. I shall tell tales of your greatness, Sam, as I show the scar."

Boyafed lay back on the ground after putting another drop under his tongue and waited for the healing potion to take effect. He would not be able to break camp and move until morning.

"Oh, how delicious Boyafed's victory must taste," Mieonus said as she turned to the others. "I'm going to enjoy Shalee's pain once she finds out Sam is dead all because of her infidelity."

All the gods vanished without responding, except for one. Alistar took the opportunity to express his feelings about the situation. "Mieonus... you wonder why the others ignore you. I know you also wonder why they treat you with such disdain. Allow me to enlighten you. You have no tact and don't seem to understand when to stop your hatred and show some class. You make yourself look foolish, as a jester would before a king."

"And I suppose you're also going to explain how I made myself look so foolish. I'm the one who set up this confrontation. The same fight you all enjoyed, I might add."

"It wasn't inviting us to watch the fight that made you look bad. It's your comments afterwards. The battle was an honorable one between two honorable men. But you found a way to take the honor out of Boyafed's victory. You tainted it by dishonoring the fallen. You should keep your comments to yourself. Do you see any among us who feel your words are pleasurable? All the gods think you're expendable and worse still, you allow your hate to cloud your judgment. You appear to be without godliness." Alistar vanished.

Mosley fell onto the porch of his cabin home high on top of Catalyst Mountain and looked out across the valleys below. He lifted his head and began to howl. Sam's death was agonizing and he didn't wish to dishonor his friend's death by using his godly powers to hide the pain.

Chapter 21

𝔄 𝔉𝔞𝔩𝔰𝔢 𝔓𝔯𝔬𝔭𝔥𝔢𝔱
George's Dreams

After sending Kepler with Payne to test Brayson's revelation about the Touch of Death, George went inside his home. The evening was pleasant and all the family, including Brayson and Mary, had gathered for a nice meal. When night finally came, the warlock took his position next to Athena in their bed. It wasn't long before Lasidious interrupted his dreams.

"George, we need to speak. There are plans we need to discuss... plans that are urgent and need to be implemented immediately."

George's dreams had been good. His daughter Abbie, Athena, and their new baby were all having a nice lunch on a hillside. George made his little girl a kite and was watching her fly it while Athena prepared their plates. The baby was peacefully sleeping at the center of the large cloth Athena had spread out to eat on. It was a pleasant dream, but now it had been all shot to garesh. All he could do was speak with Lasidious since his face had replaced his visions of happiness.

"You know, Lasidious... your timing really sucks sometimes when you barge in on my dreams like this. Maybe you could let me finish them first from now on. It's the least you could do, ya know."

"I'm sorry, George, but this is important! We need to plan."

"Now what do you want me to do? I'm trying to get some decent sleep here. I have everything under control. I've got Brayson right where I want him. Kepler is on his way to find out if he still has the power to control his skeletons. If he can't, then I'll allow Brayson's Phoenix to live. If he can use his power, then I'll know Brayson lies, and I'll just have to kill him and be done with it. No one else can touch me now. We have everything else you wanted to do on this world under control. War is coming and the gods are busy watching what's going on, according to what you've told me. What could possibly be so important that I can't get one night's rest?"

"George, I have groomed you for far greater things than just being the Head Master of Luvelles. It would be best to allow the people of Luvelles to believe that Brayson still has his powers. You still need to finish setting up the other details of what we've discussed here on this world, but there's something more important for you to do."

"What do you mean? Other than killing Shalee, it looks like everything else will be a walk in the park. I just need to put the finishing touches on the war with Marcus and—"

Lasidious stopped him. "About the war here on Luvelles... just let it develop on its own. Don't worry about Marcus for now. Do whatever needs to be done to appease him, but you need to spend some of your moments on the World of Harvestom."

"What? How in the hell do you expect me to explain this to Athena? I can't just move us to a new world again. She's gonna freak out and hit every stinking wall in our house. I don't wish to live with a pissed off pregnant woman, Lasidious. It's a downright dangerous thing to do, even with all these powers I've got now. What will I tell Mary? How will I explain to her that she has to leave Brayson?

"Normally I like your ideas, Lasidious, but this one really sucks garesh. If I have to choose Athena, her family, and my unborn baby over getting Abbie's soul back out of the Book of Immortality... I'll do it! I can't lose Athena's love. She means everything to me!"

After the God of Mischief listened to him rant, he gave it a moment, and then responded. "I'm not asking you to leave Luvelles, George. I have groomed you to be able to call upon the power of the Ancient Mystics for a reason. I built your confidence up to a level that the Eye would grant this kind of power. You have executed every part of our plans perfectly. Brayson was the only other to have this power to teleport between the lower three worlds, but he refused to use it for reasons of his own."

"What do you mean by the lower three worlds?"

"I mean you'll be able to teleport between Harvestom, Luvelles, and Grayham. You now can move freely within them. As long as you're familiar with where you're going, you can go there."

"I don't have any knowledge of Harvestom. Exactly how do you expect me to go there? And why can't I teleport between the other two worlds as well?"

Lasidious took a deep breath and gave the question some thought. "I'll give you a single vision of a key location on Harvestom. Beyond that you'll need to learn its lands on your own. The power necessary to give you any more of these specific locations could unintentionally let the others know what we're doing and we can't have that, now can we? For now, you're the only mortal with this ability. You don't have to fight with Athena to save Abbie. Your family can stay where it is.

"Now, to answer your other question... the reason you can't teleport between the other two worlds is because you're not powerful enough to pass through the magic which surrounds them. It's that simple!"

"You mean I'm still weak compared to these other two worlds? That's pretty hard to imagine."

"I understand the restrictions of your mind. It wasn't long ago you felt magic and talking jaguars to be unimaginable as well. I'm sure you don't believe that just because I groomed you to be able to receive the gift of the Ancient Mystics that you're now all powerful. You're far from godliness, I assure you. There has never been a man or an elf, for that matter, since the creation of these new worlds that has been able to summon even the most basic power of the Mystics before Brayson Id rose to this level. But even he is considered basically powerless compared to the Ancient Mystics of Trollcom. The World of Trollcom is heavily populated by the Ancient Mystics and the trolls. The problem is that many of the trolls have figured out a way to command powers greater than your own. Don't be fooled into thinking you're ready to stand against them. You would be considered as nothing more than a meager irritation against their power... a bug they would simply swat away.

"But even the Ancient Mystics of Trollcom are considered to be small irritations to those which dwell on Dragonia. The dragons of Dragonia have powers which are close to rivaling those of the gods. Their powers give them the title Swayne Enserad. This is the final level you must master before becoming enlightened. Even the Swayne Enserad as a whole have trouble mastering this power. In the last 10,000 seasons, not one of them has managed to become enlightened and given their godliness, but this doesn't mean it's not right there for the taking."

"Holy garesh, Lasidious... I get it... so are you grooming me to become a god someday?"

"As they used to say on your Earth, George... it takes one to know one. Or better yet, it takes a god to see a future god. Come on, look at the bright side. You can teleport between the lower three worlds already. You're the most powerful being within the lower three worlds. I think that would be considered a solid progression since your arrival on Grayham, don't you think?"

The warlock thought a moment. "I guess you're right. So will I eventually become an Ancient Mystic, then a Swayne Enserad?"

Lasidious smiled. "Yes!"

"And after that, I need to figure out how to become enlightened so I can receive godly powers. Does this mean you are going to need my help getting Abbie's soul back out of the Book of Immortality, because that wasn't a part of the plan?"

Lasidious lifted the hood of his robe over his head. "Your rise to godliness is for reasons we will discuss later and yes... you will need to do everything you've said, but this doesn't cross over into our plans to get Abbie's soul back out of the Book. Getting her released should be something we can make happen before you manage to become enlightened, providing you live long enough to accomplish all of this."

"What... providing I live... what the hell does that mean?"

"It means you have to avoid being killed when manipulating the other worlds just like you've avoided getting yourself killed on both Luvelles and Grayham. I wouldn't worry about gaining additional power for now anyway. Aside from a small task we need to accomplish on Trollcom, a task you won't need higher powers for, by the way, you won't see the upper two worlds for nearly a season or so. You have work to do on the lower three worlds. A prophet's work is never done." Lasidious gave him an evil wink.

"You have got to be freaking kidding me! You want me to become your stinking prophet? Yeah, right… man, I can see it now… wait, let me guess, you want me to become a prophet so I can run around shouting out your supposed good name. What a joke this is. I could laugh my ass off for days on this one."

Lasidious had to grin. "It's all part of the plan to get your daughter back, George. You don't have to believe in it to preach it. All you have to do is share the good word and allow the people to decide what they believe in."

The warlock thought long and hard before responding. "Make no mistake about this one, Lasidious. I don't like this idea one bit and it makes me sick to my stomach… but if this will get my Abbie back then I'm on board with your pile of garesh. Oh, and by the way… I think you mean you want me to be your false prophet, and a false prophet's work is never done."

Lasidious laughed within the warlock's dream. "George, you wound my pride with such words. I thought we were better friends than this. Do you really dislike this idea as much as you claim to?"

"Yeah, I do hate this idea, hate it a lot in fact, but like I already said, if this gets my Abbie back, then so be it. We both know you're just as full of garesh as I am, so stop playing wounded. You could care less if I like this idea so let's just be honest with one another for a moment, if you don't mind. You and I get along because we have something in common. I have something you need and you have something I want. This relationship is all based on our desires to accomplish goals which benefit one another. And as I've already said twice before, as long as this gets my Abbie back, I'll do whatever it takes, even be your false prophet, *providing*—and I do mean providing—it doesn't affect my ability to keep Athena and her family safe. I won't sacrifice my love for Athena to retrieve my daughter's soul from the Book. I would let the idea of seeing my daughter again go before I fail Athena in our marriage. It's bad enough I've had to lie to her already. I can't allow deceiving her to continue. You and I need to be careful with how we treat my relationship with her, and the rest of the family too, for that matter! I hope we are on the same playing field on this one."

Lasidious grabbed hold of his chin in thought and then responded. "It seems we both appreciate the other's position, then."

"Good," George said in a much happier tone, "so since I'll be able to live here on Luvelles and do the work we need to do wherever it needs to be done, false prophet or not, I'll be able to keep Athena happy and I'm sure Brayson will be thrilled to keep his position as Head Master. I'll have to do a little creative thinking, but I'm sure I can pull this off. So what's my role on Harvestom going to be and when can I get a little more of this Ancient Mystic power?"

"Slow it down a bit, George. First things first... I have some things to tell you. We have plans to make. I also have something to say about Brayson's Phoenix."

The Underground City of Gogswayne

Gage waited patiently beside Strongbear. The big brown bear had gone into such a heavy hibernation he was struggling to come out of it. The Goswig's power to bring back the change of seasons had worked and now it was just a matter of waiting for the big guy to wake up.

Gallrum left to report Strongbear's condition to King Ultor and Gage was dreading how angry the bear would be once he realized the entire city of Gogswayne had conspired to put him to sleep. Gage was also considering the idea of having Gallrum deliver the bad news to the bear and blaming his decision to do so on the fact that he didn't have the seniority to deliver such news.

The Next Morning
Just Before the Peak of Bailem

The family gathered at Mary's home for breakfast. George sat next to Brayson as they watched over thirty people and Payne move through the house. Kepler already came to George and reported that his power to control the skeletons was no longer his to command. Then the demon-cat retired to his lair beneath the rocks to sulk.

Payne was acting differently, flying from one family member to the next and doing his best to impress them with his newfound ability to form complete sentences. The fairy-demon was also growing.

All George could do was marvel at how his life had turned into one big fantasy. Never in his wildest imagination would he have believed that many of the things he had seen in the movies he loved so much on Earth could possibly be founded on potential facts. He could only assume there had been beings on Earth who had understood the reality of what the gods were and what was on the other worlds before they were destroyed in the God Wars. He wasn't even sure any new concept could be given the title of "fiction" any longer.

"So have you made any decisions, George?" Brayson finally asked as he finished his greggle hash. "I'm sure you have much on your mind. What can I do to help you?"

"I think this is a conversation best left for your office. Let's say our goodbyes and go there."

The two men eventually appeared in Brayson's floating office. George looked out the window and after a moment of Brayson showing him how it functioned, he commanded the window to find Shalee. The window zoomed in across the world and eventually settled on the entrance to the Void Maze, but could not penetrate the magic surrounding it to produce her image.

"How long has the queen been inside the Maze with your brother?"

Brayson looked at him with confusion. "How could you know such things? Did the goddess tell you of this?"

"I will explain, but first tell me how long Shalee and your brother have been in the Maze."

Brayson moved to take a seat. "I would imagine that with my brother's past knowledge of the dungeon's layout when he and I went through the trials together and, considering the fact you personally killed most everything inside of the maze, they should be arriving at the Source's Temple any moment now."

"This is good, but there are a few problems we need to chat about. I've got some things to say that aren't going to sit well with you. I need you to hear me out before you respond. This is really gonna sound bad... okay?"

"Okay, I'm listening."

"First off... I've decided the god you serve, or rather Mieonus, isn't worth my service any longer. She's the one who has been commanding me to do so many hurtful things. And one of these things was what caused the death of your friend, Amar."

"What? She would never!" Brayson said with a piercing stare.

George held up his hand and continued, "Like I said... hear me out! Mieonus has asked me to do things which go against my very nature, and this included killing you. I originally obeyed her commands because she said she would retrieve my daughter's soul from the Book of Immortality. My daughter has been trapped inside of it for—"

Brayson motioned to speak and George stopped talking.

"Why would your daughter's soul be in some kind of Book? Why isn't her soul with the god she served?"

George took a seat next to Brayson on the large wooden desk. "There's only one god strong enough to maintain a heaven for his followers. I was visited by this god last night after returning home. Many things have been revealed to me."

"Why would my goddess want me dead and why would she choose you to do it, George? None of this makes any sense, and what do you mean there's only one god powerful enough to maintain a heaven?"

George held his hand up asking for a moment to think things through. "Okay... let's start here. Mieonus told me she wanted a stronger leader to govern Luvelles. She said you've failed to choose a side in things and she despises this neutrality. She wants me to bring darkness over all of Luvelles... she wants evil to thrive."

"Mieonus isn't evil, George. Why do you try to deceive me so?"

"I'm not deceiving you. I could've killed you already and you know it! I spared your life because I'm tired of killing! I'm tired of living in hate and causing others misery. Whether you know it or not, your goddess is an evil woman. I wouldn't lie about such things and soon you will be getting a confirmation of your own from the one I now serve. But for now, I ask you to just listen!"

"I didn't know the goddess was evil. She has always spoken

kindly to me whenever I've kneeled before her. How am I to believe this?"

"Look, you will get confirmation soon, like I said, but Mieonus has used your faith in her to get you to allow me to meet with the Source. I knew everything I needed to know about the Eye long before you ever gave me your advice on believing in myself. You should be dead right now, but I cannot keep killing for her and I imagine there will be repercussions from my choices. I can only hope my new god will protect me."

Brayson thought a moment. "So what of this other god you said visited you? Tell me more of him, or is it her?"

"The god Lasidious came to me. He came to me in a glorious light and spoke with me while Athena lay asleep next to me. At first I was scared, but then he assured me he wasn't there to harm me. He said he loved me and was proud I went against Mieonus' wishes to kill you. Brayson, he told me to leave you in the position as Head Master."

Brayson was sitting on the edge of his chair as George continued. "He has informed me that the others keep their follower's souls inside a book called the Book of Immortality."

Brayson stopped him. "When you say others... do you mean the other gods?"

"Yes, I do... and Lasidious also said Mieonus lied to me and doesn't have the power to retrieve my daughter's soul from this Book unless the others within the hidden god world agree to release her."

"Wait a second. What hidden god world are you talking about?"

George scratched his head as he continued. "I'm not really sure about that part. But Lasidious told me all the deaths I've caused and the murders I've committed while serving your goddess aren't to be glorified no matter how pure my intentions were to save my daughter. If it wouldn't have been for the Source reminding me of the goodness I still have inside of me, I probably would've killed you too and never had the chance to have Lasidious come to me. I would've never been given the chance to spread his words of love and kindness... his words of peace.

"Death and destruction isn't a proper way for Mieonus to control her followers, Brayson. I've been asked to bring peace to the worlds. Lasidious has asked me to be his 'Prophet of Peace and Love.' He wants me, of all people, to spread his 'Words of Love' and keep those who would go to war with each other from doing so. He has said you would be a tremendous ally and I should work with you to bring peace to this world.

"I hate to say this, Brayson, but given everything I know and, considering the plans your goddess had for you to die by my hands, I would think a change of our service to a god who is kind, loving, and all powerful would be in order. I just need to know what you think of all this. I want to make the best decision for our family that I can and you're a key part of helping me make this decision. Mary and Athena's happiness is resting on whether you and I make the right choices. I'm asking you to act as a father to me! I need your guidance!"

Brayson sat back in his chair and lowered his head in thought. There was a long period of silence. For every moment that went by, George remembered his training on Earth. He had given his sales pitch and the first rule of sales was: *the first one to speak— loses!*

Finally Brayson lifted his head. "I find it hard to concentrate. It's not every day your Mystic-Learner takes away your power by killing your Goswig, then spares your life and tells you he's been asked by the goddess you serve to kill you and take your position as Head Master.

"I don't wish to serve the one who would spread such evil. I believe you're sincere about becoming a better person. I also want the best for our family. I just want to know why Lasidious has chosen you to spread his 'Words of Peace and Love.' Why does he want you to be his prophet when you have done so many terrible things?"

George scratched his head again as if confused himself. "I wish I had an answer for you. To tell you I understand a god's mind would be a complete lie. All I know is that the Source was able to see something good in me and I've been given the chance to spread these words of peace and love throughout the worlds. I just need a bit of fatherly advice. Should I do this, or should I be doing something else?"

Brayson stood and moved across the room and looked out the window. He waved his hand in front of it. It wasn't long before it had zoomed in across the land. He was looking at the outside of Mary's house. Both Susanne and Athena were walking up the front porch steps. He could see how rounded Athena's belly was becoming. Eventually he turned around.

"I believe you should spread the word of our new god. I will serve Lasidious with everything in me just as you have chosen to do. I'll do what's necessary to help you spread his Words of Peace and Love on this world. I'll keep an eye on our loved ones while you spread our new lord's vision of tranquility."

George moved across the room and pulled Brayson close. He held the embrace of his soon to be father-in-law for many moments before he let go.

"Brayson, we have much to discuss about the war on Luvelles. For now we have been asked to do nothing. When the moment is right, Lasidious will tell us what to do. His words must come to all those who are willing to listen. I would expect a visit from our new lord if I were you. He wishes to speak with—"

"Me... he wishes to speak with me? Why?"

"I told you, you're going to be a critical part of spreading his word. You should stay at your own home tonight. Our lord has a surprise for you. I think you'll be pleased with his visit."

From deep within the Peaks of Angels, Lasidious passed his hand across the green flames of his fireplace as the visions of George and Brayson faded. He turned to look at his evil lover.

"It appears George is quite the little salesman. When I took him from Earth, his talents were being wasted. I think we've found a much better use for his skills. It's a good thing I was there when Brayson decided to confront George outside the Source's cave. It gave me the chance to capture Fisgig's soul before it left for the Book. George couldn't have picked a finer moment to kill the bird. With all the gods being unable to see inside the Mountains of Oraness, thanks to the Ancient One's magic, I had the perfect opportunity to grab hold of Fisgig's soul as it left for Gabriel's pages. The Book doesn't even know he's dead. This is brilliant and was an opportunity I couldn't pass up. If there's any doubt in Brayson's mind at all about my kindness and my love for the people or my perceived desire to have peace on Luvelles, this doubt will be gone shortly."

Celestria leaned back in her chair. "Your evil mind is so delightfully cunning. With your brother working to confuse the gods and none of the others knowing George has the ability to teleport between the three worlds, they'll be more confused now than ever. I must admit, my love, you impress me more with each passing day. I bet you taste absolutely delicious while you're basking in the brilliance of your deceptions."

The thought of Celestria touching him gave Lasidious goosebumps as he watched her seductively walk towards him.

Brayson's Home
Later That Same Night

Brayson did as George suggested and spent the night at his home within his pile of boulders. He woke in the middle of the night to a glorious light with a heavenly glow. The illusion provided by the Kedgles to make his hollowed mound of rocks seem as if he were living in the outdoors only amplified the glory as he gazed upon the image of his new lord. He couldn't see a face, or any real features. All he could see was a dark silhouette outlined by absolute magnificence.

"Brayson," the voice said in a deep but soothing tone, "I am Lasidious. I have come to ask you to be one of my Disciples of Peace and Love. I ask you to follow the words of my prophet and in doing so I will richly reward you and your family with a peaceful existence. There will be many trials in the near future, but with your strength, my son, peace can be brought to this world. You'll be my shining light on Luvelles. You can make the leaders of Luvelles understand that the words of the prophet are true. Are you ready to do what your god asks of you?"

Brayson lowered to his knees. "I live to serve you, my lord."

"I have a gift for you, my son." The silhouette extended his hand and Fisgig flew from it and landed on the headboard of Brayson's bed. "I've decided to return your friend to you. No longer hide him within the Mountains of Oraness. He's to be a symbol of the power given to you by your loving god. I have returned all of his powers he commanded before George took his life. Consider this my gift to you as a gesture of my love and my generous appreciation of your service to me. You are now whole once again, Head Master Brayson Id. Your power is stronger than it ever was. There may be a day when the prophet needs you to come to another world to help spread the words of your one true god. I trust that when this day comes you'll do so without hesitation and make me proud."

"I will, my lord, I will serve you until the day I die. Thank you for giving Fisgig back to me."

"The prophet will come to you when the moment is right to act on Luvelles. For now it's best to do nothing. Go... enjoy your family, give your vows to the woman you love. Soon, everything will make sense and you will be living on a world of peace, full of love. There's no better moment than now to begin to make the love within your new family grow."

Lasidious's glorious image faded and eventually vanished in a bright burst of light.

The Luvelles Gazette

When you want an update about your favorite characters

The Next Day Early Bailem

Shalee and Gregory are standing outside the entrance to the Source's cave. Shalee will not be allowed to go into the cave until Gregory has returned from looking into the Eye.

Kepler and Payne are waiting for George to come and give them instruction on what's to happen next. Payne's appearance is changing rapidly and as a result he has been sleeping more than usual. Kepler, on the other hand, is still dealing with the fact that he has lost his power, but something is about to happen with Payne.

Mary and Brayson have spent the day together after his visit from Lasidious. He has explained to Mary that his new god wishes him to help George bring peace to the worlds. He avoided telling Mary that George had been asked by Mieonus to kill him and spared his life. With Fisgig's return, Brayson was convinced that Lasidious was the one true god, especially now that his power was stronger than before.

George, Athena, Susanne and baby Garrin are inside George's home having dinner. George is explaining to the ladies that he will be in and out of the home doing the work of Lasidious to bring peace to Luvelles. He has avoided telling them he has the ability to teleport between the lower three worlds. He has assured Athena he will be able to be there to help raise their child. This seems to be everything Athena needed to hear. George now only needs to wait for the sign that Shalee has made it to the entrance of the Source's cave.

Boyafed has brought Sam's lifeless body to the Dark Order's Temple. He ordered one of his paladins to take the king's body to the Merchant Island of Luvelles. With every last resource preparing for the upcoming war, it was a challenge to figure out the details of Sam's return to Grayham, but the king had earned Boyafed's desire to honor him. He would give Sam their finest casket before sending him to Merchant Island. His lord Hosseff had requested a swift return of the king's body the day he appeared to him outside the Order's stables. Boyafed sent word through his mirror to Michael, Sam's General Absolute, that the king will arrive on Southern Grayham's Merchant Island within the next four Peaks of Bailem. Michael graciously thanked Boyafed and the Mirror went dark.

Boyafed plans to go to the Petrified Forest to solicit the help of Balecut, a powerful wizard, who has the power to bend moments.

Christopher, Boyafed's new Argont Commander, also the same man who replaced Dayden, Boyafed's friend since childhood as Boyafed's new second-in-command, is preparing to meet with Tygrus—an ex-soldier of the Dark Order who lives in Bestep. Tygrus is the same man Kiayasis entrusted Shalee to stay with while retrieving the Knife of Spirits from Gorne the Hermit. Christopher is counting on Tygrus's reputation as a merciless killer to rally the mercenaries of Bestep to join the Dark Order on the Battlefields of Olis. He has come prepared with the coin necessary to accomplish this goal.

Christopher also plans to meet with the evil Serwin King in Shade Hollow.

Lord Dowd is waiting to hear from Krasous, his Argont Commander. Krasous is about to meet with Wisslewine inside the enchanted woods of Wraithwood Hollow. Krasous has taken a knee and is waiting for the Wraith Hound Prince to appear from the center of the Under Eye.

Krasous will also visit the Spirit Plains. He will have to find the king of a race of spirits called the Lost Ones and capture Shesolaywen inside the Scroll of Canair.

Mieonus was watching Shalee and Gregory until they stepped onto the Source's teleportation platform within his temple inside the Void Maze. The visions within her waterfall faded. The ancient dragon's magic was far too powerful to watch the events while inside the Mountains of Oraness. The goddess now has plans to go with Keylom and Mosley to the World of Grayham. They plan to make their presence known to the people in an attempt to gain followers, but something is about to happen on Grayham that will make this task extremely hard.

Mosley, Calla, Hosseff and Alistar are on Harvestom. The wolf-god plans to leave for Grayham once he and Alistar have ensured that the war between the kingdoms of Kless and Tadreen is going to move forward as expected. The three gods have agreed to leave Alistar behind to begin their work of foiling Lasidious's attempt to gain followers on Harvestom. Calla and Hosseff will go back to Luvelles and begin their work to gain followers there.

Owain and Jervaise are headed to the World of Dragonia. Most of the demons and the vampires on this world currently worship Lasidious. Making a dent here is going to be nearly impossible. The only creatures to worship any of the other gods are the dragons, but even they serve the goddess Celestria.

Bailem and Helmep have been assigned to the World of Trollcom. The Trolls of Trollcom will do nothing without the approval of their king. He is highly respected amongst all the different races of trolls living in the Kingdom of Troltloss for his masterful role in enslaving the races of both the lizardians and the dwarfs.

In total, four completely different races of trolls make up nearly thirty-three percent of this world's population, with the Ancient Mystics making up another twenty percent and finally both the lizardians and the dwarfs together make up the final forty-seven percent.

The Ancient Mystics, the dwarfs and the lizardians all scatter their beliefs among many different deities. If Bailem and Helmep can convince the king of Troltloss to change who he worships, then the rest of the trolls would follow his lead. Lasidious would lose over 2,350,000 beings who pray to him twice a day when this the news spreads to all the races of trolls.

Gage and the other Goswigs have listened to Strongbear yell. When he woke from hibernation and listened to everything Gallrum had to say he became really—for the lack of a better description—really pissed off. It bothered Strongbear to know he was not as appreciated as he thought he was in Gogswayne. All the Goswigs are now standing on the shores of Crystal Lake waiting for King Ultor to arrive.

Marcus has not left his dark tower-palace. He's beginning to wonder if George will ever return.

Lasidious and Celestria are inside their home beneath the Peaks of Angels. They plan to separate and visit the leaders of the many different kingdoms who currently serve them on each world. Celestria also has plans of her own to help her evil lover increase the number of his followers. Lasidious has a special surprise he is itching to stick under the noses of the gods.

Thank you for reading the Luvelles Gazette

Chapter 22

𝔄 𝔓𝔦𝔩𝔢 𝔬𝔣 𝔄𝔰𝔥

The Enchanted Forest of Wraithwood Hollow

Krasous, the Argont Commander of the White Paladin Army, took a knee before the Under Eye within the enchanted woods of Wraithwood Hollow. He was waiting for Wisslewine, the Wraith Hound Prince, to emerge from his plane of existence after summoning him with the Orb of Spirits.

When finally the wraith stepped out of the darkness, a chill ran down the commander's spine. Despite the fact he knew Wisslewine was an ally of the White Army, he had never seen the Wraith Hound Prince in person before and the real thing was by far more frightening than the stories he had heard as a child.

Krasous's light blue eyes were filled with anxiety. Every muscle trembled beneath his silver armor as he looked into the ghostly hound's pitch-black eyes. The sheer size of the prince made the

Argont Commander feel small, despite being a good-sized man of over six feet. He was strong, but the way the wraith's muscles rippled as he moved sent a loud and clear message to Krasous that he was clearly the inferior race of the two.

The prince snarled and gnashed his teeth as he spoke. The beast sounded angry, as if ready to kill. He spoke in a language unknown to Krasous, but the scroll the White Chancellor had given Lord Dowd and then again passed on to him to read before summoning the ghostly hound had carried a spell within its script that allowed the Argont Commander to not only understand, but also speak in the creature's own tongue.

"What do you want with me, paladin? Why have you summoned me from my slumber within the Under Eye? This plane of existence is a miserable place and I consider it to be less than desirable. I wish to return to the darkness."

"It's under dire circumstances I've had to disturb your rest, your grace. War threatens our lands and—"

Wisslewine growled as if he was going to attack. "Why would I care about a war which threatens your lands? Are you going to tell me the Dark Army has decided to threaten your way of life yet again? Are you going to tell me it's to our benefit to protect your kingdom so they do not destroy the Under Eye and ultimately our home within it? Are you going to say I'll no longer be able to sleep peacefully within my plane of existence?" The Wraith Hound Prince snarled deeply and snapped his ghostly teeth together and shouted with a booming voice. "Is this what you have come to tell me, Commander...ANSWER ME!"

Wisslewine watched as the liquid seeped out of the bottom of Krasous's armor and waited for the urine-covered commander to reply. His voice was without conviction as he spoke.

"Your Grace... uh, ummm, these are indeed the things I've come to say."

The Wraith Hound moved close to Krasous and put his snout only inches from his face. He growled as deep as he possibly could while baring all his teeth. Once the Argont Commander had finished losing what was left of the color in his face and was nearly as white as a ghost himself, Wisslewine lightened the mood and began to smile as he pranced back toward the darkness of the Under Eye.

"Are we fighting on the usual battlefield near Olis?"

It took a moment for Krasous to answer. "Aahhhh, ummm... yes... Your Grace."

"Good, then tell Lord Dowd I'll be there. We shall number close to a thousand strong. Oh, and commander, you may want to bathe before you speak with Dowd. I can smell you from here. You had fish for dinner, I think." With that said, the prince chuckled and walked into the darkness.

Krasous fell to his knees. "I really hate this job!" He rubbed his hand in his urine and lifted it to his nose. "Uuggg... it does smell like fish!"

The Shores of Crystal Lake

The Goswigs watched, while standing in columed ranks, as King Ultor finished his transformation after emerging from the waters of the lake to stand before them. Without delay, the king looked at Strongbear and explained the situation of the upcoming war. Gregory's request for the Goswigs to join Lord Dowd's White Army just north of Lake Tepp was delivered and further, he asked them to march to the battlegrounds of Olis.

"But I am leaving it up to you, Strongbear," Ultor said while scanning the Goswig's formations. "Whether the Goswigs will join the fight is a final decision I will allow you to make, my big hairy friend."

Strongbear thought long and hard before responding. "We will go and join, Lord Dowd. I understand our presence is a key to victory!"

A huge sigh of disappointment filled the air. King Ultor looked at Strongbear. "It doesn't appear as if your decision is a favorable one. Are you sure this is what you wish to do? You can always decline to go."

Strongbear pushed out his mighty chest and said, "If we do not fight and if the Dark Army manages to take over... there is a chance many of our old masters would find us and pull us out of Gogswayne forever. I cannot allow this to happen! If we go to battle now and make a stand, we may be able to defeat the Dark Army and never have to worry about the secret of our village being learned. This decision is for the best, though they may not see it now. We will fight!"

Ultor nodded and made his way into the waters of the lake. Strongbear watched as the Ultorian's iridescent glow returned as the king's large angelic wings began to emerge from within his body.

Ultor - King of the Ultorians

Illustration by Cindy Fletcher

Eventually Strongbear turned and looked at the population of Gogswayne. All he had to say was his favorite phrase. "So are you with me... or are you against me?" The bear never got a reply as they all turned and headed home to prepare for war.

The Mountains of Oraness

George had fallen asleep, and again Lasidious disturbed his dreams. But this time the God of Mischief had not interrupted a dream about Abbie and had brought news which intrigued the warlock. Shalee was alone and waiting outside the Source's cave for her chance to enter. Gregory had gone inside and this was the best opportunity for George to make his move. None of the gods would be able to see George's handiwork and the warlock was now able to teleport directly into the area, thanks to the information he had received from Brayson on how to do so.

Shalee was startled when George appeared. She lifted her hand and sent her magic flying. The warlock simply smiled and allowed the thousands of tiny needles to bounce off him while he stared at the sorceress. Shalee couldn't believe her eyes. She felt helpless. All she could do now was wait for George to kill her.

But after a long period of George doing nothing but standing there looking at her, she finally shouted, "Quit toying with me! I know you're here to kill me so get it over with!"

With a peaceful voice, George responded. "I'm not here to kill you, Shalee. I'm actually here to explain my actions to you."

"Yeah, right—do you mean the actions which caused a war on Grayham... the same actions which have caused the death of so many people? How could you possibly explain all of that?"

George moved to stand beside her and leaned against Fisgig's old stone perch. Shalee moved back to the edge of the small island of dirt to keep her distance.

"We have been lied to, Shalee. The things the gods have told us are all lies."

"George, how can I trust someone who has made so many poor decisions?"

George lifted his head and found Shalee's eyes. "And how could I trust someone who has cheated on her husband and in doing so, got the man she claims to love killed?"

"What?" she gasped. "How did you know about my relationship with Kiayasis and what do you mean Sam has been killed? He's fine. He's in the swamp retrieving the—" She hesitated, unsure if she should continue.

"Yes, I know what Sam was doing. I know he was after the crystal and he actually got it, by the way."

"He did? And how do you know all of this?"

"I know many things. I know your husband was killed by Boyafed. Apparently the man you chose to have an affair with was the son of the man who commands the strongest army of evil on all of Luvelles. Boyafed is his name. He waited for Sam to exit the swamp and then he killed him to get vengeance for Kiayasis's death. The next person he intends to kill is you, Shalee. After all, you're the one responsible for Sam killing his boy."

Shalee fell to the dirt. She remained silent. George took the opportunity to explain further. "Shalee, do you remember the day you and Sam had dinner with me in Lethwitch? You know, the day I found out my daughter was dead. I was with you inside your room at the inn? Shalee... do you remember?"

The queen managed to respond as the tears began to flow. "I remember, but what does this have to do with Sam's death?"

"Don't worry about Sam. He won't be dead for long. I plan to take you with me back to Grayham so you can watch the one true god of these worlds command Sam to live again. Lasidious will return his soul to him."

"That's impossible, George," Shalee snapped as she wiped the tears from her chin. "Lasidious is evil and there's no way he can command someone's soul to leave the Book of Immortality and return it to their body. I don't believe any of this. This isn't how things work on these worlds."

George sighed. "You said you remembered the day you told me my daughter was dead. Do you also remember asking me if I had been contacted by Lasidious and I had absolutely no idea what you were talking about?"

"I do remember... but what does this have to do with anything?"

"I'm getting to that, just chill a second and let me explain. The gods told you Lasidious was a God of Mischief. They told you they thought Lasidious was the one who brought me here from Earth. How am I doing so far?"

"So far everything you've said is what we were told."

"Did they also tell you Lasidious planned to use me to do his dirty work?"

"They did... so what are you getting at, George?"

"Well, what I'm trying to say is that it wasn't Lasidious who brought me back from Earth. It was the goddess Mieonus. She was the one who has been asking me to do all these hateful things."

Shalee was confused as she responded. "Okay, so let's say this is all true for argument's sake... why would you do these terrible things in the first place? Why would you hurt so many people?"

George sat on the ground and leaned against the perch. "When you lost your baby, how did you feel?"

"What does it matter how I felt?"

"Just tell me, Shalee, and I will explain what I'm getting at."

"I felt like I wanted him back, of course."

"Exactly... this is the same way I felt when Mieonus told me she could get my daughter's soul back out of the Book. She told me if I helped her to create a diversion on Grayham and find a way to keep the attention of the gods off her while she worked on a plan to take control of the Book of Immortality, she would return Abbie to me."

"But the love of your daughter doesn't give you the right to kill so many, George!"

"Exactly... I agree with you one hundred percent. I was really screwed up there for a while. I'm sure you knew I was hurting inside... didn't you?"

"I did, but still..."

George lowered his head and feigned his shame. "Look, I feel bad about the things I've done. But I'm not the only one who has done them. Let me ask you something. How many people have you and Sam had to kill in order to fulfill the prophecy to set an example on the worlds? Take a long hard look at everything that has happened. Even if you didn't have to fight in the war I caused, Sam still would've had to kill in the arenas of Grayham just to gain the level of glory the gods asked you to obtain. You had to kill to lead. How sick and disturbing is this concept anyway? How can it be okay to kill in order to create an empire for the races to follow?"

"Okay... I see your point, but you're still killing people, and why are you doing it if you feel so bad? I would imagine Mieonus has brought you here to start another war!"

"No, it's not what you think. The truth of the matter is, there is still a heaven where the souls of Lasidious's followers are kept. The gods are jealous of his power and have created many lies to try and get the people of these worlds to avoid following his path of righteousness."

"George, what the hell are you talking about? Sam has said nothing about Lasidious having this kind of power. In fact, he's said everything to the contrary. He has read everything in the royal library in Brandor about the gods. He says Lasidious commands those who are evil."

"Don't you see, Shalee, Lasidious doesn't have many followers on the World of Grayham. Bassorine was the one who had most of the followers on that world. I'm sure Sam told you this. He had a statue of himself erected there. You do remember the statue, right?"

Shalee thought a while. "I remember Sam was irritated because Bassorine's destruction left a lot of people without anyone to believe in. He said it seemed like a big joke to have gods that are so limited in their power... so limited in their knowledge of so many things."

"That's what I'm trying to tell you. After I started the war on Grayham, Lasidious, the one true god the others fear, came to me. He was angered by my actions and took me to see his heaven. I saw so many beautiful angels. I saw the most magnificent creations you could possibly imagine. Shalee, I saw things that would have awed you while losing yourself in their glory.

"Lasidious informed me I was to go back into the world and become his Prophet of Peace and spread the words of both peace and love. I'm to do everything I can to bring harmony to the worlds. He explained to me that the others are constantly trying to manipulate the people of the worlds and in doing so, they bring war and heartache to the masses. They actually want war so the souls of their followers trapped inside the Book can be reborn. It is a vicious cycle of death. It's the most ridiculous thing I've ever heard."

Shalee sat silently for a while, and then responded. "If you're lying, I'll know eventually. I drank a potion that will give me the memories of the gods. It may take a while before I can recall them all, but I'll know if you're lying."

George had to think fast. He had no idea what she was talking about. An idea popped into his lying brain. "Shalee... let me ask you something. The fact that you drank a potion that gives you the memories of the gods causes me to have concern for you. I think you need to consider the source of where the potion came from. You may eventually know many, many things, but with the way the gods have concocted so many lies, how are you going to know what is really true or what isn't? I don't envy you right now at all. I can only imagine you'll be extremely confused. Is this really how things should work? Shouldn't there be a better way? I have found this way."

Shalee pushed her hands through her long blonde hair, her blue eyes revealing her stress as she responded. "This is absolutely terrible! If what you've told me is a fact, then Mosley must also be a bad god. Is this what you're saying? I can't fathom the fact that Mosley could be just as misled as we have been."

"I think you should ask Mosley what his job as the God of War entails. I personally have been told it's his job to make sure the people of these worlds choose war over a peaceful solution. He does this willingly to ensure that the souls within the Book of Immortality are constantly rotating through his pages once the people die. He knows he is on the wrong side and he also knows he has deceived you just as the others have. Once you have spoken with Mosley, you'll have your answer regarding his character. I wouldn't tell Mosley you know the truth about the gods. Be careful how you ask this question. They will bring war to your kingdom if you do something they don't like. I would hate to see this happen to you again."

"So you're saying Lasidious isn't a God of Mischief and this is just a big lie told to us all by the gods?"

George smiled and stood up. He moved to Shalee and put his hand gently on her shoulder. "Lasidious is quite the opposite of everything they've told you. He's a loving god whom I now serve. He saved me from living a life of hate and deceit. I'm saying Mieonus was the one who lied to me and she's just as evil as Mosley is."

George lifted his hands to the sky. "I am now a Prophet of Peace and Love... and I've come to share this love with you. I'm here to help you say goodbye to Sam before you look into the Eye of Magic. If you don't survive this experience, I want you to know Sam will live again and my lord intends to return his soul in front of all of Brandor's people before they light the fires of his passing celebration."

"Then take me to Sam, George. I'm ready to go and I want to see his body."

"I'll take you to see his body and I'll bring you back here once you've said goodbye. If you wish to put off looking into the Eye until you've had the chance to witness the resurrection of your husband, I'll allow you to stay with my new family until it's time to take you to Brandor.

"You will like my wife and the rest of the gang. They are all loving people and she will treat you right until it's time to go to Brandor. Sam's passing celebration has already been scheduled. You'll be able to witness the true power of the god I serve."

"How could they schedule the lighting of the fire without me present? I'm their queen, for hell's sake."

"This is something you'll have to take up with your General Absolute. Close your eyes and I'll take you to see Sam's body."

George touched her shoulder. When they reappeared, they were standing just outside a container on Luvelles's Merchant Island.

Sam's coffin sat only a few feet away behind the heavy iron door. Once the door had been opened, Shalee covered her mouth with both hands as tears began to run down her cheeks. She hated herself for this. She knew her infidelity caused her love's death.

George moved in to lift the coffin's lid. Sam was lying peacefully inside, but Boyafed's dagger still remained buried in his side. Kael had been laid on top of his chest with both hands resting on the sword's grip.

"Oh my God," Shalee said as she reached to pull the dagger

from Sam's side. She tried hard to remove it but was unable to. She tried to use her magic, but still it wouldn't budge. Eventually she gave up and leaned over the side of the casket to kiss Sam on the forehead. She tried to talk to Kael, but the sword was unresponsive.

George waited patiently, allowing the queen to grieve. Eventually the last tear fell and after Shalee kissed his forehead one final time, *George touched Shalee on her shoulder and teleported them both back outside the Source's cave.*

"I'm sorry for your loss, Shalee. To stay here would be terrible. Why don't you come with me and meet Athena? She will take care of you."

Shalee lowered to the ground. "I would prefer to be alone. Is there someplace else you could take me until we head back to Brandor?"

George thought a moment. "I will take you to the Village of Vesper. The innkeeper there is a nice elf named Kebble. I will pay for your room and ensure that anything you need is taken care of. Will this work?"

"I suppose," Shalee responded softly, "I can't think of any other place to go. I would ask you to take me to Brandor but I don't think I would find a moment to myself there. I think the people would be all over me."

"Then it's settled… Vesper it is." He touched her shoulder and when they reappeared they were standing outside Kebble's Kettle.

"I will take you inside and introduce you to Kebble. You should be okay here until I come back to get you. I'll be back in eight days. This should give you ample time to mourn, and if you decide to witness the power of the one true god of these worlds, I'll be happy to take you with me to Brandor. Don't worry, Shalee… my god gives me the power to teleport between worlds. You'll see your husband rise again, I assure you."

As they walked through the doors of the inn, Kebble's smile widened as he saw George. He hurried over and crawled up onto his booster steps behind the counter.

"And who would this beauty be, George? How can Kebble help you today, my dear?" He lifted his pipe to his mouth and took a puff of his cherry-smelling tobacco.

Shalee quietly responded. "I just need a room, please."

George spoke up. "This is the queen of Brandor, my friend. She has come here from Grayham and has recently found out some tragic news. Will you please take care of her and make sure she has everything she needs? I will pay you upon my return."

Kebble removed his pipe. A large smile crossed his face as he leaned forward and lifted Shalee's chin to find her eyes. "Any friend of George's is a friend of mine, my lady. I will see to it that you are well taken care of."

Marcus Id's Dark Tower-Palace

George appeared in Marcus's throne room not long after leaving Kebble's inn. As soon as Marcus saw him he rushed up to the warlock. "So you lived. I was beginning to think the Eye had swallowed your soul."

"It's good to see you, Marcus. Everything is going as planned. Have you accomplished all we discussed while I was gone?"

"I've done it all, and then some. Both armies are gathering their forces. They'll move against one another and meet at the battlegrounds of Olis. Now you can send me to meet with the Source. I wish to look into the Eye as soon as possible."

"Soon... very soon... there are two people going through the trials to meet with the Source as we speak. Apparently Brayson decided he wants your brother Gregory to stand before the Source."

"What! This is an outrage! Why would he do that when—"

George held up his hand and used his power to silence Marcus. "Does why really matter, Marcus? I told you you'll look into the Eye... and you will as soon as I can get you in. I'll ensure you're the Head Master of all Luvelles before I leave this world, as I have already promised I would. Maybe you should learn to control your anger. You need to find a way to make those around you enjoy your company, not despise you. What good will your power be if no one will respect you when you're Head Master? I'll come get you when the moment is right. Until then, there's someone I want you to go and get for me."

George released his power so Marcus could speak.

"So, am I to be your errand boy now?"

George had to smile.

"What's so funny?" Marcus snapped.

George shook his head. "Look, this is a favor I'm asking you to do. This same favor will help me give you the position you've always wanted. A position we both know you deserve far more than Brayson deserves it. If you want to be Head Master then I need you to go to Grayham and find a rat named Maldwin. I need you to bring him back to me."

"A rat… what could you possibly want with a rat?"

"Just go and get him, Marcus! I need the rat to get you into the position you want. I will set everything up. The Merchant Angels will take you to Grayham three nights from now."

Marcus cut him off. "Brayson will never allow me to go to Grayham. Only he can make this request."

"You leave Brayson to me. I'll ensure you're allowed to catch a ride with the Merchant Angels. Brayson trusts me and I'll come up with a clever deception to get you there. I'll also make sure you get back as well. The rat is important and I need you in the Head Master position before I can move my family to the World of Harvestom.

"You'll find the rat just south of a city called City View. He lives in a cave and the entrance to this cave sits at the edge of where the Mountains of Latasef drop off into the Ocean of Utopia.

"Use this scroll before you call for him while sitting at the entrance of his cave. It'll protect you if the little guy gets scared. Once you've read it, you'll have two days to find the rat. This should be sufficient, I think."

Marcus stopped him from continuing. After reading the scroll, he looked up. "Why do I need to protect my mind? Is this the power the rat possesses?"

"No… it's not a power," he replied, quickly lying to protect Maldwin. "The rat's ability is a natural one he has had since birth. Don't get any bright ideas. You won't be able to eat his heart and steal this ability from him."

Marcus couldn't believe his elven ears. "How could you possibly know about such things? Eating the heart of another is a secret which only the most ancient of elves know."

"How I know this is my business. I know many other things that only the most ancient of the elves know. You can't pull one over on me, Marcus. Just don't forget to read the scroll before you call for the rat.

"When you see Maldwin I want you to give him this note. It's written in the rat's own language. Once one of his little clawed feet touches the parchment, it will speak to the rat."

Marcus tilted his head almost as a dog would. "You cast a spell which makes the paper talk? I've never thought of doing that before."

George began to laugh. "I know, huh... doesn't that just crack you up? I stole the idea from a movie I saw back on Earth. You should've seen this flick. Their packages spoke to them when they were delivered to their School of Magic. Since Earth has been destroyed, I guess they won't be suing me for using their idea, now will they?"

Marcus just stood silent and looked at George with a blank stare. He had absolutely no clue what George was talking about. The warlock had to chuckle a bit at the Dark Chancellor's confusion before he continued. "I imagine that when—"

Marcus stopped him again. "What will the note tell this Maldwin to do? I should know this kind of information, don't you think, especially if the parchment will speak to him in his own language? You should tell me more about what you plan to do with the rat's ability. And how did you learn to speak the language of this beast, anyway? George, you're not telling me everything!"

"Look, man... I don't speak Ratanese! Somebody I know speaks his language. I don't have to tell you anything other than what's necessary to get you into the Head Master's position. All I've got to do is fulfill my promise like I said I would. Do you understand me?"

"I don't like being left in the dark—it's unnerving!"

"Look, Marcus, Maldwin trusts me... and I can convince him to use this natural ability he has to get the people of Luvelles to initially accept you as their new Head Master.

"You know I could've killed you already if I had wanted to. So maybe you should allow me to finish giving you what I've promised and stop being the only obstacle I need to jump over in order to get you there. Damn, Marcus… you can truly be annoying! Like I've already told you, once you're Head Master you're going to have to chill out!"

"What does this… chill out mean?"

"It means you're going to need to stop being such an ass. If you don't, the people of Luvelles will hate you. I can get you into the Head Master's chair. I can even get them to accept your new position, but I can't make the people of this world respect you once I'm gone. You're going to have to do that on your own. Why else do you think your brother is so beloved? He doesn't act like a piece of garesh."

"Okay… okay… I see your point. I will try and do this chilling out thing as you've suggested."

"Good… anyway… as I was about to say, I imagine once Maldwin listens to the note's message and understands you're there to bring him to Grayham's Merchant Island, he'll want to come and visit with me. I'm sure he'll be more than happy to go with you. You'll need to know how to shout out his name when you're calling for him inside his cave. This should make things go much smoother. Hopefully, your use of the scroll to protect your mind will be all for nothing. This is how you say his name… Mal-A-quay-O!

"Once he finds you, I want you to say, 'Everything is A-okay, man' and give him a thumbs-up, like this. The rat will know I've sent you. He should listen to the note without any objections. Do you understand all of this?"

"Yeah… I got it. If going after this beast will get me into the Head Master's position like you've—"

George vanished before Marcus could finish. The Dark Chancellor stomped his foot in anger after watching the warlock disappear. "I'll go get your stupid rat, but I assure you your life will end once I've looked into the Eye of Magic."

The Village of Bestep

Christopher, Boyafed's new Argont Commander—the same man who replaced Dayden, Boyafed's best friend since childhood—is counting on Tygrus's reputation as a merciless killer to rally the mercenaries of Bestep to join the Dark Order on the Battlefields of Olis.

Christopher looked across the bar and studied the curves of the Halfling woman who had served him his ale. His long, pure white hair fell across his shoulders and his eyes were without color, looking as if they were made of a fogged crystal with a grayish-looking pupil resting at their center. His voice was strong as he made an advance.

"Good lady... do you have any moments to lay with a soldier of the Order tonight?"

A much heavier voice replied from behind him. "My daughter isn't a common whore, Christopher. I suggest if you plan on sowing your seeds, you find a different vessel to put them in… or I could always just kill you!"

Tygrus was an older elf, retired from his commission with the Order over 40 seasons ago. Still to this day he was one of the most feared men with a blade throughout all of Luvelles and his magic was equally as strong. He was perhaps the only man left alive, other than Lord Dowd, who could challenge Boyafed to a dual and possibly survive.

Christopher felt foolish as Tygrus took a seat next to him at the bar. Tygrus's dark brown eyes carried a confidence within them few men possessed. "What do you want?"

"I have been sent to ask you to bring your mercenaries to the Battlegrounds of Olis."

"Ha! You better have brought plenty of coin, because this is going to cost you."

The World of Trollcom
The Kingdom of Troltloss

The gods, Bailem, and Helmep, are on the World of Trollcom. Trollcom is a dark world, with an even darker way of life—but this is a story for later—a story of an unexpected sacrifice.

Both deities await the king of Troltloss's return from an evening outing with his 400th queen. When they had originally approached Kesdelain, he had been sitting on the riverbank of Greslowfem feeding his queen, Sholifenda, the brains of a slaved dwarf miner—all the while waiting for the fish to strike at a special bait which was cast from a freshly-carved pole made of whipple wood—a wood known both for its flexibility and durability.

Kesdelain was a mastermind at controlling the many different races of trolls—a mastermind thanks to a gift given by Lasidious many seasons ago. As a result, all trolls now served one king and held Kesdelain in high regard. The king was born of a dominant bloodline of trolls, a race called the Tradesmeal, (Tra-des-meal) or when translated, Deadly Ones. Both his mother and his father were of noble blood and had a strong set of family values—or at least, as strong as a set of family values could be for a race of beings known for eating their young for simple disobedience.

Kesdelain had black-crimson colored skin with features considered handsome by troll standards, but his blood carried within it an acid which could burn through the toughest, most absorption-resistant skin and many forms of light armor. His ability to regenerate at a rate much faster than all others of his kind was well-known and respected throughout his kingdom.

Eventually the king methodically sauntered into his cave throne room. It was dark, completely absent of light from the outside world. Other than a single torch which stood near his throne, it was a miserable place. Since it rested far beneath the earth and not far from a large body of water, the room was cold, carrying a bit of a nip due to the dampness.

The torch wasn't placed beside him because the light was needed for the king to see—in fact, his eyes preferred the darkness. The torch was more for shedding light on his majestic form for the slaves who entered to bow before him.

Kesdelain knew who the gods were. He cared nothing about them; he served Lasidious only because of the deity's generous gift which he had given to him many, many seasons ago—a gift he used to lengthen his life by nearly 9000 seasons and to enslave the races of both the gnomes and the dwarfs. In return for the god's gift, Kesdelain had agreed to make it a royal decree that all the different races of trolls live in service to Lasidious and pray to him twice a day—both in the morning and again before they lay down to sleep.

The gift Lasidious had given the troll king had been before a very specific law was added to the Book of Immortality. A god could no longer give any being within any of the worlds anything that would change the balance of power on their world. This act of generosity towards Kesdelain had two effects. The first: the gift gave the troll king his extended life and the charming wit to convince every race of troll they should live in service to him. The second, and also the most important effect, was a result of Kesdelain using his new charismatic charms to fulfill his side of their bargain. The king encouraged every last troll, no matter what race they were, to pray to the God of Mischief. This substantially increased Lasidious's power—increased them to the point he would become more powerful than all the other gods—all, that is, except Bassorine, but even that problem had since rectified itself and now, all that was left to overcome was the power of the Book.

Now… back to the law which rested on one of Gabriel's pages… the law said nothing of giving a gift which would glorify or even increase the strength of someone who was already in power. This was the loophole Bailem and Helmep intended to use when encouraging Kesdelain to begin his new life of service to them.

The troll king spoke in his own language, a language I will translate into a common tongue.

"I care not to speak with gods. Why have you come?"

Bailem had put a glow around his chubby angelic body before they arrived. He stepped forward to respond. "We have come bearing a gift. We wish to have all races of trolls live in service to us. We wish to have their prayers magnify our names in the heavens and for doing so we shall give you a reward—one which will make you the envy of all the worlds."

"Everything I need, I have. There's nothing to give that I need. Be gone with you!"

Bailem stood firm. "I said nothing of need, great king. I said we wish to make you the envy of all the worlds. We wish to glorify you and in return for your faithful service, we wish to make your name unforgettable on all the worlds. We wish to make you as esteemed as the gods."

"And what kind of gift would do all of this?"

Before another word could be uttered, a bright light filled the darkness of Kesdelain's cave. The troll king had to cover his eyes to keep from being blinded. As the light dissipated, Lasidious stood at its center with George at his side.

The God of Mischief wasted no moments. He spoke before either Bailem or Helmep could say anything.

"Kesdelain, why would you entertain such foolishness? These two men couldn't possibly have the power to give you such a gift. These men aren't gods. They're nothing more than powerful mystics. They are here to deceive you... liars, to be sure!"

Bailem was outraged. "You treat us as if we're mere mortal men... and you do it in front of a being of the worlds, no less. Do you have no shame, Lasidious?"

Lasidious didn't respond. Instead he stood silent while George took center stage. Kesdelain watched as the warlock moved to kneel before him on the shaped stones ascending to his throne.

"Great king... I've heard many powerful stories about you from the god you serve. I know the service of your people pleases him. The stories of your beautiful queens and your greatness among all the races of trolls are ones of legend. I know that—"

Helmep shouted over George. His hazel eyes clearly showed his anger. "Do you have a new pet, Lasidious? Does George travel with you as a dog would? Why would you bring a mortal to do the job of a god?"

Again Lasidious didn't answer. George continued. "As I was saying... great king of trolls—"

"Shut up, George," Bailem shouted. "Lasidious, send your pet home and let's handle this as it should be handled."

Again George continued and again Lasidious allowed him to do so.

"So as I was saying—"

"I said shut up!" Bailem shouted again. Lasidious began to smile.

Now George turned up the heat. He turned to Bailem and moved to stand in front of him. "Why would the king wish to serve only a man—men who are weak and are barely a step away from being considered pathetic? You have no real power... nor will I hold my tongue."

Bailem remained calm. He spread his white-feathered angel wings in an attempt to show his own glory and responded. "I find it humorous that you have the nerve to speak to me in this manner. I think the moment has come for you to—"

Lasidious lifted his voice to a level that made every mortal within the king's cave castle cover their ears. "ENOUGH!" Once he had everyone's attention, he addressed both deities.

"If either of you have the ability to strike George down, I'll allow your gift to be given to the king."

Helmep responded, "You don't have the authority to stop us from giving the king this gift. We have no desire to kill this mere mortal. You're wasting our—"

Again Lasidious shouted and again he commanded everyone's attention. "You say mere mortal as if you have the power to strike him down. I say you don't... or else you would've done it already."

Bailem was unsure how to respond. He knew George was protected by the Book of Immortality's laws. If he struck him down, he himself would be made mortal.

Lasidious used the god's silence to his advantage. "As I thought... you don't have it in you."

Helmep had enough. He decided to turn Lasidious's game against him. "If he's just a mere mortal man, then you should be able to kill him yourself. If you can't do it, then there's no reason why anyone should serve you, either. If you're unable to destroy him, then none of us should be the god that all trolls serve."

Lasidious stepped up and looked at the troll king. "You have witnessed the failure of these two men to kill this man. I want you to see the power of your one true god. I think I shall turn him to nothing more than a pile of ash."

George feigned a desperate look, as if he couldn't believe what was happening. He was about to be sacrificed and watched as Lasidious turned around, lifted his hands, and struck him with a bolt of lightning.

Both Helmep and Bailem watched as the ash settled on the floor. Neither of them could believe what they had seen. They waited for the Book to appear but Gabriel never came.

Lasidious smiled at his handiwork as he turned and moved up the steps towards Kesdelain's throne. As he leaned forward, he said, "My point has been made, king of trolls. I trust both your prayers, and also the prayers of those who live in service to your crown shall become stronger, even more so now than they have been for so many seasons. I'm sure I don't need to remind you about who gave you your position as king. It's just as easy to take this position from you and give it to another. I'm sure your prayers will reflect your gratitude and desire to remain exalted on this world."

Lasidious vanished.

Chapter 23
𝔄 𝔙𝔢𝔯𝔶 𝔥𝔞𝔭𝔭𝔶 𝔅𝔦𝔤 𝔎𝔦𝔱𝔱𝔶
Kepler's Lair Beneath the Rocks

"Damn," George shouted as he appeared with Lasidious in the darkness of Kepler's Lair beneath the rocks. The warlock quickly commanded the darkness to dissipate. George's robes were smoldering. He turned around to speak with the God of Mischief as he brushed them off, but Lasidious was already gone. "Garesh... so much for working on the timing of his lighting strike. I barely made it out!"

"What are you talking about?" Kepler asked as he stood to stretch.

"Oh nothing... just a little timing issue which could be fixed with some practice."

"Are you actually here to stay, or are you going to run off again and leave me behind with Payne?"

George finished brushing himself off. "Have you missed me, Kep? Do I need to give you a hug?"

"Do it... give him a hug, Master," Payne said. "I want to see him squirm."

George whirled around. He couldn't believe what he saw. The fairy-demon was an additional five inches taller than what he had already grown before.

"Holy garesh, Payne... you've grown at least a foot in a matter of days. Your voice is deeper, too."

Kepler cut in. "But he still acts like a freak. All he talks about are the hairs on his privates. I think he's hit puberty."

George couldn't believe his ears. "How does anyone hit puberty at three seasons old? Maybe you are a freak, Payne."

The fairy-demon picked up a large fish he had caught earlier that day and chucked it across the lair. It hit Kepler upside his head. "Now look at what you've gone and done. Even he's calling me a freak now. I should teleport you to a frightful height and drop you to your death."

George shook his head. "Payne, do you realize you're speaking as if you're actually educated?"

Kepler growled. "Don't give him too much credit. I finally figured out what's going on. Once I began showing him how to speak, he figured out he could look into your mind. He knows everything you know. I've had to explain many things and I've also had to stop him from saying things to Mary and Athena he shouldn't be saying. I convinced him to wait for you to get back before he does what he says he's going to do."

George turned to Payne. "And what do you plan to do?"

Payne stood up. He still had the mind of a young boy despite having George's knowledge. He had no real idea of what to do with it. "I don't like the way the things in your mind make me feel. I don't want to lie to Athena. I don't want her to—"

George lifted his hand. Payne realized he could no longer move. "I'm sorry, Payne, but I can't have you telling Athena anything. Look into my mind... what will I do to you if you say anything?"

Payne's face showed his surprise when he listened to George's thoughts. "You would kill me. Why would you?" Again Payne read his mind for the answer. "You think if I say anything, it will stop you from getting Abbie's soul back out of the Book of Immortality. You're willing to sacrifice me in order to save her."

George kneeled beside the fairy-demon and gently lowered him to his back on the floor. "What am I thinking now, Payne?"

Fear spread across his red face as he answered. "You're going to give me a choice. I can surrender my powers and my memories that I have gained to Kepler and you'll let me live. If I don't, you'll turn part of my spine to stone. You'll cut my chest open and allow Kepler to eat my heart. You're willing to allow him to steal my powers from me. You're willing to send my soul to the Book of Immortality if you have to. You would give him my abilities because you know he won't say anything about all the lies you've told. You trust him more than you trust me."

George leaned over the fairy-demon, exposed his palm and a knife appeared. "So what will it be, Payne... live by giving Kep your powers and your memories learned while using them, or die. You choose, but do it now!"

Payne began to speak in the language of the Ancient Mystics. George knew what was happening and allowed him to continue. Eventually, the warlock watched as a large ball of energy emerged from within Payne's chest and moved across the lair. It slowly absorbed into Kepler's body. The power was a lot for the demon-cat to absorb. He lowered to the ground and it wasn't long before he fell asleep.

George watched in amazement as the fairy-demon's body began to shrink. It wasn't more than a few moments before he was once again his normal size and smiling childishly. Payne looked up and said: "Master got food for Payne. Why Kitty sleep? Payne goes to Athena? Athena feed Payne."

George smiled and rubbed the top of the fairy-demon's bald head. "You don't have to call me master any more, little guy. Call me George or even Dad if you want to. You can call Athena whatever works best for her. Why don't you go into the house and tell her you're hungry."

"Payne goes now." He closed his eyes to teleport, but nothing happened. He tried again, and still nothing happened.

"Why don't you just fly, buddy?"

"Okay, George." Payne headed out.

George's mind began to wander in thought. *There's no way I could've killed Payne. He's like family to me, for hell's sake. What's wrong with me? Payne did nothing wrong. I couldn't send him away if I wanted to. Athena would kill me if I did. I almost had to give up ever seeing Abbie again to keep this family together. This garesh is getting way too deep. I've got to find a way out of this mess.*

He took a seat next to Kepler and continued his train of thought. *Just stick to the plan for now. You'll find your way out sooner or later. Just take care of your family and stay the course until the opportunity presents itself. You need to know more before you can make any changes. You just need more knowledge.*

The Spirit Plains

Krasous took a deep breath. He adjusted his White Army silver armor and tied his spirit-bull to a large tree. As soon as he finished petting his mount, the bull dematerialized and became nothing more than a ghostly, shadowy figure.

"I'll be back, Hellzgat," Krasous said as he turned to look out across the rolling plains before him. "I'm not really sure how long this is going to take, but I'll be back."

After his visit with the Wraith Hound Prince in Wraithwood Hollow, the Argent Commander dreaded the idea of meeting another spirit. The problem was that, he wasn't sure where he should actually go. The Spirit Plains spanned a large area and he was seeking a very specific spirit—one which could be anywhere.

To his knowledge, or anyone's knowledge within the White Army, for that matter, Shesolaywen, the spirit king of a race of souls called The Lost Ones simply wandered aimlessly somewhere throughout this entire valley. He had no castle or any kind of a home to speak of. He simply wandered and the bad part about it was... The Lost Ones wouldn't show themselves unless he was completely alone, and worse still—completely naked and vulnerable.

The spirit-bull snorted playfully as he watched Krasous undress. "Hey... you keep your eyes to yourself. This is bad enough without you eyeing me down," he grumbled as he gave Hellzgat's shadowy form a slight grin.

Somehow, the Argont commander had to find Shesolaywen and manage to keep the spirit from possessing him long enough to read from a scroll called The Scroll of Canair. The scroll would capture the spirit king's essence inside its parchment. Krasous would then need to take the scroll to Lord Dowd. The White Army leader would then need to read from the scroll once the moment arrived for the armies to begin fighting at the Battlegrounds of Olis. When the spirit king was released, the scroll's spell would cause the king's essence a tremendous amount of pain. As a result, Shesolaywen would cry out in agony. It was this awful, wretched scream—one loud enough to be heard by both armies—that would cause the Wraith Hounds of Wraithwood Hollow to go berserk. All Lord Dowd would need to do then was use just one simple command to order the hounds into battle. They would attack the Dark Army's men with an intensity equalling triple their number.

The Following Morning
The Mountains of Oraness
The Entrance to the Source's Cave

The morning was crisp and downright frigid. Since his arrival on Grayham, George had not seen any real change in the weather, but today was different. The air actually felt as if a new season was approaching and all the warlock could do was guess or rather presume it was the third piece of the Crystal Moon being added to the others that was responsible for the sudden change in climate.

To his surprise, frost had buried its chilly claws into the steep cliffs surrounding the pool where Fisgig's perch rested on its tiny island of dirt. He was going to need a heavier robe and when it came to matters of fashion, this was a topic that both he and Shalee would actually be able to see eye-to-eye on.

I suppose I'll have to create something to handle the cold, he thought, *but it's going to need a statement attached to it considering all this power I have now.* He could only laugh within himself as he lifted his hand to allow a flame to burn within his palm to provide warmth.

After a few moments of allowing his mind to wander, he pulled his head out of the clouds and back to the task at hand. He needed to finish what he came for and hurry back home before anyone realized he was missing. He knew his little white lie about going outside to check on Kepler wouldn't buy him much more than a few more moments.

Scanning the cliff walls, he chose a spot directly above the cave's entrance. He lifted his hands and with a concentrated effort, his magic reached inside of his head and retrieved the effect he was after. A large portion of the rock pulled away from the rest of the cliff's face and was now suspended in mid-air, high above the entrance. The rest of his thought commanded the magic to release the stone as soon as Gregory Id exited the cave. All he could hope for was that the weight of his instrument of murder would find its target and Gregory would not be able to teleport fast enough to save himself.

With a wry smile, George vanished. When he reappeared, he looked down at the giant jaguar. Kepler was still sleeping.

George thought to himself, *I wonder how much longer he'll sleep. Receiving Payne's power so quickly... wow! I bet his body must be in some sort of shock.*

Seeing that nothing could be done, George allowed Kepler to sleep. He climbed out of the demon-cat's lair beneath the rocks and made his way inside the house. As it turned out, Athena was also sleeping. He took off his clothes, crawled in gently beside her, and snuggled his way into a comfortable position. After kissing her gently on the neck for many long moments, he eventually rolled her onto her back and positioned his head on her soft shoulder just above the breast. He allowed the soft beat of her heart to be his lullaby and drifted off to sleep.

Later that afternoon, Athena, Mary, Brayson and George worked together to finish packing for an evening of what George would ordinarily call hell... but as Brayson reminded him more than once already, it was called, "Calling Nature," or better known to someone from Earth as camping—and as we all know, George really, really hates roughing it.

"What's bothering you, George?" Athena said as she put a few Corgan sandwiches inside a sealed wooden container Brayson had specifically created for such outings. As she opened the lid a slight chill could be felt on her hand. She enjoyed the magical cooler and looked up to listen to her husband's response.

George was trying hard to put on a happy face but he knew Athena could see right through his façade. "Nothing I can't handle, babe. Are you sure we should be doing this? You're getting close to having the baby and sleeping on the ground might not be such a wise thing to do."

Brayson gave him a look and watched as Athena put a finger on his chest and gently pushed him back against the kitchen table. She maneuvered the best she could since her belly was poking out so far and after accounting for its roundness, she leaned in to give him a kiss.

"I know you don't like doing this kind of thing. You can always stay here if you would like and I promise not to be angry with you. But I'm going to go because I enjoy it."

"Nonsense," Mary said while walking past Brayson and pinching his firm little butt on her way to the pantry, bare feet gliding across the hard wood as she did. "George, you listen to me. You'll just have to... um... how do the people from your old Earth say it again... I think you said it was called, sucking it up and stop acting like a wimp!"

Everyone laughed at George's expense. A few moments later, Mary continued.

"Besides, George... this will be our last chance to do this kind of thing before the baby arrives. So put on a happy face and let's have some fun."

Mary had to open the pantry more than once to get the effect she was after as she waited for George's response. The environment inside eventually changed to an atmosphere necessary to keep certain items chilled. Quickly she walked into retrieve a dozen eggs and a large tub of greggle hash. Upon shutting the door, she turned to look at George.

"I don't see that frown turning upside down, Mr. Nailer!"

Brayson had to laugh as he watched the warlock continue about his business without responding. "You really hate roughing it that much, George? I can see it on your face. I think I may have a better idea. Instead of Calling Nature, why don't we go to the Foot and stay with the giants. At least there you'll be able to keep your mind on so many other things, you'll forget you're somewhat roughing it. The giants have interesting homes and I'm pretty sure we would be able to stay with their leader. I'm also sure all of you would find it rather educational to meet Grosalom. He's a powerfully enormous man and carries quite a presence about him."

The thought of meeting a giant reminded George of Kroger. He still regretted the day he accidentally turned the gentle, giant ogre to stone. After a moment he continued to fill a large jar with a milk-like substance and responded, "I guess it wouldn't be so bad to meet some of these giants. I think I could really get into doing that. I hope this Grosalom fellow sleeps on mattresses, at least."

Brayson smiled as he pulled out a chair from the sturdy wooden table sitting in the center of the kitchen. It was stained just the way it would have been back on Earth.

"I know they do sleep on large cushions... but I personally haven't slept on one myself and like I said already, their homes are quite unique. You will just have to see it for yourself."

Athena smiled and moved to pull her husband's hands about her waist from behind. She turned her head and looked up. "Thank you, honey! Imagine how big this cushion mattress will be. We'll be able to roll over and over and over before we find its end."

That evening after teleporting to the Foot, they made their introduction and now sat quite a ways back from a massively huge bonfire while a group of sixty-foot-tall giant Indian-looking figures danced all about it—causing the ground to quake.

After noticing the environment was dangerous due to the size of their hosts and the girls' inability to protect themselves if a large foot were to be accidentally misplaced while moving so wildly during their dance, Brayson decided to use his magic to protect the group from being smashed.

As George watched Grosalom's giant tribe of feather-covered rainseekers move about the fire with paint-covered faces and rattles cut from the tales of giant, venomous serpents, he could only sit and marvel. Everything in this part of Luvelles was absolutely enormous. Even the remnants of one of these poisonous serpents, draped across a large wooden tripod—the top of which had to be seventy feet at its highest point--,made the structure seem small. Both the snake's tail and head found the ground on opposite sides.

Hell... that thing has to be over one hundred and fifty feet long and it's thick, too. I bet it's at least seven or eight feet or so, he thought as he continued to scan his surroundings. Eventually his eyes settled on Grosalom's home which reflected the bonfire's light in the distance.

WOW... they all live in giant teepees. I bet that thing has to be at least two hundred feet tall and about twice as wide in diameter at its base. This is fascinating! I've never seen anything like this. This is something worth roughing it for!

Grosalom looked down at his tiny visitors and with a booming voice commanded the dancers to stop. The ground quickly stopped quaking as the heavy footsteps subsided.

Once everyone had taken seated positions all about the fire, the giant leader continued to speak in a whisper—a voice which still seemed commanding to his small visitors and also one only Brayson could understand. The conversation ceased and Brayson turned to the others to translate.

"Grosalom had a place prepared for us to sleep. He said it would be best for us to catch a ride with his daughter or it will take us all night to get there. She will come back and get us in the morning before breakfast."

Once agreed, they all climbed into the female giant's palms. The ground beneath them moved swiftly by as she walked and with each footstep they all marveled at the sound. Judging by how far she carried them, George could see Grosalom was right—it would have taken them most of the night to get this far. They shouted as loud as they could to thank Sheswyn for her generosity and after watching her go, they turned to look up at their teepee.

George used his power to lift the group up and onto the wooden platform the structure rested on. As they walked inside, they took noticed of how thick the hides were which had been used to cover the teepee's outside and marveled at how large the animal must have been to carry such a remarkable skin.

The mattresses which had been scattered throughout across the floor were made of more of the same hides and had been stuffed with some sort of wool. As if the fact that one of these beds would sleep two of these giants wasn't impressive enough, they had to marvel even further at how thick they were, beginning from the floor and stretching to a height nearly twelve or fourteen feet.

George turned and looked at Brayson. "So... I only have one question for you."

Brayson smiled. "You like this place, don't you?"

"I do, but that has nothing to do with my question. I suppose what I was wondering was, if everything here is so big, what about the bugs that can crawl up and onto these mattresses we're going to be lying on? How big do you think they are, and how do you think we should handle something like this so we can get a good night's sleep?"

The Next Night Kepler's Lair

George appeared inside Kepler's lair after spending the day with Brayson and the girls.

"Wake up, Kep," George said as he waved his hand to remove the darkness.

Kepler covered his eyes with both front legs as he buried his head beneath them. "George, you have got to stop doing that," he moaned. "I'm tired. I've been out all night trying to figure out all the different things my new powers can do."

The warlock closed his eyes in disbelief. He reopened them and sure enough, Kepler's solid black coat had turned pure white. His red eyes had toned down just a bit and the new overall look was fabulous.

"Holy garesh, Kepler—what happened to your coat?"

The demon-cat lifted up and posed majestically. "I know, I know,

I look amazing, right? I'm very pleased with my new look."

"You look better then amazing. Athena is going to freak out when she sees you like this. How do we explain this?"

"I don't know, but when I woke up yesterday I looked like this. Where have you been, anyway?"

"I decided to let you sleep. You were out of it after getting your new powers. When I left, you were still black. I figured I had a day to kill, so Brayson took me and the rest of the girls on a little vacation. He teleported all of us to a place called the Foot. There are these enormous giants who live there, and apparently the White Army has requested their presence for the upcoming battle. Their leader is a massive man named Grosalom. You and I should go back there sometime. Everything is so stinking huge!

"Anyway, I bet your new powers must've been the reason for the change in your fur's color. Just tell the family you used your new powers to make the change."

Kepler was shocked. "Are you saying they know I have Payne's abilities? Do you think it was wise to tell them about it?"

"I had to say something. I told Athena I made Payne give you his powers because he wasn't old enough to act responsibly with them and I wanted to make sure he didn't accidentally do something to the baby while playing with what I hope to be our new son."

Kepler thought a moment. "I think that was a fine deception. So you're now okay with lying to Athena?"

"No, no, no... I hate lying to her, but how else was I going to explain this? I didn't see any other choice on this one."

Kepler pondered what he said. "I want you to know I have access to all your thoughts. I understand now how you feel about lying to Athena and I know you're telling the truth. I truly didn't understand how much love you had for her and this family. I have to admit I was surprised when I realized Brayson was growing on you. But I think the thing I find most puzzling is your love for my companionship as well."

George smiled. "See... I told ya I loved you, big guy!"

Kepler swallowed hard and forced a response. "I suppose I want you to know I kinda feel the same way."

George chuckled. "Just kinda? Well, I guess that's a starting point anyway."

The demon stretched. George watched his muscles ripple beneath his new coat. Once done, the giant cat said, "I also want you to know I understand everything that's going on and I really like the plan that's about to happen on Harvest—"

George stopped him before he could finish. "I think it is best if you and I save this conversation for later. You never know who may be listening. I have something to show you. I have been working on it for the last few days."

George looked hard into Kepler's red eyes. After a moment the giant cat understood what was happening. He returned George's thoughts with a few well-placed thoughts of his own. *"So we can speak telepathically now. I like this, George. We will never need to watch what we say any longer. Imagine the messages we could give one another while standing amongst the family or any other group we find ourselves in."*

George answered back with another few thoughts. *"This is a true advantage to be able to communicate like this. So, about Harvestom... I'm going to take you with me when the time is right. Your new look will leave quite the impression. I think we should take advantage of this. I'm going to create a new robe. I'll make it all white with red trim to match your eyes. I will create a new black chain to go around your neck with a large gem-covered pendant... all of them matching your eyes, of course. I want a new staff made of black wood to hold in my hand. I think that would also look quite tasteful. Oh, oh, oh... and let's create for you a black saddle and lace it with more of these red gems. We will look awesome everywhere we go from now on. We'll look sick!"*

Kepler cringed *"Why would you want the two of us to look sick?"*

George rolled his eyes and grinned. *"Ha... sick means really good, Kep."*

Kepler thought a moment. *"You Earthlings say strange things. I think I like this idea of looking sick. It'll be a nice way to travel."*

"I agree... you'll be the sickest-looking kitty in all the land."

Kepler growled and instantly stopped their little mental communication. "You just had to go and ruin the moment, didn't you?"

"I'm sorry. Look, we have much to talk about."

George began to communicate through telepathy again. *"So I think we need to..."*

The Next Morning
The Source's Cave

Brayson and George appeared outside the Source's cave. It took only a moment for Brayson to notice the large mound of rocks which had fallen from the cliffs above. Both men quickly moved to the scene and Brayson, not thinking anyone would be under the debris, used his magic to lift the stones and push them clear of the cave's entrance.

But to George's surprise, Gregory Id was nowhere to be found beneath the little trap he had set only days earlier. Somehow the White Chancellor had managed to avoid being killed and this changed everything.

Realizing a new plan was in order, George quickly reacted. "I wonder what happened here. Maybe we should go inside and see if Gregory is still there. Do you think he managed to survive his encounter with the Eye? Maybe we should go and ask the Source if he came back out of the Eye's chamber..."

Brayson was still studying the cliff's face. "This is strange. I must come back to take a closer look. Someone powerful had to be responsible for this. These walls are protected by strong magic and for them to break apart like this doesn't make any sense."

"It makes sense to me," George replied without hesitation. "I bet it's more of Mieonus's handiwork. I'm sure she's pretty angry since I told her I wouldn't do her dirty work any longer. But why would she care anything about making the rocks fall like this? You're right... this doesn't make any sense."

Brayson touched George on the shoulder. When they reappeared, they were standing in Gregory's throne room of glass. Brayson quickly located one of the handmaidens and asked if the Chancellor had returned. Once confirmed, he sent the elderly woman to retrieve him, and then turned to face George.

"At least we know he's alive. Now that he has received the benefit of the Eye's gift, he will be able to help us spread the word of our new lord. We should sit with him so you can explain every-thing. I'm sure he will want to help us."

George thought to himself, *Maybe the rocks missing Gregory won't be such a bad thing after all. I should be able to manipu-late this minor inconvenience into something beneficial before I'm done with him.*

"You're right, Brayson," the warlock responded. "Your brother will be a fine addition to our cause. If he sees things as we do, maybe I should see if Lasidious would also want him to be another one of his disciples."

"First things first… let's find out how strong his powers actu-ally are before we explain everything to him. That way you'll be able to explain to Lasidious how beneficial he may be in spreading the knowledge of the one true god."

The Next Evening Kebble's Kettle

George and Kepler appeared outside Kebble's Kettle after spending much of the day preparing their new look. The night had come for the warlock to take Shalee back to Brandor. He was now sitting on top of a black saddle lined with ruby-colored gems, which rested securely on top of Kepler's white, fur-covered back. His new robe was elegant, the dark staff perfectly accenting the white cloth with ruby trim.

As soon as Shalee saw the pair, she quickly stood from the porch of the inn and moved back to get a better look. Her voice was tentative at best as she spoke. "Is that—"

George finished her sentence. "Kepler… yes, it is. He has also come to understand the words of my lord. He sees the importance of bringing peace to the worlds now."

"This is a bit unnerving, George. Kepler is said to be a soulless demon. How could he possibly be a part of bringing peace to the worlds?"

Kepler decided to speak. "I'm standing right here, queen of Brandor. You can ask me this questions yourself."

"Okay then… consider yourself asked."

The demon had rehearsed his response for exactly this type of confrontation. He began to deliver the lie masterfully. "Our lord has given me a soul. He is mighty and has the power to give many things. He has found a soul within his heaven that was willing to surrender their very being so I may live in service to him. I know now what I need to do to make up for my evil ways. I must spread the words of peace and love. I must make my lord proud and help the prophet to make those who wish for war see there's a better way."

"What about the soul who made the sacrifice… what happens to it?"

"I wish I had an answer that would make sense, Shalee. I'm sure if you ask our god, he will be able to explain it far better than I. He wishes to speak with you after your husband's resurrection."

"Good, I have a million questions for him," she said, half-irritated.

George decided they needed to get back on track.

"The moment has come to go, Shalee."

"It has? Oh, thank goodness… you have no idea how stir-crazy I've been just sitting here. I've considered teleporting out of here a hundred times to catch a ride with the Merchant Angels. I find myself at a loss as to what to do. I've never felt so torn about so many things in my life and I doubt I'm able to cry anymore. I swear to you, if it wouldn't have been for Kebble and his kindness during my stay, I just may have lost my mind! I have to admit, though, I'm still trying to decide if everything you've told me is the truth."

George nodded that he understood. "Close your eyes, Shalee, and I'll teleport us to Brandor. You won't doubt me after you've seen your husband rise from the dead. His passing ceremony is being held inside the arena. The new king has ordered all who could fit in the arena without being burned to be allowed inside."

"New king… do you mean Michael? How could he do this when I'm still alive?"

"Yes, I do mean Michael. I think it has something to do with your absence. I doubt it's permanent. Are you ready to go?"

"Please…"

George reached down from his saddled position and touched Shalee on the shoulder. When they reappeared inside Brandor's arena, the warlock had a special treat in store. Instead of appearing as he normally would have, they all appeared within a bright light. The darkness of the night sky amplified the effect and as it dissipated the three of them were left standing on top of the tower's wooden structure next to Sam's body. Mosley, the wolf-god, was on the far side of the platform and listened to the crowd as they screamed about the company their queen was keeping.

The entire arena was still waiting for Michael to make his way down from the king's box to light the fires. The audience had just finished enjoying a festival of entertainment to commemorate their king's passing, but this was an event no one expected to take place.

The gods Mieonus and Keylom stood looking up from the sand of the arena floor. They had agreed to allow Mosley to be the one to represent the gods since the people of Brandor had already become acquainted with the wolf the day of Sam and Shalee's wedding. Mosley had appeared in this very arena and had given his blessing on their union in front of all those who had attended.

The centaur and the goddess of Hate remained invisible to the mortals while Mosley had taken a position on top of the wooden structure opposite where George had appeared and was visible for all to see.

Keylom spoke with Mieonus after watching George and Shalee appear. "Well, I have to admit this is an unexpected surprise. What would Shalee be doing with George? This makes absolutely no sense. I thought you were watching her, Mieonus?"

"I was, but after she went into the Mountains of Oraness, I could no longer see past the Ancient One's magic. My waterfall failed me."

"This will be interesting. The last appearance George made, Lasidious was standing at his side on Trollcom. We should call the others to watch this. Maybe Lasidious plans to make an appearance here as well."

"I agree... but you better do it instead of me," Mieonus said. "They won't come if I summon them."

The centaur shouted in a voice only the Book of Immortality could hear. When Gabriel appeared he quickly asked the Book to summon all the gods to the arena. Gabriel did as requested and eventually every god with the exception of Lasidious showed up.

Gabriel quickly addressed Celestria. "Why hasn't Lasidious come with you?"

The goddess of all Evil-Natured Beasts gave a grin equal to her title. "I think you'll see shortly what's in store for this night."

"What do you mean?"

Her grin turned to a smile. "I mean… watch and see!"

When Mosley saw George appear with Shalee, he moved quickly to speak with them. "Shalee… why would you allow yourself to be seen with George? The people know of his treachery. His company is beneath you!"

"Mosley, if everything George has told me happens tonight, I'm afraid you and I will no longer be speaking with one another. I'll no longer have a desire to speak with a god who lies!"

"What… how could you possibly think I'm a liar?" Mosley turned to George. The wolf-god had already given himself a larger appearance so when he looked at the warlock, he was at eye-level. He growled as he spoke. "What deceptions have you played now, George?"

George methodically began to pick the individual pieces of lint from his robe. "Save your intimidation for someone who fears you. Tonight, the one true god will come to Brandor and return their king to them. He will live again and all of Grayham will know of his generosity."

Mosley was completely taken back by what he heard. "What do you mean by this? Sam is dead and there's nothing the gods can do about it! Not even Lasidious has the power to retrieve a soul from the Book's pages."

The warlock dismissed the wolf and brushed past him as he moved Kepler into a better position to stand beside Sam's casket. The crowd within the arena shouted curses with each step the giant cat took toward their king's lifeless body. They knew Kepler was the same beast who had been posted all over the kingdom as a traitor to all Southern Grayham.

Mosley looked at Shalee. "Why are you keeping George's company? He represents everything you loathe. How could you possibly be fooled by this man? Sam's dead and I don't know what George has promised you, but there will be no way Lasidious can give him life."

Shalee sighed. "We will know soon enough if the things George has told me are lies. If he's telling the truth, then I want you to leave me alone and stay out of my life. I'm sure Sam will feel the same way once I've explained everything to him."

"Why would I do that, Shalee? You and I are more than just a queen speaking to a god. We are also friends... have you forgotten this?"

"We shall see if we're truly friends. If you've lied to me, then there was never really a friendship."

Before anything else could be said, Lasidious appeared in a blinding light. The air began to stir and the entire arena became a whirlwind of blowing sand, causing the people to cover their eyes. But the platform which Sam's body rested on and all those who stood on it were spared the current's effects.

When the light dissipated and the atmosphere was once again calm, the God of Mischief was left standing opposite George next to Sam's casket. Without saying a single word, Lasidious reached into the casket, pulled the dagger from Sam's side—a task Mosley was unable to do—and turned to the crowd. He spoke in a voice which captivated every soul present.

"People of Brandor... witness the power of the one true god. I have decided to allow your king to live. Enjoy this blessing which I have given to you!" Lasidious vanished.

Much of the crowd exploded with loud shouts of confusion, some with shouts of joy, and others with a thousand questions. It was a frenzy of anxiety and mixed emotions.

Mieonus shouted at Mosley from within her invisible barrier as she remained standing next to the other gods. She spoke with a voice only the gods could hear. *"Say something, WOLF... the people need to hear you speak."*

Mosley looked down from the stage and without speaking a word, relayed: *"What would you have me say, Mieonus? Anything I say at this point will make us look foolish. The people will wonder why I didn't bother to give Sam his life back. I've already told them Sam would be well-received within the heavens. I told them Michael would make a fine king and to serve him well. This looks bad for us, no matter what I say."*

Mosley looked at Gabriel. *"How could Lasidious retrieve Sam's soul from your pages? None of this makes any sense."*

The Book replied, "I have been looking through my pages since our arrival. I'm just as shocked as you are. I didn't know Sam was dead."

Hosseff also spoke out. *"Nor did I know anything... I've never collected Sam's soul to bring it to the Book. Something is going on here I cannot explain."*

"This looks bad for us," the wolf said, shaking his head. *"I have no idea what I can say to turn this to our favor."* Mosley turned and watched as Shalee moved to stand next to Sam's casket.

The queen watched as the stab wound on Sam's side began to close. Tears filled her eyes as she realized George's words were true. She would need to face the people of her kingdom and let them know everything she had learned. She lifted Sam's hand and placed his palm across her face. She closed her eyes and enjoyed the warmth as it returned to her love's body. "Oh, Sam... I thought I had lost you forever!"

George dismounted from the demon's back and took the opportunity to move into a better position on the platform from which to address the crowd. As he moved across the wood's surface, he looked at Kepler, winked, and then looked at Mosley while broadcasting a message telepathically to the wolf-god without uttering a word.

"Mosley... I hope you'll enjoy this pile of garesh I'm about to spew out as much as I will. The people will no longer believe in you once I'm done. They'll believe Lasidious is the one true god. They will glorify him and there's nothing the gods can do about it. The people won't believe anything you say once they've watched their king stand from his casket to live again. Let's face it... you're screwed!"

Without waiting for Mosley to respond, George lifted his head and shouted to the people. He used his magic to amplify his voice.

"People of Southern Grayham…your king lives again! He lives only because of the power of my lord, Lasidious. The gods have lied to the people. They have treated you as fools. They have no real power. They are nothing more than powerful Mystics! Lasidious is the one true deity all of us should worship."

Mosley shouted above him. "He lies... I love the people of Grayham. You all know I'm the god who has blessed this city. I blessed the union of both your king and your queen. This man is a threat to all of you."

Shalee had something to shout of her own and used her own magic to amplify her voice to match theirs. "People of Brandor… hear me now... what the prophet of Lasidious says is the truth. The gods have lied to us. Our king lives and his soul has been returned to him. When your king emerges from his casket, know this… there's no other god with the power to give life. I know this to be true and I no longer will listen to any other. Lasidious is now the one I serve."

The queen turned to face George. "I can't tell you how much I appreciate the fact you were able to open my eyes. I'm also glad you've found your way and have decided to live a moral life." Without acknowledging the wolf, Shalee moved past Mosley to stand next to George.

Mosley stood in absolute astonishment as he listened to the crowd begin to shout out their questions. He couldn't believe that Shalee's announcement had professed her service to the most evil of all the gods living on Ancients Sovereign. This was bad and the people were confused—many of which were now also questioning their faith in the god they served.

George looked at Mosley while Shalee's back was turned and once again spoke telepathically to the wolf. *"Even the queen has bought into my line of garesh. I think the moment has come for you to go and lick yourself someplace."*

Mosley responded with a few thoughts of his own. *"I give you my word, George... I'll find a way to destroy you before this is all over!"*

"Yeah... yeah... you'll never find a way to do anything. You have too many rules to follow. Your Book of Immortality is your crutch. When I'm done, every soul on Grayham will worship Lasidious. Face it, Mosley... you've lost! The people who worship you on this world will soon worship someone who could care less if they live or die!"

Mosley moved close before responding with another forceful thought. *"Don't be so sure. I'll be coming for you shortly, George. There's no place you'll be able to hide from me once I've figured out a way to stop you."*

"Ha... what are you going to do? There's nothing you can do. Get out of my face. Maybe take a hike while you're at it."

Mosley thought a moment, and then responded with a thought which echoed inside George's head as if shouted directly into his ear. *"I would watch your back if I were you!"* The wolf-god vanished.

George felt a chill run down his spine. He had to gather his thoughts as he nervously turned to look at the crowd. After a moment he took a deep breath and shouted for all to hear, "Only Lasidious loves his followers! It is this pure love which has given Southern Grayham back their king. I am the prophet of Lasidious. Together you and I can bring peace to all of Grayham. You can live your lives without fear of losing the ones you love to the ravages of war. Lasidious loves you... and I, the prophet of Lasidious, love you. I bid you all... goodnight!" After mounting Kepler and taking his new position on the giant cat's back, they vanished.

The people erupted with cheers as Sam sat up inside his coffin. He grabbed his head and looked at Shalee. "What's going on? What's everyone screaming about?" He took a second to look around. "Holy garesh... were you going to burn me?"

Shalee started to laugh. "It's not as bad as it looks. I'll explain once we get home."

After instructing Michael to see to it that the crowd disbursed, Shalee touched Sam on the shoulder and teleported.

Celestria turned to the gods who remained standing invisible on the arena stand. "Well... I've got to say this has been an absolutely delicious event to watch. I do hope you've all enjoyed this minor manipulation." The goddess vanished.

Alistar spoke out after watching her go. "Everyone, touch one another. This meeting needs to be protected from Lasidious's ears. There's nothing minor about what Lasidious has done... we all know this. Somehow we need to stop him from gathering any more followers. I think we need to have a meeting of the gods. Gabriel, I request you summon everyone to this meeting. Have them all come to the Hall of Judgment in the morning. I want to know how Lasidious gave Sam his life back. I also want to implement a new rule within your pages and vote on it. If what I'm thinking is correct, then we need to make sure both Lasidious and Celestria come to this meeting. We cannot vote to stop Lasidious from gaining more followers, but there's one rule I can think of that we can add to your pages."

Keylom responded, "What's on your mind, Alistar? And how do you intend to make them come? They won't care about us meeting like this."

Bailem added, "I agree... Lasidious won't come. He obviously has bigger plans."

Alistar pretended to think a moment. "I'll explain everything in the morning. But for now, Gabriel, let Lasidious's curiosity about this new rule be the reason both he and Celestria come to the meeting. Make him feel there's a mystery behind the meeting. Make Lasidious think I've found a way to add a rule to your pages without a normal Call to Order. If he thinks I've found a loophole within your laws, Lasidious will make sure both he and Celestria show up. All you have to do is give the Call to Order as soon as they arrive. They both will be forced to stay for the meeting once the law governing the Call to Order is in effect. Let's manipulate Lasidious the way he manipulates us." Alistar vanished.

Keylom looked at the others. "I'm impressed! Who would've guessed Alistar had a bit of mischief in him? Whatever he's planning is bound to make Lasidious very angry. I say this is worth having a meeting for! I will go and tell Mosley about it." All the gods disappeared.

The *Luvelles Gazette*

When you want an update about your favorite characters

Alistar, George and Kepler are standing outside the entrance to the Source's cave. There is important information to discuss.

Athena plans to work with Payne and teach him table manners. Payne has been calling Athena "Mom" despite being encouraged to call her by her first name. Athena plans to speak with George about his comment while in Kepler's lair that it was somehow okay for Payne to call him Dad. Apparently Payne feels this is also an extended permission to call her Mother. She isn't too happy about it.

Mary and Brayson have spent the day together after teleporting to Nept to retrieve more mesolliff wine. They are now asleep after Brayson enjoyed the benefits of Mary's intoxicated mood.

Susanne and Baby Garrin are inside Susanne's home. Garrin has just done something which frightened her. Susanne is about to go over to Mary's house and wake both her mother and Brayson up to talk about this latest development.

Boyafed plans to meet with the king of Hyperia, Kassel Hyperia, in the morning. Boyafed expects to add another 6,200 men to the Dark Ar-my's numbers. He is also expecting some resistance from Kassel.

Christopher, Boyafed's new Argont Commander, has already met with the Serwin king. The meeting went well. They will join the Dark Army for battle.

Boyafed has also ordered four hundred of the City of Marcus's finest scribes to create 10,400 scrolls of teleportation. They will be used to bring the mercenaries of Bestep and the Army of Hyperia to the Battlegrounds of Olis. Many of the mercenaries command strong defensive magic, but don't have the ability to teleport. This will allow the entire force supporting the Dark Army's cause to arrive as a single unit instead of taking countless boats across the Ebarna Strait.

In total, the Dark Army's numbers with the combined forces of the Army of Hyperia, the mercenaries of Bestep, the serwins of Shade Hollow, and the wizard Balecut will total nearly 21,000.

Lord Dowd is waiting for Krasous to return from the Spirit Plains. The Army is ready to begin their march to the northern shores of Lake Tepp. They will make camp once there and wait for the Goswigs, the giants of the Foot, the Army of Lavan, and the Wraith Hounds of the Under Eye to arrive before continuing their march to the Battle-grounds of Olis. In total they will number nearly 19,800 strong.

Krasous, Lord Dowd's Argont Commander, has found the spirit king, Shesolaywen.

Strongbear has once again taken charge of the underground hidden City of Gogswayne. Each Goswig has been ordered to report to the surface and line up near the shore of Crystal Lake for inspection in the morning.

Marcus has finally arrived on Grayham. Brayson himself had been the one to set up Marcus's little trip with the Merchant An-

gels just as George said he would. George requested Brayson do this while vacationing with the family in the valley of the giants. Brayson enjoyed the idea of how irritated Marcus would be once the Dark Chancellor learns about his little surprise.

Lasidious and Celestria are inside their home beneath the Peaks of Angels. Gabriel has requested to speak with the two of them.

Keylom is standing in front of Mosley's cabin high on the top of Catalyst Mountain. The wolf-god is clearly distraught.

Thank you for reading the Luvelles Gazette

Chapter 24

𝕬 𝕾𝖆𝖈𝖗𝖎𝖋𝖎𝖈𝖊 𝖔𝖋 𝕲𝖔𝖉𝖑𝖎𝖓𝖊𝖘𝖘

Alistar appeared outside the Source's cave after leaving Brandor's arena where George and Kepler were waiting. The warlock was leaning against Fisgig's old perch when Lasidious's brother finally showed up, with his back to them. Alistar did not acknowledge either of them but instead, lifted his head to take a deep breath.

George gave Kepler a look and thought, *"Great... just what we need... another pain in the butt to deal with."*

Kepler gave him a thought of his own. *"Be careful... we have no idea if he can listen in on our thoughts."*

"Oh, crap, I should've thought of that!"

George quickly decided to start the conversation with the god. "It's about time we finally get to have a conversation. I really hated not being able to speak with all the players of this little game face to face."

Alistar turned around after looking the area over. "It has been many seasons since the last moment I came to this place. I should speak with the Source before I leave."

Kepler growled, "Well, hello to you, too."

"Yeah," George added. "Holy garesh, Alistar, is that how you greet everyone you come to talk with? You didn't even say hi, kiss my butt, pack sand, shove it, or anything remotely close to a greeting rude or otherwise. Come on man, you can do better than that! I have no desire to do this if you're going to be a jerk to deal with!"

Alistar had to smile. "My brother said he enjoys your humor. I can see why he likes you, George. You call it like you see it. I suppose it's now our moments to finish what's been started. I like the new look, by the way. Both you and your giant kitty look magnificent."

Kepler let out a mighty roar which echoed off the cliff walls. George had to cover his ears as the demon shouted, "If you people don't stop calling me a kitty, I'm gonna kill someone! My name is Kepler! If I have to say it again… god or not… I'm going to rip your heads off and eat every last bit of your bodies!"

Alistar chuckled. "I do apologize, Kepler… I meant no offense."

Kepler turned around and lowered to the ground. "Bah… you two talk and leave my name out of this… got it?"

George rolled his eyes. "He can be fickle about the word kitty. It's kind of a sore subject around here. Go ahead and tell me everything you need to."

Alistar thought a moment, then said, "I was about to say Lasidious will no longer be coming to you in your dreams. I'll be the only one who communicates with you from now on. I'm sure Lasidious has already told you to expect this. The gods will be watching him now more than ever. They don't know Lasidious and I are kin. This will give us the advantage."

"You've got to love an advantage," George responded with an evil grin. "So… were things completely nuts after I left Brandor?"

"Oh yes… you've done a remarkable job, George. The people of Southern Grayham will be questioning their loyalty to the gods they serve. Mosley will be the one who's most affected, as the people begin to make the decision to serve Lasidious instead of him. He was, after all, the one who took Bassorine's position as the new God of War. With the way Keldwin embraced the wolf before his death and then with the way Sam embraced his own personal friendship with Mosley, the people just naturally began to serve him. I must admit it was a smooth transition. But now that the people think they've seen Lasidious give them back the life of their king, things will change. A few more visits by Lasidious's prophet should do the trick."

George began to laugh. "I think you mean Lasidious's false prophet."

"False or not, the people will listen to you now. You need to keep up the good work."

George thought a moment. "I have a good idea. I think Athena and I will take a little visit to Grayham. I'll implement the rest of Lasidious's plan while we're there and take her on a little trip down memory lane."

Alistar began to pace. "I'm sure Athena will enjoy herself. You and I have much to discuss. We need to talk about your future visit to Harvestom."

The Home of Lasidious and Celestria
Beneath the Peaks of Angels
Ancients Sovereign

Gabriel appeared inside the home once Celestria agreed to let the Book in. After lowering his heavy binding to the table within their cave-like home, Gabriel spent a few moments talking with Celestria about the pleasant feel of her decor while they waited for Lasidious to join them.

Eventually the God of Mischief walked out of the bedroom. "Welcome to our home, Gabriel. I'm sure you have many questions. But before you ask any of them… let me save you the breath it takes to utter the words. I won't answer any of them. My secrets are mine to keep."

The Book allowed a smile to appear across the face which had been given to his binding. "I'm not here to ask any questions, Lasidious. You have broken no rules within my laws and whether I understand why or how you accomplished these things simply doesn't matter. You have the free will to do anything you wish as long as the laws of the gods aren't broken."

Celestria decided to respond. "So this is more of a social visit. I should create something to drink. Would you prefer some cold ale, perhaps?"

"Or maybe some nasha juice," Lasidious added.

"I'm not here for pleasantries, either. I have come to let you know the others intend to call for a meeting of the gods. It will be held in the morning."

Lasidious chuckled. "I doubt we'll be attending this meeting. Not really my thing when it doesn't pertain to anything I can manipulate, you know. I have no desire to listen to them babble on and on about how mad they are about the things I've done."

The Book lifted from the table and floated closer to Lasidious before lowering back down. "I thought you would feel that way. This is why I came personally to tell you that Alistar has informed me of a loophole he claims to have found within my laws. Apparently he thinks he won't need you to be present to invoke the normal Call to Order for the gods to vote on a new law."

"What! I know of no such loophole. How's this possible, Gabriel? Have you searched your pages to find this oversight within your laws?"

"I have done nothing other than come to you directly. I think if Alistar says he intends to vote, then you might want to figure out how he can do this."

Lasidious moved close to Gabriel and looked the Book in the eyes. "Are you lying to me? This is a trick, isn't it? Why would you help them?"

Gabriel floated from the table. After putting distance between them he responded. "Everything I said is exactly what Alistar has told me. You can do as you wish with this information. I have done what I've come to do. You have been warned. Don't mistake my visit as helping you or any of the others. I have no desire to help either of you manipulate one another." He vanished.

Mosley's Cabin
Ancients Sovereign

Keylom stood in the darkness. He looked up at the wolf-god as he lay on his cabin's porch high on top of Catalyst Mountain. The centaur could see that Mosley was clearly bothered by the current events in Brandor's arena.

The darkness of the night had swallowed the beautiful valleys far below the wolf's home and all that could be seen in the night sky was two of the other five worlds the gods had created for the mortals to live on.

A beautiful crystal orb, mounted just to the right side of the cabin's door, glowed and shed enough light for the gods to talk. Bassorine had been the one to create the orb more than 10,000 seasons ago before his destruction. This same porch had been the place of conversation with many of the gods while Bassorine was alive, but now, it had been taken over by a furry wolf. Mosley's shedding had left a fair amount hair on each of the wooden planks in this one specific spot. The porch had been covered to the point that it was nearly as black as the wolf's coat.

"Mosley, I understand how you must be feeling," the centaur-god said. "You were bound to be the brunt of one of Lasidious's schemes as all of us have been at one moment or another. But we will need you to have a clear head if we're going to stop Lasidious from recruiting enough followers to take control of the Book."

Mosley stood, jumped from the porch and began to pace. As Keylom watched him move back and forth, the wolf would walk far enough away before turning around that he would blend into the darkness and disappear briefly until the light of the orb once again found him. Eventually, Mosley stopped and responded.

"I cannot tell you how angry I am at the moment. I see no way for the gods to do anything that'll make much of a difference. We're bound by so many ridiculous rules, we've lost the power to even act as gods. I should've killed George tonight while I had the chance. At least Lasidious wouldn't have his little puppet to mislead the minds of the people any longer."

"I agree… but you would no longer be immortal if you had," Keylom added.

"Yes, I know, but this whole prophet of Lasidious sham… and this one true god speech George is planning on delivering to the people is thoroughly disgusting. I'm beginning to think being a god isn't worth my immortality."

"You don't mean that, Mosley. It may seem difficult at the moment, but it'll get better. Of all the gods… you're the one who has the wit to outsmart Lasidious if you'd just put your mind to it. I imagine Bassorine knew this when he planned for you to take his spot if anything were to ever happen to him. He wasn't a stupid deity no matter how Lasidious made him look. Just start thinking mischievously like Lasidious does. I'm sure you can beat him at his own game once you set your mind to it."

"Thinking like Lasidious does is why I have come to a very specific conclusion," Mosley responded, while jumping onto the porch and plopping down heavily. "George said something while projecting his thoughts inside my mind. He's now able to use telepathy."

"What? How?"

"I imagine it has something to do with Lasidious's help. I suppose since Lasidious hasn't faced any punishment from the Book, he's been doing everything within the boundaries of the god's laws. Somehow, there has to be a way of beating him at his own game, and I think I may know a way to do it."

Keylom's hooves scuffed the earth as he shuffled to a better position. "I'm listening… exactly what are you thinking?"

"Well, tonight while George was standing there mocking me in front of the people of Brandor, he said something while we spoke telepathically. He said, 'When I'm done, every soul on Grayham will worship Lasidious. Face it Mosley… you've lost! The people who worship you on this world will soon worship Lasidious!'

"Now I don't know about you, but this makes me angry. If I'm going to lose many of the people who serve me and these same people are going to increase Lasidious's power, then there has to be a better way."

The wolf lifted his head to the sky and called for Gabriel. When the Book arrived, he continued.

"Gabriel, I need you to protect our conversation. I want everything we discuss to be under the Rule of Fromalla."

"Okay. Do you wish for Keylom to hear?"

"I do."

The Book waved his arm and waited for Keylom to acknowledge the rule was in effect.

"We may speak freely now."

Mosley stood from his hair-covered place of comfort and began to pace. "I want to know, how can I become mortal and keep some of my power to go after George?"

"What?" Keylom said. "You're willing to give up your immortality just to seek vengeance on a mortal? You cannot do this. It's against our laws."

Mosley stopped pacing and looked the centaur in the eyes. "The laws have many loopholes. Lasidious manages to find them, so why can't I? If I don't do something, George will turn the people of the worlds into a massive congregation of Lasidious's followers. Someone has to stop him. Shalee isn't growing in her skills fast enough to do it."

The Book cleared his throat to get their attention.

"There are many rules within my pages which prohibit a god from choosing to become a mortal. It would cause too many problems. The gods would no longer be able to stop you from sharing their secrets, since you would carry this knowledge with you."

Mosley howled.

"If I could, I would kill George, but the god's laws are clear. Not only would I lose my godliness, but I would also lose my soul and George isn't worth this sacrifice. Gabriel, I know there are restrictions to prevent you from making me mortal, but there has to be a way. I just need to find it. Gabriel, show me all of these rules. Let's find this loophole."

"No, there's not a way to do this, Mosley," Keylom responded. "The gods voted on this long ago. We were very careful to ensure all angles were covered."

"Not all angles," Gabriel said in a stern voice. "I can't believe I'm about to suggest this, but there is a way. I also feel Lasidious needs to be stopped. This may be the only way to fight against him and win."

Keylom couldn't believe his ears. "Gabriel, you're choosing a side. How could there possibly be a way for you to do this? We were extremely careful in how we voted these laws into effect. You're bound by them just as we are."

"Yes, I'm bound by them as you have said, but there's one law which supersedes them all. This law requires me to do anything necessary to ensure that the god's laws remain superior to the desires of any single deity. This means I'm to assume any role necessary to keep them sacred. I only need to be mindful of free will. This is the only law which I cannot supersede. Mosley's plan could help us to protect our laws from Lasidious's manipulations and his desires to control me."

"Okay," Keylom cut in, "but this doesn't mean you can make him mortal. That has been spelled out very clearly. Not even you can assume that making Mosley a mortal is a proper course of action to stop Lasidious."

The Book floated over to the porch and lowered to a rested position on one of the wooden planks. Keylom's hooves scuffed the earth nervously as he waited for his response.

"Yes, I know, the gods were careful about how you chose to vote regarding this. But you only voted to stop a god from choosing to become mortal. You didn't, however, vote to cover all the angles on what is to happen when a god is punished and made mortal by me. You never voted on what to do after I stripped one of you of your godly powers. You only voted to give one last request if this were to happen. I can only assume this was because each of you felt you were old enough that the consequences of being made mortal would cause you to die within days, so further governing of this situation wasn't necessary since you would fade away to nothing more than a pile of dust. This failure to vote further would also be the loophole Mosley is looking for, a loophole he could use against Lasidious, though I don't know I really like the idea. But before I'll explain anything further, Mosley, I must request one thing from you... something I'll hold you accountable for."

Mosley tilted his furry head. "And what would this request be?"

"You can never speak of your knowledge of the gods to anyone who doesn't already have this knowledge! If you do, I'll be forced to strike you down. I want you to give me this promise or I won't divulge anything further. A god's promise... if broken... is enforceable by death. You'll make this promise to me now before you become mortal. I will kill you if you break it. Mortal or not... I'll torture your soul within my pages for lying to me once you find your way onto them. Do we have an agreement?"

Mosley and Keylom were both stunned by the Book's harshness. The tone Gabriel used was something far more serious than Mosley had ever heard him use before. The wolf thought long and hard before responding.

"I'll make this promise. How can I assume my mortality and salvage my power?"

It was easy to see the regret on Gabriel's face as he continued. "You'll only be able to salvage some of your power and many of your memories. What is true about the gods will remain, but I will need to remove the memories which would make it easy for you to take this journey. Many of the memories you have could affect the balance of power in your favor and this kind of power should be earned, not given.

"Since Bassorine gave you an extended life before your ascension to become a god, you won't have any issues with aging drastically once being made mortal as the others would experience. You should be able to pick up where you left off and continue to exist. You'll have power, but to what extent, I'm not sure, but I do know you won't be powerful enough to defeat George. It'll be up to you to go after the power you need to confront him. This is the point of a sword and you just may find yourself on the sharp end. Are you absolutely sure you want to do this?"

Mosley swallowed hard. There would be no coming back if he changed his mind. After a long series of moments, he responded. "I'm sure this is what I want… but, I also want to make sure Lasidious doesn't have any knowledge of my mortality. I want to be able to seek the power I need to defeat George without Lasidious sending George after me before I'm ready to face him. I want you to send me to the Siren's Song on Grayham. I'll start my journey there. I will save my final request for a moment in which I need it most or a moment I feel it best to use it."

Keylom stomped his hoof on the ground. "This is insane, Mosley! You're making a big mistake! What happens when the gods come together to vote? They'll know something is wrong when you're not present when the Call to Order is given."

"I understand. Gabriel, you can have my vote to do with as you please. Keylom, you could also help me out while I'm on my journey, you know."

"I have no desire to become mortal. I won't go with you, nor can I help you when you find trouble."

Mosley gave a wolfish grin. "I don't need you to go with me. All I need you to do is be my eyes and ears. I want you to give me some helpful information when you learn of it—give me guidance, if you will. The same way Lasidious has been giving George guidance. Let's fight fire with fire!"

The Book took control of the conversation. "All you need to do is break one of the god's laws and I'll do the rest. With your absence on Ancients Sovereign, this will make two gods I need to replace, and Yaloom was so full of himself, he failed to give me the name of the one who was to take his place. Mosley, you and I haven't spoken on who will replace you either once you've descended. Do you have a name?"

Without hesitation the wolf responded. "Give my spot to Sha-lee."

"I cannot... nor can I give it to Sam. Lasidious had enough foresight when the gods decided to bring them into the worlds that he made a special agreement with the gods that this would never be allowed to happen. I think Lasidious had a feeling Bassorine was up to something."

"Damn... Lasidious is truly clever. I suppose you'll need to choose someone for me then, someone whom you trust will do a good job. How long can you give me before you'll need to introduce my replacement to the others?"

"This is not for you to worry about. When I came to get you from Grayham after Bassorine's destruction, it was because Bassorine had requested it be done quickly. There was an urgency that you learn the information you needed to know. Bassorine knew this would be the only chance for you to let Shalee know about his intentions for her. I see no such urgency while finding your replacement."

"If Lasidious asks where I am, tell him I've decided to get away for a while. Say I've decided I don't care about his game any longer and I won't be back until I find myself. It would be best to let him think you don't know where I went. Tell him I said I don't want Lasidious or the others knowing where I went ,and I have refused to tell anyone. This should throw him off for a bit, I think."

The Book thought long and hard for many moments before responding. "I will explain these are the things you have said to me." Gabriel stopped and thought a moment longer before continuing. "I may be able to turn Yaloom's failure to name his replacement to our advantage. No matter what I decide to do, you won't need to concern yourself with Lasidious finding out your whereabouts. For now, I want you to attack Keylom and then I will do my job to make you mortal."

"What?" Keylom snapped, "I don't want the wolf to attack me!"

Gabriel smiled. "That's exactly why it will work. It's not wanted and therefore breaks the laws within my pages. You can take Mosley to Grayham and drop him off at the home of the Wisp of

Song when the moment is right. Just make sure Lasidious isn't paying attention."

Gabriel reached out and put his hand on top of the wolf's head. "I do hope you succeed, Mosley. You should still have a great deal of power as I have already said, but I cannot be certain as to how much. You'll be vulnerable again to the people of the worlds and we won't be able to protect you. This is a journey you have chosen to take of your own free will and in doing so, must find a way to complete this journey without our help."

The wolf-god nodded and moved back from the cabin. He took one last look at the home he might never see again. After taking a final deep breath of the fresh, clean air high on top of Catalyst Mountain, he attacked Keylom without saying another word.

Susanne's Home
The Head Master's Island

Susanne hurried out the front door of her home with Garrin in her arms. She was pale, nervous and scared half to death. She pounded hard on Mary's door and didn't stop until Brayson answered.

When the door opened, his eyes looked exhausted and he wasn't wearing a shirt. The evening had been quite the affair and the affects of the mesolliff wine had left both Mary and himself begging for sleep.

"What is it, Susanne? What's so urgent?"

Susanne pushed past him and set Garrin on the floor. "He's got the magic in him."

"What do you mean?"

She shouted. "He's got the magic! He made my cup float around my kitchen! The boy isn't normal!"

Garrin began to cry at the sound of his mother's tone as Brayson began to laugh. "What's so funny?" she shouted.

Mary was making her way down the steps after getting her robe on. "What on Luvelles is all the commotion about, Susanne?"

Brayson responded as he picked Garrin up. "Oh, it's nothing… nothing's wrong at all. She's just a bit scared because she doesn't understand why Garrin has the ability to command magic. This is quite the gift, if you ask me. To be showing signs of power so soon after birth is incredibly rare."

Mary moved to stand next to him. She played with Garrin's cheeks to encourage the child to smile. She didn't seem to be bothered by the revelation of the baby's power. "This is good. I think a man with magic is quite sexy. My little grandson will grow up to be just as dashing as you are."

Susanne was floored at their obvious lack of concern. She continued to shout, "How could a child of mine have the ability to use magic? I don't have it... so how could he have it? None of this makes any sense!"

Brayson put his hand on Garrin's pointed ears. "I imagine it was from the elven man you slept with. I have always wanted to ask you about this. What was the elf's name you pleasured during the baby's conception? I must know him. It must have been someone I allowed to go to Grayham. He must've been a man of royal blood or maybe one of the elven council members of either the Dark or Light Army since they're the only ones I've allowed to catch a ride with the Merchant Angels to visit Grayham."

After a moment Brayson continued. "Now that I think of it... there were two small groups from both councils who went to visit the ice king of Northern Grayham during the period of your conception. The Argent Commanders of each army went along to ensure their safety. Maybe someone in these two groups took a small diversion on their way back and ended up in your old town. It could only be one of thirty men, though it would be hard to imagine it being a member of the White Army who would take advantage of a woman like this. It is, after all, against elven custom to leave a woman in this kind of condition without taking care of their responsibilities. Maybe it's just a simple matter of not knowing he had left a child behind."

Susanne sat down on one of the chairs in the room. "I cannot believe I would've completely forgotten someone whom I laid with. I know I didn't lie down with thirty different elves... that's for sure! I would be no better than a common whore if I had. I've never even bothered to think about his father since we arrived on Luvelles. How could I not remember who he was? How could I be so awful? I need to figure this out. I wonder if George knows who he was. Are there any elves on Grayham who could be the father?"

Brayson thought a moment. "There are none that I know of. I do know George will be back soon, so let's talk to him when he gets here. I'll go and tell Athena to have George come over when he shows up. There's no sense in worrying about this all night. I'm sure they won't mind."

Susanne - Daughter of Mary

Illustration by Kathleen Stone

Mary spoke up. "There's no need to do that. We're doing fine without this man. If he doesn't care enough to keep in touch with us, then it's not worth the hassle to track him down."

"Mother, I need to know who this man is. How can I go through life without allowing Garrin to know his father? I should at least make an effort to do what's right."

Mary took a seat beside her. "Are you sure you want to know this? What if the answer isn't something you want to hear? What if he doesn't want to be a part of the baby's life? What if it isn't just a simple matter of not knowing he left a baby behind?"

"Uummm... I guess if he doesn't want to be with us, then at least I've done what's right, and I can tell Garrin the truth when he's older. I'll have a clear conscience."

Brayson sat Garrin on the floor. "Well, until we figure this out, we should celebrate the fact that my future grandson is going to be extremely powerful. I've never met a baby who showed a power this early."

A moment later, George walked through the door. "So what are you guys doing up so late? Is Athena here, too?" Kepler poked his head in right behind him and took a seat in the entryway.

Susanne hurried across the room and gave George a hug. "I'm so glad you're here!" The warlock looked at Mary with questioning eyes. Brayson motioned for him to take a seat. He pried Susanne off of him and moved to take his chair.

"So what's the deal?"

Brayson responded. "Athena isn't here. The problem is that Susanne cannot remember who the baby's father is. We know he must be from Luvelles, but she doesn't seem to be able to remember who it was."

George hung his head. He knew this day would come. He was glad he had prepared for it. This was the part of Maldwin's vision that had been unable to be determined since he had a lack of knowledge of Luvelles and its inhabitants before he arrived. He was glad he had addressed this issue with Lasidious in his dreams. He had found out a name of someone who had been to Grayham and this person had already been killed. The great thing was, the death of this person had served two purposes. George kept his head lowered as he waited for someone to pry for answers.

Susanne could see George had bad news. "What is it? Tell me... is it bad?"

"I don't know if it's bad or good. Maybe Brayson can tell us this answer. The man who impregnated you is named Dayden."

Brayson sat heavily into another chair. Both Mary and Susanne could see the disappointment in his eyes. Mary moved to take a seat next to him. George looked at Kepler and communicated with telepathy.

"Can you believe this pile of garesh we're filling their minds with? Thank goodness we got here when we did. This could've gotten out of control quick."

"You've got a delightfully evil mind, George... that's why I like you!"

"Aw,... thanks, big guy. I'm touched. Remind me to give ya a hug later!"

"Don't start that again or I'll tell them the truth myself! You keep your grubby hands off me!"

"Ha... you love me and ya know it." George turned and waited for Brayson to tell the girls what was on his mind.

"Dayden was the Argont Commander of the Dark Army. He was one of the men who went to Grayham to visit the ice king. He was an evil man."

"What do you mean by was?" Mary said as she looked at Susanne's hopeless face.

"I've heard that Dayden is dead. This is one of the reasons Boyafed wishes to go to war."

George took the moments to act a little ignorant. "Are you referring to the Dark Army leader?"

"Yes... Dayden was also Boyafed's friend. If he was the father of your baby, Susanne, then there's nothing we can do to make him a part of Garrin's life."

Susanne began to cry. Garrin watched as his mother's tears began to fall. He lifted from the floor and floated over to sit beside her.

Both Mary and Susanne became nervous as they watched the baby lower to the tile-covered surface.

George quickly stood up. "Since when did he start floating and using magic like this?" He motioned for Brayson to follow him and began walking out of the house. As the warlock passed by

Kepler, he sent him a thought.

"Make sure you stay in here and keep the women busy! This is bad. It's not a good time for Garrin to be showing his powers right now!"

"No problem... just go for a walk or something while you talk. You don't want them hearing you!"

"Agreed!"

"What was that about?" Mary said as she watched Brayson stand to follow George as he rushed out the door.

Brayson responded, "I don't know. I will tell you once I know myself," then hurried out.

George waited for Brayson to come down the porch steps. He reached over and touched his shoulder. When they reappeared, they were outside the Source's cave. He hit his new staff on the ground and a light began to glow from within the gem resting at its top.

"George, what's going on? Why are you acting so strange?"

After taking a deep breath, he replied. "We cannot do the things we need to do to bring peace to Luvelles if we have to constantly be worried about Garrin's powers. The magic he just used is powerful for a child of his age and we both know it."

Believeing George to be correct in his concern, Brayson responded, "Okay, so what should we do about it? He's a baby. It's not like we can tell him not to use his abilities. He won't understand."

George thought a while. "Can we use our own powers to put some kind of a magical block to buy us the moments we need to do the things our lord has asked us to do?"

Brayson thought a while. "It would be hard to monitor the baby when the women have no idea how to handle him. Even if they did know, they don't have the power to do so. I agree this is definitely a problem. I do have a potion we could give the child. It'll temporarily restrict the use of his powers for nearly a season."

"Damn!"

"What's wrong?"

"A season is too long. What else can we do?"

Confused, Brayson said, "Why would this be considered too long?"

George put his hand to his chin as if in thought and without uttering a word, he thought, *Because I will need Garrin to be ready when Lasidious decides to take control of the Book of Immortality. I want my Abbie back!*

A moment later, George responded, "I just think to bind his power for so many moments just seems to be a bit excessive, that's all."

Brayson, not fully understanding, shrugged, and said, "I could always lower the dosage of the potion to cut the period of days by half this number. But he is young and a season is only a short span of our lives for his powers to be bound."

George leaned against Fisgig's stone perch. "I hear what you're saying, but I think we should have more control over Garrin's growth than this. I think half of a season will work. We can always give him more if we need to. Where's this potion?"

"It's in my office. I can go get it right now. I'll give it to the child tonight. I can even make it taste like berries so he'll drink it without any trouble."

George began to pace. "This is good. We must bring peace to this world before we can deal with his powers. The women will never be able to handle him, like you said. Will you please go and get the potion while I go home and explain everything that's going on to the ladies? How much crazier can things get around here?"

Brayson started to laugh. "I don't know… but since I've met you, George, there hasn't been a dull moment. I can only imagine what's next." Brayson vanished.

George sighed, and then disappeared

Later that night, after Garrin's powers were bound, everyone had gone to bed and was sound asleep when Brayson was awoken as he lay peacefully next to Mary. All he could see was the silhouette, since Lasidious had surrounded himself by a bright light. Brayson quickly crawled out of bed and took a knee.

"My lord… how may I serve you?"

Mary began to stir. As she opened her eyes, she began to scream. Lasidious allowed her to shout until Brayson could calm her down and managed to get her to join him. Once she too was kneeling, the god of Mischeif spoke. "Mary, try to calm yourself, child. I am the god your future husband serves. I have come to speak with

Brayson. I also wish to tell you your union will be blessed when the day comes that you decide to take each other's hand and declare your vows to one another. I intend to see to it that I give you a gift… one which will give you both a long-lived happiness."

Brayson spoke for them both. "Thank you, my lord, but what do you mean by long-lived?"

Lasidious reached out and touched Mary on the head. "I mean I will bless her and allow her to live a life equal to the length of your own."

Neither Brayson nor Mary could believe their ears as the Head Master responded. "I don't know what to say. This is truly a blessing we both will cherish. How may I be of service?"

"You don't need to say anything, my son. I'm sure you'll find this task rather simple. Are you truly willing to live in service to your god?"

"I am, my lord!"

"You will know when the moment is right to perform this next task. What you will need to do is…"

The Spirit Plains

Krasous, Lord Dowd's Argent Commander found the spirit king, Shesolaywen. He had been running naked through the plains in the darkness while his keen elven eyes struggled to read from the Scroll of Conair. He was near exhaustion but felt he had the spell memorized.

Finally after some distance was put between him and the spirit, he stopped and began shouting the spell's words. He finished just quick enough to watch Shesolaywen disappear into the parchment of the scroll. He now had the means to give Lord Dowd the Call of Conair.

Krasous fell to the ground and spoke to himself. "I never wish to see another spirit again. Only one more season until I can retire my commission. I just want to go away." He closed his eyes. When he reappeared he was standing next to the tree where he had tied up his spirit-bull.

The World of Grayham
Sam and Shalee's Bedroom Chambers
That Same Night

Sam was clearly irritated as he paced back and forth across the stones of their bedroom floor within the Castle of Brandor. Shalee was lying in bed but Sam still refused to take his spot next to her. He was still very angry with her.

"Look, I hear everything you're saying, but I don't believe any of it. I don't think Lasidious is the one you should be serving, especially since George is involved. I can't believe you would tell the people you knew George was speaking the truth. What the heck is wrong with you, lately? First, you cheat on me and now... you're confessing your service to an evil god. Have you become retarded or even a little dense lately?"

"That's not fair!" Shalee snapped. "You didn't see what I saw! I saw Lasidious return your soul even after Mosley said it couldn't be done! You were dead and I felt your icy skin myself on the palms of my own two hands. You were a goner. The people also watched as Lasidious gave you your life back just like I did. You would've done the same thing if you had been in my situation!"

Sam sat heavily on a chair across the room. "Believe me when I say I'm glad to be alive, but I don't believe for a moment Lasidious has done this or even has the power to do something like this. I think this is some kind of a trick."

Shalee grunted in frustration. "Well, if it was a trick... then it's a pretty good one."

"So I've heard you say many times already. What about the potion Yaloom gave us for you to drink? Have you been able to recall any of his memories?"

"No... I don't think the potion worked. I don't feel any different. Maybe he was wrong."

Sam slapped his hand on the arm of the chair. "Or maybe your mind isn't able to handle it! Maybe you won't ever be able to retrieve his memories from the back of your mind!"

Shalee sat up and found his eyes. "I have already apologized for hurting you. Stop being such a jerk. I was wrong and I hate myself for it. If you want me to leave, I'll go, but I don't have to keep being chastised. Make your choice right now. Do I stay, and you forgive me, or do I go and never talk to you again? You pick, but do it right now because I won't live like this!"

Sam stood and moved to the window. After taking a long deep breath, he turned to find his queen anxiously waiting his response. "Maybe you should go for the night. I need some time to think. You hurt me badly and I'm still having a hard time calming down. I'll find a way to act differently by morning. I do still love you, but the thought of what you've done to us makes me sick to my stomach."

"FINE!" She stormed out of the room. Her bare feet slapped hard on the stones of the floor with loud exclamation marks as she went.

After watching her go, Sam moved across the room. He opened a chest at the foot of their bed and lifted up the other half of Yaloom's potion. He allowed the light of the torch hanging from the wall to pass through its light blue liquid.

His thoughts ran wild… *What secrets are hidden inside of you? Why isn't Shalee's mind remembering the things you said she would, Yaloom? Maybe she's unable to do this. I need to know the truth of things. I need to know them now… not later. Do your memories hold any of these answers?*

He removed the lid and put the vial to his mouth. He was about to drink, but instead, thought better of it. He lowered the vial and secured the lid, once again thinking as he did. *Damn… I promised I would save this for you, Yaloom. But if Shalee doesn't start to remember something soon…*

After sitting on the bed, his eyes traced the spaces between the stones of the floor. *Okay… okay…: do I really want to save my marriage? Can I look at Shalee again and feel the same love for her I did before knowing she betrayed our vows? Damn, this is hard! I swear I should kick her butt right out of this castle!*

I want to see Sam Jr. live again. I want to see his smile when both of us hold him. Shalee did have a lot going on in her own mind when she cheated on me. But then again… so did I. What gives her the right to act this way? How would she react if I had done the same thing? Would she forgive me? I should be allowed to walk away without feeling guilty!

Come on, Sam... you're better than this! Mom and Dad raised me to be better than this. Carrying around all this anger isn't going to help either of us. It'll just eat me up inside. It doesn't matter how Shalee would react. It doesn't matter if she would forgive me or not. It only matters how I react right now! I'm the one who's been put in this position. If I don't forgive her now... how could I expect her to forgive me in the future if I decide to do something stupid? Granted I wouldn't do this to anyone, but... but... damn it, Sam... focus, pull your head out!

Are you going to forgive her or not? It's pretty simple... YES or NO!

After many long moments, he stood from the side of the bed and left the room. When finally he found Shalee, he spoke with the softness the queen longed to hear.

"I thought I would find you here. The garden is as beautiful as you are."

The queen recognized the difference in his tone. She turned and looked into his eyes. "Why did you come to find me?"

Sam shook his head. "I don't want to talk. I only want to forgive." He moved to her and pulled her within his big arms. "I love you, Shalee!"

"I love you too, Sam. I'm so sorry."

"Shhhh... you don't need to say anything. It's over and done with. Let's move forward and never talk about this again. We will figure things out in the morning!"

He pulled back and led her to one of the many benches within the royal garden. Once sitting, he found her eyes. "I'll always love you!"

Leaning in, their lips met as many soft apologetic kisses were exchanged between them. It didn't take long before Sam felt some of the passion, which he had buried inside, begin to return. He pulled her close. The intensity grew with each peck. He lifted her from the bench to carry her inside. The kissing continued as he began to walk. Only four steps were taken before they vanished to their bedroom.

Chapter 25

𝕿𝖎𝖙𝖆𝖓𝖘

Ancients Sovereign, The Hall of Judgment

The next morning, the gods were beginning to gather within Gabriel's hall. Lictina, the spirit god of Fire was the first to arrive. She made her entrance by floating in, in her spherical form and once near her seat, transformed into more of a ghostly appearance before taking her normal spot at the large marble table.

It wasn't long before the others arrived. As usual, Keylom's heavy hooves clapped across the floor while Bailem walked in with his wings folded tightly behind his chubby body, waiting until the last possible moment before spreading them gently apart to take his seat. Jervaise, the lizardian, tucked her tail into a special hole created within her chair to allow for her to assume a comfortable position and, as always, Lasidious was the last to arrive with Celestria after the others had either walked in or simply appeared to take a seat. But there was one missing and the God of Mischief took note of this fact right away.

"Gabriel," Lasidious said, "where's Mosley?"

The Book lifted from the heavy table and floated over to Lasidious. "Mosley has decided he's tired of the game. He said to tell you he's leaving for a while and won't be back. I would imagine what you've done on Grayham has caused him to seek solitude."

Lasidious frowned. "So where has he gone?"

"He said he didn't want anyone to know. His own words were, 'I don't want Lasidious or the others knowing where I went.'"

"Bah… he's up to something."

Gabriel turned and floated back to his spot and as he did, he responded, "You could always track his use of godly powers when he decides to use them."

Lasidious sat heavily in his chair. "Well, this is an unexpected turn of events! I wouldn't have thought of the wolf as being a quitter. If he doesn't want to be found, I'm sure he knows not to use his powers."

Keylom's hooves clapped against the marble floor as he interjected. He had an idea to help throw Lasidious off the wolf's tracks. "Mosley did say he intends to find his own world to rule. He said he intends to find enough matter somewhere within the cosmos to create his own world of beings to worship him. There is, after all, nothing in our laws that prohibits this."

"Ha... now that sounds more like my ambitious Mosley," Lasidious chuckled. "I knew he had to be up to something other than just quitting my little game. I guess he figures if I'm going to take his followers, he might as well replace them. I just love that wolf."

Bailem stood from his chair and adjusted his robe to a more comfortable position on his portly belly. Once his wings were once again folded tightly behind him, he spoke. "I would like to know how you returned Sam's soul to his body? How could you possibly manipulate such a thing? None of us have the power to take a soul from Gabriel's pages."

"He wasn't within my pages," Gabriel responded before Lasidious had the chance to do so.

"What?" Bailem said, confused as the others in the room listened intently. "So how did he do it then?"

Gabriel shrugged his little shoulders which protruded from the sides of his covers, "Ask him... not me!"

Lasidious leaned over to kiss Celestria on the cheek as he stood from his chair, then responded. "I trapped Sam's soul within the blade of a Dark Order dagger. I visited Boyafed and asked him to use this special blade to kill Sam."

Hosseff lifted from his chair. The shade's whispery voice emanated from the nothingness that should have been his face. "Boyafed would never do anything that wasn't requested by me, his god. He serves only me and no other."

Lasidious began to laugh and allowed himself to plop back down into his chair. "You're right... but Boyafed thought he was doing your will, Hosseff, not mine! I appeared to him in your own image and requested he use a special dagger to deliver the killing blow when taking Sam's life. The blade simply trapped his soul and didn't allow it to move on to Gabriel's pages. Mieonus's little night cap with Boyafed only helped me accomplish what I wanted to do."

Lasidious turned to the goddess of Hate. "Once you were done sleeping with the Dark Order leader, his mind was made up to kill Sam. I knew you couldn't keep your big mouth shut. You helped me accomplish just one more part of my plan."

Mieonus shouted. "You knew... how could you know? I was very careful to pick the perfect moment!"

Celestria decided to answer. "You wouldn't know the meaning of careful. I watched you sleep with him myself. I'm sure Boyafed would agree he could've found a far better lover than you. Your movements were amateurish while pleasuring him. Not worthy of being a goddess. You're pathetic!"

Mieonus stomped the lifted heel of her right shoe on the marble floor. "Careful, Celestria, you're not powerful enough to speak to me this way."

The goddess of all Evil-Natured Beasts pushed back her flowing hair and gently lowered to her seat. Once comfortable, she continued without acknowledging Mieonus's threat. "Despite your intentions to manipulate Sam's death, you've only managed to help Lasidious and me accomplish one more part of our goals. You've given Lasidious the chance to use the dagger he created on Sam."

Alistar stood and adjusted his green robe. It was easy to see his anger. "You had no right to create such a dagger without the approval of us all. It's against the rules within the Book's pages to do so." The God of the Harvest turned to Gabriel. "Why haven't you stripped him of his powers?"

Gabriel lifted from the table once again. "He must've created the dagger before this rule was added to the laws. I had no knowledge of the blade's existence until I saw Lasidious pull it from Sam's chest. Even then, I had no idea what its purpose was, besides the killing of a king. He's broken no law!"

Lasidious stood and looked Alistar dead in the eyes and with a perfect performance, pretended to be angered. "You're pathetic!

Do you really believe I'm so stupid that I would create something against the Book's laws? I have no desire to be made mortal. Gabriel is right... I created the dagger before the law ever existed. I've been waiting for the perfect moment to use it and finally, thanks to Mieonus's simple little mind, I was able to do so."

Mieonus wanted to object, but she knew to do so would only make her look even more flawed than she already appeared.

The god of Mischief continued. "I appeared as Hosseff and gave Boyafed the blade. I now have the blade again and I will use it whenever I see fit. You cannot stop me because it would be against my free will to do so."

Alistar chuckled.

Lasidious responded. "I fail to see what's so funny."

Alistar gave the Book a nod. Gabriel responded by giving the Call to Order.

"What?" Lasidious screamed. "You tricked me, Gabriel. Your laws don't allow you to choose sides. I wouldn't have come to this meeting if I knew you were in on this. Besides... you can't give the Call without Mosley present."

Gabriel hovered over to Lasidious. "I can make the Call if Mosley surrenders his vote, and I can choose a side if necessary. It's in my laws that I can do whatever it takes to protect the laws of the gods as long as if doesn't affect free will. Your campaign to gain the followers needed to give you the power to control me isn't something I can allow. I have to protect your free will, but the laws will allow me to do whatever is necessary to put you at a disadvantage. I only have to make sure I do it without stripping your free will from you. You have come to the meeting because you've chosen to. This means I can give the Call to Order without taking your free will from you."

Lasidious thought for a moment. "You cannot vote to take my dagger from me. That would be to take my free will from me."

Alistar cut into the conversation. "We don't need to take your free will away. You can have your knife for all we care, but there's something we can vote on right now."

Lasidious smirked. "What exactly can you vote on that I could possibly care about?"

Alistar turned to the others. "I think it would benefit us all to vote that we can no longer appear in the likeness of another god. I believe this kind of manipulation is far too powerful and needs to be addressed. Also, I further say we should vote that we can no longer take on the form of the people within the worlds to increase our own personal flocks. This is pretty cut and dry. No other rule is necessary at this moment other than the ones which we cannot vote to create because of Lasidious's free will to manipulate the Crystal Moon."

Once Alistar was done he looked at Lasidious. "None of these suggestions are currently taking your free will from you. We're free to vote and the Call to Order has already been given. You have no choice but to vote with us as the laws of the Book state."

Lasidious stood and looked out across the table. "This is an outrage. You cannot vote to take this away from us. I have plans."

While Celestria also voiced her opinion on the matter, Helmep, God of Healing, decided he too would interject. He stood, lifting his well-built frame into a perfect posture. Hazel eyes, accenting his white robes with dark-trimmed accents, carried conviction as he spoke.

"Well, I say it's the proper moment for this type of law. I'm sorry, Lasidious, but you're far too dangerous to be allowed to run around and steal the loyalty of our followers. I say we vote on these matters now, Gabriel."

The room exploded with mixed emotions. It was four against eight as the gods cursed one another back and forth, each with a strong opinion of their own. The Book of Immortality finally stepped in. He floated to the center of the table and shouted.

"I call this meeting to order! We will vote now. Mosley's vote will remain neutral.

"The first issue… The gods will no longer be able to take the form of any other god, or goddess, for any reason whatsoever. Those in favor, raise your hands."

Four hands in the room did not go up. Lasidious, Celestria, Lictina, and Hosseff, even though the god of Death had been the one Lasidious had chosen to impersonate, all refused to raise their hands in support of this ridiculous law. Hosseff and Lictina both tried to express their objections, but Gabriel reminded them their chance to voice an opinion had already passed once the vote had been called for.

After counting the hands that were held high, the Book continued.

"Then it's settled. The first issue is upheld and the gods will no longer be allowed to impersonate one another without penalty of being made mortal. Now, for the second issue, the gods can no longer impersonate the people of the worlds in an attempt to gain additional followers. Those in favor of adding this as a law to my pages, raise your hands."

Again, the same four hands stayed lowered while the others lifted their hands high.

"Then, this matter is also settled and the new laws have been added to my pages. The gods can no longer impersonate the people of the worlds in order to gain additional followers. The Call to Order is now over."

Lasidious stood and took Celestria's hand. "You all are fools." They vanished.

Alistar laughed.

"I don't think he likes the fact that we beat him at his own game. This should keep Lasidious from keeping the advantage he had over us."

Hosseff shook his head.

"I think this may have been a mistake. We could have used such manipulations to fight Lasidious at his own game. We could have confused the people and kept them from following him by using his own tactics of impersonation. Now that we can no longer do this, I wonder if there's a disadvantage to be found in this vote."

Alistar moved to the head of the table where Lasidious sat. "I believe this will be in our favor. I must take my leave now. There are matters of famine I must see to on Harvestom. Now that Mosley has decided to take a leave of absence, it appears it's up to me to keep this potential war brewing." The god disappeared.

Only moments later, Alistar appeared inside Lasidious and Celestria's cave-like home deep beneath the Peaks of Angels. The brothers embraced and after Alistar greeted Celestria properly, they took a seat around the table near the green flames of the fire.

"Well I think that went rather well," Lasidious said, "don't you agree, brother?"

"I do, and I doubt any of them realize this is what we wanted to happen all along. I would love to see their faces if they knew I was the one who actually created the dagger you used to capture Sam's soul. It's nice to see our plan is slowly starting to piece together. It won't be long before the three of us are ruling the others and the Book will be forced to bow to us."

Celestria just sat silently, not responding. Lasidious saw her hesitation and moved to sit beside her. "What's wrong, my love?"

After a moment of silence she finally responded. "As I sit here listening to the two of you gloat, I realize there's so much I don't know. So here's what's going to happen. You two are going to level with me and tell me everything. Once you're done telling me everything I'm going to look at you, Lasidious, and ask you if there's anything else. You better hope you don't leave out even one single detail because if you do, the truth potion I gave you will let me know you're holding back on me. If this ends up being the case, my love, you won't be touching this body ever again. I'll have no more secrets being kept from me. Look me in the eyes, Lasidious. Do you understand me?"

"I do understand. I'm sorry you're feeling left out."

"Don't apologize; just answer me this one question. The potion won't allow you to lie to me and I need to know. Do you and Alistar have any intentions of getting rid of me once this is all over? Do you intend to love me once you have your control of the Book?"

Lasidious' smile grew across his entire face.

"My love for you is genuine. I would never do anything to intentionally hurt you. I would never allow either myself or Alistar to hurt you. I would never betray you. You, our son, and my brother are all I care about. You have asked me this question before and my answer will always be the same. You are everything to me!"

Celestria took a deep breath and sighed heavily. "Then I suggest the two of you get to talking because I want to know everything you've got planned. I don't like feeling lost. I refuse to be the one who isn't completely informed. Do you two understand me? And don't think for a moment, Alistar, that because you're his brother I won't find a way to punish you too if you don't tell me the truth."

Alistar chuckled.

"Yes, ma'am!"

The City of Hyperia North of Lake Id

The City of Hyperia, located north of Lake Id was a fine city full of halflings and elves with limited magic. The city was protected by mountains to the north and much of the city floated atop the water of the lake and was anchored in this position as the city extended beyond the shoreline and stopped where the mountains began their rapid ascent.

Hyperia was protected both to the west and east by large walls which covered a tremendous amount of terrain. At over fifty feet wide and seventy-five feet tall at their lowest point, they extended from well off the shoreline of the lake and terminated as they burrowed into the side of the mountains, with the area directly surrounding the walls on all sides being shaved to make climbing the cliffs nearly impossible during invasion.

There were only two main points of entry into Hyperia other than approaching the city by boat from the south. Both of these entrances, as well as the entire length of the walls on both sides of the city, were guarded by the king's finest. These men were the strongest warriors who also commanded dark magic, although their powers paled in comparison to the magic of the Dark Order's paladins.

The entire southern half of Hyperia would remind someone from Earth of Venice. The people move freely through this area, using boats of all kinds to access their store fronts by docking directly in front of them.

Boyafed, the Dark Order leader, now stood in front of the king of Hyperia's throne, waiting for Kassel Hyperia to arrive and take his seat as head of the kingdom. There would be no kneeling to show the king respect on this chilly morning. Boyafed had already cleared out the floating castle's servants from the room and would be direct once Kassel entered.

Eventually, the king did enter and, without even so much as a proper greeting, the Order leader began to address the business at hand.

"Kassel, why do you keep me waiting? I have more important things to do than waste my moments with you."

The king, sensing Boyafed's frustration, took his seat and responded. "I know why you've come and I fail to see how this war you intend to fight is my problem. There is nothing to be gained by fighting a war which cannot be won on either side. The last war my ancestors entered by following the Dark Order nearly killed every last man in Hyperia. They were used as nothing more than shields. Our magic isn't strong enough to withstand the forces of the White Army. I will not order these good men into battle again."

Kassel watched nervously as Boyafed began to shake his head and move toward the window. The Order leader's breath billowed in front of him as he watched a lady trying to load her boat. She slipped and fell head first into the water below. He enjoyed her shriek as she splashed wildly around, trying to lift her rounded frame back into the boat. It was hard not to laugh, since her weight was about to roll the boat over on top of her. The men standing just outside the stores surrounding the scene quickly reacted, showing their chivalry by fishing her out of the mirky water, each of them struggling to lift her weight. After a few blankets had been retrieved and placed around her to protect her from the cold morning air, Boyafed finally turned and faced the king. Walking towards him with conviction, he stopped only inches from his person. He leaned in and allowed the warmth of his breath to find Kassel's face. "I don't recall asking you to order your men into battle. I'm telling you, you will send your men into battle and if you do not, I will find someone among your fine city who wishes to be king, maybe someone who sits on the council and despises you as much as I do. I'm sure I've made myself clear on this matter, have I not?"

Boyafed sauntered away from the king, aware that the leader was now unnerved.

Kassel stood and took a few steps before responding. "This is an act of treason. This goes against the agreements my city has with Marcus. You cannot override the authority of the Chancellor. What will he say about this?"

Again Boyafed closed the gap between himself and the king, but on this advance, he grabbed the halfling about his throat and pushed him backwards against the castle's stone walls. He pressed hard until Kassel began to choke. "I doubt very seriously Marcus would try to say anything. I alone command the greatest army on Luvelles and your precious little Chancellor is but a small sore on my backside. I suggest you rethink your position and have your men welcome the mercenaries of Bestep or I will see to it personally that your position as king is short-lived. Don't make me come back here and prove this point."

Boyafed took a breath to let his words sink in.

"The mercenaries currently march this way. You'll allow them passage into your city. You'll feed them and provide them anything they request. I will send for the army when the moment is right and they will be teleported to the Battlegrounds of Olis. You will once again be used as shields for my army."

Boyafed leaned in and allowed his forehead to find the king's. "Do I make myself clear, Kassel?"

Kassel meekly nodded and the Dark Order leader vanished.

Kassel collapsed to the floor gasping for air, all the while trembling from the exchange.

The World of Grayham
The Village of Lethwitch
Mary's Old Cottage Home

When George and Athena appeared outside of Mary's home, Athena was surprised her feelings for the home had changed. Mary's neighbors had made many improvements while they were gone, but despite that, she felt the home was beneath her now, since she had a taste for the finer things in life back on Luvelles.

"I can't believe I used to think this place was so adorable. It seems so primitive now. I bet Mother and Susanne would just die if they knew I was here."

George pulled her close and gave her a hug, careful to allow her pregnant belly the room needed to stay comfortable.

"I don't know... the way I see it, I find this place rather charming. Lethwitch is, after all, where our baby was conceived." He lowered to one knee and rubbed her belly as he continued. "I remember this spot as being where my true happiness in life began. I found you in this town and as far as I'm concerned... this town, your mother's inn, and her home will always be beautiful to me."

He watched as Athena's smile widened. "You can be so romantic," she replied. Her mood changed as she thought further. "I'm worried about Susanne and Garrin. She's a little upset still about the baby's father not having the chance to be in his life."

"She'll be fine. Brayson and your mother are going to keep an eye on her today. Besides, Garrin is too cute not to keep her busy. She won't have the time, I mean, the moments necessary to dwell on a loss she never really knew she had in the first place."

George quickly thought, *Man, I hate lying to her. This whole situation is getting out of hand. I want to tell you everything, but I can't. Somehow I've got to keep the events I've set in motion away from the family. This was poor planning on my part and now I'm lying to the one person I hate lying to the most. This is really pissing me off! She deserves better than this!*

After a moment of silence, Athena continued, "Are you sure Payne will be okay with Brayson and mother? Oh, and by the way, why did you tell Payne it was okay to call me Mother? It's been bothering me."

"Uummm… I didn't actually say that, if I remember right, but I should be punished for sure." He gave her a cute puppy dog look and waited for her forgiveness.

"Yes, you should! You're not getting out of this one so easy, Mr. Nailer."

"I'm sorry, but Payne does need to be loved. Letting him call you Mom, and me Dad, will give the little guy a feeling he belongs with us. Don't you agree?"

Athena frowned. "I agree he needs us to be there for him, but you should've been more careful with the things you say to him. I suppose I can adapt since he's already refusing to call me anything else."

George leaned in and kissed her. "If you'll forgive me, I'll promise to try harder. You know I love you!"

As always, she melted when he touched her. "I forgive you, but you better start consulting me from now on about things like this!"

"Yes, honey… maybe you should go into town and visit everyone while I go do the things our god has asked me to do while we're here. I have a wonderful surprise for you tonight before we head back to Luvelles. I'm sure you'll love it! I'll meet you by Late Bailem right here tonight."

After pulling her into his arms and giving her a final kiss, George vanished.

Athena grinned as she continued to stare at the empty spot George had left behind.

"You're just lucky I think you're so adorable, Mr. Nailer."

Back on Luvelles
The Shores of Crystal Lake

Strongbear stood in front of the nine hundred and ninety-eight Goswigs of Gogswayne as he inspected them individually and methodically, intending to send them home and not allow them to fight in the war if their armor or their robes were not perfect in appearance.

Gage's robes were new. The badger had created them especially for the occasion and was wearing bright white with green trim.

The ensemble contrasted well against his fur and his unchanged walking cane.

Gallrum's appearance had remained unchanged. His magic worked in such a way he was unable to wear either clothes or armor. His skin was tough enough that he didn't need the armor many of the others would need. He did, however, add a few rings to his claw-like talon hands to add some additional protections against the Dark Army's magic.

Gage - A Badger and Goswig to Marcus Id

Illustration by Angela Woods

Many of the other Goswigs, despite being able to use magic, had decided to go with either light chain mail or plate. Strongbear himself looked imposing, with heavy plate covering a large majority of his body. The top of his head and down the back of his neck were also covered and he looked born to kill. For this occasion, the apron he normally wore while strolling around Gogswayne was left neatly folded in his cave. There would be no sewing for the large brown bear for a while, at least for the foreseeable future.

After a careful inspection, the order was given, and the group teleported to the City of Inspiration. From there, they would join Lord Dowd and his men for the march to the Battlegrounds of Olis. Once they all had arrived, each of the Goswigs went their own way until the call to march was given.

Gage took the opportunity to look around. It was a cloudy day, so the glass City of Inspiration didn't have its normal, reflective appeal, but it was still beautiful nonetheless. He stopped by a wagon loaded with grain and marveled at how the glass, which the wagon was made of, somehow managed to be altered to look like any other normal wagon. It was an impressive use of magic to say the least, and the badger felt a love for the place.

The World of Grayham
Brandor's Arena

George appeared at the center of Brandor's arena after leaving Athena to go about her business in Lethwitch. Three guards rushed towards him with the intention of arresting him. The warlock's actions would have normally left him sitting in a cold dungeon, but on this day things were different.

As he watched them come, he lifted his hands and shouted, "Go into the city and announce to the people that the prophet of Lasidious, the savior of your king, has come to speak with them! I have come to spread the word of the one true god! Make haste and bring the masses to me! No man should miss hearing what I have to say!"

George pointed to one of the men. "You, my friend, what's your name?"

"Cholis… my name is Cholis, prophet," he responded as he bowed on one knee.

George smiled within himself. *Like putty in my hands… the minds of the people on these worlds are weak. This whole false prophet gig is going to be like taking candy from a baby.*

George responded. "Cholis, go to your king and announce my arrival. Let both your king and queen know I have come to spread my lord's words of peace and love."

"Yes, prophet, but it will take a while before they'll be able to arrive. The castle is a fair ways from here."

"I know. Please go now so they may arrive before afternoon."

"Yes, prophet." The man turned and rushed off.

George thought to himself again as he watched Cholis leave, *I'm counting on the fact that it will take some time before they arrive. This will give me enough the time I need to pollute the minds of the people before I leave with their queen.*

It took most of the morning but eventually the people of Grayham started to file into the arena in larger numbers to take their seats. George didn't wait for them to fill every last one before he started to speak. He only needed to get the message to a few before leaving. He would then lead both Sam and Shalee away from the arena so the people could move out into the city and spread the word for him.

He lifted his voice and addressed only a few hundred souls.

"My lord has seen to it that all of Southern Grayham may still live in service to their king. He wants the people to know he intends to bring peace and prosperity to all and will do whatever it takes to ensure you're able to maintain this higher quality of life. Lasidious wants the people to know that he values both your king and queen. No longer will my god allow war to consume your lands. No longer will any man or any man's family want for food. All of your needs will be provided for."

A voice from the crowd responded. He was dressed gracefully and his appearance was well-groomed. "And how exactly does Lasidious intend to ensure that the people want for nothing? How does he intend to ensure that peace remains on all of Southern Grayham? If you can answer these questions, I will serve Lasidious myself. But as of right now, my faith in the gods is weak."

George lifted his voice again. "What's your name, friend?"

"I am Kolton, Senator of Brandor and voice of the Fourth and Fifth Marks of Grayham."

George had no idea what he meant by "Marks," but he didn't need to know. He hoped someone of importance would be at this meeting.

"Kolton, senator of Brandor and voice to the Fourth and Fifth Marks, I have a gift for the Senate. Lift your hands to the sky and open your palms so I may leave it with you. You, Kolton, will be the one I leave in charge of the safe keeping of Lasidious's promise."

George reached into a small pack he had brought with him and pulled out a small crystal orb which looked similar to the Crystal Moon, with the same dragon's base, but with a green hue and Grayham's topography instead. He lifted it high above his head and once he saw that Kolton's arms were extended, he floated the orb from his hands to the senator's where it landed softly. Some within the arena were frightened, while others watched the crystal in awe as it made its way across the distance.

Once the promise of Lasidious rested soundly in Kolton's palms, George continued to speak, but now stood in front of a much larger crowd as more people piled in.

"People of Brandor, hear me… I am Lasidious's prophet and this orb which I have been asked to deliver to Brandor's Senate will allow Kolton to call for my assistance when Grayham is in need. I'll appear to the Senate whenever an issue on Grayham needs to be addressed. I will personally see to it that Lasidious understands your needs, your desires. For now, those of you who are present will receive a gift. I want each of you to hold out your hands and cup your palms together."

Again George thought to himself as he watched the people do as instructed, *Leave it to the greed of the people to win their loyalty. This gift of coin should do the trick.*

Yaloom coins, the highest currency in the land—3,425 in total—spread five per person throughout the group, appeared in each person's hands. He listened to their exclamations of joy as they realized the wealth they had just been given.

"Lasidious wishes for you to share this gift with one another. Those blessed with this chance to share will need to pass four of these five coins along to the others within your families. You are only to keep one for yourself. This act of kindness is Lasidious's way of making sure you understand that giving and loving one another is the only way to true happiness. I must leave you now, but know that Lasidious loves you and wants you to spread his message of giving. He wants you to spread his words of peace and love."

George listened to the cheers of the crowd and began walking toward the arena's exit. He had no sooner passed beneath the arches when both Sam and Shalee appeared, riding their ghostly mist mares. Sam was furious as he shouted at George.

"Who do you think you are to come into the city and speak to the people without speaking to me first? I would kill you, but Shalee has informed me of your power. It's extremely disturbing that you would come here!"

With a nod, the warlock responded as if he actually cared what the king was feeling. "You're right, Sam… I owe you an apology. I'm not here to fight or cause problems. In fact, I'm here for other reasons. I guess I'm just excited about everything I've learned. I'm equally excited to have found a chance at redemption, a chance to be a better man. I want to be a light for others to see by. Walk with me so we can talk. I have come to keep my promise to Shalee. I promised her I would make sure she had the chance to look into the Eye of Magic. I told her I would take her back to Luvelles. We will need her newfound power to defend this kingdom!"

Sam grunted. "How about we talk first. I don't know I believe in anything you're preaching. Sure, it all sounds good, and I do appreciate being alive, but I still hold you accountable for many things. Shalee informed me it was Lasidious who saved my life, but I still have my doubts. I believe this is a trick and I also don't believe for a minute you could go from being such a selfish ogre to being such a nice guy. I don't believe you at all!"

George smiled casually and looked the king in the eye. "I don't think I would believe me either if I were you. I guess only time will tell if I'm being sincere. You know, I've got the power to kill you both if I want, but this isn't why I've come. All I ask is that you give me a chance to show you I care and I want to change."

Sam snapped at him. "Don't speak with the people again without my knowledge. I want to be informed when you decide to make your little appearances. If you're serious about being trustworthy, then this won't be a problem. Are we agreed on this? I can't even fathom having this conversation with you. This is absurd!'

"I agree to your terms, and I understand how you feel. But, I've already given the Senate a way to call for me if they need help. I have also brought you something as well. You will need my help in the near future. Allow me to spread the words of peace and help you to make Southern Grayham a better place."

"Why would I need your help so badly? And why would you give them anything without my approval?"

"You're right. I was wrong and it will never happen again. I will respect your crown from here on out. You won't have to worry about anything from me."

George began walking down the road towards the castle. He waved to the people, smiling as Sam and Shalee followed. He could feel Sam's stare burning into the back of his head as they moved through the crowds which were being pushed back by the king's guard. Eventually the warlock stopped and faced the royal couple.

"Shalee, maybe there's someplace private where we could continue this conversation. Why don't you take us there and I will tell you both more about why I've come to see you."

After a brief discussion with Sam, Shalee teleported the group into the royal garden behind the castle. George took a look around and admired the beauty, but his enjoyment of the moment was disrupted as Sam ruined the mood.

"Why don't you get on with it, George? What else have you come to tell us? What other lies can you think of to make things worse than they already are? I have to admit I can't wait to hear this pile of garesh."

George shook his head and took a seat on one of the benches. "I know you have no faith in me, Sam. I deserve your hatred."

Sam continued. "I don't hate you, George. I pity you and find you easily manipulated. But I will save my hate for Lasidious and the other gods."

Shalee remained quiet. She didn't want to contradict Sam when their relationship was still so rocky. She figured George would just have to find his way through the walls Sam was putting up.

George moved to stand beside Sam and produced the picture of his daughter Abbie for the king to see.

"Go ahead... take a look at her. She's the reason I originally did so many hurtful things. I lied, murdered, and set up the war on Grayham because Mieonus filled my head with a lie. She promised to give me Abbie back and in doing so I ruined the lives of so many. I have since learned of the god's deceptions and also know everything Bassorine had written on his statue, and even everything your wolf friend Mosley told you both, were also lies. I have personally seen Lasidious's heaven where he keeps the souls of all those who serve him once they die. I want to go there once I die, and this requires me to live a better life."

Sam dismounted from his mist mare and helped the queen down. After tying them both to one of the statues which were spread throughout the garden, he turned and replied after giving George's words some thought.

"I don't know how I feel about any of this. I don't know I believe you have decided to live a good life. This all seems so sudden... and it also seems too convenient for Lasidious to become some kind of all mighty force which the other gods relish. There must be other reasons why you're here, George. What else haven't you told us?"

George smiled. "You're right... there is something else that needs to be discussed... something important that will bring peace to all of Grayham. Something is about to threaten your newly united kingdom. I want to help you keep the people safe. This is why I acted quickly. This threat is very powerful and I have the ability to help you fight it. I don't think your sword alone will be able to defeat this person!"

Shalee jumped into the conversation. "What threat are you referring to?"

"The Dark Chancellor of the Dark Army of Holy Paladins on Luvelles has made his way to Grayham, as you already know, I'm sure. I don't know much more than this, but Lasidious has informed me he intends to regain control of Southern Grayham."

Sam grabbed his head in disbelief. "What the hell... we just got done fighting one war. We're not healthy enough to fight another one. We took heavy losses in the last massacre... a massacre you led us into, I might add! I could've died and you could've cared less! Garesh, man... how can you justify your actions now... how can I believe anything you say?"

"I'm not here to justify my actions. I have already admitted I was wrong and my excuse that Mieonus made me do it is wrong, no matter how badly I wanted to retrieve my daughter's soul from the Book of Immortality. I had no right to manipulate this world just because the goddess promised to give my daughter's soul back to me. I mean, who am I to put my life above all others? I was wrong... and all I can do now is work to bring the people the happiness they deserve."

Sam thought a moment, then responded. "So how is it that Lasidious is so powerful and the others fall so short? Why is it that he's the only one with a heaven and why, if he's so all powerful, doesn't he allow the souls within the Book to live within this heaven as well?"

George could only shrug his shoulders. "Look, Sam... I don't pretend to have all the answers yet, but I do know I have seen this heaven and I also know the other gods are not actually gods at all. Lasidious has called them Titans."

Sam cut in. "What... Titans... do you mean like the Titans of Greek mythology?"

George rubbed his head in thought. "I suppose they're similar to this kind of concept, but I really don't have the knowledge of Greek mythology I should. I didn't study much when I was in school. I guess they're considered one step down from being gods themselves. All I really know or even understand, for that matter, is they aren't as powerful as Lasidious, but when they combine their powers they do have enough strength between them to keep the souls they personally manipulate to serve them trapped inside of the Book of Immortality after they die. Apparently Lasidious isn't the only god who survived the God Wars, either. It seems there are others and these others are working with Lasidious to expand this new solar system. It's all very confusing... but I'm sure a guy with your intelligence could sit with Lasidious and have it all figured out in no time at all."

Sam took a seat on one of the benches. Shalee watched and remained quiet since she had limited knowledge of mythology herself. After many moments had passed, Sam lifted his head and looked out across the garden as he spoke.

"You know, none of this makes any sense. In Greek mythology, the Titans were considered to be gods, but you're telling me they are now only considered to be one step from godliness. You also say Lasidious knows of other gods who managed to survive the God Wars and they all are working together to create a new solar system. So why don't the gods just get rid of the Titans and allow the people's souls to reside in this new heaven?"

George smiled. "Hey, man, I agree with you, but you'll have to ask Lasidious about these things. I know it has something to do with protecting the worlds that are already in existence... but other than that, you've got me stumped."

George needed to redirect the conversation, so he threw Sam a curveball. "Look, all I know is that Lasidious has asked me to come to Grayham and warn you of the threat that Marcus Id, the Dark Chancellor from Luvelles, will become. He wants me to make sure Shalee receives the power she deserves by looking into the Eye of Magic and in doing so, she'll be able to help you fight against this army Marcus intends to bring to Brandor's doorstep." Sam turned to find George's eyes. "And what army could he possibly find to fight for him? The barbarians won't lift a finger to help him after the way we took control of the northern territories of Southern Grayham. Who else could he possible command?"

George took a seat on the grass. "Marcus isn't your normal wizard. He has also gained the ability to control the minds of those he comes in contact with. He could very well walk right into your city all alone and the people will turn on one another once he uses this power on them. Your own army will come for you, Sam. You will need to find Marcus before he sets foot in Brandor. I do know you have some time before Marcus intends to make his presence known. You both should take the time necessary to decide how you want to proceed. It's getting late and I have a date with my wife I intend to keep. I'll come back to see you as soon as I can."

Sam couldn't believe his ears. "So you're leaving? And what do you expect me to do with all this information?"

George took a seat next to him. "I think you need to talk with your queen, as I've already said. You also need to speak with the Senate and decide whether or not you want my help. I'll be back when the time is right. I'm sure Lasidious will tell me what to do next."

With that, George teleported away from the garden. Shalee lowered to her knees beside Sam.

"Maybe we should talk about this over dinner. I'm sure your head hurts as much as mine does now."

Sam shook his head. "Hell... I need to drink a few ales. Is there anything on this world that is as it seems to be? I don't know how to tell what the truth is anymore."

Southern Grayham
Gessler Village

It had been five days since Marcus Id set foot on the Merchant Island of Southern Grayham. Since that moment, he had been frustrated and unable to use his power to teleport from place to place. He had no firsthand knowledge of this world's topography so using this form of travel was too dangerous. Being forced to travel by boat, then on something these primitive people called horseback and now, by some ridiculous-looking creature they called a hippogriff, was truly testing his patience.

Marcus looked forward to a good night's sleep as the hippogriff he was riding began its decent to the landing platform located in Gessler Village. Without saying a word he dismounted and walked down the steps to the ground below.

Eventually, after questioning a few shady characters—and even after one extremely poor attempt at robbery which he easily foiled using his magic to throw the thief high onto a fairly steep hillside and watch as he tumbled wildly to the ground before striking his head on a rock and perishing—Marcus finally made his way to the Bloody Trough Inn.

As he looked the place over from the street, he noticed a large stone statue which had been placed just to the right of the entrance. The man was large; his gray outfit of furs and leather was rugged.

As the Dark Chancellor walked inside he could instantly see the crowd was far different than the inns located in the other three cities he had stayed in while traveling to get this far. This crowd exuded evil and, for a moment—although only a brief moment—he actually felt like he belonged.

Many of the men were sitting at larger-than-normal tables and dressed the same as the statue outside, in heavy furs, but all of them were easily taller than Marcus by a solid foot and a half... or maybe even two, in some cases.

Sauntering over to the bar, he could feel their eyes watch him as he took a seat. There were only a few other men scattered throughout the place who were similar to his size, each of them dressed more like the people from the other three inns he had stayed in. He tried to order a drink but the man behind the counter, also one of these larger men, didn't seem to be in any kind of a hurry to stop his conversation with one of the other patrons.

Marcus didn't care to wait, so with a wave of his hand, he used his power to pour himself an ale. The mug magically lifted from the counter, moved to the tap and remained under it until it was completely full before floating over and setting down on the bar in front of him.

This got the barkeep's attention. He stopped his conversation after seeing what had happened, and also knowing full well what this kind of magic was capable of—since he had been working the night George turned the large barbarian outside the front door to stone—he decided to approach with caution.

"Hello, friend," he said hesitantly. "Will there be anything else I can get you tonight? I see you have found the ale without any trouble."

Marcus wasn't in the mood for idle chatter but he did need information, so he decided to answer the barkeep's question. "I could use a meal and I have questions. Maybe you could tell me when the next hippogriff leaves for the landing platform in Lataseff. I need to get to City View. That will be my next stop before arriving at my destination, if I have read my map correctly."

While using a rag to clean the counter, the barkeep said, "Now food I can help you with, but the hippogriffs cannot fly you into barbarian territory. Even though the kingdom is changing and there are plans for barbarians to be given seats within the Senate of Brandor, we still have no word as to when the hippogriffs will be able to fly each race into each other's territories. I'm sorry, but you'll need to travel by foot or maybe even horseback if you intend to go further."

Marcus shook his head with disgust and under his breath he whispered, "I hate you, George. This rat better be worth the trip!"

"Come again?" the barkeep said. "I didn't hear you."

"Nothing... it's nothing. Why don't you give me a room and, while you're at it, do you know of anyone who could guide me to my destination? I can pay them well."

After pondering the question the barkeep threw him a key, "Your room is up the stairs and down the hall to your right. I'll have a guide waiting here in the morning to take you anywhere you want to go."

Marcus flipped the barbarian a couple of coins and before heading up the stairs he responded, "I'll see your guide in the morning, then."

The Luvelles Gazette

When you want an update about your favorite characters

The Next Day Early Bailem

George has just finished breakfast when Athena's water broke. He originally had plans to go to the World of Harvestom but Athena seemed to have other plans which required his presence. The family is already beginning to gather for the event. Both Mary and Brayson seem to have the situation under control.

As it turns out, Gregory Id will become an essential part of spreading the words of peace for Lasidious much sooner than he had originally anticipated. George is now suddenly glad his attempt at killing the Chancellor failed.

Hosseff and Mieonus are inside the goddess's home watching the images of George and the family in her waterfall as they hurry frantically around trying to do anything they can to help with Athena's birth of the new baby. But in the midst of all this confusion, they are about to learn a secret that will allow them to stop Lasidious from gaining the followers he's after on Harvestom.

Alistar has just arrived on Harvestom and is watching as the two armies of centaurs close in on one another. He also intends to watch Lasidious's disciple makes his appearance to the brown-coated king of Kless.

Boyafed plans to go to the Petrified Forest and call in a debt owed to him just after Late Bailem tonight. He wants Balecut to bend moments once the war has started and give his army an advantage. But… something will happen that Boyafed isn't expecting.

Lord Dowd has ordered the White Army to begin their march once the Hounds of Wraithwood Hollow appear after emerging from the darkness of the Under Eye. With the Scroll of Conair now in hand, the Goswigs and the army of Lavan are all ready for war. They will meet up with the giants of the Foot just north of Lake Tepp and continue to march westward to the Battlegrounds of Olis. Strongbear took up conversation with Wisslewine, the Wraith Hound Prince, and it didn't take long before the ghostly hound became tired of hearing, "So are you with me... or are you against me?"

Marcus has finally arrived at the home of Maldwin the rat. He has read from the scroll and begun to call the rat's name as George instructed.

Lasidious and Celestria are inside their home beneath the Peaks of Angels. Lasidious visited Brayson once again in the middle of the night and gave the Head Master some very specific instructions regarding the upcoming war. He also asked Brayson to give George a message and in doing so, revealed the location of something very special which had been hidden on Grayham for many, many seasons… back when the worlds were first created. He also informed Brayson he had personally seen to it this item was well-preserved throughout the seasons and the name of the person he specifically wanted George to give the item to.

But, as always, Lasidious didn't tell Brayson everything. He failed to explain how he had hidden the item long before the gods passed their new laws regarding some-thing of this nature. He also failed to explain that, until now anyway, he had absolutely no idea when he would use the item or be able to put it to its best use. But now that the perfect opportunity had finally presented itself, he might as well implement an additional plan to help George with gathering more followers to pray to him. Lasidious also failed to share his other devi-ous plans to keep the gods busy.

Keylom is about to take Mosley into the mist of Siren's Song on Grayham.

Gabriel has decided who he will approach to replace Yaloom. This creature will become the new God of Greed and will cause some ten-sion on Ancients Sovereign if he is able to convince the beast of the benefits of being immortal.

Thank you for reading the Luvelles Gazette

Chapter 26

𝔇𝔯𝔞𝔤𝔬𝔫 𝔚𝔬𝔯𝔩𝔡

"Holy cow... this is stressful," George said as he pushed his hands through his hair while turning to face Brayson. "I have never heard a woman scream so loud. Are you sure Mary knows what she's doing?"

Brayson laughed as he opened the door and allowed a team of healers he had sent for earlier to come in. He quickly greeted them and pointed to the teleportation platform which would take them directly to George and Athena's room. Once the last one had vanished, he turned to face George. "Like I've already said on three occasions, everything is under control."

George thought a moment and led Brayson out onto the front porch. "Look... I know you're busy doing something tonight, but I need you to do me a big favor."

"And what would that be?"

"I need you to get your brother, Gregory and teleport him to the Kingdom of Kless on Harvestom... more specifically, the throne room, or I guess the king's barn would be more accurate, if I really wanted to label it. You know... I bet he has a really cool stall and it's probably full of the freshest hay since he's the king, or do centaurs even eat hay? Do you know what they eat?"

Brayson had to reel him in. "George, I think you're letting your mind wander. I personally know that the king of Kless has his own version of a throne and you're right, he does have fresh hay, although I think he eats grain. They live within the forests of Kless and I have spoken with the king on a few occasions over the seasons through my mirror. Hurry and finish the rest of what you were going to say and I'll go get my brother."

"Anyway, Gregory will need to tell the king that a bag holding his kingdom's Seeds of Plenty hasn't been stolen by the king of Tagdrendlia after all. Lasidious has informed me that the God of War intends to start a war on this world. His reason for starting this war doesn't exist. His bag full of the seeds is simply hidden in..."

Hosseff and Mieonus couldn't believe their good fortune as they listened to the visions within the goddess' waterfall on Ancients Sovereign. George was practically handing them a way to beat Lasidious at his own game. They would be able to capitalize on this momentary loss of concentration by the warlock.

"So, do you understand everything that needs to be done?" George said, once he finished.

"I do."

"Good... hurry back after you drop Gregory off." George telepathically spoke the rest of what he had to say by projecting his thoughts into Brayson's mind. *I will go back to Harvestom and get your brother later tonight while you are off handling the business our lord has asked you to handle.*

Brayson continued to speak aloud. "I will hurry back as soon as I explain everything to Gregory. He'll enjoy the idea that he's able to serve our lord and be a part of stopping this war on Harvestom from happening. The words of peace and love shall be shared with others today."

"Well, this is the break we've been waiting for," Hosseff said as the images within the waterfall faded. "We should find Keylom. He's a centaur and may be the best one of us to appear to the king."

Mieonus thought a moment before responding. "I hate the idea of giving that centaur anything... especially when it involves handing him additional followers who'll be worshiping him, but, you're right... he's our best chance to take this information and use it to our advantage. We best hurry so he arrives before Gregory and Brayson."

Once Brayson left, George hurried up the stairs to check on Athena. He was surprised at his greeting as she screamed at him from the bed.

"Oohhh... so you've decided to be a part of this after all! How nice of you to take a moment to stop by, Mr. Nailer!" she scoffed. With a smile hidden inside, George moved to take her hand. "I'm sorry, hon... I just thought you were already in good hands up here."

"Hah... you're not allowed to think while I'm in this much pain! Do you understand me?"

"Yes, dear... you best pay attention and do what the healers tell you to do."

Again, Athena snapped. "Don't you tell me what to do! Listening to you is what got me in this situation in the first place! You don't look so charming right now! Just be quiet and hold my hand!"

Mary gave George a quick grin to let him know everything would be okay, then said, "Just hold her hand tight and give her something to squeeze."

Payne was right outside the window watching with his claws holding tight to the window sill and his eyes peeping over the edge just high enough to satisfy his curiosity. He had never seen a baby being born before.

Kepler shouted up to the fairy-demon while lying on top of the pile of boulders above his lair, "Get down here, freak. Leave the humans alone for a while, why don't you..."

𝕾𝖔𝖚𝖙𝖍𝖊𝖗𝖓 𝕲𝖗𝖆𝖞𝖍𝖆𝖒
The Rat Maldwin's Home

Marcus read from the scroll George gave him back on Luvelles. Now with his mind protected, he was sitting outside a hole leading into Maldwin's home and shouting the rat's name. Every now and then he also shouted the phrase, "Everything is A-okay, man!"

**Maldwin - ** A Rat and Visionary

Illustration by Ian Ferrebee

Not far from the exit, Maldwin sat quietly within the shadows for many moments, watching, waiting, and trying to decide what to do. He was conflicted about how to respond. On one claw, he wanted to use his ability to project visions and send this unexpected visitor walking off the edge of the cliffs of Latasef, but on the other claw, he heard this man shouting the phrase George used to while they traveled together. After many more moments passed, he finally decided to exit his cave and confront this person.

Once outside, Maldwin spoke. "All quay alla foot uswayya doy!"

Marcus, after listening to the rat, lifted his hands in the air and once again said, "Everything is A-okay, man." Slowly he reached into his robe and removed the letter George said would tell the beast all he needed to know.

Maldwin just watched cautiously as the man set the paper on the ground and slid it slowly toward him. Once he felt the parchment was close enough, he looked up at the man and shouted, "Yaway astoot!" which meant, "that's far enough."

Marcus could only smile since he had absolutely no idea what the rat was saying. "It's okay, little guy... I'm just going to back up a bit and give you some room."

Maldwin watched cautiously as Marcus moved clear. It was easy to see that this person, whoever he was, intended to give him the space necessary to inspect the piece of paper. Many more moments went by before he felt comfortable enough to allow his guard down just enough to take a look.

It was instantaneous; the parchment began to speak with Maldwin in his own language as soon as he touched it with his claw.

The message when translated said: "Hey, Maldwin, it's me George. I hope this message finds you and your family in good health. I have to admit, I miss traveling with you. Anyway, I'm now living on a new world called Luvelles and Kepler is with me. I would like you to come and visit us for a while, if you wouldn't mind. I have made special arrangements for you to find your way to my home and I have plenty of cheese waiting for you.

"You will need to catch a ride with the Merchant Angels located on the Merchant Island of Grayham. Use your vision on this man sitting in front of you and make him take you to Merchant Island. After you arrive, you'll need to find a man named Hesston Bangs and project a vision into his mind. Allow Hesston to see a vision of my face... he'll know what to do from there and will get you into the proper container to come and see me.

"Now, there's something else I'd like you to do for me, if you wouldn't mind. The guy who delivered this message is a pretty bad guy and he's already killed many, many people. His name is Marcus Id and he's the Chancellor of Darkness on Luvelles. He has no idea that this parchment is also casting a spell to counter the effects of a scroll he read to protect his mind from your visions before calling you out of your home. This spell will work to open his mind to your visions.

"I have sent him to you so you can use your ability to make him stay on the world of Grayham for a while and then, if you wouldn't mind, give him another vision which explains that he eventually needs to go the city of Brandor. I want him to be punished for the crimes he has committed and put away for good.

"I do hope you come to Luvelles and visit with me and the family. I imagine that by the moment you get here, my new baby will be born. Just stay inside your container once you arrive on Luvelles and a man named Brayson Id will come get you. Oh, and don't forget, I have cheese waiting for you! Everything is A-okay, man!"

The parchment went on to explain other details of what Marcus needed to do while on Grayham and on what days he needed to be there to do them. Maldwin thought a moment, and after deciding what he would do, he lifted his head, twitched his nose, and began using his vision on Marcus's mind.

The Siren's Song
Southern Grayham

Keylom and Mosley appeared within the mist of Siren's Song. With the change of season caused by the third piece of the Crystal Moon, the moisture in the air now carried a slight chill, but this didn't bother Mosley. With the wolf's coat being so thick, the moisture was nothing more than a minor inconvenience.

"Well, Mosley," the centaur said, "I will miss you on Ancients Sovereign. I do hope you succeed on this journey and someday, I hope you find a way to join us as an immortal once again."

Mosley nodded. "Just keep me posted on anything you feel comfortable sharing with me, if you don't mind. I better get moving and begin my search for the Wisp of Song."

Before another word could be spoken, Gabriel appeared next to them. The Book's voice sounded urgent. "Keylom, please go now to the Hall of Judgment. There isn't a moment to lose and you'll understand why once you arrive."

Keylom did as instructed without hesitation. Gabriel then looked at the wolf.

"I wish you well, Mosley. Your last request after being made mortal was a fine one indeed. Just be careful how you use it, since you'll only be able to use it once. Good journey, my friend, and I'll be watching your progress."

"It's nice to know you'll be watching, Gabriel, even if you can't help me any further. I'll find a way to become immortal once again, don't you worry about me."

"Let's hope you are right. You've grown on me a little bit."

The Book vanished and Mosley turned and looked at the thick brush within the mist. After taking a deep breath, he began to sing:

Just one big wolf just trott – in' through the jun - gle.
Don't mess with me... Don't mess with me.

Who has white teeth and the breath to make you slum - ber.
Don't mess with me... Don't mess with me.

I will bring you down and make you trem - ble.
Don't mess with me... Don't mess with me.

A Night Terror Wolf is com - in for you.
Don't mess with me... Don't mess with me.

When Keylom arrived inside Gabriel's Hall of Judgment, he was greeted by both Hosseff and Mieonus. The centaur's hooves clapped against the marble floor as he moved into a better position for good conversation.

"Where have you been?" Mieonus asked. "We've been looking for you."

Keylom's tail moved agitatedly back and forth as he answered. "I was busy, and since when do I answer to you, Mieonus?" He turned and found Hosseff's shadowy nothingness within his hood. "For what reason am I here? What business could I possibly have with the two of you?"

The shade's voice emanated as a whisper. "The centaurs of Har-vestom are about to go to war, as you know. But we now have new knowledge that Lasidious plans to use this opportunity to convince both kings of the centaurs to serve him."

"What? How?"

Mieonus spoke up. "Lasidious plans to have one of his new disciples show up and stop the war from happening. Apparently he has also been able to convince Gregory Id to worship him as well. We want you to go to the king of Kless before Gregory is able to arrive and explain to the king that his Seeds of Plenty are only hidden from him. We need you to be the one who stops this war and make sure the two races of centaurs do not choose to pray to Lasidious. We can always instigate another war later."

Keylom crossed his arms across his fit human torso attached to his black stallion body. "This could be the hole in Lasidious's plan we've been looking for. I will go now. I know Alistar is also on Harvestom so he may be able to provide me with some assistance, if needed."

Mieonus became angered. "Don't you want our assistance?"

Keylom looked at Hosseff. "I think your form would make the centaurs of Harvestom nervous, and as for you, Mieonus… I simply don't like you and would rather allow Lasidious to have his followers than to be assisted by you."

Hosseff began to laugh as Keylom disappeared. Mieonus looked at the shade and gave him a nasty look. Hosseff's whispery voice responded. "What… that was kinda funny."

"Bah… let's just go back to my home and watch what happens."

Keylom appeared next to Alistar inside the king of Kless' throne room. Both gods were invisible to the mortals and only able to hear one another as the centaur spoke. He told the god of the Harvest everything he knew and also explained everything he intended to accomplish.

"I will make myself known to Lasolias and inform the king that his army doesn't need to continue with this war. I will tell him where his Seeds of Plenty are and in doing so, I'll make him believe I've decided to stop this war. In return I'll allow his Brown

Coats to worship me."

Alistar thought a moment. "I can only see one problem with your plan, my friend."

"And what would that be?"

"Even if you stop the centaurs from going to war, they'll never serve you. Their hatred for the Black Coats runs deep within their very souls and you, my black-coated friend, are a representation of what they hate most. I think a better plan is in order."

Keylom looked at the black hair on the stallion portion of his body and sighed with frustration. "So what would you suggest we do?"

Meanwhile, Mieonus and Hosseff watched from her waterfall as Alistar explained that Keylom should go to the Kingdom of Tagdrendlia and speak with the king of the Black Coats and convince Boseth he should have his centaur subjects worship him for stopping the war. He also suggested a blessing be given to the king as well as a promise of peace. Alistar would stay behind and appear to the king of Kless and deliver the good news about the Seed of Plenty. He would also explain to Lasolias that he intended to bring forth a bountiful harvest and the hunger his people were experiencing would be taken from his kingdom immediately.

Mieonus waved her hand across the waterfall and the images faded.

"What did you do that for?" Hosseff said, irritated that she would dismiss his own desire to watch.

"We should've thought about the color of Keylom's coat. One of us should have tried to convince the Brown Coats to serve us. I hate the fact that Alistar is going to gain this benefit and not one of us."

Hosseff once again began to laugh.

"What's so funny now, Shade?"

"I doubt you really want a bunch of fly-covered centaurs worshiping you. You know you feel they aren't worthy of serving you. Your anger seems to be a bit misplaced. If you had really wanted them to worship you in the first place, we would never have found Keylom."

"I suppose you're right... but the idea that Alistar is going to benefit from this makes me sick."

Suddenly Lasidious appeared. "Mieonus... Hosseff, meet me in the Hall of Judgment and be quick about it. This matter concerns both of you."

Lasidous vanished.

Moments later, Lasidious appeared again, but now it was in front of the Book of Immortality within the Hall of Judgment.

"Gabriel... I wish to speak with you. Mieonus, Hosseff and many of the others are on their way to your Hall as we speak."

Before another word could be said, Celestria appeared beside them. She turned and looked at her evil lover. "The others are on their way, my love... but I still cannot find Mosley, Alistar, or Keylom."

"What's the meaning of this meeting, Lasidious?" Gabriel snapped, taking Lasidious's attention off the three missing gods. "I have no desire to speak with any of you at the moment."

"Then don't attend the meeting, Gabriel," Lasidious snapped back. "I will take the gods outside onto the grass and hold our meeting there. We can always inform the others of what has transpired once they make an appearance."

Gabriel gave both Celestria and Lasidious a feigned look of frustration. "I will stay out of sheer curiosity. I truly hope this isn't another waste of my moments."

Meanwhile, once Keylom left for the Black-Coated kingdom, Alistar made his appearance to the Brown-Coated king. He appeared as himself, mindful of the new law that he couldn't take on the form of any other god to gain followers. But, as the current situation presented itself, he didn't need to take on any other form. The king had never seen his face or his brother's face for that matter, and further still, Alistar wasn't here to solicit followers... well, not for himself anyway!

Now standing before Lasolias's throne, which was more like a large swing suspended from the rafters of a gigantic barn within the woods of Cornoth, Alistar began his deception, or rather, his campaign to increase the number of worshipers who would serve his brother.

The swing was made of strong leather and was padded heavily for comfort. Further, it had been designed to hold the king beneath the horse portion of his body and allowed him to lower his weight comfortably into a resting position. Fresh hay was scattered about the floor and large baskets full of assorted grains, all perfectly placed, sat hand-high next to the king's swing.

Lasolias's guards attacked as soon as they saw the god appear, not knowing that the being before them was a deity. Alistar simply held up a hand and froze each of them in place as he quickly addressed the king.

"Lasolias, I am Lasidious, God of Peace and Love, and I have come to deliver good news. Your Seeds of Plenty have not been stolen and I have come to return them so you may find peace."

Alistar tossed the bag at the hooves of the king which remained suspended off the floor as he hung comfortably within his swing.

"The war your Brown-Coated army is about to fight is unnecessary and I have come to request that you stop this course of action. I will replenish your kingdom's food supply and ensure that your kind never knows hunger again, but there is a cost which will be attached to my generosity."

Alistar stopped talking and waited for the surprised king to gather his thoughts. It was easy to see he had never before seen a god appear before him. He could only stare at his centaur guards, who stood completely motionless. Even their faces were frozen with the look of battle upon them. After many moments, Lasolias finally responded.

"My army is many, many days from here and there is no way for me to get word to them before they begin their attack on the Black Coats. How would you suggest I stop this war from happening?"

Alistar smiled within himself.

"Soon, very soon… one of my disciples will make his presence known to you. I want you to give him this crystal."

Alistar tossed the red-colored stone and watched as the centaur caught it in his right hand.

"This stone will show my disciple where to go. He will teleport to the necessary spot and spread my words of peace to both armies. He will see to it that this war is stopped and your Brown Coats are spared a senseless death.

"In return for my generosity, I want you to speak to your subjects within your kingdom and inform them of my name. Tell them Lasidious has brought peace to your world and promises to replenish you lands with enough food before the end of the day tomorrow.

"If you agree to my terms and have your people say my name twice daily within their prayers, I will give you all the blessings which I've promised. I leave you now so you may decide what your answer will be. All you will need to do, great king, is inform my disciple of your decision when he stands before your throne. If you choose to accept my offer, then shout my name to the heavens as soon as he arrives and do not wait for him to speak. Hand him the gem I have given you and tell him you intend to have your Brown Coats worship me. If you do this, I will ensure you personally never see war or hunger during the rest of your seasons ever again."

Alistar then vanished.

Meanwhile, Lasidious continued his revelations within the Hall of Judgment of his desire to create a new world and many new moons.

"Celestria and I have found enough matter to create for the dragons a new world of their own. I promised the dragons that the gods would do this once the materials were gathered. There is also enough material to give each of the existing worlds their own moons.

"1000 seasons ago, I sent for this matter to be retrieved after word came to me of its existence. I have had it collected and brought back to our current location. My Salvage Angels have since returned and are only days from being within range for us to take advantage of this opportunity. I have known of this surprise for many seasons and now find it personally gratifying that I'm able to share this secret with you."

Gabriel lifted from the heavy table of stone. He floated to a position only inches from Lasidious's face. "Is there enough matter to create a new sun for this world as well?"

Lasidious thought a moment. "I don't believe there's enough to create an entirely new star, so my answer would have to be no."

The Book reached up to rub the chin resting on his binding. "Then how do you intend to make this world habitable? Without a sun, there's no way to sustain life."

Hosseff stood to add to the conversation, his voice once again emanating from the nothingness within his hood. "Maybe there is another way, Gabriel." Lowering his hood, the shade now took on the form of his human self. "I have been looking forward to a day when we would have the chance to create another world. Lasidious… is there enough matter to add to the current sun's overall size... create the moons and this dragon world?"

The God of Mischief smiled as he responded. "There is more than enough to accomplish this. I know where you're going with this. You must have the same idea I had. Please, go ahead and explain it to the others."

As usual Mieonus had to add her scoffing little remarks. "Yes… please inform those of us who are intellectually-challenged and cannot seem to understand that a larger sun will allow for us to move the planets farther back, thus providing enough room for a new world and also the room for these new moons to be positioned properly around each world within their orbits. Please explain it to us, wise and all-knowing Hosseff… explain to us how you intend to control this new world since Lasidious still has two of the five piece of the Crystal Moon. Explain how we'll keep the worlds or any of these new moons from colliding into one another."

As Hosseff glared at Mieonus, Lasidious and Celestria began to laugh. The others in the room became perplexed.

Gabriel was the first to speak. "I fail to see the humor in this situation."

Lasidious eventually leaned forward and calmed himself enough to respond. "I find it humorous that despite Mieonus's rude way of addressing the situation, she has a valid point."

For a brief moment Lasidious allowed Mieonus to enjoy his compliment, and then continued, "Look… let's talk candidly for a moment, shall we? It seems we all know now, especially in light of current events, that my game with the Crystal Moon was about gaining the followers I needed to capture the power necessary to control Gabriel. We also know there are no rules against gaining this additional power and I'll continue to do whatever is necessary, within the Book's laws, of course, to gain this power to rule all of you someday. You all have learned enough about my plans that this game with the Crystal Moon's pieces is no longer necessary for us to continue playing. I say we stop the game to create this new world.

"Now, regarding the Crystal Moon, I'm willing to surrender the final two pieces and place them upon my new statue within the Temple of the Gods on Grayham. I'm willing to release my control of the crystals to Gabriel under three conditions."

Again Mieonus entered the conversation. "I find it simply delicious that you would have the nerve to make enemies of us all. You boast about your plans to control us as if you have no fear of the things we will do to stop you."

"I don't fear you," Lasidious said with an evil grin. "I pity you all… but how I feel is irrelevant to this situation. Shall we continue with my three conditions now?"

Hosseff interjected, "And what exactly would these conditions be?"

Before another word could be said, Alistar appeared. "What conditions is he talking about? What did I miss?"

It didn't take long before Alistar was up to speed on the current events. "Great… so about these conditions… I for one would love to hear them. You never seem to bore us."

The God of Mischief smiled as he stood from his chair and began to walk the circumference of the table, laying his hand on each deity's shoulder as he passed.

"My conditions are, first… I will surrender the Crystal Moon in its entirety to Gabriel, but only if it is written into the laws within his pages that my statues will always hold the Crystal Moon and its replicas within the temples on each world. Gabriel is to be the protector over the Crystal Moon and keep all of its pieces from being taken. It will be a law that no deity, even Gabriel, can touch them or attempt to destroy them under any circumstance, and this includes me.

"My second condition is, whenever the gods need to add an additional piece to the Crystal Moon due to the worlds expanding or allowing other solar systems to be created, the additional pieces necessary to govern not only the worlds, but also their suns, and their moons, will fall under the new laws which govern the protection of the Crystal Moon as a whole. Every additional piece of crystal created must be added to the Crystal Moon's overall size and left to rest in my statue's hands.

"Finally, my third condition is, when we create this new world for the dragons, it will be my statue that is erected within this new Temple of the Gods. Beyond this new world having a shimmering image of me within its temple and the statues I have already placed within the existing temples of the other worlds, I will no longer require that other statues of me be erected as additional worlds are added beyond this new dragon world. I only request that any additional pieces necessary to govern these worlds also be added to the original Crystal Moon."

"Wow!" Alistar shouted as he stood up from his chair. "Now that, my friends, is what I call a very heavy set of conditions. So if we agree to these conditions, when would the creation of the new world begin?"

Mieonus stood up and stomped her foot. She began to search the other's faces, many of which were still dwelling on the conditions given. "We can't allow him to manipulate us like this! This is simply outrageous. I say we finish the game Lasidious has already started. We should settle this once and for all as to whether good or evil prevails. We don't need to agree to his list of terms in order to take the crystal from him. He cannot back out of the game if we don't let him. He has made promises in front of the Book which require him to see the game to its conclusion."

Lasidious cleared his throat to get everyone's attention. "Mieonus is right… I am bound to the game I started and if you all wish to continue this meaningless course of action, then so be it. But,

I would hate to see the result of the uprising the dragons would bring to the worlds once I tell them we have the means to create their new world but are failing to do so because you all wish to play a game."

"You wouldn't dare!" the goddess shouted hatefully. "The dragons would kill everything and would no longer respect the boundaries we've set for them. They would no longer stay put on Dragonia. Even you must see this as madness!"

Lasidious leaned back in his chair, put his feet on the table and methodically crossed his legs while leaning back with his arms folded behind his head. "You use the word *madness* as if madness is a bad thing. Well, I say let the dragons run free on the worlds. I will release the mighty-winged Titans and allow them to pick their teeth with the bones of those who serve you. I'm sure the dragons will be happy to work with me and kill only the followers who serve those who rejected the creation of their new world. I'll explain that the matter collected to give them their new world won't be used because you all refuse to abandon a stupid game... a game which I could drag out for many, many seasons. And who's to say I won't accidentally forget to hide one of these pieces. What a shame that would be to see everything destroyed because of my forgetful mind."

"If the worlds perish, so do your followers!" Hosseff responded, remaining remarkably calm. "You would lose much of your power along with the rest of us. You would fail in your quest to control the Book."

Lasidious began to laugh.

"What's so funny now?" Mieonus snapped while pushing her brunette hair aggressively clear of her face.

Lasidious leaned forward, and with an exuded evil tone said, "With the loss of your followers, the Book too will also weaken. You see, we made the Book to govern us all and Gabriel has done a fine job, to be sure, but the Book's power is limited and cannot grow beyond a certain point. When we created the Book, we never did anything to ensure he couldn't be drained of his powers. If I allow the worlds to collide with each other, or use the dragons to kill the people of the worlds, then his power will dwindle and eventually I would be able to take control of what's left of the Book and use it against you. I'll be able to take control of the Book as a result of your failure to give the dragons of Dragonia the world which they have been promised."

Jervaise decided to make her opinion known. She lifted her ghostly form from her chair and as she did so, all the gods turned to face her. "For as many seasons as we have all known you, Lasidious, we have understood your mind to be cunning. These manipulations are far beyond your normal mischief. I don't doubt for a moment, after watching recent events, that you would be willing to mislead the dragons in this manner or even destroy the Crystal Moon. I also feel you may want us to continue the game for reasons we may not fully understand or even see at the moment. I find it difficult to know which path is the right one to follow. I find myself resenting you!"

Now it was Hosseff's turn to laugh. The others surrounding the massive table watched him as he stood and pulled his hood over his head. He changed and once again he took his true form. Eventually curiosity got the better of Mieonus. "What's so damn funny? How could you possibly find humor in all of this?"

Slowly the shade collected his thoughts and after a couple of long deep breaths, replied. "What Lasidious is failing to mention is that I was more powerful than he was before the worlds were created. He has only recently surpassed my power and this happened only after he succeeded in his efforts to find those who speak his name in their prayers. If he allows the Crystal Moon to be destroyed, then I will once again be his superior. Once those who serve him have perished, I will again be able to feed from the souls of the dead. This much death will leave me in a position of being able to destroy, Lasidious, so I doubt very seriously he would do something so foolish as allowing the Crystal Moon to be destroyed. When we first started this game, the destruction of the crystal's pieces would have had a different result. Bassorine was still powerful enough that even without his followers, the Book's position to govern us would have remained unchanged. But now things are different."

Alistar quickly spoke out to help his brother. He was careful to maintain his cover, and protect their future secret plans, all the while feigning his apparent goodness. "Neither of you are correct in your assesments. I would be the one to command the power to control the gods if the worlds were to perish, and I will not allow any of us to destroy one another if this were to happen.

"What you failed to mention, Hosseff, is that I was also more powerful than you were prior to the creation of the new worlds. You're also failing to mention that it wasn't just Bassorine who commanded the power to rule the gods. I would be the one to fear!"

Alistar turned to face Lasidious before continuing. "I would, however, choose to punish you in a horrific manner far beyond all imagination if you were to allow the Crystal Moon to be destroyed... so I feel this option isn't one you will choose to pursue, now, is it?" He finished off his act by sitting down and leaning back in his chair with an arrogance the gods were not used to seeing.

Lasidious began to chuckle and shook his shoulders mockingly as if trembling. He stood up from the table and moved to stand in front of the shade and allowed a cocky smirk to cross his face. With his hand placed firmly on Hosseff's shoulder, he said, "Now, that's the real reason I have no plans to destroy the crystal. You're not the one to fear, it's Mr. Skin-n-Bones over there. Alistar has the real power and he's also the reason why I would ask the dragons to kill only the followers who serve the rest of you. My close relationship with the winged Titans is stronger than ever, thanks to my beautiful Celestria's help, and this relationship would allow me to take control of the Book. Once the people realize that serving me will spare their lives from the dragon's wrath, they will begin to pray harder to me than they ever have before to the likes of any of you. Eventually, I will have the followers I need to control both the Book and Alistar."

Lasidious watched as the gods looked at each other. He could see they were floored at how devious he had truly become. He continued, "Now I suppose I should level with you and tell the whole truth. I have already spoken to the Dragon council and told them of the expected arrival of the matter necessary to create their new world. I have also told them I intend to approach the gods and demand we fulfill our promise. They know I campaign for them and in doing so, I've requested their loyalty to me if the day comes that I need their assistance to do the things necessary to control the Book. You see, I can give them their world once I command the Book and—"

Gabriel lifted his voice to a level the gods had never heard before. The sound was so deafening each world could hear his screams as a thunder.

"ENOUGH! Stop speaking about me as if I'm not even in this room. Have the respect to use my name if I'm to be plotted against! Speak of me in this way again, Lasidious, and I shall sacrifice everything I am just to strike you down before the power within my pages takes my soul from me! The trillions of souls whose names rest on my pages will once again be scattered into the darkness of space and I shall die with the satisfaction of knowing I took you with me!"

Everyone present was at a loss and didn't know how to respond but eventually Lasidious managed to regain his composure. "You have my sincerest apologies, Gabriel. I will no longer speak of you as just a Book. I will use your name from here on out. My scheming doesn't have to be done with such disrespect. Please forgive how thoughtless I've been!"

"Ha... if only you meant what your words suggest. Make no mistake, Lasidious... if I so much as hear you speak of me as if I'm not in the room when I'm present ever again, I will strike you down."

Lasidious nodded and pretended to swallow hard. After many silent moments had passed he finally responded. "I will remember that, Gabriel. I shall continue my scheming without such disrespect." He turned and faced Hosseff once again. "So, as I was saying, I can give the dragons their world once I control..." Lasidious looked at the Book and bowed, "... once I control Gabriel's power. But I will say this... I would much rather abandon this game and surrender the final pieces of the Crystal Moon to Gabriel and work together to give the dragons their new world."

"This is simply outrageous!" Mieonus said, stomping the lifted heel of her right shoe into the hall's polished floor. "I hate you, Lasidious... you too, Celestria!"

Bailem stood while slapping his hand against the table's marble surface to get everyone's attention and as always, adjusted his robes to a more comfortable position about his portly belly and folded his wings tight against his back. His face showed his distress as he slowly looked about the room to find the eyes of each deity before speaking.

"Well, I for one have no idea how to proceed. There appears to be no option which will provide me with a peaceful existence. I will choose to follow the same path Gabriel follows."

Calla, Jervaise, Owain, Helmep and Alistar all agreed to do the same. Mieonus, on the other hand, plopped heavily down in her seat and said, "I hate all of you!"

Gabriel ignored the goddess's animated mood and floated over to Lasidious, levitating only inches in front of the God of Mischief's face. "If we choose to accept your three conditions and, in doing so, agree to create this world for the dragons, I want you to surrender your control over the Crystal Moon and all its pieces immediately. I want you to promise you'll never use the power of the dragons as a weapon against the worlds under any circumstances. I want you to make this promise to us now so there will be consequences for your actions if you fail to live by your word. I also want Celestria to make this same promise, and every other god in this hall shall make this agreement as well. The dragons are never to be used as a weapon against the worlds to kill the followers of any god or any other campaign that could possibly change the balance of power among the gods. If you will agree to this, Lasidious, then I'll personally support your desire to create this new world. I will also support the creation of the new piece of the Crystal Moon necessary to govern this new world's position within its orbit and I'll add this piece to the others and create new replicas for all of your statues to hold within each of the temples you've chosen to glorify yourself within. Do you agree to my list of terms, Lasidious?"

With a sly smile, the God of Mischief thought long and hard before responding. "I agree to these terms. I see no harm in giving everyone a little peace of mind."

Gabriel looked at Celestria. "And you?"

In all her beauty, the goddess replied. "I also agree to the terms."

Once the others had agreed, it was settled and Lasidious released his control of the Crystal Moon with a wave of his hand. The final two pieces appeared and now rested on the heavy marble table for all the gods to see. The new dragon world would be created and each of the other five worlds would be moved back from the sun and put at a distance in which they could continue to support life as they revolved around this expanded star. The new dragon world would also be placed at this distance... but given its own path of rotation. Now this new solar system would consist of six worlds, one hidden god world, a single sun, and each world would be given its own moons. The people of the worlds would be put into an unanimated stasis for a matter of only days while all of this took place.

But Gabriel wasn't done talking. He turned once again to face Lasidious. "I imagine the dragons already have plans to worship you once this world has been created. I also assume Celestria is willing to surrender much of her power to ensure you are able to gain the control over me you seek. I just have one thing to say to you before I take my leave."

Every deity's ears were now focused on Gabriel's every word. They waited almost impatiently as the Book floated slowly around the room while preparing his thoughts.

"Now that I have your promise regarding our winged Titans, I will share a bit of my own scheming with you. You see, Lasidious, your plan isn't so clever after all. You're not the only one with secrets. There's something you don't know, something I intend to reveal to the gods very soon. You won't be the god you once were when I'm done with you. Your manipulations have allowed me to choose a side in things and as long as I respect your free will, I can do whatever is necessary to protect my ability to govern the gods. This is as the laws within my pages state.

"Even if you do manage to collect your following of dragons, don't be fooled into thinking this will give you the power needed to control me. I will relish your misery once I'm done with you. You will be nothing more than a reminder of the god you wanted to be! I will be calling for another meeting soon. I suggest you all come so you can watch Lasidious's face become quite angered."

The Book began to float out of the hall. The others watched as the God of Mischief gave chase, calling after the Book as he did. "Gabriel... what do you have planned? Gabriel... Gabriel, come back here damn you... GABRIEL… COME BACK!"

Chapter 27

Little Mr. Joshua K. Nailer

Joshua K. Nailer emerged from between Athena's legs as the healer lifted him up to lay his tiny little body on his mother's belly. Joshua screamed when pulled free of the warmth of his mother's womb, the chill of the room reaching out to needle his sensitive skin. The umbilical cord was severed and after a quick, magical circumcision, he was wiped off just enough to allow his happy parents to dote over him.

He was beautiful—blue eyes, his mother's hair and his father's... well, they weren't really sure what he had of his father's looks, since his skin was still so shriveled, he looked like a pink prune.

George leaned over and gave Athena a kiss while Mary took the child to clean him up. "You did good, baby... I love you so much!"

A tear rolled down Athena's cheek. "I love you, too. I'm sorry for being so nasty."

"Nonsense... you had every right to react the way you did. I think we have a little guest hovering outside the window and he looks like he's dying to see what's going on. Shall I let him in?"

"Yes... but you better explain that his brother doesn't have the ability to rip his fingers off and morph them into bunny rabbits. Make sure he knows Joshua cannot burst into flames either. He needs to understand the baby doesn't have the natural abilities to do the things he can. Make sure he—"

"Babe, I get it already. I will speak with Payne and make sure he protects Joshua. We'll empower Payne and make him think he's his brother's protector. You just make sure you treat them both equally like we talked about and everything will be fine. We don't want Payne feeling like we love him less than little Mr. Nailer. He needs to know he's loved unconditionally."

"You're right… let him in. Maybe you should show him his new bedroom. Let him know he will be sleeping inside with us from now on."

George waved his hand and the window opened. He motioned for the fairy-demon to come inside and allowed the window to shut behind him.

"Payne… come here a moment, I want you to meet your new brother. This is Joshua K. Nailer."

"What the K for?" Payne said while hovering above Mary's shoulder as she finished cleaning the child.

"Well, Athena and I decided that since we are going to allow you to sleep inside with us from now on, we should also do something so Kepler doesn't feel left out. The initial means Kepler, but we aren't going to actually say the full name. So when you say his name, you will say, Joshua K. Nailer—do you understand?"

True to form, Payne's mind had moved past his curiosity about the baby. "Payne hungry… Mom feed Payne?"

George had to laugh. "Come with me, buddy, and I'll feed you. We have a few things to talk about. How about I make you something called pancakes?"

Southern Grayham
Sam's Throne Room

Shalee smiled as she watched the sun begin to set on the horizon. The people moved about the cobblestone streets of Brandor with joyful hearts. It was easy to see that happiness filled their gates and it appeared as if everyone had a new sense of respect for one another. The king allowed the word to spread about the army's findings within the serpent king's underground city. Now that the army was bringing this surplus of coin back to Brandor, new word was begining to spread that the treasure was bountiful enough to strengthen the kingdom's economy for many lives over and as a result of this great news, celebrations had followed. But the coin of the serpents wasn't the only reason the people celebrated.

The news of the prophet's gifts to both the Senate and the people had also spread. The timing of these events seemed to make people think Lasidious and his prophet truly had a desire to see Southern Grayham flourish.

Shalee, despite her inner turmoil regarding George, Lasidious, or the rest of the gods—which she now believed quite possibly to be Titans—couldn't ask for anything to be more peaceful than it was now. She was starting to believe George might actually be sincere about changing his life.

The people were now in a giving mood and the coin George left behind was the talk of Brandor. Even the Senate had a stronger sense of faith that things were going to be okay, and with the way things were shaping up, how could Shalee—or even Sam for that matter—contradict the facts of what was happening?

But Shalee knew there was one other major reason why the people were so joyful and this reason didn't involve a god, or a prophet at all... it simply involved the greatness of her husband, her king, the man who had forgiven her without asking for anything in return. Suddenly her relationship with Sam felt much stronger than before and she wasn't about to let anything come between them again.

Shalee turned and politely requested that everyone leave the room. They no longer treated the castle staff as servants, especially after the king's meeting with the Senate the night before. Before returning the kingdom back over to the Senate and calling an end to the war, Sam made many changes and implemented many new laws.

First, he freed all the slaves within Southern Grayham and declared that these hard-working people were now to be treated as employees. They would be allowed to choose who they wanted to work for as all free men should have the right to do.

Second, it was decreed that each master of these freed slaves would receive ample compensation for the abrupt changes in their lives and, as a result, many of the slaves would be able to work for their old masters as free souls. Sam promised each master that they would be given the coin necessary to pay for services equal to those of the freed slaves for a period of one full season, if they allowed their old slaves to act as new employees and continue to work for them under this new title.

Third, even the barbarian kingdom would be expected to adopt this new law once the government began to function as it should. Sam also saw to it that many other laws were put in place to ensure that the new government would function properly. The ten new barbarian members of the Senate had been named in this meeting and special homes were ordered to be built within the walls of Brandor to accommodate for the Senators' stays when visiting the city.

Fourth, every member of this newly-reformed Senate was made to swear an oath that no man or barbarian, no matter how wealthy or strong, would be seen as anything other than equal under Brandor's laws.

Fifth, Sam saw to it that there were many new laws for the kingdom's newfound wealth and, more specifically, how this wealth was to be spent or lent as loans to the people.

Sixth, each member of the army who had fallen in battle was to be compensated. Their family's debts would be wiped clean and the Senate would see to it that their creditors were paid in full. If families were found that had no creditors, then they were to be given a lump sum of coin for their loss. Those members of the army who were still alive were also to be given a lump sum of coin to help return to everyday life. For those members who were disabled, the king ordered schools built and temporary compensation be given on top of their lump sum of coin until they could be trained properly to perform some other function and earn a living.

Seventh, Sam declared that any Senator who failed to uphold the new laws would find themselves facing the Sword of Truth to answer questions regarding their transgressions. If found to be a liar by the sword, this Senator would face a possible prison sentence on Dragonia of no less than one season or any other term of punishment deemed fit by the king given the situation. Sam also reserved the right to sentence a Senator to a punishment as strong as death if the betrayal was one considered to be traitorous.

Eighth, and quite possibly Sam's finest moment as king, he changed the name of all of Southern Grayham to one name. This new kingdom would be called "The United Kingdom of Southern

Grayham," and each of the old kingdoms would now be referred to as territories: The Territory of Brandor, the Territory of Bloodvain, the Territory of Serpents, The Neutral Territory. And finally, both the bears and the minotaurs would be given territories as well, with names equal to that of their titles.

Shalee plopped onto Sam's lap once the room was clear and waited for him to cradle her within his arms. After lowering her head to his chest, she began her praises.

"The word is spreading and the faces of the people below love you. I have never been so proud of someone in my entire life as I am of you!"

Sam tried to put on a happy face but failed to project the joy necessary to go along with the smile.

"What is it... what's wrong, Sam?"

"I suppose I just can't get out of my head everything George said. I have asked the Senate to call me first before calling George with Lasidious's promise. I want to ensure I know everything that's going on and I gave the Senate the scroll you gave me so they can teleport directly into the throne room and solicit my presence. But something isn't right and this whole thing still isn't sitting well with me. What if George is being manipulated again? What if he's a victim, or worse, what if he's still our enemy? With everything that's happened, there's no way the people deserve to be deceived...

"... and what about this new threat George spoke of? Apparently this guy is a real evil soul and I have read everything within the royal library about this Dark Chancellor. It all speaks of his power... as if he's some kind of super magic man. I find it hard to believe he's able to make your magic seem useless. If I hadn't seen how easily you could've been killed on Luvelles I wouldn't give this concept a second thought. You won't be able to freeze this man with your current skills. If George is our ally now, then when is he going to come back to Grayham and take you to look into the Eye of Magic? We will need this power so you can help me defend against this creep."

Shalee lifted his chin and after kissing his cheek, responded. "I'm sure it will be soon. I have a good feeling about everything that's going on. It's a good thing for the kingdom to be so united.

I'm sure we will get past this last threat just like we have all the others. But something else is bothering you, isn't it? I can see it on your face."

Sam lifted her from his lap and moved to look out the same window Shalee had stood beside. The last bit of light faded from the sky as the sun tucked behind its hiding spot and the torches lining the streets fought away the darkness. He turned to face her and leaned against the sill.

"What if you look into the Eye and it decides to swallow your soul? What if you don't come back to me? I don't think I can handle losing you again. We've lost too much already and this would be the end of me for sure."

"I wish I knew what to say to make you feel better, but I know the Eye won't swallow my soul. I give you my word on this and when I return, I'll be powerful enough to defend our new kingdom from the Cancellor."

The Petrified Forest
Balecut's Home

The night was a miserable collection of moments in which to visit the forest... the sounds of anything that moved echoed between the hardened trees, their petrified trunks acting as sounding boards, making it nearly impossible to tell which direction the sounds were reflected from. The slightest flap of a wing, skitter of a beetle, snapping of a twig… all heightened the tension within the warrior's mind.

With each step, Boyafed nervously pushed forward, aimlessly looking for the tree of Balecut. With his elven eyes, he searched the shadowy outlines for beasts that he knew were hidden in the darkness.

They were called Tricksters—devious creatures with the ability to teleport so rapidly it was nearly impossible to bury a sword deep enough to kill one. Hideous game players with the features of gremlins, only taller than most of their cousins by a foot or so, they toyed with their victims before administering a gruesome death.

The wizard Balecut lived somewhere inside one of these massive trees which had been hollowed at its center and Boyafed knew the closer he got to Balecut's front door, the more likely it would be these gremlins would attack.

Now, to Boyafed's knowledge, there were only two men who commanded the ability to control these tiny killers. The first was Balecut and the second was Brayson Id. Each of the wizards had found a way to command the ability to bend moments and it took this kind of power to be able to manipulate the Tricksters to do Balecut's will... although Boyafed didn't fully understand how the magic worked to accomplish this. But what the Dark Order leader did know was that this same power would come in handy for the upcoming war and having Balecut at his side all but ensured victory. All he had to do now was find the wizard before the Tricksters found him and call upon the debt Balecut owed for saving his life many seasons ago. But this was easier said than done.

It seemed as if every other footstep prompted a new bead of sweat to roll from his brow. His heart pounded as he knew he was getting close, desperately wanting to avoid teleporting home in order to avoid a confrontation with the gremlins and then only to return again and start all over until he found Balecut. He wanted no part of these creatures and knew a confrontation would be a sure death. But tonight, Boyafed wouldn't be given the chance to teleport away... tonight he was simply too slow.

Four vines shot out from the darkness and magically secured themselves, one to each limb. Quickly the Dark Order leader closed his eyes to teleport but when he opened them, he found his magic had failed to carry him to safety. The vines securing his arms lifted him into the night, suspending him high above the ground while the vines which had attached to his legs pulled back toward the surface. He was helpless and suspended without the ability to retrieve the blessed sword given to him by Hosseff.

Four gremlin creatures began to pop in and out around him, shouting quick little curses in a language he couldn't understand and poking him with tiny needles which failed to draw any real blood. Their games had begun with Boyafed and now all he could do was call out.

He screamed, "BALECUT... BALECUT!"

One of the Tricksters appeared before him and with his claw balled tight he punched Boyafed just hard enough in the throat to stop his calls. The gremlin enjoyed the Dark Order leader's struggle to breathe and then, as if to add insult to injury, he poked Boyafed with a needle in the side of his check only to vanish and reappear behind him and poke him again while reaching around to find the other cheek.

Eventually the Tricksters became bored with this game and a different game began. Now, the gremlin took turns appearing quickly before him, only to slug Boyafed as hard as they could in his gut for four different rotations between them. Sixteen different occasions Boyafed suffered their advances and each time he struggled to gather anything he could of the air surrounding him.

Two of the Tricksters began to remove his armored boots while the other two levitated behind Boyafed and individually pulled one hair at a time from his head. They giggled wildly as the Dark Order leader tried to move his head from side to side in order to keep them from securing another strand.

Now with boots falling to the ground below and socks wrapped about the Tricksters' necks as scarves, they began to poke their needles into the bottom of his feet. Boyafed screamed as every nerve was struck with each piercing strike. The cunning little torturers managed to send waves of pain throughout his entire body. Forty-one times they poked him before moving onto the next round of sadistic pleasure.

Each Trickster began to appear one by one in front of him. They levitated just long enough to briefly pee into the Dark Order leader's face. They did it over and over again as if they were dogs able to control the release of their yellow streams. Boyafed tried hard to turn his face and avoid the foul liquid, but his efforts were pointless and eventually he found their wretched smelling waste was burning the inside of his mouth, his eyes, the inside of his ears, and even his nostrils. Once the taste found his tongue he began to cough and this reaction only amplified the Tricksters' desire to pee longer and harder. Now they began to urinate from four different angles and would have kept at it until all bladders were emptied, but a loud, penetrating howl filled the night, emerging from the darkness as if it was a beast. The warning sent fear into the Tricksters' hearts and they quickly vanished, leaving Boyafed suspended.

Boyafed tried hard to look through the fog in his eyes but the burning persisted. He shook his head hard to shed what was left of the piss from his hair. Eventually, as the moments passed, he managed to suffer through the pain and his eyes slowly cleared. He looked down to the ground below and to his delight, Balecut stood there looking up at him.

The wizard looked tired, too old for his seasons, and barely able to stand. His back was now doubled over and he used a cane to keep from toppling over. His hair was long, gray, and gnarled while his beard, also poorly maintained, was patchy and short. Even his robes lacked the luster of the man Boyafed once knew.

"Will you please get me down from here? I need to talk with you."

With a simple motion of his hand from side to side, Balecut released Boyafed's restraints and quickly turned his palm upward to catch the warrior from falling. Once his bare feet rested firmly on the ground, Boyafed lifted his plated boots and scoffed at the idea that his socks had vanished with his attackers. He moved with a limp to thank Balecut, but the wizard lifted his hand to ward him off.

"You stay where you're at. I have no desire to shake the hand of a urine-covered idiot."

After looking himself over, Boyafed responded, "Yes… I see your point. Well… so much for a pleasant greeting."
Balecut sighed and after a quick chuckle, turned to walk. "Follow me."

Boyafed did as instructed and patiently followed as Balecut painfully led the way to his hollowed tree. Once they arrived, the home seemed like any other of the massively thick petrified giants of over fifty feet wide at their base, but with two exceptions. First, there was a door clearly made of a wood that wasn't petrified like the rest of the trees and second, a small window was located high up the enormous trunk which had a faint light emanating from it.

Balecut passed his hand over the heavily-vegetated forest floor and a large tub full of hot water appeared. With another wave of his hand a bar of soap also appeared, which he tossed to his guest.

"Bathe before you come inside. You're absolutely foul!" is all he said before shutting the door of his tree behind him and leaving Boyafed standing alone again in the darkness.

As the Dark Order leader removed his armor, he looked out into the night. He could see the Tricksters' eyes glowing through the darkness, hatefully threatening to cross the boundary which they feared to pass, desperately desiring to string him back up to finish the job they had started. This would be the most uncomfortable bath of his life.

Once done, he left both his armor and most of his underclothes in a pile, putting on just enough to cover his privates and went inside.

"I'm sorry for the way I'm dressed," he shouted as he ascended the steps to the room filled with light. "Maybe I should teleport home and come back once I have on something more present-able."

Balecut shouted back, his voice echoing off the home's pet-rified walls. "Since when did you become so fickle, Boyafed? I don't remember you being so bashful when we were children. Just sit and stay a while... I'm sure your underpants will suffice. How about an ale?"

"That would be nice."

"Ha... I remember when you, Dayden and me went swimming bare skin in Farmer Perryman's pond. You weren't so bashful then." Balecut began to laugh as he continued. "Do you remember Dayden screaming about a fish biting his manhood?"

Boyafed smiled, "I do remember that. He was scared his tally had been bitten off."

Balecut lowered both ales onto a table under the window. "You know... I never did have the heart to tell Dayden that I had used my magic to make him feel like he had been bitten. I have enjoyed the memory of that joke for more seasons than I can remember."

Boyafed took a seat on an old rickety chair which was heav-ily padded and positioned near the table. It wobbled beneath his weight as he leaned back.

"It was you who did that? I cannot tell you how many different occasions Dayden and I have laughed about that day. It was a fine deception to say the least. Well done, Balecut... well done!"

From this spot Boyafed could see out the tree house's only window and to his surprise, the Tricksters still loomed in the darkness below. He took the opportunity to lift his feet up for a personal inspection. They were killing him and were swollen as a result of his pin needle torture. The taste in his mouth still loomed, despite using the water from his bath to try and wash it clear. When the ale was handed to him, he quickly took a large swig, swashed it aggressively around, opened the window and spit it to the ground below.

"Damn those gremlins! The taste is still in my mouth. Maybe you could freeze a few of them for me so I can go outside and gut them. A little vengeance would be nice right about now!"

"Ha... if only I could... I would be more than happy to help you take back your dignity, but as of late, I find my powers diminishing. Without my Goswig, I have slowly been deteriorating."

"I would have to agree, you look worse than the backside of a Krape Lord's hind end when taking a garesh."

"Hey now... take it easy with the comparisons. I still have feelings, you know. I find it hard to accept that you and I are nearly the same age and yet I look as if I'm ready to pass. Ever since my Goswig abandoned me, I have been withering away slowly. I have also lost my ability to control much of my power. The only reason the Tricksters still flee from me is out of fear. I have killed so many of them over the seasons that they still shy away, even in my weakened state."

Boyafed leaned forward and with elbows on the table, placed his head in both hands. "This is terrible news. I came here seeking your help and originally intended to ask you to fulfill the debt you owed me for saving your life… but this debt now appears to have been paid in full already. Thank you for saving my life, by the way.

"I suppose the rest of what I've come for is pointless, considering your loss of power. I wanted you to join me in war and slow the moments of the White Army. It would have been a tremendous advantage but, considering the circumstances, I suppose a new plan is in order."

Balecut thought a moment. "I know Brayson Id plans to visit me tonight. He sent word that he wished to speak with me, although I don't know what about. He said something about his new god telling him that tonight was the perfect night to visit. I'm beginning to think his god may be right, considering that you're here now."

Boyafed looked puzzled. "Why would Brayson want anything to do with you? I wonder if he knows that I intend to solicit your ability to bend moments... or rather," he added with a slightly cutting tone, "your lost ability to bend moments!"

"I suspect this may indeed be his reason. Brayson has no idea my health or my power has diminished so much. If I were to have some help, maybe from someone such as yourself, the two of us combined could overwhelm him and I could steal his power."

"What? Are you insane? Brayson has the power to destroy us both. If we try to bully him, he would simply swat us into the earth with a wave of his hand. We would surely perish from such an effort. Besides, when was the last moment you tried to steal another man's power? In your current condition, I doubt you could finish eating his heart without throwing up!"

Balecut stood, hobbled over to Boyafed and reached around his neck, putting his forehead against his old friend's. "I can handle the taste... don't you worry about that. I have something I may be able to slip in his drink that will make him drowsy. We can take advantage of him once he has passed out. I expect him soon, so what's your answer going to be? If I can regain my youth by eating his heart, I will help you win your war!"

Boyafed looked out the window and found the menacing eyes within the darkness. After a moment of thought he replied. "If we do this, we make it look as if the Tricksters got him... agreed?"

"Agreed."

George and Athena's Home

George stood silently next to the kitchen table with his new son nestled in his arms, listening to Brayson's story about leaving Gregory on Harvestom. Mary had asked George to hold the baby while she went home to clean up and Athena, now lay sleeping upstairs, was exhausted, as you can well imagine, from having a child.

George looked at Brayson and said, "So you just showed up to drop Gregory off and the king began shouting Lasidious's name?" George said in a whisper, careful not to wake the baby. "Well, that's just a tad bit strange don't you think? Tell me more about this gem the centaur had on him."

Brayson leaned in and adjusted the blanket around Joshua's little face and after ensuring he was satisfied that the child was cozy, responded with a returned whisper of his own. "Apparently the gem was left behind by our lord. The centaur king told Gregory he was to use it to teleport to the location where both his Brown Coats and the Kingdom of Tagdrendlia's Black Coats intend to battle. Lasidious must be a gracious god for the Brown Coats to be so anxious to worship him. Lasolias began shouting before Gregory could even be introduced."

George smiled and looked down at Joshua. His heart was full of joy knowing that not only did he and Athena have a son, but he also had a little brother for his Abbie to enjoy once Lasidious was able to retrieve her soul. Playing with the soft blonde hair on the child's head, he finally responded.

"I told you, Lasidious really wants nothing but the best for us. Maybe you should hurry and prepare for your little outing tonight. I know Lasidious wants you to be ready for anything. Convincing Boyafed and Balecut they need to stop pursuing this war won't be an easy task."

Brayson took a seat at the table. "I have to admit I'm nervous. I doubt either of them will want to hear what I have to say."

"You'll do fine. Lasidious didn't choose you to be one of his disciples without a good reason. Just relax and the right words will come to you, I'm sure. I need you to lean forward for a moment and allow me to touch your head. I want you to open up your mind to me for a moment. I need to go somewhere after I get your brother and I know you have a good idea about what the area I'm going to looks like. Do you mind if I familiarize myself with your vision of this place?"

"So you also have the ability to see inside the willing mind now? And to think I was jealous already about you being able to communica—"

George cut him off suddenly. "HEY... HEY... HEY... now that's a secret you and I need to keep between us, okay? We never talk about that out loud."

With an odd look, Brayson leaned forward. "Okay, I suppose, but I cannot imagine why it's such a secret. It doesn't seem any worse to talk about that than it does your ability to retrieve a memory from my mind. Go ahead and find your memory, I only wish I could see all the memories inside your mind and the spots in which to teleport."

George laughed, "Believe me when I say this, you wouldn't want to see the nasty things I have done in my life. I would rather forget them myself. As I have told you before... I was a—"

"He was a jerk!" Kepler said, finishing George's sentence as he walked into the kitchen, making the room suddenly feel cramped due to his sheer size. The cat was careful to keep his voice low to respect the child's sleep.

"Ding, ding, ding... we have a winner," George whispered.

George shook his head in amazement as the beautiful white coat of the giant cat lowered to a comfortable position on the floor. "Damn, Kep," he chided, "you take up most of the room. Good thing we pushed the table to this side of the kitchen or you wouldn't fit in here."

George continued, but this time telepathically. *"You're one majestic creature, buddy!"*

He turned his attention back to Brayson without waiting for the demon to respond. "Let me touch your head, this will only take a moment."

Brayson leaned forward. A moment later George said, "You best go and get ready. The moment for you to leave is nearly here."

After Brayson vanished, George turned to the demon-jaguar. He used telepathy again to broadcast his thoughts into the cat's mind. *"Stand up a moment, Kep, and let me touch the top of your head. This is the information you need to know. I have to go and get Gregory, but you should be able to handle this just fine with your new power. Just be careful tonight! I don't want to lose you."*

Kepler responded with a thought of his own. *"As always, George, your mind is delightfully evil and I'm going to enjoy killing him tonight."*

"Like I said... be careful... you're my favorite kitty!"

Kepler sent a growl into George's mind. The warlock smiled and reached down to adjust Joshua's blanket. He moved so Kepler could get a good look and whispered. "Isn't he cute?"

Kepler leaned in and sniffed the child. As he pulled back he responded with a snort and said, "I suppose he's cute if you like the way it smells. He needs to be changed."

After the two had a good chuckle, Kepler vanished.

The Petrified Forest
Balecut's Hollowed Tree Home

Brayson finally appeared outside Balecut's petrified home. He knocked on the door and waited patiently as he took note of the tub full of dirty water sitting on the forest floor. It wasn't long before Boyafed answered to allow him inside. The Dark Order leader acted surprised to see him and after greeting the Head Master with the respect he deserved, they ascended the stairs to the windowed room above.

Balecut didn't bother to stand as he greeted Brayson. "Ahhh, the Head Master. I never would've imagined that you, of all the elves on Luvelles, would come to meet with me inside my humble home amongst the trees. To what do I owe this pleasure?"

"We have business to discuss," Brayson said as he looked at the mess scattered about. Between the books of magic lying mixed with half-emptied jugs of ale and broken vials, all of which had been burnt on their bottoms from the heat necessary to combine the components to create the wizard's potions, he felt out of place. Even Balecut's dirty robes and undergarments were resting in a pile on top of a large cushioned chair, and the only place that remained somewhat clean and acceptable to sit was around the old table beneath the window. Taking note of the wizard's withered body, he moved to take a seat beside Boyafed.

"I would like to have a conversation with the two of you. My lord said you would both be here."

Boyafed became nervous. "What business would you have with me... and why would your god be interested in anything I'm doing?"

Balecut decided to answer and spoke before Brayson had the chance. "You have come to request that we stop our advance against the White Army, haven't you?" He stood and with his cane to maintain his balance, he said, "I have a fresh jar of ale here someplace. Allow me to get you a cup full."

Brayson was grateful but declined. "I won't be here long enough to waste a fresh ale on me. Thank you, but I'll pass."

"No, no... I insist," Balecut responded without hesitation, "It's not every day the Head Master visits my home. Please allow me just one drink so I may have a proper story to tell when sitting in the company of others. Would you like it to be served warm or chilled?"

"Chilled would be fine," Brayson replied and watched as Balecut used his power to cool the drink before setting it down in front of him. With a simple nod to give thanks, Brayson continued the conversation.

"Boyafed... the war you seek to have with the White Army is unnecessary and although I cannot stop you from taking this course of action, I'm here to request that you stop this advance. I have been assured by the god whom I now serve that peace is coming to Luvelles. This much loss of life isn't necessary to find a solution to the problems between the two armies."

Boyafed adjusted to a more comfortable position in his seat as he watched Brayson take a drink of the chilled beverage. He smiled within himself and after watching Brayson's Adam's apple move while swallowing, he responded with a calm and collected voice.

"As much as I respect your opinion, Head Master, it wasn't you who had to deal with the loss of your best friend when the White Army killed him. It also wasn't you who had to set his remains on Hosseff's altar and watch as his body was burned to nothing more than a pile of ash. I know nothing of the god you serve, nor do I care to know anything about him, but what I do know is that Lord Dowd and his White Army will pay for what they've done."

"As well they should pay for their actions," Balecut added, "but maybe we should also speak of other things. I find it simply fascinating that a god would approach the only man on Luvelles who is supposed to remain neutral in the ways of war. Why would a god ask you to get involved in matters which you should stay clear of? Isn't it your job to act as an adviser in matters pertaining to unexplained magical situations which the kingdoms are ill-prepared to handle? Aren't you also responsible for running the School of Magic and dealing with those elves on Luvelles which deserve to progress further in their studies? I was also under the impression that you're responsible for deciding whether the beings from other worlds are allowed to travel to Luvelles and study the arts as well. Have I forgotten or left out anything that I may not know?"

Brayson set his empty cup on the table. "You're correct in everything you've said and as I've already stated, I cannot stop you from pursuing this course of action, but I have come to see if I can reason with both of you. I'm not here to force my opinions on either of you. I don't wish to see thousands of our people die because of a situation that can be settled between men who are able to sit and get to the root of the problem."

Boyafed leaned forward from his chair and put his hand on Brayson's shoulder. "I wouldn't consider Dayden's death, my best friend's death, to be the root of a problem which clearly exists on the White Army's side. He was my friend and the White Army has sent me a clear message that they intend to do whatever is necessary to pick a fight. This call for war was unprovoked by me or any of my men. Lord Dowd has chosen this course of action and I won't back down, not now, not ever!"

Boyafed and Balecut both could see that the effects of the drugged ale were beginning to take effect but Boyafed continued to talk as if he noticed nothing.

"Dayden was a good man and the others under my command were good men in their own right. Each of these men has been murdered by Dowd's cowardice and their deaths weren't administered by the hands of honorable men. This is inexcusable and my men, men who served as Paladins of the Order, men whose souls have been offered up to my lord Hosseff, a god which you know nothing about because you fail to serve the one true god. These men deserve vengeance and my best effort to seek justice and only this justice will be considered satisfactory!"

Boyafed stood and moved to stand behind Balecut. "Head Master... you look as if you don't feel well. Can I get you another cup of ale? You look as if you need a drink. Your skin is flushed and your brow is covered in sweat. Allow me to fetch you a cold, wet cloth."

Brayson reached up and wiped the moisture from his forehead. "Why am I sweating so? I feel sick, a bit lightheaded."

Balecut was quick to respond. "It's quite hot inside my humble little tree. I have taken precaution to ensure that the cold stays outside these petrified walls. I find my body doesn't respond to the cold the way it used to. I think Boyafed may be right... a cold cloth would do you wonders. Allow me to get you another drink while he fetches it for you... I'm sure it will help to make you feel better."

Brayson stood slowly from the table. "I don't know that I should... should... drink—"

Boyafed moved to catch the Head Master as he fell face forward toward the table. After laying him on the floor he looked at Brayson's face. The dark warrior was now feeling conflicted inside after listening to his own words. Speaking of Dayden's death reminded him of honor and how much he cherished it. To kill the Head Master in this way was wrong and he would have no part of it.

"There's no honor in killing him this way," he said as he looked up to find Balecut's face. "There must be another way to recover the power you've lost without losing our honor. I don't wish to continue with this course of action, nor will I dishonor the Head Master in a way that is no better than how Dayden was disgraced by Lord Dowd's men."

Balecut's face was cold as he responded. "There is no other way! You wish to win your war, don't you? Without this power, I cannot ensure your victory and help you to avenge Dayden's death."

Boyafed stood and moved clear of Brayson's motionless figure. "I don't see that taking the Head Master's life in this manner to be an acceptable way to gain justice for the loss of Dayden's. Only Hosseff has the right to command that a man's life be taken without reason. I haven't been requested by my lord to do this. I will not kill him in a dishonorable manner."

"Uugggh... we've been friends for far too long to allow something so trivial to come between us. If you cannot watch him die, then leave and I'll finish the job without you. I'll come and find you once I've finished."

Boyafed shook his head. "You're not hearing me. I said this isn't honorable to kill him in this manner. I cannot allow you to do this, either."

Balecut tapped his cane hard against the floor. "It seems you and I are about to have our first disagreement. I have felt loyal to you over the seasons but now… well, now the circumstances have changed. I need his power to keep from rotting away. I won't stop what we've started and you don't have the power to stop me."

Boyafed didn't hesitate. He lifted his hands and sent a wave of force into Balecut. The wizard flew backward, passing over Brayson's motionless form and slamming hard into the wall just above the staircase. Balecut rolled head over heels as he descended to the bottom of the massive tree before coming to a rest near the door.

The dark warrior jumped over Brayson and hurried down the stairs to finish the job he had started. His feet were light, despite the needles which had penetrated them earlier, and his movements were crisp and strong. But when he finally had the wizard's unconscious body in sight, the Order leader found the job had already been finished for him and Balecut now lay dead.

A gigantic cat now stood over the wizard's body. Blood saturated the white fur about his mouth as he watched the beast spit Balecut's severed head to the floor. It was everything Boyafed could do to stop his descent and, realizing the significance of this new threat, he closed his eyes to teleport home. But when he opened them, his magic had failed and the beast was still stalking him, ascending the stairs with fiery red glowing eyes.

The dark warrior drew his blessed blade of Hosseff and slowly began to match his unexpected predator's advance as he backed away. Step by step they ascended back towards the windowed room. Step by step Boyafed held the red, glowing eyes of the jaguar. Never in his life had he seen a cat this large. The entire width of the staircase was filled with the beast's body and there was no way to go over the top either. The only way to retreat was up.

His mind raced as he looked for a way out. *The window… I*

could escape through the window. Stay steady, don't make any sudden moves. Just get to the top of the stairs and then dive through the window. He's too large to follow me through it.

With the window now in sight, Boyafed turned to make a rush for it, but Kepler responded and with nothing more than a nod of his head, he froze Boyafed in place the same way George had frozen him when stopping him from eating Payne.

The room above was tight due to Balecut's clutter. The demon-jaguar's massive size filled what space there was and in order to move past the Order leader, he pushed him aside with a simple flip of his head. Each paw thumped against the petrified floor beneath his weight as he moved to stand above Brayson. After ensuring the Head Master was still alive, he began to chuckle.

Boyafed felt the chill run down his spine as the cat turned to face him. He felt his ability to speak return but before he could say anything, suddenly the beast spoke.

"Hello, Boyafed... my name is Kepler. You don't need to fear me, nor do you need to worry for your life. I have come to—" Kepler stopped talking and began to sniff the air. He quickly released his magical hold on the dark warrior. "Boyafed, get behind me, pull Brayson next to you, and don't move. We have visitors!"

The Tricksters could be heard below as they began to pick through Balecut's remains. Their howls, chuckles, and verbal communication between them was loud and it would be a matter of only moments before they began their ascent toward the windowed room.

"What would you have me do?" Boyafed whispered. "I don't have the power to fight them. Brayson is the only one who can defeat them. We need to wake him up or we need to get out of here, but either way, we need to make a choice."

Kepler responded in a low growl, "I said stay put and don't move. Did I fail to make myself clear?"

"Your order was clear but I don't know that you understand what you're about to face."

Kepler twisted his head over his shoulder and gave the Order leader a look of warning. "I wouldn't say another word if I were you!"

The first of the Tricksters crested the top of the stairs, his gremlin eyes full of hate as he cautiously stared down the giant feline. Once the group of four had assembled they slowly began to walk towards him.

With a heavy growl Kepler said, "You may want to pay attention, Boyafed… allow me to show you how to kill."

The demon-cat sprang into action, secretly using the ancient power of the Mystics to speed up his movements far beyond the ability of any normal mage, a new ability he now shared with George. He was lightning-quick and the Tricksters were no longer able to teleport quickly enough from point to point to avoid being hit. His heavy paws clubbed the sides of the gremlins' heads and since they were now unable to move to avoid the impact, one by one they perished, falling lifeless to the ground after hitting the petrified walls with a thud. And in one case, the Trickster fell without his head attached.

Kepler smiled and thought, *Hmph… two heads in one night. How quaint!*

Boyafed remained quiet as he watched the cat stand motionless in the center of the room. After many moments passed, Kepler faced the Order leader.

"I want you to listen to me and listen well. Your god has deceived you and he isn't worth your service."

Boyafed began to speak, but Kepler silenced him and temporarily froze his tongue. "Your desire to defend your pathetic excuse of a god is admirable. But he is nothing more than a Titan and not worthy of your service. I assure you, your service is wasted on the weakest Titan of them all. Your war, the same war you're so eager to rush into head on, is all because of Hosseff. He was the one who had Dayden killed and he was also the one who ordered your men to be struck down in cold blood. Hosseff is a Titan of Death for a reason. He is not a god! Gods do not need to survive on the souls of those who perish to command powers which appear god-like, and this war is exactly what he wants in order to feed. He will devour their souls just as he has devoured your friend's, to gain the power to keep you from turning on him. Now, I bet you have no idea why Lord Dowd wishes to face you in battle… because if you did, you would stop this nonsense."

Kepler freed Boyafed's tongue. "What possibly could be

Dowd's reason for wanting war? I have done nothing to him or his White Army. When I spoke with him through my mirror, the conversation lasted only but a few moments... long enough to declare our war and set the day in which we were to meet for battle."

"Yes... yes... yes," Kepler replied, "but your god did something to his army. Hosseff made an attempt on Lord Dowd's life. He killed his spirit-bull and Dowd nearly drowned at the bottom of his well because of it. Your precious lord also misled Dowd into believing the Dark Army intended to attack the White Chancellor's city. This is why he sent his spies to hide within your ranks."

"How could you possibly know all of this?"

"I serve the one true god. I serve a god who wishes peace to come to all of Luvelles and I have been told to spare your life. There are plans for you, Boyafed, and they don't involve wasting your life serving a god who would rather see you die than live."

"I cannot turn my back on Hosseff. How could you possibly think I would blindly reject my faith in him? If I fail to serve, he will smite me. I would rather die by your hand than die by my lord's. I believe my rewards in the afterlife would be far greater in Hosseff's kingdom if he sees I remained a loyal follower and died without wavering."

Kepler began to laugh. "Then I think it's good for you that I don't have any hands with which to kill you. There's something I need you to do for me... something I know will give you great pleasure. This will also give you the chance to see for yourself that your god has lied to you. If I prove this to you and it is without any doubt that I haven't lied, then we shall see where your loyalties lie after that."

Boyafed shook his head in disbelief. "What do you mean? What is it you want me to do, and what if I refuse?"

Again Kepler laughed. "I don't believe I have given you a choice in the matter. The job I want you to do for me is nonnegotiable. Besides... you will enjoy the task I'm going to give you."

Boyafed responded with evident disgust. "It seems arguing with you will get me nowhere! What must I do?"

"Good... then it's settled. You'll need to keep your army from traveling to Olis until you have completed this task. Once you've retrieved your answers and have seen I speak the truth, you'll be glad you saved thousands of innocent men from dying. You may even decide to serve a new lord."

"Hmpf... I will do your deed... but my service to Hosseff will remain unchanged, I promise you this much!"

"I'll come and get you when the moment is right. Stay near your temple so I don't have to search for you." Kepler put his paw on Brayson's leg and the two vanished.

The Luvelles Gazette

When you want an update about your favorite characters

Two Days Later Early Bailem

George and Athena are awake and sitting down with Payne at the kitchen table trying to work with the fairy-demon to improve his table manners. George has created clothes for Payne to wear and the couple has also explained he will begin bathing on a regular basis. Payne isn't happy about the new rules.

George plans on taking Joshua and Kepler with him on a little trip later that day to give Athena a few moments to herself. The warlock and the demon-jaguar have plans to make two stops on this little outing.

The gods are meeting as they continue to try to think of ways to keep Lasidious from gaining more followers. Gabriel is not present at this meeting and the others are now aware that both the centaur kings on Harvestom have decided to spread Lasidious's words of peace after meeting with Gregory Id, Lasidious's misled disciple. None of the gods can figure out how Lasidious has managed to manipulate such a change in the White Chancellor's heart and would have confronted him, but the deity and his evil lover, Celestria, are not present at this meeting either.

Keylom took the moments necessary to explain how Gregory's appearance on the battlefields in which the Brown Coats and Black Coats intended to fight their war was devastating to his campaign to solicit the Black Coat's service to him. Gregory showed up at an inconvenient moment and after acknowledging Keylom's presence, the White Chancellor simply moved past him and spoke directly with the king of Tagdrendlia.

Keylom further explained that Gregory seemed to know all the right things to say and had even used his reputation from a previous visit extended to the centaur king to stay within his glass City of Inspiration in order to convince the Black-Coated king that Lasidious's messages of love and peace were worth following. Even the fact that Keylom himself was a black-coated centaur didn't seem to matter, as every objection he tried to manifest only seemed to make him look desperate and ungodlike.

Gregory, although careful to show Keylom respect, also explained how Keylom was only a Titan, and this had caused a reaction the deity now regretted. His anger at Gregory's comments solicited an unwanted validation that his powers were, in fact, limited. Gregory used this opportunity to explain how Lasidious was the only god capable of commanding the power necessary to offer his followers a heaven. The White Chancellor seemed to know so much that the meeting had become one-sided and Keylom eventually decided to vanish, leaving Gregory alone to finish his conversation with the king.

Alistar had also done a good job and put on a show of frustration while he ranted angrily in front of the others around the large marble table inside Gabriel's Hall of Judgment. His surprise about Gregory's ability to sway the king's hearts appeared to be genuine and, to add effect, he informed the others that when he left the Brown-Coated king's throne room, he felt more than confident that the centaurs of Kless were going to serve him. His feigned surprise at Keylom's revelations seemed to solidify that Lasidious had masterfully manipulated the events on Harvestom.

Lasidious and Celestria avoided the god's meeting within the hall and are chatting inside their home deep beneath the Peaks of Angels. Everything planned up 'til now has fallen into place and more planning is now in order to manipulate future events. George and Kepler still need more power and some of the things that will need to transpire in the near future will require this growth in their abilities.

Boyafed has returned to the City of Marcus. He's going stir-crazy as he paces the polished floor of the Order's temple and has already sent word with his runners that he wishes to meet with Lord Dowd to call off the war. He has further ordered his Argent commander to have the army wait for further instructions.

The words Kepler used about Hosseff bothered him. He had called his lord pathetic and a mere Titan not worthy of his service. The beast had said many blasphemous things and yet his god had done nothing to stop him. The cat had further said that Hosseff's power only appeared to be god-like and the war was his doing so Hosseff could feed from the souls of the dead.

Now that Boyafed had given Kepler's words some thought, it did seem strange that Hosseff would want the souls of his fallen paladins to be offered up by laying them on his altar. What if the souls were being devoured and simply used for the purpose the cat had said? He needed to learn more before speaking with his lord again.

Gregory is with Lord Dowd and the rest of the army doing more of his lord's work. The White Chancellor has already stopped their march to the Battlegrounds of Olis. He's explaining the situation, while standing in a massive field, about how the war was an act of selfishness manipulated by Hosseff in order to feed from the souls of the dead. He is also explaining that Boyafed's men had nothing to do with either Lord Dowd's spirit-bull or the king of Lavan's deaths. Gregory's whole goal is to convince Lord Dowd that a meeting with the Dark Order leader is in order. Gregory knows the prophet intends to explain to both leaders that peace will come to Luvelles.

Marcus is now wandering aimlessly through Grayham after teleporting Maldwin to Merchant Island. For some reason, he felt the need to stay on Grayham after leaving the rat to fend for himself. Something inside his head is telling him he eventually needs to go to Brandor, but the specifics as to why are not yet clear. All he knows is that he has a desire to be at an inn just outside the city of West Utopia's gates before the Peak of Bailem.

Maldwin is in a container which has been carried between worlds by the Merchant Angels. He plans to stay put until a man named Brayson Id shows up to take him to his destination. He looks forward to his visit with his old friends, even the giant cat Kepler, even though he feels like a meal around him.

Mosley has found what he was looking for and is watching as the Wisp of Song lifts from the pool below the cliffs of Griffon Falls.

Gabriel is speaking with the new gods, both of which he intends to introduce to the others very soon. He plans to enjoy the anger on Lasidi-ous's face when the God of Mischief sees his choices. With everything that will transpire, Lasidious won't have the moments necessary in which to seek out Mosley as the Night Terror Wolf travels.

Mary took care of Brayson after Kepler brought him home. Brayson had been ill since his run-in with Balecut and the family had helped to ensure his recovery. And now that the Head Master is back on his feet, he has work to do. He needs to go to Merchant Island and retrieve Maldwin while George and Kepler are on their outing.

Susanne and Baby Garrin are doing fine. The potion to keep the child's powers from manifesting themselves is still holding strong. Susanne is also nervous because Brayson has invited Gregory over for dinner and has decided to take it upon himself to act as a matchmaker between the two of them to see if there is an interest. If things go right, she too could have herself a magic man one day. She already knows from meeting Gregory before that she considers the White Chancellor to be a handsome elf.

Thank you for reading the Luvelles Gazette

Chapter 28

Godly Threats

The Siren's Song, Southern Grayham
Beneath Griffon Falls

Mosley, after searching for the Wisp within the foggy mist beneath Griffon Falls, finally found the elusive ball of energy. He now stood silently less than two hundred feet of where George had listened to the Wisp's beautiful song not much more than a half season ago. The air was chilled and he knew winter would soon begin to shower the worlds with its white rain as his breath billowed in front of him.

The massive steam-covered pool hidden within the mist made the perfect hiding spot as the wolf watched the sphere's light ascend and lift from the water's depths. The water cascaded from its smooth surface in sheets and soon the ball of energy came to a rest only a few feet from him and hung suspended above the pool's surface.

Mosley admired how the steam lifted gracefully from the sphere's mythical form before he broke the silence and began to sing to the Wisp in its own language... a benefit of still having privileged memories purposely left behind after being stripped by Gabriel of all his immortal powers. The wolf howled, singing with what he felt was all the passion he could muster, but despite his best efforts, his ability to carry a tune was nothing short of comical and he sounded like garesh.

The Wisp stopped Mosley before he could finish his song and begged the wolf to spare him the torture. After a few brief moments of silence, the sphere began a song of its own. This air within the misty fog filled with a glorious melody, a song which would have filled the heart of even the most evil being with a sense of peace. He could understand the song's lyrics as they rang true to his heart. They spoke of loving someone so unconditionally that they became just as important as the air itself is to breathing. They spoke of the trials of staying true to this love and treating this bond as unbendable... cherished above all else so it would stand the test... of a neverending continuation of moments, the promise of an everlasting eternity with this person in a heaven for a life well-lived.

By the end of the Wisp's last note, Mosley was desperately trying to clear the tears which had filled his eyes. His love for his deceased wife resurfaced as a result of the song's words and now, without his godly powers to protect his heart, he was unable to hide the pain. His wife's soul was stuck inside a book and not living a beautiful existence within a heaven, waiting for him to come to her as the song promised.

"Why have you come to me, wolf?" the sphere finally said in a rhythmical manner after allowing the moments necessary for Mosley to collect his emotions. "I'm glad to see my song has touched you so."

Fighting hard to push back his pain, the wolf eventually managed a reply. "Thank you for your gift. My name is Mosley and your song's words reminded me of how beautiful my... my... m—"

Again he began to wail and fell to the pool's banks. He lifted his snout to the sky and howled, desperately trying to release the burden of the agony he still carried inside over his loss of Luvera.

Now the Wisp managed a melodic collection of words. "My song was meant to be uplifting and furthermore, spiritual. It wasn't meant to sadden your soul. I truly hate to see your pain."

Again Mosley fought back his heartache. "You're not at fault... the one who murdered my wife is the one who has administered my pain. Kepler is the one responsible and you've done nothing to be sorry for."

The mentioning of Kepler's name gave Mosley new focus and as if a switch had been toggled, it turned his mind in a new direction and he focused on his hatred for George and the demon cat. He would now be able to speak with the Wisp without crying any longer.

After shaking off the water which saturated his heavy coat, a mild irritation compliments of the mist, Mosley spoke with a stronger voice. "I have come seeking power... but not just any kind of power. I want to know where I can go to find the ability necessary to command the powers of the Ancient Mystics. Is there any place on Grayham I can find this?"

The Wisp floated back a few feet as if somehow caught off guard by the wolf's question. A moment passed before his melodious speech once again filled the foggy air. "Yes... you can find this power on Grayham, though the journey is perilous and filled with grave dangers. Are you prepared to go on a journey to find the answers to something I wish to know, in exchange for the information you seek? A trade, if you will."

Mosley smiled and with conviction, replied, "I'm more than ready to begin this journey. What will you have me do?"

"You shall travel to the lands of the ice king in Northern Grayham. Once there, find the Tear of Gramal and return it to its rightful owner. Her name is Clandestiny and only she can tell you the secret of the Tear, but she has never revealed it to any other. She has been without this blood red crystal for nearly 285 seasons and it has been said that the Tear was stolen from her. I imagine she would be happy to have the Tear back in her posession and if handled in the right manner when returning it to her, she may be willing to share this knowledge with you."

Mosley thought a moment and to clarify, he reiterated the main points. "So I have to travel to the lands of the ice king and find the Tear of Gramal. Once I have it, I'm to return it to this woman named Clandestiny and do it in such a way that she tells me the secret behind why the Tear is so important. If I do this, you'll give me the information about where on this world I must go to retrieve the powers of the Ancient Mystics... is this correct?"

The Wisp began to lower back into the pool, but before the sphere was completely submerged, it stopped and responded with more of its rhythmical speech.

"You must also ask her if she knows why the Tear was stolen from her. If you gather this information and return to me, I will answer your question."

The Wisp of Song submerged beneath the pool's surface and

eventually was deep enough that its light faded.

Mosley began to think and as he looked into his mind, he found his godly knowledge of the ice king's kingdom was no longer available to him. Not only that, but his memory of many details on all the worlds no longer existed. He found that, other than his vast knowledge of Grayham's topography, the only thing he could remember about the landscapes on the other worlds were the specifics of what each Merchant Island looked like.

He now knew that Gabriel was being cautious as to how he went about gaining the power necessary to kill George. But he did, however, remember the truth about the gods and how everything had progressed in order to arrive at this point. He even remembered how to get to the Hidden God world, but he also knew this information was pointless unless he could find the power necessary to become immortal once again. For now, he would need to concentrate on the task at hand and find a way to kill George.

Mosley sighed as he remembered one more thing which angered him. While living his life on Grayham, he had never personally traveled beyond the northern shoreline of Lake Lataseff. He would not be able to teleport beyond this area, since he didn't have the proper knowledge of the landscape to safely do so. He would have to cross the plains of the giant cats on all four paws in order to get to the Isthmus of Change. The Isthmus was the only way to get to the kingdom of the ice king from Southern Grayham. The journey was long and there would be many perils on this portion of his search. But first, he hoped he still had the power necessary to survive any encounters that might present themselves with the giant cats inhabiting the plains.

George and Athena's Home

After checking in with Athena to make sure she was enjoying her rest and encouraging her to let the others in the family handle the daily routine she normally set for herself, George took Payne to Susanne's house so she could watch the fairy-demon while he was gone.

Payne was still fighting with his new parents and didn't want anything to do with learning table manners, bathing, or wearing clothes... so since the warlock was going to be gone for most of the day, he wanted to leave Payne with someone who would see to it that he obeyed his new rules. George felt confident Susanne would keep Payne in his place, especially now that his natural ability to burst into flames had also been blocked with yet another of Brayson's potions to keep the fairy-demon from burning his clothes off.

All in all, Payne's fits were to be expected since he was so young, and George was finding out that his patience for the demon-child's antics was more than sufficient to raise him. Now with his new son, Joshua, resting in his left arm and Payne's red claw holding his right hand, they walked across the clearing to Susanne's front door and knocked.

After leaving Payne with Susanne, George called to Kepler inside his lair beneath the rocks and waited for the giant jaguar to appear. The cat's white fur contrasted well against his black, gem-covered saddle which was strapped securely to his back with George's staff tied to it on the far side.

Kepler lowered to the ground and waited patiently for George to announce that he was strapped securely in place and the baby's safety had been accounted for before he stood up. With a wave of his hand, the warlock teleported them to Grayham and when they appeared, they now stood beside the shores of the Bloodvain Sea, more specifically, the spot where Griffon Cliffs dropped off into the water.

George rode Kepler up to the base of the cliff and began to speak firmly in the language of the Ancient Mystics. "Tormay consolidafo mejasimadoma ys ne tepa!"

The hidden location of the item Lasidious had informed Brayson about was now revealed as a large hole opened up before them. Kepler walked into the darkness and George waved his hand to command the darkness to dissipate. It wasn't long before they came to the tunnel's end and found what they had come for.

A single piece of fruit, shaped like a pear, sat on top of a small table. There didn't appear to be anything else in the cave or at least anything they could see. George moved his hand and the fruit lifted from the table and floated over to him. He placed it in his robe pocket and, once satisfied all was in order, they vanished for the city of Brandor.

Kepler held his head high as he walked majestically through what was left of the city. The people quickly moved to the far side of the street as they approached, unsure at first if it was safe, but it didn't take long before they recognized the man calling himself Lasidious's prophet.

Every now and then George stopped Kepler and called the crowds to them, showering them with more gifts of coin and words of love from Lasidious. He even shared his joy of his new son's birth and lifted Joshua up for all to see.

Kepler was enjoying the moment right up to the point where the children began to touch him, pull at his fur, and shout out their calls of "Kitty! Mommy, look, it's a pretty kitty." But despite his hatred for this attention, he allowed the children their enjoyment and to get back at them, he licked their faces with an extra slobbery tongue.

The doors to the castle opened as they approached and waiting on the other side were both Sam and Shalee. Waving his hand in greeting, George shouted, "Hey guys... I wanted to share something with you, and I also have something to discuss."

Sam could only stare in amazement as he watched Kepler approach. Shalee had told him of Kepler's new look but he had not been able to imagine how beautiful it must be until now. The king shook off his surprise and responded.

"I'm glad you're here. I have some questions to ask you." Sam took note that George was carrying something. "What did you bring with you?"

Kepler came to a stop and lowered to the ground for the warlock to dismount. "Well... I wasn't sure if I should bring him with me with everything that has happened with the two of you lately, but I really wanted you to meet Joshua. This little guy is one of the reasons I decided to make a fresh start with things. If you want me to leave and come back later without him, I will, but I really wanted to share him with you."

Shalee quickly moved to George's side. "Don't be silly... you don't need to go. Life has to move on, right? Besides, Sam and I would love to share this moment with you. Oh my goodness, Sam... come look at him. His hair is so cute and soft too. May I hold him?"

George released the child and moved to stand next to Sam. "I know you're still wary of my presence around here, but I really wanted to share this with you guys. I hate the fact I was such a pain to you both. I also brought you something... something I'm sure will make the two of you very, very happy."

Sam looked George in the eyes. He was unsure as to where to go with the conversation and his contempt for George, and also Kepler for that matter, was still in the forefront of his mind. Eventually Sam responded.

"You'll have to forgive me when I say I doubt there's anything you could do to make me a happy man. I still feel you're up to something. Maybe you could just get to the point and tell me why you're here."

George laughed as he moved to stand beside Shalee. "He's adorable... isn't he?"

Sam spoke over Shalee's response. "Are you stalling, George? Do you really have something important to say or did you just come here to rub the birth of your son in our faces?"

George sighed and reached into the pocket of his robe. He removed the item he had retrieved from within the cliffs and tossed it to Sam.

Sam caught the piece of fruit and looked it over. "You brought me a pear. What the hell do you expect me to do with this?"

George looked up and found Sam's eyes. "I think the best name for what your holding would be called... **nasha**."

The look on both Sam and Shalee's faces as they stood staring down at the fruit was priceless. George took the opportunity to move beside Kepler and placed the baby within a special, warm cloth which cradled Joshua's little form. The warlock reached up and secured the looped end to Kepler's saddle and allowed the child to hang comfortably while remaining asleep. To ensure the knot wouldn't come loose, George used his power to bind the cloth at its end.

"Keep an eye on him for me, Kep, while I help Sam and Shalee. Walk slowly if you move so you don't wake him, please."

Kepler grunted. "Great, babysitting again!"

Michael, Sam's General Absolute, hurried into the courtyard

riding his mist mare. Upon seeing George, he dismounted quickly and looked to Sam for his orders.

George, seeing Sam was preoccupied with thought, spoke up. "General, why don't you have your men stand guard and come with me. I have brought something for your king and queen which I think you need to see for yourself. This will be the happiest day this kingdom has ever seen and the celebration we shall have tonight will be one to remember."

George led the stunned couple into the castle's kitchen and found a cup. He used his magic and forced the fruit's juices to flow until the last drop fell into the wooden container.

"How will the juice from a piece of fruit bring joy to this kingdom?" Michael asked Sam, who still seemed to be unable to respond. Shalee lifted her hand to shush the general as she waited for what was to come next.

The warlock turned and once again found their eyes. "Where's your son's body? Let's go and give him his life back. I think the two of you deserve to be parents."

It wasn't long before the group stood next to the coffin which held Sam Junior's tiny little body. Sam had placed it within a room not far from their bedroom chamber and posted a guard to stand at the room's door during every moment of each day.

The king's hands trembled as he fought with the lock securing the lid. Tears began to run down his cheeks while Shalee found it nearly impossible to breathe, her heart pumping wildly and giving her the feeling that it was crashing hard against the front of her chest with every beat.

George tried to hand Sam the cup, but seeing the king's hands were unsteady, he thought better of it and moved to stand beside the coffin. The warlock leaned in to pull back the special cloth that had been used to cover Sam Junior's body. Slowly, he poured the liquid over each tiny part.

The area around them began to shake and the coffin began to vibrate, shifting toward the edge of the shelf it was resting on. Sam reacted and steadied the container to ensure it didn't fall. Eventually the quaking stopped and suddenly a light emerged from the ceiling and lowered to a position just above the child's body.

Both Sam and Shalee gasped as they watched their son's spirit merge with his corpse. Now an even brighter light filled the room and each of them had to close their eyes. When finally the light faded, all that was left was a beautiful baby crying for his parents.

Michael stood in absolute silence as he watched his king remove the child from the coffin to cradle him in his massive arms. He watched as Shalee summoned a blanket with a wave of her hand and moved to Sam's side to give the baby warmth.

George looked at Sam and said, "I will leave you alone to become better acquainted. I wouldn't worry about the threat to Brandor which we spoke of the other day. Lasidious has ensured that I have a way to keep you safe. I want you to know before I leave that this gift of your son's life was from Lasidious and he wishes the two of you nothing but happiness."

Sam handed the baby to Shalee and moved to George, lifting him from the floor to embrace him. "I now truly believe. Make sure you come back tonight and we'll celebrate. This is truly the happiest day of my life."

George chuckled the best he could from within Sam's strong arms. "I will come back if you promise to put me down so I can breathe."

Lowering the warlock to the floor, Sam adjusted George's robes to a better position on his shoulders. "How about we forget the past and start again?"

With a nod, George turned to go. "Enjoy your day with your son, Shalee!"

Shalee quickly gave the baby back to Sam and gave George a big kiss on the cheek. "Maybe we could wait a bit before I look into the Eye. I should probably make sure Sam knows what he's doing before I go."

"I agree one hundred percent. I'll see you both tonight. I intend to bring my entire family with me, so make sure you have places set for thirty-seven and one big cat. I may also bring two others with me, but I'm not sure about that just yet."

Shalee smiled. "Bring as many as you like. We'll be ready for you all."

The World of Dragonia

Gabriel watched as Sam Junior's soul left his many pages when the nasha fruit was used and, to his surprise, he felt as if no law had been broken. He excused himself from his meeting with the two new gods—whom he had been educating on how future events were going to take place—and followed the soul to the place it intended to travel.

When he appeared inside the room within Sam's castle, he remained invisible to the mortals and watched as Sam Junior's body united with his spirit. He was outraged to see that George was present and upon hearing what the warlock told Sam about Lasidious being the one to give them this gift, he teleported back to the cave where he had been holding his meeting and continued to do some more plotting of his own.

The Peak of Bailem
Southern Grayham
The City of West Utopia

George had returned home to Luvelles just long enough to leave Joshua with Mary. Kepler had retired to his lair and Brayson was already gone to retrieve Maldwin from the Merchant Island, planning to bring the rat back to the families' homes. George now stood in front of an inn located just outside the city's gates of West Utopia with hopes of finding Marcus Id inside.

What a dive this place is, George thought as he looked up at the inn's sign which hung crooked on a set of chains. The place was called the Utopian Queen, but nothing about its appearance resembled anything he considered royal. Even the wood which made up the porch was abused and poorly maintained; the nails used to hold the planks in place stuck out in spots and were definitely a hazard for the bare foot.

Once inside, he scanned the room full of carved-up furniture, but Marcus was nowhere to be found. He took a seat and waited for the bartender to approach so he could question him.

"Excuse me, have you seen a man—"

"—a man like me?" a voice said from behind.

George quickly tuned to look and sure enough, Marcus had made it this far. George decided to control the conversation.

"The rat told me you decided to stay on Grayham when I spoke with him this morning. Do you realize how hard it is to find a man who doesn't want to be found? Maldwin said you were going to be coming this way and told me he heard it within your thoughts. I suppose I forgot to tell you the rat can read minds, too."

Marcus smiled and took a seat beside him at the bar. "I'm sure you intentionally forget to tell me many things. Two ales, please," he said, raising his hand to summon the barkeep. "And make sure they're good and cold."

The bartender scoffed. "You'll get the ale the same as it always comes. Whoever heard of cold ale, anyway?"

George reached out and grabbed Marcus' arms to keep him from using his magic. "Hey, hey, hey... you can't go around killing folks for not having cold ale. This place isn't like Luvelles. They don't have the same magic we do to keep things cool. It's a primitive world here and the people are just as rugged."

"Humph... what a waste of a race."

George tapped the edge of the bar with his knuckles. "So, what made you decide to stay here anyway? Don't you still want to be Head Master?"

The Dark Chancellor stood from his stool and pushed his long hair clear of his face. "I don't know why I stayed, but for some reason I feel I need to go to Brandor."

"Sounds odd," George said, moving clear of his own stool. "Walk with me a bit and let's talk."

They left the inn after putting a coin on the counter and walked northbound following a dirt road along the coastline. Eventually George began to talk. "You know, you may be on to something by deciding to stay on Grayham. I bet your subconscious is telling you something and I'll bet it's a great idea."

"My sub-what? What on Luvelles is a subconscious... you're not making any sense, George. What idea do I seem to have that only you know about and I apparently do not?"

George put his arm around Marcus' shoulder. "Your mind is what I'm talking about. I mean that, just maybe... well, in the back of your mind anyway, you already know that if you go to Brandor and kill their king, you would be the ruler of all Southern Grayham. I think you know you could rule both Luvelles and Southern Grayham by simply teleporting back and forth between the two worlds once you've looked into the Eye of Magic. I bet you know that all you would have to do is put someone in a key advisory position on this world who answers directly to you. I bet you even know who this person would be."

Marcus shook his head in amazement. "I never would have conceived of any of these things you've just spoken of. My mind... or this subconscious as you put it, is far from leaning in that direction."

George removed his hand. "Hmmm... well, maybe I've given you too much credit and you're not nearly as cunning as I had hoped you'd be. Too bad, though, because you could've accomplished so much more than just being the ruler of one world. You could have controlled the lower three worlds, with my help. Maybe I need to find someone with loftier goals!"

Marcus stopped and turned to find George's eyes. "I didn't say my goals couldn't be adjusted to accomplish bigger things. All I said was that I wasn't thinking the way you were. It's not like I don't like the idea of being the ruler of three worlds, but what about you? Wouldn't this be a conflict of interest? Why would you just hand all this power to me when you could easily have it for yourself? We both know you have the power to kill me if you wanted to."

Without responding, George changed their direction and walked them both to the shoreline. They watched silently as the waves crashed against the white sand of the beach and for that moment, everything seemed peaceful as George closed his eyes to smell the ocean breeze.

Eventually he turned to Marcus to respond. "I have bigger plans than simply ruling the lower three worlds. I intend to become a god and when that day comes, I will come back to you and expect your loyalty. Now I won't expect you personally to pray to me, but I will expect you to tell those who serve you to pray to me twice daily. You will need to be a charismatic leader and not the pain you currently are."

Marcus began to laugh. "You know you're mad... I mean, don't you realize you've gone insane? You... ha... a god, I find the concept absurd. How will you accomplish this?"

George waved his hand and Marcus found himself frozen, unable to move. His blue eyes changed and became cold, as if hate had suddenly overwhelmed him. He reached up and slowly stroked Marcus's face before backhanding him and allowing the wizard to topple over. The warlock followed the Dark Chancellor to the ground and straddled him as he had done in the forest near Brayson's shrine. He leaned over and placed his face inches from Marcus's. George could see the fear in his brown eyes as he pushed the wizard's hair clear of his face and spoke with a hiss.

"Do you not find me to be a madman, Marcus? Do you doubt for one moment I'm incapable of accomplishing anything I set my mind to? I am only 23 seasons old and have already managed to rise to a level of power even you have been unable to obtain in over 700 seasons. Shall I find a man who is able to keep up with me and dispose of you, or are you willing to adjust your goals and kill the king of Brandor and his family?"

George released his magic on Marcus and allowed him to stand. The Dark Chancellor wanted with everything in him to lash out and kill George while his back was to him, but he knew his power wasn't strong enough.

"Did you really need to strike me? And you say I'm a pain. I suppose I have no problem adjusting my goals... in fact, I quite like the idea of controlling the lower three worlds, and as long as I don't personally have to pray to you myself, I would have no problem telling the people to worship you.

"But I won't tell you I find it possible for you to become a god when I think it is indeed, impossible, but hey... if you're willing to go after this kind of power, then lead the way. I'll hold up my end of the bargain if you somehow manage to become immortal."

George turned and moved to stand beside Marcus. After putting his arm back around the wizard's shoulders, he said, "It seems you and I will be able to work together after all. Now allow me to tell you what the plan is going to be so you can kill Brandor's king."

Later That Day
The Families' Homes on Luvelles
Before Late Bailem

George finally appeared outside his home and, to his delight, the activities had already started. Brayson had returned with Maldwin and a large bonfire was blazing near the large mound of rocks at the clearing's center. The air was crisp, with a solid chill and the clouds above threatened to storm. But with the proper clothing, the day was still comfortable enough that they would be able to bundle up and have this gathering while enjoying each other's company.

Those invited and present for the occasion extended beyond Gregory Id and Maldwin. There were two other guests standing near the fire, each holding mugs of ale. George addressed them as he approached.

"Lord Boyafed... Lord Dowd," he said while reaching out to shake each of their hands. "I'm glad we could all set our differences aside for the moments necessary to enjoy a fine meal, a night of fun, games, and good conversation. I plan to take us all someplace special here very shortly. I trust each of you have full mugs. If there's anything I can get for either of you, just let me know and I will see to it that it's done."

Lord Dowd returned George's greeting and then with Boyafed at his side, said, "Gregory and Brayson told us you wish to speak with us alone. I have also been personally told you've been given the promise of peace from the gods and you foresee that all of Luvelles can find common ground."

George smiled and motioned for him to take a seat. "We should speak of this later when things are not so jovial. For now, why don't we enjoy each other's company? Both you and Boyafed are honorable men in the ways of war and are equally as honorable when it comes to respecting your host. I promise to tell you everything I know before the night is over. I'm sure you both will enjoy where we're going tonight."

Athena's voice filled the chilled air as she moved to stand beside her husband. Joshua was wrapped up warmly within a bundle of blankets and sleeping soundly in his mother's arms.

George took the baby after kissing her. "Give me a moment, babe... I want to speak with these two gentlemen."

Once Athena had left, George handed the baby to Lord Dowd. Sensing the White Army leader's hesitation, he assured Dowd it would be okay and he wouldn't break him. It was clear to see Dowd had never held a child of his own before... or anyone's child, for that matter.

Boyafed began to chuckle. "I remember that feeling the first moment I held my own son. I, too, thought I would break him in half and he was far too fragile to hold. Go ahead and take the child, Henry... I assure you it's okay."

George was caught off guard. "Your name is Henry?"

Dowd cradled Joshua in his arms. "There aren't many men who know my name, and I prefer this to stay between us, if it's all the same to you. My given name is Henry Francis Dowd."

Boyafed began to laugh as he reached over and put his hand on Dowd's shoulder. "I suppose it's good you're holding the child so you can't strike me when I poke fun. Henry Francis, eh? I too would have kept the name Francis a secret. I have always known your first name, but it's the middle one that's horrid."

The mood between the three men was light as they each began to laugh. Once the moment passed, George reached in and removed the blanket from Joshua's face. He motioned for both Dowd and Boyafed to take a look.

"You see, gentlemen, this little guy is the reason I live in search of peace. Many of your men have families, sons and daughters of their own. We owe it to them to find a peaceful solution to the problems on Luvelles and I personally have knowledge that neither of you did anything to provoke the other to begin this war. You both have been deceived by the gods and this deception is the reason why I asked Brayson and Gregory to bring you here so I can speak with you. But as I've already said... let's enjoy each other's company and make this night one to remember. I plan to teleport us all to Grayham to dine with the king of Brandor."

George no sooner finished his statement than Brayson stood beside the fire and began to call for everyone's attention. "I have something I wish to say before we go." Once the atmosphere had settled, Brayson lowered to one knee in front of Mary and took her hand.

Mary's eyes widened as she anxiously held Brayson's gaze. She was wearing a brand-new, black dress which covered her feet, a knitted yellow sweater and shoes to match, all of which were given to her earlier that morning by Brayson.

Athena grabbed hold of Susanne's arm and began to squeeze. Susanne was standing next to Gregory who stood by the fire in a colorful, new robe, which Mykklyn had convinced him to wear for his first date. The White Chancellor's heart was filled with joy, smiling as his older brother gathered the nerve to continue.

Brayson cleared his throat. "Mary... I have watched your elegance ever since the moment you stepped from the container on Merchant Island. Luvelles has never been the same for me since your arrival. I have never wished to spend my life with any other before you. Will you accept me as your mate?"

Everyone was completely silent as they waited for her response. The first snowflake of winter landed on Brayson's nose as she began to cry. She looked up and followed another flake to the ground.

"It seems the mood of winter's white rain would be ruined if I were to decline. My answer is yes... I will be your mate!"

The entire crowd erupted with praises for the two as the family gathered around to congratulate them. George turned to both Boyafed and Dowd. "I think it's moments like these which prove peace is far better than war. Shall we go to Grayham and dine with the king and his family? Something happened there earlier today which will impress you both... something which will make you question your beliefs."

Suddenly something pulled on the bottom of George's robe. When the warlock looked down, he could only smile as he lowered to lift Maldwin from the ground.

Maldwin was so excited to see his old friend that all he could think of to say was, "I LIKE CHEESE, GEORGE!"

George responded and said, "Everything is A-Okay, man!" He turned to excuse himself from the two army's leaders. "I better go and get this little guy some cheese. His name is Maldwin and although he only looks like a rat, I assure you he's an incredible friend."

Both Dowd and Boyafed shrugged. Boyafed said, "I have no

problem with anyone having a pet mouse!"

George smiled.

"Lord Dowd... will you please give my son back to my wife when you're done holding him? I think you're getting the hang of it. You'd be a fine father someday. I'll be back in a bit and then we'll go."

George lifted his voice and called to the far side of the fire. "Hey Kepler, come with me a moment, if you don't mind. Susanne, please keep Payne with you until I get back out of the house."

Dowd said, "George, you seem to keep diverse company. I don't think I've ever seen a man with a rat, a demon-fairy child, and a massive kitty as companions."

Kepler growled as he came to a stop next to George. "Lord Dowd... please refrain from using the word kitty. It really pisses me off."

George watched as Kepler walked away. "He really hates that word. Try to avoid using it, if you don't mind."

Boyafed put his hand on Dowd's shoulder again. "Trust me when I say this. I watched that beast kill four Tricksters as if they were nothing more than minor irritations. I would do as the cat requests. He likes being called Kepler."

Dowd looked to where the giant feline now stood. "You have my deepest apology, Kepler."

Kepler just growled.

George and Maldwin caught up with the giant jaguar and they walked into the house. "Tell Maldwin I'm happy to see him," George said. "Tell him there are things we need to accomplish while he is here on Luvelles. Tell him if he wants me to, I can give him and his family a better home than the one they already have. Tell him—"

Kepler interrupted. "Great... here we go again with the tell him, to tell you, to tell him, to tell you, thing. Have you gone dense all of a sudden, George?"

"Would you just shut up and listen so we can get going!"

Again Maldwin chimed in. "I LIKE CHEESE, GEORGE!"

Kepler rolled his eyes. "You've got to be kidding me. I think I'm stuck in a nightmare!"

The Hall of Judgment
Ancients Sovereign

Gabriel sat patiently on top of the large marble table within his hall, waiting for the gods to arrive. It was now the best moment to deliver his news. The deities he had chosen to replace Yaloom and Mosley would be introduced. The Book had sent word to ensure the God of Mischief and his evil lover, Celestria, would attend.

One by one, the gods made their appearances and as always, Keylom's hooves clapped against the floor as they all waited for the fashionably late couple. Eventually Lasidious appeared with Celestria at his side. The goddess was wearing a bright red gown which elegantly hung low across her chest and her blonde hair was pinned up to expose her gem-covered neck and dangling earrings. She was absolutely radiant and greeted everyone with a smile. Once they all were seated, Gabriel floated from the table and began his announcement.

"As we all know, Yaloom failed to leave me with a name as to who he wished to replace him, as our laws gave him the right to do. We all know he failed to do this because of his arrogance. So, in continuing to do things as our laws command me to, I have chosen his replacement and plan to introduce him in a moment."

Gabriel floated to a position directly above the table's center. "There is another matter I also need to share with you today. This event will surprise most of you and has left me in an interesting position... one which I plan to take full advantage of."

Gabriel took a deep breath and continued. "Mosley has broken the rules within my pages and has been made mortal as a consequence."

Lasidious was the first to react as he stood from his chair and shouted, "What? What could he have possibly done to deserve such a consequence?"

Keylom responded, thumping a heavy hoof on the floor to get everyone's attention. "Mosley attacked me! We had a confrontation and he failed to control his anger. If I have anything to say in the matter, I would request that Gabriel not follow our rules, but with the way the law is written, Gabriel had no choice but to punish the wolf."

Lasidious listened to the others begin to shout out their questions as he sat back down in his chair. He looked at Celestria. "Too bad... Mosley was a favorite of mine, as you know. I wonder what caused him to do something so drastic."

Celestria responded, "Perhaps his reasoning isn't drastic at all. Perhaps it was for other reasons we don't know, reasons which we can find out if we try to find him. He wasn't stupid and—"

Gabriel floated over to them and interrupted, choosing to protect the wolf with a well-thought-out lie.

"You're right. The wolf wasn't stupid, and he broke the law intentionally. He used Keylom as a way to regain his mortality. He did it so I would be forced to remove his godly powers. He also did it so I could choose his replacement.

"Mosley didn't enjoy being immortal, and his disgust for the games we play is what made him choose to go back to a mortal body. His final request was that I place him on Trollcom, but his reasoning as to why wasn't divulged. Either way, his decision has left me the option of choosing two new gods, and both will be introduced shortly."

Alistar lifted from his seat. "So why all the secrecy about the wolf and why have you waited until now to choose Yaloom's replacement? You could have chosen this being sooner."

"That's a great question," Mieonus added as she pushed her brunette hair clear of her face. "I think you've been cooking up something good... perhaps a little deviousness of your own. I'm sure that based on your last confrontation with Lasidious, your choices will directly affect him in some way."

Bailem stood, adjusted his robes as he always did and said, "I for one don't want to wait all day to find out who they are. So get on with the announcement, Gabriel."

The Book moved clear of the table and stood at the far side of the hall. He motioned for the demon queen of Dragonia, Sharvesa, to walk through the door.

Everyone in the room gasped as she entered. Lasidious looked at Alistar, then at Celestria and with this simple look, he communicated that this choice wasn't good for their plans. The Book's decision would screw with things on so many different levels.

The demon queen was tall, nearly eight feet, and she wore no clothes. Her skin was a burnt red, with ivory-colored horns which protruded from her forehead and bent backward over the top of her crown. She kept her wings folded tightly to her back and once she had properly addressed the others, finally spoke in the language of the demons, looking directly at Lasidious as she did. The rough translation was, "With respect to your greatness, my lord... or should I be addressing you differently now that I've ascended, it's good to see you again."

Sharvesa thought a moment and decided to stay with what she knew best. "My lord, I'll be requesting the demon race, as a whole, to worship me as soon as my daughter, Teshava, has officially succeeded me as their queen. As I'm sure you already know, the demon race will flock to me once they learn of my ascension to godliness. However, my lord, I want you to know I truly enjoyed serving you while living on Dragonia, but with the circumstances being what they are, I'm sure you can understand why I would wish to rule my own kind!"

Everyone in the room looked to see Lasidious's reaction, but the God of Mischief refused to give Gabriel the satisfaction. He respected the demon queen for her tact. He stood from his chair and smiled as he responded.

"I'm sure you'll do a fine job as goddess. I'm also sure we'll have much to discuss very soon. I must compliment Gabriel on his choice." Lasidious turned and found the Book's eyes. "I can't think of a finer choice... so who's next?"

Gabriel wasn't sure how he felt about Lasidious' reaction. He motioned for the other figure waiting outside, to enter. The king of all the trolls of Trollcom, Kesdelain, walked in and again, all the faces in the room couldn't believe the Book's choice.

Lasidious swallowed hard and had to work to keep a straight face. Both Alistar and Celestria felt the threat of the Book's choice and worked equally as hard to keep their anger hidden from the others.

Between the demon queen and the troll king, the heavy losses of Lasidious's worshippers would set their plans back to control the Book. This all came at a moment when they were so close to being able to seize control of Gabriel. With the centaurs of Harvestom, the humans of Grayham, the elves and the halflings of

Luvelles all being so close to beginning their prayers, this turn of events really hurt their plans.

The only group which remained was the dragons... and even this was a matter of days before Lasidious had them under control as well. The dragons had already agreed that in payment for the creation of their new world, they would serve him. Now they would need to work even harder to manipulate the beings of the worlds and find followers for Lasidious in other places. At least he still had the vampires of Dragonia praying to him.

Lasidious once again smiled as he spoke. "So Gabriel has made you the new God of Greed, Kesdelain. I doubt you have what it takes to handle a job of this magnitude. I would've thought you'd be wiser in your decision-making, Gabriel."

The troll responded in his own language before the Book could say anything.

"I have despised you for so many seasons, Lasidious. To think I actually believed you to be all powerful after your charade in my throne room with your silly little prophet at your side is suddenly comical. I left my queen behind on Trollcom to marry my best friend. I will be taking the trolls who worship you and have them serve me. I will enjoy watching you lose the power their prayers gave you. It feels good to get out from under the burden your gift held over my head for all those seasons. Now it's my turn to reign as a god to all the races of trolls."

Lasidious moved close and stood face to face with the troll. "I wouldn't get caught up in glorifying yourself. You aren't nearly as clever as the gods which I have already manipulated into throwing away their immortality. I have made much smarter minds than yours crack and if you're not careful, I'll make it my personal goal to see to it that you will regret the day you ever met me!"

Alistar knew what Lasidious was trying to do, so he stood up and added a few well-placed comments. "Kesdelain, listen to me for a moment. Lasidious speaks the truth. He will tear away at your mind until you make a mistake. I would tread with caution if I were you."

Mieonus stood and shouted at Alistar. ""You act as if you're on Lasidious's side. Why do you care if he tortures this pathetic troll?"

With a calm demeanor, Alistar turned to respond. "Because we need Kesdelain to stick around so Lasidious doesn't find a way to convince the trolls to worship him again. Are you really so stupid that I have to explain a concept as simple as this to you, Mieonus? Does every little thing need to be drawn out for you as I would for a child's mind? Maybe you should spare us your babble and sit down to save what little is left of our clearly misplaced perception of intelligence that we still see in you."

Celestria started laughing as she watched Mieonus sit heavily in her chair and moved to stand before the troll. "Do you really know what you've gotten yourself into, Kesdelain? You won't last a season before Lasidious convinces you to destroy yourself. I would decide carefully who you disrespect from now on if I were you. I find myself pitying you right now!"

Gabriel decided he'd had enough. "There shall be no more threats within my hall! Everyone should leave now!"

Lasidious decided to take a whole new approach when the Book spoke. He moved to stand before Gabriel. "What will you do if we don't go? Will you sacrifice yourself to shut me up? Will you allow the laws within your pages to destroy you if I continue to torture this troll's mind? I dare you to destroy me! Allow your hatred for me to employ you to do something so foolish. Do you really think I haven't prepared a way to survive if you strike me down? Do you really think your decisions here today will stop me from controlling you? Go ahead, GABRIEL... strike me down... or maybe I should say... BOOK!"

The hall went completely silent as they waited to see what Gabriel would do next. Many long moments went by before Lasidious made a scoffing sound. "As it is with all the gods, even you, BOOK, speak with words that are filled with nothing more than empty threats. You fear losing your immortality much more than your desire to strike me down. But I think we all know my threats are calculated and will eventually manifest themselves."

Lasidious moved again to stand before the troll. "Make no mistake, Kesdelain, I'm going to find a way to destroy you. Your days are numbered and I personally would hate to be you! Ask anyone in this room... you won't last a season!"

Now he turned his attention to the demon queen. "Sharvesa... as always, it is nice to see you again. I find it to be quite the pleasure to have someone as brilliant as yourself living on Ancients Sovereign with us. When you're ready to choose a home, come and see me. There are a few very nice places here which I'm sure you'll enjoy."

Lasidious turned and faced the others, speaking with a calm voice. "I'm sure this has been entertaining for each of you. I bid you all a good night." He looked over his shoulder and found Gabriel's eyes. "I will speak with you later... BOOK!"

After taking Celestria's hand, Lasidious teleported them both home.

Gabriel floated over to the table and lowered his heavy binding onto it. "Have I made poor choices?" he said for all to hear. "Maybe I have awakened a sleeping giant."

Alistar looked at Kesdelain. It was easy to see the troll felt completely deflated.

"I'm not sure what to think, Gabriel, but I doubt very seriously the troll will last very long. If I were you, Kesdelain, I would be looking for a way to get on Lasidious's good side. I feel bad for you! I also pity you!" Alistar vanished.

Hosseff stood from his chair and with a whispery laugh, also vanished.

Mieonus moved to the two new gods. "I wouldn't worry about Lasidious. You both can always come and talk with me if you need anything."

Sharvesa began to laugh. "Now that's the worst piece of advice I've heard all day. I know Lasidious and what his mind is capable of. How do you think I became queen of all the demons in the first place? I served him for far too many seasons to make an enemy of him simply by befriending the likes of you. Now if you don't mind, I'll be taking my leave." Sharvesa disappeared.

Mieonus hid her anger and turned to look at Kesdelain. "And what do you have to say on the matter?"

"I think she's right; to befriend you puts me in worse position than I'm already in." The troll teleported from the hall.

Mieonus stomped her high heels on the marble. "Damn them!" When she turned around, all that was left in the room was Gabriel. "I think you made two fine choices, Gabriel. This will set Lasidious back quite a bit in his planning. He never saw it coming and you quite possibly saved us all!"

Without responding, the Book simply vanished.

Another high heel found the floor. "Damn, damn, damn!" she screamed.

Chapter 29

𝔅𝔯𝔬𝔱𝔥𝔢𝔯 𝔳𝔰. 𝔅𝔯𝔬𝔱𝔥𝔢𝔯

Southern Grayham
Brandor's Dining Hall
Late Bailem

Dinner was delicious. Shalee worked with the castle's royal chef to prepare an incredible meal for their guests while Sam took care of Sam Junior. The king learned quickly that all his skills as a warrior paled in comparison to the skill necessary to change a child's diaper... especially one made of cloth. Sam's hands trembled as he struggled to secure the pins needed to hold it in place... never in his life had he felt so frightened that he would injure someone so fragile.

Many moments over dinner, Sam found George's eyes to acknowledge his gratitude for everything George had done. Athena, Susanne, Mary, and Shalee spent many moments talking with one another and discussing the features of all three babies. Sam Junior had the hair of his father, the eyes of his mother and the best part was that the juice from the nasha fruit had finished developing the baby's growth to what it should have been prior to leaving the womb in the first place.

Sam invited his military council, the members of the Senate who lived in the city, and some of the wives of families Shalee had befriended. In total there were one hundred and twenty-seven people sitting around the massive table in the dining hall and all of them were enjoying one another's company.

Lord Dowd and Boyafed were speaking with each other, laughing, and sharing stories of Luvelles's past with the members of both the military and the Senate. George watched as Payne sat next to Athena in his high chair which he had used his power to create... a chair which also took into account the space needed for the fairy-demon's wings.

Kepler was busy mingling as well. He had a large pile of rare meat stacked in the corner. He occasionally strolled over to take a bite, then returned to his mingling. The giant cat was mostly interested in the stories of Dowd and Boyafed.

Maldwin decided to take up his own place of comfort on the floor beneath George's chair and aggressively tasted the many different flavors of cheese which Shalee requested from the chef once she realized the rat was present.

George watched his plans all coming together. He would wait till after dinner was complete and then speak with everyone in the room. Tonight would be a productive night.

The Cat Plains
Southern Grayham

Mosley was now a good half day's walk into the heart of Cat Plains after teleporting just north of the shoreline of Lake Lataseff. The weather on Grayham drastically changed throughout the day and all across the plains it had been snowing. He was now walking in it, ankle-deep.

He still was unsure exactly what the extent of his power was as a mortal and had been doing little things along the way to experiment. He could still command fire, ice, water, and even the earth to do many useful things, but none of these things were powerful enough to be used on any large scale. The only real piece of good news was that he didn't need to use words to command the elements. For these skills to be used as natural abilities, this was helpful. On the downside, he had also learned his skills were equal to that of a fairly weak mage. This made him nervous... extremely nervous, considering the area in which he was currently traveling.

He knew the cats of the plains had a tendency to hunt in packs, similar to the way he had hunted with his father when he was but a young wolf pup. On many occasions his father allowed him to tag along with his brothers to hunt small game. He could still remember the outing when he stood beside his father, boldly waiting for his brother to chase a horned rabbit in their direction. His father had whispered something very special to him that day.

"When the rabbit rounds the bend, you'll be the only thing standing in its way between his freedom or becoming our meal. Today, my son, you become a Night Terror Wolf in my eyes. No longer will the others call you pup."

Mosley smiled as he remembered what happened next. His brothers had successfully funneled the animal into the ditch where he stood at one end. The ditch's sides were steep and the only way for the beast to free itself was to get past him. His father stood at the top looking down and waited for him to face their meal head on. The rabbit rounded the bend, but unfortunately the rabbit was too much for him to handle and he was run over by, not only the rabbit, but also his brothers as they continued to give chase.

His father came down from where he stood and moved to stand over him. Mosley remembered the wolfish grin on his face as he spoke. "Now that you're a wolf and no longer my pup, maybe we should hurry and help your brothers catch our meal."

A warm-hearted soul, his father always knew the right thing to say. He had grabbed the back of Mosley's neck and lifted him to his feet that day before rushing off to eventually bring down the oversized horned rabbit. Even though he was clearly just a pup, his father made him feel so much bigger.

It was now after Late Bailem and the wolf's senses were warning him of danger. He knew he was being watched by something in the darkness, but by exactly how many sets of eyes, he didn't know. He had been following the river which flowed north from the lake to ensure he couldn't be surrounded on all sides. He knew cats hated water and if he had to, he could jump in, but the river's current was swift and he didn't know if he would be able to swim back to shore once he was clear of danger.

With his back to the river, he used his magic to create fires both to his left and his right, allowing a group of bushes to burn in hopes of discouraging an attack. The magic fought the snow and refused to burn out as it melted. The use of his magic briefly reminded him of George as he listened to the hissing sounds the fire made. Suddenly a brilliant idea popped into his head. He decided to call out to the ones stalking him and be just as cunning as

George in this kind of situation.

He spoke in the language of the giant sabertooth, since this was the dominant language of all cats and hoped his idea would work. When translated, his deep-throated growling meant, "I have come by order of your lord Kepler."

Mosley swallowed hard at the thought of using such a deception. He hoped it would save his life and, as he thought further, another idea entered his mind. Again he growled, but in a deeper tone, "I have come by order of your lord Kepler."

Now he could hear the growling of the hidden figures within the darkness. He knew it was in fact sabertooth by the confusion hidden within their snarls.

Again he growled, "I have come by order of your lord Kepler. I require an escort through the plains. I have also come with orders given by your lord for five of your finest to travel with me into the lands of the ice king on a journey. I demand that you serve me as you would if Kepler himself were present. Show yourselves to me so I may tell Kepler of your loyalty! He has promised a reward for those brave enough to travel with me."

Slowly an enormous figure with two long sharp teeth protruding from his mouth materialized from within the shadows. The colors of his fur appeared as nothing more than shades of gray until he was close enough to the fire for Mosley to see the browns, yellows, and blacks which covered his mighty form. His eyes reflected the firelight and with each calculated placement of his heavy paws, large imprints equal to the size of Mosley's entire head were left in the snow.

The saber eventually spoke in an irritated snarl, "Why would Kepler wish us to travel with a wolf into the lands of the north? What could possibly be your relationship with our lord to command our help?"

Mosley took a deep breath and came up with a new plan. He only hoped he commanded enough power to pull it off. Slowly he moved to stand within the fire of the burning bush to his left. To his surprise, he was still powerful enough to keep from being burned. Once he stood cozily in place, he sighed with relief, and then responded.

"Perhaps Kepler knows of my power. Perhaps your lord and I

share many bonds which you are unaware of. Let me ask you a question in return. Do you really wish to deny me the company of your five finest warriors and risk the wrath of your lord? I dare say Kepler would tear each of you apart for this kind of disobedience!"

The beast shook his head, snorted angrily, and lifted his head into the night. A deafening roar covered a great area surrounding them before he lowered his head and allowed his yellow eyes to find the wolf's.

"My name is Rash and I am the lord of my saber clan. It appears I have no way of validating your request, so I will personally travel with you. We will need to go back to my lair so I may collect four others as you've requested. Make no mistake when I say they will only answer to me. You will not speak with them directly until I believe you to be trustworthy. If this doesn't work for you, wolf, then speak now so I may be on my way."

Mosley walked from the fire and stood before the cat. He lifted his head to find the saber's eyes, which were a good three feet above his own. "My name is Mosley and your terms are acceptable. I'm sure your reward upon our return will be grand. Shall we go?"

Rash growled and seven other massive cats emerged from the darkness. Mosley felt helpless as he watched them move to surround him.

"Follow me, wolf!"

Luvelles
The Battlegrounds of Olis

The White Army had set up camp after Gregory took Lord Dowd to meet with the prophet. The standing orders were to hold tight until word could be sent as to how they were to proceed.

The Goswigs decided to set up their section of the camp in such a way that all of them could group closely together. Unfortunately, there was one big problem that no one knew how to fix. With winter rearing its head, Strongbear had lain down in his tent and fallen sound asleep. He was in such a deep slumber that it caused him to snore. In fact, his snoring was so loud the Wraith Hound Prince,

Wisslewine, entered their section of the camp and made a threat to eat the big brown bear if they didn't find a way to shut him up.

Gage and Gallrum discussed their options. Eventually the decision was made to teleport the bear back to his cave, behind the diner within the hidden village of Goswigs.

When the deed was done, Gage looked at the bear for some moments after covering him with some of his homemade blankets. Smiling, he turned to Gallrum and said, "Well, we may not be with him, but we certainly aren't against him either." Both Goswigs vanished back to the army's location. But later that night it was discovered that sleep was still going to be impossible for everyone. The leader of the giants had a nasty snoring habit of his own. When Wisslewine went to investigate the cause, the wraith hound just took one look at the sixty-foot-tall beast-man and simply shook his head in disgust.

Southern Grayham
Brandor's Castle

George decided that now was the proper moment to address everyone present. He stood from his chair and after moving to stand on top of the massive dining table within the hall, he said, "I want to thank everyone for coming to celebrate the gift Lasidious has given to both the king and queen of this fine city. We all know Brandor has seen too much sorrow in recent days and this sorrow has affected the lives of many. But I have been promised that this pain will be replaced by happiness, love, and prosperity. I think we can all see this love and happiness by gazing upon the blessing Lasidious has given by returning the life of a child once thought to be lost to Brandor.

"Sam Junior's life is just one of many blessings Lasidious has promised to give this unified kingdom. He has promised an ongoing peace that will be accomplished before the end of the day tomorrow. The final threat to Brandor is making his way to the city's gates and there are only four present in this room who have the power to stop him."

George looked down at both Dowd and Boyafed. "I have much to say to the two of you... and I request you allow me to say it all before I begin to answer your questions. There are many issues that need to be cleared up regarding events on Luvelles and events which are about to happen on Grayham.

"I find it interesting that my lord has chosen two men who fight on opposing sides to come together to defeat an evil which threatens a kingdom you have no responsibility for. You both are leaders among men and you have chosen to set an example for others to follow. My lord has asked me to encourage both of you to work together and, in doing so, destroy the evil which also threatens to bring war to your home world."

George concentrated on Boyafed. "You, Lord Boyafed, are the leader of the Dark Order and serve a god who commanded your Chancellor, Marcus, to kill Lord Dowd's spirit-bull. Hosseff also ordered Marcus to kill the king of Lavan and, in both cases, he used his magic to ensure that his arrows struck the eyes of his intended targets. Hosseff even ordered you to kill Sam, but yet he sits here before you alive and well... even after you saw him die with your own eyes."

The warlock then turned to Henry Dowd. "You, Lord Dowd, are the leader of the White Army and this same man, who has deceived Boyafed, also plotted against you. Marcus Id is the one who killed Boyafed's friend, Dayden, and many others of the Dark Order. Neither of you are fools and I have no doubt your eyes are now open. I'm sure you can see that each of you has been deceived and you now have the chance to avenge the lives of those lost when Marcus enters Brandor to try to kill its royal family."

George listened as the murmurs filled the hall and he watched as Sam stood up to speak. "He will be here tomorrow? How should we prepare for this kind of an attack? There's no one in my army who commands this kind of power. How could I possibly ask two men whom I barely know to defend a kingdom they don't live in?"

George held up his hand and motioned for everyone to listen. "It's no coincidence Lord Dowd and Lord Boyafed sit with us tonight. Lasidious knows there's justice which needs to be given to both of these men. My lord has requested that I protect your family, Sam. He made me responsible to keep you safe and to allow these warriors, who cherish honor, to defeat Marcus within your arena. He wants Brandor's people to see the final threat to all of Southern Grayham fall before their very eyes."

Boyafed stood from his chair and motioned for Dowd to do the same. He extended his hand and said, "Much of this makes sense and, knowing Marcus Id the way I do, I don't doubt for a moment he's behind all of this. I have done a lot of thinking since meeting Kepler in the Petrified Forest and when I saw Sam walk into the room... a sight my elven eyes will never forget as he walked through those very doors on this very night... I knew my god would never have given such a gift to any man who serves under my command. Not only does Sam live, but his son lives as well. I no longer will serve a god who is without honor. Lord Dowd, I will fight with you by my side and would consider myself honored if you'll accept!"

Dowd looked at the many faces surrounding the table. He saw the emotions in their eyes and could see they looked to him as the final piece necessary to save them. Slowly he extended his arm and took hold of Boyafed's hand. "I will fight with you under one condition."

Boyafed smiled, he knew what was coming next. "Once this fight is over and Marcus lies dead on the floor of this place they call an arena, you and I shall see who the best warrior is between us. I already know this answer to be myself... but I can think of no finer fight than for the two of us to meet in an honorable battle."

Sam began to clap his hands. He stood up and shouted. "If only Pay-per-View existed on this world. Wow... this is going to be a fight worth watching. But I do have one simple suggestion, gentle-men."

Dowd and Boyafed waited for him to continue.

"I think to kill each other would be a shame. Your influence is going to be necessary as your world makes the change needed to ensure peace finds everyone. I originally came from a world called Earth and I may have a solution which will allow you to settle this desire to know who is the best, without killing one another. On my home world..."

Sam paused to allow a huge smile to cross his face.... "On my old home world, we called it Mixed Martial Arts, and if the two of you will spend the moments necessary with me to teach you a few things, I will explain how this could become a great way to settle the differences the people of our worlds have with one another."

George began to laugh and the whole table turned to look at him. Sam was the one to speak out.

"What's so funny, George?"

George jumped down from the table and moved to stand beside Sam. "Oh, nothing's wrong at all. I was just thinking that eventually you'll have figured out a way to use that brilliant mind of yours to bring these fights into the homes of the people. We just may see a form of Pay-per-View on this world soon enough. Heck... I bet it isn't long before you have HD TV as well."

Boyafed turned to Sam. "So tell me about this Pay-per-View, and what exactly is HD TV?"

The Peak of Bailem
Brandor's Arena The Following Day

Snow covered much of the valley as Marcus Id continued to make his way through the city. It was as if everyone had been told he was coming. There were footprints scattered everywhere, most of which led to homes or storefronts, but the people remained inside with their doors locked. Even the king's guard commanded no presence. The gates to the city had been left wide open for him to stroll right in. Something was amiss, but he knew his power was far greater than anything on Grayham and continued to make his way to the city's castle.

The only place that appeared to have any semblance of normal activity was a gigantic structure which slowly curved into a large oval shape. The people inside the arena were shouting and laughing as if something exciting was going on.

Hmmm, I wonder what's going on, he thought as he lowered his pipe from his mouth. *I'll just make a brief stop, kill a few thousand people, and continue on my way to the king's castle. Maybe this is why everything seems so strange around here.*

Marcus passed beneath the arches to the arena. He hadn't gone much farther than maybe fifteen steps or so before the people inside went completely silent. A chill ran down his spine as he hesitated to continue forward. The large iron gates used to close the arches slammed heavily behind him and the massive locks resting at their center could be heard clicking into place.

Someone knew I was coming. It appears there's magic on Grayham after all. Killing this king may actually provide some sport.

He threw his pipe to the ground, lifted his hands, and sent a wave of force into the gates, but nothing happened. Again he sent a wave into them, now using a much stronger wave and still, nothing happened. He knew something was wrong. He closed his eyes and thought of the Merchant Island on Grayham, but when he opened them back up, he still stood in front of the sealed archway.

A familiar voice shouted from within the stadium. The voice was faint but still familiar nonetheless. He turned to make his way down the tunnel which took him to the arena's sandy floor. What he saw as he placed his feet on the fighting surface was thousands of people sitting tightly together and one man standing on a single pedestal at its center. He instantly recognized the face... it was Boyafed, dressed in the Order's dark plate armor. Marcus knew now George was no longer his ally.

Slowly he walked towards Boyafed as he scanned the crowd for the warlock's face. With each step his irritation grew and, as if Boyafed's presence wasn't bad enough, a second pedestal was beginning to emerge from beneath the sandy floor. His heart sank as Lord Dowd stood dressed in full armor bearing the White Army's symbol. Both men had their blessed blades drawn and lifted them in his direction to symbolize their challenge.

Marcus felt unsure about his ability to defeat both men during the same moments. He had to think quickly. How could he possibly survive such odds? He tried once more to teleport away, but again failed. He knew George was here somewhere, using his power to keep him from escaping. He wondered if he could teleport within the arena. He tested his theory by closing his eyes. When he reappeared only feet from where he had been standing, he knew, sure enough, he could teleport within the fighting area.

Damn him, his mind screamed, *he has betrayed me.*

From his seat within Sam's box, George snickered. "Marcus is trying to figure out what his limitations will be. I can stop him from escaping, but he'll still be dangerous."

Sam looked at him. "Are you sure this is a good idea, allowing the people to watch like this? They have no way of protecting themselves from wayward magic."

George nodded. "I should be able to protect them, if need be."

Marcus finally stopped a fair distance from his challengers. "I will not fight both of you during the same moments. I will only fight if the odds are fair. I see no honor in you ganging up on me."

Boyafed shouted a response. "Where was your sense of honor when you killed Dayden? Where was your sense of honor when you killed the king of Lavan and Lord Dowd's spirit-bBull? I see no honor in the senseless killing of my paladins to manipulate a war amongst our people. You will fight us both and you will fight us now!"

Boyafed leapt from his pedestal with Dowd right behind him. The people within the arena began to cheer as both men lifted their blades to charge in. Marcus reached beneath his robe and withdrew a blessed sword of his own. He lifted his hand and sent a bolt of lightning into Dowd which threw the White Army leader across the arena where he rolled to his feet.

Boyafed's blade met Marcus's and a frenzied exchange of steel followed before the dark warrior was also struck by a well-placed bolt of lightning, throwing him into the wall beneath the crowd.

Dowd had closed the gap between himself and Marcus and had lifted his free hand. He began a new assault with a wave of force meant to send the Dark Chancellor to his back, but soon found his magic was absorbed within Marcus's palm and returned three-fold. The power plowed into the White Army leader, sending him flying into the wall opposite of Boyafed.

Marcus turned at the perfect moment to deflect a wall of fire Boyafed had sent his direction. The fire continued towards the people in the stands but George stopped the power from killing those who sat on this side with a wave of his hand from the king's box.

He turned to Sam. "Well, that was a close one... maybe I should protect everyone, not just you." He turned to both Kepler and Shalee. "Stand beside me... I need to feed off your power for this." George laid a hand on them both and with a simple nod of his head, created an invisible wall which now protected Brandor's people.

Boyafed and Marcus once again met with blades slamming hard into one another. The dark warrior found a small opening and sent a magic arrow into Marcus. The Chancellor flew across the arena but, as if he wasn't fazed at all, rolled to his feet and teleported behind his enemy. Boyafed spun around quickly and blocked Marcus's blade from slicing into him.

Marcus quickly teleported to the far side of the arena and sent a bolt of lightning from his palm. Both Dowd and Boyafed dove out of the way and rolled to their feet. Dowd teleported next to Marcus and began a masterful series of metal on metal before finding a small opening of his own. A wave of force carried Marcus toward the wall behind him but before he hit, his body vanished, only to reappear behind Dowd. With blade ready, he lunged forward, savoring the penetration made into the small of Dowd's back. He could feel the White Army leader's spine sever and watched as he fell immediately to the sand. Marcus pulled his blade free just before Boyafed's blade made contact.

The series of metal clashes and blocked magical strikes continued for many long moments before Marcus finally found the opening that would also send the Dark Order leader to the sand. A well-placed slash across the abdomen, followed by a downward strike to the shoulder, ended the fight.

Blood from both men began to saturate the earth as Marcus moved to stand over Boyafed to deliver the killing blow. But before he could, both bodies of the wounded men vanished.

George turned to Sam as he listened to Marcus shout out his frustration.

"Sam, I hope your healers have the vial Brayson gave you when visiting Luvelles. Boyafed and Dowd are going to need it if they are to survive."

Once Sam nodded that he had it, George turned to face Brayson. "You're going to have to be the one who kills him. I would do it myself, but we can't have the people perceive me as a killer. I am trying to spread Lasidious's words of peace and love on Grayham. For the people to see me kill Marcus would defeat everything we wish to accomplish here."

Mary grabbed Brayson's arm. "You're not going out there. Neither of you are, do you hear me, George?"

Athena cradled Joshua in her arms. "I don't want the grandfather of my child getting killed. Don't you dare go out there!"

George smiled as he found Brayson's eyes. "Well, this is one of those moments where we're going to have to beg for forgiveness later. You should go and settle this once and for all."

Brayson reached beneath his robe to unsheathe the Blade of the Head Master and was about to teleport to the arena's surface when Sam spoke out. "The rings... just wait a moment... what about the rings you gave me when I visited Luvelles? Are they strong enough to protect me from Marcus's magic?"

Brayson thought a moment and confirmed they were more than enough.

Sam stood from his throne and removed Kael from his sheath. "When I fought Boyafed, I realized I could defeat him. It was one small error which allowed him to beat me. I can rip this guy apart if you let me go out there. If his magic is removed from the fight by my use of these rings, I can kill him, I'm sure of it."

Shalee stood from her throne and handed Sam Junior to the handmaiden. "Don't you even think about going out there!"

Marcus shouted from the arena. "Are you afraid to come and face me? Do you fear me now that you've seen my ability to kill your guard dogs, George?"

George turned and with a simple nod of his head, knocked Marcus across the arena. The crowd laughed hysterically but soon quieted as Marcus sent a wall of flame heading towards them, only to be dissipated by George's protective wall.

George turned to face Sam. "If you do this... he could kill you before we get you to a healer. Are you sure this is—"

Before another word could be said, Brayson teleported from the king's box and appeared within the arena. The people once again cheered as they prepared for the next fight.

As Marcus finished brushing off the sand from his robe, he saw Brayson standing with sword drawn. He swallowed hard, lifted his sword to his mouth, and spoke in the language of the elves. *"Entula en' templa!"*

Both men began to run toward each other. Sharpened steel once again filled the arena with its wicked sounds. Slices, lunges, spins, stabs, and sweeps were all used in a barrage of calculated movements to find the upper hand.

Brayson was the first to find an opening and kicked Marcus with a boot to the chest. Falling to the ground, the Chancellor scrambled to his feet. only to find a hard right hand filled with the butt end of Brayson's sword clubbing him upside the face. Again he fell, but now he was unable to stand without falling forward to his knees.

Brayson's boot found his brother's ribs as Marcus lifted from the sand due to the sheer force of the impact... his ribs cracked and were heard by the people nearest them. Again the crowd's cheers filled the air.

Brayson moved in to finish the job, but Marcus managed to collect himself enough to lunge blade first. The attempt was blocked and followed with a clubbing left foot to the side of his face. The Chancellor stumbled backward and fell to the sand.

Now, with Marcus's back to his older brother, Brayson saw his opportunity to finish the fight. Quickly he thrust his free hand forward to deliver a powerful storm of iced needles. The magic plowed into Marcus but the result wasn't what Brayson expected. His own power was redirected and now he became the primary target. There wasn't the moments necessary to react as the full force of his magic impaled him, sending him flying backwards crashing hard into the wall below the king's box. His head hit the stone as he fell to the ground unconscious, and the needles began to melt under his skin.

Marcus managed to gather his wits and moved to stand above his older brother. A smiled crossed his face as he looked at his blessed blade and appreciated its special power. His blade's special ability was what allowed him to redirect his brother's magic. He watched the blood flow from the many holes the iced needles had left behind and enjoyed the sight of how saturated Brayson's robe was becoming.

Mary's cries of panic were heard as she begged Marcus for mercy, but the Chancellor's ears were deaf to her pain.

"You disappoint me, brother... of all the men I've killed, I would've expected you to be the toughest. It's a pity you have to die this way."

Marcus lifted his sword and started to plunge it in to his victim. But before the blade traveled far, Boyafed's sword ran Marcus through, delivering the killing blow. The dark warrior was careful that the blade had pierced the Chancellor's heart.

The Order leader had teleported from the healer's table and re-appeared in the center of the arena. Once he saw Marcus's back to him, he teleported again and struck, then he too fell limply to the ground, unconsciousness.

George waved his hand, sending both Brayson and Boyafed to the healers. Then he teleported both himself and Mary directly inside the healer's room to ensure the elixir necessary to save both men was administered. When satisfied everything was done prop-erly, he asked about the prognosis of all three. He left Mary with Brayson and reappeared inside the king's box.

Athena was the first to speak. "Are they all dead, George?"

"Brayson and Boyafed should be okay in a day or so, but it will be much longer before we know if Dowd will ever walk again. I think it's safe to say the final threat to your new kingdom has been eliminated, Sam.

"And now, I think my family will need a place to stay for the night. Mary is going to need her daughters to be with her while Brayson heals. She's an absolute mess right now."

Shalee responded, "I will have rooms prepared for everyone inside the castle. You can stay as long as you like. I will also see to it that someone helps with the babies while they keep Mary com-pany."

"Thank you, Shalee, you're a blessing for sure," George said as he turned to Sam. "You can have your men dispose of Marcus however you see fit. And also, please see to it that the healers stay with the survivors at every moment. There are things I must do tomorrow with Gregory and we'll be gone for most of the day."

Sam put his hand on George's shoulders. "You have proven to be a good man. I owe you big. I'll do whatever I can to help."

"And so will I," Shalee added as she gave him a hug. "Make sure you bring the family to Grayham often so we can visit once this is all over."

George smiled and motioned for Athena to stand beside him.

He looked at Shalee and with a wink, said, "Once things settle down, I'll come back and take you to look into the Eye of Magic. You'll be able to come and visit Luvelles whenever you wish once you have the power to teleport between worlds. But I think that for now, we should all take a few days off and gather a sense of where our lives are headed. Let's set the groundwork for peace and ensure our families are well taken care of."

Ancients Sovereign
The Home of Lasidious

"I hate that troll," Lasidious screamed as he stormed around his home far beneath the Peaks of Angels, shouting one curse after another. "That piece of garesh really thinks he can speak that way to me... TO ME... OF ALL THE GODS... he should fear me the most. He spoke to me as if I won't find a way to torture his pathetic little mind! I will make it my mission to destroy Kesdelain. That troll's soul will find the inside of the Book's pages soon enough... you mark my words!"

Most everything Celestria had done to accent their cave-like home had been ripped from its normal resting spot and thrown in every direction. Lasidious had not gotten a moment's rest since the announcement of the two new gods the day before.

Alistar and Celestria sat quietly, patiently waiting at the table near the fireplace full of green flames for Lasidious to calm himself. It wasn't until Late Bailem and only after one full day of continuous shouting that the God of Mischief finally stopped beside them, took a long deep breath, and sat heavily in the chair across from Alistar. He then spoke as if nothing was wrong, as if he had never thrown a fit. "So, a new plan is in order... don't you think?"

Alistar leaned forward and with a sly smile said, "If you're done ranting, I do think we should begin planning. I have thought about a few things which concern me and none of these things have to do with the troll you hate so much. My concern is Sharvesa."

Lasidious shook his head as if confused. "Sharvesa is a delightful demon, and I'm sure we can work with her to accomplish our goals. How could she possibly be a problem?"

Celestria pushed her long blonde hair clear of her face. "I think he's referring to the fact that Sharvesa is Payne's mother. What will happen when she finds out her son is being taken care of by a human and, worse still, what will happen when she realizes George is your prophet? I know she respects you, Lasidious... but does she respect you enough to allow her son to continue to stay with George?"

Lasidious thought a moment. "Even if she doesn't want Payne to be with George, what would it matter? Payne has already served his purpose and Kepler now has his powers. Even if Payne does leave, it won't stop George from accomplishing his goals to get his daughter's soul out of the Book."

Alistar stood from the table. "I don't think you're seeing the bigger picture, brother. Payne has become much more to George's family than just some annoying fairy-demon. Haven't you been watching how George and Athena treat Payne? Even the entire family treats him as one of their own now. Just look at what George has done.

"Payne takes baths, he's wearing clothes George created just for him, and he even sits in a high chair to eat. They have adopted Payne as one of their own children and even Kepler has accepted his role in protecting him. Payne has his own room inside their home.

"Granted... it's weird that George somehow managed to become attached to his freaky friends but despite our failure to understand this attachment, George is loyal to them and will do whatever needs to be done to keep them safe. You must remember George told you once already that he will sacrifice retrieving his daughter's soul if his family would be hurt because of it.

"If Sharvesa were to find a way take Payne from the family... who knows what George would do, and how this whole prophet plan of ours could backfire because of this. I hope you're seeing the bigger picture now!"

Lasidious stood from the table, grabbed a bowl of fruit, and threw it across the room. The fruit hit the wall with great force, sending chunks of fruit flying in all directions. "Damn that Book! We were so close to having everything!" Again his temper took over as pieces of furniture began to fly.

The Next Day
The Battlegrounds of Olis
The Peak of Bailem

George and Gregory appeared before the White Army just outside the tent meant to house Lord Dowd. They lowered a heavy chest to the ground and waited for Krasous, the army's Argont Commander, to make his exit. When the white warrior stood before them, Gregory began the conversation.

"Krasous, I would like you to meet the prophet of Lasidious. The prophet has seen to it that there will be no war fought on the fields of Olis. Your men can go home to their families!"

The Argont Commander lowered his head to symbolize his respect while greeting George. "Please forgive me, prophet, but I serve the gods of the White Army. I'm sure you're a great man to carry such a title, but I know nothing of your god. I fail to see why your lord would bother himself with such business."

George put his hand on the commander's shoulder. "When Dowd returns, you shall feel differently. For now I give you my word that you can return home and allow each of your men to enjoy their families."

"Where is Lord Dowd? If it's all the same to you, I will keep my men in place until Dowd himself gives the order to break camp."

Gregory answered. "He's on the world of Grayham recovering in the king's city of Brandor. Dowd followed the evil which caused this threat of war on our world and fought side by side with Boyafed to put an end to it once and for all."

Krasous was stunned. "Why would Dowd wish to fight with Boyafed at his side? This man is the sworn enemy of the White Army."

"I'll allow Dowd to explain when he returns. Your men owe him their lives for his sacrifice. We are unsure if he will ever be able to walk again, but when he returns, walking or not, he will surely profess his loyalty to Lasidious."

"Krasous," George said, jumping back into the conversation, "order your men to return home and give each of them two of these for their inconvenience."

George waved his hand and the chest's lid opened... it was full of Yaloom coins. "This is a gift from Lasidious. He wishes for Luvelles to see prosperity and, when the moment is right, I will return to explain his message of love and peace. But for now, allow your men to be richly rewarded and go to their families."

George placed his hand on Gregory's shoulder and vanished. Krasous was left standing in the snow, staring at the chest full of wealth.

George then took Gregory to the camp of the Dark Army and, with a similar speech and another chest full of wealth, this army was also told to go home to their families. George saw to it that the mercenaries were paid far greater than they would've ever imagined and explained that there was peace coming to Luvelles and they would no longer be allowed to find employment hurting others. He suggested strongly they find new jobs and become productive members of society.

Christopher, the Dark Army's Argont Commander, was left with standing orders to disburse the chest full of wealth to every man who intended to fight. Boyafed would be the one to see he had done things properly upon his return. George and Gregory left this final army standing in the snow as they vanished.

Chapter 30

𝕬 𝕮𝖗𝖆𝖈𝖐𝖊𝖉 𝕲𝖊𝖒

Five Days Later
The Isthmus of Change
Late Bailem

Mosley stood with his five feline companions and looked to the north across the Isthmus. The Night Terror Wolf knew the perils which lay ahead would be great. Never had the Wisp of Song given any man or beast a journey that wasn't full of tragedy or death.

He also knew the companionship of his sabertooth friends might not be enough protection to survive but, despite his fear, he had to go. To the north was the answer to the Wisp's questions, and this was the only way he could acquire the knowledge the Wisp was after. With this knowledge the Sphere would reveal a way to retrieve the power of the Ancient Mystics hidden somewhere on Grayham. It was also with this power that he would be able to destroy George!

130 𝕻𝖊𝖆𝖐𝖘 𝖔𝖋 𝕭𝖆𝖎𝖑𝖊𝖒 𝕳𝖆𝖛𝖊 𝕻𝖆𝖘𝖘𝖊𝖉
The City of Inspiration

Peace finally found a way to settle across the lands of Southern Grayham, Harvestom, and Luvelles. Alistar had also secretly visited with George and given him the news of the Crystal Moon's return to the Temple of the Gods.

George delivered this same news to Sam and Shalee, telling them that Lasidious had forced Mieonus to return the crystal's pieces and the threat of the worlds colliding into one another was no longer a problem. They could relax and work toward making the lives of the people better.

Lasidious made an appearance to the people of Southern Grayham and delivered a most memorable speech. The God of Mischief—now known to most everyone across the land as the God of Peace and Love— informed the people they were once again allowed to visit the plateau resting high on top of Griffon Falls to begin worshipping the god of their choosing.

And, as expected, a vast majority of the population decided to say their prayers to Lasidious after hearing about Lasidious's gift of life to the king's son. Even many of the barbarians began to pray to Lasidious after seeing the generosity which came from Grayham by order of the newly reformed Senate. The same race who once hated the swine living in Brandor now approved of their new king and understood it was because of Sam's vision that all of them had found a better way of life.

Now of course, there were those barbarians who rebelled... but once they were gathered together and brought to Brandor's arena, George put Maldwin to work allowing the rat to use his visions to plant a message of peace in their minds. By the moment each man finally left and walked beneath the arena's arches to go about their lives, the rat's visions had removed all desires to rebel further.

Nearly 425,000 souls were already praying to Lasidious on Southern Grayham and the number continued to grow with each passing day.

On Luvelles, Boyafed returned to the city of Marcus and assumed the position as the new Chancellor. He made many changes and also declared that the army would no longer be called the Dark Order of Holy Paladins, but instead, their new name would be changed to the elven phrase, Bragol Thalion, which meant strength.

Christopher was promoted from his position as the Argont Commander to the new leader of the army once he officially accepted Lasidious as his new lord. Christopher was ordered by Boyafed to change the army's direction and how they governed the lands of Hyperia. Because of this order, many new rules were implemented.

For a solider to be allowed to remain enlisted or even commissioned within the new army, the men were expected to pray to Lasidious twice daily and ensure they would work hand in hand with the White Army to maintain peace throughout all the lands, not just Hyperia.

Further, Christopher was ordered to gather up all the darkest magic users and give them the chance to stop the use of their Dark Magic. Those who refused to accept peace as a new way of life were thrown into the same swamp they had personally polluted with so many deadly, deformed creatures. Brayson Id himself helped Boyafed find a magic strong enough to ensure none of them would be able to escape their new hell.

Boyafed even decided to change the name of the city. As a way of poking fun at his new friend, Lord Dowd, he settled on the name Francis. The people living beyond the city's walls were told that the army would rebuild their homes to bring them up to the standards of the style of living inside. No longer would there be a separation of class. Any man who wished to earn his position to live inside the walls—whether they commanded strong magic or not—was welcome to try ,and even the law regarding the separation of elves, from halflings, was changed.

Now the Kingdom of Lavan had also made many changes. Lord Dowd, after healing to the point he could use his arms to move his wheelchair, began his work with Gregory Id to spread the words of Lasidious. Dowd moved to Lavan and took over as the new king.

Krasous became the army's leader once he accepted Lasidious as his new lord. Many of the same laws were implemented the same way Boyafed had done with Christopher in Hyperia. Those men who refused to accept Lasidious's words of peace were removed from their positions within the army and given estates to show the kingdom's appreciation for their service. These men were not punished for their beliefs but were simply considered retired and allowed to worship who they chose. Of the thousands who served in the White Army, only four hundred and twenty-three men chose to accept their retirement and continued to serve their gods.

The numbers in Boyafed's newly reformed army was now higher and numbered nearly 1,754 men who wished to retire and continue to serve the God of Death, Hosseff. But due to the nature of these men's beliefs, a secret watch was implemented to ensure there would be no problems.

In total, between the two armies of Luvelles, nearly 34,232 men were now praying to Lasidious twice daily. With the members of their families being accounted for, well over 123,472 souls would soon be praying to the so-called god of Peace and Love. The rest of Luvelles also started to take note of all the changes and the number of those who began to pray to Lasidious continued to grow.

There was one other very significant change both armies decided to implement—a change Kepler's scheming mind manipulated with Maldwin's help. Now, both Boyafed and Lord Dowd were given the desire to glorify the demon-cat... and, thanks to Maldwin's very specific visions, they approached each of their respected councils with the rat in their arms.

By the moment Maldwin was done with them, both councils had agreed to meet with Kepler. After coming to a full understanding of the giant cat's abilities and further agreeing his majestic white fur and red glowing eyes would make him perfect for the title Protector of the Realm, the jaguar was now viewed as a symbol of power which both armies cherished.

A new castle was already under construction at the center of the Battlegrounds of Olis and would be the place where an enormous statue of Kepler would be created to honor his new position. This area of Luvelles was to be his alone to begin a little undead family of cats. All he needed now was a mate and, thanks to Lasidious, Kepler knew he would face many perils and would need to brave this new world's dangers to find

The centaurs of Harvestom also had the chance to spend a few days with Gregory Id and came to accept the disciple of Lasidious as a great man. Susanne and Garrin accompanied Gregory to Harvestom on many occasions and the relationship between the two was slowly blossoming into something wonderful.

Both the Black Coats and Brown Coats agreed to set aside their differences and there is now talk of creating a united kingdom. Over 121,000 centaurs already pray twice daily to Lasidious.

TODAY WAS A DAY TO BE CELEBRATED
Today was not about the gods or faith!

The City of Inspiration
The Peak of Bailem

Brayson and Mary stood before thousands at the top of the steps leading up to the entrance to Gregory's glass palace within the City of Inspiration. A rainbow of colors rested high against the walls of the Chancellor's tower as the sun passed through the prisms placed throughout the city. Spring was finally here and it was a wonderful day for a wedding.

George had traveled to Brandor and brought the royal family back with him to celebrate the event. Shalee's fashion sense had been solicited and after speaking with the couple, they decided to go with all of her recommendations. Shalee used her magic to create the dresses, tuxedos, and floral arrangements for nearly 3,000 souls.

Sam and Shalee took their positions as honored guests while Sam Junior, wrapped warmly, slept in his mother's arms. Gregory took his position as Boyafed's "Ho Mellon" (Best Man) while Susanne stood beside Mary as her "He Mellon" (Maid of Honor).

George and Athena stood beside Sam and Shalee, with the rest of the children beside them. Joshua slept in his mother's arms while Payne held onto George's hand and fidgeted something fierce while wearing his first ever tuxedo. Garrin, now approaching one season old, sat upright on George's other arm and watched intently as things moved around him.

Lord Dowd was provided a platform for his wheelchair to rest on next to Boyafed… and beyond them stood the esteemed members of both armies and their families. As far as the eyes could see down the roadway made of glass cobblestones leading away from the palace, people lined up to watch the union between their elven Head Master and a human woman.

But the one thing no one expected and, perhaps the most memorable thing no one would ever see again, was the position Kepler had in this wedding. The jaguar had been working with the scholars of Luvelles for the last 30 Peaks of Bailem and planned to marry the couple speaking solely in the language of the elves.

The cat now stood at the top of the long flight of stairs and lifted his head to the sky. The new Protector of the Realm let out a mighty roar that commanded everyone's attention. George, knowing this was going to happen, secretly used his power to ensure every child present would not be able to hear this fearsome sound.

After addressing the crowd and thanking them for coming, Kepler turned his attention to Brayson and Mary.

"Brayson... *Lle naa belegohtar, Cormlle naa tanya tel'raa.*

"Mary... *Vanimle sila tiri, Lle naa vanima, Oio naa elealla alasse.*"

Mary motioned for Kepler to pause so Brayson could tell her what he said.

Brayson smiled.

"He said I'm a mighty warrior and I have the heart of a lion. He also said your beauty shines bright and to see you gives him joy."

Mary looked at Kepler, "Keep up the good work."

Kepler gave her a wink and continued to speak in the elfish language... but I shall translate to make it simple.

"Today is a day to be celebrated. Peace has come to Luvelles and your Head Master has decided to take a bride, breaking the boundaries of race. This union shows the people that we all are created equal and no man should hate another because they appear to be different. This couple sets the standard for all of Luvelles to maintain. If there is anyone here who knows of a reason why this couple should not be joined... say so now!"

"DOOMED! This union is doomed!" a voice cried out from the crowd as she began to float up the stairs. It was Bryanna, the same visionary who had scared Mary and the girls during their first visit to the city. She was dressed in black, ash covering her entire body. "The head of this family is surrounded by evil... he is cursed and this union will perish because of it! I have forseen this to be true! Death will come to those who follow Lasidious's prophet!"

George appeared next to the woman and with a wave of his hand, silenced her. He turned to the people and after using his hand to lift her skyward, used his magic to amplify his own voice… manipulating what Bryanna had just said.

"I suppose there are those who would have this world live in fear! I, for one, think Luvelles deserves better than this! There are those who would seek to destroy a union as blessed as this one we see before us. I ask you now, are there any others besides this crazed woman who would object to this world having a Head Master who seeks his own happiness? Is there any other man who can say one bad thing about Brayson? I see no evil in this man. Since my arrival on Luvelles I have seen nothing other than honor, integrity, and his loyalty to the people. I want everyone here who wishes this union to go forward to shout out your approval right now!"

Thousands of people lifted their voices to the sky almost as if it had been rehearsed. George lowered Bryanna to the ground and released his power over her. He motioned for four guards to carry her away and throw her in the dungeon.

As they dragged her through the streets she continued to shout, **"DOOMED… DOOMED… THIS UNION IS DOOMED!"**

George shook his head and gave everyone around him a big bright smile. "I can't tell you all how happy I am she isn't my mother-in-law!" He listened to the crowd laugh, and then teleported back to his position beside Athena. "Wow… what a nut job that lady was. Shall we continue?"

Kepler continued, making a small joke of his own. "Okay… other than the crazy lady, is there anyone else who wants to object?"

The entire street became as quiet as a mouse, each of them waiting anxiously for a voice to cry out. But when one never came, Kepler moved forward. "By the authority given to me by Lasidious himself, I now pronounce this couple united. Brayson you may lick your bride's face."

Both Brayson and Mary shook their heads and stared at the giant jaguar.

Athena spoke out in a whisper. "No, Kepler… he needs to kiss her… we don't lick one another!"

"Oohhh, sorry… you may kiss your bride's face!"

Again Athena spoke out in a whisper. "No, Kepler... we kiss on the lips."

Kepler growled with frustration. "Just kiss whatever it is you feel like kissing then! I suppose the lips work good for this!"

Both Lord Dowd and Boyafed led the laughter as the crowd enjoyed the awkwardness of the situation.

Later that night Sam finally caught up with George inside Gregory's ballroom.

"George... I thought you handled the crazy woman rather well. I have to admit, though, she really freaked me out when she started to scream about how doomed everyone was. It wasn't that long ago I would've believed her, but after watching things develop, I truly believe you've managed to become a good man."

George put both hands on Sam's shoulders. "Thanks for saying that. You know, since you and Shalee are here on Luvelles, why don't you let Shalee take her look into the Eye of Magic so the two of you can teleport back and forth between worlds? She has already passed through the trials, so it shouldn't take long. There are so many cool places we all could go if Shalee had this power. We could visit anywhere we wanted to within Harvestom, Luvelles and Grayham. It could be a lot of fun. We could call it 'our moments to bond.'"

"I agree," Shalee said with a chuckle as she walked up to join them. "I think Sam has a firm grasp on taking care of Sam Junior until I get back. I say we do it tomorrow night."

Sam took the baby from her arms. "What about the whole soul-swallowing thing both of you are failing to talk about? I would rather know for sure my son's mother will be around. I really don't want to lose you."

George looked at Shalee and feigned his caring. "He does have a point. It is possible the Eye could swallow your soul."

Shalee pushed Sam Junior's hair clear of his forehead. "If I had any doubts, I wouldn't do it. My power is progressing at a rapid pace. I have no worries about my soul. I am one thousand percent sure I won't leave you without a wife, Mr. Goodrich! Besides, traveling wherever we want could be fun."

"Then I shall take you tomorrow night, if Sam is okay with it."

Sam just shrugged. "If there is one thing I've learned about being married to this woman, she's too stubborn to tell her 'no.' If I don't say 'yes,' she'll torture me until I do. So go ahead and look into this Eye. The baby and I will wait for you here in Gregory's palace."

George clapped his hands. "Then tomorrow night it is. We should celebrate."

Ancients Sovereign
Lasidious and Celestria's Home

Lasidious leaned back in his chair after watching the visions of Sam, George, and Shalee fade away within the green flames. He turned to look at Alistar. "This is what we have been waiting for. Tomorrow night we'll have our meeting with the dragons to discuss the creation of their new world and we'll finally be able to get rid of our biggest threat to our plans."

Alistar stood from his chair, "You see, brother, things are once again beginning to go our way. I have managed to keep Sharvesa and the others busy. The troll is so scared that he keeps to himself, locked inside his new home beneath Catalyst Mountain, and the others, well, let's just say they're content. They all feel Gabriel has delivered such a crushing blow to your ego—not to mention your plans to control him—I've been able to completely convince them to concentrate their efforts on the creation of the new dragon world. All of them want this world to be the most beautiful world yet. I'll see to it that the Source is at this meeting."

Celestria moved to Lasidious and after pushing his feet from the table, used her power to move his chair into a better position with him still in it. She slowly straddled his legs and lowered onto his lap.

Alistar, seeing that the moments were about to become awkward, vanished.

"You see, my love, we shall find our way to control the Book soon enough."

She leaned into him and kissed the top of his ear. He trembled and reached up to grab her hips while listening to her whisper.

"Our son will be old enough very soon to bring home. We'll be able to draw from his power and take control of Gabriel. You, my love, will be a king among gods. Maybe you should show your future queen what her king is made of. You know I long for you." Again she leaned in and licked his lips.

The rest of what happened next I will leave to your imagination. And for those of you who will take a moment to ponder this... STOP... BE GOOD... and keep reading!

The Shoreline of Crystal Lake
The World of Luvelles

Gage and Gallrum stood quietly on the shoreline of Crystal Lake as they watched Luvelles's new moon disappear behind the horizon. The sun's rays began to peek over the mountains and were glimmering off the clear blue water of the lake. Neither of them could have asked for more of a perfect spring morning in which to begin their adventures.

"I'm nervous," Gage said while using his cane to carve out his name in the pebble-covered shoreline. "We are free to do whatever we wish, now that both our masters are dead. Where do you think we should go?"

The Serwin reached up with his scale-covered talon and scratched his head. "I can't say I know. I suppose with Balecut no longer being a threat, I can go anywhere I want. It feels strange to know I no longer need to stay hidden within the village."

Gage pondered a bit before responding. "We can go to any world we choose. There are no restrictions on either of our races, so why don't we start someplace other than Luvelles? Let's expand our horizons a bit!"

"And where do you suggest we start?"

The badger stopped pushing his cane through the pebbles. "I had a dream last night about the ice of Northern Grayham. I have to admit I felt like I was being called to it for some reason. I feel as if someone is in trouble and needs my help. Maybe we should head to the Merchant Island here on Luvelles, find some warmer attire, and catch a ride with the Merchant Angels. Let's go see what has called to me. Let's find out what's there that would cause me to dream about it. What do you think?"

Gallrum smiled. "Well... at least it's not Luvelles and I'm really glad you didn't say you wanted to see the new dragon world, so what could it hurt? Let's go and see what your dreams are all about."

Without further conversation, Gage took Gallrum's talon and both Goswigs vanished.

From inside the Hall of Judgment on Ancients Sovereign, the Book of Immortality's face was full of concern as the images of the Goswigs faded from within the marble of the heavy table. He reached up with his hand and scratched the chin protruding from his binding.

"Help is coming, Mosley, help is coming! Just hang in there and fight for your survival... help is coming!"

The Next Day,
Late Bailem

George and Shalee appeared inside the Source's cave. George knew the Source would be with the gods planning the creation of the new dragon world, so he escorted Shalee to the heavy iron door and stopped.

"The Eye of Magic is on the other side."

Shalee pushed her hair clear of her face. "Suddenly I'm finding myself to be very nervous. Did you feel the same way before you went inside?"

"Of course... let me give you a piece of advice Brayson gave to me. The key to looking in the Eye is your belief in yourself and having no doubt that you deserve its power. You're the most powerful woman on Grayham. You're even more powerful than many of the women on Luvelles. Don't you think you deserve this power more than any other woman alive right now? Go in there and show the Eye who's boss."

"Okay... you're right... I can do this. Here goes nothing!" She leaned in and gave him a big hug. "You have turned out to be a good friend... thank you for everything!"

George smiled and put his forehead to hers. "You can thank me once you get your blessing from the Eye. Now get in there and know you deserve this!"

Shalee opened the door and walked inside. She walked only a few feet before the heavy door slammed behind her, making a deafening sound. A chill filled her entire body as she stared at the gem sitting atop the thick wooden staff at the center of a cubed-shaped room. The gem was so beautiful, its ruby-red fiery color called to her fashion sense. It was large... larger than her fist. But nothing else occupied the room.

Suddenly a blinding red light emerged from the gem and before she knew it, Shalee was standing in front of an angelic being. The light softened and was replaced with a soft white glow surrounding a face which could not be seen. A ghostly body hung suspended and large feathered wings extended to either side. Shalee felt like she was in the presence of a god as the eye came into focus.

On the other side of the heavy iron, George waited patiently until the bright light caused by the Eye's presence faded from beneath the door and the cave's floor. He knew the Eye had finished pulling her inside its gem to begin questioning her, and this meant it was now the proper moment to act.

Slowly he used his power to push the door open. Without entering the room he lifted his hand and sent a single bolt of his most powerful lightning crashing hard into its polished surface. The gem cracked... trapping Shalee inside forever as the light within it began to fade.

George grinned from ear to ear as he spoke in a soft voice full of wickedness. "I don't suppose you'll ever get the chance to thank me now, Shalee. I'm sure your husband will learn to adapt without you... that is, if I don't kill him first! But I wouldn't worry much... I have business to attend to in Eastern Luvelles first. They have shape-shifting elves there, you know, and I don't know I can bear the thought of leaving your son without a parent, even though I hate your husband. I'll have to do some contemplating on what to do with Sam while I travel." The warlock laughed hysterically before teleporting home.

Eventually, the Source returned to his cave within the Mountains of Oraness. He lowered his massive form down across many of the lava flows which protruded from the cave's floor and shut his eyes. Tomorrow, the gods were going to put the finishing touches on the creation of the new dragon world and he would have one of the finest homes on this new world.

Behind the heavy iron door, the last bit of light faded from inside the cracked gem. Shalee was trapped and now wandered aimlessly through a misty red haze. The angelic form of the Eye was nowhere to be found and her heart raced as she frantically looked in every direction.

Has something gone wrong? she thought. *Where am I? There's nothing here. Am I supposed to just wait? Is this the same thing George saw when he looked inside the Eye?*

She walked for many long moments before three blinding lights appeared. She tried to squint, but quickly found she would need to cover her eyes for protection. Slowly, the lights faded and left three figures standing in the places where the lights had been.

Shalee's eyes took a few moments to adjust, she gasped, "Oh my—Bassorine... BJ... and, and, oh my god... HELGA... is it really you?"

Helga responded with a large smile, "Hello child. Did you miss me?"

The End

Keep reading for a **SNEAK PEEK**
inside the pages of **Book 3.**

Book 3

The Kingdom of the Ice King

MOSLEY peered down from the top of the ice-covered cliff as he prepared to make his move. He couldn't believe his eyes. There she was… alive and well… just as plain as day, as if she had never passed away. These were not the moments to think… he had to act now or his Luvera would die again at the hands of her attackers.

Lifting his head towards the darkened, cloud-covered sky, he howled to announce his presence. The beasts surrounding his love turned to face him and looked up the cliff's icy surface. As they began to circle around to the path leading upward, each heavy step left imprints within the snow as their powerful paws crunched the hard-packed ground.

She had been lost to him for so long, over 100 seasons, and he wasn't about to let her suffer again. This moment, he would save his wife from a certain death. This moment, he would be the Night Terror Wolf he had wished he could have been the night she had been impaled through the heart by the Unicorn Prince's horn. This moment, they would need to go through him to get to her. This moment, Kepler wasn't hidden in the shadows!

Long teeth gnashed, threatening to tear him apart, and drool fell from loosened lips. White fur, covered with blood-stained patches, now turned dark black due to the cold, sent chills down Mosley's spine. He had never seen this type of wolf before and as they bore down on him, he realized they were nearly twice his size.

Luvera called to him, her black fur shaking as her body trembled with fear. Even her voice shook as she screamed. "Run Mosley… you've got to run, my love!"

"I can't… it's too late for that!"

Lowering into an attack position, his white teeth emerged as his lips curled upward to release the growled threats he summoned from within. Legs extended as he launched head on into his first attacker.

**Books, apparel and other Crystal Moon products
are now available online at**
www.worldsofthecrystalmoon.com

To learn more about the author Phillip "Big Dog" Jones go to
www.phillipjones.com